The Romero Brothers (The Complete Collection)

Shadonna Richards

Published by Shadonna Richards, 2015.

This is a work of fiction. Similarities to real people, places, or events are entirely coincidental.

THE ROMERO BROTHERS (THE COMPLETE COLLECTION)

First edition. December 9, 2015.

Copyright © 2015 Shadonna Richards.

ISBN: 979-8230533825

Written by Shadonna Richards.

Table of Contents

The Romero Brothers (The Complete Collection) 1
CONTENTS 5
THE BILLIONAIRE'S SECOND-CHANCE BRIDE (The Romero Brothers, Book 1) 9
PROLOGUE 10
CHAPTER ONE 12
CHAPTER TWO 18
CHAPTER THREE 22
CHAPTER FOUR 28
CHAPTER FIVE 30
CHAPTER SIX 32
CHAPTER SEVEN 43
CHAPTER EIGHT 47
CHAPTER NINE 51
CHAPTER TEN 56
CHAPTER ELEVEN 63
CHAPTER TWELVE 66
CHAPTER THIRTEEN 69
CHAPTER FOURTEEN 71
CHAPTER FIFTEEN 75
CHAPTER SIXTEEN 76
CHAPTER SEVENTEEN 79
EPILOGUE 84
A BRIDE FOR THE BILLIONAIRE BAD BOY (THE ROMERO BROTHERS, BOOK 2) 85
PROLOGUE 86
CHAPTER ONE 87
CHAPTER TWO 90
CHAPTER THREE 93
CHAPTER FOUR 99
CHAPTER FIVE 102
CHAPTER SIX 107
CHAPTER SEVEN 109
CHAPTER EIGHT 112
CHAPTER NINE 116
CHAPTER TEN 123
CHAPTER ELEVEN 130
CHAPTER TWELVE 134
CHAPTER THIRTEEN 137
CHAPTER FOURTEEN 139
CHAPTER FIFTEEN 143
CHAPTER SIXTEEN 144
CHAPTER SEVENTEEN 146
EPILOGUE 148
THE PLAYBOY BILLIONAIRE (THE ROMERO BROTHERS, BOOK 3) 150

CHAPTER ONE	151
CHAPTER TWO	156
CHAPTER THREE	159
CHAPTER FOUR	169
CHAPTER FIVE	179
CHAPTER SIX	182
CHAPTER SEVEN	186
CHAPTER EIGHT	188
CHAPTER NINE	192
CHAPTER TEN	198
CHAPTER ELEVEN	201
CHAPTER TWELVE	208
CHAPTER THIRTEEN	210
CHAPTER FOURTEEN	212
CHAPTER FIFTEEN	214
CHAPTER SIXTEEN	216
CHAPTER SEVENTEEN	217
CHAPTER EIGHTEEN	219
EPILOGUE	221
THE BILLIONAIRE'S ISLAND ROMANCE (THE ROMERO BROTHERS, BOOK 3.5)	224
CHAPTER ONE	225
CHAPTER TWO	229
CHAPTER THREE	234
CHAPTER FOUR	238
CHAPTER FIVE	242
CHAPTER SIX	246
CHAPTER SEVEN	249
CHAPTER EIGHT	251
CHAPTER NINE	261
CHAPTER ELEVEN	267
CHAPTER TWELVE	268
CHAPTER THIRTEEN	272
CHAPTER FOURTEEN	273
CHAPTER FIFTEEN	274
THE BILLIONAIRE'S PROPOSITION (THE ROMERO BROTHERS, BOOK 4)	277
CHAPTER ONE	278
CHAPTER TWO	285
CHAPTER THREE	289
CHAPTER FOUR	292
CHAPTER FIVE	294
CHAPTER SIX	296
CHAPTER SEVEN	298
CHAPTER EIGHT	301
CHAPTER NINE	307
CHAPTER TEN	311

CHAPTER ELEVEN	313
CHAPTER TWELVE	317
CHAPTER THIRTEEN	324
CHAPTER FOURTEEN	326
CHAPTER FIFTEEN	331
CHAPTER SIXTEEN	333
CHAPTER SEVENTEEN	336
CHAPTER EIGHTEEN	341
CHAPTER NINETEEN	343
EPILOGUE	347
THE BILLIONAIRE'S BABY (THE ROMERO BROTHERS, BOOK 5)	349
CHAPTER ONE	350
CHAPTER TWO	355
CHAPTER THREE	361
CHAPTER FOUR	365
CHAPTER FIVE	370
CHAPTER SIX	378
CHAPTER SEVEN	386
CHAPTER EIGHT	390
CHAPTER NINE	395
CHAPTER TEN	396
CHAPTER ELEVEN	400
CHAPTER TWELVE	403
CHAPTER THIRTEEN	410
CHAPTER FOURTEEN	413
CHAPTER FIFTEEN	417
CHAPTER SIXTEEN	421
CHAPTER SEVENTEEN	422
CHAPTER EIGHTEEN	423
CHAPTER NINETEEN	425
CHAPTER TWENTY	428
EPILOGUE	431
THE BILLIONAIRE'S ASSISTANT (THE ROMERO BROTHERS, BOOK 6)	432
CHAPTER ONE	433
CHAPTER TWO	438
CHAPTER THREE	443
CHAPTER FOUR	447
CHAPTER FIVE	453
CHAPTER SIX	459
CHAPTER SEVEN	464
CHAPTER EIGHT	469
CHAPTER NINE	472
CHAPTER TEN	475
CHAPTER ELEVEN	478
CHAPTER TWELVE	481

- CHAPTER THIRTEEN 483
- CHAPTER FIFTEEN 490
- CHAPTER SIXTEEN 492
- CHAPTER SEVENTEEN 493
- SNOWBOUND WITH THE BILLIONAIRE (THE ROMERO BROTHERS, BOOK 7) 497
  - Chapter One 498
  - Chapter Two 503
  - Chapter Three 508
  - Chapter Four 513
  - Chapter Five 515
  - Chapter Six 516
  - Chapter Seven 521
  - Chapter Eight 526
  - Chapter Nine 527
  - Chapter Ten 528
  - Chapter Eleven 533
  - Chapter Twelve 535
  - Chapter Thirteen 537
  - Chapter Fourteen 539
  - Chapter Fifteen 543
  - Chapter Sixteen 545
  - Chapter Seventeen 549
  - Epilogue 552
- THE BILLIONAIRE'S MARRIAGE PROPOSAL 554
  - Prologue 555
  - Chapter 1 557
  - Chapter 2 560
  - Chapter 3 563
  - Chapter 4 565
  - Chapter 5 570
  - Chapter 6 572
  - Chapter 7 577
  - Chapter 8 580
  - Chapter 9 583
  - Chapter 10 585
  - Chapter 11 587
  - Chapter 12 591
  - Chapter 13 593
  - Chapter 14 596
  - Chapter 15 599
  - Chapter 16 604
  - Chapter 17 608
  - Chapter 18 612
  - Chapter 19 615
  - Chapter 20 617

Chapter 21 620
Chapter 22 622
Epilogue 624

THE ROMERO BROTHERS BOXED SET
(Books 1 - 8)
Shadonna Richards
Copyright 2014 by Shadonna Richards

Author Contact:
Website: www.ShadonnaRichards.blogspot.com[1]
Email: Shadonna@ymail.com
Facebook: http://www.Facebook.com/AuthorShadonnaRichards
Twitter: @Shadonna[2]
Cover: Keri Knutson

All rights reserved; no part of this publication may be reproduced or transmitted by any means, electronic, mechanical, photocopying or otherwise, without the prior permission of the publisher.

This book is a work of fiction. The names, characters, places, and incidents are products of the writer's imagination or have been used fictitiously. Any resemblance to persons, living or dead, is entirely coincidental.

ACKNOWLEDGMENTS

Thank you, God, for all my blessings. To my cherished son and husband for your unconditional love. With gratitude to my family and friends for your endless support. To Solomon, Jermaine, Merdella, Nesitta, Monica, and Percell. To my editor M.M. for always being brilliant. To M.H. and K.D. for your wonderful support.

---

1. http://www.ShadonnaRichards.blogspot.com

2. https://twitter.com/shadonna

Books by Shadonna Richards

THE ROMERO BROTHERS
The Billionaire's Second-Chance Bride, #1 (Antonio III & Lucy)
A Bride for the Billionaire Bad Boy, #2 (Lucas & Maxine)
The Playboy Billionaire, #3 (Zack & Blue)
The Billionaire's Island Romance, #3.5 (Christian & Arianna)
The Billionaire's Proposition, #4 (Carl & Venus)
The Billionaire's Baby, #5 (Jules & Amber)
The Billionaire's Assistant, #6 (Dion & Jenna-Lynn)
Snowbound with the Billionaire, #7 (Troy & Pamela)
The Billionaire's Marriage Proposal, #8 (Alonso & Britney)
BILLIONAIRES OF BELMONT (The Belmont Family)
The Billionaire's Bride for a Day #1 (Dane & Olivia)
The Billionaire's Promise #2 (Brandon & Faith)
The Billionaire's Housekeeper #3 (Chase & Abbi)
The Billionaire's Lost & Found Love #4 (Cole & Hope)
The Billionaire's Redemption #5 (Leo & Honesty)

THE BRIDE SERIES
An Unexpected Bride
The Jilted Bride
The Matchmaker Bride
His Island Bride (Free)
An Unexpected Baby *(The sequel to An Unexpected Bride)*
The Billionaire's Second Chance Bride
The Belmont Christmas Bride
THE BRIDE SERIES COLLECTION (Books 1-5 and other stories)
WHIRLWIND ROMANCE SERIES
Accidentally Flirting with the CEO (Free)
Accidentally Married to the Billionaire
Accidentally Falling for the Tycoon
Accidentally Flirting with the CEO 2
Accidentally Flirting with the CEO 3
THE BILLIONAIRE'S WHIRLWIND ROMANCE (Books 1-3)

PRAISE FOR THE ROMERO BROTHERS

The Romero brothers are perfect!! It's nice that they actually get to know each other before they jump in to bed with each other! Too many books now are just all about the naughty bits but these aren't, yes there are naughty bits going on but there's more of a story too! Zack in particular when he speaks with Blue, he is so seductive in normal conversation!! Three great stories lovely reads, will definitely read the rest!
–5-stars (AMZ) Reader Review

Anyone who has read Shadonna's series on the Romero family knows the guys are all super hot, successful, and upstanding citizens, even if rather commitment phobic. But Jenna-Lynn, her backstory was a surprise. Can't reveal too much without having to give a spoiler alert, so read the Billionaire's Assistant. It's another good one. I hope a boxed set is in her fans' future!
–5-stars (AMZ) Reader Review

I love the story line and how it kept you guessing. Who would've thought that Jenna would be who she was. You have your suspicions but the story was written so well that it kept you hanging. Great job. I can't wait for the next book just the first paragraphs of it have me drooling already. This is going to be a good one. :-) –5-stars (AMZ) Reader Review

I love this author. I love the series too. Definitely romance at its best. These guys are a woman's dream come true. Too bad they really don't exist, but it's still nice to dream. That's why I read.—
–5-stars (AMZ) Reader Review

I loved this book. It keeps you on edge!! And to top it off, gives you hope of happily ever after!!!! Must read –5-stars (AMZ) Reader Review

As usual Shadonna has met and supersedes my expectation I couldn't put it down –5-stars (AMZ) Reader Review

This is some very good reading..a great story line and some wonderful mystery..Not to mention some steamy Love making..I enjoyed...
–5-stars (AMZ) Reader Review

I loved this book. It keeps you on edge!! And to top it off, gives you hope of happily ever after!!!! Must read –5-stars (AMZ) Reader Review

This series is wonderful. I have bought every one of them, and they just keep getting better
–5-stars (AMZ) Reader Review

I really enjoyed this book. The characters were great and the story line was great. I couldn't put this book down until I finished it. I recommend this book to everyone. –5-stars (AMZ) Reader Review

I have been reading the Romero brothers series and everyone of the books hold my interest. Looking forward to the next book. –5-stars (AMZ) Reader Review

Suspense, family support, a proposal to be considered!!! If I were in Venus's situation, I would definitely seek the pleasure and say YES!!!
–5-stars (AMZ) Reader Review

Another GREAT story line!! Exceptional read with an amazing twist that keeps you wanting more!! Shadonna, you never disappoint. Alot of sizzling romance details that we all crave!!
–5-stars (AMZ) Reader Review

I've read all of the books in the Romero Series and they just keep getting better and better! Another heart warming love story! –5-stars (AMZ) Reader Review

I will always look forward to Shadonna's next love story! She writes from her heart and consistently comes up with interesting storylines.
–5-stars (AMZ) Reader Review

Very well written leaves you waiting to see how this family pulls together when one is in trouble a very lovely family –5-stars (AMZ) Reader Review

This whole series about the Romero Brothers is awesome! I hope the next book comes out very soon. The details are enticing and you feel as if you are there in the story. I read the entire book in one setting. I could not put it down until I finished the story –5-stars (AMZ) Reader Review

Loved this book and am loving the Romero brothers series. Roll on the last 2 books. Great story line, brill characters. Lost of sexual tension. A must read. –5-stars (AMZ) Reader Review

I am loving the Romero brothers series. Looking forward to the next book. They are very passionate, sexy and powerful men. I would happily marry any of them. –5-stars (AMZ) Reader Review

I loved this book as i have done all the others. Was hard to put it down until i had finished it. Brilliant Series and great Author. –5-stars (AMZ) Reader Review

What a man! I want me one! –5-stars GOODREADS reviewer

Enjoyed..have to read the entire series. –5-stars GOODREADS reviewer
What can I say but wow. Everyone wants a man to protect and defend them –5-stars GOODREADS
Hot!!!!! Read it twice. It makes me want to go to Jamaica now!!! Good descriptions. Wow i was surprised at the twist at the end. can't wait to read the next romero in the series. short but fun, fun read. –GOODREADS reviewer

Excellent – 5-stars (AMZ) Reader Review
I love how she created the family to be real and have hearts rather than pretentious little selfish rich boys! –5-stars (AMZ) Reader Review
The Romero Brothers books are fun, fast-paced romances. Each story featured a new couple and the main hero was one of the Romero Brothers. It was nice to see it all connected yet have each story remain separate. The Romero Brothers are hot, powerful, billionaires. The stories each have happy endings which I am a fan of! They are a perfect escape from the world.
– 5-stars (AMZ) Reader Review
I love the Romero Brothers series!!! Great story lines. Great family. I've enjoyed all the books in the series so far. It was nice to read the first three in the series in this box set. The stories are captivating with some page turning suspense thrown in. The characters are loveable and I love Granpa Toni. He's a ton of fun. The books have great supportive characters. The stories are well written.
–5-stars (AMZ) Reader Review

CONTENTS

THE BILLIONAIRE'S SECOND-CHANCE BRIDE (BOOK 1)
A BRIDE FOR THE BILLIONAIRE BAD BOY (BOOK 2)
THE PLAYBOY BILLIONAIRE (BOOK 3)
*THE BILLIONAIRE'S ISLAND ROMANCE (BOOK 3.5)
THE BILLIONAIRE'S PROPOSITION (BOOK 4)
THE BILLIONAIRE'S BABY (BOOK 5)
THE BILLIONAIRE'S ASSISTANT (BOOK 6)
SNOWBOUND WITH THE BILLIONAIRE (BOOK 7)
THE BILLIONAIRE'S MARRIAGE PROPOSAL (BOOK 8)

Dear Reader,

Welcome to The Romero Brothers, the hot series by USA Today bestselling author Shadonna Richards. They're hot, sexy, powerful and eligible! The wealthy, handsome bachelors of the Romero dynasty have had their share of heartbreak and tragedy, yet they make their waves in the trendiest industries. Come enjoy their journeys as each brother finds the right woman to tame his heart.

A special limited time offer! *Read all eight books in the popular series in one collection: The Billionaire's Second-Chance Bride, A Bride for the Billionaire Bad Boy, The Playboy Billionaire, The Billionaire's Proposition, The Billionaire's Baby, The Billionaire's Assistant, Snowbound with the Billionaire, and The Billionaire's Marriage Proposal.*

The Billionaire's Second-Chance Bride (The Romero Brothers, Book 1)

Betrayed by Mr. Wrong. Could she ever trust Mr. Right?

After losing her fiancé, Jeff, in a tragic accident (with his mistress!), Lucy Shillerton throws herself into running the company her eccentric aunt has left her: Dream Weddings Inc. Her current project is to present an outrageous wedding for her latest client, a wealthy, older tycoon who wants to marry his young nurse.

In comes sexy, rich, dripping-with-charm and sworn bachelor, Antonio Romero III, the grandson of said tycoon, who has a good reason to shut down Lucy's "scam wedding" business. However, when he meets with sweet, wounded Lucy, shutting her down is the last thing on his mind.

A Bride for the Billionaire Bad Boy (The Romero Brothers, Book 2)

She needs security...

When Maxine Summers took over Dream Weddings, Inc., her friend's former business, she had no idea what a nightmare she would have. It is believed a past disgruntled client is making attempts on her life and she can no longer return to her apartment. Feeling alone, Maxine has nowhere to turn—until the sexy, notorious bachelor, Lucas Romero, offers her a proposition. Her heart says yes, but her mind is saying "no way!"

He needs stability...

Scandal-ridden billionaire, Lucas Romero, knows his reputation with women could cost him everything he's worked for. He previously met Maxine when she helped plan his grandfather's remarriage, a fifth one at that, so when Lucas discovers she needs protection, he is all too willing to help. Except, falling in love was never a part of the arrangement.

Will Maxine be the one to tame his bad boy ways?

The Playboy Billionaire (The Romero Brothers, Book 3)

Blue Monroe needs to get her life together. The once-promising TV reporter was wrongfully fired by *Channel 31 News*, thanks to her jealous ex, and newly hired by the wealthy Romero family. She desperately needs this job. All she's got to do is keep out of sexy, hot playboy Zack's way and everything will be fine. Blue's got other things to worry about like putting food on the table, taking care of her younger sister and keeping her dark family secret secure.

Sexy philanthropist and playboy billionaire Zack Romero's seductive past may soon catch up with him. Skilled in his taste for fine wine as well as fine women, he does a smooth job of running the Romero family's prestigious award-winning winery and vineyard. But his world is soon rocked when a scandalous sex-tape with an ex-girlfriend threatens to surface. Zack's grandfather and the Romero patriarch, Toni's ultimatum...control his love life! No sex for at least thirty days! But when Zack is forced to hire Blue Monroe to work closely with him to produce a documentary for the vineyard, will it be sour grapes or a sweet pairing from heaven?

The Billionaire's Island Romance (The Romero Brothers, Book 3.5)

Bonus Short Novella featuring Zack and Blue's Island Wedding!

A romance, hotter than the island sun...

Coming from one of the world's wealthiest and most influential families, the Romeros, Christian Romero knows better than to turn down an invitation to a mega family reunion in Jamaica for his cousin's wedding. The family is gathering at the exclusive Duponte Hotel & Resort in Montego Bay for the highly anticipated nuptials of former playboy billionaire Zack Romero and ex-reporter Blue Monroe. Christian's ex-girlfriend, Arianna Duponte, who walked out on him over a month ago just when things were getting hot, happens to be the general manager of the five-star palace resort where the family is gathering. No woman has ever turned him down before. Yet, sweet Arianna wasn't just any woman. She'd given him her virginity and he'd given her his heart. So what went wrong? Will this be a bitter reunion or a better opportunity to find out if there are truly second chances?

Arianna Duponte has always had a special place in her heart for sexy, hot Christian Romero, her first true love, but getting close to him would be too risky given her past and a scandalous family secret. She refuses to break his heart again. She tries to keep her distance while preparing for the big Romero wedding but it's not as easy as it looks. As the wedding bells echo in the sultry island air, will they rekindle the union they once had?

The Billionaire's Proposition (The Romero Brothers, Book 4)

Sworn bachelor and sexy charismatic billionaire, Carl Romero, needs to find himself a wife and child before he announces his run for mayor—but only for a one-year commitment. He's determined to win in the next election but being a young, single man is his only obstacle to gaining the voters' confidence. In politics, image is everything. He has his eyes set on his delightful executive assistant, a single mom, Venus Jackson. His troubles compound when he realizes winning votes isn't all he wants, so is winning Venus's heart.

Struggling single parent, Venus Jackson, has a dark secret in her past and too much emotional baggage. She simply can't handle any more drama in her life, but when her irresistible boss, Carl, offers her a proposition to play his doting wife for one year as he embarks on a political career, her mind is telling her to run the other way, yet her heart is pulling her in his charming direction.

The Billionaire's Baby (The Romero Brothers, Book 5)

Pregnant and alone, Amber Johnson-Murray, aka "Miss Always-Careful," never in her life thought she'd end up single while expecting a child. After leaving an emotionally abusive relationship, she has sworn off men until further notice. That is, until she bumps into an old friend, hot and delicious property developer, Jules Romero. The baby growing inside her is a precious miracle. But how can she control the feelings growing inside her for too-hot-to-handle Jules?

High-flying billionaire Jules Romero is determined to bury himself in his work acquiring properties after suffering injuries from a near-fatal accident, but meeting up with sweet Amber has thrown a kink in his plans. Though Amber is determined to keep the identity of her baby's real father a secret, he wants nothing more than to take care of Amber and her child.

The Billionaire's Assistant (The Romero Brothers, Book 6)

When it rains, it pours. Swoon-worthy billionaire bad boy Dion Romero knows this all too well. It's bad enough to get thrown into a crisis that threatens the survival of Rom International, one of his lucrative business interests, but now a frivolous lawsuit by an ex-girlfriend who worked with him has surfaced. He needs to focus on getting his business in order and keep as far away as possible from women. The trouble is, he's falling hard for his wonderful new assistant, Jenna. She's a sweet and innocent, yet deadly distraction to his heart. But he's finding she's too irresistible to avoid.

Jenna-Lynn Macchiasso knows what it means to have a crushed heart and suffer betrayal from those close to her so she no longer has men on her agenda. But her new oh, so sexy boss Dion Romero is giving her a run for her money. The secrets of her past make her life too complicated for her to get close to another man. What should she do? Forfeit her mission to her work, or forfeit her heart's desire?

Snowbound with The Billionaire (The Romero Brothers, Book 7)

Baby, it's cold outside...

Pamela Alvarado, the Romero family's loyal press secretary, finally plucks up the courage to tell her deliciously gorgeous eligible boss, Troy Romero, how she truly feels about him. But when she goes to share her feelings with him one evening, she bumbles into a humiliating and heartbreaking situation when she learns that he's...getting married!

But it's warm in here...

Sexy billionaire philanthropist, Troy Romero, is reluctantly entering into a loveless marriage to spoiled heiress, Cilla de Montagio, so she can keep her fortune. Yet it is his faithful, yet feisty, press secretary, Pamela, who really has his heart. So, stranded in a blizzard during a power outage with Pamela over the holiday season can only spell trouble. The blizzard brings the chill, but it looks as if Pamela will melt Troy's defenses. Now he's got one heck of a storm brewing inside him, too. Does he fulfill his obligation to the heiress who once saved his life, or does he follow his heart to the woman of his desire?

The Billionaire's Marriage Proposal (The Romero Brothers, Book 8)

Sexy, tall, dark and handsome Dr. Alonso Romero was scarred in childhood from losing those close to him, including his first girlfriend, to whom he'd proposed marriage. When she died, he took that as a sign he should never marry. Losing a loved one hurt too much. His remedy? Never get close to another woman—and never wed. To his tycoon grandfather, Toni Romero, Alonso is the only disappointment in the family who has not tied the knot and settled down like his other once-professed bachelor brothers. But that's just fine with Alonso, until...

Beautiful and feisty street nurse, Britney Andropolous, walks into Alonso's office late one night and straight into his heart. She's on the run from a dangerous past. He wants to help her but the trouble is, he's falling for her. Will he keep his distance and his declaration to never get close? Or will Britney's dainty curves and warm heart melt Alonso's defenses?

THE BILLIONAIRE'S SECOND-CHANCE BRIDE (The Romero Brothers, Book 1)

ROMERO FAMILY TREE

Antonio Romero, Sr. (5th marriage to) Shelly Munro

/
Antonio Romero II (deceased) m. Ruby Ann Devereaux
> Antonio Romero III (m. Lucy Shillerton)
- Alexander

Jack Romero m. Janissa Milano (deceased)
> Lucas Romero (m. Maxine Summers)
- Mary-Louise
> Zack Romero (m. Blue Monroe)
- Jefferson
> Carl Romero (m. Venus Jackson)
- Tristan
- Daniel
> Jules Romero (m. Amber Johnson-Murray)
- Crystal
> Dion Romero (m. Jenna-Lynn Greene)
- Cherry-Rose
> Troy Romero (m. Pamela Alvarado)
- Janissa Marie
> Dr. Alonso Romero (m. Britney Andropoulos)
- Joshua Elijah

George Romero
> *No known children*

Santos Romero
> *No known children*

PROLOGUE

"Four children. Eight grandchildren. All successful college grads and professionals yet no great-grandchildren. No wedding invitations on the horizon. What is wrong with this picture?" Antonio Romero, Sr. wasted no time in chastising his grandchildren as they were seated in the cozy study of Romero Manor on the grand Romero Estate.

Seated in his temporary wheelchair, Antonio, Sr. looked out at the verdant garden through the French doors of the study. He had gathered the group for a family meeting to discuss his wishes following his fall down the marble staircase the previous week. He was lucky to have survived the ordeal. He had just finished riding his horse and had gone inside the mansion to change. Eager to get going to a meeting, the eldest Antonio lost his balance and toppled right on over the hard stone of the stairwell. His bones were fortunately strong but apparently not strong enough.

His nurse Shelly had just finished changing his dressing on his knee when the meeting was called.

"Grandfather, you know it's not that simple. We don't want to just bring anybody into the family," Antonio Romero, III, his grandson, chimed in. He leaned over by the fireplace with his elbow resting on the counter. He had just finished work in the city of Toronto and flew in by helicopter and landed on the family property. The Romero estate was situated two hours from Toronto and was a four-hour drive from Buffalo, New York. They truly had the best of both worlds. The family owned real estate across the globe-buildings, skyscrapers, clubs, restaurants and hotels but the real estate Antonio, Sr. had in mind was the property located within the heart. When would his scions ever settle down and provide heirs for the Romero dynasty? It was a coincidental disaster that none of his eight grandchildren from four different children had settled down with anyone.

In addition to being philanthropists and mighty good-looking young men, if the patriarch may say so himself, the boys were gifted in their own areas of expertise. Antonio III was highly successful in property development, while Lucas founded a highly in-demand app and software for the medical industry. Zack owned and ran the vineyard and winery, while Carl and Jules operated world-renowned fitness centers. Dion and Troy were leaders in the global online educational community, and Alonso, a top med school graduate, opened medical clinics around the world. All talented trendsetters. But were any of them hitched? Not even close. They dated plenty and often made headlines in the tabloids but if only Antonio, Sr. could get them married off before he put one foot in the grave. If only.

Were the Romeros blessed with success in business while cursed in love as to their personal lives?

No.

Antonio, Sr. refused, absolutely objected to any notion to believe that.

"Baggage, Gramps. A lot of girls have baggage these days," Lucas added as he fiddled with the display on his smartphone.

"That's rubbish. I know you've been heartbroken before and for that I am sorry. I've had broken bones many times in my life but that's nothing compared to a broken heart. The bones heal faster, I agree," Antonio, Sr. rebutted. "But you will never be happy if you continue focusing on the terrible things you've gone through and judge everyone as if they've hurt you. You'll find whatever you look for in life, grandson. Remember that. Too many times you see a nice young woman or a girl in her thirties and you assume the worst. You look for the worst. And trust me, you will find it. Everyone has something unfavorable about them, but they also have redeeming qualities. If you keep thinking something's wrong with people, you'll end up alone. And that would sadden me immensely."

The old man continued, breathing hard.

"You should probably rest now, Mr. Romero," Shelly urged.

"No. I'm not finished yet," he declared, waving her off before turning again to his grandchildren. "Stop trying to find the perfect soul mate and start trying to think of ways you can *be* the perfect soul mate to someone else. I'm telling you this for a good reason. You don't want to end up alone in your advanced age because you're looking for someone who will never exist. A flawless human being. Heck, you are my grandchildren and I love you more than I love anything else, but you sure as heck aren't flawless either. Nor am I. I've been married so many times already. People aren't perfect, but love…love is. A woman may not be perfect but that doesn't mean she won't be perfect for you. Your other half. The yin to your yang. Give love a chance."

"Sorry to interrupt," Shelly said, looking at Antonio, Sr. Her voice sounded urgent. "There's a call for you, Toni." Shelly often addressed Antonio, Sr. by his short name. "It's the secretary from the Dream Weddings agency. She called to remind us of our upcoming consultation."

"Consultation?" Antonio III interjected, obviously perplex. "What is that about, Granddad? Consultation? Dream Weddings?" He shifted his position from the fireplace and stood erect. A fierce expression on his face.

Antonio, Sr. sighed. "Yes, that's right, boys. I don't just talk the talk, I walk the walk. And I'll be taking that walk right down the aisle. I didn't want you boys to find out this way, but as you know, I'm quite fond of Shelly here, and well, life is too short—for me, life could be shorter still. We have been spending a great deal of time together, and so, Shelly and I are getting married."

Antonio III's body stiffened in response. Shock, and a hint of horror, filled his dark eyes. But Antonio, Sr. did not wait for his grandson's reply.

"I'll be taking this call in the den. If you will excuse me," Antonio, Sr. concluded. And with those final words, he walked away, accompanied by his new fiancée, to the disbelief of his grandsons.

CHAPTER ONE

"We're being sued for *how* much?" Lucy Shillerton asked over the speakerphone. Her jaw fell open. She could feel the air being sucked out of her lungs. She dared not take a breath.

"Twelve million dollars." The voice sounded cold on the other end of the phone.

Lucy closed her eyes and placed her hand on her forehead. Her heartbeat pounded fiercely in her throat.

Twelve million dollars? My life is so over.

She was dead.

She was so dead and it wasn't even funny.

She could not believe her burning ears. Her company could never recover from a civil suit of that magnitude. Heck, it couldn't recover from a twelve *thousand* dollar suit. Her insurance alone would fly through the roof! Lucy hunched her shoulders as she sat down in her leather chair at Dream Weddings Inc. Welcome to your new, and possibly the last, job as its CEO.

It hadn't been six months since her eccentric late aunt left her the business in her will to take over and Lucy barely knew said auntie. And now?

How in God's name had she gotten herself into this business?

Why didn't she contest her aunt's will?

For all she knew, Lucy didn't even believe in the institution of marriage. Her own father had left her mother for his secretary when Lucy was in her teens. Later, her mother, who had suffered from a rare congenital heart defect, died of a broken heart. Then, just when Lucy was about to embark on happiness with Jeff Samuels, her first and only love, he perished in a car crash two years ago—along with his mistress, apparently. So much for happy endings. It seemed as if Dream Weddings was nothing more than nightmare weddings for her now.

"Okay, let me get this straight. We're being sued by the bride *and* groom-"

"No, dear. The parents of the bride *and* the parents of the groom are suing the company for endangerment."

"But it was *their* dream wedding. We warned them about the dangers of bungee jumping off a bridge while screaming their vows. It's all written in the disclaimer, Mr. Petri. We can't possibly be liable. I'm truly sorry that the bungee jump off the bridge didn't go as planned but-"

"Sorry, Lucy. You're a sweet girl. You really are but such are the dangers of running a business like Dream Weddings. These days brides and sometimes the grooms want to go all out to have the most unusual adventurous nuptials, and they don't think about the consequences or the risks involved."

Lucy was beset with a massive headache at that moment. She rubbed her throbbing temples while talking on the speakerphone of her new corner office. The headquarters of Weddings Inc. was situated near the lake on Front Street in Toronto's artsy business district. The loft-style office was on the top floor of a four-story building and had the shiniest hardwood flooring she'd ever stepped on. The walls were adorned with the coolest artwork she'd ever seen. Apparently, her elusive actually great-aunt, who really knew how to decorate, had won some lottery draw in the province and invested in helping others secure the weddings of their dreams. The company was previously called Weird Weddings Inc., then it was changed to Have It Your Way Weddings, but her aunt received some sound legal advice about changing its name. If Lucy could have it her own way, she wouldn't even be in this situation right now.

This whole scenario was getting weirder by the moment.

Regardless, Lucy would always be eternally grateful to her aunt for sending her some of her winnings so that she could secure her own place and finish her studies. That was so kind of her, even if they weren't close. Her aunt was ever-so-elusive and travelled considerably. The saving grace was that her aunt's assistant, Maxine Summers, who knew the business very well, still stayed on after Lucy took over.

It wasn't as if Lucy currently had much of a life. She wasn't in touch with her father, had very few friends and rarely went out. She recently graduated with her Masters in Philosophy and Psychology and was about to complete her PhD. Since teaching jobs at area universities were scarce it seemed like a blessing in disguise at the time to have this opportunity to turn over her aunt's business and perhaps complete her studies later.

At twenty-nine, Lucy wasn't exactly a social animal but she really needed to get a life. A proper one.

"Okay, fine. I will get in touch with my lawyer, Mr. Petri, and someone will get back to you on that one." After Lucy hung up the phone she rubbed her temples again.

"Girl, you are not having a good day, are you?" Her assistant, Maxine, walked in as if on cue after she'd disconnected the phone call. Maxine juggled two steaming lattes in her hands.

Thank God for Maxine!

"Thanks, Maxine," Lucy said and took one of the cups from her assistant. Maxine always knew what to get Lucy when she really needed it.

"Oh, no worries, Lucy."

Maxine plopped in the chair in front of Lucy and surveyed her. She was five-ten and had dark hair with a touch of blue and blond highlights and wore a pencil dress with tights and thick dark-rimmed glasses. Her long hair was pulled up into a ponytail. She was fun to work with and catty enough when she needed to be to keep Lucy on track and full of valuable knowledge about the business. Of late, Maxine was in talks with the Home network. She was trying to secure a spot so their business could do a segment on one of its popular reality TV shows, but Lucy could not even entertain that thought with the recent chaos in her life. Yes, she had other proverbial fish to fry.

"You sure you're okay?" Maxine continued. "You really don't look too good."

"Maxine, I...I don't know what to do. Was this what Aunt Chris went through every day?" She gave her left temple a break from massaging and picked up the latte and took a sip of the warm, smooth drink. Its rich, creamy texture melted down Lucy's throat and soothed her inside. That was just what she needed.

"Oh, every day, girl."

"Okay, that's all I needed to know." Lucy hadn't had a chance to go through all the paperwork when she took over. Mr. Petri, the part-time business manager and bookkeeper, had only informed her of her current contracts that had to be fulfilled but still went through other business matters and tax documents that needed to be processed.

"What do you mean by that?" Maxine placed her latte on the table and pulled out her iPad.

"Aunt Chris must have really hated me."

Maxine chuckled. "Really, I don't think it's that bad, honey. Besides, this business really gave your aunt a lot of love."

"Yeah, I'll bet."

"You know what your problem is?"

"Oh, boy! Yes, Dr. Phil?"

"No seriously, girl. When *was* the last time you got laid?"

"Maxine!"

"No, really. Have you even been on a date this century?" Maxine playfully arched a brow.

"Um...when was the last time *you* got...some?" Lucy shot back, knowing full well Maxine hadn't been on a date as long as she had.

Maxine shot her a playful scorn. She reminded Lucy of the little sister she never had. When things got stressful around the office, Maxine was always there to lighten the mood and remind her not to take herself too seriously all the time. It just wasn't worth it.

"Besides, you know I was engaged two years ago," Lucy's voice trailed off as she continued. The memory was way too painful to conjure up right now. The conversation was going to a darker place she'd rather not revisit.

"Sorry, Lucy. I totally forgot. But listen, just because you lost love, it doesn't mean you can't go out and find someone else who would really appreciate you."

"Maxine, you're a sweetheart. Ever the romantic enthusiast. But seriously, I've learned that marriage is not for everyone." And boy, did Lucy really mean it. It hadn't worked out for her own parents, and although her heart still ached over losing Jeff in such a horrific accident, he *was* with another woman at the time. Imagine that! He was with his mistress. Apparently, according to news reports, they were in a compromising position, both partially undressed below the waist in the car, when the collision occurred. Jeff was definitely distracted when that accident occurred.

Lucy squeezed her eyes shut as if to push that horrific scene out of her mind.

No. I will not go back into the past. It's gone. The past is gone. I will not let the past hurt me. It's gone. I will live in the present and dream about the future.

At least that was what months of therapy had taught her during that time period.

She had to move forward. But Maxine, as well-meaning as she was, was wrong about marriage. It really wasn't for everyone. And it certainly wasn't for her. Okay, so she'd create dream betrothals for other people but that was as far as it would go for her. No dream weddings for Lucy Shillerton. No way in hell.

"Okay, now tell me about the outstanding contracts my aunt left…I mean, that we at Dream Weddings have left," Lucy corrected herself.

Maxine started fingering across the screen of her iPad and pulled up a few files. She sure was quick with her fingers on the tablet. Thank God for technology. It wasn't long ago Lucy remembered digging through stuff in a regular file cabinet and pulling out stacks of paper files on documents she needed at one of her old summer jobs.

"Okay, so we have at least three or four left and then we can take that much needed break that you so crave, girlfriend," Maxine said.

Lucy grabbed her old-fashioned notepad and braced herself to take notes.

"Okay, what have you got?" Lucy prompted Maxine.

"Right now, we have Debbie and Luke."

"And their wedding theme is…?" Lucy asked, taking another sip of her coffee.

"Mud-style wedding."

Lucy spewed her coffee all over the desk.

"Girl, you okay?" Maxine got up and immediately went around the table to pat Lucy on the back as she choked.

"I'm good," Lucy said after she composed herself. "Mud. Style. Wedding?"

"Yeah, it's supposed to be a popular theme."

Lucy sighed.

"Listen, I've got to be heading out soon," Maxine said. "Got a dentist appointment and I don't want to miss this one."

"Okay, who are the other wedding contracts?" Lucy asked quietly sucking in a deep breath. *Breathe, Lucy. It'll be okay. Just breathe. You are granting wishes here. It's not about you, it's about these wonderful people who want a chance at a happily-ever-after. And who could fault them, right? Maybe a little thing called…fate!*

"Well," Maxine continued, leaning back in the chair with a grin. "Crystal and Randy, who still don't have a theme, but they want us to decide."

"Really?"

"Really."

For some reason, Lucy felt a small sense of relief. She thought of doing a risk-free romantic celebration.

"If you want, I can take that one over." Maxine raised a brow with a wicked grin on her face.

"Okay, Maxine. I know it's always been your dream, so..." Lucy breathed in then exhaled calmly. "We'll do that one together. Okay?"

Maxine frowned. "Fine."

"What's the timeline on these?"

"Well, the mud-style is in two months and the unknown one is in two and a half months."

"Great!"

"We're not done yet, hon."

"We're not?"

"Nope."

Maxine suppressed another wicked grin.

"Okay, Maxine. Cough it up."

"Antonio Romero, that wealthy real-estate tycoon."

"Romero? Romero Realty? No. Way."

Maxine nodded slyly. "Yes. Way. And he'll be the biggest client your aunt ever secured. God rest her soul."

"Wow. I don't believe it. But wait a minute. Isn't he like, ninety?"

"Not quite. He's seventy-six." Maxine paused for a moment. "But he looks fit for his age and does scuba diving and stuff like that. Oh, this dude is young at heart. He's got the body of a forty-nine-year-old. You know—like Joseph Pilates had."

Lucy leaned back and relaxed in her soft-leather seat of her executive chair. Finally. A safe wedding. So, what could they do for a sweet elderly man and his equally senior bride? Perhaps they were both widowed and wanted a second chance at love. Maybe Dream Weddings could set up a romantic, authentic forties-style old Hollywood wedding theme from the era of the silver screen. That would be appropriate.

"Have they chosen a theme?" Lucy asked eagerly.

"Fun Birds!"

"Huh!" Okay, Lucy did not see that one coming. "Fun Birds?"

Maxine nodded emphatically. "It's sort of like Angry Birds, only it's not!"

Lucy could not imagine two seventy-something-year-olds having a Fun Bird wedding. "Okay, you've lost me. Exactly *how* are we going to do this?" Lucy leaned forward in her chair and pressed her elbows on her desk.

"Well, the bride wants to meet her groom at the altar by way of a human-sized slingshot."

Lucy thought she was going to collapse. "Just...*how* old is this bride?" *Or how young?*

"Forty-six."

Lucy flopped back in her chair and placed her palms on the edge of the desk. She pinched her lips to either stifle a hysterical laugh ... or a hysterical cry.

"Okay." She nodded and hunched her shoulders. This was about the couples. This was about granting wishes to happy couples. "Okay," she said again quietly.

"Are you sure you're not having a meltdown?"

"Yep. Yep. I'm...sure. I think. Have fun at the dentist, Maxine. See you in the morning."

"Um. Tomorrow is Saturday."

"Right. See you Monday, Maxine."

Maxine grinned and got up slowly. She grabbed her iPad and coffee and proceeded to walk about but paused at the door. "You know, Lucy. For what it's worth, I'm proud of you."

"You are? Why?" Lucy asked.

"For not contesting Chris's will. She was an odd one at times but this business meant the world to her. She was able to make dreams come true for people just like her, I guess. You're sort of cool. I thought you were some prude Miss Proper who was going to sell this company to the highest bidder and here you are..." Maxine seemed as if she was going to be teary-eyed but Lucy could tell she was only teasing her. "Doing your best to make this work. Kudos to you, girlfriend." She strode out of Lucy's office.

Lucy smiled and shook her head. She glanced at the clock on her computer screen and it was almost four-thirty in the afternoon. The young receptionist outside her door would be leaving soon, too. Lucy continued her aunt's tradition of letting employees leave earlier than five o'clock on Fridays.

Just then the receptionist buzzed her office.

"Yes, Darla?" Lucy called out over the speakerphone intercom.

"You have an appointment, Lucy."

"I do? I thought I was all clear for the afternoon." This was the last thing Lucy wanted to hear. She was looking forward to going home early on this Friday after a hectic week at the office and soak in a nice aroma-therapy Epsom salt-soothing bath, sipping champagne to celebrate that she was still alive after a crazy week. Heck, just celebrating breathing.

"You have a Mr. Antonio Romero here to see you," Darla answered back over the intercom.

Antonio Romero? Antonio Romero? Lucy glanced down at her notepad. *Holy shit! The seventy-six- year-old tycoon with the Fun Birds themed wedding!*

"Right. Please send him in, Darla."

"Will do."

Lucy straightened out her skirt, which had ridden up while she was seated. She looked as if she'd just worked a busy workday but she knew how respectable she needed to look for her clients, especially the elderly ones who were used to prim and proper back in the day. When the door swung open, Lucy's jaw fell wide open.

Lucy was stunned, dazed, confused.

Standing before her was the most gorgeous, possibly six-foot, dark-tanned and sexy as hell *young* man she'd ever seen in her life. He was dressed in a stunning, expensive-looking suit that seemed to complement his obvious muscular frame and broad shoulders. He had dark, silky cropped hair and deep, rich dark eyes and high chiseled cheekbones. He was to die for. She wasn't good with ages but he sure as hell was nowhere near seventy-six. There must have been a mistake. The other thing Lucy noticed was that Mr. Drop-Dead-Sexy was not smiling. He appeared not in a good mood. He glared at her through dangerously dark eyes framed with the longest lashes she'd ever seen on a man.

"Mr. Romero?" Lucy queried, still stunned!

"I'm his grandson, Antonio."

Oh. My. God. "You're Antonio Romero the third?" Lucy extended her hand then quickly withdrew it when she saw his jaw was clenched. *Did he bite?*

"I'm sorry, I thought it was your grandfather. We're not allowed to discuss contracts with anyone other than the client and his or her spokesperson, sir."

"Miss Shillerton, I'll make this short. I know you're probably as pressed for time as I am but I want you to cancel this wedding of my grandfather's. And I want you to do it pronto."

"What?" Lucy almost fell over. *Who does he think he is?* "What are you talking about?"

"I'm aware you took over the business from your aunt and I appreciate what you are trying to do." Antonio sounded more curt and authoritative, if that was possible. "But I will pay you any amount of money for your inconvenience to prevent my grandfather from making the biggest mistake of his life."

"Do tell. What makes you think he's making a mistake?" Lucy was growing hotter by the second. Was the heat climbing in the office all of a sudden—or was it the tension between them? It wasn't merely the fact that this bossy man just barged into her office uttering commands for her to follow but, yeah, he was hot as hell. *Focus, Lucy. Focus.*

Lucy fought hard to keep her composure but it wasn't easy when someone so good-looking and sinfully sexy was distracting your professional thoughts. "L-l-listen. My clients *are* my business. I'm sorry you are having family issues but-"

"Family issues?" Antonio repeated as he shoved his hands in his tailored pants pockets, swiftly pacing side to side in her office. Oh, she caught the soothing scent of his delicious cologne and it stirred some naughty feelings inside her. He smelled good! She noticed the way he moved. Powerful. Manly. It *had* been too long since she'd been with someone. Maxine was right.

Focus, Lucy. Focus.

"This has nothing to do with family issues, Ms. Shillerton. This is my grandfather's life and I'm protecting him from some two-bit gold digger."

"Gold digger?"

"Are you planning on echoing every select word I speak, Ms. Shillerton, or do you plan on following through on my wishes?"

"I'm sorry, Mr. Romero." Hell, even his name sounded sexy. It just rolled around and off her tongue. Mmmm. "But your grandfather is my concern. I work for him and his bride-to-be. We're here to make *his* dream wedding come true and who are we to tell him he can't have it or to tell him he can't fall in love? Besides, why didn't *you* tell him to call it off?"

For a moment, Antonio paused. He locked gaze with Lucy causing a wave of hot emotions to spring through her body. She was shivering inside. Holy cow! No man had ever had that effect on her body. And just from one look. There certainly was some sort of indescribable magnetic pull between them. She just couldn't quite pinpoint it. This man oozed sexual power and something else.

He pulled his gaze from her and left her cold for a moment. How odd. He glared her as if undressing her with his eyes but then he stopped himself and regained his composure.

"I did," he admitted curtly. "I asked him to halt this foolishness and come to his senses but your agency had already convinced him that this was the best decision he was making. You need to undo this! You have until the end of next week to call this thing off. This is not a request. It is an order." He spoke so calmly and quietly and so deadly cool that Lucy's knees weakened and almost buckled.

What the hell was that about?

Antonio Romero, III, the hot and sexy grandson of her client uttered some sort of ultimatum and stormed out of her office as quickly as he'd blown in.

The end of next week?

What would this man do to her then?

CHAPTER TWO

Moments later, Antonio headed to his BMW parked outside the headquarters of Dream Weddings Inc. What just happened? His intention was to really put Ms. Shillerton in her place for taking his vulnerable grandfather's money and planning some high-risk, embarrassing wedding that would probably aggravate his grandfather's heart condition but he just couldn't.

That was so unlike Antonio.

Antonio was always a man in control. And he'd seen plenty of beautiful women in his lifetime and dated the most eligible high-society bachelorettes, but Lucy Shillerton? Damn! She was stunning!

She had almost thrown him off balance. Good thing Antonio caught himself and got back on track with his demands. Antonio slid into the driver's seat of his car with his jaw clenched. No way in hell was he about to be that easily distracted by a pretty face. A beautiful face.

He thought back to her smooth-looking, tanned skin and her large, brown, beautiful eyes framed by long lashes, her high cheekbones and well-defined, full lips that looked so damned kissable. Her long, dark hair looked so silky he was almost tempted to reach over the desk and run his fingers through it.

When she rose to greet him, Antonio noticed she was nicely filled out. She had optimal proportions. Lucy didn't look like some of those malnourished and boney models he'd seen. She had the hour-glass shape. Small waist, shapely hips and a full bosom. He was an expert at detecting boob jobs. She, thankfully, had no sign of plastic surgery that he could discern. Lucy was the real deal. But it wasn't just her physical assets, it was her aura. Yes, that's what it was. Her aura.

Antonio could tell there was something sweet and humble about Lucy. The way she extended her hand so sincerely, and despite his coarse introduction, she retreated humbly and recomposed herself. She didn't seem to hint at all at having an attitude or being hostile. Antonio could not be sure, of course, but he was often right in his assessments of people he'd meet.

"Start car," Antonio commanded in a deep, forceful voice using his sophisticated voice-control engine-start system. The engine of his luxury vehicle promptly revved. He then navigated his way through the streets of downtown Toronto towards his high-rise condominium near the waterfront.

Still, his mind was on pretty Ms. Lucy Shillerton. He'd caught the fact that her ring finger was completely bare and had no sign of a ring ever being on it.

So there was a strong possibility that she was *available*.

Just then a tone rung from the speakers of his vehicle.

"You have a call from...Lucas," the disembodied female voice stated through his speaker.

"Answer," Antonio directed. He was still deep in thought, but he could take a call from his cousin and business associate.

"Hey, man. You okay?" Lucas Romero's voice pierced the speakerphone.

"Just a little distracted right now. I'm on the road."

"I see," Lucas hesitated at first. "Listen, I just wanted to check on the latest with our granddad. Any news? He's still not going through with the crazy wedding, is he?"

"Not if I can help it," Antonio answered coldly.

"Did you speak to the people at the agency to get them to stop it?"

"Not quite. I got...a bit distracted. But I gave her an ultimatum."

"*Her*?" Lucas sounded surprised. "*Ultimatum*?"

"Yes, it's a young woman who has apparently taken over from her late aunt who owned this agency. They grant wishes to couples to put on interesting wedding ceremonies."

"But you told them they can't go through with it, right?"

"I gave her till next Friday to break it to him gently ... or else."

"Or else what?" Lucas paused. "What a minute. Is she cute?"

"Lucas." Antonio's tone was sharper than he had intended but he was so not going there. Usually, he would entertain his playboy cousin's juvenile sense of humor but he wasn't in the mood for it now.

So why had his crotch jumped when Lucas pried as to whether Lucy was cute? Just thinking about Lucy made Antonio hard. Because she was hot as hell. He'd never seen anyone so stunning, so naturally beautiful. And then there was that sweet perfume she was wearing. What was it called? Angel? Yes, she certainly *was* an angel. How fitting.

Damn! Why did Lucy have to be so good looking in every way? That would only serve to complicate matters. Antonio was a man who usually focused on a mission and got it done. Period. But Lucy Shillerton was proving to be a distraction already and he hadn't even known her long.

Still, he had to shift his focus back on track to his grandfather. The old man meant the world to him and he sure as hell wasn't going to let some broad in her forties take his grandfather to the cleaners and leave him cold.

Antonio has had his own share of gold diggers in the past. Every society woman he'd ever met wanted to date him or would take "selfies" on their smartphones if they were with him. Subsequently, they would post to their Instagram accounts or Facebook pages with captions of "me and my boo" or something childish like that. Or "out with my baby on a date." Those women would often give the impression that something serious was going on between them when he was only there at a party or event and even though they may know each other, there was nothing going on between them. The only way he'd found out was through his cousin Lucas who happened to be a social networking fanatic and would happily flirt with women online, exchanging hot poses of themselves.

Mind you, Lucas happened to go into one of the women's online albums and saw a picture of Antonio there and promptly alerted him. That was another reason why Antonio wasn't a huge fan of some social media sites. In fact, he tried to stay off the Internet most times unless he truly had to be "connected." Business was crazy enough with him. He'd left all that online work to his associates or the assistants who worked in his organization.

"Now that I have you on the phone," Antonio continued, "how is that deal going with the community center?"

"Oh, that?" Lucas changed his tone. "Well, we still have a ways to go before we can get the green light. Something about zoning issues in the area. Everything is on schedule otherwise, so we'll make the deadline."

"Right. Keep me abreast if anything changes."

"Will do, cuz, but I am sure we are fine."

"And did you get any more information on this Shelly character?"

"Oh, right. The lovely lady who will be our forty-six-year-old step-grandmother."

Antonio was thirty-three years old so he cringed at the thought of having a grandmother thirteen years older than he was. "Lucas. Enough of that!"

"Sorry, cuz. Yeah, she's coming up all clean so far."

"Well, no information doesn't mean she's in the clear yet. I want to know what forty-six-year-old would want to marry a seventy-six-year-old man. End of story."

"Gotcha."

"Besides, Granddad's not doing so well and this would be his fifth marriage. We know how the others ended after Grandmother passed away."

"I know. They took him to the cleaners every time. It's amazing he still has any assets left. Don't worry, cuz. We'll protect our grandfather from any more heartbreak."

"The thing what bothers me the most is that I don't think he realizes what he's getting himself into. He only just met this woman three months ago."

"Well, she *is* his nurse, cuz."

"Yes, I know. But she is also aware that he has that heart condition. Any unnecessary excitement and that would be it for him."

"I know," Lucas agreed.

"Keep your men on it, Lucas. I want to find out everything about this woman and how she got to know Lucy Shillerton and this Dream Weddings company. I want to find out if there is a connection. Something is not adding up and I don't like loose ends."

"I hear ya, man!"

After Antonio finished his phone conversation he pulled up at one of his glass condominium high-rise buildings. He had already inherited his share of the Romero Realty from his own father but had merged it with his own investment firm and created his own corporation. It wasn't like him to pull himself away from his work, but after hearing that his grandfather was going to tie the knot with a woman old enough, or young enough, to be his granddaughter, Antonio gave his right-hand person and chief administrative officer, Mariam, the go-ahead to take charge of his affairs for a while as he tended to "personal business."

He was going to focus his energies on making sure no harm came to his grandfather. None what so ever. The doorman nodded to Antonio as he entered the marble lobby of his building. "Good afternoon, sir."

Antonio absentmindedly nodded back while taking out his smartphone. He couldn't wait until he got upstairs to his suite. There was something he had to Google and fast. As he entered the private area where his own personal elevator would bring him to his penthouse waited, he moved his fingers fast across the screen in the search box and typed in "Lucy Shillerton, Toronto, CEO."

And sure enough, hundreds of sites popped up. He tried to see if she was on Facebook or LinkedIn. He went to her Facebook page to see if she had left it open for anyone to see who was on the system. Since he'd already logged in he should have no trouble if it was not private. Sure enough, there she was. She posted a beautiful photo for her profile picture yet it was not recent. The photo looked as if it was a few years old. Maybe from her college days. There was that reaction again. The cloth covering his groin area grew snug. Why on earth did that girl have that kind of effect on him? This was all too crazy. He wasn't looking her up to stalk her. He was trying to see if he could see her Friends list to see if she knew Shelly, his grandfather's new fiancée. Lucy had 127 friends and most of them were women. He scanned her page to see if she was one of those women who took selfies of themselves posing in sexy photos. None. Good. She wasn't a complete tart.

Why was he even going there? This was about business. This was about keeping his grandfather safe from scammers after his fortune. After all, his grandfather had made some Top 100 Wealthiest billionaire list some time this year, so it was only natural he would be concerned about gold diggers popping out from under rocks to be with him.

His grandfather's last wife used him while she had her own boyfriend on the side. It was no wonder Antonio did not trust the not-so-fair feminine gender. All his life he'd seen them claw after his family's money, fame and fortune. The sprawling estate north of Toronto hosted some of the finest parties—his father bequeathed him that home. But his parents had a bitter divorce and Antonio himself was hurt one too many time by opportunists. That was why he swore he would never marry. He would let his girlfriends know up front that it could never be anything more than physical and that was that. Sex but no love suited his lifestyle just fine, thank you very much.

Antonio entered his suite before long and continued to glance at the screen of his phone looking at any evidence or useful information he could find on Lucy. Who was she? What were her interests? He quickly scanned her likes, her friends list again, the type of quotes she posted on her wall and the type of stuff she in fact posted. The more he wanted to find something about her to dislike the harder it was. How on earth could he hate this woman?

One of her shared quotes caught his eye: "It's not about who is real to your face...It's about who stays real behind your back!"

Antonio's gut clenched. He didn't know why he reacted to that post but he did. He'd known all too long how much he could trust very few people. And that post really grabbed him. He was utterly amazed at the fact that Ms. Lucy Shillerton loved that quote enough to post it on her page.

Again, he was always assessing people. What you choose to like and post says a lot about you as a person. He thought Lucy was going to have only pinups of hot looking men or crazy, self-serving tenets but no, Lucy seemed different. She was a woman who thought deep. Antonio couldn't argue with that. But it meant he would have to tighten up his game plan. She seemed like a woman who wouldn't change her mind that easily with what he had to say. Still, he was going to do what he had to do. Whether or not he liked her. Business was business and his grandfather was his business and she'd better not go through with her plan to give him a heart-attack-inducing wedding to the gold-digging girlfriend he'd found ... or else.

Antonio powered down his phone and attached it to his charger in the kitchen before grabbing a drink from the fridge and heading to the solarium. He sat down on his patio chair and scanned the gorgeous Toronto skyline with all the skyscrapers and the lake nearby. The sun was setting and the sky was a reddish hue now mixed with blue. He leaned back and took a swig of his lager. He should be out with his cousin Lucas winding down at one of the exclusive clubs in the city for guys like them. But then that would be a distraction he didn't want right now. His mind was on one subject. And it killed him inside to think about it.

Lucy Shillerton.

He wondered what she was doing now—on a Friday night?

CHAPTER THREE

Lucy did not have a good weekend.

It had all gone to hell.

It was Monday morning and she was still worked up over the events of Friday afternoon. All she could do was think about Antonio and his threat to her and her business. What on earth was she going to do? She'd just finished up a general meeting with the rest of her team in the boardroom to prepare for the outstanding weddings they had upcoming. She was not happy about the report from Mr. Petri, their bookkeeper. Their company was a little behind in some of their payments with their contractors. Thankfully, the deposit Mr. Romero, senior, had given them for his Fun Birds themed wedding helped pay their lease or it would not have been renewed.

"Okay, so what's going on, girlfriend?" Maxine probed as she crossed her legs in a chair across from Lucy.

"What do you mean?"

"Oh, come on now. I can tell something's on your mind."

Yeah, I need to get a life. Heck, maybe she's right about me needing to get laid, too.

Lucy didn't want to admit it but as much as Antonio Romero, III terrified her, she was deeply attracted to his charm and his seemingly sexual prowess. There was something present she just could not describe. Heck, she'd fantasized about him all weekend when she wasn't lying awake wondering how she was going to pull off the next weddings without any more possible lawsuits from stunts gone wrong.

"It's nothing."

"Yeah, right. You're talking to *me*. Maxine!"

"Okay, fine." Lucy spilled it to Maxine as to what happened on Friday night after Maxine left for the dentist.

"Oh, that guy I saw coming out of his Beemer? I knew he looked familiar. He was Antonio Romero the third, wasn't he?"

"Yes," Lucy said evenly, trying to hide the shaking in her voice.

"Girl. He. Is. Hot!" Maxine gushed, fanning herself with her right hand. She then grinned leaning forward in her chair waiting to hear more.

"Girl. He. Is. A. Hot. Head!" Lucy shot back.

Maxine leaned back shaking her head and playfully rolling her eyes. "What is wrong with you? He only wants to do what's best for his grandpa. Who can fault him?"

"I can. We have a business to run, remember? Wait a minute. Aren't I supposed to be the one avoiding these unusual weddings and you're supposed to be the one defending them?"

Maxine laughed. "Listen. You're right. We have a business to run, but really, what's the worst he can do?"

"I don't know, and I don't want to find out."

"So what are you going to do? Dump the poor old guy and send him into shock and heartache?"

Lucy thought about that for a moment. It wasn't going to be as easy as it sounded, was it?

"Look, we have until the end of this week, right?"

"I guess." Maxine shrugged her shoulders.

"Get out your notepad or iPad. We're going to go through what we need for this wedding first and consider all the options and start looking at the vendors."

"Okay. It's your funeral."

"Maxine!"

"I'm only teasing, girl."

Lucy really had to get used to Maxine's wry sense of humor. It wasn't always easy. But she did have a point. Lucy had to look at this thing from all angles. The last thing she wanted was for it to blow up in her face. Or worse, her client's face. Heck, she really didn't want to face Antonio III again. Then on second thought, maybe she did want to see him again. Maybe she secretly loved the way his presence revved up her temperature and made her heart pitter-patter in her chest and caused butterflies to explode in her belly. Maybe, Lucy really liked the way he gazed into her eyes making her tingle between her thighs. Oh, God!

They discussed the Fun Bird ten-tier wedding cake that the bride-to-be, Shelly, requested. And the human slingshot, the location of the trees involved, the plate holders, napkins, decorations, the dressing ensemble for the wedding party and so on. It was to take place on the 16,000-square foot Spanish-style winery and estate. It was a beautiful sprawling acreage with breathtaking views. The mansion had a massive flower garden, a park, a five-hole manicured golf-course, state-of-the-art gymnasium and tennis court. The main house consisted of a 22-bedroom luxury mansion and plenty of guesthouses and employee quarters. How convenient for the live-in staff at the estate.

The Romeros were also one of the few billionaires in that area that had a private helipad for their lavish home. Their own helicopter was housed there within minutes in case they wanted to, or needed to, fly off at a moments notice.

Imagine that! A helipad.

Lucy could not wrap her head around that one. How decadent it must be to live like that. She had heard that the elder patriarch of the family had grown up impoverished as an immigrant and had to fight hard, study hard, network hard and create the empire that he currently owned from the ground up. Literally.

Lucy hadn't actually been to the estate as of yet but she saw the beautiful pictures on the Internet. It was intimidating. Breathtaking. Surreal. Yes, these folks were certainly out of her league. If it weren't for taking over her auntie's business, she would have probably never brushed shoulders with the Romero clan. She felt blessed to have had this opportunity. And she also prayed to God that she would not screw this up for Mr. Romero, senior or his grandson, either way.

As hot and sophisticated as Antonio Romero III was, Lucy still could not believe how a man who had such privilege growing up in a world that was foreign to her and in a world that seemed more like a fantasy than reality, was now accessible to her.

He still had this sort of down-to-earth, prosaic feel to him. Or maybe, slightly more than mere common. He made her heart flutter in her chest when she was near him. Heck, he had that effect on her all weekend when she kept thinking and fantasizing about him.

Hot damn!

Just dreaming about Antonio lifted Lucy's mood. It was true then that a little healthy fantasy could go a long way in improving one's attitude.

"Listen, we'd better get back to business at-hand," Lucy said shuffling some of the loose sheets on her desk. Her table was an utter mess. She had opened files and brochures spread out everywhere.

Lucy placed the file containing Romero's wedding to the side.

"Okay, let's deal with the other outstanding weddings." Lucy picked up the pages and the contract signed by the next couple. "I'm going to be meeting with the venue manager for Debbie and Luke's mud-style wedding."

"Oh, that should be interesting."

"Yes, it should be and you'll be coming with me."

"Sweet. I'm looking forward to that. I've never planned a mud wedding before."

"I'm sure they haven't either." Lucy grinned. "Well, we need to have an idea of the floor plan and speak to the person in charge of designing the hall. I believe they want to make it exotic, right?"

"Yes, something like that," Maxine concurred as she ferociously typed away on her iPad. "Good, how does this look?" Maxine showed Lucy an idea on the screen and Lucy gave her the thumbs-up.

"What would I do without you, Maxine?"

"Probably nothing," Maxine teased.

Lucy rolled her eyes in jest and shook her head.

After an hour of discussing what they would be doing for the mud-style wedding of their client, they sent off some emails and had Darla arrange the appointment for the following week with the venue manager of the hotel where that wedding's reception would be hosted.

"Great!" Lucy said as she placed the file aside. "Now, what do we have planned for this week?"

"Well, there is the Bridal Show at the Convention Center."

"Already?"

"Yep. And don't forget we have someone from our company there in a booth. They'll be handing out flyers and other enticements while we look around."

"Oh, wonderful. Can you have Darla make all the arrangements for our business cards and other swag that would be needed?"

Maxine tapped away on her iPad and whipped off an email to Darla, their receptionist and administrative assistant. "Done. Now what are we going to do about the ball, Cinderella?"

Lucy looked lost for a moment. "Ball? What ball?" Her heart palpitated again. All she could do was think about a glass slipper, and for some reason, Prince Charming was that hot and stubborn Antonio Romero III. Lucy blinked hard and tried to push the naughty thoughts about Antonio out of her head. He was way out of her league. And a super sexy distraction she did not need nor want at this time. Back to business. "What ball are you talking about, Maxine?"

Maxine feigned being shocked. Her mouth opened into a perfect O. "You mean you forgot about *the* ball of the year?"

"Maxine, what are you talking about?" Lucy sighed heavily.

"Girl, it's the Diamond Ball and Fundraiser for Economic Empowerment."

Lucy waited to see if Maxine was going to elaborate. Should Lucy even know about this ball thingy? She'd been briefed on so many of her aunt's old business dealings and projects during the past few weeks but this one did not ring a bell. Perhaps she'd forgotten. She hoped it wasn't something in which she was supposed to be involved. "Maxine. I...I don't know anything about the Diamond Fundraiser."

Maxine rolled her eyes in exasperation. "It's the event of the year, Lucy. Besides, your dear aunt Chris had agreed to do her part this year...before she passed away, of course."

"Oh. I see."

"The Diamond Ball and Fundraiser is about helping young people from all kinds of backgrounds from disadvantaged to the privileged. Basically, it helps people with great ideas thrive in life and do something to change the world."

"Sounds good. And?" Lucy knew there must be something else forthcoming.

Maxine grinned sheepishly. "And, girl, the hottest, sexiest businessmen in the industry will be in attendance."

Lucy leaned back, shook her head and laughed. "Now how did I know that was coming?"

"We have to go, Lucy. It's for a good cause."

"Why do I get the impression that if this was a fundraiser to help ants in the wild you'd still want to attend?"

"Honey, with all those rich, eligible hotties in one place. Hell yeah!"

Lucy leaned forward with a grin. "Fine. We'll attend but only because it's a good cause. How much are the tickets and how are we involved?"

"Well, they're about one thousand dollars for the cheapest."

"One thousand dollars? A little steep for our budget. Are you insane?"

"No, but I will go insane if I can't be there."

"Maxine!"

"Lucy!"

"Okay, fine. It's going for a good cause so okay. I'll try to make it work. Now how are we involved?"

"Well, each year somebody helps out with the planning or donates ideas. And your aunt and I had already made suggestions to some of the song selection for the dance." Maxine swayed her hips on the seat as if she could hear music pumping through some imaginary speakers. "I thought we could open up with a song about making a difference in the world or making a change...'"

"Yeah, and it seems as if we're gonna have to make a bit of change, too, if we want to afford this thing. Literally. Our cash flow has decreased over the past few months according to Mr. Petri. I hope you know what we're doing."

Maxine stopped moving and glared at Lucy. "Of course, I know."

Maxine then showed Lucy some of the lineup and playlist she previously approved. They would play some oldies and some new music to please the entire crowd that would consist of A-listers in the Toronto area and icons in the industry. The age of the participants would be mixed. Somehow, Lucy felt good about having a break this week to take her mind off things. It would be good to get out and dance for a change. She couldn't honestly remember the last time she had fun at a musical event of any sort. She really needed to get a life, like seriously. Like yesterday.

"Okay, fine. The ball is when?"

"Thursday evening starting at six."

"Thursday? That's so soon." Lucy glanced at her desk calendar and scanned her other commitments for the week. Her heart turned over in her chest when she saw Friday. She had scribbled down something about Antonio and a decision that had to be made. Why had she written that? She wasn't about to cower to this man's ridiculous demands. Or was she? No. It was her business and his grandfather was her client and that was final. She worked for Antonio I not Antonio III.

So then why had images of him slid into her memory? Her mind drifted back to his tall, muscular frame. The man obviously worked out—a lot. He was built like a Greek god. A sex god. Why was he suddenly dominating her every thought? She had to learn to control that. She had to learn how to squish thoughts of him out of her mind. But it wasn't as easy as it sounded. Antonio Romero III.

The smooth, silky deep voice that danced from his beautifully defined lips. The way he said her name, smooth like warm honey and how it slid down her spine and brought shivers of delight coursing through her body.

Stop it, Lucy! He's only a man.

And a hot, sexy one at that. One who would ruin her world if she didn't meet his demands this Friday.

This Friday.

This Friday.

Oh, why was she both terrified and eager to see this Friday appear?

She was terrified of what he might do to her or her business. He acted like a man not to be reckoned with. At the same time, she would be seeing him again this week, right?

Stop it, Lucy! You're not that desperate, are you?

Lucy and Maxine both went through the playlist one more time. Journey's Don't Stop Believin' would be amongst the tunes blaring through the speakers in addition to some classical tunes, the Beatles' Come Together,

Avril Lavigne's Hot, some Beyonce, Britney Spears, Motown artists, Nat King Cole, and all other tunes including Bob Marley's One Love near the end.

"Wow, that's quite a collection. So...eclectic."

"Thanks." Maxine blushed. "Your aunt was an eclectic-loving woman, you know."

"I just hope the crowd is okay with that."

"Oh, trust me. They'll love it. It's a mixed audience, you know. A lot of young folks will be in attendance."

"Okay." Lucy just thought about something. "What are we going to wear? I haven't been to any black-tie affairs in so long..." What she had meant to say was that she could not ever remember going to a black-tie affair.

"Don't worry, girl. I've got it covered."

"You do?"

"Yeah! We're going shopping before the Bridal Show anyway. We're going to Yorkdale Shopping Center."

"I hope this is all in our budget, Maxine." Lucy sighed deeply. She wanted to look good but she'd recently taken over her auntie's business and right now finances were tight. Not to mention that impending lawsuit from one of their former bride clients.

"Here's the invitation." Maxine handed her a digitally-designed sheet of parchment paper.

Lucy paused.

Romero Realty Inc.

Cordially invites you and a guest to attend its annual Diamond Ball fundraiser to benefit the

Society for a Brighter Future: Helping Young People Succeed

Thursday, September 30th

6:00 p.m. – 11:00 p.m.

The Romero Estate - Banquet Hall

18550 Young Street

Black tie.

A night of dinner and dance.
Cocktails 6:00 pm
Dinner 6:30 pm
All proceeds will fund the Society for a Brighter Future: Helping Young People Succeed

If Lucy had been standing, she knew she would have probably collapsed. She felt weak in her limbs. Her mouth was as parched as a desert landscape. She was sure her jaw had dropped to the ground. It sure as hell felt like it. "Maxine, you didn't tell me that the Romeros were hosting this thing."

Lucy read over the heading of the invitation: Romero Realty Inc.

It could not be. How could it be? How had she missed this? Romero Realty hosted the annual Diamond Ball fundraiser? An event they were committed to attending but she had no idea about beforehand?

"But I thought you knew. I mean, everyone knows it's the RR Diamond Ball fundraiser. Romero Realty."

"I didn't," Lucy said quietly trying to swallow the hard lump surging in her throat. She thought she would choke any moment. This entire situation was getting to be more difficult than she imagined. No way could she attend now. And then what about Antonio I's wishes? And Antonio III's crazy demands that she end it for his grandfather?

"Girl, you look as if you're turning blue. You okay? You need oxygen or something?"

Lucy let out a deep breath. She hadn't realized she'd not inhaled.

As if things could not get any worse, Darla pinged her on the intercom.

"Yes, Darla?"

"Hi, Lucy. Antonio Romero is on the phone."

Fear and anxiety knotted inside Lucy. A sense of inadequacy swept through her but it was too late. She couldn't handle this. She should have never gotten into the business. There went her heart fluttering about in her chest again.

She sucked in a deep breath.

"Lucy speaking," she said answering the phone.

"Hello, my dear," the other voice on the end of the line was the cheerful voice of Antonio Romero I. "It's Toni here. Antonio Romero."

She was relieved it was the elder Romero on the line. She didn't know if she could possibly handle speaking to anyone else right now. Certainly not his gorgeous, overbearing grandson who was about to make her life a living hell. That much into the future she could see.

"Hi, Mr. Romero."

"No. Please, call me Toni. I feel like a young man again. It's Toni." A hearty chuckle followed on the end of the line.

Toni.

Okay, I'll call the older Romero Toni from now on. Good. That makes things easier.

Lucy felt as if her heart plummeted to her knees. How could she possibly ruin this happy man's life? How could she turn around and tell him she wasn't going to do his high-risk wedding to his young sweetheart? It wasn't for her or his grandson to decide. He was, after all, a big boy. But then again, she saw Antonio's point about not wanting any harm to come to his grandfather. She could just see it. The older Romero having a heart attack after being slung from a gigantic human slingshot to the funny tune of Fun Birds and then Romero the third fuming mad and holding her fully responsible for his death.

Lucy blinked her eyes shut and opened them again. She fought hard to stifle a tear.

"Yes, sir. Yes, Toni."

"Listen, I need to see you right away. It's very important. How soon do you think you can come over to the house?"

House? Come over to the house? Well, if that isn't the understatement of the year. Try mansion or palace.

"Um. We'll be there as soon as possible."

When Lucy concluded her phone call, she collapsed into her chair and held her head in her hands.

"You okay, Lucy?"

Lucy shook her head. "What have I gotten myself into?"

CHAPTER FOUR

"We need to tighten things up, Antonio," Mariam told her boss, Antonio Romero III, at his headquarters. "Your expenditure on the Brighter Future project has gone through the roof. I know you want to help our community's younger people but-"

"The matter is closed." Antonio's reply was curt. His tone was sharper than he had intended. After all, Mariam had always been his faithful assistant and advisor for as long as he was in business. A friend of his own late father. She had been in the family forever. She was an older woman but charming and had her days. But she was stellar at keeping the family assets in tune with changing times. They'd even survived the great economic meltdown that had adversely affected the real estate market in Toronto many years ago, all thanks to her astute financial planning and management.

"It is for a good cause," Antonio continued.

"I know it is, sir." Mariam grew more defensive and formal. "But every little Tom, Dick and Henrietta who comes to your project with a business idea gets your approval for a sizable grant to fund their new business venture and you haven't even looked at any of their business plans to see if they are solid."

Antonio leaned back in the leather executive chair behind his oak desk. He gave thought to what Mariam was saying. It was true that during the past year he hadn't bothered to see if the recipients of his grant program had solid plans but he was extremely preoccupied for some reason. And just this morning he had given more funding to groups of university students who had requested additional sums of money. Why had he done that? Was he displacing emotionally? No. It must have been something else.

Maybe he was tired of the underdogs being kicked and he wanted to overextend himself to give them a good start. Something they would have difficulty securing anywhere else. Or maybe he was simply rebelling against his own grandfather and everything his materialistic family stood for.

Perhaps he secretly wanted to give away every dime he inherited to the underprivileged because he knew it would tick off the gold-digging leaches that sucked the lifeblood from his family. And even though Mariam was a loyal associate and assistant, she was a throwback from his father and grandfather's time and she seemed to worship money more than people and that irked him more than anything.

Antonio's mind drifted to the flowers he'd sent for his biological mother earlier that day. The mother who turned her back on him and abandoned him many years ago.

His biological mother made it clear to him when she was young and married his father, producing a child in the marriage was part of a business deal. A way for her to earn some extra cash. In fact, she told Antonio that she never really wanted to have children and that she was hired to be a bride for his father. When his father died, Antonio thought for some reason he would be able to get close to his mother but she was cold and hard as he'd ever seen her. She maintained that she would keep her distance from Antonio and that he should do the same.

So much for love and money.

So much for true love and marriage.

The thought left a bitter taste in Antonio's mouth. Perhaps that was why he never truly trusted women. Because it was always about what a man could do for them. Men were to be providers and nothing more. Still, the pain of the rejection was too much for Antonio, who had always craved his mother's approval. Why would a mother reject her own child?

At least sending the flowers to her anonymously assuaged his soul in a way no one could possibly understand. It was just his own crazy way of coping. It was wrong for a woman to give birth for money and the hell if he was going to think of himself as some purchased object, some stock option.

Still, Antonio vowed he was never going to get married.

And he was never going to have children.

Heck, if he could change his last name and live anonymously somewhere else in the world—somewhere exotic and unknown, he would do it.

"Are you okay, Antonio?" Mariam's voice pierced his thoughts. And it was probably a good thing, too.

"Yes, I'm fine," Antonio lied with conviction. He recomposed himself. He knew what this was all about now, didn't he? That woman marrying his grandfather.

And then there was that other woman who was running through his mind and his system from the day he laid eyes on her. The girl who owned that crazy wedding agency. Lucy Shillerton. There was something about her he just couldn't shake off and it drove him out of his mind.

What was it about her?

He'd never felt that way about any woman before. Was it because she didn't seem to give a damn about his wealthy background or his assets? And the fact that she was so hot? Not only that but whenever he spoke and gave a command, women, especially, heeded it. That was because they were all about men and power. He could clock their reactions automatically.

But Lucy Shillerton.

She was unpredictable. She was different. She really didn't seem to give a damn. The thought of him shutting down her business by Friday if she didn't heed his order to stop his grandfather's risky wedding to the young opportunist didn't sit too well with Antonio because that would mean he would have to hurt her.

The thought then ran through Antonio's mind about seducing Lucy Shillerton.

However, he wasn't into breaking women's hearts on a whim. He would always be upfront about what he wanted. Sex. No love. Just pure, physical, hard sex. But this wasn't about sex, it was about destroying her business and all that she had worked for after taking over for her aunt's enterprise. Could it be Lucy was so different from every woman he had ever known? Could it be that there really are decent, honest, hardworking women who cared about people and not solely material things?

Antonio rubbed his throbbing temple after his lengthy meeting with Mariam once they discussed the last minute preparations for their annual Diamond Ball and Fundraiser Dinner on Thursday and Mariam's role in taking over for him for the next short while as he attended to other matters.

He sat there alone. Thinking. Pondering over Lucy Shillerton. She was like a song he could not get out of his mind. What was the term they use? Earworm, oh right. But, oh, worms or not, that song brought a smile to the corner of his lips. He wasn't into skinny girls and he loved a healthy-looking woman with curves in all the right places—and she was that girl.

Yet, he still felt that he had to get this pretty young thing out of his mind and out of his system if he knew what was good for him. It was just way too dangerous. All he knew was that Lucy Shillerton had better follow his orders.

CHAPTER FIVE

Lucy Shillerton's jaw toppled open as she and Maxine drove up to the sprawling luxury estate of the Romero family later that afternoon.

Oh, Holy Grail!

This was not somebody's home; it was a palace, a fortress, a kingdom! It looked even more impressive in real life than it did on the Internet.

Lucy and Maxine stepped out of the car with their mouths wide open gawking at the massive estate and the multi-level, white-brick mansion that sat behind the golden-gated entrance. There was a concrete flowing water feature in the main garden in front of the house that looked more like an enchanted fountain. The water spurting out of it was richly blue and forceful.

God, it was mesmerizing. Right behind the water fountain dozens of wide steps led up to the main house with its beautiful French doors. There was something about the double French doors that captivated Lucy. The whole scene looked like something out of a movie. So surreal.

This was a far cry from her humble old brick apartment building complex in the suburbs. Heck, the elevators were inoperable virtually every other day. When you had to walk up the steep, dark stairwell after finishing up a 12-hour workday, it was no fun.

But Lucy was still sincerely grateful to have a roof over her head, so she rarely complained.

"Girl, this is hot!" Maxine commented as she took out her smartphone to take a picture.

"Maxine!"

"What?"

"You cannot take a picture. This is private property. There are laws against doing that."

"The paparazzi do it all the time."

"Maxine!" Lucy scowled at her assistant.

"Sorry," Maxine pouted as she slid the phone back in her handbag.

Lucy felt guilty for snapping at her assistant in such a rigid tone. "Listen, if we ask permission later we can probably take pictures of the ballroom area and the garden for the wedding planning."

"Oh, right. Of course. That was the reason I *was* taking pictures, Lucy." Maxine playfully rolled her eyes.

Lucy grinned and shook her head. The excitement of being in a place such as this really got to them. In a good way, of course. They both felt exhilarated. It was as if they were in Hollywood or some sort of paradise.

"So this is what forty acres looks like up close, huh?" Maxine remarked as she and Lucy walked up the stone pathway to the palatial abode. They pressed a button and the intercom sounded. No doubt cameras were planted everywhere. Hidden cameras in addition to the visible ones. Lucy looked around and saw green land stretching far and beyond. The house was slightly on a hill so she could overlook the town. She had never seen this side of outer Toronto before. It was as if she was on an island, secluded from prying eyes, yet she could see all. She was so used to the city life and city living that she'd never imagined being near fresh, uncongested open air with hundreds of acres of land unfolding before her. She knew there was also a winery on the estate. It was amazing. Lucy appreciated that her client worked so hard his entire life to have all of this and she wanted more than ever to give him the dream wedding he so deserved—just as long as it didn't cost him his life!

The thought of his grandson's threat loomed large. This dream wedding could turn into a nightmare affair if she wasn't careful and she knew that all too well.

"Yes, Miss Shillerton. Mr. Romero will see you in the study." A man with a waiter's tuxedo greeted them after opening the door.

"Thank you," Lucy said warmly. She felt so out of her league and intimidated by the premise and the staff, which was so weird. Why should she be? They were just as human as she was, right?

The inside of the grand entrance boasted golden marble and the ceiling was the tallest she'd ever seen. It seemed to go on forever. An enormous chandelier dangled from above and the walls were adorned with beautiful yet subtle artwork. Lucy felt like she'd just stepped into an art gallery, not somebody's private residence.

She also noted that this would certainly be an ideal place to take some of the pictures for Toni's wedding to Shelly. The backdrop would be so romantic. So royal-looking.

Later, they received a brief tour of the beautiful premise and the enormous ballroom where the reception would be held. Maxine ferociously typed away on her iPad taking notes and snapping pictures of the setting. Then they were introduced to the official photographer so they could go over the layout and photo settings.

They had spoken with Shelly, who seemed so full of life and humor. She kept hugging Toni and held firm on his arms. Clearly, the couple seemed as if they were in love. Toni showed Lucy and Maxine his iPad with his Fun Bird scores and told them that while Shelly was caring for him after his second stroke, she'd showed him how to play the game to cheer him up and he hadn't stopped since. He showed Lucy and Maxine their scoreboards with the names Mr. Romero and Shelly Romero. Of course, they had given Shelly his surname as a joke. Mr. and Mrs. R. Bird they nicknamed themselves.

"Beautiful," Lucy commented. She was gushing now. This all seemed so perfect, except the fact that they still wanted to go ahead with the Fun Bird slingshot down the aisle.

"Well, you know there are risks involved, right?" Lucy warned the doting couple.

"Of course we know that. Life is a risk, wouldn't you say?" Toni shot back before bursting into laughter. He seemed to be a jolly old fella who really did look more like a fit forty-something-year-old. Shelly and he looked roughly the same age—almost. His upbeat attitude was so infectious. It was obvious that one of the reasons Shelly loved Toni was because despite his age, he was young at heart and he rarely took things seriously, including himself.

"You know, Lucy, I want to thank you and your aunt...er...God rest her soul, for this wonderful wedding you're putting on for us. It's a dream come true," Toni said as he looked lovingly into Shelly's eyes.

Lucy exchanged a glance with Maxine. It translated to I-really-hope-this-works-out-for-them-because-they-are-such-a-nice-couple. Maxine appeared to have swallowed hard. Lucy could also feel a lump in her throat.

"Come. Let's go out into the garden where part of the ceremony will take place." Toni escorted them outside to the patio then led them down a pathway to the fertile garden.

Lucy noted the two trees near the pond where Shelly wanted to be tossed from the slingshot to the aisle and they had already worked out with the videographer and DJ how they would film it to the Fun Birds soundtrack and quirky bird sound noise complete with slingshot. Lucy felt a migraine coming on and she really didn't know why. Perhaps it was the whole litigious angle not to mention the safety-risk involved.

"I've already gotten fitted for the harness that will go with the gown," Shelly beamed. "I'm so thrilled to be doing this. My friends are going to have a blast. We're going to post this on YouTube. It will be great, won't it?"

Oh. No.

"Um. Oh. Yes." Lucy hesitated. *It's about the client. It's about their happiness. It's about them, not me—or Antonio! God, there was that Antonio again.* Lucy's thoughts were distracted by the sound of rotors in the distance. What the—?

She'd thought it might be some news chopper overhead but then realized that the helipad off in the distance was empty. It must be someone family related. Who could be flying at this time?

"Oh, great!" Toni seemed excited. "My grandson Antonio is here. You've met him, haven't you?"

Lucy felt her stomach plunge to her feet.

CHAPTER SIX

And what an entrance *that* was. Toni, along with Shelly on his arm, walked over towards the helipad and his grandson. Lucy and Maxine followed closely behind. Lucy was chewing her lower lip so much so that she thought she tasted blood. Her heart thrashed about in her chest. As the blades slowed down and stopped, Antonio, looking hot as ever in his Ray-Ban aviator shades and expensive business suit, stepped off the chopper, along with another gentleman. Antonio wasn't looking particularly pleased when his gaze met Lucy beside his grandfather while Shelly was waving maniacally at his grandfather's side.

"Welcome home, my boy! I see you wanted to avoid the evening rush-hour traffic again."

"Grandfather," Antonio formally greeted Toni. He then nodded to Shelly and glanced at Lucy and Maxine. He arched his eyebrow when his gaze met Lucy. Though the corner of his lips turned up slightly, the smile definitely did not reflect in his eyes. He pulled off his shades to reveal his dark and dangerously sexy gaze before re-focusing on the property.

"What is all of this?" Antonio asked as he scanned the area around him. Some of the decorating team had already begun the work on the garden for the upcoming wedding, getting the new gazebo reconstructed among other things.

"Have you met Lucy from the wedding agency?" Toni asked.

"Yes. We met last week." Antonio's voice was void of any emotion; his dark gaze was fixed on Lucy.

Lucy realized from staff at the estate that Antonio no longer resided there full-time but he had his home in the city, a penthouse in a luxury high-rise building that he owned, by the lake and would visit his elder periodically whenever business allowed.

And today had to be one of those days.

"Well, grandson, Lucy…along with her assistant, is just getting the setting for the wedding in place. She has her entire crew here and it looks as if we are going to pull this thing off, eh, pumpkin?" Toni then turned to Shelly and they smooched.

Lucy could see the queasiness on Antonio's face. Then the look on his face turned to a scathing one directed towards Lucy. He narrowed his eyes and walked closely towards her. Lucy felt the penetrating heat of Antonio's gaze and it was making her feel weak in the knees. But somehow she just didn't feel threatened. It wasn't a look of hate, it was something else. Perhaps annoyance that she dared disobey his command or the raw hurt that a lover gives to his love when she was about to do something cruel. But the difference was that Lucy and Antonio were nothing more than acquaintances.

"Why don't we all walk back to the house?" Toni suggested as he and Shelly proceeded towards the main house from the helipad. The ground crew appeared on the scene and tended to the chopper. It must have been for maintenance, Lucy noted.

What a way to live.

As they traversed back on the well-kept grass, Antonio strolled with sophistication, his hands shoved in the pants pocket of his suit. His friend flanked him and Maxine walked closely beside Toni and Shelly as she held her iPad up chatting to them about locations on the estate for the ceremony.

"So, I see you're following through on my orders very well," Antonio said through clenched teeth.

"I can explain everything," Lucy offered softly. Her voice trailed off and she wondered if Antonio even heard her. The others were busy talking so they seemed oblivious to the vibes between her and Antonio.

After having refreshments in one of the main dining quarters of the house, Antonio, who had been quiet through most of the meal, got up. "Grandfather, I would like to speak to Lucy alone in the study, if you don't mind."

"Oh, sure, Antonio. Is everything all right?"

"I have a few things to discuss with her. Things we'd spoken about last week."

Maxine gave Lucy a peculiar look but his doting grandfather and his fiancée seemed unaware and carried on with their cuddling. "Very well. And Maxine?"

"Oh, I must be getting home."

"But you don't have a ride," Lucy blurted out.

"We can have one of our drivers take her home. Or better yet, you can let her drive your car and I will take you home."

"Sounds great!" Maxine enthused before Lucy could say anything.

Was it Lucy or was the heat climbing up in this place?

"Fine," Lucy acquiesced. Great! Now she was at Antonio's mercy and she had no other means to get home. But something told her Antonio wouldn't leave her inconvenienced in any way. He seemed like too much of a gentleman to do so.

Lucy watched as Maxine departed the luxury living area and waved giving Lucy a salacious wink. Why that—!

It didn't take Lucy long to realize that Maxine was thrilled she was leaving Lucy alone with Antonio. With the elder Romero gone to another part of the God-knows-how-large-this-place-was mansion, she was practically alone with Antonio, save for a few of the staff about the premises.

"After you," Antonio offered as he directed Lucy down the tiled corridor. Artwork decorated the cream walls. She noted that the place had imported Italian molding top and bottom of the walls. It really seemed as if she were in some sort of museum. The place was quiet now, too.

They walked into the book-lined study. Lucy was in front of Antonio but when she spun her head around, she caught his salacious gaze that seemed to have fallen to her derriere. He didn't even seem embarrassed when she caught him looking.

"So, you wanted to speak with me about your grandfather's wedding?" Lucy cut into his gaze, feeling the heat rise to places in her body she wished it didn't.

"Can I get you something to drink?"

"I'm fine, thank you. I'm still sort of full from the pastries and that *delicious* fruit tray."

"Will you be staying for dinner?" he spoke softly.

"I..." would love to. "I can't. I have so much work in the morning and-"

"Very well. I won't keep you too long then. I'll cut to the chase."

Oh, no. Had she offended him? She just refused to have dinner with one of the hottest, eligible, affluent bachelors in the world. Was she crazy? Foot-in-mouth disorder. Arrgh! *Stupid. You should have said hell, yeah! No wonder you are still single.*

"You seem to have given my grandfather the impression that the wedding is still forthcoming, Lucy." Was that a question or a statement? Either way, his rich, deep tone of voice—that silky voice and the way he said her name *Lucy* in a low timbre captivated her.

"Listen, Antonio. I have no disrespect for you but..." This was not going to be as easy as she thought. A lump as large as a boulder seemed to have lodged in her throat. Damn, why the heck did Antonio have to look so hot? She was burning from the sexy heat of his delicious gaze. Even his name Antonio Romero was seductive.

Antonio Romero. Antonio Romeo. Antonio Romero. Lucy Romero. Stop it!!

That irresistible scent of his sweet cologne tickled her nostrils and lulled her into a dizzying calm state. But it wasn't just that. It was his aura. There was something about being in this man's presence. Heck, even looking at his tall, muscular-built frame. His excellent physique and his skin! His skin was almost flawless. He was blessed with good genes and good bone structure. She again noted his high cheekbones and chiseled features. His beautiful large, dark eyes and softly defined lips. Oh, those lips!

Okay, I've so got to focus here or that's it for me. Game over.

Lucy closed her eyes for a moment feeling utterly incompetent. Why was Antonio Romero having this crazy effect on her? This was absolutely insane. She barely knew the guy. But, oh, she wanted to know him better. Much better. Even biblically. *Stop it!*

"Antonio," she said almost breathless. "I realize how difficult this may be f-f-for you. We may not fully understand your grandfather's happiness. But it is *his* to have…to decide on how he wants to be happy." Oh, God! Why was she sounding like an incoherent idiot? "He obviously cares for Shelly. I want him to be happy."

"You want him to be happy?" Antonio echoed. "You don't know anything about my grandfather, Lucy. Loneliness and love are two completely different animals."

"Loneliness?" Lucy repeated, incredulously.

"Yes, Lucy. My grandfather always had this fear of dying alone. Since my grandmother passed many years ago, he has been on a rollercoaster of indiscreet relationships and bad marital decisions. All of them ending bitterly in divorce. And all of them ending with my grandfather getting nothing but slapped with exorbitant spousal support. And what has he been left with?"

"A broken heart," Lucy whispered, her voice trailing off. She swallowed hard. Her heart was pounding in her chest again. She could see raw hurt glittering in Antonio's dark eyes. She really did not want to be responsible for Toni suffering more heartbreak, but on the other hand, what if this marriage did work out for him? But would young Shelly stick around for Toni until his final days, whenever that would be?

"Love is one heck of a ride, Antonio. It's never easy. You never know how bumpy or smooth it's going to be. You never know if you'll have enough fuel to go the distance or if you'll crash and burn." Lucy bit down on her lower lip.

She noticed Antonio's body language changed ever so slightly. He'd become more rigid. Then his eyes trailed to her lips. Damn! She must stop that awful habit of biting down on her lower lip. What must Antonio think of her? That she was some shy, awkward school girl who was indecisive?

"I like what you just said," Antonio finally spoke in his deep, throaty voice. "It's true."

"I take it you've had your share of-" Lucy decided not to probe further. She thought it would be way too inappropriate at that time.

"Broken hearts?" Antonio interjected for her. A grin touched the corner of his lips. "Not exactly. I've been very disappointed, Lucy. But I don't give my heart to just anyone."

Whoa!

"Oh. Um…I didn't mean…I mean…" Lucy didn't know what to say and she bit down on her lip again. "I meant to say that love is one heck of a ride. But we won't know if we'll enjoy it or not if we don't take the driver's seat and punch the gas pedal. We need to steer ourselves where we want to go." Okay, wow, that sounded awkward. Lucy chewed on her lip again.

"Please don't do that," he said quietly.

"What?"

His gaze fell on her lips again. "Never mind." He exhaled sharply and moved over by the French glass doors leading to the garden from the study. The view was spectacular. There was so much greenery outside and the hills in the distance created a picture-perfect painting of the outdoors.

"The view is very nice," Lucy said to break the tension.

"It's okay. It was there when the house was built in the 1940s."

House? That's an understatement.

"Oh, nice. I absolutely love the view over there. God, it's beautiful."

"Want a closer look?" Antonio invited in a low, sultry voice that caused a little explosion of butterflies in her stomach.

God, that man could say Atlas and it would sound sexy as hell. The truth was, she would like a closer look at him.

"Do you want a tour?" he continued.

"Well, I've seen quite a bit of the property."

"I'm not talking about the estate."

"Oh," Lucy answered, stunned. To what exactly was Antonio referring?

"I'm talking about the part beyond that stretch over there." Antonio raised his hand to motion to the area beyond the hills. "I know my grandfather wouldn't have anyone take a tour there. Well, not just anyone. It's actually an area we keep away from most people."

"Oh, and you want me to see it?"

"I'm a spontaneous man, Lucy," Antonio proffered. "I don't always plan things. I act on things."

Like acting on the moment, Lucy guessed. "I'd love to. Thanks." Lucy got up and reached for her handbag and her cardigan on the chair. This was not about to screw up any more opportunities to be in Antonio's presence. She really wanted more than anything to just be with him. Just to be near him. There were few people in her life who could command that sort of reaction from her. And Antonio was one of the few!

"Are you seeing anyone?" Antonio asked.

Whoa. Where did that come from?

Her knees just got light and her heart went pitter-patter in her chest. There was that funny tingling sensation in her belly again.

"E-excuse me?"

"You didn't understand the question? Or you didn't hear me?"

"Yes, I just can't believe you..." *Think about what you are going to say before you say it, Lucy. Don't put your stiletto in your mouth again.* "I mean, am I seeing anyone? What kind of question is that? I could be happily married with three children."

"You didn't put that up on your Facebook profile and you don't wear a wedding band."

Oh.

"You're stalking me on Facebook?" she asked as she gave a nervous chuckle. *Oh, my God! He's interested in me?*

"You attached your Facebook address to your business card, Lucy."

Oh.

"R-right. Of course." Lucy blushed. She was sure she was beet red. How embarrassing. Why was she acting like a school girl speaking to her crush ... again?

Heck, she was looking at Antonio's Facebook profile, too. Only she wasn't one of his friends so she could not see anything on his page. Set to private, no doubt. Antonio certainly was elusive.

"Besides that, I always make it my point to run a check on everyone who comes into the family circle."

"A check? You mean a security background check? You do surveillance on everyone you meet?"

"Just those who work closely with me or my family. I am very protective of those close to me, Lucy."

She felt his words resonate inside her heart. She certainly could relate to that. Who could fault a man who only wanted to protect his family and those close to him? Heck, if she had that kind of money, she'd probably do the same. Or, maybe not. Either way, she was stoked that he took interest in knowing about her. What else had he found out about her?

Oh. My. Goodness.

"Come, let me take you to the slopes."

"The slopes? Now? In the fall?"

"Yes," he murmured as they walked through the French garden doors.

Before long, they had walked to a driveway where a two-passenger red convertible was parked. "We'll drive up to the hillside. It's quite a way," Antonio explained as he opened the passenger side of the car for Lucy.

"Thank you," she said with sincerity.

The interior smelled like fresh, new leather. The car itself sparkled under the sunset sky. It looked more like a showroom model than a car driven by anyone on a day-to-day basis. Maxine earlier mentioned that she saw Antonio exit a BMW. This was obviously a different vehicle. It would be no surprise that a man of Antonio's stature would have several luxury vehicles, no doubt. Probably each one for a different occasion. What a way to live!

"Very nice," she commented, almost breathless.

"It gets me around," Antonio virtually dismissed the compliment as he sat in the driver's seat. He turned the key in the ignition and the car started with a smooth, quiet start.

Lucy's old sedan certainly never started that way. It was often obvious that her engine could use a bit of help or at least some fine-tuning. Heck, some mornings it never started.

They drove through the verdant hilltop path taking in the scenic view. "I didn't know there was so much pristine land out here."

"It's a break from the city," he said, casting her a sideways glance. His lips curled into a sexy grin. He looked adorable as the wind whisked through his dark, short mane.

"For sure," she agreed as she held down her own locks of hair as the wind tousled it. She tucked the sides behind her ears but it was no use, the warm early autumn breeze continued to sweep her brunette hair into her face.

"The scenery is so beautiful." Lucy's eyes drank in the greenery as they climbed higher up the hilltop.

"Not half as beautiful as you," Antonio murmured in a low, deep voice.

Lucy turned to him. She was, in a word, stunned. Did he just say she was beautiful? Oh, God! Her belly was really bubbling up in a tingly way. Oh, God! "Thank you," she replied sheepishly as she looked out at the scenery, trying to avoid his gaze. This was stupid. She was a grown woman. What was she afraid of?

"You want on some music?" Antonio asked with a dimpled grin.

"Sure. Can you get one of those oldies station or easy-listening channels?"

Antonio reached over the satellite radio and set it to a station.

Before she knew it, the song "Never Knew Love Like This" by Stephanie Mills boomed through the speakers. Lucy thought she would faint. Good thing she was sitting. The smooth, soul ballad with the catchy melodic tune sounded: "I never knew love like this before, now I'm lonely never more...since you came into my life..."

Oh, God! Lucy felt as if she could sink into her seat. What a coincidence for that song to play! How embarrassing. The song was one of the most beautiful ballads she'd ever heard. An old eighties tune but it certainly couldn't have spoken for the mood any more than it did. It was as if Antonio's car was alive and played music to what a person thought inside his or her mind.

Antonio glanced in her direction and his grin grew wider. Great! He sure was enjoying this, wasn't he? He probably thought she was in love with him or some such nonsense. Egotist.

"Nice choice. The station, I mean," he quipped.

Lucy resisted the urge to playfully slap his muscular arm. She wanted to pinch him but she didn't.

She rolled her eyes and shook her head in amusement. By the time that song ended, the beautiful ballad "Lost in Your Eyes" by Debbie Gibson played. It had to be one of her all time favorites. Both of them were quiet in the car for a moment as they pulled up to the top of the hill with the gorgeous view of the mansion and the enormous green spread below.

"Well, we're here. What do you think of the view?" Antonio seemed a bit more mellow. Was it the music? Could a beautiful ballad really tame the beast, so to speak?

She got out of the car slowly as he held the door open for her. "Thank you," she said.

"You're a very polite woman," he commented. "You must have said thank you at least three hundred times since this afternoon," he surmised with a boyish grin. "But who's counting?"

She would not say thank you to that comment. She willed herself not to. Gosh, he was right. She was very over-thankful for everything, if one could call it that.

Antonio took that opportunity to grill Lucy about her life. What she enjoyed and what she didn't and how noble it was for her to take over her auntie's business, though he still wanted to discuss letting his grandfather down as gently as possible. He loved that old man. Lucy asked him about his own family since clearly he knew much about her.

Antonio was closed at first but as they meandered around the hillside they got to talking more. He loved to capture the beautiful scenic images, and in fact, he owned a mini gallery in one of the cottages where he displayed his artwork and nature photography. He even showed her some images on his smartphone. Lucy was awestruck.

"That is so beautiful, Antonio. You really have a good eye for capturing nature's best."

"It takes a lot of practice. But I can't take the credit, of course. Nature does its thing. I'm only a fan."

"A fan?"

"Yeah. Why does that surprise you?"

"You just don't seem like the…" *type to appreciate things like Mother Nature?* Lucy's mouth felt dry and brittle. All the moisture had dried up. Why was she nervous around this good-looking, obviously caring man? Why did she feel so comfortable around him yet so nervous at the same time? Her heart pounded in her chest.

He was interested in just spending time with her, wasn't he? They had some sort of chemistry. She felt it deep into her core.

"You think I don't have time to appreciate the sunrise on the horizon or the fields of greenery around here?" he said with amusement, his brow arched. He had read her mind!

"No," she said sheepishly, feeling heat rise to her throat. The truth was, she was seeing a different side of him. Such a contrast from the overbearing executive who stormed into her office when they first met. "I do think it's sort of cute though. I mean, I love sunsets and vivid scenery. I could stare at it all day. I used to do that a lot on my lunch hour but everyone thought I was crazy."

"You're not the one who's crazy, Lucy. We all need to take time out to appreciate breathing once in a while. To look at our surroundings while we can. What's the point of life if we take everything around us for granted?"

"That's so true." Lucy had never met a man like Antonio. Certainly, her ex was nothing like him. She and Antonio had a lot more in common than she had originally thought.

"Oh, look at this one," she said, browsing through more images on his smart phone. It was a snapshot of a beautiful puppy with golden fur and large brown eyes laying comfortably by what looked to be an apple tree. "He's adorable," Lucy said, her voice cracking with emotion. The lovely pup reminded her of Baily, her own little mutt.

"Is everything okay?" Antonio's smooth deep voice interrupted her daze. "You seem upset."

"No. I'm fine…thanks. I…this little guy reminds me of my dog."

"Oh? What happened to him?"

Lucy swallowed hard. Her throat was closing in. She could not breathe again. "He...he passed away."

"I'm so sorry, Lucy."

"It's okay."

"He was a cross-breed? Like the one in the photo?"

"Yes. A beautiful Labradoodle." Lucy smiled with appreciation. "The best thing that happened to me at that time. He was my little friend. My son. He was a gift from my mom. A cross between a Labrador retriever and a poodle and he had the finest, softest fur ever. Honey golden with the largest brown eyes I'd ever seen on a dog. My neighbor was pet sitting for me at the time but there was an accident when they were outside. A car..." She swallowed hard. "Oh, God I miss him."

Antonio seemed genuinely sorry about her loss. "What a tragic incident for you. I'm really sorry you went through that. Did they find out who...was in the car?"

She shook her head. "No," she said, quietly. "The driver never even slowed down! Everyone was so shocked, no one had the presence of mind to note the license plate or even the type of car." She willed the tears to not flow. It took her forever to get over that.

"So sad. Nothing can ever replace someone or something you love," Antonio said.

Those words captured Lucy's heart and tugged at her. She looked up at Antonio, startled. "Thank you."

"For what?"

"For empathizing with me. My ex...he couldn't understand why I was so overcome with grief at the time. He told me Baily was just a dog."

"Baily was no doubt like a wonderful companion to you. Your ex seems like the dog."

In spite of her mood, Lucy almost burst out laughing. What was with Antonio? He really had a wry sense of humor. He knew how to make her laugh. That was another score for him. Not that she could ever really be with someone like Antonio. Geez, she felt more chemistry with Antonio than she ever had with her ex. Wasn't that weird? It wasn't the quantity of time you spent with a person, it was also the quality. Jeff and she had been together for a while but they rarely had talks like the one she and Antonio were having. And it was interesting how easy she felt she could speak to Antonio about anything. In fact, she could not recall a single heart-to-heart conversation like this with Jeff.

"Well, I wish he had half the feeling over Baily's death as you do. I mean, it means a lot when someone else shares your pain. Understands you."

"We all need that, Lucy. Life is one heck of an emotional ride."

"Agreed."

Antonio and Lucy spoke about the other pictures in his digital portfolio. She didn't even realize the time. She was having the most fun. Their conversations jumped all over the place covering many different topics.

She noticed that his mood darkened somewhat when she asked him about his father. He didn't want to delve too deeply into his father's passing and what type of man he was. And what Lucy noticed more was the pain in Antonio's eyes when he answered a question about his mother. She was alive but it sure didn't feel like it. He didn't want to discuss anything about his mother. She was off limits apparently. Period. Done with. A nonissue. Lucy wondered in horror about what type of relationship they might have had for him to never want to trust women. Perhaps there was more to the story than the little she had heard. There must have been. Antonio was a sweet, resourceful man who gave a lot to the community, though he never spoke directly of it. While questioning him on his projects, she learned that most of it was to help young people succeed in life on their own regardless of their backgrounds. He seemed to be quite passionate about that. Obsessed even. It was one of the forces that drove him daily. To turn underdogs into top dogs. Who could blame him for wanting to do that?

Was it because he didn't have much himself growing up? Not in material things, obviously, but in love. Companionship.

Lucy had explained to Antonio that the reason she wanted to continue the agency, despite having her own reservations about some of the stunts the brides and grooms wanted to pull off, was it was a way to grant dreams to deserving people. Antonio commended her on her intent but still made it clear that by Friday, he wanted her to resolve the issue with his grandfather's wedding.

Way to ruin the moment, she thought.

They enjoyed the scene of the lake below and Lucy also noticed the chairlift to the side going all the way down to the bottom of the hill.

"You guys own all of this land?"

"We do."

"But it's like cottage country up here. Is there a resort nearby?" Lucy felt so out of her league and so out of bounds. How could she not have known this? She knew that Romero Realty owned plenty of properties and land but never envisioned this. Unlike Antonio, it wasn't as if she went around ordering background checks on everyone with whom she did business. Although it would probably be a good idea. Everything she knew about people was reduced to whatever she could Google about them. Ha! That made her feel so amateurish compared to the Romeros.

"During the winter months, we open up the cottages over there and we pretty much run a ski resort. We do a lot of student packages."

"Can the students even afford this?"

"We do complimentary packages, Lucy. We give back to the community and to the young people."

"Oh, right."

"I trust you will be present at the Diamond Ball this Thursday evening?" Antonio's tone made the sentence sound more like a command than a question or invitation.

"Well, I do have a lot of projects this week," she answered with a grin. "But I think I will try to squeeze it in."

"Good," Antonio answered curtly.

The sun was setting and the sky was turning into swirls of red and purple in the distance. When she looked at the lights of the town below, it was a picture-perfect image.

"You must love coming up here, Antonio."

"Like I said, I like to get away from the city when I can. And from people."

"From people?"

"Yes. Why, does that surprise you?"

"Well, you seem like such a people person."

"I do?"

"Yes." Lucy then thought back to their first meeting at the office. He didn't exactly seem people-friendly at the time but that was obviously because he was peeved with her about his grandfather's wedding.

Oh, no. His grandfather's wedding. Just then, Lucy's feelings took a serious nosedive.

Lucy kept directing her gaze to the chairlifts going up and down the steep hill, empty. It was sad in a way. Here, Antonio had all this land and it was practically empty. It was like owning an amusement park and not allowing admittance.

"You want a ride?"

"On the chairlift?"

"Come." Antonio didn't wait for her to answer.

Oh, my. This was so not how she had planned her evening. It was better. Too bad it was a work night.

Lucy didn't know why but she just wanted to spend the whole evening with Antonio. Heck, she wanted to spend more than just the whole evening with him. There was something about him that lulled her senses. Something about Antonio that she just couldn't quite pinpoint.

What was it about Antonio Romero? This man was as elusive as he was sexy and hot as hell. His presence captivated her every time she saw him. Whether in person or in her dreams or her fantasies. And there he was. With Lucy. Alone. Just the two of them.

He had some sort of magical effect on her emotions. Like some sort of sedative that mellowed her mood and relaxed her at the same time. She glanced at his softly defined lips. What would they feel like on hers? As if he could hear her, Antonio escorted her to the chairlift, but before he got on, he glanced into her eyes.

Her legs weakened.

Please kiss me.

Just then, the image of him touching her, caressing her, making love to her, engulfed her mind. God, she really needed to get a life. She really needed not to be celibate right now. How long had it been since she'd been intimate? Way, way, way too long.

Antonio's cell phone buzzed and shattered the moment. He paused. She thought she heard him curse under his breath. He turned away to answer. It had a distinctive ring so it must have been somebody important.

"Yes, Grandfather. You have a good night, too."

"Sorry, I wasn't listening, but that was so…sweet." There. She said it.

"You're really something else, you know that?" he said, guiding her to the chairlift.

"Why do you say that?"

"You're sentimental, for one thing."

"Thank—" Lucy stopped herself and watched as Antonio's lips curled into a smile.

The scenic chairlift ride was extraordinary. She grabbed on to Antonio's arm as he casually leaned back in the luxury seat of the lift gliding all the way down at a swift pace. Lucy was breathing hard, catching her breath but enjoying the sights. How could Antonio be so calm when dangling in the air from a thin cable?

She gripped his biceps and could feel the steel hardness of his muscles. Good God! This man was built solid like a sculpture. Oh, my. What could he be like in bed?

"Are you going to be okay, Miss Shillerton?" Antonio turned to her, grinning.

She playfully rolled her eyes. "I'm afraid of heights."

The grin vanished. "Why didn't you tell me?"

"No. It's okay. I'm…I'm with you so…"

He held on to her. "We'll be down soon."

Lucy leaned into Antonio. She really did enjoy the scenery, it was just the thought of the cables holding them up so high off the ground worked on her nerves. They must have been at about two-thousand feet above sea level, she guessed. Of course, who cared about sea level? To Lucy it looked like a million mile plummet to earth!

Antonio turned to Lucy and lifted her chin up so that their gaze met. Lucy looked into Antonio's dark, sexy eyes and she felt oddly protected. He gave her the look that he would not let anything happen to her. But there was also something else in his eyes. Oh, those beautiful dark eyes framed by long, thick lashes.

Then as if time had stopped, he leaned down and pressed his soft lips to hers. Lucy felt electricity pulse delightfully chaotically through her blood. He slowly slid his tongue inside her parted lips and twirled and sucked on her until she felt heated between her thighs.

Holy crap!

Lucy and Antonio were locked into the hottest, most passionate kiss she'd ever experienced in her life. He held her closely and sucked on her lips and pleasured them in a way she never imagined.

This. Man. Can. Kiss!

She didn't know where she was she was so lost in the moment. She couldn't care less if she were dangling from the Empire State Building in New York or the CN Tower in the downtown Toronto core. Her mind buzzed, her body convulsed.

What a kiss!

Antonio's lips tasted as sweet as they looked. His lips tasted of savory wine and were divinely intoxicating. Heat coursed through Lucy's blood. Her blood pumped fast and hard, and she didn't know whether she was coming or going. She was in a trance. When he licked her lips and pulled away from her, she was still buzzed, dazzled, discombobulated. Her lips tingled from his soft, intimate touch. Her body reacted like crazy. Her nipples were hard as if she was in the Arctic and her inner thighs pulsed and pounded from want.

Oh, God!

Oh, God!

Antonio's lips. His kiss.

Lucy was breathless, she was dazed and needed oxygen ... like yesterday.

"Are you okay, Miss Shillerton?" Antonio's low voice slid into her.

She took a minute to catch her breath and realized that they were already at the bottom of the slope. She was still panting, breathing hard and fast.

"Well, I'm glad you didn't pass out on me up there." He grinned.

Lucy gazed into his eyes, her mind was still reeling from his soft, sensual kiss. This man oozed power. Sexual power and lots of it. Yet he just claimed that he didn't fall in love. That was what he said, wasn't it? She was aware he was never heartbroken but he must have broken a hell of a lot of hearts.

Lucy was shaking. She was shivering and it wasn't because of a cool night breeze.

"Lucy, come on. I'd better take you home."

"M-m-my car," she stuttered.

"Maxine drove it home, remember?"

"Oh, right." Lucy clutched her forehead. Superman CEO here just stole her breath away and all her senses and her memory, too, with just one hot, memorable kiss.

"Sorry, I shouldn't have done that," he murmured.

"Done what?"

"I sometimes get ahead of myself. I just didn't want you passing out on me there. You know, just trying to distract you."

"Yeah, I...I know. Thank you." So that was all it was? Antonio was saving her, not seducing her?

Then why was her body still pulsing and reacting to him?

It wasn't anything, Lucy. Don't get ahead of yourself. It was only a kiss.

No. It wasn't just a kiss. It was freaking the best feeling I'd ever experienced sexually and he hadn't even undressed me...yet.

Later, when Lucy arrived at her apartment, she pressed the remote for her iPod dock and the first song that loaded really spoke to how she felt at that moment. It was a hot, soulful ballad from Deborah Cox titled "Nobody's Supposed to Be Here." That woman sure could sing. And she was singing just what Lucy was feeling. Lucy crouched down on the floor by her door after closing it. She grabbed her knees to her chest.

Shit!

She was falling for Antonio Romero.

That was so wrong on so many levels.

He wasn't relationship material. He told her that. Not just told her, screamed it from the mountaintops.

She didn't want to get her heart slammed into pieces again. But yet, he made her feel the way no man had ever made her feel before. Not even her first love.

Lucy had to get Antonio out of her system and fast. This was all wrong. She craved the way he made her feel. She craved him. But she could not, should not give her heart to him.

Once bitten, twice shy.

Once betrayed, twice afraid.

She had to try to un-fall in love with this guy. He was so out of her league. Besides, she swore off men—for now, anyway. Look what Jeff did to her. And she really had trusted Jeff.

So why was her heart telling her that she needed Antonio, that she should be with him?

She squeezed her eyes shut. She was shivering all over. She was still buzzing from Antonio's sexually charged, passionate kiss. Her lips still tingled from his touch. Those soft, hot lips of his. His amazing tongue twirling. How did he do that? She was stoked by him. Captivated by him. She was…in love with him.

CHAPTER SEVEN

Antonio kissed me.

Lucy was reeling over that seductive kiss. She was still thrilled about Monday's erotic brush of the lips with Antonio Romero. It was two days ago and yet the fantastical touch of his lips remained as a phantom sensation. *Ah, those lips of his.* Soft, sweet, tender. She'd never met anyone like Antonio. His kiss could bring a woman to dizzying heights of sensual pleasure. What would it feel like to be even more intimate with him? Lucy's body was still pulsing over the naughty thoughts swirling in her mind. So there really was such a thing as sparks flying when you kissed the right person? Lucy had never felt that way before with Jeff. Never.

But the words that followed after her close and personal encounter with Antonio left a bitterness in the pit of her stomach. He said he didn't want her passing out on him. It was merely a distraction. It meant nothing to him, yet she was having these crazy whirlwind feelings about him. Her body desired his touch, his passion. What was wrong with her?

The Diamond Ball Fundraiser was the following evening and Lucy honestly didn't know if she could handle seeing Antonio again. The thought was overwhelming in more ways than one. Then there was the decision regarding what to do about his grandfather's wedding.

Oh, God! His grandfather's nuptials. She was going to have to hurt one of the Romeros and the mere thought scorched her heart.

This was not going to be easy.

"Penny for your thoughts." Maxine raised a brow coupled with a wicked grin. She and Lucy headed up the grand escalator of the Metro Convention Center towards the Bridal Show.

Lucy came out of her daydream and drew in a deep breath before answering. "I've just got a lot on my mind, Maxine."

"I'll bet you do. And I bet his name is Antonio Romero, the third," she said, rolling the R in Romero.

"Maxine!"

"What? I'm just saying."

"Antonio is the grandson of one of my clients. Nothing more."

"Yeah, if you say so. I saw the look on your face when he asked to be alone with you on Monday. Come on. You must have gotten some."

"Maxine! I would never just...I'm not easy. Besides, that would be just so unethical."

Maxine grinned and rolled her eyes playfully as they both stepped off the escalator and walked towards the carpeted corridor towards Showroom A.

"Lucy, you're a woman in love. You may not want to admit it, but I see the way you are around that dude."

"And just how am I around that *dude*?"

"You're always blushing and incoherent for one thing."

Lucy stopped walking for a moment and turned to face Maxine. She could not believe her ears. "Excuse me?"

"You know what I'm talking about, girl. And then, you're like, not letting anything around the office bother you as much. You're always daydreaming and thinking about something and there's that silly grin on your face."

Lucy felt heat soar through her body, her face must have been cherry red by now. "Okay, Maxine. That's enough. I don't know where you got those ideas from-"

"Okay, you can run, girl, but you can't hide."

"Hide?"

"Yeah. You can't hide from love."

Just as they approached the entrance of Showroom A, music wafted out from the loud speakers. And as if some coincidence, the song was none other than "Love Makes Things Happen" by Pebbles and Baby Face.

Oh, hell no, Lucy thought to herself.

The words "love can pull you deep into a spell...." resonated loud and clear as a wedding bell in the hall.

Okay, why on earth do they have to play that song now?

Then Maxine, as if on cue, unsuccessfully stifled her giggle as she held her iPad up to her nose to hide her wide grin.

Lucy and Maxine explored the exhibit with the Fun Bird wedding invitations in the themed wedding section. Next to the Twilight themed wedding, it was the most popular there by far. They carefully selected items that would be more elegant and stunning for the various weddings they would be planning this year.

There was a one-of-a-kind Fun Bird themed boutonnière and bouquet that caught Lucy's attention on a display in addition to slingshot pens and golden eggs and a treasure chest for notes to be penned by guests. Lucy and Maxine were even treated to a video tour of one of the weddings that contained the designer's supply so they could see firsthand. To say they were impressed was an understatement. Going to bridal shows and conventions was a productive way to actively sample the products they would be buying in addition to networking with contractors and future business associates.

The supplier had a display of Fun Bird sugar cookies and a tutorial as to where the special decorations should be placed in the wedding reception. They contained various decorations including themed flowers, three-tiered cakes, placemats, buttons, flags, balloons, red confetti in the shape of tiny bird feathers and the whole works. The vendor even displayed samples of the Fun Birds deviled eggs decorated with one red bird in the center of the tray on the sample dessert table along with fresh strawberries and whipped cream. Lucy tasted the sweet strawberries and scooped up a delicious deviled egg.

Lucy felt the excitement for any bride and groom who would make this a fun wedding. It really took the seriousness out of the occasion. The couple who used these products would have to have an excellent sense of humor and a mentality steeped in fun to pull this off.

The products from this designer would be perfect for Toni's wedding to Shelly, Lucy thought. But then as if right on cue, that awful feeling in the pit of her stomach about the risks involved to pull off such an elaborate ceremony sunk her like a rock in the lake.

Her excitement waned for some reason, though she had less fear of Antonio than she had before. Was Maxine right? Was she really having those symptoms of a person who had caught the magical love bug? Or was that *lust*?

The noise level in the auditorium was quite high but they could still hear the enthusiastic speaker hawking off all the unique elements in their themed-wedding booth. Lucy used many suppliers in the past but she was always glad to attend these shows to meet upcoming designers and view the latest hot trends in the biz. Keeping up with the best and most current trends was the name of the game in the wedding planning industry. You wanted to let people know you had everything to offer them to make their dream ceremony come true.

"Oh, look, this is interesting," Maxine said pulling Lucy away from the booth an hour later after they placed their orders.

"What is this?" Lucy said looking around for the display sign for the tent they were approaching.

"It looks like a tent booth for a DIY wedding," Maxine replied.

"Oh, do-it-yourself. Really? That's not so good for us." Lucy walked inside the open white tent and her vision captured the beautiful decorations and mannequins with various wedding gowns. The tent booth had tons of gorgeous wedding decorations, a conference-length table with sample foods, and various photos on stands with the countless wedding themes. It felt so surreal to be there. For the first time since her fiancé had died, Lucy actually dreamed of becoming a bride again. She squeezed her eyes shut momentarily then reopened them. It was all too much. She came so close to happily-ever-after with Jeff but now?

Maybe she would never become a bride again.

Perhaps planning weddings for others was the closest she would ever become to being a bride. She'd heard the saying always a bridesmaid, never a bride. Well, Lucy thought she might be always a wedding planner and never a bride.

"Hey, cool! And don't worry, Lucy, there's plenty of couples getting married and remarried to go around for all of us in the industry. And look! You can build your own dream wedding here on their computer," Maxine said as she scurried over to the interactive display screen. They were lucky the area wasn't as crowded as the other parts of the booth.

"I...I'm not really interested," Lucy lied.

"Yeah, right. Come on. How could you not be? We plan weddings for a living, don't we? Let's check out the competition!"

Lucy breathed in deeply and the pain of inhaling almost squeezed the air out of her lungs. This was all too much for her. It was like looking at pictures of babies and being told you could never have one of your own. Good heavens! What on earth was she doing in this business? Torturing herself?

No. Making others happy makes me *happy.*

"Okay, fine. You're right. I'll have a look," Lucy finally agreed.

Both girls sat down and were asked to log into a section of the screen where they could design their own dream wedding and have the information forwarded to them in their email inbox. Lucy rolled her eyes and shook her head. Marketing 101. What a great way to collect email addresses of potential clients.

Lucy followed the prompts and filled in her details, then for the hell of it she had fun with it and planned her dream wedding. She paused for a moment when the groom's initials were requested. She did not know why but she decided to have a bit of daring fantasy fun and keyed in AR. Antonio Romero. Yeah, right. Like that would *ever* happen.

Lucy felt silly after she'd gotten up from the display screen and looked around to see if anyone was close enough to see what she entered. She quickly decided to delete the information.

It was useless.

Fantasies were not going to make her real life any better—it was only an illusion, she tried to justify to herself. What was she doing here? Lucy decided that after planning the next three weddings that she had already been contracted to do, she would turn over the keys to a new CEO. She was done with planning weddings for others. It was too heartbreaking for her. It would only serve as a reminder of how much she had failed in her own love life.

Oh, Lucy felt down on herself for even thinking such notions. When she thought about the look on Toni's face or that of her other clients who were in love, she realized that saying something and doing something were two completely different things. It wouldn't be easy to give up Dream Weddings, Inc.

Just as most people who have difficulty in their jobs, they stick it out for one reason, because deep down inside it is their passion. Either that, or they need money to pay their rent and buy food. Still, she wasn't hurting as much as she was financially two years ago and she could always try to get a job in psychology, research or teaching but it wouldn't be as much fun.

If Lucy was honest with herself, then she would know what the real obstacle was. Antonio Romero. She was going crazy out of her mind thinking about him every waking second. And of course there were the dreams! She just couldn't flush his charm, the memory of his sweet kiss, his touch out of her mind. Oh, she tried. But she just couldn't and because he was as emotionally detached as a slab of steel (hmm, speaking of abs of steel), she knew he was unavailable to her in the way that she would need him to be.

The truth was, as embarrassing as it was, Antonio hadn't even called her since Monday. Not that she expected him to. Not that he told her he would but after such an intimate lip-locking session, she thought he would at least have tried to reach her or reach out to her.

Damn Antonio!

Why hasn't he called me?

He should have called me.

He should have tried to send me a text message or an email to see how things were going with his grandfather. Or maybe even make an excuse to drop by the office, just as he did last week.

What was it with him?

Was he seeing someone? No. He said he wasn't.

Lucy then realized that Antonio was hot and sexy and bad in every sense of the word where raw physical attraction was concerned and although she almost went into cardiac arrest when he almost sucked her breath away with that sizzling kiss, it obviously meant nothing to him. At least that's what Lucy believed. She anxiously bit down on her lip while thinking about Monday night.

"Come on, Maxine," Lucy finally uttered. "We need to get going. We have a million things to do before the end of the week."

"Oh, and we *must* get an appropriate outfit for the ball tomorrow."

"I don't think I'm going again. I've got too much on my agenda for our upcoming weddings."

Maxine turned to her as if Lucy had morphed into a vampire or a zombie. "Are you feeling alright? You can*not* miss the Diamond Ball, girl. We have to go!"

"Oh, you can go. You can represent the agency. I don't think we both need to be there. In fact, why don't you ask one of your friends to go? Or, you and Darla can go in my place," Lucy murmured, her heart squeezed at the thought of not going but it was for the best.

There was only one solution to prevent Lucy from heartbreak again.

I've got to get Antonio Romero out of my system.

CHAPTER EIGHT

"You seem preoccupied, grandson," Toni commented as he hobbled with his cane into the den. He didn't always walk with a cane but at times when his arthritis acted up, he would use his walking stick on the advice of his physiotherapist to help stabilize him while ambulating and help to reduce the pressure on his ankle.

Antonio was gazing outside through the French glass doors in the room. He had his hands shoved inside the pockets of his dress pants. His tie was loosened at the neck and his blazer was opened up. He was leaning against the antique oak desk, just glaring as if his vision was fixed on an object. Only it wasn't. It was his mind that was fixated with a subject.

Lucy Shillerton.

He loathed the fact that she was dominating his every thought since he'd met her. She was nothing but trouble and Antonio knew that. Yet his mind and body were not in unison where thoughts of her were concerned. A surge of heat raced through him just visualizing her in his mind. The rounded curves of her hips, her intoxicating fragrance and thoughts of what her slender legs would feel like around his waist.

He had kissed her. That was memorable. There was something about the softness of her lips. She seemed so inexperienced, yet a breath of fresh air at the same time. Antonio had admittedly kissed a lot of women in his time to know about the individuals. Much like James Bond, he could tell a lot by the way a woman kissed, including her sincerity. He didn't know how but he was always spot-on.

There was something that was in sync with his body and soul when his lips touched Lucy's. His mouth literally watered to taste her sweetness all evening before he finally kissed her. But why had he done it then? Was he just curious to see if she tasted as good as she looked? He had found her fragrance so damn intoxicating at the same time, it drove him wild.

Antonio was simply captivated by Lucy's chaste beauty. And not just the physical beauty. The attraction to her was one thing but it was the kindness that rested within her that struck him. It wasn't as if he'd met women like that every single day. There was always an agenda with other women, followed by emotional baggage attached to the ones he'd met.

So now he was hooked on Lucy's taste and that was bad, very bad for him. He didn't like the feeling of being hooked or dependent on anyone. Certainly not some hot-looking woman. He had too many negative experiences in his past with Velcro-women who liked to cling on for dear life to him. He didn't want the responsibility or the emotional commitment they required. They wanted what he could not, would not give them. All of him. Where his heart was concerned that was off-limits. Period.

Then why was she dominating his thoughts all of a sudden? Antonio wasn't a relationship man, so his feelings regarding Lucy brought him to the brink of cognitive dissonance. He needed to do something about that quick.

Antonio turned around to face his ailing grandfather. "Granddad, we need to talk about...your health." Antonio said quietly, shifting the topic in his mind to the real reason he decided to pay his grandfather a visit.

"My health?" Toni sat down on the plush chair by the fireplace. "There's nothing wrong with my health," he continued cheerfully as he leaned back and reclined the chair. He pressed a button by the side and within seconds a staff member entered the study.

"Yes, sir. Can I get you anything?" one of his butlers asked as he entered.

"Yes, my usual, Sam. And for Antonio...?"

"Nothing. Thank you." Antonio wanted nothing more than to get off his chest once and for all what he came to say.

"Very well. Now what is this about my health that you're concerned with?" the elder continued the conversation.

"I've said it before, Grandfather, and I'll say it again. I really think you should reconsider getting married so soon."

The older man's expression darkened slightly. Toni pinched his lips before answering. "Listen, Antonio. We're not going to go through this again. I want to marry Shelly and that's final. It is not subject to negotiation."

"Negotiation? Grandfather, we're not talking about a business merger."

"That's right. We're talking about a marriage merger. You should try it sometime."

Antonio respected his grandfather so much but resisted the urge to be flippant. If it were any other person with whom he was speaking, he may have responded with a "try it four or five times, like you did?" but he could see the old man was simply trying to prove a point.

"Everyone has an agenda, Grandfather. You haven't even known Shelly that long."

"And just how much time do you think I have to get to know her?"

"That's just the point! Don't you question the fact that she is so young and interested in spending her life with you?"

"What's that supposed to mean?"

"Grandfather, you're a noble man, a great person. It's not about you. The fact that you have four alimony payments going out to your ex-wives should set off some red flags. Won't you even consider a pre-nuptial agreement?"

"Now you stop that, Antonio!" Toni sat up straight in his chair, his trembling index finger jabbing the air towards his grandson.

"Granddad, listen to me. I don't want anyone to take advantage of you. For one thing, why did she choose to have such a risky ceremony? She, of all people, should know what too much excitement could do to your heart."

"I went through the entire procedure with the wedding planning agency..."

Damn, them!

His gut clenched at the thought of how they pumped up his grandfather with all these stupid ideas about dream nuptials and outrageous ceremonies.

"They told me that those sorts of weddings are the in-thing now and they are fun," Toni continued, as the butler came in with a tray filled with his evening snack, fruits, biscuits and a steaming cup of coffee. "You know how much I like to have fun, Antonio."

"I understand, Grandfather. But do you remember what the doctor said to you after-" Antonio hesitated for a moment.

"Yes. After the stroke. I do remember. And I also remember that I may not have all the time in the world but that doesn't mean life has to be a bore."

"Grandfather, I don't want you to rush in to things. If you really want to marry this woman, at least give it a little more time. You don't have to wait years, just don't jump into another marriage without thinking about it. What do you even know about this woman?"

"This *woman* is going to be my future wife and that's that. I don't require your approval or anyone else's."

"Fine. But you left me in charge in case you couldn't make decisions for yourself."

"Please don't remind me. Besides, that's not the case now." The older Romero paused for a moment as if in deep thought. "I know you care about me, Antonio. And I know you haven't exactly experienced the joys of marriage or seen it with your own parents," Toni's voice softened, "but trust me on this one. It's not as bad as it seems. Just because you've been hurt or just because I've been hurt by other relationships, do you think I'm going to want to miss out on potentially finding true happiness because of some bad decision I made in the past?"

Antonio closed his eyes and listened. His lips were clenched. He tried to suppress the emotion that had overcome him. Yes, his grandfather touched a raw nerve where marriage was concerned. His own mother was a self-professed gold digger and his former girlfriend had more than betrayed him.

It was a bitter betrayal. The one girl he thought he was in love with when he was younger used him and then went on to sleep with his so-called best friend. Antonio chose to block memories of her from his mind but the fact that his grandfather remembered how much it almost killed him at the time when he was still in college brought the reality back that it had happened and it was real.

Antonio didn't get love from his own mother nor from the women in his life he had dated and add that to the fact that his own grandfather had been strung through the alimony cycle several times didn't make it any easier.

Antonio wasn't like his grandfather, though. Hurt him once and no one would ever get the opportunity to pull that again on him. He was through binding himself or tying himself down to one woman. Sex not love was his motto. And that was good enough for him.

No one would ever get the opportunity to hurt him again. Antonio would make sure of that. And if his grandfather wanted to make a fool of himself and risk his health, then that would be his prerogative.

"I've made bad decisions in the past, Grandfather, and so have you. Yes, I agree with that. But I don't agree with making similar decisions that could lead to the same results," Antonio opined. "When you believe you're in love, isn't it possible to think things are better than they really are? Isn't that why they say that love is blind?"

"Perhaps, grandson. Perhaps. But it is still my decision to make. I really wish you would change the way you feel about love and marriage. I really don't want to see you have all this success and no one to share it with. I want to see you happy with someone who makes you happy, Antonio. There really is someone for everyone. The world is a big place. It is our thinking that can make it small. Please think out of the box where love is concerned." With those words, Toni got up from his chair and pressed the button near his elbow. When the butler returned, Toni motioned to him to take his tray upstairs. "I will be having my evening snack in my room, thank you."

The butler nodded and picked up the tray.

"Well, Antonio, I need to get some rest. We have the ball tomorrow night and I have some business to attend to during the day. And by the looks of it, you could do with some rest yourself." Toni patted Antonio on the back and walked out of the study.

Antonio moved over to the desk and pressed his elbows on top of it, resting his chin on his folded hands.

He gave thought to what his grandfather told him. It wasn't planned that way, yet it had turned out to be a heart-to-heart, man-to-man talk, didn't it? So why hadn't he mellowed a bit?

A flash of loneliness stabbed at Antonio's heart.

The words of his late father's surfaced in his mind. "Fall in love when you're ready, not when you're lonely," his old man once told him. The truth was, Antonio didn't want to mess around with anyone's feelings just because he was unsure of his own. That was what it all boiled down to, wasn't it?

Antonio was sure of many things in his life but knowing when you meet the right person wasn't one of them. Who could tell the difference? No one. Antonio took great risks with business decisions, stock options and game plans to do with the family business, but with his own personal life, that was no longer something he wanted to risk.

He squeezed his eyes shut then opened them again as if tortured by his own emotions as he stood in the dimly-lit study while the sun set outside.

Antonio was in the dark, emotionally and physically. Tormented by his own turbulent feelings and his own secret desires and his own...fears.

The worst thing a woman could do to a man was to damage his pride. Trample his male ego.

Emotionally, he was damaged.

Was Antonio merely lonely and longing for someone who cared for him for who he was and not for the material things he possessed or the lifestyle he could offer the so-called fairer sex? Was he fearful that Lucy could be the one but may not be the one? Or that he may end up ruining her just as he had been ruined? If she was looking for someone to love her completely then she shouldn't look his direction. He would be all wrong for her. No one would be right for Antonio.

Emotionally damaged.

Antonio was a heartbroken, walking wreck.

He didn't need nor want anyone to complete him. He just needed someone to accept him for who he was. He needed someone to be who she was and to allow him to be who he was inside. Unconditional love. That was what his father once spoke about. Someone who loved you in all conditions and was appreciative of you regardless of external circumstances. But that wasn't possible in his books. Something or someone would always end up destroying that beautiful love.

Had he been acting on his grandfather's behalf from the viewpoint of someone who had been emotionally ruined by all the women in his life he'd ever cared about? Antonio was beginning to question his intentions. He was beginning to re-evaluate the rationale behind his thinking and dealing with the patriarch of the Romero dynasty.

How awful to be in a position where you couldn't trust a soul. If only no one knew about his background, then it would be fair game, wouldn't it?

What was with him? Was it because Antonio had seen his grandfather this happy before, four marriages ago? And was it because when the old man was heartbroken after his young wives extracted enough out of him and decided it was time to leave him in the cold, that he was the one to pick up the pieces for his grandfather? It was Antonio who had to talk his grandfather out of killing himself after each wife cheated on him with a younger man then left him in the dust, requesting alimony in the process, wasn't it? It was Antonio who was taking time away from work to take his grandfather fishing, golfing and scuba diving to bring him into a different world and teach him that there was more to life than being married.

Antonio swallowed hard. He sat and leaned back in the leather executive chair and pondered what to do next. His grandfather was right in some regards. His men could not find a damn thing wrong with Shelly, at least not yet. Her character was reportedly impeccable. So then why did Antonio carry this sick feeling in the pit of his stomach about her marrying his grandfather? And why did Lucy's face flash through his mind?

Not her again.

Antonio picked up the phone on the desk and dialed. He knew what he was going to do to fix this situation. He was going to call Lucy Shillerton. He glanced at the antique clock in the study. He knew she often worked late at the office. His men informed him of that when he was checking out her background. It wasn't too late but what if she had already left the office? God, he hoped not. He wasn't about to call her at home.

CHAPTER NINE

The following evening, Lucy sat down in the office at Dream Weddings Inc. Earlier that morning she was stoked when she got into her office and saw there was a missed call from the Romero residence on her caller ID. At first her fingers hovered over the dial pad of her phone. She was contemplating calling the number back but how sad was that to call back a number?

Oh, why didn't he leave a message? Whoever it was.

Perhaps it was an error. Perhaps they really didn't need to speak to her after all.

So she didn't bother to call back since whoever it was didn't leave a voicemail. Still, she wondered if everything was okay with Toni.

Or, dear God, was it Antonio trying to reach her?

Lucy's heart thumped hard and fast in her chest again. Just by thinking about oh-so-sexy Antonio.

No. It could not have been him calling. Why would he?

Lucy was not about to raise her hopes to a false high only to come crashing back down in a balloon of embarrassment. He was just not *that* into her and there was nothing she could do about it.

End of discussion—with self.

"Well, I'm leaving now, Lucy," Maxine called out before walking into Lucy's cluttered office.

Maxine had already gotten dressed to go to the ball from her office. Luckily they had amenities at the loft office complex including a plush gym that included shower facilities and ample change rooms. Since she had been working with Lucy late at the office, she had no choice but to bring in her gown to change into later. They already arranged to have a limousine pick them up at six o'clock.

"Are you sure you're not coming?" Maxine added. She looked vibrant in her yellow beaded empire-waist strapless evening gown that was accentuated by her lovely diamond custom necklace with matching earrings. Actually, she looked more like a bridesmaid than a guest at a formal dinner party.

Lucy thought to herself, *Maxine really deserves to meet someone special at the ball, but knowing Maxine, she probably will find someone.* Maxine was always the go-getter type who could strike up a conversation with anyone and come away with a new friend.

Lucy, on the other hand, would take a lot of convincing. She could be fierce in the office and while hitting the books and in the classroom but in social situations, like formal dinners and dances, she was a wallflower, a bashful soul who would much rather fade into the background.

"You look very nice," Lucy offered, sifting through papers. She then picked up several files from her desk and shoved them in the nearby filing cabinet.

"Thanks." Maxine spun around in her dress as if showing it off at a runway show. "I hope Mr. Right thinks so, too."

Lucy smirked. "Now, how do you know you'll meet Mr. Right tonight, Maxine?"

Maxine placed her hands on her hips. "Well, duh! I didn't go through all this trouble for nothing, girl."

"Maxine, we're there to help raise funds for the Diamond Ball's charity, remember?"

"Yeah, I know that, girl. Just kidding."

Lucy chuckled. "Right. Of course."

"Seriously, though. Lucy, you don't want to miss out on this. You're always busy working so hard, slaving away in here. I mean, life is more than just work. All work and no play...you know what they say, right?"

"No. I don't." Lucy arched her brow to humor her.

Maxine grinned and shook her head. "All work and no play makes Jill a dull cow."

Lucy almost laughed out loud in spite of herself. "Hey! There's no such saying."

"How would you know?" Maxine played back. "I thought you've never heard the saying."

"Fine. Maybe I am a dull cow but I am my own dull cow. Okay?"

Maxine pouted. "Lucy, please don't let me show up alone."

"I thought you were going with our illustrious receptionist. You know, you could both represent the company, then maybe meet a nice guy there." Lucy winked.

"Very funny. You know Darla isn't exactly a going-out-type of girl. Besides, she's not as much fun as you. And you know I'm stretching the truth a bit, right?"

"Maxine! Now, go!"

"Seriously, I really thought you would change your mind, Lucy. That's why I hadn't bothered to ask her or anyone else."

"The limo will be here soon. Don't forget to expense this under Special Events."

Maxine shook her head. "You're really not going, are you?"

"No. I'm not. End of discussion. So, go!"

"Fine."

Lucy felt her heart squeeze. Maxine seemed genuinely disappointed. What was with Lucy? God, she was going to miss out on the annual Diamond Ball—the event of the year to see and be seen, just because what's his name, kiss 'em and leave 'em hanging was going to be there?

She sighed deeply as a horrible dark shadow clouded her mood.

After Maxine left, Lucy felt cold in the office but it wasn't because of a faulty heating system. It was because of her emotions. Did Maxine have a point? What on earth was she afraid of? Besides, how many hundreds of people would be in attendance? She probably wouldn't even have to see Antonio.

Lucy quickly flung the rest of the files down on her desk and grabbed a self-sticking note to place on top of the pile. "To do immediately," she scribbled on the paper.

She would tend to the pile first thing in the morning. It was six o'clock and the refreshments were already being served at the ball.

Lucy left her office and closed the door behind her, locking it with her master key. She walked out of the building and down the street towards her parked car and got in.

Driving back to the suburbs, she knew she would be late. She blasted the music on her radio and "Wrecking Ball" by Miley Cyrus boomed.

She didn't know how long it took her to reach her apartment building but she practically zoomed up the flight of stairs and to her suite. She threw her bag on the kitchen table and stripped her clothes and hopped in the shower.

I have to do this.
I can't hide like this.
Who am I kidding?
Why wouldn't I go?
What am I afraid of?
Who am I afraid of?

As the warming water splashed down her soapy skin, Lucy thought about Antonio holding her from behind. She squeezed her eyes shut and then opened them again.

No. She could not go there. He was out of her league. Was she going to make a fool of herself over him? No. Perhaps she was going to see if she could see him only to show him what he missed out on or what he could miss out on by avoiding her.

Why do women do these things? Why was it that impressing the guy of your dreams was such a huge deal? Girls of any age wanted to look their best when they knew the object of their desire was going to be around, just like in high school, right?

Oh, she was crazy. She was crazy in love with this guy. She could feel it. Her body was heated up and not because of the steamy shower. She was hot for him. She was obsessed with thoughts of him, loving her, kissing her again. Oh, his electrifying sweet kiss. The way his strong arms felt around her waist. His touch. That soul-satisfying caress. His firm, powerful embrace. She'd never in her life met a man like Antonio Romero III. She'd never been captivated by the presence of a man or the anticipation of seeing a man again, a man as hot and sexually potent as Antonio Romero.

Would he ever kiss her again?

Twenty minutes later, Lucy had her cordless phone pressed to her right ear. "Yes, I would like to know if you could send the same driver to pick me up," Lucy inquired, while in her lace bra and matching underwear. Her gown was laying on the bed. She wanted to assure she would have a ride in time for the dance.

"That would be no problem, Ms. Shillerton. Thank you again for your business. The driver will be there shortly."

Lucy's sigh was one of relief. It was as if she'd been holding her breath, wondering how on earth she would get a last minute limo to take her to the ball. The last thing she wanted to do was to drive there herself and show up in her old car while the valet directed all the limos present there.

It was a good thing that the limo driver from their favorite company was already booked for the entire evening. They were technically paying for him by the hour, anyway, and since Maxine was already inside the ballroom, the driver would be free, right?

Lucy could not believe the image she saw in front of her as she stood in front of her full length mirror. She barely recognized herself.

Oh, my God!

Was that really her?

She was no beauty queen and certainly no super model but she really could not believe how transformed she looked. Maxine was right. There's a time for work and a time for play, to relax and unwind and maybe dress up and feel good about yourself. Every woman should do that once in a while. Take time and nurture themselves and take good care of themselves. They were so programmed to taking care of others, whether in business or family life, that sometimes they forgot to take care of themselves or felt guilty when they did.

Lucy spun around slowly in her gown to make sure everything looked okay. She never had the opportunity to go to her high school prom. She wasn't particularly popular and didn't even have a boyfriend or a date at that time. It was as if she were going to her prom now. How silly was that?

She glowed in her floor-length, satin emerald green dress. It was sleeveless, strapless, sexy. The off-the-shoulder look and full flowing bottom gave her silhouette the accentuated appearance that she'd always admired in other women. She looked like a modern-day Cinderella going to the ball.

Yeah, right. She sure didn't feel like a princess-to-be.

Lucy was still tired and stifled a yawn. Her makeup was tastefully light and her dark long mane flowed down her back and off her shoulders.

Suddenly, her legs weakened again. *Damn that feeling!*

Butterflies tickled her stomach at the mere thought of seeing Antonio. She thought about Antonio Romero's eyes capturing her. Or his lips reclaiming hers. What would he say? Would he even notice she turned up at the ball? There would be hundreds of guests and probably many beautifully dressed women there. What would he even think of her? Would he even care to see her again?

Insecurity gnawed at Lucy. She looked down at the hemline of her prom-like gown. Who was she kidding? She could never pull this off. She wasn't the confident, outgoing type. At least not as far as socializing was concerned. And to top that off, she'd be showing up alone! How pathetic would *that* look?

The buzzer sounded through her phone and she picked it up. Her driver was waiting downstairs.

Okay, it was show time.

Antonio glanced at his watch. It was already seven thirty. He had scanned the ballroom several times. He spotted Lucy's associate, Maxine. But where was Lucy? So she decided to bail, huh? She dared not show up to his annual function. Just what exactly was she playing at? He had spoken to her about it on Monday.

Just then Antonio's groin ached. Of course, he had kissed her. That was not his original intention during their meeting but it was something he had to do. Had to. And she all too well kissed him back hungrily as if she wanted more. She could not have expected him to call her after that, could she? Was that her problem? Antonio sensed something might have been wrong. Still, the thought of being slighted by a woman unnerved him. He was used to women calling him all the time, caving to his demands, begging to see him. Not the other way around. Oh, no. What was it with that woman? She was certainly different than any woman he'd ever met in his life, that was for sure.

Antonio stood on the second level in the Imperial ballroom at his family's estate. The room was two-tiered so he could survey from the main floor and watch the guests while enjoying the sights and overseeing that everything was the way it should be.

The first part of the evening had gone well so far. The night was still going to be long. And he had other things to attend to. Still, he would be handing out several prestigious scholarships later, then he would leave. He looked over to the far corner and saw that his grandfather was having a great time, dancing with his young fiancée. Antonio's stomach clenched.

Where was that woman?

Was she trying to avoid him?

Did Lucy think she was going to get out of his demands so easily? Antonio loved his grandfather, even though they didn't always see eye-to-eye but he wasn't about to lose him to some foolish, rushed, high-risk wedding to a young woman he barely knew. And Lucy Shillerton was going to make sure that didn't happen. At this point he knew his grandfather would only listen to Lucy if she convinced him that he should hold off for now.

"You seem preoccupied, cuz. Got a lot on your mind, I see," Lucas commented with a wine glass in his hand. He was gently swaying to the beat of the song and leering at the women as they brushed past the two bachelors on the second level of the grand ballroom.

The dance had already begun and music was booming through the speakers as the live band played. Shortly before, Antonio and Lucas were discussing a potential merger plan with one of their offshore businesses.

Antonio breathed deeply. "I've always got business on my mind, Lucas. You should know me by now." Antonio realized he sounded more agitated than he intended. A wave of apprehension swept over Antonio. Should he tell Lucas what was really bothering him?

"Oh, I get it," Lucas said as he lifted his wine glass to his lips to take another taste. Antonio's held his glass on the rail as he leaned against it and peered out at the guests. "You're not thinking about that little missy from the agency, are you?" Lucas continued, gazing over the balcony. Lucas playfully gave a wink to a young woman walking by who met his gaze. She seemed to have gushed and smiled at him then waved. Antonio noticed Lucas never missed an opportunity to flirt. No matter what the occasion was.

"Now what makes you think I'm thinking about Lucy?"

"Well, for one thing, you didn't say 'that girl' like you would often say. You used her name."

"And your point?" Antonio quizzed as he lifted his wine glass to his lips.

"My point is, cuz, she's the first woman I know you've been so preoccupied with and you haven't even slept with her."

"How would you know that?" Antonio was trying hard to hide his agitation with his young playboy cousin.

"I know. Besides, you don't usually see them afterwards. You avoid them like the plague."

Antonio was glad no one else was around to hear their conversation. "You really don't know me that well, Lucas. For one thing, I always let a woman know upfront that there will be no relationship. It is their problem if they persist after the fact."

"Oh, you are good, cuz. Really good. But I know when you've fallen for one."

"I don't think you do. I'm more concerned right now about getting our grandfather away from the clutches of that opportunist nurse of his, and Lucy seems to have the right influence on getting him to come to his senses. Nothing more. Nothing less." Antonio was getting ready to walk away from the conversation. He felt heated up under his dinner jacket.

Antonio proceeded to walk towards the short staircase to the lower level of the ballroom when his breath ceased.

Lucy Shillerton.

CHAPTER TEN

Antonio didn't even bother to look at his cousin, whom he could see from the corner of his eye looking where his gaze was fixated. Lucas glanced from Lucy to Antonio then back to Lucy with his mouth open. So what? Antonio didn't care how foolish he might look at that moment or how awestruck he appeared. The truth stood that he *was* awestruck. And it took a lot to get that sort of reaction from him.

My God! This woman has been transformed.

She is a goddess.

Antonio felt the mild twitch in his groin. A surge of heat raced through his body. A grin of amusement touched his lips as he watched Lucy make her way through the ballroom looking lost, unsure of herself. She looked like a beautiful homecoming queen yet she did not exhibit any of that confidence.

Antonio's eyes clung to the stunning emerald green ball gown she wore.

Breathtaking!

Emerald green was one of his favorite colors. Actually, it was his only favorite color. He had positive association with that beautiful hue of green and it had little to do with finance. There was something calming, seductive and captivating about emerald. It was, as Lucy was, precious!

If he could remember correctly, that color was the symbol of balance and harmony, renewal and rebirth. It had been said to be an emotionally powerful color as far as love was concerned.

Love?

Why did *that* word love seep into his mind?

Her floor-length evening gown hugging her tiny waist and accentuating her beautiful curves and voluptuous bosom drove him virtually insane just looking at her. It was so tempting not to reach out and hold her close.

She's beautiful. Oh, God, she's amazing.

Lucy was certainly more pleasing to his senses than any other woman he'd ever laid eyes on.

Don't go there, Antonio. You're damaged, remember?

Damaged.

She doesn't deserve you. She'll only get hurt by you.

Those haunting words forced an emotional battle to rage within Antonio.

Lucas moved close to Antonio on the steps of the stairs and continued to watch his cousin's reaction to seeing Lucy.

"Man, I hate being right. Kidding! I don't and I like to gloat." Lucas grinned and shook his head. He then raised his wineglass to his lips.

Just then, one of Antonio's associates walked over to Lucy and struck up an animated conversation. Antonio noticed the dude even had the audacity to place his hand on her lower back. Antonio narrowed his eyes. The image of another man flirting with Lucy struck a dangerous chord within him that caught him by surprise. Why should he care? Why *did* he care?

"I'll be right back," Antonio dismissed Lucas as his gaze followed Lucy and his associate. Antonio made his way through the crowded dance floor but not before being stopped by several guests.

"It's a fine party here, Antonio. Thanks," a woman said to him as she grasped his dinner jacket. He'd turned around and recognized that it was one of his contract employees at his realty branch in the suburbs.

"Thank you," Antonio said with an air of distraction. He could tell the woman wanted to chat him up but his dark gaze was still fixed on Lucy. It was as if she was his companion and somebody was trying to step into his territory.

His blood felt as if it had reached a boiling point. His heart pounded hard and fierce in his chest. He gently placed his hand over the woman's hand on the breast area of his jacket and placed it by her side with as much courtesy as he could.

"Thank you so much for coming...Amanda," he said, recalling the woman's name at the last minute. His tone had an air of finality to it. He could see the woman retreat with disappointment. He hadn't even looked at her again.

His eyes scanned and noted that Lucy was now hidden in the sea of well-dressed guests at the affair. Music continued to blaze through the speakers and the dim ambiance of the ballroom didn't make it any easier. The noise level was extremely high considering he was amongst three hundred excited guests. Chatter and laughter, the epitome of people having fun. Why wasn't Antonio enjoying himself at his own event? Was it because as much as he chose to deny it, something was missing? Or some*one*?

"You look lost, Antonio." It was his assistant, Mariam. She was wearing a long dark blue evening gown and looked more stunning than she ordinarily did. She'd put in a lot of effort for the occasion. Mariam was typically conservative and rarely wore makeup.

"Everything is okay, Mariam." Antonio sighed heavily. "I'm just looking for someone," he replied sharply. Bitterness spilled over in his tone. He didn't like being interrupted, no matter the situation. How on earth did Lucy manage to vanish from his view so suddenly?

He needed to speak to her at once. He was so sure she would have sought him out upon her arrival. Or perhaps she *was* about to contact him before being rudely interrupted by his associate.

"Oh," Mariam said, sounding surprised as she looked around. "Who are you looking for?"

Just then, Lucy appeared in front of him. Antonio's body reacted to her stunning presence. She appeared even more enticing up close. Her sweet perfume wafted to his nostrils. She smelled as good as she looked. His mouth watered to taste the sweetness of her lips again. Her gentle, soft lips.

His gaze fell to her cleavage and he throbbed. She was arousing him right there on the dance floor in the presence of hundreds of guests. Heat continued to race through him. He had a sense of urgency to pull her into his arms right there and then and make passionate love to her.

He noticed out the corner of his eye that Mariam's posture had changed to rigid but he chose to ignore it. "Oh," Mariam seemed to have snarled, curling up her lip.

"Lucy, good to see you!" Antonio's voice was reserved. "You look beautiful. Stunning."

"Thank you," Lucy murmured.

"Mariam, this is Lucy Shillerton," Antonio continued with a tone of authority.

"Yes, I know. From that marriage agency." Mariam seemed annoyed more than anything. Antonio was getting impatient with his so-called loyal assistant. Why was Mariam reacting to Lucy that way? In fact, if Antonio could remember correctly, she would always react that way to any dazzling female he would introduce to her, whether in a business setting or social situation. Perhaps he should be looking for another assistant.

"Actually, it's a dream wedding planning agency," Lucy corrected with a hint of humility. She seemed to flush at that moment. *Was she embarrassed or nervous?* Antonio wondered as his gaze continued to enjoy the sight before him. She radiated vitality that enticed him. There was just something about her that resonated with him and that pleased him very much.

"Yes, of course." Mariam paused for a moment and as if eyeing her up and down surreptitiously she moved in closer to Lucy.

"Oh, wait a minute," Mariam said as she reached into her satin clutch purse and pulled out a handkerchief. She then moved closer to Lucy's hemline near her bosom. "Oh there," she said wiping something off, perhaps an imaginary stain.

Antonio held Mariam's arm and gently pulled her back. "I believe you will be making an announcement soon," Antonio said with an underlying chill.

Mariam flushed. "Yes, Antonio. I...I'll be going then. Nice to meet you, Lucy." Mariam made her way through the crowd.

"I apologize for my assistant or soon-to-be former assistant's behavior," Antonio murmured. "She's apparently a little insecure at times."

"Oh, no worries. Actually, I didn't notice anything strange. She seems really helpful."

Antonio could tell Lucy was embarrassed by her expression and redness of her cheeks. But her reaction brought a delightful warmth to him. Lucy. Had. Class!

She certainly knew how to brush off an embarrassing situation and let it slide off like water off a recently waxed car. Antonio was becoming more fascinated by Lucy each and every time he met her. He was always a good judge of character and the way a person reacted in a negative situation was a greater testimony than the way he reacted in a positive one.

It wasn't how you treat your friends that makes you a powerful person, it's the way you treat your enemies—with compassion. That revealed a lot about a person's heart.

Just then a ballad began to lilt through the speakers and many guests took to the center of the dance floor.

"May I have this dance?" Antonio asked Lucy.

Lucy hesitated. "I...I've never danced like...um...in this situation...in a formal..."

Antonio grinned. "Don't worry," he teased her, "we're not doing the waltz. I'll take the lead, just follow."

Lucy's heart thumped erratically. She was all thumbs or toes when it came to dancing, even slow dancing. Heck, she really didn't think she would have to dance at the Diamond Ball. What if she tripped over her floor-length gown and ripped the seams off and had to have Mariam come rushing to the rescue with her needle and thread that was probably stashed away in her clutch purse?

Breathe deeply, Lucy. It's only a dance.

But that wasn't the only thing that was making her heartbeat thump hard in her throat.

Antonio Romero.

My God!

She was getting up close and personal with the most eligible bachelor at the ball! He asked her to dance. Her!

After fretting she heard the song playing. It was that beautiful ballad again, "Lost in Your Eyes," by Debbie Gibson. What an uplifting love song. The melody was one of the prettiest she'd ever heard. If that sultry serenade couldn't tame a beast, Lucy didn't know what could.

Lucy's body was heating up. She could not do this. How could she slow dance for the first time in her life with a hot, sought-after billionaire in the presence of hundreds of affluent guests? This was utterly insane. She was going to trip and fall and make a complete ass of herself. She didn't slow dance but she dare not tell Antonio this.

Once in elementary school, a boy named Peter asked her to dance and she complied, only to accidentally step on his bad foot. Long story short, neither of them knew what they were doing. They both became the laughingstock of the school and Peter had to have an operation on his foot (though minor) later that week. Of course, she hadn't known beforehand that he had a serious issue with his baby toe. Lucy felt so awful and hadn't even bothered since. Besides, it wasn't as if she went to her prom or had any invitations to go formal dancing since that time.

Antonio was different, of course.

This situation was a billion times different.

Antonio was hot and charming and really knew his way around women and social settings of high class.

Antonio looked Lucy over seductively and her nipples hardened under his touch of her hand as he guided her to the center of the dance floor. He was dripping with delicious charm and this man really oozed powerful sex. She could feel the sexual magnetism between them. She genuinely could and this was not her imagination at play. She could see it in his eyes. It reflected from his soul. She was lost in his dark, enchanting eyes.

Lucy found herself studying Antonio's tall, muscular frame and his sexy profile. He was angelic in every way imaginable. Built like a Greek god.

He looked dazzling in his formal black attire and filled out nicely with his broad athletic shoulders and his height. God, he towered over her and yet she wore her six-inch heels.

Antonio wore a rich black single-breasted tuxedo dinner jacket with satin facing and neatly pressed matching trousers, a la sexy, dangerous James Bond. There wasn't a crease in his attire. He was immaculate.

He sported a crisp white shirt with a black bow tie to match his lapel facings. Hot. "Very nice ensemble," she whispered breathlessly.

"Thank you," Antonio murmured in a deep, rich silky voice that made her spine tingle. A delicious shudder heated her body and she licked her lips. Antonio's sexiness captivated her every time she was close to him.

She glanced down briefly while making sure she did not step on her dress and noted his black, highly-polished expensive leather footwear. She knew what to look for and appreciate because she studied menswear while working with clothing designers for her wedding planning agency with regards to the reception dance room events they'd hosted in the past. And oh, French cuffs. She adored French cuffs on a man. There was something rich and sophisticated about a man in that style shirt.

When the lyrics of the song came to "something's there we can't deny" Lucy's heart fluttered in her chest. Her belly tingled with a thousand tiny butterflies. Waves of excitement washed through her body and coursed through her veins.

To take her mind off feeling nervous around Antonio, she briefly glanced around at the marvelous ballroom. It looked more enormous than she previewed on the Internet. This would be a perfect setting for a wedding reception. The ballroom exuded grandeur. She loved the stunning two-tiered design of the hall. She could see silhouettes of people standing on the upper level looking down at the dance floor. She noted the musician's section over by the left side and there was also some sort of gift table. Perhaps that gift table was where the organizers arranged to host the upcoming prize draw.

Lucy was taken away by the high ceiling, the eye-catching, gold-leafed ceiling with the magnificent crystal chandelier. The soft colors and ambient lighting of the room (if she could call it that) made for a truly romantic fest.

She felt like an honored guest. Maxine was right. Lucy was glad she'd changed her mind about going and showed up. Speaking of Maxine, Lucy wondered where she was. Probably chatting with a hot guest, no doubt.

"You seem nervous," Antonio murmured into her ear, interrupting her thoughts. His deep silky voice sliced through her.

A sense of inadequacy gnawed at Lucy. Oh, why didn't she accept those dance lessons offered gratis from one of their contractors? She was extended an invitation from Dazzling Dance Studios, a client her wedding planning agency used to teach grooms and brides how to prepare for their big day (if they so chose that option in their wedding package) so that they hit it off at their reception while dressed in their best.

A surge of heat rushed through her. She would have been treated to lessons in Ballroom dancing, Salsa, West Coast Swing, Argentine Tango, Latin, and even the Country Two Step. Silly girl. That's what she got for being too busy to socialize and have fun beyond work. Maxine begged her to go along

for the longest time. Now Lucy was about to have her first lesson in front of witnesses—and the hot Mr. Romero.

"I'm not nervous," she denied, biting down on her lip. She noticed that Antonio's hungry gaze slid towards her lips and she tingled between her thighs. *Oh, God! I must stop doing that.*

"Good," he grinned then slid his soft hand over hers. "You're far too beautiful to be nervous."

Lucy's knees weakened at his tender touch and soothing words.

Antonio slid his right hand around her left hip side then towards the center of her mid-back. His left hand gently took her right hand and moved it towards his shoulder. He stood close facing her and she could not help but blush. Heat raced to her throat and to her cheeks. Was it hot all of a sudden? No. It was Antonio who was sizzling.

Her heart raced like mad in her chest. Lucy was terrified and thrilled at the same time. Was he aware of that? Oh, God! How embarrassing that would be. She sure hoped he wasn't as perceptive as she thought he was.

I can do this.

It's only a dance.

Yeah, right. With the hottest bachelor she'd ever met in her life.

Lucy met his gaze again, oblivious to the others in the ballroom. Heck, she couldn't care less who was watching her. The most important person right now was Antonio. She felt the firmness of his hand on her back as he held her snug as if they'd been lovers.

Oh, my!

Soon they were both swaying and moving to the music as they slow danced to Lost in Your Eyes, which then broke out into a string quartet version.

All Lucy could think about as he grinded his hard hips into hers was, this man can move! She had read somewhere that the way a man moves on the dance floor says a lot about how good he can move in the bedroom.

Fire scorched through Lucy's blood at the thought.

This man is sex. He is the embodiment of sexiness.

Antonio was an expert in his movements and in taking the lead. Thank heavens for that!

He whispered in her ear on occasion and told her she was doing very well and how gorgeous she was.

"You're the most beautiful woman I've ever laid eyes on, inside and out."

Lucy was gushing inside, wavering with self-consciousness. Was he just saying that? Had it been the intoxicating atmosphere of the dance floor or did it come from the heart? Right then and there, she knew that *she* was also sedated from the music. Lucy felt pleasantly seduced by his soulful movements, his touch and his aura.

But what about Monday night? He was all hot and heavy with her then and cooled off her like a slab of ice the next day.

An adorable boyish grin touched the corner of his lips. Her palms were getting sweaty from her bungled nerves. Lucy had stopped breathing momentarily. She was only inches away from Antonio's sweet lips. But she felt the solid hardness of his manhood pressing against her inner thigh as they grinded their hips vertically on the dance floor.

If only I could taste your lips again. Oh, God! Kiss me, Antonio. Kiss me again. Please.

His cologne tantalized her nostrils and she was dizzy with excitement. She was enjoying her first real slow dancing experience with Antonio.

The image of Antonio releasing her from her ball gown and pressing his lips to her naked skin slipped inside her mind causing her heartbeat to escalate. It was a wonder she didn't have a heart attack from all the heart racing. She squeezed her eyes shut for a moment and re-opened them, hoping the image would vanish. She didn't want it to, but she sure didn't want to raise her hopes for nothing.

Lucy didn't know what had gotten into her but the urge to rest her head on his chest as they continued to dance was overpowering her. As if he could read her mind Antonio pulled her close and she nestled her head on his tuxedo.

"I want you, Lucy," he whispered in her ear. His breath was warm on her skin and she felt a light sensation.

Lucy pulled her head away from him momentarily and gazed longingly into his dark eyes.

"W-what?" Her voice was oddly hoarse. She could not believe what he just whispered to her. Was it her imagination or did he just say what she thought he said?

"I need you, Lucy. I need you now." His voice was raspy in her ears.

The first silly thought that slid into her mind was, what type of lingerie am I wearing underneath my gown? She often didn't wear sexy lace panties unless it was a special occasion. Thankfully, she did tonight and she breathed a sigh of relief.

I want you, too.

She could not tell him this and her startled gaze must have put him off.

Great going on ruining the moment, Lucy.

Once the music stopped, Antonio pulled away from her slightly and lifted her right hand to his lips and kissed the back of her hand so sophisticatedly. The feeling of ecstasy raced through her blood from the soft touch of his lips. She wanted him. She wanted Antonio now. Her body was begging for him to touch her body. The thought of him being inside her dominated her whole being and it was driving her crazy.

"Thank you for this dance," he had finished his moment of seduction. A grin curled the corner of his lips.

What was he thinking? What was on his mind? Lucy wondered ferociously. Was Antonio trying to smooth-talk her into seeing things his way where his grandfather's wedding was concerned? Was he playing a game with her? Or was she going crazy out of her mind?

"May I escort you to your table?" he offered.

"Um...I...I don't really have a table." Actually, she was sure that staff from Dream Weddings, Inc. was seated at table seventeen, come to think of it, but the words would not depart from her lips. She wanted to say, *Take me anywhere you want to take me.*

As if he could read her mind, Antonio took her hand and guided her through the crowded ballroom dance floor and up the steps of the stairwell. They moved away from the noise of the gala event and walked through a cordoned off corridor leading towards the main house.

"Where are we going?" she whispered, dizzy with anticipation and excitement. They walked through an area that reminded her of an art gallery with fancy paintings adorning the walls and a plush Persian rug cushioning their footsteps. It all seemed so surreal. She was with Antonio Romero. Alone. Lucy nervously clutched her purse in front of her as the bottom of her ball gown swept the floor while she hurried to keep up with Antonio.

"Somewhere more quiet," he murmured. She noticed Antonio's eyes seductively traced her silhouette as he stole a sideways glance in her direction her as they walked.

That nagging sense of inadequacy swept over Lucy. What was with her? Why was she suddenly nervous? She bit her lower lip anxiously. She wanted this. She had been fantasizing about being with Antonio for so long. She wanted him more than ever.

But she felt so unprepared. It wasn't as if she'd done this many times before. Oh, could she possibly live up to his standards? Whatever his standards were?

Oh, to hell with it! She was going to be with him. She had already decided that the moment he gently eased her onto the dance floor and seduced her vertically.

She just hoped, prayed that nothing would interrupt their closeness tonight.

"Okay, everyone," Mariam announced as she held the microphone to her lips. "We're now going to have the next prize draw for those holding a lucky ticket."

The crowd gathered in her direction as she stood by the musical section and in front of the prize table.

"Now, as you are all aware, when you received the invitation to the Diamond Ball and RSVP'd there was a number on the invite and you were notified that all invitees would be eligible to win a door prize."

The guests murmured excitedly. The music had already stopped so all attendees would be able to hear.

"Now. The ticket stub I have here belongs to…" she fumbled with a card that she had pulled out of the glass draw box. She almost got her hand stuck in the opening. Many of the guests cheerfully prodded her on, eagerly anticipating winning one of the prestigious door prizes from the Diamond Ball. They were famous for giving away many luxurious gifts from a new sports model car, a newly built cottage, all-expense paid vacations and a grant of up to $50,000 to be used in a business venture startup, a scholarship to the university of the winner's choice or cash! Many visitors attended for the prestige and excitement but the generosity of the Romeros was staggering compared with many other balls and charity functions. Oftentimes, Mariam thought the Romeros were far too generous and far too kind but she realized that it wasn't her decision to make.

"Well, let me see here," Mariam hesitated. She paused for a moment and narrowed her eyes. She realized that all eyes were fixed on her and she quickly changed her expression. "Lucy Shillerton!"

She heard a shout from the audience but it could not have been Lucy, could it? She thought she saw that girl leave with Antonio after the slow dance. Not that she was spying on or stalking them. It was just so obvious that she was making a fool of herself trying to seduce poor, unsuspecting Antonio on the dance floor in the middle of the ball in front of all these elite girls.

Mariam tasted bitterness in her mouth at the thought but stopped herself. She knew Lucy Shillerton would be trouble the moment she'd first met her.

But still, Antonio's a big boy, she consoled. Why surely, he could take care of himself from gold-digging opportunists? Why was Mariam worrying? She'd been around to protect his father and she would do anything she could to ensure that he didn't get himself wrapped up with the wrong type of girl, much less distracted from the family business.

Soon Mariam realized that the call out came from the girl who worked with Lucy at the agency. She'd been introduced to her earlier that evening as Maxine.

Mariam's eyes scanned the room and she raised the microphone to her lips again. "Lucy Shillerton. Lucy, are you here?"

Everyone looked around and shrugged their shoulders.

"Lucy. Shillerton. Are. You. Here?"

CHAPTER ELEVEN

"It's beautiful," Lucy commented as Antonio led her into a spacious guest room on the ground floor of the west wing.

"It's okay," Antonio murmured as he closed the French doors behind them.

Finally. They were alone. At least for now.

Lucy didn't think she could breathe again. Her heart was pounding fiercely in her chest, the thrill of anticipating what was to come overpowered her.

Breathe, Lucy. Breathe.

Antonio looked even more ravishing in the dimly lit presidential-like suite. She quickly looked around, trying not fall into a trance from his penetrating gaze. "Nice. Do presidents come to stay here?"

He grinned. "Presidents of companies. Yes."

"Oh."

"Can I get you anything?"

Just you. "No. I'm good, thanks."

Antonio leaned in to Lucy and gently pulled her closer to him. "I've been waiting for this moment for a long time, Lucy," he said, tilting her chin up slightly so that he could gaze into her eyes. He seemed to carefully survey her features and a grin of approval touched his eager lips.

"You have?" she whispered.

"Why does that surprise you?" he asked in a hoarse voice. "You're a very beautiful woman, Lucy. Surely, you must know that deep inside. I realize that baggage of humility you like to carry with you can be overbearing but any man who doesn't see how gorgeous you are has to have something seriously wrong with him."

Nervously, Lucy chuckled. If only Jeff could have heard that.

"Who hurt you?" he said, his tone shifting dangerously cold. It was as if the warmth of the moment had chips of ice thrown in.

"W-what makes you th-think someone's hurt me?" she said breathless, close to his lips.

He pulled away and his eyes searched her countenance. "I'm good at reading facial expression, Lucy. Even if someone tries to deceive me. I noticed a change in your eyes when I told you that a man has to have something seriously wrong with him to not appreciate you."

"It's that obvious, huh?" Lucy nervously tried to brush it off.

"What happened?"

She really didn't want to go into it with him. She felt as if she could trust him but she really didn't know if she could open up about...that night. The night she found out she had been duped by her ex's cheating behind.

"It doesn't matter. It's over. Right now, I care about now."

"Fine. But eventually, I will know who did this to you."

"Who did what to me?"

"Made you doubt yourself. Second guess yourself. The man who made you believe that you were not good enough for him or any other man. I can see it in you, Lucy. Whoever it was that shattered your self-confidence isn't worth a damn!"

"Thanks, Antonio but...It's over. It really is." She didn't want to bring up what had happened to him then either.

Antonio loosened his bow tie and unbuttoned his tux jacket as he paced the grand suite. She could see the outline of his muscular chest through his shirt. He must be ripped underneath all of that. She moved over to the bed and sat down.

Over to the side she admired the marble fireplace. It gave the room a cozy appeal. She also noted that there was a seating section with two recliners facing each other by the fireplace and by the far left a maple door opened up to what appeared to be a gorgeous en suite bathroom.

She was even stunned to see a tiny bar area in the room and a mini fridge. It was as if this was a VIP hotel suite rather than a private room in a massive mansion. She guessed the Romeros thought of everything.

So this is how the other side lives. Nice!

She peeked at the shiny marbled floor inside it and a viny green plant. God, this was beautiful. Lucy felt so out of her element. Not even the finest hotel suites she'd seen on her business travels came close to this room. In fact, this entire suite could house her studio apartment.

The ceiling-to-floor windows in the bedroom were opulently covered with plush drapes and another prestigious painting hung over the wall by the fireplace. The bed was the biggest she'd ever seen. It was a four-poster bed and must have been larger than king sized. But looking at Antonio, it wasn't surprising that he'd chosen a large bed even if it was for guests. Perhaps he'd spent some time in there, too, when he didn't feel like going up to his own room or to his penthouse. Heck, he could really have any room in the mansion, couldn't he?

An uneasy thought plowed through Lucy's brain. Was she the first woman he'd taken there? Were there others before her who enjoyed being pleasured in this room by Antonio?

She immediately squashed the thought from her mind. She didn't want to ruin the moment with insecure thoughts of what might have been. She was going to live in the present and enjoy the gift of the moment.

Antonio had gone into the bathroom to splash his face with water before drying it with a towel. For a moment he paused over the sink as if his mind was darkly preoccupied. Outside the room, a heaviness settled over Lucy's mind. Had he changed his mind about her? Oh, God! She hoped not. He then came back out as if nothing had bothered him. His mood seemed to mellow slightly.

Antonio reached over to the table and grabbed a remote control and pointed it at a set of speakers. The iPod system in the room played a seductive soulful ballad called "Tonight is Right" by Keith Washington. Oh, talk about setting the mood.

Antonio made his way over to the fridge and scooped up what seemed to be a tiny piece of ice from the freezer and slid it inside his mouth.

What was he doing?

"Come here," he whispered throatily as he snaked his strong arm around her waist when she complied. Electricity pulsed from his touch to her body.

Oh, Antonio.

The thought of being with Antonio set her afire. A sense of urgency and want surged inside her. She ran her hand up his strong, hard, muscled biceps. She could tell he was fit under his suit. She melted under the heat of his seductive gaze. Those dark, beautiful eyes of his. Antonio was dripping with charm and sexiness. As she pressed her body to his, she felt the hardness of his erection behind his zipper. His manly cologne drove her crazy. The way he made her body feel was intoxicating. Could she really do this? Would she have the strength to consummate their affair?

Hot!

She was ablaze and needed him now like she needed air to breathe.

"Oh, Antonio," she murmured huskily as he lowered his head to hers.

When Lucy parted her lips and arched her neck, Antonio slowly pressed his soft, hot lips to her neck and erotically sucked on her flesh before kissing the area. His lips caressed the nape of her neck sending shivers of delight down her spine. He then moved his mouth to her lips and slid his tongue inside.

Oh. My. God!

So that was what he had in mind putting ice chips in his mouth. Lucy felt the heady sensation of the melted ice in his mouth. The stimulation of the chill on her body sent her senses rocketing.

Antonio really knew how to set a woman on fire. Lucy never experienced such a dizzying sensation before. He kissed her in more places than one. His lips trailed to the sensitive part of her neck and down her arm to her inner elbow and her pulse jumped! Her body trembled with an uncontrollable want. She tingled and throbbed between her legs by his sensational erotic foreplay.

Oh, Antonio was so good with his sexually powerful lips. His cologne also had a soothing effect on her.

He sucked on her lower lip then slid his tongue inside her parted lips. Antonio's lips tasted of sweet red wine. His tongue of delicious mint. Fresh and clean.

Lucy's breathing became labored. She'd never desired a man as much as she desired Antonio. She thought she was going to go crazy out of her mind if he didn't get intimate with her. Her head was spinning out of control. They were alone. In a romantic bedroom. Just the two of them.

Oh, my God!

Meanwhile back in the ballroom Mariam was growing frustrated. "Okay, I'm going to make one more announcement and if no one comes forward, we'll move on to the next prize. Lucy Shillerton, are you here? Please come immediately to the podium to see what you have won. Lucy Shillerton?"

She pressed her lips together as she glanced around the ballroom. "Very well. We'll have to move on to the next prize."

Mariam thought it odd that Lucy would suddenly disappear and there was no sign of Antonio either. But she was not about to let that go so easily.

CHAPTER TWELVE

The anticipation of what was to come made Lucy dizzy with desire. She was overwhelmed. Secretly, she wondered if she was okay underneath her garment. Was everything in place? Should she hold her tummy in when he stripped off her gown? Thank God, she was wearing her sexiest, most expensive undergarments.

Antonio's erotic touch sent Lucy's pulses racing. Spinning out of control. He continued to pleasure her with the expert touch of his soft lips and twirl of his tongue. It gave French kissing a delightful new meaning.

"God, you have no idea what you do to me, Lucy," he moaned into her neck, breathing hard as he sucked on her soft skin. Blood pumped hard to her inner thighs.

Lucy's pulse roared in her ears. She groaned from the erotic pleasure. She felt a cool draft at her back realizing that somehow he smoothly unzipped her dress leaving her exposed. How *did* he do that so fast? He was slick with his hands, she noted. Lucy's heart pumped hard and fast. Before long her emerald green ball gown was heaped on the floor at her feet. She stepped out of her dress and Antonio pulled her onto the silk bedspread. There, he was on top of her. His fully-loaded kiss made her forget her name or who she was and where she was. She felt as if she would faint from the pleasure to which her body was treated.

Her nipples tightened as Antonio slowly unhooked her lace bra before pulling it down, exposing her hard, round nipples. He gazed into her eyes. "You are so beautiful, Lucy," he breathed, his voice so hoarse she hardly recognized it.

Antonio then lowered his head to her bosom. His lips ravaged her breasts and he slowly tantalized her hard bud with his lips sucking on her nipple before moving to her other breast. Lucy arched her back on the bed and grasped the sheets. The sensuous brush of his lips on her breasts sent signals of desire rushing through her veins.

"Oh, Antonio," she cried out as the touch of his lips sent her blood pumping. Lucy shuddered with delight as a low moan caught in her throat.

The heat between her thighs was so overwhelming she thought she couldn't wait any longer to go all the way with Antonio.

"Oh, God!" she cried out. *You feel so good.* She savored the feeling of intense pleasure with Antonio. She didn't have a care in the world at that moment. Her thoughts were she was his. She wanted Antonio and he wanted her. He wanted to pleasure her as much as she desired to do the same to him.

Antonio continued to delight Lucy as he moved his lips down her belly, sucking on her navel before sliding lower while she writhed with ecstasy beneath him. He removed her lacy panties and she dug her hands into the firmness of his strong arms. She then moved her fingers to his head and slid them through his dark, silky hair as she continued to be sated.

Lucy spread her legs apart to give Antonio better access, groaning in delight. He French kissed her sex with a hungry passion. This caught Lucy by pleasant surprise. She'd never been fulfilled there before. She didn't know what to expect. His soft tongue slid in between her wet swollen folds, twirling and circling until she came with a sweet orgasmic tremble, arching her back and moaning in satisfaction.

"Oh, God!" Lucy moaned in pleasure, breathless. After another jolt of sweet release she cried out his name. Antonio was hot! The man rocked her world in ways she could never have imagined! Where did he learn to be such a skilled, erotic lover?

She was still buzzing from the sensual experience of feeling his tongue between her legs. Her body was trembling.

Antonio then shifted position and got up, breathing hard. She could see the tented erection through his pants. He gazed lovingly into her eyes and a warm smile touched his lips. He seductively swept his eyes over her nakedness and her body tingled everywhere. He seemed to be admiring her curvaceous form.

Oh, God! I'm naked. He can see my naked body fully exposed. He is enjoying this.

The thought fueled a sexually powerful urge within her. It was highly empowering, more than she ever would have thought watching him admiring her body and her defined curves. She had always been self-conscious about having a little extra weight and not being a super-model size but Antonio made her feel as if she were a precious treasure. She could feel the soulful appreciation in his dark, deliciously sexy gaze.

He wants me. Me!

Still, she was grateful that the low lighting of the room created a warm, romantic ambiance. The beautiful ballad "On the Wings of Love" by Jeffrey Osborne played on the iPod. She was memorizing the gorgeous physique of Antonio's hot body as he removed his attire.

Her body was highly aroused as she trembled with desire. God, he really knew how to turn on a woman and keep her fire stoked.

He reached into the pocket of his dinner jacket that was tossed on the bedside and pulled out a shiny, silver-foiled package.

A condom.

Oh, thank God! She hadn't thought of carrying one in her purse because it wasn't as if she'd ever planned to get some any time soon.

For a fleeting second, Lucy respected that he was in control and sensible enough to never take chances. They really were going all the way. And there would be nothing to stop them. Nothing.

By the time he unzipped his pants and exposed his tented silk boxers, Lucy was heated to the boiling point. Ready to explode if he wasn't inside her soon.

Oh. My. God.

Antonio really did have a well-sculpted body beneath his clothes, as she had imagined. Lucy gasped as she surveyed his herculean physique. *This man takes care of himself.*

Antonio was drop-dead gorgeous in every way. Her heart turned over in response to seeing him almost naked. His dark toned muscular build and well-defined body was impressive to say the least. There wasn't an inch of fat anywhere. He obviously worked out a lot at the gym.

Her eyes devoured his broad shoulders and defined biceps and his impressive six-pack.

Oh, my! He had a real six-pack. She'd only seen stuff like that in sports magazines with certain athletes or body builders. Not the large type but the medium-to-lean built athletes who made it a point to sculpt their physique. Lucy felt a little intimidated by this sex god in front of her but that melted away when she saw his smile of approval and that look had warmed her heart.

Antonio was devilishly handsome. He had the smoothest skin she'd ever seen and a radiant glow about him.

As the heat of expectancy filled her, Antonio moved closer to her and pressed his lips to hers again as he devoured her on the bed. She dug her fingers into his naked flesh. He then shifted his position and stripped off his boxers. Lucy's eyes widened. "Oh, God!"

"Something wrong?" he teased her in a hoarse voice, a wicked grin on his lips.

"No. Everything's…right," she whispered sheepishly, feeling the scorching heat rise to her cheeks and to her nether region. Lucy secretly wondered if she could really accommodate Antonio's huge manhood. He certainly was blessed with porn-star proportions. Nature had been good to him, she observed with delight.

Right then, Lucy wanted him inside her. She wanted to pleasure him with the moistness between her lips the same way he pleasured her moments ago. She lowered her head to his impressive manhood and wrapped her fingers around his long, hard shaft before taking him into her mouth. He tasted sweet, she thought with delight as she motioned her tongue around his hardness while moving her hand up and down his length simultaneously. She enjoyed the low groans of delight as he reacted to her soft tongue over his flesh. She could tell that she was close to bringing him to release but then he stopped her. His voice was hoarse when he told her he wanted to be inside her.

Yes. Make love to me, Antonio.

After she pleasured his body to the brink of orgasm, Antonio ripped open the condom packet and rolled it over his long erection. He was ready to take her to ecstasy.

Antonio was on top of her now and Lucy moaned uncontrollably as he slid deep inside her between her thighs, thrusting his manhood firmly and powerfully as she tightened around him. Her hands tightened around his back as he moved inside back and forth, over and over sending sexual currents through her. Lucy couldn't believe how good Antonio felt. She cried out for more as he gratified her sexually. This was the craziest, mind-blowing sex she'd ever experienced in her entire life. Not that she had much experience to begin with. What had she been missing out on?

Her heart pumped fast and hard as she came. Soon after, Antonio came before collapsing on top of her, breathing heavily. She relished in the drowsy warmth of his embrace, savoring the moment.

She was feeling deeply satisfied and richly desired while Luther Vandross's hauntingly beautiful ballad "So Amazing" played through the speakers. Yes, Lucy concurred with "truly it's amazing...it's so amazing to be loved..."

Now the only feeling drifting through Lucy as she lay on top of Antonio's muscular chest listening to his strong heart beating rhythmically was that Antonio was amazing. He made *her* feel amazing. And she didn't want it to end. Ever.

CHAPTER THIRTEEN

Antonio was incredible, Lucy thought to herself waking up a short time after they'd made hot, passionate love. She turned her head to glance his way and saw that he looked like he was dreaming in his sleep, a sexy grin curled his lips. She admired the beauty of his dark long lashes as he lay with his eyes closed.

He's stunning!

She wondered what time it was. Her eyes caught the display of the digital clock on the bedside table. It was five o'clock in the morning.

Mon Dieu!

Why was she thinking in French all of a sudden? Was it because it was the language of romance? She quickly got up off the bed and gathered her clothes from the floor. Her long, satin ball gown.

What had she done?

She was supposed to have attended the charity ball then leave that evening, not the next morning from Antonio Romero's bed.

But it was what she'd dreamed about for so long.

Antonio Romero.

He looked as if he was in a deep sleep and she didn't want to wake him. Not just yet, anyway.

The naughty thoughts of last night's remarkable sexual adventure were more than overwhelming. Lucy was grinning from ear to ear. The memory of his silky touch on her skin left her feeling on top of the world.

Incredible!

Just as Lucy headed to the en suite bathroom, she stopped dead in her tracks.

Footsteps.

She thought she heard the sound of feet shuffling outside the door. It must have been her imagination. She carefully walked closer to the door and her heart flipped in her chest. She spotted a shadow underneath the door but that shadow vanished.

The corridor lights were on outside so it was obvious to her she wasn't imagining things. Her stomach churned with anxiety.

Was somebody spying on us?

Lucy squashed the thought from her mind. No. That wasn't possible. Who could have possibly known Antonio and she would be there, together? Lucy drew in a deep breath and continued to the bathroom to shower.

An hour later, Lucy and Antonio sat down in the breakfast nook near the kitchen. "You didn't have to do this, Antonio," Lucy said, grinning. She was seated before a plate of delicious scrambled eggs and crisp bacon with fresh slices of tomato. A breakfast fit for a queen compliments of her gracious host. Or new boyfriend.

"It was my pleasure," Antonio said, looking stunning wearing his dress pants and undershirt showing off his rippling biceps. Only moments ago, those strong arms of his were wrapped around Lucy making passionate love to her.

"This is so delicious, Antonio. The eggs are so fluffy and tasty. I had no idea you could cook."

"It's only breakfast."

"Not the way you prepare it. A lot of love went into this. I can tell."

Antonio tilted his head back and laughed. "You're too funny, Lucy. You act as if you've never had breakfast in bed before or had anyone make you a meal."

"I haven't," she said, looking down at her plate. She tried not the kill the mood and perked herself up. That was the least she could do since Antonio was being nothing but overwhelmingly attentive to her.

"Well, I figured you had the staff tend to those mundane duties like making meals," she continued.

"Please. I'm not sure what impressions you have of my family, Lucy, but I can assure you, we take care of ourselves and those we care about."

Those we care about? Lucy loved the sound of that. Come to think of it, Jeff had never cooked her breakfast or anything, ever. It felt so good to be pampered for a change. She was always the one to do the pampering. Not that it did much good in her past relationship.

CHAPTER FOURTEEN

Later that day, Lucy sat at her desk in her office at Dream Weddings, Inc. sipping on her French vanilla latte. She had a mound of paperwork to go through but oddly enough, her mood wasn't as dark as it had been during the week.

She ran over the events of the morning in her mind and a smile warmed her heart. She couldn't help but feeling mellow inside. She was feeling dizzy with excitement. She felt so on top of the world. Love did that to a girl.

Antonio Romero. Had she fallen, God forbid, in love with Antonio? She couldn't have. But she cared so deeply for him. Her mind was dominated with thoughts of him with her, inside her, around her. What were these feelings she had for him nestled in the cushion of her heart?

Love.

She was like a school girl again. Or more realistically, she was more like a girl who had fallen head over shoes in love since she hadn't actually fallen in love in school. She had never had feelings like this for Jeff or anyone else for that matter. Lucy gave Antonio her whole heart. Would he give her his? She knew Antonio cared deeply for her. He told her so many times when they'd made love last night and the way he looked at her and treated her with such high regard and respect. And the way he lovingly made her breakfast this morning and told her he wanted to make sure she had proper nutrition going into work today. Breakfast was the most important meal of the day, yet she had skipped it so many times to begin a grueling long day. No wonder she was always spent by noon. It was nice having someone fuss over her for a change. And more importantly, someone who cared about her and wasn't afraid to show his feelings to her.

He took her home early that morning and made sure that she was okay before tending to a business meeting at his office.

It was midday and she would be expecting Maxine to come in any moment. Maxine had a meeting with the vendor dealing with the upcoming mud-style wedding couple. So far everything was in place and safety measures were set. Yes, even mud weddings needed to have safety measures in place.

Not even *that* bothered Lucy.

Lucy also had a productive meeting with the legal team regarding that dreadful twelve-million dollar lawsuit the company was facing. On advice of her bookkeeper she decided not to get an ulcer over it and let the powers that be handle it. That legal mess had torn Lucy up when she had first heard about it but the matter was out of her hands now and dealing with her current clients and making sure the business ran as smoothly as possible was on the top of her list of priorities. Besides, the case could take forever in the court system which would give her enough time to gather the right documents and help her company's defense team. She had to make sure not to dishonor her aunt's memory. Even though that disastrous wedding occurred while on her aunt's watch.

Then another thought struck Lucy. She and Antonio had been so busy in each other's love that they hadn't even brought up the whole wedding fiasco with Toni's dream Fun Bird wedding to his young bride. Had Antonio changed his mind? Would he call off his silly little ultimatum to shut her down if she didn't find a way to cancel Toni's dream wedding? She understood how much he loved his grandfather and wanted to ensure that he was not taken advantage of and that no harm would come to his health in any way by planning such a risky ceremony, but really, he needed to look at things from his grandfather's perspective. His granddad was in love and Antonio needed to accept it. Why, surely now that Antonio and she were "seeing" each other he would understand and mellow his temperament towards Shelly, his soon-to-be step-grandmother.

"Well, look whose sitting pretty at her desk!" Maxine burst into Lucy's office with a wide grin.

Lucy rolled her eyes and smiled. "Good afternoon, Maxine. How did it go at Robertson Hall?" She tried to dodge any insinuation.

"Oh, no, girlfriend," Maxine persisted, pulling up a chair right in front of Lucy's desk. "You are going to spill the goods."

"What goods?"

"You know what I'm talking about. You. And Antonio." Her eyes widened, excitement brimming over.

Lucy sighed deeply, her heart was fluttering about in her chest again. Thoughts of Antonio did that to her. "There's nothing to tell, Maxine."

"Oh, yeah, like heck. I saw you walk away with Mr. Hot and Sexy after that dirty dancing y'all did."

"Dirty dancing?!"

"Yes. You were grinding and swaying," Maxine teased her as she swayed her hips in the chair. "Then, that assistant of his called out your name after the prize draw and you weren't around. Where'd you sneak off to?"

"What?" This was the first time Lucy heard any of this. "W-what are you talking about?" Anxiety seized her throat and tightened its hold around her windpipe.

"The door-prize, Lucy! You won. Your name was drawn and when she, Miriam, I think, went to announce it, you...and Mr. Hot Guy weren't around." Maxine let out a cackle, clearly enjoying herself.

Lucy felt feverish all of a sudden. So everyone knew that she wasn't at the ball very long. Oh, God! How mortifying.

Then another thought sent daggers to her heart. Did Mariam come looking for Lucy? Was she the one who was snooping outside the bedroom door after she and Antonio...? Oh, God!

"Lucy, are you okay, girlfriend? You don't look too well."

"I'm...I'm okay," Lucy eked out. She swallowed hard and looked down at the file in front of her, scooping it up in her hand, as if to avoid talking any more about the possible fiasco. Her lips were pressed into a thin line. Her mood deflated in an instant.

That week, Antonio and Lucy had managed to avoid talking about Toni Romero's upcoming nuptials as they spent more quality time together, getting to know each other and enjoy each other's company. She was amazed at all the interests they had in common. They caught a basketball game at the Air Canada Center in downtown Toronto. Antonio also took Lucy to see Disney's The Lion King at the Princess of Wales Theatre. As crazy at it sounded, it had been the first time in years since she'd gone to a live show. She talked about how much she really missed seeing Shakespearean plays and Antonio took her to Stratford to see A Midsummer Night's Dream. It was always her dream. She sat cozied up beside Antonio feeling so in love. So secure. She just realized that she had very little in common with her ex. They hardly went places together. It was amazing how they had gotten together in the first place. The only thing they had in common was that they worked at the same place of employment but that was it, apparently. She thought she could never date someone who was so compatible with her on so many levels. Antonio and she just hung out together, enjoying each other's company. She thought to herself, she could really see herself spending the rest of her life with him. But that—was a far off dream. She wasn't going to raise her hopes just yet.

But she sure was enjoying every moment with Antonio. At times he seemed preoccupied. He often had his phone ringing nonstop, as busy as he was but he would always snap back to the moment with her.

Antonio was called away on an out-of-town meeting in New York. "It will only take a day or two. I'll be back soon," he told her.

It was weird feeling but she hated to be away from him. Even though they'd been unofficially dating for short period. Short but sweet and fulfilling. She wanted so much more from him. Yet, she knew they both had busy lives. She had a lot of upcoming wedding assignments to complete for her clients, especially her complex client Toni Romero.

"And don't go arranging this wedding for my grandfather while I'm gone," he told her, but his voice was not as threatening as it had been in the past.

"I told you, Antonio, I'm not getting into that again with you." That was the only thing they hadn't agreed on. "I won't tell you how to run your business and you won't tell me how to run mine," she reminded him before pressing her lips to his at the airport hangar before he left on his private plane to New York.

The following week, Maxine sat in the office with Lucy going over some more last minute details for an upcoming wedding gig for a client. Her mind ran on Antonio. Like what else was new?

She hadn't heard from Antonio in over a day and a half, which was odd, since they'd spoken almost daily since the ball. She didn't want Antonio to feel as if she was crowding him in any way. She knew he had an upcoming bid on a large strip mall in a New York suburb. The municipality was giving him a hard time as it was. As much as she craved every part of him, Lucy wanted to take things at a reasonable pace. The last thing she wanted was to chase him away or suffocate him.

Just then, their receptionist came bursting into her office. Why hadn't she pinged on the intercom?

"Lucy, it's Shelly on the phone."

"Shelly?"

"Yes, Toni's wife...I mean fiancée. She's at the hospital. Toni had an MI."

"An MI? What's that?" Lucy asked as horror crept into her voice. That sure didn't sound favorable, whatever it was.

"I'm sorry," Darla shook her head. "I'm in nursing school part-time so I sometimes revert to medical terminology."

"Darla, what is that? What happened?" Maxine chimed in, anxiously as she leaned forward in her chair gaping at Darla.

Why did Darla have to be so dramatic?

"Myocardial infarction," Darla said as if they should know what that meant. *Didn't they ever watch TV?* Darla had the look of sorrow in her eyes. "He had a heart attack."

Lucy felt the blood drain from her face.

"What?" she cried out. She shot up from her chair, almost toppling it.

"He suffered a big one, he's at the General in the ICU. Intensive Care Unit."

"Oh, God! I...I hope he's alright. We have to go."

"I don't think they'll let us in. Not in the ICU. Only close family are allowed in," Darla explained apologetically.

Lucy paced her office frantically. "Antonio. Oh, God! He must be going through hell." She picked up her cell phone to call him but she received a busy signal which meant he probably had two calls coming in at the same time.

"Listen," Lucy sighed, "since Shelly called us, we'll go to lend our support."

Lucy's stomach sank to her knees. So Antonio had been right about not letting his grandfather get involved with a high-risk wedding ceremony. Oh, God! What had she done? Why hadn't she listened to Antonio in the first place and cancelled the whole darn thing in the beginning?

When Lucy and Maxine arrived at the hospital on the fourth floor, they were seated outside in the visitor lounge. Shelly had already brought them up-to-date with the events of the morning. Lucy could not believe how quickly things could change in a heartbeat. Literally. She had spoken to Toni and Shelly early that morning to confirm details of the placemats for their upcoming nuptials and now this.

Antonio was in the ICU with his grandfather. Lucy could see through the glass how broken and crushed he appeared. Guilt tore through Lucy.

Oh, Antonio. I'm so sorry for not listening to you. Please forgive me.

Tears stung her swollen eyes as she sat there, trembling under the air-conditioned area. It was the end of September yet the chill of early fall had already touched them.

Oh, why didn't I listen to you, Antonio? Maybe he would have been resting in bed instead of dealing with last minute details of his weird wedding adventure. Maybe the thought of being up in a human slingshot got to him.

Lucy hugged herself while she gazed through the glass partition of the ICU. Hoping, wishing, praying that Toni would pull through.

"You know, he told me he still wants us to get married," Shelly cried into her tissues. "I told him that I will always love him and it doesn't matter about a piece of paper." Shelly continued to sob as Lucy wrapped her arm around her.

"It's okay. It'll be alright," Lucy consoled.

Just then, the temperature of the visitor lounge dropped significantly again when Mariam walked in. She eyed Lucy with such contempt she could have frozen under the icy gaze.

Mariam said nothing but spoke to the nurse who came in and was later escorted into the ICU after gowning up. Lucy remembered Antonio mentioning that Mariam had been a faithful assistant to his father and in the family for decades. Perhaps that was why she had the right to go into the ICU as a family member.

"Wow, she's really nice," Maxine commented.

"Maxine, shh!" Lucy shot back. "She's probably upset about the whole situation."

"So upset that she could not say hi? Is she blaming us?"

"Maxine!"

"Sorry." Maxine shrugged her shoulders and reached over to console Shelly.

Then Maxine's words dawned on Lucy. Having a high-energy wedding ceremony planned would be a lot of excitement for an old man. Was Mariam really blaming Lucy for what happened to Toni?

CHAPTER FIFTEEN

The next few weeks were a blur...

Lucy saw Antonio quite a bit during that period but they spent time getting caught up with Toni's progress as he moved from the ICU to the Coronary Care Unit then to the Medical ward. Antonio footed the bill for the best private care for his grandfather. Lucy had been as good as support as she could be while running her business.

She also had the opportunity to speak with Toni.

"I still want to do this, Lucy. Please help us make this happen. I want to marry Shelly. She's truly amazing," Toni pleaded. He was frail but his spirit was soaring through any weakness.

Lucy swallowed hard when Toni told her that from the hospital bedside. Antonio was standing close by leaning against the wall, his hands shoved into his pockets and his chin tilted upwards. Did he even care about his grandfather's wishes? Even if it might be his *last* wish?

"Grandfather, you need to get some rest" was all Antonio uttered during that conversation. Ignoring anything else that was said.

Later, his grandfather became slightly more confused as the hospital staff tried a different type of medication for his nerve pain.

"Well, that settles it," Antonio declared.

"That settles what?" Lucy was confused.

"My grandfather is not in the right frame of mind to make any decisions. And I'm officially his POA."

"POA?"

"His power of attorney, dear. Do you not know what that means in this province?" Mariam's wicked smirk grinded at Lucy's nerves. "That means that all decisions pertaining to finance and living declarations are to be made by Antonio. Period."

"Okay, so?" Lucy challenged.

"The wedding is off," Antonio announced so coldly that Lucy felt an icicle stab right through her heart.

CHAPTER SIXTEEN

Events the next day rendered Lucy gasping for air. She fixated on the email in front of her.

Lucy,

My apologies for communicating via electronic mail but please understand. I think it is for the best. We should no longer see each other. I thank you for all that you were trying to do for my grandfather but the matter has been settled. I also appreciate the time we had together. Please do not try to communicate with me after this.

Respectfully,

Antonio Romero, III

Romero Realty Corp.

Respectfully? WTF? Lucy was fuming. She was boiling at a dangerously hot level. She could feel her blood sizzle in her veins.

I hate Antonio!

What was he thinking? Who was he to blindside me like that? What a creep!

Lucy could feel her breath getting short as she hyperventilated. Oh, God! She was going to lose control. Of her mind. Of her faculties. She thought things were good between the two of them. She really believed they had a spectacular chemistry. She thought he was the one she could possibly spend the rest of her life with. She really thought the universe was giving her a second chance at love. At happiness with a man of her dreams, someone who cared so deeply about her, cherished her, empathized with her sorrows. Her mind flashed back on the day she'd told him about her dog Baily dying, and how sorry he was, feeling her pain. What was that all about then?

So she would not be getting a second chance at love as she had foolishly thought.

Antonio used me!

I will never, ever, ever trust another man again!

Lucy's heart palpitated hard in her chest, her lungs burned when she inhaled. Oh, God! What was happening to her? She poured herself a glass of wine and flumped on her couch in her living area of her bachelor apartment. Drowning her sorrows. She closed her eyes. *I'm so through with the male species!*

* * *

"You okay, cuz?" Lucas turned to Antonio as they sat in the study at Romero Manor.

"I'm fine."

"No you're not. Why don't you just call her."

Antonio turned to Lucas, obviously perplexed. "Excuse me?"

"This is about the wedding planner girl. You're taking out all your anger over Granddad's health on Lucy."

"I'm not having this conversation with you, Lucas."

"Oh, yes you are, man."

"Lucas, I don't know what's gotten into you but really, this is getting old fast. I have no time for your games."

"You've been miserable since you stopped seeing each other. You two were so happy together. What's this going to Stratford and seeing shows and taking her to games? Come on, cuz. Since when have you really taken the time to mellow out like that or take a girl on a guy trip? I've never seen you so hung up on a girl."

"A guy trip?"

"You know what I mean, cuz. You hang out at the court with someone you can chill with. Someone you can talk about anything and everything with. It's not every girl you can talk about the play by play on the court or go sight seeing in the hills. You two really had me there for a moment. I thought you were both mad but then I see you're madly in love and made for each other. Don't let her go over something that none of you have control over. You know Granddad is his own person. If it wasn't Lucy's agency it would be some other agency."

Lucas did have a point, but right now, Antonio was too messed up to even entertain that thought. He didn't know what was going on inside him right now. He was torn. In every single direction. He was right about Lucy being so compatible with Antonio. The short time they spent together meant more than those hot dates he'd had in the past with the superficial women who only cared about the latest designer ensemble on the market. Lucy was passionate about wanting to get involved in everything he was involved in, not just his community work, but his quirky pastime hobbies. Still, he had a lot on his mind. He needed more time to sort out his own feelings and think things through. Right now, his grandfather's full recovery was high on his priority list.

* * *

Four weeks later and Lucy still hadn't heard from Antonio, not that she was really expecting an apology for breaking up with her via "electronic mail." Heck, who spoke like that? *It's email, stupid!*

She was having difficulty focusing on anything these days. It was crazy. She felt as if her mind was going. Antonio. He used her. There was no chemistry after all. Except maybe the chemical imbalance in her brain making her think she had found her soul mate!

She sat in her office typing her latest contract and perhaps her last. She was going to train Maxine to take over her aunt's business in the near future. She really didn't want to have anything to do with arranging asinine weddings for people too-stupid-in-love to see that love didn't work one iota!

She had already given Maxine the reins to guide the ambiguous wedding of their clients Crystal and Randy.

"Well, this is it!" Maxine bubbled as they drove up to the garden wedding party they helped planned. Or that Maxine helped arrange. All on her own. Lucy had no part of it.

Everything seemed pleasing upon inspection. They both carried a clipboard to ensure that the flowers were properly displayed and all the decorations were up to standards and the waiters were present to serve the guests. The reception would also be in the garden.

"I heard one of the guests is planning to get his vid up on YouTube. Think of the publicity," Maxine beamed.

"Yeah, it would be great." Lucy tried to sound as enthusiastic as Maxine felt. But it was no use.

Antonio Romero.

It had been over two months since they'd been seeing each other and four weeks since that god-awful email he slapped her with. Emotionally slapped her in the face with.

Lucy caved under Maxine's badgering and spilled to her what had happened between them, not to mention that infamous email.

Maxine truly provided the support Lucy desperately needed at the time and for that she would always be grateful. It wasn't as if she had many friends. Heck, her friends tended to be the ones she spent the most time with like her colleagues. The nice ones, of course.

"So what is this theme?" Lucy said glancing at her clipboard. "It doesn't say."

"Oh, it's a dance theme. It should be fun."

"Oh, okay, cool!" Lucy said in a low voice. They were both dressed in wedding guest attire so they would at least fit in and blend in with the crowd as they surveyed the scene to ensure everything ran smoothly. They stood over to the side in front of rows of white chairs and the altar nearby decorated in white roses. The sky was blue and the sun shone, though there was a slight chill in the autumn air.

Lucy knew then that this would be the closest she would ever get to being in a wedding. She felt she would never become a bride. Ever. The feeling tore at her inside. Still, she was happy for Crystal and Randy since this was what they wanted.

Lucy grabbed a glass of wine from the waiter walking by as the guests filled up the wedding area.

The groom, Randy, walked down the aisle with his brother as soft music played. So far, so good.

Then the bridesmaids started in and the music changed to some dance-hall sort of heavy-beat song. It seemed so inappropriate but Lucy shrugged her shoulders as she watched from the sidelines.

Six bridesmaids with knee-length dresses glided down the aisle calmly at first then they broke out into a gymnastic-like dance. Lucy's eyes widened. One of the older guests started fanning herself looking as if she would pass out at any moment.

But then it all went downhill.

The bridesmaid, in tune with the heavy beats, started doing this phenomenon known as "twerking" and Lucy almost choked on her drink and spurted out the wine that was in her mouth, coughing so hard that a waiter had to come by and attend to her.

She saw another older guest cover the eyes of a young attendee. The older woman who was fanning herself fainted while the elder gentleman beside her put on his glasses and started dancing too. He, at least, seemed to be enjoying the show.

A commotion soon broke out as the bride in question came dancing down the aisle, but then she tripped over one of the twerking bridesmaids.

I'm dead.

I'm so dead.

Maxine is dead.

She is so dead.

It was a PR disaster, but since it was modern times dominated by social media, disasters could turn out to be a good thing. The next day, the video captured on the cellphone of a guest garnered 50,000 views and 3,000 thumbs-up, 400 thumbs-down.

"Well, at least we got the publicity we needed," Maxine boasted the next day.

"We don't need *that* kind of publicity, Maxine. Not like that." Was Lucy a fool to leave the agency to Maxine? But who else was enthusiastic about continuing her aunt's dream?

"Okay, you can plan the next one," Maxine chimed in. "It's Mr. and future Mrs. Smithson. And they want a simple garden wedding. Nothing fancy. Just beautiful. Paradisiacal."

"Okay, good. When are they getting married?" Lucy took her notepad and grabbed her pen as they sat in her office.

"This one's a rush job. Two weeks."

"Fine. I'll be in charge. No one else."

CHAPTER SEVENTEEN

Thank God this will be the last wedding I will have to plan, Lucy thought.

She was all too grateful for this day to come. The sun shone bright in the blue sky. It was much warmer than previous fall days. Lucy was glad for that. Mr. and Mrs. Smithson would be so happy. She had met them last week for the first time since Maxine originally managed them and they seemed so sweet and appreciative.

Right. The checklist.

Lucy glanced at her notepad and clipboard in her hand. She'd already spent the morning and last two days obsessively checking the wedding day forecast. It was forecast to be a cloudless fall day. An unseasonably warm day, at that!

Lucky for the Smithsons.

I wish it were me getting married.

A longing so sharp and painful settled inside Lucy's heart but she tried to squash the thought. It was a good thing this *would* be her last planned wedding.

She confirmed securing necessary permits, as well as a backup locality for the wedding ceremony and reception in case it rained unexpectedly. Catering was organized. Easy access to bathroom facilities was checked and so was access to parking. The sound system was checked by the DJ and they had a hard surface for the dance so that lady guests would not get their heels stuck in the grass. Not like that last "twerking" wedding disaster weeks ago.

Lucy drew in a deep breath. She glanced around her surroundings. It was breathtaking. A gorgeous Edenic garden nestled near a wooded area outside of Toronto belonging to a rich owner who was generous enough to allow them to use the facilities. Maxine located the venue when the Smithsons requested a specific setting. The trees looked angelic adorned with warm fairy lights that created an inviting ambiance. So romantic. So soothing to the senses. Flowers of every kind decorated the area and lined the aisle leading up to the makeshift altar. Lace curtains were also present. It was spectacular. Lucy spun around and froze.

She caught the silhouette of a tall, well-built man in a suit near one of the trees.

Antonio Romero?

No. It couldn't be. What was he doing there? If this was his property, she would be leaving like right now.

She started to walk away.

Perhaps it was her imagination. She'd been working so hard these past few days, training Maxine to take over while planning this wedding, amongst other things.

"Lucy," Antonio's deep, rich silky voice called out to her from afar and she stopped. Her breath was labored, her heart pounded hard, fast, erratically in her chest. She thought it would explode.

She spun around on her heels. The look of disdain evident on her face.

"I guess I deserve that," he said moving closer to her. He seemed so much better looking than she had remembered but there was a five o'clock bad-boy shadow that gave him edge she'd never seen him sporting before.

"I should have called you before today," he said in a low, deep voice.

"Should have called me?" Lucy could barely contain herself. "Last month, you left me that stupid email saying that we shouldn't see each other anymore… I don't even think we should talk right now. I…I have a wedding to arrange."

"I'm sorry about the email, but I fired Mariam."

"What? What? What are you talking about, Antonio?" Lucy's head was spinning. None of it made sense. "What on earth does Mariam have to do with any of this?"

"It was she who sent you that breakup email from my account. As my personal assistant she had access to send messages on my behalf. Unfortunately, I didn't know until your friend Maxine contacted me recently. Apparently you shared that information with her about the message."

Lucy froze.

She was speechless.

So it *was* Mariam who was the culprit.

She squeezed her eyes shut then re-opened them. Disbelief clouded her mind. Why would Mariam go through so much trouble to ruin their relationship? How evil was that?

"I should have fired her a long time ago. She was always the jealous type. She's lucky that was the only legal action I took with her. But that's another matter. How have you been?" His voice was low, seductive and sincere and brought that familiar shiver of delight down her spine.

She'd missed him. She missed the way he touched her. The way he had made her feel in the past.

"Oh, Antonio. I...I don't know what to say. I guess I should have verified the information. I guess-"

"You should know that I'm a man of class and taste. I would never send such a despicable message."

She giggled. "By email or by electronic mail?" Lucy raised a brow to humor him.

He grinned.

Antonio reached over to bring her body closer to him and he leaned down and pressed his lips to hers. "I've missed you, Lucy. I've spent every waking moment thinking about you."

"Then why didn't you even call me?"

"Because, my dear, I didn't want to bring this up but Mariam is good in an evil sort of way."

"What do you mean by that?"

"She sent me an email on your behalf as well," he growled.

"But she doesn't have access to my account."

"She hired someone to hack into it. That's why I said I could have taken legal action but I decided that she suffered enough when she was plagued by a mild seizure shortly after I caught on to what she was doing. It was then I had realized she played both of us. But I don't want to waste any more of our time speaking of someone who's not worth a second of our time. I need you, Lucy. I need you in my life."

Lucy glanced down not sure of what to say or how to reply. Heat flared up to her cheeks. She was so torn and confused. Would she end up being hurt again as she was demolished by Jeff? Would Antonio be different? Was she fooling herself by trusting him again? Could Antonio really be the one?

Lucy shot Antonio a wicked grin. "You should have known I would never write such a lame email."

He chuckled.

"Listen, about your grandfather..."

"He's recovered. Doc says he still has to take it easy."

"So the wedding is off then?"

"Actually," Antonio said, leaning into the breast jacket of his suit. "He told me to give you this when I see you."

"What is it?" Lucy reached to take a card from him.

"A thank you card."

Lucy opened the card and covered her mouth with her hand, stunned. A picture of Toni and Shelly, at what looked to be the registry office, both dressed in Fun Bird themed outfits. She fought to stifle a giggle. "It's beautiful. I'm so happy for them."

"They thought it best to keep it simple, given his...condition."

"Are you okay with them...getting married?"

"I have to be. As you said, it's their life, not mine," he murmured, gazing into her eyes. He brushed his long finger on her cheek and Lucy shivered. Butterflies tickled her belly.

Then a loud yip from the nearby tree startled Lucy.

She turned her head and saw a gangly puppy tangled in a decoration attached to one of the trees. He was caught on a branch. "How on earth did he get there?" Lucy asked, dropping her clipboard and making her way over. Antonio followed closely and stood and watched her take hold of the brown, fluffy, four-legged beast.

"He's so adorable," she cooed and stroked his fur. The puppy reminded her of Baily. Her beloved beautiful mutt that was taken from her too soon. Oh, God! He reminded her so much of Baily. Her heart squeezed hard in her chest. She was overcome with emotion. "Where did you come from, sweetie?" Lucy paused. Her heart pounded harder and faster now.

There was a festive satin emerald green bow around its neck. Emerald green was one of her favorite colors. And Antonio's too, she had learned.

She saw a little box tied to the chain part of the bow. Her heartbeat pounded in her throat. She opened the box and there was a folded card.

LUCY,

WILL YOU MARRY ME?

XX ANTONIO

Lucy almost collapsed into Antonio's arms. "What?" She was breathless.

"I believe the answer should be yes or no, Lucy. Not *what*?"

Lucy giggled and snaked her arms around Antonio's neck. She squealed with excitement!

"Yes. Yes." She hunched her shoulders and gushed, "Yes!"

"Good. I love you, Lucy. I love you more than I love anything in this world. I hate to sound cliché, but you complete me. You mean the world to me."

Lucy was overcome with emotion and tears of joy welled her eyes. "I love you so much, Antonio. You...you mean the universe and then some to me."

Antonio gave her a grin of approval and got down on bended knee to complete the proposal. Lucy's heart fluttered. Waves of happiness coursed through her blood. She was overcome and overwhelmed with pure unadulterated joy!

This was what it felt like to be in heaven, Lucy was sure.

She was breathing hard and fast now.

"Take it slow there, future wife. I need you to be around for a long time."

Lucy tried to calm herself. This was all too much. Was she dreaming? Should she pinch herself?

"Sorry for the deception, by the way."

"What deception?" she asked him after he placed the most gorgeous diamond wedding ring she'd ever seen on her finger. She didn't even know a rock could be cut so huge and sit on a woman's finger. The ring certainly must have added to her weight by just wearing it.

But it wasn't the size of the ring.

It was about the size of Antonio's heart. And his love for her was huge! Oh, God! He even remembered how much she had missed her dog Baily and she had described him to a tee, down to his alternating white and black whiskers, and now, this little bundle of fur looked just like the one she had lost.

There she was doubting Antonio all this time and he had this elaborate staging of events to get her to marry him.

"So you had all this planned?" she clarified.

"Of course. Well, some of it. This little fella here," he said snuggling the spirited pooch, "was a gift to you from Shelly. So, I thought I'd bring him along. Well, I helped Shelly pick him out. I know how much you loved and missed your little mixed-breed friend."

Lucy gushed. She looked lovingly from Antonio to the puppy and back to Antonio as she weaved her arm through his while they walked on the grass towards the parking area.

"This is one of the properties we own. I figured you wouldn't know about it."

"So the Smithsons…?"

"Sorry, those guys are great. They are married by the way and they were up to having a second ceremony if you had said no to my proposal," he grinned, arching his sexy brow.

Lucy flushed sheepishly. "And you planned all this with Maxine, right?" Lucy grinned and shook her head. She thought no one really cared about her but Antonio cared. Maxine cared. She wasn't alone.

"Pretty much."

"You know I owe her a lot," Lucy quipped.

"Don't worry, we'll make it up to her." He flashed his boyish smile.

We'll make it up to her.

Yes, Lucy loved the sound of "we." Togetherness. Two souls in one. Yes, Maxine certainly deserved some recognition in all of this. Lucy was glad she was handing over the agency to her. This was the ultimate planned wedding.

She was betrayed by Mr. Wrong in her past but now she was with Mr. Right. And nothing could be more fulfilling.

"So I ended up planning my own wedding?"

"And what's so wrong about that?"

"Nothing, except…when is the ceremony? The invitations have to go out."

"Done. Maxine and I took care of all that, Lucy. You needn't worry about a thing."

"I'm speechless. So I got engaged and will get married in the same day? What about my gown?"

"Hey, people are doing it these days. Nothing wrong with that. Why waste time and headache with all that long-term planning? Besides, you already laid the groundwork. Maxine told me about the do-it-yourself wedding booth at the convention. And your gown was fitted when you tried on that dress at the same booth."

"Maxine!" Lucy grinned, shaking her head.

"I thought it was a great idea. So she showed me the email and we took it from there making sure that you planned the Smithsons wedding how you would want your own wedding since they were leaving it up to you to design."

"Thanks!" A warm feeling nestled in her heart.

"I'm so completely in love with you, Antonio."

"I love you, too, Lucy. I don't know how I would manage to spend another day without you."

When they arrived at their cars, Antonio firmly kissed Lucy and the puppy he had cradled in his arms planted a sloppy, wet one on her chin.

Lucy laughed. "I think he's trying to tell us something. Here, let me hold my little guy." She carefully took the pup into her arms and cuddled him. "He's so adorable. Maybe he could be the ring bearer."

"I think that might be pressing it. He may run off with the wedding bands," Antonio teased.

"No. We can't have that now, can we?"

Later that evening…

The garden looked picture perfect.

The flowers decorated it in such an enchanted way that Lucy felt as if she was the princess from a castle wedding at sunset. The sky was turning a purple orangey hue. It was breathtaking. The blooms smelled of sweet perfume and filled the air with their fresh aroma.

Lucy walked down the aisle to the soft, sensuous ballad "Evergreen" by Barbra Streisand. It was perfect given the floral setting.

And what a sweet ambiance!

Though the day was turning to night, the trees all had the warm glow of the lights in the fairy lights that decorated them. Then the aisle was gorgeously lit with tea lights in safe glasses glowing in a warm orange. Gold and cream were the colors for the ceremony with a touch of emerald green.

What gave it its breathtaking ambiance was the fact that the four-place round tables on the property had lanterns underneath the tablecloths to give off the sensation of orange balls of sun glowing beneath the evening sky.

Beautiful.

Lucy wore a white, full length, Cinderella wedding gown with a plunging neckline that accentuated her body as her emerald green gown did the day she first danced with Antonio. She was choked by emotion over her small, close-knit guest list. Her good friends.

Maxine sat near the front since Lucy decided not to have any bridesmaids. She noticed Maxine eyeing Antonio's cousin Lucas who was seated near to her. Lucy grinned. Then there was Toni, Antonio and Lucas's grandfather who sat in a wheelchair alongside his new bride, Shelly. Darla, from the office, and Mr. Petri and others watched Lucy with loving eyes as she made her way down the aisle.

Antonio, of course, was stunning!

There was something so desirable about a groom in a white, crisp, shiny tux.

Breathtaking.

And he was all hers.

Proudly, she embraced with him when she reached the altar. The minister was in place and the ceremony commenced.

Moments later...

"I do," Lucy answered, raw emotion controlling her voice.

"I now pronounce you...husband and wife," was all she remembered hearing before Antonio leaned down and swept her in his strong arms. He bestowed on Lucy the sweetest, most sensual kiss. She thought she would forfeit her breath.

The cheers from the guests and the yapping from Sugar, their new puppy, brought the celebrations together in a spectacular way.

Confetti glinted as it danced through the evening air. And the party began.

And Lucy and Antonio would begin their happily ever after...together.

EPILOGUE

Two hours later...

Besides the occasional influenza bug, Maxine rarely caught anything. But tonight, she caught the gorgeous bouquet of flowers from her friend and former boss, Lucy! She also caught the attention of Antonio's sexy-as-hell playboy cousin, Lucas.

"Beautiful!" Lucas grinned as he gave Maxine a salacious glance. Maxine was playing with the flower petals of the bouquet when he approached her at one of the tables on the lawn.

Of course, he was dangling the lace garter that his cousin Antonio pulled off his new bride using his teeth. That was quite a hot sight to see.

Did sexiness run in the family? It certainly looked like it. Lucas had a few glasses of wine and seemed quite mellow tonight.

The music was blazing from the speakers in the dimly lit garden reception. The night was fresh and crisp. And Lucas was, well...fresh!

"Thanks, Lucas!" Maxine said, flushing. Lucas was not her type. He was a player. Period. She saw the way he flirted with every other girl at the Diamond Ball a couple of months ago. Why surely, he didn't think *she* was some fly-by-night girl, did he?

Lucas?

Lucas caught the garter?

Good grief!

Marriage material, he was not!

"Would you like to dance?" he invited in a deep, smooth voice as if to challenge her to say no. It was more of a statement than a question.

Oh, God, there was the flirtatious thing going on again.

Hell no! Players are just not my type.

She'd heard too much about Lucas's reputation with the women. He was smooth as warm caramel and could be just as sweet with his mouth.

Maxine felt terrible having thought that. What harm could one dance possibly do? It wasn't as if he'd asked her to go to his private yacht or anything like that. Heck, it was her good friend's wedding. People dance at weddings. Nothing wrong with that.

"Sure," Maxine finally agreed. Her mind was telling her one thing but her heart was speaking a whole different language.

It's just one dance, she told herself. Nothing more has to come of it.

Why did she get the feeling this would not be the last time she would see Lucas?

***

A BRIDE FOR THE BILLIONAIRE BAD BOY (THE ROMERO BROTHERS, BOOK 2)

She needs security...

When Maxine Summers took over Dream Weddings, Inc., her friend's former business, she had no idea what a nightmare she would have. It is believed a past disgruntled client is making attempts on her life and she can no longer return to her apartment. Feeling alone, Maxine has nowhere to turn—until the sexy, notorious bachelor, Lucas Romero, offers her a proposition. Her heart says yes, but her mind is saying "no way!"

He needs stability...

Scandal-ridden billionaire, Lucas Romero, knows his reputation with women could cost him everything he's worked for. He previously met Maxine when she helped plan his grandfather's remarriage, a fifth one at that, so when Lucas discovers she needs protection, he is all too willing to help. Except, falling in love was never a part of the arrangement.

Will Maxine be the one to tame his bad boy ways?

PROLOGUE

Six months earlier...

Besides the occasional influenza bug, Maxine rarely caught anything. But on this night, she caught the fragrant bouquet of flowers from her friend and former boss, Lucy! She also caught the attention of Antonio's sexy-as-hell playboy cousin, Lucas.

"Beautiful!" Lucas grinned as he gave Maxine a salacious glance. Maxine was playing with the flower petals of the arrangement when he approached her at one of the tables on the lawn.

Of course, he was dangling the lace garter that his cousin Antonio stripped from his new bride's thigh using only his teeth. That was quite an x-rated sight to behold!

Did sexiness run in the family? It certainly looked like it. Lucas had a few glasses of wine and seemed quite mellow on this eve.

The music was blazing from the speakers in the dimly lit garden reception. The night was fresh and crisp. And Lucas was, well...fresh!

"Thanks, Lucas!" Maxine flushed. Lucas was not her type. He was a player. Period. She saw the way he flirted with every other girl at the Diamond Ball a couple of months ago. Why, surely, he didn't think *she* was some fly-by-night girl, did he?

Lucas?

Lucas caught the garter?

Good grief!

Marriage material, he was not!

"Would you like to dance?" He extended his hand. And his voice, it was oh so deep. It commanded respect and oozed sexiness at the same time. It was as if to challenge her to say no. It was more statement than question.

Oh, God, there was the flirtatious thing going on again.

Hell no! Players are just not my type.

She'd heard too much about Lucas's reputation with the women. The countless women. He was smooth as warm caramel and could be just as sweet with his mouth.

Maxine felt terrible having thought that. What harm could one dance possibly do? It wasn't as if he'd asked her to board his private yacht or anything like that. Heck, it was her good friend's wedding. People dance at weddings. Nothing wrong with that.

"Sure," Maxine finally agreed. Her mind was telling her one thing but her heart was speaking a whole different language.

It's just one dance, she told herself. *Nothing more has to come of it.*

So why did she get the feeling this would not be the last time she would see Lucas?

CHAPTER ONE

This is a nightmare!

Reporters gathered outside Toni Romero's black chauffeur-driven SUV as his driver pulled up to the gate of his sprawling estate, Romero Mansion in the quiet town of Mayberry Hill. A place that was often dubbed a beautiful scenic paradise with breathtaking views of the hills and stretches of green land just north of the city of Toronto. A few hours drive from Buffalo, New York. A tranquil escape and stark contrast from the hectic bustle of the concrete jungle. And now? The center of unwanted media attention!

Toni was seventy-six, after all. He didn't need this type of ridiculous scrutiny. Especially resulting from the behavior of one of his own grandsons, Lucas!

Lucas!

Why couldn't Lucas stay out of trouble and out of the headlines once in a while? Would that be too much to ask?

"Would you like me to turn around and go to the west entrance instead, sir?" the driver asked Toni.

"Oh, no. I'm not going to hide. We'll use the main entrance. They're not going to intimidate me that easily." Toni stiffened his upper lip.

The Romero family's grand estate covered forty impressive acres of sweeping land with scenic surroundings protected by several gated entrances. You could drive to the location from any direction since it housed several properties, including the main house between four different roads. One of the roads was not even accessible to the public.

But the last thing Toni wanted was to give the impression that he was hiding or cowering from disgrace. The Romero family did not hide … from anyone. Not a true Romero, anyway. It was *his* home and he would not be using any back entrances to enter.

"Will they ever go away?" Shelly, his forty-six-year-old wife number five turned to him, her brows furrowed.

"Probably not for now," Toni sighed deeply. "They're like vultures, you know."

"The reporters?"

"Yes. They feed on scandal. Where are they when the Romero men raise millions of dollars to house poor families and feed children from broken homes?"

Toni grasped his cane as the driver drove through the open gates. "Where are the reporters on our good days? One misstep with one of my grandsons and they go crazy." He waved his hand in the air. "And they totally ignore all the good we do for our community." He frowned, pinching his lips tightly as he leaned back into the leather seat of the vehicle.

Once the gates opened, the reporters raced through to follow the SUV that drove slowly up the driveway towards the main house.

"This is intrusive," Shelly called out as she shook her head and gaped at the press through the tinted window.

Once they pulled up to the steps outside the main doors, Henry, the driver, switched off the engine and opened the driver's door. He was a burly man of six feet, five inches who could easily pass for a bodyguard for the stars. It was only recently that Toni's grandson Lucas insisted he hire a driver to take him around after a stroke.

Lucas had made all the arrangements and hired Henry himself.

The good thing about Lucas was, like the rest of Toni's grandsons, he was fiercely protective of his grandfather—and anyone who was vulnerable for that matter. That was why it irked Toni so when Lucas took the initiative to help curb the skyrocketing unemployment rate among young people from various backgrounds by creating jobs in his company and opening up centers to train those who lacked job skills, the same hoards of reporters were pretty much absent from the opening—not that Lucas cared much for hype. He acted out the goodness of his heart, never for publicity. But still, a press release was sent out and very few thought it was as newsworthy as the current headline scandal of the day that often rocked ratings to soaring levels.

Lucas even went as far as personally mentoring many of the community youth. He had such an amazing rapport with youngsters who needed guidance. Lucas's main love was for the Healthy Start Program that operated out of many walk-in clinics around the province, especially in low-income neighborhoods—in addition to Funds for the Future, another program he launched with his brother, Zack, and his cousin, Antonio III. Lucas had taken one rundown clinic that was about to close down and turned it into a flourishing program encouraging people from all economic backgrounds to do various health screening and preventative medicine practices. He'd made it fun by investing in incentive programs to get people to come in.

Then it was soon followed by that cringe-worthy scandal when he'd arranged to have free condoms delivered to local community colleges to promote safe sex—only it was taken way out of context. So this recent scandal only made matters look worse.

When Lucas was growing up, he didn't have the privileges he currently had. Toni never knew he even existed up until his teens.

When Lucas received his inheritance, he'd done a lot of things with the cash, including purchasing fast cars and dating fast women but he'd also invested a lot of his money in all sorts of programs. Following the Romero tradition, of course. Every living person in Mayberry Hill knew about the Romero family's Annual Diamond Ball and Fundraiser. It was the place to be every September.

Lucas was certainly down-to-earth and easily approachable. *Ha! And that was his problem! Easily approachable by gold diggers!*

Lucas could be a hardhead sometimes, actually most of the time. Always out to prove himself. Always taking chances. Doing the unconventional. Making strides. Creating waves. The press dubbed him the Romero Poster Boy for Bad Behavior once when he'd been mixed up in a scandal involving one of his ex-girlfriends who turned out to be some notorious jewel thief.

Toni had made sure to take a hand in raising his grandsons when he learned about his son Jack's existence later in life. Jack was Toni's illegitimate son with a relationship he'd had after one of his divorces. When Toni first met his son, Jack already had five sons and was going through difficult times.

"He said he didn't have anything to do with that woman's claim, so why are they here?" Shelly pursed her lips in disbelief.

"Because, he's a good looking, single man who parties too hard and often with the wrong crowd."

"But Lucas *is* a workaholic, Toni. He works hard so what he does outside of business hours is his own business."

"His own business? No. It's the family's business. The family's name. He has to think about that every waking moment. Like it or not, he's a role model in the community."

"Toni, don't you think you're being a bit harsh on your grandson?" she tried to soothe him.

"He thinks he can just date any pretty woman who bows to him. I warned him that he needs to think about settling down early instead of dating these opportunists. Every year he has a different woman. It's like he gets bored easily and thinks the New Year change means a New Woman. There's bound to be trouble. Now this young lady has a paternity suit. What else is new?"

"Don't be too upset with him, Toni. He's just an easy target. You know that. Lucas is way too careful for get himself into that position. You raised your grandkids well, Toni. They would never put themselves into danger like that."

Toni scoffed. Those words didn't seem to ease his anger. It was the last thing he wanted to hear. "I'm going to settle this once and for all," he murmured under his breath.

"And just how will you do that?" Shelly looked taken aback.

Toni said nothing more as the passenger door to the SUV opened and the noise from the cameras clicking and the reporters all shouting questions besieged his ears at the same time. "Mr. Romero, do you have any comments on the latest allegation regarding your grandson, Lucas?" one reporter shouted.

"No comment," Toni replied firmly and as politely as he could while he hobbled out of the vehicle with his cane at his side. He then walked up the steps, trying to ignore the commotion surrounding him. His chin was raised proudly. If there was one thing about a Romero, it was that they were a proud and confident family. Even in the midst of adversity or scandal. Shelly held on tightly to his arm as they walked inside the foyer of their home.

Shelly and Toni had just returned from a weekend excursion to Niagara Falls when the news broke about the latest scandal surrounding his grandson. He'd summoned his entire family to the estate, those who could make it, to conduct an emergency family meeting. Jack, his son, was still in hiding somewhere in Paris and hadn't stepped foot in the country the past few years. Jack was the father of Lucas, as well as his brothers, Zack, Jules, Troy and Carl. All in their late twenties and early thirties. Toni's eldest son, Antonio Romero II, died at the age of fifty-five, but his grandson Antonio III and his new wife Lucy Shillerton-Romero would be present.

Toni was so proud of his enterprising family; they'd inherited his good business smarts and established their own names in the community, but of course, scandal and controversy seemed to follow them everywhere they went.

A long running feud with the Romero and the Bronson families didn't help either. His old rival, Larry Bronson, was the former mayor of Mayberry Hill and also the patriarch of the Bronson Media Corp.

Surprise. Surprise. The Bronson family owned most of the newspapers in town. Larry made his dislike for the Romero family very clear from the early days—since the Romero family won claim to a piece of land that the Bronson family had insisted was theirs.

But Toni was not about to entertain that idea right now. He had other more important things to tend to. Like, once again, clearing his family's name. He ignored the scores of reporters, knowing full well who owned the papers and TV channel they were reporting for. Talk about media bias.

But somehow his ears zoomed in on a raspy voice of one TV reporter. "So there you have it...Toni Romero will not be making any statements about his grandson Lucas Romero over the latest allegation. I'm Blue Monroe reporting for Channel 31 News."

He'd seen that reporter many times before camped out at his functions. He shrugged and moved up the steps carefully as his wife, who happened to be his former nurse, assisted him.

Shelly whispered in his ear. "You still didn't answer my question, Toni. Are you planning on telling me what you're planning to do to settle this problem with Lucas?"

Toni wouldn't dare admit it, but he'd always had his eye on Maxine Summers who, along his other grandson, Antonio's new wife, Lucy, made glorious arrangements for Toni and Shelly's wedding to happen through their Dream Weddings, Inc. agency. Maxine seemed like a stable, well-adjusted young woman. He had already had her checked out through his contacts. And as if fate couldn't have done a better job, Maxine caught the bouquet from Antonio's wedding while Lucas, of all men, caught the garter. Well, that could only mean one thing. Two birds with one stone. He didn't know how he was going to pull it off, but he was going to do something about getting Maxine and Lucas together as fate had intended. Yes, he hated to meddle, but for the good of the family, sometimes it was necessary. That would help Lucas's wild-partying image and also provide some stability in his life. Maxine didn't know it yet but Toni already considered her part of the inner circle. Trustworthy.

"You'll see," he whispered back, and he raised a brow.

CHAPTER TWO

Somebody is stalking me.

Maxine Summers sat dazed in her office at Dream Weddings, Inc. Heat shot through her veins and boiled her blood. It hadn't been six months since she'd taken over the position of CEO of the company from Lucy Shillerton and, ever since, she'd been plagued by a series of hate mail in her inbox.

Trouble was—she didn't know she even had enemies!

"Well, this one's new," Maxine whispered looking at the screen of her laptop on her desk.

"What does it say?" Betty, the new receptionist who took over for the previous secretary, Darla, seemed as anxious as Maxine.

Maxine read the message out loud. "I know where you live. Your apartment is 11C at the Westwood."

"Wow! That's crazy! Maxine! You have to call the cops. You will call them, won't you?" Betty asked; her mouth fell open as she glared at the screen behind Maxine's desk. There was more to the message Maxine hadn't read aloud. Much more. And it was explicit to say the least.

"I'd say I have no choice." The previous emails seemed like pestering and more of a nuisance, so Maxine was hesitant to call the police for what could have been simply spam or a hoax. But now these creepy people, whoever they were, had her personal information. Heck, they had her home address!

How on earth did they manage to track her down like that? She was a nobody. She wasn't famous or even widely known.

Not like the Romero family!

And thank goodness for that! She'd read the latest scandal surrounding Lucas Romero, whom she'd met at Lucy's wedding. Lucy was the previous owner of Dream Weddings, Inc. and Maxine's good friend since she worked for Lucy before taking over. Lucas was hot but thank goodness she'd stayed clear away from him! How awful to be in his shoes. She pitied the girl who would be his next arm candy.

Maxine wasn't a politician, a reality star or an entertainer. Not that those people deserved to be stalked. But who on earth would have that kind of interest in her? Heck, she was barely making ends meet at the moment, so blackmail was out of the question. It was June, the so-called high season month for weddings and yet—business was unusually slow.

Sure, she was the CEO of the small business owned by Annie, the eclectic woman who'd started the Dream Weddings, Inc. agency to grant the most unusual weddings to deserving couples. Only trouble was that most people were scaling down expenses during this period of economic uncertainty.

"Girl, you look exhausted," Betty commented.

"I am," Maxine murmured. She was drained. Exhausted, really. This was the last thing she needed. "I was at the nursing home late last night."

"Oh, no. What happened? Is your mother all right?"

Maxine sighed. "She'd fallen off the bed."

"But how? Don't they have rails?"

"She's confused again. You know how it is with short staffing."

"Right. I see."

"Well, sometimes it's better for family to be there to make sure things are done. I always try to make sure I'm there at meal times to assure she's fed. Sometimes her meal tray is left untouched. I try to read to her while I'm there, too. When she's having her good days."

"Doesn't it bother you that she doesn't know who you are?"

"Yeah, but I know who *she* is and every day I'm going in to be with her. She took care of me since she adopted me when I was a toddler. She's the only family I have." The words scorched a hole in her heart. Maxine didn't want to see anything happen to her mom. She just couldn't bear it.

And that was why Maxine needed this job like crazy. How else could she afford to keep her mother in the nursing home—as imperfect as it was, if she didn't have a decent salary? If business ran downhill, where would she be? What would happen to her mother?

That's why this latest stupid hoax letter didn't help matters. Could things get any worse?

"Just try to avoid caregiver burnout, Maxine," Betty offered while scrolling down the screen on her iPad with her finger.

"Oh, I will," she sighed wearily. "Now I've just got to try to figure out who the hell would want to send me these nasty letters!"

Maxine thought for a moment. There was that twelve million dollar lawsuit from the couple suing the agency after their bungee jumping nuptials took a nosedive. Maxine squeezed her eyes shut and re-opened them. But it could not have been them—could it? The matter was in the hands of the court system and they were warned beforehand by the previous CEO of Dream Weddings, Inc. of the risks involved and not to take on such a crazy stunt but they wouldn't listen. Maxine racked her brain again. What? What? What?

Was it her ex, Jiles? He was a former co-worker whom she found out had real issues prior to dating him. Her first real boyfriend. But then when she ended it with him as gently as she could, he couldn't let things rest. He was emotionally abusive towards her and would often cause her to doubt herself. That was until she broke away from his hold. Really weird. But somehow, Maxine didn't think it could be him. Or, could it?

This was no time to play Russian roulette with her life. She was not about to take any more chances.

She picked up the phone and dialed the local police station after Googling the information.

"Eighty-fourth division. How may I direct your call?" the operator sounded on the other end of the phone line.

"Yes, hi, I need to speak with a detective. Right away."

***

While waiting inside the Romero mansion for his grandfather to return from his trip, Lucas Romero finished pumping weights in the gym with his brother Zack by his side. The fitness facility was situated on the Romero estate.

He pressed the towel to his moist skin and pondered the latest allegation. He felt a vein throb in his temple. The more he dwelled on the ridiculous accusations, the more the heat of contempt scorched his blood.

The nerve of that woman! Trying to trap me like that. Extort money from me. Well, she's got another thing coming and it won't be cashable.

His biceps were more pumped than before and the adrenaline was still shooting up. He wasn't a man who did the commitment thing unless you counted committing to working out at one of the many gyms owned by his family, or to dedicating all sorts of hours to help run Romero Realty Enterprise and Romero Foundation, the multi-national organizations founded and built from the ground up by his seventy-six- year-old grandfather when he was Lucas's age of twenty-eight.

He was serious about his workout regime, especially since his motor vehicle accident some years back. He'd almost lost his life and his limbs. He was driving a friend to the hospital after she'd experienced dizzy spells. Out of nowhere they were struck by an intoxicated driver. Luckily, they survived. Lucas was given a second chance and thereafter he took nothing for granted. Yeah, he played around a lot but he made it clear up front to the women he dated.

He wanted a no-strings-attached good time. Period. Take it or leave it. He was happy for his cousin Antonio who got hitched six months earlier to that CEO of Dream Weddings, Inc. and he was happy his grandfather found love with his much younger nurse but marriage was not something he was going to touch with a long pitchfork any time soon. He had a brief engagement right out of college but it didn't work out. Said "fiancée" was using the young Mr. Romero for his name. So much for finding someone who cared about you for who you were.

And now?

This crazy scheme from a woman he'd never even dated who claimed he was the father of her child? Yeah, right. Lucas was a lot of things but a deadbeat dad wasn't one of them. No way in hell would he not claim a child who was his.

He loved sex. He loved bringing his women to all kinds of sexual heights. What man with a pulse didn't? But the safer the sex, the better. He always used protection.

Lucas, like his brother Zack, loved the adrenaline rush that also came with fast cars and living in the fast lane but figured getting adrenaline from working out was best at the moment.

Anything to release the pent-up pressure he was feeling. He loathed deceitful women and wondered what the hell put that woman up to her shenanigans. He'd met her at a club once, yes. But she was all over him and Lucas just wasn't feeling her. He guessed it was true that hell hath no fury like a woman scorned—by a Romero.

Right now, he didn't even have his mind on a specific woman, unless he counted that woman he'd met. The hard-as-hell-to-get-her-attention Maxine Summers.

Maxine was that hot chick he'd met through the agency that hooked up his grandfather's fifth wedding to the younger nurse Shelly. The wedding didn't exactly go as planned but his granddad was sure glad they had made arrangements for him to get hitched in style.

He'd always thought it was crazy the way Maxine seemed to ignore him every time he was near her. She wasn't stuck-up or anything remotely close to hoity-toity. Lucas could tell she was interested in him, but she was perhaps shy about expressing herself around him. She'd even told him she'd heard about his reputation with the women and seen it for herself and that's what piqued his interest in her. She was brutally honest. He hadn't met too many girls who carried those qualifications. That really turned him on.

"That's twenty-eight reps, man. Sure you wanna go on?" Zack commented as he handed Lucas his bottled beverage that was ever present by his side while he worked out.

Lucas replaced the weights on the rack and sat up to take a good swig of his energy drink. "Thanks." He wiped the sweat off his face with the white towel and then flung it over his shoulder.

"Granddad's going to want to meet with us soon," Zack said, leaning against the treadmill sipping on his bottled water.

"I can't wait," Lucas said, his tone sharp as acid. He growled knowing full well that a scolding would follow very soon.

"Let Granddad know I'm coming," Lucas added. "I'm going to hit the shower first."

"Sure thing," Zack agreed. He then grabbed his cell phone and headed towards the main area of the mansion.

CHAPTER THREE

A few moments later, Lucas stripped off his gym vest and track pants and headed to the shower of the home-built gym. He turned on the faucet, making sure the water was cool enough. He knew full well that it wasn't good to shower immediately after working out. He should let his body cool down a bit first. Trouble was, he knew damn well nothing could cool him down. He was fired up. Seething. Beside himself. He rubbed the stubble on his chin and got inside the stall allowing the water to splash on his skin before lathering up. All the while thinking. Women. Nothing but trouble. He turned cold inside thinking about the latest headlines he'd seen in the morning papers:

"Another Romero Weasels Way Out of Trouble with Family Connections."

"The Bad Boys of the Romero Family," followed by a caption of "Lucas and Zack at it again!"

"Romeros Want to Rule," followed by a story about how the family was likened to modern-day barbarians who seek to buy up as many properties and take over as many businesses as possible to "take over" and "now they want to sow their wild oats!"

Tabloids!

Didn't they have anything more newsworthy to cover? Like the massive layoffs and high unemployment rate? Growing up, he and his family didn't have much until they'd found out about their long-lost grandfather, Toni. When Lucas's father Jack was unemployed, their family home was repossessed by the bank and they were forced to live out of their dad's old minivan until the authorities got involved. That was why no matter how successful or rich they were, they never forgot where they came from and would do everything in their power to help those up.

What was that saying again? "When you have more, you should give more!" That being said, he also knew one didn't have to be rich to give.

Yeah, he lived on the edge at times! Sure, he wasn't perfect. He sometimes could be a real jerk in the business arena but he still couldn't get his head around the press mentality.

Anything to feed the story-making machines! The Romero family sold papers! That was something he would never get used to.

"When Money Affords Everything…Even Bribery!" was the headline that irked him the most. The same woman claimed that Lucas was trying to buy her off from coming public—which was completely fabricated. She even took a selfie on her camera phone at the time while they were entwined in some exotic dance move. Yeah, the music was pumping and the energy at the club was electric. People go to clubs to have a good time, let loose. Unwind. Unfortunately, when snapshots are taken and a little airbrushing on a photo manipulation program is applied, things can look ten times worse than they are.

Damn those camera phones! Lucas thought bitterly.

The brothers, along with their cousin Antonio (prior to his tying the knot recently), would often unwind at an exclusive nightclub in the downtown core of Toronto every so now and again. Unfortunately, many opportunists and wannabe reality stars would take their phone recording devices and cameras and take all sorts of snapshots of them or with them and post all sorts of stories online.

Lucas thought little of it at the time but every time there was a community program he was involved in on a workday or a major deal to clinch, random images would surface in the media at just the right time in an attempt to discredit his reputation as trustworthy or professional. Like he needed that sort of help. It was bad enough his old man left him a legacy of a tainted name from which he had to distance himself.

His father, Jack, was caught up in some fraud and mishandling of funds scandal some time ago but the media never eased up after he was cleared on a technicality. Reports even went as far as to accuse the Romero family of using their influence and money to buy off witnesses—which was completely false. But that didn't help much.

He had already gotten into a heated discussion with his grandfather over the phone last night about the situation as it unfolded in the media. His grandfather's solution was to issue a written statement, yet again. But Lucas sure as hell wasn't going to apologize or try to explain himself every single time a ridiculous insinuation came to light in the papers. He had better things to do with his time than to consistently play into games.

But a few things were true about Lucas Romero.

He didn't bow to pressure.

He didn't care what the hell people thought about him—as long as he was true to himself.

He didn't believe in marriage.

***

An hour later, the Romero clan was seated in the plush study on the main floor.

"Have you read the headlines this morning?" Toni spoke up as he sat by the grand marble fireplace facing his grandsons. He was, in a word, furious.

"Granddad, I'm sorry this all happened but I had nothing to do with that girl. I'm not issuing a statement," Lucas asserted.

"Do you even care about your reputation, Lucas?"

"I care about not wasting time," he responded with rigidity.

"Lucas, I've told you before and I'm telling you again. In business, reputation is everything. Without it, you're nothing."

"You can't control what people say about you, Gramps!" Zack shot to Lucas's defense.

Toni gave his grandson a stern glare. He sighed deeply before answering. "That is true, Zack. But it doesn't mean that you live in such a way that makes it darn easy for people to say horrible things."

"Now what's that supposed to mean?" Lucas's voice hardened. He felt his muscles tense as he pulled away from the oak table in the study he was leaning against. His hands were still shoved in the pockets of his trousers. His blazer was opened and his tie loosened around his neck. He was on his way to the office downtown after the meeting.

Antonio and Lucy looked on with mixed expressions. Lucy rubbed her hand over her swollen belly as if she felt her baby move. She was five months pregnant with Toni's first great-grandchild. Something that should be the delight of his world right now but unfortunately it was overshadowed by the current nonsense. At least Antonio III was doing something valuable with his life. He had some stability being married to a good woman, expecting a child. The way things should be.

Jules, Troy and Carl, Toni's other grandsons, were present and had already proffered their share into the matter when the family meeting commenced without Lucas while he showered. Occasionally, the men would exchange glances with each other as the elder Romero spoke. It wasn't often a family emergency meeting had to be called at Romero Mansion to brainstorm on what move to make after the family name was being sullied. Toni was at least grateful for that. But one time or twice was one or two too many.

"I'm saying that this isn't the first time you had some...indiscretion. Remember that time at the hotel in Vegas?"

"You're not seriously blaming *me* for that?" Lucas fired in a clipped tone. He leaned back against the desk again, his hands shoved in the pockets of his dress pants as his blazer hung loosely. Toni resisted the urge to tell him to button up his suit. What he wanted to tell him instead was to button up his attitude.

Toni's pet peeve was the casual business look his grandsons often sported. He always thought it was better for a young man to have his suit done up and neat to give the impression of professionalism. But that was back in his day. Was Toni being too old-fashioned regarding his grandsons? For heaven's sake, they were two generations apart. Toni grew up in a much different era from his grandsons. Very different.

"Granddad, I'm sorry you've had to endure inconvenience with all this press intrusion but I'm not taking responsibility for other people's actions. I think we're all wasting our time trying to address this. And as for Vegas, I don't go around judging people by their backgrounds."

"Lucas! You need to be more careful with whom you associate. I'm warning you." The tension in the study was beyond palpable. Toni recomposed himself, feeling guilty for tearing into Lucas the way he did. "Lucas, I didn't mean to raise my voice like that," Toni's voice softened.

Lucas's gaze was fixed outside through the French doors overlooking the massive garden. Luckily it was a private area and tranquil so they were unaware of what was going on outside at the main entrance. It was a quiet area of the estate. A perfect place for family gatherings. At times, one of sorrow. Toni's other grandson Antonio III was an emotional wreck when the family was called in to the study years ago to address the tragic death of his father Antonio, Jr. The family attorney was the one who delivered the heartbreaking news.

"What do you propose we do, Grandfather?" Antonio III chimed in, his eyes narrowed in anger. He was just as fed up with the series of bad press as the rest of them.

"We must act fast in order to mend the damage," Toni responded with an air of authority. He then redirected his attention to Lucas. "Lucas, you've done so brilliantly with your Healthy Start Program. You've not only created jobs with that spectacular software and the initiative walk-in program. I want you to focus on the launch of your new product line. I just don't want this perception of your being reckless and dishonest to tarnish that."

"He has a point, Lucas," Carl added, his deep voice cut through the tension in the room. Carl himself owned the successful string of fitness centers around the city and was quickly branching out to the west coast and to the U.S.

"I'm not disputing that we need to uphold the family honor, Granddad," Lucas growled. He moved from the spot where he was resting and paced by the fireplace. "I'm disputing the fact that we need to keep playing into this publicity game when every Jane, Mary and Sue comes forth with ridiculous allegations. There's a time to do damage control and there's a time to let things go and focus on what really matters. What's that saying? Time spent on getting even is time wasted for getting ahead."

"Good point!" Lucy spoke up. Since coming into the family circle six months ago, she rarely spoke up at family meetings such as this.

"I second that," Zack concurred.

"Yes, you do have a point, Lucas. I understand you don't want to play into the publicity game, but you must understand that we have a reputation to uphold. I don't want you to be the easy target and prey of every young woman out there." Toni rose from his seat with cane in hand and hobbled over to his grandson. "I just wish you were more steady in your life. I wish you would settle down. I wish you would…" Toni broke off. His voice choked.

"Settle down?" Lucas felt his blood drain . "What does this have to do with me settling down?" Fury erupted inside him. He felt his muscles tightening again and it had nothing to do with the rigorous workout he had over an hour ago. He was fit as an Olympic athlete but had a temper like a volcano when certain topics were thrown at him—such as his issues with commitment.

Now just what was his old grandpa up to this time? Lucas was beginning to get suspicious. He didn't like where this conversation was headed one bit.

"Perhaps I didn't choose the right words, Lucas. Forgive me," Toni backed down. His voice was more curt than before but his eyes were downcast.

Lucas's jaw clenched. His lips were pressed together in a thin line. He knew his old gramps was only trying to make things easier for him, but there were just some places he wasn't willing to go and a wife with kiddies waving from behind a white picket fence was one of them.

"I know you wanted me to give you more time, Toni, but I think we should make an announcement soon or tell the reporters there will be no further comment. We need to say something to quiet the commotion outside," Pamela interjected softly.

She was a younger woman who'd been hired as the Romero family's new spokesperson and informal press secretary. She did indeed look anxious as she waited for a response. Pam was seated with her notepad and pen in hand. The room was packed with family members and the temperature level was off the chart. The heat was sizzling, and not from the sun beaming through the window!

"She's right, Lucas and Gramps," Zack added. "We look guilty as hell right now. We need to say something."

"I realize your job is to help my family maintain a positive public image, Pamela," Lucas spoke with cool authority. "And it is appreciated. But I think I will handle this one my way."

His stomach clenched at the thought of finally getting even with the scandal-hungry media that had taken great pleasure ignoring his hard work while digging up all sorts of juicy stories at his expense. Did they even check out the women's claims before posting their news online? Anger seared through his body.

"What?" Toni called out. The rest of the clan looked just as shocked as Toni. "That's nonsense, Lucas. What has gotten into you?"

"I'm heading to the office, and when I leave this house, I'm going through the main entrance and I'll be giving them a piece of my mind so that I can have peace of mind and this can all be done with."

"Don't, Lucas. You're upset. You'll say something you may end up regretting. Let me be the one to speak," Pamela urged.

"I see where Lucas is coming from, Pam." Zack also paced nervously by the fireplace. "It looks bad that Lucas is always seen in compromising positions and always seems to hide behind sugar-coated prepared statements by our spokesperson. He's never spoken up for himself. Maybe this would put an end to this media circus."

"Or feed it further!" Toni growled.

Lucas's jaw tightened. He was damned if he did and damned if he didn't. "Fine, Pam. Say whatever you want." Lucas's gut was telling him to give the press a piece of his mind but right now he'd already been caught saying enough in public. Maybe it was time enough for him to lay low.

"In the meanwhile, I suggest you focus on all that good stuff you're putting into the new software from Healthy Start, Lucas. You're doing such a fine job with that."

"Thanks," Lucas responded half-heartedly. Like any good he'd done ever got noticed. He worked hard to make systems better. Luckily, he'd been a bit of a tech genius and when he'd aced his courses in college, a rival accused him of hacking into the institution's main computer. Of course, that was untrue. He could crack most passwords if he wanted to but he'd much rather be doing more productive things with his time.

"In fact, Lucas, I need to speak with you privately. I have a job I would like you to personally oversee. This will take a bit of time, but it will get you away from the office and away from the office gossip that is sure to follow after today."

Lucas narrowed his eyes. He was often a man in control, feared even in the business arena but around his family he was just little Lucas—at least that's what his granddad always called him when they'd met because he was one of the youngest, though also one of the tallest in the family at six-feet-four inches. So that was ironic. Still, he had to remember that he wasn't always going to win battles with his dear old grandfather.

Just what did his old man have up his sleeve? He hoped it wouldn't be some inane publicity stunt planned with Pamela, this neophyte image consultant and advisor. As much as Lucas liked Pamela as a person, he often wondered why the family needed an employee in her position twenty-four-seven.

"Listen, Granddad, we can all leave so that you two can have some privacy," Antonio said as he helped Lucy up from the leather recliner seat.

"Very well," Toni responded. "And, Pamela, please let me go over the draft before you make your announcement to the media."

"I will, of course, sir," Pamela said before leaving the study with the rest of the clan.

"Hey, Lucas! Are we taking the chopper into town or are you driving?" Zack called out from the foyer after exiting the study.

The Romero family was one of the few residents of the town that had access to its own spacious helipad right out near the east entrance. It would take a couple of hours to drive through the morning traffic to Toronto but the chopper would get them there as the crow flies. Lucas was already running behind and had several meetings to attend during the course of the day.

"Sure, I won't be long," he assured his cousin. Zack winked and grinned before turning towards the corridor of the left wing.

"Okay, let's have it, Gramps! What's this all about?" Lucas probed as he turned to his grandfather. He eyed Toni skeptically at first, then by looking at the elder patriarch of the family something inside him melted. He resisted the urge to grin. He didn't know if he should be annoyed or amused at what his grandfather was about to do. He could almost predict every little scheme he had up his tailored sleeves.

"You almost say it as if you expect something awful, my dear grandson." Toni sat back down on the recliner.

"Because I know this is about something I'm probably not going to like."

"You see, Lucas, how do you expect to achieve positive results if you expect negative ones?"

"Aren't those my words, Gramps?"

"Yes, and I'm giving them back to you, grandson, because sometimes we all need reminders."

"Fine." Lucas's lips melted into a grin as he pulled up a chair and sat opposite Toni. He leaned forward with his elbows on his knees and looked into his grandfather's tired, dark brown eyes.

Lucas had to hand it to him. The man looked great for his age. Lucas hoped he would look as fit when he reached that age. Except for the fine, silver strands of hair on his head, you'd never know Toni was pushing eighty in a few years. He barely looked half his age. He had smooth olive skin, a family trait that was a blessing...and sometimes a curse.

"Do you remember Maxine Summers from Dream Weddings, Inc.?" Toni asked casually as he dusted imaginary lint from his tailored blazer sleeve.

Lucas's gut reacted. He didn't know why. But it just did. The sound of her name. Maxine Summers. There was something about that woman that switched him on and he wasn't all that pleased about that right now. Why would his grandfather bring up Maxine? What did she have to do with anything? Funny thing was that Lucas was thinking about Maxine earlier. In fact, she crossed his mind with naughty thoughts on a few occasions.

"I remember Maxine. Why?" Lucas got up and shoved his hands in his pockets again. He often did that when he was compelled to pace or think. Right now, he wanted to get the heck on out of there if he knew where his grandfather was headed with this.

"Well, as you know, she's a good friend of your cousin by marriage, Lucy."

"I know." Lucas gazed out at the garden outside. "And?"

"Well, she needs to revamp the business. The Dream Weddings business to make it more interactive for a new generation of clients. Most people prefer to interact online these days and well…she needs a bit of help."

"Okay. So what does this have to do with me?"

"The Healthy Start Program is interactive, isn't it?"

"But it wouldn't apply to her business."

"Oh, it just might. I thought maybe you could tailor it for her. Spend some time with her and-"

"Oh, no! Wait a minute. If she's looking for new software for her company, she can have one of my tech guys come in. I'm way too busy-"

"Lucas! Let me finish!"

Lucas rolled his tongue in his cheek and decided to let his elder carry on. "Fine. What is it that you have in mind, Grandfather?"

"She's a nice girl, Lucas, and I think she could do with a bit of help."

"Don't you think I should be steering clear of women right now?"

"Yes. The wrong kind. But this isn't a date, Lucas. This is business. Good business. If it hadn't been for that agency's wonderful encouragement, Shelly and I would not have had our happily-ever-after."

Lucas felt his heart squeeze. And that didn't happen often. At times, he may challenge his grandfather but he loved the old man more than his own life. It gave him immeasurable satisfaction to see Toni happy after his stroke and certainly the fact he moved on after four failed marriages was an accomplishment in and of himself.

His old man was right. It wasn't a date. It was a personal appointment with a client. Heck, CEO of world-renowned companies often went to celebrities to launch their products or personally show them how to use the latest gadget. It was the least he could do. And he would never forget who saved his life—practically saved his life, when his father lost everything and was forced to live out of their old minivan before they even found out about the famous Toni Romero being their own flesh and blood. Who knew where he would be if they didn't have that saving grace. Sure, he'd help out Maxine. She was pretty much one of the few women he could probably trust. She didn't seem to have any tricks up her sleeve.

"Okay. I'll have my secretary hook us up with an appointment."

"Good. That's all I ask, Lucas."

Lucas wasn't sure but it looked as if his grandfather had a smug grin on his face. But he let it go and rolled his eyes playfully.

"I'm heading to the chopper now. Can I get you anything before I leave?" Lucas added.

"Just stay out of trouble, Lucas. I beg of you."

CHAPTER FOUR

"Hey, don't you go getting this one knocked up, either!" Zack teased his brother as the helicopter landed safely on top of the Romero skyscraper in the downtown core. It seemed like a perfect summer day. The sky was cloudless and deep blue. The wind was blowing a mild beginning-of-summer breeze. The temperature outside might have been mild but there was nothing mild about the way Lucas was feeling at the moment. The rotors settled down and the motor quieted.

"You're not freaking funny, Zack!" Lucas shot back.

"Hey, lighten up, bro. You can't take everything so seriously."

Zack was always the prankster and the one to come out with the most hilarious things but this time Lucas was too much on fire to be cooled by even his brother's sense of humor.

"I've got a lot on my mind, Zack," Lucas sighed heavily. He placed on his Ray Bans and prepared to exit the Romero1, the name given to the blue and orange helicopter, one of the first gifts the boys gave to themselves after they'd reached their first major business milestone on their own.

Their first billion dollars in worldwide sales for their software programs and successful stock options.

It was also the time they set up their own wing at the Romero Foundation unique from the other sectors their grandfather managed. They were a strong part of the Romero empire yet had their own independent successful ventures.

"Yeah, I know," Zack replied grabbing his shades from the dashboard. He placed on his sunglasses and unstrapped his seatbelt after powering off the equipment.

As soon as they entered the building, Zack hit the elevator button to head to the executive floors of the corporation while Lucas pressed the main floor button to get to one of his BMWs parked on the premise and left there for days like today when he flew into the city but needed his own vehicle to get around. "I should be back by late afternoon so you can have admin prepare the report for me in time for our meeting," Lucas added, swiping the screen of his iPad while he made arrangements. It was a good thing they were in a private elevator so they wouldn't have to deal with any onlookers or undercover reporters. His grandfather was right. It was better to be out of the office for a while, given the latest hoopla in the media.

"Have fun, but not too much!" Zack playfully slapped Lucas on the back before exiting the elevator on the 43rd floor.

Lucas growled and mock punched his brother in the arm. Of course, they were both athletic and had iron biceps, so it wasn't as if he could really hurt his darling big brother. Zack was only one year older than Lucas but he looked up to him. They always looked out for each other. Of all the brothers, they loved each other and fought for each other but Zack and Lucas seemed to hang out the most. Their interests were more similar than the other siblings.

***

Later, Lucas pulled up to the offices on Front Street for Dream Weddings, Inc. He had already called ahead of time to speak with security about having access to the private back entrance in case any reporters were lurking about. That way, they wouldn't see which office he would be going to. Luckily security and he were tight and it wasn't the first time they'd done favors for his family. Lucas had to always think two steps ahead. That was the blessing, or the curse, of being a Romero.

When he got to the loft offices at Dream Weddings, Inc., Lucas was shocked to see a detective there. "Is everything okay here, officer?" Lucas's deep voice commanded authority.

Maxine felt as if her limbs were going to give way. Heat rushed through her body. *Lucas Romero?*

Oh, my God! What is he doing here?

Why was she always captivated by this…sexy Adonis? *Oh, no. Not Lucas too-hot-for-his-own-good Romero. Anyone but him.*

"Yes, everything is fine, sir," the officer said to Lucas. "Just a routine report."

"Oh, good," Lucas's voice was edgy and curt as he responded to the officer.

The detective nodded and left. It was evident that somehow the officer knew who Lucas was. There seemed to be that air of respect there. The Romero family was well-known in the city. They were a prominent family for a reason.

Maxine was stumped. She still couldn't get her head around this.

Lucas Romero?

She knew Toni Romero had said he was going to assist her in helping her secure new software for her company but she had no idea Lucas Romero would be the man in charge. Why hadn't Toni warned her?

Her mind was mush all of a sudden.

She couldn't think. She was in a daze. Giddy like a school girl with a massive crush on the captain of the football team.

Maxine stood in the reception area of her office when she caught sight of his tall, lean frame and his broad shoulders accentuated by the expensive looking dark blue suit he was wearing. It looked like an Italian designer cut from what she had studied in that workshop on selecting the best tailored suits for grooms. His dark cropped hair and sexy stubble caught her off guard. The man had a sexually-charged rugged bad boy appeal, that was for sure.

"Hi. Are you okay?" Lucas's deep, rich voice caused a surprising reaction in Maxine. She was in a momentary trance from the moment he said "hi." His dark, rich caramel eyes melted her inside like warm butter in a pan. Oh, his eyes were so sexy.

Oh, no. I can't be around this guy. Not now.

"I'm fine, thank you," she replied a little more breathless than she intended. Her heart rate must have been climbing by the second. "I'm surprised to see you. Did you have an appointment?" Maxine tried to compose her voice and quiet the internal trembling.

Maxine, he's just a guy. Just an ordinary guy.

Yeah, one who's headlining every tabloid in town right now. And he's here. In my office.

"Well, I'm here by special request. But what was that all about with the police?"

"Oh, I just…it's nothing. Just some prank notes."

"Prank notes?" His voice grew dark. Lucas seemed very much concerned. Angered even. Was he that worked up over something that happened to her?

"Um…I'll go to Starbucks to get some coffee," Betty interrupted, sounding uncomfortable as she eased out of her chair in the reception area. Maxine almost forgot Betty was present.

"Sure. That would be great, Betty. Lucas, can we get you anything?"

"I'm good. I just want to know if you're going to be alright." Lucas's voice was baritone low and edged with steel. His jaw was clenched. He was fired up all right.

She would be fired up too, but his aura and the scent of his cologne was irresistible to her and lulled her senses. *Oh, heavens.*

Were all the Romero men hot, sexy and this bad?

There was an electrical current between them. Maxine didn't know if she was coming or going. She really wanted to be going…away with him, into his burly arms. She wanted him to carry her away but she could never let on to that.

Maxine hugged herself feeling so self-conscious.

Here was Lucas Romero and she should be thinking about that darned letter. Instead she was fretting about how awful she must look since she barely slept a wink while tending to her mother at the nursing home and at the same time figuring out how to balance the books late into the night so that she wasn't the one responsible for running the company into the ground.

Man, she really needed to get a life. Her thoughts were all over the place. Was this the effect this Romero man had over her? So it was true what her friend Lucy said. Lucy mentioned about how Antonio made her feel and she recalled how dazed and giddy Lucy had been since dating Antonio. This thing the Romero men had was hereditary for sure and it wasn't just their charm, aura and hotness.

Maxine was all over herself. She was a nervous wreck. She didn't know what got into her but she turned to go into her office not caring if Lucas followed or not. She needed to grab a seat fast.

She sat down, placed her elbows on her desk and pressed her hands to her head. "No. I'm not okay, Lucas. But I'll be fine. I think we should probably reschedule our meeting for another day."

Lucas stood rigid at the doorway to her office. "I'm afraid you're not going to get rid of me that easy," he said in a low, controlled voice.

CHAPTER FIVE

Lucas didn't know what got into him at that moment. He stepped inside Maxine's office and gently closed the door behind him to give them some privacy.

Maxine. Maxine. Maxine.

He didn't think he would be seeing her so soon. Here he was in the midst of a public relations scandal whilst reporters camped outside his family's estate and currently his only sole focus was on Maxine Summers and her safety.

Damn, she looked finer than he'd remembered. Her dark, shiny locks cascaded down her back. She was simple beauty personified. A natural. No caked-on makeup. Her lips were full and red as a ripe pomegranate. He wondered if they'd taste as sweet as they looked.

Lucas, that's what's gotten you into trouble in the beginning. Enough already.

He was there to do business not poke his nose into her personal life. But he couldn't help himself. He was a man who acted on impulse and followed his gut instincts. Everything else that occurred as a result, he would just deal with.

This girl had some sort of hold over him. He honestly didn't know how or why. She wasn't wild or flashy. Not his type really, but the way she dressed, the way she swayed her rounded hips when she walked into her office, obviously unaware of the view he was left with of her behind when she turned her back on him. She wore a dark fitted pencil skirt, low heeled pumps and knitted light purple vest with matching cardigan with what appeared to be custom jewelry. Lucas always took note of his surroundings and people. He often studied them and within seconds could sum up a lot of things. It was an old habit of his he'd learned from his cousin Dion who owned a private detective agency. At family gatherings Dion would entertain them with tips from his trade. Maxine was simple and elegant without even trying. Not like those women he'd been unfortunate to cross paths with during his weekend rendezvous at the hottest clubs in the downtown core. They had their place and time, but the scene was getting old.

He realized this ever since he'd danced with her at his cousin's wedding. And even before that she'd captured his interest while he was surreptitiously checking her out. She was a fine young woman. That was for sure. But there was something else about her.

"Now. Are you going to tell me what's really going on or am I going to have to drag it out of you?" Lucas looked directly into Maxine's beautiful dark eyes. He could tell she was anxious. Was she nervous because of his presence or because of what just happened to her—whatever that was?

Now he'd like to get hold of the creep who did this to her. She was much too fine to be going through this sort of hell. Was somebody threatening her? Was that why Officer Lindle dropped by the office?

Lucas was no fool and he happened to be an acquaintance of Lindle since his foundation hosted various events and donated to the Police Community Relations Initiative to help troubled youth.

"I...I'm fine really," she stammered, dropping her gaze to the desk.

Lucas moved in closer and casually pulled up a chair opposite her. "No. You're not. Don't lie to me, Maxine." His tone was more curt than he intended.

"You're here for a business arrangement, I gather." Maxine looked up to meet his gaze once again.

Lucas noted the dark circles under her eyes yet he could still see beauty beyond the fatigue. She looked weary, no doubt, yet so innocent and harmless.

"Are you trying to brush me off, Miss Summers?" Lucas arched a brow.

"Yes." Maxine cocked a brow and a grin touched the corner of her lips.

He liked that. Oh, those lips of hers. When would he get his chance to taste them? he wondered. Was she trying to be brave all of a sudden? Well, this was certainly a charmer. Often women flocked to him, played at his feet and sucked up to him. But no, not this one. She couldn't care less about his name or who he was or what he had. She treated him like any ordinary Joe on the street.

Good.

Maxine was a breath of fresh air. His grandfather was right about sending him personally to help her with her software program. It would take his mind off his own troubles and he would enjoy her heartwarming company. She could try to be as mean to him all she wanted but he could see something in her eyes, hear it in her tone of voice. She wasn't about to admit it, he gathered, but he knew when a woman was interested in him. But he knew she had other pressing matters on her mind.

"We'll talk business in a moment," Lucas stated. He tried to avoid grinning in amusement. She was a feisty one, wasn't she? God, this woman was causing a sexual reaction inside him right now. If only she'd known how much he wanted to take her, right across her desk.

"If you know anything about me," he continued, leaning forward with his elbows resting on his knees, "people come first with me, not business. And right now, Maxine, your well-being *is* my business." His tone was cool and to the point.

Maxine trembled inside. Butterflies exploded in her belly and there was that weak, giddy feeling again. Oh, his voice resonated through her body. Maxine had to get a hold of herself. After all, Lucas was in the midst of a scandal that highlighted his womanizing ways.

Wait a minute. Did he just say my well-being was his business? Oh, my God! The thought both thrilled and terrified Maxine simultaneously. Lucas Romero was interested in her personally? In her well-being? Maxine had never really had any man want to stand up for her like that. Especially not a man so important and larger than life like Lucas Romero.

What had she done to deserve the honor of his...honor?

She had better watch out, though. The last thing she needed was more trouble. And Lucas Romero was the epitome of trouble with a capital T. But oh, he was so irresistible. How could she not want to be around him? Oh, why did things have to be so complicated?

Her eyes drank in his magnificent form. Lucas was very tall. He must've been way over six feet maybe six-four she guessed. And he had the most beautiful dark, smooth skin she'd ever seen on a man. He filled out nicely in his suit with his broad shoulders.

She could tell he was muscular and heard that he worked out at the gym quite often as much as his cousin and brothers. Okay, so she admitted to herself that at times she would stalk him online by simply reading the news articles about him, admiring his photos.

The man was photogenic, yes. But oh, he was so much better looking in person. He was GQ or Sports Illustrated cover material. And that lovely boyish grin on his face and the dimpled impression in his cheek when he smiled. He was quite a charmer. He sure knew how to ring her magic bell. He made her want to scream out, "Seduce me."

His lips looked so kissable. Man, she could really use the touch of his lips on her right now. She wondered what his strong arms would feel like around her body. Heck, she wondered what he would be like in bed.

Okay, her thoughts were all over the place. She really had to round them up and get them out of the naughty gutter soon or she would say something that could make this morning's debacle in the papers seem like a quiet day at the press.

"I...It's nothing really," she hesitated as she rung her hands in her lap. She sighed deeply and decided she could not hide it from him. What was the point? Clearly this man was not going to let up any time soon. And neither of them would get anything done. The sooner she came out with it, the better. Then he'd realize that it was all a silly situation not worthy of additional attention.

Maxine spent the next few minutes explaining everything to Lucas. She noticed his poker face and then later his grim expression.

"But it's nothing really. Detective Lindle is going to look after everything and that's that. Probably some hoax. Maybe one of our competitors got my address somehow and simply wanted to scare me off."

Lucas said nothing for a moment then stood up, shoving his hands in his pockets. "I'm going to look into this myself. I know people who can check this out. In the meanwhile, I don't think you should be alone."

"Alone?" Maxine was offended. "What makes you think I'm alone?" Which she was, but how dare he insinuate that she was frail and vulnerable and had nobody else in her life who was capable of supporting her.

"Don't you live alone?"

"How did you...?"

"You just told me."

"Okay. So I live alone. Doesn't mean I'm vulnerable. I live in an apartment complex. We do have security. It's not like anyone will try to break in to the building and come up to the eleventh floor and try to abduct me or anything."

"Do you realize what you are saying? This is a little bit dangerous for you, don't you think?"

"Maybe, but it's up to me to make that decision. Thank you so much for your interest, Mr. Romero." Maxine was tormented by conflicting emotions. What was with this guy? Her emotions were out of control. Strange and disquieting thoughts raced through her mind. A part of her wanted to beg him for help. But she was way too independent for that. She was no damsel in distress, that was for sure. Oh, it was tempting all right. A sexy, rich guy like Lucas Romero wanting to help her out. He didn't actually say it, but she knew what he was implying. She'd heard about his reputation. And that was something she wasn't going to touch with a ten-foot pole.

He looked intently into her eyes and her heart flipped in response. She could feel the sexual magnetism between them; it was undeniable. The same way he'd made her feel at Lucy's wedding only six months earlier.

Besides, she also had her mother to think about. Her home may be modest but it was her place and the place where she and her mother stayed for so many years.

"So you're just going to go back to your apartment knowing that someone knows where you live?"

"I'll be fine ... really," Maxine stuttered. Gosh, the man was making her nervous as hell. Her mind was drawing a blank. She was about to say something else but then she was completely distracted by his refined assets.

"I don't think you'll be fine. I want to help you, Maxine. Let me help you," he ordered.

Maxine was attracted to this gorgeous hunk in front of her, but man, he seemed as if he wanted to control her. *No, thank you, sir. I can take care of myself, thank you very much.*

"Thank you so much, Lucas. I really do appreciate it, but really, I'm good," Maxine murmured. "Now, about this new software program," Maxine shifted the topic. "Your grandfather mentioned you would be able to help Dream Weddings, Inc. revamp into a more digital-friendly service?"

Lucas looked more annoyed than anything else. Did she just offend him?

Maxine surveyed Lucas's sexy, dark eyes. There appeared to be a mischievous twinkle in his dark eyes. It was delicious but seemingly dangerous. She hoped he wasn't going to do anything behind her back.

Lucas moved behind the desk and he leaned over Maxine. His palms were spread out on the desk as he bent over her laptop. Oh, that sexually charged scent of his heady cologne. It was tantalizing Maxine's nose. She wanted to ask him what cologne it was. But she stopped herself. The last thing she wanted him to feel was that she was flirting with him. Rumor had it he had enough women throwing themselves at his feet. She did not want to be one of them.

She was inches from Lucas. This was crazy. She didn't know if she could actually contain herself How would she be able to focus with Mr. Sexy so close to her, inches from her? His voice was husky when he spoke to give her instructions on which webpage to log on to.

"I already had my men set up things for you on this unique Web server," Lucas instructed.

"Great. Do I go from here?"

"Click on that link where it says download," he advised in a velvet-deep voice.

"Okay. Done."

"Now. Once it's done downloading, save to a location on your desktop."

Maxine did as he advised. Everything seemed to be going so smoothly but she knew this was only the beginning of the setup.

Lucas surveyed the screen to ensure that everything was downloading as intended. "Good. Let me take over from here." He rolled Maxine's chair out of the way so he could hover over her keyboard.

Maxine was blown away by the speed of his fingers. It was rare to see a man who could type so fast. She'd read somewhere that he was some sort of a hacker but then again those were probably just rumors. She didn't believe everything she read in the tabloids.

When Lucas was done he leaned back and surveyed the screen. "Now, over the next few weeks we'll be working closely with you to develop the program fully. I'll send my tech guy over to spend some time with you going through the interface."

Maxine's heart sank to the ground. "Tech guy? I thought..." she broke off.

"You thought what?" Lucas's voice was commanding.

She was about to say that she thought...or hoped, Lucas would be the one to be spending time with her over the next few weeks to go over the software program with her but she stopped herself.

You don't want him, remember? So why do you care if he's going to be around you for the next few weeks are not?

"What was the name of that bungee jumping couple?" Lucas fired up the question so quickly she didn't really have time to think about it.

Her answer just flew out of her mouth before she could stop it.

"I shouldn't have told you that," Maxine said flatly after she revealed the couple's surname.

"You don't have to worry about me breaking your confidence, Maxine." Lucas's tone was brittle yet a smug grin touched his lips.

What was he going to do now? She hoped to God that Lucas was not about to interfere with the investigation. What was she doing talking to a Romero like that? She should've kept her mouth shut. This was *her* private business, not his.

"Oh, God, look at the time. It's so late," Maxine commented.

Lucas glanced at his expensive watch. He then reached into his breast pocket and pulled out a business card. He handed it to her so smoothly as if he was James Bond. A grin touched his lips.

"Be sure to call me if anything comes up." His tone of voice was hard. *If. Anything. Comes. Up.* He had spoken the words so deliberately that it caused a chill to slither down Maxine's spine. She'd read about his dangerous ways, too. He could be a real friend but woe be it if anyone messed around with his family...or his friends, she guessed.

Lucas Romero had connections everywhere.

She took the card from him. "Th-thank you. I...I don't think I'll be needing it, though."

"Don't count on that, Ms. Summers." With those words, he extended his hand to shake hers. Their meeting was officially over, she supposed.

He gave her a firm handshake. So firm that she felt a surge of power shoot through her body.

Have mercy! This man had a lot of strength. He caught her by surprise by lifting her hand slowly and pressed his lips to the back of her hand. This well-dressed human deity was not only sexy but so charming as well. Electricity jolted through her body at his sexual touch. Oh, what a soft kiss. Was he teasing her with a sample of what he could offer?

It was a wonder that he wasn't accused of getting more women pregnant, she humored.

Maxine was melting inside. How was she to respond? "Thank you," she said softly. She felt a surge of heat rush to her cheeks. She hoped she wasn't blushing. She wished she had access to a mirror to be sure.

He eyed her salaciously before making his way out of her office. "I'll see myself out."

Maxine was beside herself. Lucas had caused so many emotions to stir within her over the past couple hours they'd just spent together. She wanted more of him. She needed to see more of him. What had she done? She should've asked him to stay longer. But no, she had work to do, a lot of work to do. And she knew he was busy and had lots of things to attend to himself. She was honored to be given a few hours of his time today of all days.

Just then Betty came back into the office with a couple of coffees in her hand. "Are you all right?" Betty placed the cups on the desk.

"I'm good, thanks," Maxine said absently. "Well, the good news is that we'll be getting a new system in place over the next few weeks."

"Yay," Betty chimed in. "It's about time. And what's the bad news?"

"Oh nothing. It's just that..." *If I don't get Lucas Romero inside me soon, I think I'm going to explode.*

Maxine thought about her hormones running wild and chalked it up to the fact that she hadn't been with a guy in almost two years. She'd been celibate way too long. Way, way too long. And now, the one guy who fueled the fireworks to explode inside her and was rocking her world without even knowing it had just walked out of her life again. How was she going to get with him now? Not that she really wanted to be involved with a local celebrity, but damn! Hot damn! She at least wanted to see him again. She was quickly becoming addicted to the way he made her mind spin and butterflies to flutter inside her.

"You like him, don't you?" Betty leaned in with a grin.

"No. I don't," Maxine shot back sharply. She felt sorry for snapping at Betty who was only trying to make light of the situation. "Sorry, Betty, I've just got a lot on my mind."

"I know. No worries."

"Anyway, we've got tons of work to do before the new system goes live. I'm going to contact the advertising agency we used last year and see if they can do a little campaign on a budget for us. It's the only thing we have going if we're going to compete in the new market."

"Tell me about it. Everything is self-serving these days. All you need is an Internet connection and a password to do anything and everything."

"For sure," Maxine said, lifting her latte to her lips. Her mind was still on Lucas, though. Would she ever see him again—besides on the Internet tabloid news?

CHAPTER SIX

Four weeks had passed since the sex scandal involving Lucas Romero became public. All eyes were on Lucas as he sat at the head of the long oval table in the boardroom with the sun beaming through the ceiling-to-floor windows. He casually leaned back in his leather executive chair with his knee propped up.

"So, what's the verdict?" He turned to his team.

His grandfather insisted on attending the meeting along with his brothers Zack, Jules, Troy and Carl. Though the brothers didn't always attend meetings together, one thing was for sure—they stuck together like a pack of wolves during tough times.

"We need to do damage control again," Toni said firmly.

It had been a few good weeks since allegations that Lucas had gotten a young woman he'd met in a nightclub pregnant.

What did Lucas do?

He reluctantly followed the advice of his grandfather and the family's spokesperson to lay low for a while.

He almost disappeared from the limelight. And it was a divine coincidence that a senator was engulfed in a political scandal that rocked the nation and dominated headlines, thus taking the spotlight off Lucas for a while. But still he would see reporters camped out at his family's home or one of his condo buildings once in a while.

But as much as he wasn't commanding headlines, he was still in hot water with some of his contractors.

Lucas sat in the boardroom of Romero Foundation on the forty-third floor of the tall glass high-rise in the downtown Toronto core. The view on the lakeside was breathtaking below. The July sky was a cloudless blue, yet Lucas's mind was filled with dark clouds.

It had been four weeks and he still couldn't shake Maxine Summers out of his system or his mind. He fought to keep his distance from her by having D'Andre, his tech, guy go over to the Dream Weddings, Inc. headquarters to personally help them get their new e-system up and running. Why hadn't he done it himself? He had to get hold of his emotions and put things into control.

He had his connections look into who the heck was sending Maxine the hate mail, too. So far, they received some lukewarm leads but nothing substantial, yet. Lucas thought of himself as her guardian angel. Invisible. Yet present. A grin touched his lips at the thought.

"I say we do business as usual and those who prefer to go by headlines and rumors can go to—"

"Lucas!" his grandfather interrupted, fuming. "We've just lost one of our biggest clients, the Carlson College! Do you not care?"

"Of course I care," Lucas fired back, leaning forward in his chair. He felt his blood burn inside his veins. He folded his hands tightly in front of him on the table.

"That program meant everything to me, Grandfather. You know it did!" Lucas asserted. He was about to break but maintained his cool. Carlson College had a very close place in his heart but he wasn't about to go there.

"Well then, I'm glad we got that settled. I'm sorry to say this, Lucas, but sometimes we need to take aggressive means to clear our good name. The college does not want to be associated with you or your program because of the recent headlines in the media. Including the most recent one. That woman has been giving interviews on talk shows right and left."

"I don't care what she wants to do with her spare time. I've got a foundation to run, Grandfather."

"And a reputation to protect. A family business to run," Toni added, pinching his lips.

"One thing's for sure, Lucas. We don't want to lose more contractors. First, the college makes the announcement they are severing ties with us. Who knows who else will follow?" Zack spoke up in a serious tone. A tone of voice Lucas had not heard from him in a while.

Was Lucas playing with fire? What else was he to do?

"Listen, she wants to play games. I do not negotiate with extortionists. We've been through this already. She's good alright," Lucas chuckled. "I wonder who put her up to this. She knows it's too risky to do a paternity test until the baby's born, which would prove once and for all she's a liar, so she figured she'd drag my name through the mud for the next few months until she delivers hoping to gain some financial advantage. Have any of you thought of how that would look even if I was crazy enough to pay her off for the sake of a pristine image?"

Zack nodded thoughtfully.

Lucas's team of close advisors were also in agreement, silently at the table. The truth was that Lucas ran that division of the foundation dealing with software developments, which included the famous Healthy Start Pre-screening programs used at dozens of clinics across the province.

"I understand, Lucas. Please try to understand my point of view as well. I'm your grandfather. I may have come from a different era where business practices differ from today but it's out of love for you why I'm being tough. I'd rather it come from inside than outside. It hurts me to see your name tarnished while your great ideas suffer negative publicity. Do you understand that, Lucas?"

Lucas could feel the tension in the boardroom.

Though the advisors and he were close, it almost seemed as if they were squirming in their seats. Talk about uncomfortable. He wondered why he allowed his grandfather to attend. Oh, right. Out of respect for him.

CHAPTER SEVEN

Toni Romero was the one who initially gave each of his grandsons their startup cash flow and the connections to get started. Of course, the rest they did on their own with their own ideas and initiatives and their own blood and sweat and precious tears.

They each opened their own division within the foundation and hired their own staff and grew business from their one million dollar startup to their multi-billionaire dollar empire. The tech world took off in ways that surprised even Toni.

Of course, they'd had a string of successful stock investments and wealth building strategies that literally soared. All in the name of helping others achieve their best potential. Still, Toni insisted in continuing to be a presence in their business from the shadows. It gave him something to live for. Something to hope for. He was still useful and wanted to be their ever-present guide. It's just that they didn't always see eye to eye on everything or agree with everything.

"You need to do damage control, Lucas. Pronto," Toni continued, "The media is painting a picture of you as an unstable young man who has a wild side and takes nothing seriously. Unfortunately, sometimes what sells isn't the good news or the good things you do day-to-day to run this part of the foundation. They love it when you make a mistake."

"Because it makes them look good," Lucas finished the sentence with a taste of bitterness in his mouth.

Lucas sighed deeply and leaned back in his chair once more. He gazed out at the view of the Toronto skyline. The other tall buildings glistened under the shining sun. It was a picture perfect day outside. He wished he could say the same about inside his office. Or inside his heart. The sun certainly wasn't shining there at the moment. It was a dark and cold place inside him. He felt as if nothing could make that gloominess go away. Nothing.

Lucas thought for a minute. Was the foundation seriously blaming him personally for the loss of their biggest contract? What was he supposed to do? Barricade himself inside his own home and become a recluse? Never to associate with anyone again? Never speak or say anything? Ridiculous. And not happening.

He remembered an old saying he'd read somewhere in college. "Well," Lucas broke the silence in the room. "You know what Aristotle once said, right? 'To avoid criticism say nothing, do nothing…'"

"Be nothing," Zack added with a smirk as he finished his brother's speech.

"And we all know, Lucas is not one to go away quietly, Granddad," he said with an air of coolness.

"What do you mean by that?" Toni leaned forward in his chair across the table.

"They'll be people who criticize me no matter what I do. I'm not playing into their game. Nor will I go away quietly. I'm truly sorry we lost the…Carlson College account," Lucas said as he rose from the table. "But we'll move forward on all the other trial programs for the new version of updated software programs across the board."

"And?"

"And those who are with us, are with us, and those who aren't…well, I bid them adieu."

"You're not leaving the meeting now, are you?"

"Yes."

"But we're not finished yet," his secretary Mary pointed out.

"I'm finished. Ever since the meeting started, the agenda has always come full swing to my behavior or my actions that cause embarrassment for the corporation and the foundation. Well, I'm taking a break…" Lucas glanced down at his watch. "Right now!"

Lucas walked over to where his grandfather was seated and kneeled beside him. "Granddad, I love you. It has nothing to do with you. I just need to work out some things."

The elder Romero did not look the least bit impressed.

"Listen, why don't we meet back tomorrow morning?" Zack posed to the team. "Lucas and Granddad, I'm sure you need to discuss a few things."

Those words provided the cue for everyone else to clear out of the boardroom.

Lucas got up from kneeling and heaved a sigh. His grandfather's face was stone cold. Lucas shoved his hands in his pockets and paced by the window.

"What is with you, Lucas? Why do you have to be such a hardhead? The more you encounter opposition, the more you try hardest to be a jackass." The pout on his grandfather's face was priceless.

In spite of himself, Lucas turned to face his grandfather and burst out with a hearty guffaw.

Soon, his grandfather's lips melted into a smile then he, too, laughed. "Lucas, what am I going to do with you, grandson?" The affection Toni had for Lucas was evident in his voice.

Lucas and his grandfather always had this understanding with each other as long as they'd known each other. It was always an inside thing that no one else could understand.

"I don't know, maybe give me back to the stork that delivered me to my parents. Probably the old bird lost direction and sent me to the wrong family." Lucas shrugged.

He watched as his grandfather mockingly rolled his eyes and shook his head. "Are you alright, grandson?"

"I'll be fine, Gramps. Don't worry about me."

"Are you sure? Lucas, you're a fine young man. Sometimes you can be a bit rough around the edges but you're so brilliant at all the work you do and the lives you've saved through that wonderful Healthy Start pre-screening program. You've made so many people happy. I just want to see you happy, my boy."

"I know, Granddad," Lucas answered softly.

"Now, what about that nice young girl, Maxine?"

Oh, boy.

Here we go again. Now how did I know he was going to bring her name up?

"Granddad!" Lucas arched a brow. "Please, drop it."

"But you two looked so happy together at Antonio's wedding. And she seems like a very nice, thoughtful girl. Remember she helped arrange Lucy and Antonio's wedding without Lucy knowing? She's a good friend, Lucas. A true friend. Friends like that don't grow on trees. I think she'd make a fine—"

"Granddad," Lucas scolded in a lovingly warning tone. "I don't think Maxine or any woman is the answer to my troubles right now. Besides, we can't just get with people because we want to fix things in our lives. It wouldn't be fair to them or to us. It should be done for the right reasons."

Whatever those reasons were, of course.

The truth was, Lucas didn't see himself following in Antonio's footsteps any time soon. He really didn't care for marriage or lifelong commitment to one woman. Period.

The thought shot a dagger straight to his heart. He had come close only once in his life when he was fresh out of high school. Then that tragic day…

Lucas blinked hard to avoid tears stinging his eyes.

He wasn't about to take that solemn trip down memory lane again. Ever. The past was dead and gone.

"Okay, Lucas," Toni broke through Lucas's concentration. "Very well. I'll let it go for now. But I'm not going to let it be buried forever, you know. I saw the way you looked at Maxine at the wedding and Lord knows she has something for you. She couldn't keep her eyes off you whenever your back was turned. Geez!" Toni feigned shock by shaking his head and slapping his hand on his forehead.

She couldn't keep her eyes off me?

Lucas thought deeply.

Really? Geez, Granddad, why didn't you tell me this before?

CHAPTER EIGHT

What a whirlwind the last few weeks were, Maxine thought to herself as she pulled up into the parking lot of the nursing home to visit her mother. Luckily, the dirty hate mail had slowed down to a trickle. The only odd piece of correspondence she'd received was from some foreign prince requesting her phone number, driver's license and banking information so that he could wire fifty billion dollars into her personal checking account. *Yeah, sure!* She automatically spammed that with the rest of said type of emails.

The bottom line was that whomever was stalking Maxine seemed to have cooled. At least for now. She wondered if Lucas had anything to do with it.

A smile touched her lips at the thought. In fact, Lucas had dominated her thoughts once too often during the past few weeks. At times she thought she was wide awake in a dream. Lucas kissed her hand. Oh, the silky, erotic touch of that soft kiss. Imagine that! What would she be feeling if he'd done more that day? She was still buzzing for his soft lips on her again. The man really knew how to kiss. She'd dreamt about him, fantasized about him pleasuring her with his lips and with his firm body. But all she had was the sweet memory of his kiss. Would she be treated with more servings of his delicious chemistry any time soon?

Maxine was hungry for Lucas. And with each day that drifted by, she'd eagerly waited for him to call her, to drop by her office. Nada. She'd been left feeling empty again. Was he avoiding her? Perhaps she shouldn't have been so unresponsive to his flirtatious attempts.

Whenever the tech guy from the foundation dropped by during the last few weeks to help her company set up the e-program online she'd casually question him. How many times had she snuck in questions about Lucas while asking D'Andre about the software program? Was he out of town? In a meeting? Would he be coming back to her office for more follow-up to see how the program was going? Her inquiring mind wanted to know. Lucas seemed to be pretty much out of the media spotlight—for now, at least. She was glad for him that the scandalous story was dying down a bit. Maxine really wished she could have spoken with him.

Heck, she was scared out of her wits to call Lucas's number and ask him anything. She didn't want to seem as if she was into him. What did she fear? Rejection? Embarrassment?

Or perhaps, she was truly out of his league and didn't want to risk being a convenient one-night stand. Maxine tried hard not to believe what she'd read about him in the newspapers. You couldn't believe the tabloids or sensationalism, could you? And that woman seemed as if she was an opportunist, appearing on every show she could to tell her story and talk about how much money she should have for her unborn child. Something just didn't ring true about that duplicity. Poor Lucas. How awful to be in his shoes.

***

Maxine turned off the engine and the car shuddered before shutting down. Okay, she really needed to take her car in to be fixed. Trouble was, she was not auto savvy and oftentimes would be ripped off by mechanics. She could not even afford to replace anything in her old vehicle. She prayed it wouldn't conk out on her in the middle of traffic.

Lucy had offered to buy her a new car but she really felt funny about accepting any of her friend's husband's money like that. It just didn't feel right. Lucy and she had only just briefly met before Lucy married into the Romero family anyway.

Lucy had taken over the agency from her dead estranged auntie who left it to her in her will. So this was new to a lot of people when Chris, the late owner of the Dream Weddings, Inc. died suddenly a couple years ago. It wasn't as if Maxine and Lucy were lifelong friends. They'd met on the job two years earlier. Maxine didn't have too much in her life right now. But her pride was one of the things she held dear.

She glanced down at her list of things to do this week, most of them to be done today.

Ask Dr. Branson about Mom's new medication

Look over incident report from Mom's fall and speak to in-charge nurse at the time of incident

Read over research study that will help Mom then give consent if agree with terms

Pay the overdue invoice from the nursing home

Settle collection notice for Mom's old cell phone service; have disconnected since not in use

Buy Mom a pay-as-you-go phone at the grocery store for emergencies

Buy something edible to put in empty fridge

Go to the department store and pick out Lucy's baby shower gift...

The eighth item on her scribbled note brought a giddy feeling inside Maxine's whole being. She was so happy for Lucy and Antonio having a baby but an added benefit was attached to that. The invitation she'd received said the July baby shower would be a barbecue at the Romero Estate along with a Jack and Jill shower. Which meant Yay! Guys and gals would be there. She was sure Lucas would attend, too.

What was with her? Was she that desperate to catch a glimpse of him again? Yes.

He'd pretty much avoided seeing her during the past few weeks, which completely irked Maxine. She'd hoped he would have at least stopped by to say "hi" again or see how she's doing since the detective showed up.

But then again, she guessed, he was probably handling things from the background. After all, the tech guy from his company was super sweet and respectful to her, as if she was Lucas's number one preferred customer or something.

Maxine was going to go crazy if she didn't see Lucas again. She needed to feel his lips on hers. Even if he only brushed his lips on her hand. The feeling he left her with still made her tingle inside. What a soft kiss that was.

As she walked across the parking lot towards the entrance of the nursing home, a smile touched her lips. She was about to visit her mother but she wished her mother knew her and she prayed things could be normal, like bringing home a hot guy like Lucas to introduce to her mother as her future son-in-law. Yeah, she wished. If only!

Maxine knocked on the door of her mother's room before entering. "Hey, beautiful princess, how are you feeling today?" Maxine asked as she entered with a smile and a Tim Horton's bag of fresh pastries. Her mother loved pastries from Tim's for as long as Maxine could remember. Especially the Maple Pecan Danish. Mmm. Delicious. She even had it warmed up for her in the pantry before heading to the room.

"Hey, welcome to my castle," Dora beamed as she welcomed her adopted daughter. She opened her arms and made gestures to show off her surroundings. "I have a table set for you over there. Would you like my servants to get you something to eat, my dear?"

Maxine's heart hiccupped but a warm feeling settled in her soul because she was hopeful for her mother. She was used to her mother's behavior.

"No, thank you, Mom. I'm fine right here beside you." Maxine smiled warmly as she sat beside her mother at the bedside. When she'd first noticed her mother's symptoms, Maxine didn't know what to do. She played along at first but was told by the doctor that it was best to gently redirect to reality if at all possible. Her mother was always fixated on being a princess and having all the love in the world. Who could blame her? She'd been through so much heartache in her life, she deserved some fantasy. Maxine wished she could give her mother everything right now.

Her mother's hair hadn't been washed yet and that crushed her spirit. She didn't even know if her mother was bathed yet. Staffing was incredibly short at the nursing home. Maxine desperately wished she could hire a personal nurse to be with her mother twenty-four-seven when she was not there. Maxine took off her cardigan and placed it over the chair back.

"Here, Mom, I brought you your favorite. Pecan Danish."

"Oh, joy!" Dora clasped her hands together. "I don't know who you are but thank you so much."

Maxine's eyes stung with hot tears. Even though she'd called her "Mom" a few times since entering the room, Dora had forgotten. Her mom had seen better days. She wasn't always pleasantly confused. There were some days when she was more lucid.

The trouble with her mom's dementia diagnosis was that it was nonspecific. Some people with dementia could get confused and be unable to remember names or places while others were impaired in their daily living routines. But it was the change in personality and her mom's social behavior that made Maxine seek help initially.

She was glad she did when she did. Her mother's behavior was becoming out of control at home and after neighbors found her climbing the tree outside their apartment building in the middle of the night things had turned for the worse. She was taken in to the local hospital.

Still, Dora had good days and Maxine was well aware that dementia was treatable but the one shred of hope she held on to was that it was also *reversible*.

"Maxine, good to see you today." Dr. Branson walked into the room with a chart in his hand.

"Oh, hi there." Maxine spun her head around after wiping the teardrop off her cheek.

"Are you all right?"

"Oh, I'm good thanks. Just tired."

"She's such a sweetie, you know," Dora chimed with her mouth full of pastry. "She is a good servant. Look what she prepared for me in the kitchen. I should give her a raise."

Dr. Branson smiled at Dora. "Well, Dora, I think you're very lucky to have Maxine here. I don't think she's a servant, though. She's a wonderful daughter."

"Oh?" Dora looked surprised at first. She looked at Maxine, then back to Dr. Branson, then shrugged and finished eating her Danish pastry, licking her fingers.

"Dora, I'm just going to speak with your daughter for a moment. Is that okay?"

"Yes, please don't mind me. I'm off to visit my friend soon."

Dr. Branson nodded and guided Maxine outside to the hallway. "How long has she been like this? All night?" Maxine asked concerned. "I thought she was getting better with the new medication."

"Oh, she is, Maxine. It's just that at times, your mother would regress to an earlier stage but we're monitoring the situation very closely."

"Oh, good."

"Listen, I don't mean to pry, but how are you doing?"

"Oh, I'm…okay. I just had a moment there when she didn't know me again." Maxine felt a lump in her throat. Her mother had days when she would acknowledge her as her daughter but unfortunately today wasn't one of them.

"I know it can be hard. I just noticed you looked deep in thought there. For the past few weeks you'd been on cloud nine."

"On cloud nine?"

Was it that obvious? That I had Lucas on my mind, fantasizing about him the whole time? Oh, how embarrassing. I must have looked like a complete idiot. And Lucas doesn't even know I exist! He's probably thinking about some other woman every waking minute.

"Well, maybe I should clarify what I mean by cloud nine," he said adjusting his specs. "It's like someone in love," he joked to her. "Not that it's any of my business, of course. I just want to see all my patients and my patient's families happy. Especially when we see you in here almost every day without fail. As I've said before, it's wonderful what you're doing but you need to give yourself a break. You don't want to burn yourself out. Then what good will that do for your mother?"

"You're right, Dr. Branson. I just..." *really need to get a life, I suppose.*

Maxine spent the next half hour discussing her mother's care with Dr. Branson before going back to spend the rest of the time with her mother. The visit turned out to be more rewarding as her mother came around at times. She then asked for some assistance in finding towels and a new gown so that she could bathe and dress her mom. She also washed her mother's hair and brushed it as if she were a princess getting ready for a royal visit. Maxine was satisfied when she'd left her mother.

When she got back to the car in the parking lot, she wiped the sweat from her brow. The sun was getting hotter but Maxine was also tired. She still had a few more stops to make before heading home.

To the department store.

Maxine picked out a beautiful gift set and a lovely bedding set for Lucy and the baby. She then went to a specialty store in the plaza adjacent to the mall where she had the gifts personalized with a message to the baby from Maxine, the baby's future godmother. It was difficult to pick out a perfect gift for someone who actually had money but she thought every mother would appreciate sentimental gifts.

Later, she pulled up in the garage of her apartment building with a few shopping bags in her hands. When she got out of the elevator on the eleventh floor, she fished for her keys in her bag and yanked them out. When she reached her door, her mouth fell open. She dropped her bags on the floor by her feet, her keys frozen between her fingers. She didn't need a key to get into her apartment. The door was wide open! Her home had been broken into and trashed.

CHAPTER NINE

"What?" Lucas fumed. He felt a surge of heat fire through his blood. If anyone laid a finger on Maxine, he would make sure they would live to regret it.

"Lucy got the call a few minutes ago," Antonio said as he spoke to his cousin in the study.

Since Lucy's difficult pregnancy, Lucy and Antonio been spending more time at the estate than downtown, which made sense since their family doctor and trusted obstetrician was in Mayberry Hill and Lucy would eventually deliver at the local hospital. The Romeros had donated a wing to Mayberry General Hospital. It was private hospital with the latest state-of-the-art medical equipment.

"So what happened?" Lucas demanded to know.

"Well, the cops took the report and told Maxine to call someone close to her to spend the night. So she called Lucy."

"And?"

"Lucy invited her to come stay with us, but Maxine told her she would prefer go to the nearest hotel. She only called Lucy to inform her in case Lucy tried to call her at home and didn't get her."

"Is Maxine crazy?" Lucas thinned his lips in anger.

"Lucas, don't do anything foolish."

It was too late. Lucas didn't know what got into him. But he was going to reach Maxine and make sure she was safe. He reached into this pocket for his smartphone and dialed one of his contacts.

How the hell did that one slip by? He had people watch her office during the first two weeks since she'd received that note but things seemed under control then. He had someone watch her building to ensure she was safe, but again, he'd been given the green light and didn't see the purpose in continuing his surveillance for her safety.

Damn! Was he wrong? Lucas rarely took missteps. That was an oversight that would never happen again. He would see to that.

"In which hotel is she staying?" Lucas asked pointedly. He was deeply agitated. He just didn't know what came over him all of a sudden. Why did he have this reaction to Maxine? This was all too crazy for him right now but he didn't have time to analyze his feelings for this woman, he just knew he had to act fast. She was in some kind of trouble and from judging her character over the past few months, she wasn't the trouble-making type of girl.

"Lucas, what are you going to do?"

"That doesn't answer my question, Antonio."

"I'm not telling you."

"She's staying at the Fairmont Hotel." Toni hobbled into the study with his cane.

"Grandfather!" Antonio spat.

"But Toni's right, Lucas," the senior Toni continued, acknowledging Antonio with a nod but not addressing him further. "Don't do anything rash that would cause a scene, or Lord help us, a headline in the news."

"I won't," Lucas assured dryly.

"That's the same thing that got you in trouble at school, Lucas. Always standing up for anyone who was getting their butt kicked. Always fighting for the little guy and getting suspended."

Lucas growled. "This is not school, Antonio. Far different. Don't even compare."

"But you don't have all the facts. Shouldn't you just leave it to the police? I know you've made an inquiry to a contact to likely interfere with the investigation, Lucas. Don't go there."

"I'm not going anywhere, except to see if a friend in need could use a little help. I don't back away when someone needs help."

"Oh, and I do?"

"Boys, boys. Please! Let's not argue over such nonsense," Toni interjected.

Lucas walked over to the counter by the door of the study and grabbed his keys off the top. "I'm heading into town, Gramps. My phone is charged so you can reach me if you need me."

Lucas thought he saw his grandfather grin but Antonio scowled. Lucas could see Antonio's point but wasn't really interfering. Yeah, it was his big cousin Antonio who had to help him out while in senior high when he would fight off bullies for his friends or stick up for someone who was being harassed by the authorities, only to get suspended in the process and take the rap for "stirring up trouble."

But as far as he was concerned, Maxine was practically family. She was a close friend of the family and they had business dealings together. Whoever attacked her, attacked him. He took what happened to her home personally. Very personally.

"Thank you," Maxine told the counter clerk as he handed her the key card for her room. She changed her mind about staying at the Fairmont Hotel. The clerk at the Fairmont could see her hesitation, and when she told him she was looking for something less expensive, he was kind enough to suggest the Hopeton Travel Lodge down the street. She just couldn't afford the nightly fee at the Fairmont even though it would probably have been more secure. But what was she to do? She had no idea how long it would be before she could return home.

Her stomach squeezed when she thought about her personal possessions being violated by some stranger. She almost felt violently ill as if she was going to throw up. Old photos of her mother when she was young and precious priceless family keepsakes were vandalized with spray paint and nail polish. Who would do such a thing? And why her?

"Enjoy your stay, ma'am." The clerk smiled at her.

Maxine smiled weakly before turning to face the elevator. The ambiance at the motel was dim and soft. It was a travel lodge more than anything else. Still, it was better than staying alone in her ravaged apartment. Darn that security system in the building. It was virtually useless. Apparently someone else had their home broken into before and the security camera image came out too grainy to make any positive identification on the culprit who entered their building from the lobby. So much for that.

Maxine turned around to look both directions before swiping her card in the door slot. She was beginning to feel more paranoid than ever.

What had her life come to? This was not really one of those moments she wanted to have a reflection on where she was going in her life but she was forced to. When she got inside she slumped down in the chair and tossed her backpack to the floor. She held her head in her hands and let out a good cry.

After a while of sobbing, she went to reach for the phone only to realize that it was two o'clock in the morning. Who could she call now? There was a passage she'd read somewhere in a book but she could not recall from where. She thought it could be from a later Hollywood screen legend. Was it Marlene Dietrich who once said: "It's the friends you can call up at 4 a.m. that matter."

Maxine grinned and shook her head. She really wished she had such friends now.

Later, Maxine ran a warm bath and dropped in some bath oils compliments of the travel lodge. She really needed to soak her troubles away. Sleeping was out of the question. She had just sent an email off to the office to let Betty know she would be in much later in the day. She had to itemize damage for the insurance company in the morning. Then a horrible thought struck her. Did she renew her renter's insurance policy?

Maxine slid down in the tub and tried to sink the worries of her day away. Her mother would tell her while growing up: "Worry don't solve a thing. It only makes things look worse." Maxine grinned. Those were the days, all right. Worrying about what happened would only give Maxine heartburn and elevated blood pressure. She would think about it tomorrow. Whatever was stressing her out.

Right then she wanted to switch her thoughts to something more pleasurable. Like Lucas sexy-as-hell Romero. She remembered what he'd said about calling him if she ever needed him. She dreamed about acting on his offer but changed her mind. No way could she do that. He was probably just being polite and routine by giving her his business card. How many other women had he given out his business card to? What about that woman from the nightclub?

She closed her mind to that thought. She thought instead of Lucas kissing her hand, only this time as Maxine closed her eyes luxuriating in the warm silky water, she envisioned Lucas kissing her nipple. She stroked her nipple under the water lightly imagining it was Lucas's tongue and waves of pleasure pulsed through her body to her inner thighs.

"Oh, Lucas," she murmured. If only she could get a guy like that. A strong, handsome, powerful man who would move earth and heaven for the woman he loved.

Oh, if only!

After her bath, Maxine grabbed her towel and wrapped it around her. Then she grabbed her white towel-fabric robe compliments from the hotel. She pinned her dark hair up into a bun and went towards the bed feeling hot inside but was distracted when a knock befell the door.

She glanced at the clock in the room.

Who could be knocking on her door at this hour? Was it the concierge desk? Oh, God! Had her credit card been declined, too?

Great! That was just the icing on the top of her cake of a disastrous day, wasn't it?

She looked through the peephole and her heart leaped in her chest. Maxine blinked thinking she was in a dream or hallucinating.

Lucas Romero?

What was he doing there?

Lucy.

It must have been Lucy who told him about her situation. But then she didn't tell Lucy she'd changed her plans to come to the travel lodge. Perhaps Lucas went to the Fairmont and that clerk told him that Maxine was directed to check in at the lodge. Or maybe it was Lucas's men. He wouldn't do it himself. Not with him being locally famous.

She pulled away from the door. Dazed. *Lucas? Oh, my God!* Lucas was standing outside the door to her room. How did he know she was there? Maxine thought she was hallucinating for sure. He looked so stunning. In a suit and tie. That much she could see from the peephole.

Maxine looked in the mirror by the door quickly and used her hands to brush the sides of her damp tendrils of hair so that she wouldn't look so...unbecoming.

"Who is it?" she called out routinely.

"It's Lucas, Maxine." Lucas's deep voice sounded curt yet soft. She just didn't want to whip the door open first without hearing his voice.

She inhaled a deep breath, her heart pounding in her throat. She opened the door and her heart nearly leaped out of her chest.

"Lucas? What are you doing here? How did you-"

"Shh," he said softly. "Can I come in?"

Her body tingled from head to toe when he spoke softly to her. It almost sounded seductive. His words, his voice alone was sexually charged. Oh, this must be a dream.

She opened the door wider. Of course, they had to keep it down given the time of night and she wouldn't want to alert anyone else that she had often-infamous company at her door. Lord knew who was in the room across from her or next door. One could never be too careful. Though it looked as if the lodge was barely half full tonight.

Maxine was buzzing. All sorts of weird and wonderful thoughts whirled through her mind. Secretly she'd hoped and wished that Lucas would be there with her, alone. But never in her wildest dreams did she think the universe would present her with her dream man right there, in arms length.

"What are you doing here?" she said, incredulously. Deep inside she was hiding her gratitude. She also subconsciously tightened the belt around her robe and hugged herself, feeling that he would be able to see her tightened nipples under her robe. Of course, he would have to have x-ray vision for that.

"I heard your apartment was broken into. I wanted to see if you were alright," he answered her in a low voice, gazing intently into her eyes. Oh, those delicious dark eyes of his. So sexy, so inviting. The man oozed sex appeal from every inch of his body.

Her eyes surveyed his hotness. He stood so tall that his head almost touched the top of the door frame. He sported a dark suit and looked as if he'd had a rugged day at the office. His sexy stubble was more prominent than she had remembered from a month ago and his dark hair was tussled in a rock star fashion but looked good nevertheless. He had the highest, defined cheekbones she'd ever seen on a man.

"You did? You came here just to see if I was alright?" Maxine was pleasantly surprised. In disbelief. Was she that important to him? Appreciation tickled her inside. She wanted to reach out to hug him but she dared not.

"I told you," he said in a low, deliberate voice. "I take care of those close to me." He arched a brow to make his point. He looked into her eyes and Maxine quivered with delight.

The words sent a rush of shivers down her back, a pleasurable sensation. She was naked under her robe and her sex was throbbing uncontrollably.

"I didn't know we were that close," she teased him, breathing hard. A grin played on her lips.

Was she flirting with him? What was with her?

"Can I get you anything?" she breathed, her voice hoarse. It had been way too long since she'd been with anyone, meaning her ex. Her only real boyfriend. Oh, the curse of being celibate so long. Now she felt as if she was ready to explode for the one guy who made her heart go pitter-patter. She felt a close indescribable connection to Lucas. She couldn't really rationalize it or understand it but it was just what it was—kismet.

He leaned in closer to her and she caught the sweet, irresistible scent of his cologne. He was delicious in every way. Maxine was dying to be with him. She was about to lose her inhibitions—or her mind if he didn't take her there and then.

"Just you," he said as if reading her silent invitation. He lowered his head to hers and pressed his sinfully sexy lips to hers causing a rush of sexual currents to race through her body.

Her body's response was automatic as she moaned in delight and hungrily kissed him back. She'd been dying for this moment for so long. To feel the silky touch of his lips on hers. His firm arms were wrapped around her body as he held her close to him. Her arms reached up to his broad shoulders.

Oh, his lips were so soft and sexually potent. Lucas's kiss made her forget who she was and where she was. His soft lips caressed and sucked on hers sending shivers of delight down her spine and a rush of blood to her thighs. She felt the hardness of his erection behind his zipper while his hips pressed to hers as he leaned her against the wall.

Lucas slid his smooth hand beneath her robe and she felt a delicious explosion of butterflies in her stomach. His hand made its way to her mound of flesh and he stroked and teased her hard nipples bringing moans of ecstasy through her lips.

Maxine pulled away breathless.

"What is it?" Lucas's deep voice captured her.

Yes. What was it? What was she afraid of? This was what she'd always fantasized about, wasn't it? Lucas's erotic touch on her body.

Maxine adjusted her robe. She was still throbbing mercilessly. Oh, heavens, she wanted nothing more than to be with Lucas so what in Pete's sake was she afraid of?

"I'm...sorry I...Lucas..."

"It's okay." Lucas was out of sorts, breathless himself. "I should apologize. I didn't come here for that. I don't know what got over me just now."

Maxine looked up, startled. Oh, no. That was the last thing she wanted him to feel—regret! My God, the man came over there—all the way over there to see if she was alright. He certainly didn't need to do that. As big and important as Lucas Romero was, he went out of his way to track her down after she'd been victimized. How noble was that?

So was he changing his mind? Who could blame him? She was probably sending mixed signals. Heck, she felt as if she *was* a mixed signal right now.

Oh, how her body craved his touch. She desperately wanted to feel his hardness inside of her. But not right here, in some...upscale motel. It just didn't feel right. And she hadn't seen him in over a month—at least not outside her private fantasies and online.

Maxine went over by the bed to sit down.

"It's okay, Maxine. I'm not going to lie to you. I've wanted you the moment I laid eyes on you at the wedding. But I'm not a creep. I'm a gentleman—despite what you might have read about me in the tabloids."

Maxine couldn't help but break out into a smile. It was the way he said it. Charming. Humorous. Was he mocking himself? She always thought it attractive when a man could make light of his troubles. Good for Lucas.

She didn't know if *she* could have such strength with people saying all sorts of stuff about her and just keeping a cool head about it as if it meant nothing. But such was the life of a celebrity, wasn't it? Or at least someone in the public eye from time to time.

Speaking of public eye, Lucas was truly a man who could bring a whole lot of media attention. And there he was, in her motel room. Oh, heavens. Maxine could just see the headlines if anyone found out.

She swallowed hard. That would be disastrous. The last thing she needed.

"I know," she said quietly, "I didn't think you were a creep." A charming gentleman and sex god, yes. A creep, no. Far from it. She was just terrified of the situation right now. Terrified of letting herself get to close to him only to find out that he didn't want a long-term relationship. He was almost thirty and according to what she'd read or learned about him, he'd never really had a steady girlfriend. At least not since adulthood.

"I think, I'd better get changed," she murmured softly. She didn't know why she hadn't thought of it sooner. There she was naked under a bathrobe and inches from the hottest man she'd ever laid eyes on. It was no wonder something almost happened between them.

"If you need to get ready for bed-"

"Oh, no. I'm not tired at all. I can't sleep," she spewed out quickly. Then she caught herself, feeling sheepish. Gosh, did she just come off as...desperate?

"I mean, I'm just going to change into some clothes. You know, street clothes."

He grinned, a sexy boyish grin that dimpled his cheek and oh, she wanted to melt. "Should I leave?" he asked quietly, looking into her eyes. He stood erect with his head slightly tilted and his hands shoved in the pockets of his dress pants.

"Oh, no!" she said almost too quickly for her liking. She covered her face with both hands and giggled. "I mean, I'll go and change in the bathroom."

Moments later, Maxine emerged from the bathroom dressed in a black pair of leggings with a long fitted designer t-shirt. She wore her black soft leather sandals and grabbed her knitted cardigan from the chair. It was summer but the nights could be a little on the cool side with the breeze.

"You look stunning," Lucas murmured, his look of approval warmed her heart.

"In *this*?" she growled. "You've got to be kidding." Maxine cocked a brow.

"Now why wouldn't you think you're stunning?" Lucas smiled. "You see, you don't even have to try."

"I just thought you'd be more into super models. I've seen your girlfriends, you know," she teased.

"Where? In the tabloids? That I've probably never even met?" Lucas grinned as he arched a brow.

Okay. He had her there. "Sorry, I didn't mean to judge," she flushed.

"Don't be. Come, I'm taking you away from here."

"Where to? I...I've already paid for my room."

Lucas glanced around the compact room. "Do you really want to stay here?"

Maxine frowned. "Hey, listen, I may not have as much money as some people but a place like this isn't half bad for someone who needs a roof over her head for the night." She folded her arms across the chest. "Besides, I'm not going to just go to your place."

"Hey. Whoa. Wait a minute. Who said anything about going over to my place?"

"Oh," Maxine said, heat rising to her cheeks. Why was she always getting ahead of herself? Was it because she was in the presence of a gorgeous, prominent businessman who made her feel giddy and pleasantly disoriented?

Maxine shook her head and rolled her eyes. "Where were you thinking of taking me?"

"Away from here. We need to talk but not here."

Maxine swallowed hard. He needed to speak with her? But not there? She grabbed her purse off the counter and held her chin up.

"Okay, I could do with a hot drink about now," she said. The truth was, the lodge might have been an upscale motel but it had no room service and no access to a restaurant. The only close eatery was a few blocks down the road. It was dark and cool during the night. And not in the busiest places in town. Lucas was right. She needed to get away from there.

The drive out of the city was a welcome sightseeing excursion. They drove along Lakeside Drive capturing a breathtaking night view of the lake under the twilight stars. Lucas drove his BMW at the speed limit, for which Maxine was grateful. She disliked when guys tried to show off by pushing the speed limit. Another plus for Lucas, she mused with delight. He had the driver's side window opened slightly, and the breezed rustled his dark, mousy hair.

"Are you cold?" He turned to her. "I can close the windows." He noticed her hugging herself. But it wasn't because she was cold.

"I'm good, thanks," she said, sheepishly. She was in awe. She was with Lucas, alone in his car. Just the two of them driving along a long practically isolated road. And she was feeling all sorts of emotions swirl through her body. Mostly that of lust and amazement and curiosity of how the night would end.

Her eyes scanned her surroundings. Lucas kept his ride immaculate, Maxine noted with pleasure. Or, perhaps his staff kept it well. Who knew? She felt guilty for passing such judgments about him when in fact, she knew little about him outside of what she'd read about him or from little snippets from his cousin-by-marriage, Lucy.

"Very nice," she commented.

"It gets me from point A to B."

She grinned at him and rolled her eyes. "Yeah, it could be better, I agree. But what can you do with an old piece of metal on wheels, right?"

Lucas grinned. "You're a cheeky one, aren't you?" he teased her.

"So where is this mysterious place you're taking me?"

"Just a hideout I frequent at times. It's perfect."

"Oh. Does it have a name?"

"The Place."

"The Place?" She looked at him incredulously.

"There are places, Maxine, that very few people know about."

"Oh, wait a minute," she said, turning to him in her seat. "I've heard of these places. A lot of..." she was about to say rich, snobby people but caught herself. "...celebrities or public figures go there to unwind or eat in peace, right?"

"Something like that."

Maxine's heart leaped in her chest. She'd heard of these places for the elite few. It was usually not in a marked building so it wasn't obvious. There was some secret code to enter or a secret password. It appeared simple on the outside but once you entered through its secure doors, it was a world in and of itself. A world of luxury beyond the imagination. Upscale everything. Menus on iPads with no listed prices. Plush, expensive seats and booths, exclusive everything. Elite staff to tend to your needs twenty-four-seven. Was he really going to take her to such a place? And to talk? Just to talk, of all things.

Excitement gushed through Maxine. She'd almost forgotten about how she'd felt a few hours ago. Lost. Alone. Helpless. Violated.

And now for some strange reason, she felt as if maybe, just maybe things would be okay for her after all.

CHAPTER TEN

Maxine's eyes captured the beautiful surroundings of the restaurant of where Lucas took her. The place was cozy and the environment was oddly soothing. Lucas had parked outside a marble-facade building and taken the side entrance to enter their destination. Strangely enough, it was an unmarked door. It appeared that video cameras were hidden within because a voice over the intercom sounded and acknowledged him. "Good morning, Mr. Romero," the disembodied voice offered.

At first, Maxine was confused about the greeting until she realized it was four o'clock in the morning. The words drifted back to her mind "it's the friends you can call at four o'clock in the morning that count."

A warmth crept into her stomach. Lucas was a true friend in her time of need, wasn't he?

"Are you okay, Maxine?" Lucas asked her in a low voice. His tone was silky, smooth and deep. But the way he said her name. The way Maxine rolled off his tongue sent shivers of delight rushing through her.

"Yes, I'm good, thanks," she replied as she captured his beauty from across the table in the plush, cozy booth. The dim light of the candle and ambiance was soothing, romantic and calm. So inviting. Oh, God! This place was way too inviting. Anything could happen right there and then. There were very few people in the establishment except when she'd entered she noticed a few men dressed in the finest of suits. A discreet place where elite hang out. Who would have ever thought that she, ordinary, unknown Maxine, could be at a place such as this?

When the waiter took their orders after she'd made her selection from the iPad menu on the table, they were finally left alone.

"Nice place. Do you come here often?" she questioned in a hushed tone, trying hard not to gaze into his dark, sexy eyes. Every time their gaze met tingles would erupt between her thighs and she could feel moisture pool between her legs. She had to get her mind off sex. Off how sexy Lucas was.

"Sometimes. When I need to get away from it all."

"I see."

He sighed and leaned back into the leather seat of the booth. Lucas cocked a sexy boyish grin that melted her inside, yet again. The place looked elegant and rich, everything seemed elite, expensive from the art work on the walls to the soothing music in the background to the ambiance but it was all nothing compared to the vision of loveliness before her. Lucas.

"No freelance photographers, no onlookers, no hassles." He grinned.

"I get it. I should have known. It must be awful being chased by...reporters every time something...um..."

"Every time a girl makes a claim against me in the media?" he finished for her, a grin of amusement played across his sexy lips.

"I'm sorry, I didn't mean to—"

"Don't be. I'm pretty much used to it by now."

The waiter came back to the table in no time with Maxine's Caramel Macchiato. A rich blend of sweet steamed, deliciously frothy milk with a shot of freshly brewed espresso and creamy caramel. A filling hot beverage and one of Maxine's favorites when she could afford it. What really grabbed her was the fact that when she brought the drink to her lips, it tasted more rich than she'd ever remembered. Holy! Was the milk from a sacred cow or something?

She'd heard of rich folks going to places like this where it appeared that the chef took extra care with preparing their meals. This gave new meaning to the term expensive taste. Mind you, she'd also read online that some rich people went to places like this to pay $400 for the world's most juiciest, tastiest hamburgers with the most expensive organic beef. Imagine that! That was a week's worth of wages for most people.

Lucas enjoyed a steaming cup of freshly brewed black coffee. Strong and dark. Like him, she mused.

They engaged in small talk about sports and other issues before the waiter came back with their breakfast. Maxine delighted in his sense humor during that time.

She enjoyed an exquisite queen sized plate of soft scrambled eggs, mushrooms, shredded cheese and Pico de Gallo toppings and American fried potatoes. She also had Cinnamon Swirl French Toast with warm maple syrup to the side—unsure of how she would accommodate the proportions. Maxine had no idea how huge the dish would be when she ordered.

She salivated over her entrée. Lucas had a similar dish with a slice of steak! So early in the morning? But then again, judging by his broad shoulders and his muscular build she knew he worked out hard at the gym so having a protein-rich meal was probably expected.

"I'm really sorry about what happened to you at the apartment, Maxine."

"So I am," she lamented. Her eyes looked downcast. "But I'll survive." A knot tied in her stomach but she had to be brave about the whole thing.

"Thanks."

"For what?"

"For this. For doing all of this. For your concern," she murmured. "I have to be honest with you, Lucas. It shocked me to see you at the motel where I'm staying. I was like...wow! What are you doing here?"

"As I said before, you're like family. I take care of my family, Maxine."

"I know." She twirled her scrambled eggs on the plate.

"Listen, I'll be upfront with you, too," he offered. "I had my men look into things for me with that note you received."

Her eyes widened. But why was she really surprised? She suspected he may have something to do with watching her back, though she didn't know for sure. She secretly hoped he would. Who wouldn't want to have a hot, eligible guy watching their back from time to time? Watching over them, sort of? Like a genuine hero. Not that she needed saving. At least that's what she fed herself daily. She was drowning in debt, overwhelmed with caring for her mom and didn't know which way to turn at the moment.

"I can't believe you did that for me."

"To be honest, it tore me up inside when I heard about it. You're way too beautiful to be going through that crap."

"It happens, I suppose. Speaking of which. I'm sorry about what you're going through," she said with genuine concern. "That really sucks when people try to make up things about you and tell the press about it."

"I know," he said bitterly. His expression lightened slightly. "Thanks for caring."

"Well, why wouldn't I?"

"You'd be surprised at how many women wouldn't even care to ask how I'm feeling or what I'm going through. Just what I can give them. Or what I can do for them...or to them." A wicked grin touched his lips and he rolled his eyes and shook his head.

"Oh, that's terrible. You've dated the wrong women!" Maxine squirmed on her seat. Why did she say that? It must have come out awful. "I didn't mean it like that, Lucas."

"Oh, no. You're right. I dated the wrong type of women in the past, Maxine." The way he looked intently into her eyes caused all sorts of emotions to swirl through her body. Were they connecting? Lucas seemed more mellow than she'd ever seen him. He was comfortable opening up to her. That was good, wasn't it? She was equally comfortable with him.

"You must have had one woman who was nice."

Lucas swallowed hard. She knew she touched a raw nerve when she saw the look of pain sting his eyes. Oh, no. Maybe she shouldn't have said anything. She should have quit talking when she was ahead.

"I'm sorry."

"No. It's okay. I did have a steady girlfriend once. We dated in grade school," he said putting his elbow up on the back rest and casually leaning back. He was looking off into the distance for a moment as if visualizing this former love.

"Grade school?" she asked. That was so long ago. Was that his only steady girlfriend?

"She was a good girl. It wasn't anything like that. I was unaware of my...status back then. I'd only...my brothers and I met our grandfather when we were in our teens. So life up until that point had been pretty much like how your life is, Maxine."

Wow. Normal. So he hadn't been raised with a silver spoon in his mouth. No wonder he still hung out sometimes with "ordinary folks" and didn't look down on those struggling to make ends meet. It made sense how they could connect like old friends. He understood Maxine and where she was coming from.

"Your life was like mine." She smiled appreciatively. Maxine leaned forward, desperate to take her mind off her own troubles and get to know Lucas better. That was what she wanted. Intimacy on an emotional level before anything else.

"So what happened to the lucky girl? Where is she now?" Maxine probed.

Lucas's eyes grew darker. Maxine flinched slightly. Was it something she said? Was she delving too deeply into a place in Lucas's life that was off limits?

"She's, Julianna, Julianna was her name, she's no longer...around," he whispered almost inaudibly. His eyes glazed over with pain and a deep, horrible anguish she'd never seen on a man and wished she hadn't. She wanted to reach across the table and hug Lucas. Was that why he hid behind his bad boy exterior and didn't give a toss what others thought of him?

"I...Oh, God! Lucas. I'm so...so sorry," she offered, her heart squeezing.

"It's okay."

"What happened?"

"It was a long process unfortunately. But we were close throughout school and then we discovered she had a rare form of brain tumor."

"Oh, God! Lucas, that's awful."

"I know. She should have been enjoying school and everything else in life but she had severe headaches throughout it all. Her parents didn't think much of it and thought she was studying too hard. They pretty much ignored it most of the time. I would get her Tylenol from my dad and give it to her. Her folks didn't really believe much in modern medicine."

Maxine shuddered inside.

"So," Lucas continued. "Before long, the pain grew unbearable. I spent most of senior high going to appointments with her because her parents worked so hard and needed to pay the mortgage. Anyway, finally, they took time off work to get her hospitalized and we rotated turns sleeping at the bedside at the hospital. But the doc said it was too late. The tumor could have been operated on and maybe radiated if she'd had an MRI done long before and they'd caught it in time but..."

"Oh, God! Lucas, that's terrible." Tears stung Maxine's eyes.

Lucas was consumed by his emotions, she could see. "So that's why I was inspired to develop a software system for clinics to get people into early signups and pre-screening for their health."

"Of course," Maxine chimed in. "The Healthy Start Program. How wonderful of you, Lucas."

"It's the least I could do. I had developed so many different programs in my line of work but that one was close to my heart."

"I'm very…honored to know you, Lucas."

Lucas shot Maxine a glance. "Well, I've never heard that before," he admitted softly with a charming grin. "Usually women say the opposite."

"Why?"

"Well, I'm not perfect, Maxine. I've made tons of mistakes. I love women. What can I say? But commitment was always difficult for me after Julianna died. I just didn't feel anything intimate for anyone else, until now."

"What?" Maxine almost choked on her drink. Something sparked inside her. Was he referring to her?

"I've been admiring you from afar, Maxine. I thought you would have known that."

"No. I…um…why?"

"Because you're different. And I can't explain it but you reach me in a spot I've never been touched before, not since Julianna."

Oh. My. What could she say to that?

"But you hardly know me," she said, rubbing her finger around the rim of her cup.

"But I know me. And I know how I feel when I'm around you. And you'd be surprised at what I've learned about you and observed about you over the past six months since the wedding, Maxine," he said with a knowing grin of satisfaction.

Maxine was stumped. What had Lucy said about her?

"Such as?" Maxine cocked her brow.

"You care deeply about those you love. You're humble. And you're sweet. You make me feel wild things inside, Maxine, and I didn't even have to touch you. That's what amazed me."

"Oh!" Maxine felt heat rush to her cheeks and to the area between her legs. She was getting breathless in there. Was it the heat? Or the magnetic energy between them? So this was what kismet felt like. She never felt this way around any other man before.

"By the way, how is your mother doing?" he asked, so sincere.

Lucas Romero cared about her and her mother? Oh, my. He was so important. Maxine thought she hadn't mentioned her mother before but then again at the wedding when they had chatted, it may have come up. But oh, God! This guy had a memory like an elephant. He remembered. That was good, wasn't it?

"She's," Maxine swallowed hard. "She's coping."

"How are *you* coping?" Lucas leaned forward.

"Good."

"Really?"

"You don't believe me?"

"I see it in your eyes. I can read eyes, you know. You work so hard around the clock, sacrificing yourself for the good of your mother and everyone else around you. When have you taken time for yourself? You know caregiver burnout is not healthy and can happen if you don't take it easy."

Maxine looked sheepish. What could she say? "You really care about me, don't you?"

"I want to help you, Maxine. Let me. I can hire a private nurse for your mother."

"Lucas, I…" Maxine broke off. She inhaled a deep breath before continuing. She really didn't want to hurt his feelings but she had her pride. She wasn't about to take a handout for nothing, especially from a rich, sexy bachelor. She didn't want him to get the wrong idea. She didn't want to send the wrong signal.

"Lucas, that's so nice of you but…" Maxine bit down on her lower lip. "I just can't accept that generous gift from you."

"And why not?" he said forcefully.

"Well, there's a price for everything, Lucas. You and I both know that nothing is free."

"Ouch." Lucas feigned a broken heart. "You really think I'm trying to buy you, Maxine? Now, that really hurt." He seemed to be having fun with it instead of taking offense, which was a welcome relief for Maxine. The last thing she wanted to do was offend him. He was only trying to help her, wasn't he?

"All I want is friendship, Maxine. Only if you want that."

"Friendship?" Now it was her turn to take umbrage. Was that really all he wanted from her? "You mean friendship with benefits, right?" She cocked a brow. She really didn't think a man as hot and sexy as Lucas Romero would only want female friends.

"You really do speak your mind, Maxine. I like that."

"So do you. Sometimes."

"Well, I try to be mindful these days."

"But you would want something more from me, wouldn't you?"

"Not if you don't want it. But yes, I would love to f—, er, make love to you over and over again, enjoying the sounds of you screaming in unbridled pleasure like you've never known before. What's wrong with that?" Lucas grinned as if nothing out of the ordinary was said.

Maxine must have flushed fifty shades of rouge. She was getting hot inside. Too hot. She swallowed hard and with shaking hands grabbed the glass of water that was by the side of the table and placed it to her lips. She needed air to breathe. She needed oxygenated water right now.

"Sorry," he laughed. "Sometimes, I get ahead of myself. But you did want to hear what I had on my mind."

"I did," she said, smiling. "I'm...glad." *I'm flattered, too.* Lucas really wants to do that to me? She visualized what it would be like writhing beneath this sex god on a bed, naked bodies entwined in an erotic fantasy. She was throbbing between her thighs.

Time to switch the subject.

"Listen, I'm very thankful...grateful that you want to help me, Lucas. But like I said, I'll find a way to help my mom out."

"It's not a handout, Maxine." His tone was more serious. He was really serious about helping her for nothing in return, wasn't he? "You do love your mother, don't you?"

"Of course, I do!" she shot back, placing her glass back on the table. "I'll do anything for her."

"Well, I can get you anything you want. Let me know. But I'll need your consent first. I can have a twenty-four hour nurse to care for your mother." He swiped his cell phone from his pocket. "Just say the word."

"Lucas! I can't have you do that."

"Why not? I can do whatever the hell I feel like...as long as I have your consent, of course." He gave her a wicked grin to melt her heart again. He was really serious, wasn't he? He was so unlike the carefree bachelor she'd read about in news reports. Which went to show that you can't believe everything you read or hear about a person.

"Yes, but—" The truth was she was worried sick about her mother's safety in the nursing home since short-staffing was always an issue at the facility.

"Self-care, Maxine. You need to take care of number one before you take care of anyone else in your life. I know it sounds selfish but there is no other way. Besides, I don't want to see anything happen to you."

Maxine swallowed. "I promise to take care of myself, Lucas. You don't have to worry about me." She tried to brush him off with a grin and a roll of her eyes.

"You know something?" he said, leaning back. "I like that about you."

"Like what?"

"The way you just seem to brush me off every chance you get."

"That's not quite what I'm doing."

"Au contraire. You're so different. Most girls would have jumped at the chance."

"But I'm not most girls, Lucas."

He leaned forward and gazed intently into her eyes and butterflies exploded in her belly. She loved the way he looked at her that way. Hungry passion burning in his eyes. A possessive interest in her. "I know," he cooed with a wicked grin.

"Come here," he said softly, getting up, reaching his hand to hers.

"Where are you taking me?"

"Over there to a better location. The sun will rise soon."

"Oh?"

Lucas guided her to another side of the venue where there was a tinted window and a breathtaking view of the city by the lake. Beauty was not adequate to describe it.

"It's a one-way visual. We can see out but no one can see in."

"Oh, this is nice, Lucas." And what a scenic view it was. She could see Lakeside Drive with a pier and a few yachts docked. Over to the left some tall, glass, high-rise buildings that reflected the glistening sunrise overlooked the rich, sparkling blue lake that seemed to stretch for miles along the coast. They didn't call it a "great lake" for nothing. Ontario was surrounded by a few great lakes the size of some cities and even some states. Glancing at the waves in the water outside was refreshing and soothing.

But it was the deep orange and red sun rising in the east that captured her as the reflection on the water was a warm orange over the blue. Darkness was melting into light. The dawn of a new day—and a new phase in Maxine's life.

"I love watching the sunrise in the morning," he whispered. "My mother used to tell us that when we rise with the sun we get more energy to start the day. It's a wonderful way to renew your strength."

When Lucas spoke, his eyes glittered with what looked like raw hurt. Maxine was sure there must be some story there but decided not to probe further. Not now. She just could not believe that Lucas was sharing this magical, intimate moment with her and it had nothing to do with them getting naked in bed. She'd never felt so sensual, so close to a man like this. He was opening up in a way that was indescribable, yet sweet.

Lucas sat beside her and placed his arms over the back of the chair around her. She wanted to snuggle in his embrace. This was so not the bad boy image the media painted of Lucas. She would never again believe everything she read about a celebrity or public person. Never again. She learned a lesson in that there was always more to a story.

To her delight, Lucas and she spoke practically through the night to early morning. They spoke about many interests and family stuff and all sorts of things while the city slowly woke until they heard the honking of horns and the busy traffic outside. Yep, the city was wide awake now. But she was grateful to have this time to feel protected after what had happened to her at her apartment.

And all through this she wasn't even tired. How weird was that? She guessed Lucas was right about getting energy from the sun. Only once before did she remember pulling an all-nighter, while studying for finals, but it was nothing like this. Maxine always slept well during a twenty-four hour period. And she knew she would have to get some sleep sometime soon—if only in Lucas's arms.

Lucas spoke fondly about his family. His grandfather, whom he adored more than anything on this earth—though they'd sometimes butt heads about issues. He spoke about the bond he had with his cousin Antonio and his six brothers. All of his family members were doing well in their chosen industries. They all worked under the umbrella of Romero Corp. and the Romero Foundation. The foundation especially brought so much to the community and it hosted the famous annual Diamond Ball that raised millions of dollars for various programs to help young entrepreneurs, fixed-income families and funded affordable housing for low-income families.

Maxine felt a pang of longing. She was happy that after all Lucas and his family had been through that he was doing well but she wished she had a large family too. It must be amazing, simply amazing to come from such a huge family—and a close-knit one at that, Maxine surmised.

Oh, how she wished she and her mother had a family. She didn't even know her biological family. That hurt her the most. She was grateful for her adoptive mother but the pain of not knowing why her real family gave her away, stung her at times.

"So you have six brothers?" Maxine was stunned. She'd read about the Romero family but didn't realize there was…so many of them.

"Yeah. And they're all a pain in the butt!" Lucas grinned.

"You don't mean that."

"How do you know?"

"Because of the way you just spoke about them. I've heard you'd do anything for your siblings or other family members."

"Oh, really? So you've been checking up on me, have you?"

"No!" Maxine cast her eyes away to look at the blueness of the lake that was now fully lit up under the early morning sun. Heat rose to her cheeks.

"So, what is it then? How did you know?"

"Aha! See. You admit it. You said *how* did you know, not *how could you be so sure*?" she said, raising a brow, a knowing grin on her lips.

Lucas grinned sheepishly. "Yeah, I'll do anything for my family and those close to me."

His words caused a wave of hot emotions to stir through Maxine. He would do *anything* for his family or those close to him.

"You know, we really should be going, Lucas. I've really enjoyed—" Maxine stopped midsentence. Her cell phone rang and startled her. She reached into her bag and fished her out her phone. When she read the display, her heart stopped.

It was the nursing home calling her.

"What is it?" Lucas was overtly concerned.

"Um…it's the nursing home." Her heart plummeted in her chest. They would not be calling her unless it was something urgent. Not at this hour of the morning.

CHAPTER ELEVEN

"Has Lucas returned yet?" Zack asked as he walked into the breakfast room. His grandfather, Toni, and Toni's wife, Shelly, alongside side his cousin, Antonio, with his wife, Lucy, were seated at the long, oval breakfast table. The morning sun shone in the area through the ceiling-to-floor windows.

What were they talking about? Zack was no fool. The family hardly used the breakfast room unless they were having an intense discussion about something.

Was this about his brother, Lucas, and getting Lucas hitched so that he could avoid another public relations disaster with an upcoming launch? He knew his grandfather wanted so badly to repair the carefree, wild images of his grandsons in the media but Zack just hoped to God he wasn't playing matchmaker with Lucas.

It was as if his grandfather saw single as being some sort of disorder that needed to be treated…a la wedding band of gold.

Well, Zack could certainly speak for his brother when he thought: "Thanks but no thanks!"

A grin of amusement touched Toni's lips. "I think he's been out all night. He was going to help that young woman, Maxine." Toni went back to eating his crepes.

Zack sighed a deep breath. "I can't seem to reach him on his cell. I'm going in to the office now."

"Very well. And oh, Zack," Toni called out, not looking up from his plate. "Don't do anything silly."

Now what did his dear old grandfather mean by that?

***

"I'm sorry, Maxine," the doctor said as he sat in the chair of his office at the nursing home.

Maxine could not sit down. She had to stand up. She stood beside Lucas with her arms wrapped tightly across her chest. Lucas was right beside her in the doctor's office.

She was glad he was there. She needed him more than anything. She just realized she had very few close people to turn to. She did have Lucy but Lucy was married and expecting a child during a difficult pregnancy. Thank God for Lucas!

"So what you're saying is that my mother has to be transferred to…another type of facility?" Maxine's voice trembled. They were going to have her mother committed. The thought brought a crushing boulder to her stomach.

"Well," the doctor continued. "She does require more supervision for one thing. As I mentioned earlier, she had a pretty difficult episode last night. She was very…" he hesitated, glancing at Lucas momentarily as if unsure if he should divulge such personal information in front of non-family members.

"It's okay," Maxine prompted him. "He's a close friend. You can say whatever you have to say in front of Lucas."

"Very well. Your mother has been more confused and agitated lately and we're quite concerned for her safety. We can try some sedative medication as I explained to you before."

Lucas shifted uncomfortably on the spot before speaking. "Is there any reason she can't have twenty-four hour supervision?" he asked in a voice of authority, yet calm.

"Well, that would be quite costly. Maxine would have to foot the bill out of her own pocket since we don't provide that sort of care at this facility."

"It's not a problem. I'll take care of all costs. Do you have a nursing agency that you use who could send an RN right away?" Lucas probed.

"Lucas!" Maxine was gob smacked. "I…We…I can't ask you to do that. It would cost a fortune."

"Please leave that to me, Maxine." Lucas held up his hand to silence her.

Maxine was taken aback at first. Who did he think he was? Just because he had…money?

While Lucas spoke to the doctor regarding making arrangements and instructing him about his billing information, Maxine re-folded her arms tightly across her chest before shifting her composure. She considered her options. What else could she do? The only other choice was to have her mother committed to a mental ward with more staffing or a psychiatric hospital, when all her mother probably needed right now was more close continuous care around the clock, something only a private duty nurse could provide.

"Thank you," Maxine said softly to Lucas while she turned the key to her apartment for the first time since her break-in. It had been two hours later after they'd left the facility. Lucas and Maxine had visited her mother in the special room prior to the private duty nurse arriving from the agency. But he told her he wanted to take her up to her apartment to get things sorted out. He said it wasn't wise to go alone. And he was right.

"I told you, I look after my friends, Maxine."

"Only friends, huh?" She grinned playfully. "Why are you so nice to me? I mean, I really appreciate it, Lucas."

"I want to do this, Maxine. I don't know why but sometimes in life you meet someone and you feel this connection. It's not really something I can explain but I feel a rapport with you. And besides, right now I'd much rather be here with you," he said looking around the trashed unit, a bitter knife twisted in his stomach.

What crazy animal did this to Maxine? He would soon find out. Zack told him that the detective agency was on the case working with the cops.

"I'd much rather be with a kind-hearted, down-to-earth friend than dealing with the gossip-hungry media," Lucas continued.

Maxine gushed inside. She was honored. But that feeling was soon washed away with sorrow for Lucas. What on earth must he be going through? His case was still up in the air in the media. She felt bad for him. His reputation was on the line and here he was, spending time helping Maxine sort through her rubbish.

Maxine felt a bit discouraged looking at all the stuff she would have to sift through. "Are you sure you want to help me out here, Lucas?"

He glanced around and cocked a brow. "Not really. Let's hire a cleaning agency."

"Oh," Maxine said, swallowing hard.

"I'm teasing you, Maxine. Relax," he said in jest.

She melted at the smoothness of his tone. Yes, she needed to learn to relax.

"I get rustled at times, too, Maxine. Don't get me wrong. Things rile me up but I've learned a long time ago that getting worked up doesn't do anything to solve a problem. It only makes you feel worse and makes the situation look worse. And even more so than that, sometimes we miss the blessing of a simple solution to our problems because we're too busy being pissed off."

"Good point." Maxine nodded thoughtfully.

Lucas's expression turned grim when his eyes scanned the apartment further. The walls had splashes of wine from the bottles that were hurled against them. "I want you to stay at the condominium on Bay Street. The one owned by my family." The words came out more like an order than a request. Maxine did not like the sound of that.

"What?" she huffed. "What are you talking about, Lucas?"

"You're not staying here." His tone was clipped.

"I'll go back to the motel."

"The hell you will. Why would you do that?"

"Because it's what I can afford, Lucas. I appreciate what you've done for my mother but I'm not…I'm not going to be some…kept woman."

"Kept woman?" he said with a stiff expression. "Who said anything about a being a kept woman?"

"Well, I sure can't afford the rent for Romero Towers, that's a no-brainer." She folded her arms across her chest.

"I'll cover it, Maxine. When are you going to learn to accept help when it's offered?"

"Because you've done so much for me and I feel as if…I'll never be able to repay you." The words caused a painful lump to swell in her throat. Maxine could not breathe or think straight. It was all too overwhelming.

Just then Lucas paused, his expression turned serious. He saw something over by the corner of her studio apartment on the ground by the overturned bookshelf and mounds of books spewed across the floor. He walked over to that area and knelt down; a grin touched his lips.

"What is it?" Maxine asked with great curiosity. She stepped over some books and overturned coffee table to get to where he was.

It was the beautiful bouquet that she had placed on top of her bookshelf. The one she caught at Lucy's wedding around the same time Lucas had caught Antonio's garter. Oh, my.

Lucas swallowed. He turned around to face Maxine and handed it to her with a wicked grin. "You may be needing this one day, beautiful."

Maxine flushed. *If only*.

***

A few weeks blew past Maxine as she spent time in her new apartment at Romero Towers on the luxury strip of Bay Street and the lake with a beautiful view of the blue water. She had never been in a place like that. Sure enough, Lucas had convinced her to stay there. She had nowhere else to turn. In the first few days, Lucas was with her at the office to ensure things ran smoothly at the agency with the new software program. It was a dream. Speaking of dreams, every night since Lucas helped her out in her apartment she thought back to watching him pick up that magic bouquet in the rubble of her trashed apartment. That bouquet. She referred to it as magic because of all the things to find. It was as if it was some sort of positive omen or maybe even fate. What had that meant? Why had Lucas grinned? A distinct feeling of lightness floated inside her belly. Love. She thought about Lucas having caught the garter that day of Lucy's wedding, too. Was that a coincidence or…kismet?

As Maxine shuffled through some paperwork on her desk at Dream Weddings, Inc. she tried to push the thought of having anything romantic with Lucas aside. The last thing she needed to do was to raise her hopes only to have them come crushing down.

She had to shift her focus back on work. Yes, work. She loved the new technology Lucas had set up for her business. That was a step in the right direction.

Betty, the receptionist and admin assistant, loved it, too. It was more self-serve for clients and meant less hassle for them. It was also cost-effective since things were headed more online much like travel agencies these days.

At least now her company would be able to keep up with technology and the changing times. So at least they stood some fighting chance of survival in the competitive marketplace. Of course, it also meant that revenue would take a small hit but that was inevitable in any case since most clients were not coming in with mounds of cash to have their weddings organized by a live person.

But to her chagrin, Lucas wasn't there much of the time. At least after things got up and running. He left Maxine to her work, sure as promised.

The high-rise state-of-the-art condo was close to her office at Dream Wedding, Inc., which in and of itself was a dream! Talk about a fast commute. And all this time, Lucas was on the West Coast handling some business merger plans for Romero Corp. on behalf of his grandfather. She felt foolish now for accusing Lucas of having her as some kept woman. Sure, he wanted to help her out a bit, but it seemed as if he had other things occupying his mind, like business, of course. He was, after all, a prominent entrepreneur and executive, right?

All the while, Maxine longed to see him again. She longed to feel the strong surrender of his arms around her again. She longed to kiss his sweet lips. She wanted him, craved him. Absence sure made the heart fonder, and hungrier for passion, too. She didn't think she could survive another day without seeing him in person—not online either. Maxine would toss and turn at night thinking about Lucas with her, on top of her. She would lie on her back and remove her gown, stroking her nipples, imagining Lucas's sweet lips caressing them until she came. Oh, how she missed Lucas. The strange thing was that she'd never even gone all the way with him—yet. She wondered if she'd ever get to that point. She wanted him. She wanted him like she'd never wanted any man before.

"The nursing home is on line one," Betty called out from the reception area of Dream Weddings, Inc.

"Thanks, Betty," Maxine answered before picking up the flashing line. "Hi, Mom!"

"Oh, darling, you are sounding much better today," her mother's steady voiced called out over the phone. Her mom was still pleasantly confused but luckily she was not sedated with drugs and she was not in a mental ward. Thanks to Lucas, she had a twenty-four hour private duty nurse who was absolutely fabulous and compassionate. This gave Maxine more time for herself to take care of herself and run the business while her mother had a wonderful support staffer with her all the time.

"Mom, I thought I always sounded good."

"Hmm. Not really, dear, but you'll improve. So how's the weather in England?"

Maxine grinned. "Mom, I'm here in Toronto with you. The weather is great."

At least now her mother was referring to her as a daughter and not as a stranger or some ancient princess. At least that was a start.

Things were beginning to look hopeful for Maxine. Except where Lucas was concerned. Okay, so she had not been rushing into his arms or anything but what was with the hot and cold signals she was getting from him? He barely called since travelling to the West Coast. Was he with another woman? Did he find a fling to kill time while he was out there, since clearly Maxine did not give it up to him at the drop of a hat?

There were only two things of which she was unsure. One: Who was the person or persons behind those hate emails and trashing her place? And, two: Where did she stand with Lucas? Did she have a future with him or not?

CHAPTER TWELVE

Two weeks later, dozens of friends and family gathered in the garden at Romero Mansion for the Jack and Jill Baby shower for Lucy and Antonio's unborn baby. Tables and garden chairs were adorned with pretty white tablecloths and chair coverings while blue and pink ribbons decorated the trees. Enormous teddy bear balloons and "Baby Shower" blue and pink balloons were hanging everywhere. There was a large table filled with gift bags and presents for Lucy's baby, of which, Maxine's gifts were amongst them.

The proud mom-to-be Lucy looked so glowing and jubilant with her swelled belly as she sat down on the "Queen" chair surrounded by close friends who were gushing over her. The official games and shower hadn't begun as of yet. Maxine was sincerely thrilled for Lucy. She'd found her Mr. Right and now she was expecting her first child. Lucy deserved every happiness. Like Maxine, she'd been alone and heartbroken for some time. Years. In fact, they used to tease each other about their celibate years wondering if they'd end up alone and spinsters into their nineties. A lump climbed in Maxine's throat. Well, at least Lucy would not end up that way. She wasn't so sure about her own fate, though.

The sound of people laughing, talking and having fun filled the atmosphere. It was a warm summer afternoon in August. The sun was shining bright against a blue cloudless sky. Maxine felt a bit out of her element though. She'd known Lucy for a while but Lucy was hanging with a different crowd now. The rich and the famous. A waiter dressed in a white tux with a black bow tie (one of many waiters) approached Maxine with a tray of refreshments.

"No, thank you. I'm fine for now," she dismissed him politely. The man walked away. Everybody seemed to be having fun socializing with people they knew but Maxine didn't really know anyone there. Except Lucas, but he was still out of town as far as she knew.

"Gorgeous, isn't it?" Lucas said to Maxine as he stepped behind her.

Maxine was caught by surprise. A very pleasant surprise! When did he arrive? She had been admiring the beautiful flowers in the massive garden. The hedge was professionally trimmed by the family's gardener into heart-shaped motifs. Maxine was oohing and aahing over them.

"Yes, they are...beautiful," she murmured after she turned to face him. "I didn't see you arrive. When did you get here?" Her heart was pounding hard and fast in her chest. Butterflies were tickling her stomach again. Being this close to Lucas did that to her, didn't it? It never failed. There was simply something about him that lifted her spirit and elevated her mood.

"Well, you know I wouldn't miss this for the world. My cousin's...ahem...baby shower," Lucas said with a charming smirk.

Maxine could just imagine the two cousins teasing each other or having a mock spat over the fact that they were both forced to attend the Romero family's first official Jack and Jill baby shower. In fact, she noticed that Toni was extra perky today. She could literally feel his joy over having a new grandchild in the family. His very first. How exciting! And Maxine got to be a part of that.

There was the pang in the center of her chest again. A longing that she wished she had a big, close-knit family such as the Romero family. She could see how much they stuck together and supported each other whether they were busy or not. They were all in attendance.

"Can I get you a drink?"

"No. I'm good, thanks. Actually, maybe a glass of water." The hot sun was making her mouth dry all of a sudden. Or was that Lucas? She was thirsting for a taste of his sweet lips. She hungered for his passion. But this was not the time, nor place, was it?

Lucas took a glass of sparkling water from the tray of one of the waiters who happened to brush by them at the time.

"So, how are you doing?" he asked as he handed her the glass. His gaze focused intently on hers.

Maxine melted inside. He was inches from her with a glass of champagne in his own hand. "Thank you," she said, taking the glass from him. "I've been...busy." She lifted the glass to her lips and felt quenched by the cool water sliding down her throat. A naughty thought crossed her mind as she licked her lips after taking her sip. Lucas's gaze was fixed on her mouth for that moment and she thought she caught a wicked grin from his lips.

Okay. She would *not* be doing that again. The last thing she wanted to do was tease him. Or appear like some sort of flirtatious tease.

"Good. How's the Dream software holding up?"

"Oh, it's fabulous. Thank you again. We've had a few good prospects who have tried the online program and were happy to have us do the rest. It's sort of some pre-screening for them. They love it and so do we."

"Glad to hear," he said sincerely. He lifted the glass to his lips while his eyes stayed on Maxine.

"I've missed you," he said almost inaudibly when he'd finished taking his swig of alcohol.

"What?"

"Why does that surprise you?"

"Um. Well, you haven't even called me since you went out west." She placed a hand on her hip.

"Sorry. I've been busy."

Maxine rolled her eyes playfully.

"No. Seriously. I wanted to call you but I've been working on this new project and trying to dodge the local media there, too."

Maxine's heart squeezed. That scandal again. How could she have forgotten? It had been a while since things died down a bit but as she knew that could change in a heartbeat.

"It's still hanging over you, huh?"

"You'd better believe it. We're opening up a family-friendly center there and all they could keep asking about was my unborn child—the one I'm denying." Bitterness crossed his handsome face.

Maxine's insides twisted. "How awful. I'm so sorry to hear that, Lucas. That's the last thing you need. Why can't they just drop it? You're innocent until proven-"

"Guilty?" He cocked a brow and grinned.

"That's not quite what I meant, you know."

"I know. I'm only teasing you, Maxi."

Did he just call her Maxi? Only her dear and close friends called her that. The few she had, anyway. The way he said it seem to resonate well with her. It felt so right. So natural. It was as if he was warming to her.

"Anyway, enough about that. I trust everything's been okay with that situation," he said in almost a tone of finality. As if he knew everything was okay.

"Yes. In fact, I haven't heard or seen any more of those dreadful emails," Maxine said with relief.

"Good. You shouldn't."

"Okay, everyone," Shelly announced over a microphone from where Lucy was sitting. "Ladies...and gents. If you would like to make your way over to this area. We're going to begin the games and opening gifts soon."

Murmurs rang from the crowd as everyone headed in the general direction of Shelly's voice.

"You go on," Lucas said to Maxine. Zack had walked over to where they were standing with a glass in his hand. He had on a dark suit, opened-up jacket. He looked as if he wanted to speak to Lucas eagerly. Brothers. Maxine guessed they had something important to exchange.

"Okay, I'll see you later then," she said.

Lucas's focus shifted to Zack. "What is it, Zack?"

"Well, brother dear, your suspicions were right about everything."

"Okay, let's talk over here." The two brothers moved over to the hedge and a corner of the garden where no one else was within earshot. "Okay, spill it out."

"Our men found out that it wasn't the couple who was trying to sue Dream Weddings back when Lucy was CEO."

"You sure about that now? They seemed a little off, didn't they?"

"Yeah. They were all right. But as it turns out, they were running some sort of scam from the get-go. They travelled from down south and apparently they would plan these crazy weddings and try to get injured so they could blame the wedding planning agency."

Lucas grimaced. What sort of crazy people were these? "Very well. So what happened to them?"

"They got caught. They've been detained for some other insurance fraud business. Anyway, our men have confirmed that they have indeed dropped the case against Dream Weddings. So Maxine is definitely in the clear about that. And no, they did not have anything to do with the notes or trashing Maxine's apartment."

"Good."

"Bad."

"I don't follow."

"It probably would have been a lot easier if they were the ones behind it."

"Oh, great. So you're telling me you know who's behind it and it's someone close to Maxine?"

Zack nodded bringing his glass to his lips. The two men were more focused on their conversation than on the laughing and clapping going on behind them at the other side of the garden where the baby shower festivities were going on.

Lucas glanced over briefly and saw Maxine sitting on a chair in the circle enjoying herself. She looked so happy. He liked that. It killed him inside that any creepy person close to Maxine would want to hurt her. If he ever got his hands on the guy...

"Was it her ex?" he said bitterly.

"No."

"Then who?"

"Betty."

"Betty? Who's Betty?" Lucas sighed heavily. He wished Zack would just get on with it and not hold back.

"Her receptionist."

Lucas froze.

CHAPTER THIRTEEN

"Okay, let's play the next game," Shelly announced to the men and women gathered around Lucy as she sat with her swelled belly on the "queen's" chair. "What words of wisdom do you have for the baby or for the new parents-to-be?"

The crowd murmured.

"Now, now. We're going to record this so the baby will know when he or she is older what messages you want to give to him or her or to the parents."

"Sounds cool," Maxine chimed in. "I've heard of this game." She directed a wink to Lucy who smiled back appreciatively. Antonio was sitting beside Lucy looking like the doting father-to-be. A longing seeped into Maxine's heart wishing one day that could be her and Lucas. For a fleeting moment she had a fantasy play in her mind of being pregnant with Lucas's love child. *Yeah. If only.*

Still, the baby shower party was a fun and relaxing way for Maxine to spend this Saturday. Just what she truly needed. And yes, Lucas was there, too. She wanted more than anything else to see Lucas. She glanced around briefly and saw Lucas speaking with Zack. What on earth were they conversing about at a time like this? The two looked deeply engaged in some sort of tete-a-tete.

"Maxine?"

"Yes," Maxine was caught off guard by Shelly's voice.

"It's your turn. You need to write down a message for the baby. It could be funny, wise, or actually, anything you like."

Maxine took the square piece of paper Shelly handed to her and thought for a moment. She then scribbled down something cute on the paper along with everyone else who had wrote their messages and placed it inside an open basket to be drawn a bit later and read one by one.

"Good." Shelly was beaming. Maxine wondered how Shelly was feeling right now. She appeared as thrilled as everyone else for Lucy and Antonio's new bundle of joy but truth be told Shelly looked great for a woman in her forties yet she didn't have any children of her own. Granted, she married the seventy-six-year-old, Toni. Were they planning on adopting? Or was Shelly content in having eight grown men as her step-grandchildren and now a step-great-grandchild on the way? Jeez! That was a lot to digest. Maxine was happy Shelly found love with Toni and she was even more glad that she had a hand in making their dream wedding come true with Lucy at the Dream Weddings, Inc. agency. Would Maxine ever know the joys of being a blushing bride? Ever?

Moments later, Lucy picked the heartfelt notes from the basket and one by one read each beautiful message. "Thank you, Shelly," Lucy smiled appreciatively at the gracious host who also left a soothing message for her.

"And now, Maxine." Lucy had picked out another note from the basket to read. All of this was being recorded. Maxine was stunned to see Zack had his camera on record. She looked around to see if Lucas was about but she did not.

Maxine frowned but quickly shifted her expression.

"This is beautiful, Maxine," Lucy said, misty-eyed. She had read the note in her mind first then proceeded to read aloud.

"Now you know we're mind readers, Lucy, but we're not that good," Zack teased her. "Come on, read it out loud so that my video can pick up the non-telekinetic sound."

The crowd burst into laughter and Lucy scowled at him playfully as she rubbed her belly.

"Learn to have fun. Lots of fun. Memories are what last forever. Love a lot. Laugh a lot. Spend a lot. A lot of time. Children spell love T.I.M.E. Cherish every golden moment and savor every precious day. And they'll never outgrow a hug because it's always one size fits all. Good luck to the lovely parents-to-be."

A boisterous "aww" rang out from the group. Lucy got up and gave Maxine a good squeeze and hug over her large belly. Maxine hugged her back tightly.

"That was beautiful, Maxine," Lucas said later in a low voice. He stood beside her and she spun around in surprise.

"Wow, do you walk or do you just magically appear whenever you want to be near me?"

Lucas grinned, his charming dimple appeared on his cheek. Maxine was whole again. She loved when he was near her. She loved the way he made her feel. All the time.

"Thank you," she then answered him back. By then, the group was already on to the next message and Lucas gently pulled Maxine away.

"Come," he said to her. "We need to talk."

"Can this wait?" Maxine said half-heartedly. She felt bad about leaving the shower, but God, she really wanted nothing more than to be alone with Lucas. She didn't know why but she just did.

"It is something you need to know about but if you want we can do this later."

"Oh no. It sounds rather important. Okay, where should we go?"

"We can walk over to the guest house on the other side."

"Okay," Maxine murmured. "I just need to speak with Lucy."

When the game had wrapped up, Maxine spoke with Lucy on the side.

"Oh, please don't worry, Maxine," Lucy said. "In fact, the shower is pretty much over now. I'm really beat. I need to take my nap now. I've told the others to carry on without me." Lucy then winked. "I insist on you spending some time with Lucas."

"Lucy!"

"Seriously, Maxine. He's a nice guy and well...he cares about you."

Maxine smiled sheepishly and hugged Lucy. "I will speak with you later, okay?"

"Don't rush," Lucy said, smiling.

Later, Maxine and Lucas strolled along the lawn while the partygoers were oblivious to their absence. What could Lucas want to talk to her about now?

CHAPTER FOURTEEN

Lucas and Maxine arrived at the guest house—a cedar-sided cottage at the west side of the estate. It had its own cobblestone walkway and meticulously trimmed hedges in front of the main door.

It was an extraordinary guest home with a breathtaking view of the hills. How Maxine loved the way the Romero family lived. It was an impressive estate for sure. The land seemed to go on forever. It must be nice to live like this. Heck, even if the family had bothersome guests staying over, they would not be affected at all since the guest house was far from the main house yet luxurious enough to keep the guests satisfied. And she noticed there were several other cottages nearby.

Lucas opened the main door and led Maxine inside. "After you, beautiful," he invited in a smooth voice that caused her to tingle inside.

"Oh, this is nice," Maxine commented as she walked inside. She was stunned. It was an ultra-functional environment. Spacious and cozy at the same time. She noticed the open area living room with ceiling-to-floor stone fireplace and sofas with a Persian rug in the center over a shiny hardwood floor.

The kitchen area in the open concept design had marble countertops and stained oak cabinets with a marble-top kitchen island with brown leather backless bar stools around it—sort of like a breakfast bar in the middle of the kitchen nook.

"It's okay. It's a place for guests to stay."

Maxine turned around in awe. She could not believe he was so casual about the opulence of his surroundings, especially since he started out life humble. "Aren't you ever simply amazed at what your grandfather has built?"

"Of course, I am. I'm very proud of my old man. But his legacy is more important than his assets. My grandfather has instilled a lot of positive values and good work ethics in all of us. To tell you the truth, I'm more impressed with that."

"Of course!" Maxine smiled. She felt warm inside. That was one of the attributes that attracted her to Lucas. He wasn't at all what the media painted him out to be. He was so much more—profound. "Well, he's done a good job, Lucas."

"Thank you. It's because of his work ethics why we are the way we are today. It's all about helping others, leaving the world a better place than how we found it and making a difference. He always told us to never look for work, create it."

Maxine nodded thoughtfully.

"Can I get you anything?"

Just you.

"I'm okay for now," she murmured.

"Come. I'll take you on a tour."

He led her through the hallway and towards the back where there was a study and a view of the swimming pool outside.

"Nice."

"Thanks."

Lucas looked deep in thought. Of course, he did not bring her there solely for a tour of one of their guest homes. They needed to talk.

"Listen," Lucas said, his hands shoved in the pockets of his dress pants. His lips were clenched slightly. "I have some news for you, regarding the notes you received."

"Oh?" Maxine's stomach was squeezing uncomfortably inside. Did she really want to hear this? Was this about some crazy ex-client who wanted to get even with her for a wedding gone wrong?

"There's no easy way to say this but Zack had his men look into it and they found out the source. You're not going to believe it. It was Betty."

"Betty? No way. Why would she...?"

"Exactly. Sometimes it's the people closest to you who can do more harm and by that I mean the people who know too much about you."

Maxine was stumped. She sat down on the recliner chair by the fireplace in a daze. "But why?" she whispered almost to herself. She racked her brain trying to figure out why Betty would pull such a stunt but then it clicked. Betty knew her home address and everything else about her.

"We had the emails traced. The couple who had that lawsuit have dropped it by the way. You'll be hearing from their lawyer. So that's good."

Maxine practically ignored the "that's good" part of his conversation. Nothing seemed good right now. Nothing. Betty? Why would Betty want to hurt her?

"It seemed as if Betty had some sort of grudge against you. She was a close friend of the former owner, Chris."

"Oh, my God! That's right. She told me Chris wanted her to run the business before Lucy came on board."

Lucas nodded. He also explained to her that Betty agreed to resign from the company and a temp would be in place come Monday. Arrangements were already made pending Maxine's approval. He had connections with an admin agency that supplied temps to Romero Corp. and Foundation. She was at least relieved to hear that part. But she just couldn't get her head around this chilling betrayal.

"Well...I don't know what to do now or whom to trust," Maxine murmured, hugging herself.

"You can always trust me, Maxine," Lucas said in a soothing voice. He gazed intently into her eyes and shivers of delight ran down her spine.

"I'll never hurt you," he whispered and the words resonated within her soul. Maxine didn't know why but she felt something pull in her heart—a good thing. A connection.

Maxine stood up and leaned on Lucas. She pressed her head into his chest and he hugged her so tightly with such a powerful emotion she felt so meshed with him. She snaked her arms around his firm waist and looked up into his dark, sexy eyes. "Thank you," she whispered.

"You don't have to thank me, Maxine," he dismissed her overwhelming gratitude. His silky voice caused a reaction inside her. A very delicious one.

"But I want to. You've done so much for me. How could I ever...?" Her breath caught in her throat. Raw emotion washed over her. "I want you."

Her breathing grew heavy. The truth was she'd never desired someone as much as she craved for Lucas's touch, his embrace, his presence. Her mind was going crazy and her head was spinning out of control.

Kiss me.

As if he could read her mind, Lucas lowered his head to hers and pressed his hungry lips to hers. His kiss was slow, deep, wanting. He sipped her lips and sucked them causing ripples of emotions to tingle inside her. Her nipples tightened when his lips kissed the silky skin on her neck. His soft lips caressed her neck and she let out a soft moan of pleasure. She could feel his arousal getting harder and harder behind his zipper while his body was pressed to hers.

Oh, Lucas.

"God, you have no idea what you do to me, Maxine," he groaned as he continued to press his soft lips into her neck. His breathing was slow and deep. Maxine arched her back in his embrace. They'd made their way over to the kitchen counter as they ravenously devoured each other with amazing kisses.

***

Lucas moaned with pleasure as he sucked on the soft skin of Maxine's neck. The erotic sounds of her groans as he pleasured her with his lips were driving his testosterone levels off the charts. His erection was straining inside his pants. He wanted her desperately. He would do anything for her. Protect her. Take care of her and bring her carnal pleasure like she'd never known before.

No woman had ever captured his heart, his soul and his mind the way Maxine did. There was just something about her. Something that resonated within his soul.

"Oh, God, you're so sexy," Lucas groaned as he rubbed his hands down the soft curves of her silhouette. He continued to kiss her gently on her neck then he moved his lips down her arms as he caressed her body. Slowly taking his time, savoring her body while she moaned and writhed with ecstasy in his arms.

"I want you so badly, Maxine," he moaned.

"Oh, Lucas, I want you too. Please, take me."

Excitement shot through Lucas's blood. He wanted to pleasure her so badly and bring her erotic delight more than anything else.

He gently led her into the bedroom a few steps away; both were breathing heavy and in no time he guided her to the bedside and continued to delight in rocking her world.

He wanted to take his time with her gently. She deserved to be treated like a princess, no, like a queen!

"I want to taste you, Maxine. Let me take you down there," he groaned as he intermittently pressed his lips to her neck and her lips.

***

Take me down there?

Intense arousal washed through Maxine at the thought of Lucas wanting to put his sweet lips between her legs. This wasn't something she'd ever done before. She was glad her bikini wax was done. What would she have done if she wasn't groomed "down there"? She trembled inside with delight and awe of what was to come. Panting and breathing hard she moaned, "Yes. Yes!"

Lucas guided her body down on the bed while he positioned himself over her. Gently he lifted up her skirt and spread her legs. To her surprise, he started gently rubbing his fingers over her folds while her lace, sheer panties were in place. The feeling was sensual and delightful as she writhed on the bed and arched her back letting moans of pleasure escape her lips.

"Oh, Lucas," she groaned in ecstasy. He hadn't even pressed his lips there yet and she thought she was going to lose control completely.

He then slid off her panties slowly, seductively, and sent her senses into overdrive. Lucas lowered his lips to her mound and gently stroked and teased her with his tongue before covering her with the moist of his mouth while she arched her back on the bed.

Expertly, he sucked and kissed her slow and soft over and over until she came with an explosive orgasm. The first time she'd ever peaked like that. It was her first time she'd ever really climaxed. Her legs were weak with satisfaction and Lucas moved up on top of her and kissed her throat before bringing his lips to hers. She could taste her sweetness on his lips as they kissed.

She wanted so badly to return the favor and she licked her lips and repositioned herself to him and unzipped his pants to free his throbbing erection.

Maxine gently stroked his shaft with her hand while he gasped in delight. Up and down she slid her fingers lightly to drive him wild. She then lowered her mouth to his manhood and pressed her tongue then covered him with her lips and took him into the moist of her mouth. Sliding up and down and savoring him while he shuddered at how erotic it felt.

On the brink of release he stopped her, breathing hard and heavy. Lucas then reached into his pocket and pulled out a condom. He tore it open with this teeth and rolled it over his hardness and before long he had positioned herself over him taking her all the way as he thrust himself inside her back and forth, hard and fast until she came first with an intense shudder, delicious and sweet. He then came soon after and they both collapsed in each other's arms.

It was late in the evening when Maxine woke up in the cottage to the sound of music playing outdoors and the laughter of people having fun.

She came to her senses and realized the after party was now in effect. Lucy was probably in the main house getting some rest. But where was Lucas? She looked around and he was not there.

The afterglow of their passionate lovemaking brought a warmth inside her and a deep connection to Lucas more than anything else.

She grabbed the sheets around her and got up out of bed; her hair was disheveled in a good way—an after-sex way. She swept her hand through her mane to tidy herself up.

"Lucas?" she called out as she went into the main area. She looked over by the fireplace and his jacket was laid over the sofa.

She heard the door unlock and waited to the side. It was Lucas who stepped inside. Thank God!

"Oh, beautiful, you're awake," he said in a low voice, a sexy grin on his lips. "I didn't want to disturb you. Did you sleep well?"

"Yes, thank you," she said, sheepishly as she looked into his dark, sexy eyes. She could not believe just moments ago they had been so intimate and done such naughty things with and to each other. Oh, heavens! But she felt closeness to him more than before. She treasured the way he made her feel. No man in her life had ever done that to her, not that she had a lot of experience to begin with.

Lucas moved over to her and embraced her, wrapping his strong arms around her before lowering his head to hers and pressing his lips on hers again and oh how electricity pulsed through her blood like never before. The man had a seductive touch that was indescribable! How lucky was she to have Lucas in her life. But did she have him now?

"What's on your mind, baby?" Lucas asked in a low voice as if he could read her mind.

"Nothing. I just…I enjoy being with you, Lucas."

"I enjoy you, too, Maxine. In fact, I can't get enough of you. I want to be with you more than anything else right now."

Maxine gushed. So where did this leave them?

Lucas and Maxine spent the rest of the evening talking and away from the party crowd. He'd made her a wicked western omelet in the kitchen of the cottage and they dined by the fireplace and sipped on sweet red wine only to make love again later into the night.

She'd gotten to learn a lot more about Lucas and his family and his hopes and dreams and the way he'd felt about her for a long time. She cherished the moment. Not realizing how stupid she'd been not to have seen the signs before. He really liked her, didn't he? Since Lucy and Antonio's wedding. And this wasn't just about flirting with the next pair of legs. He really had feelings for her. Maxine had never gotten this kind of attention from a man before. Not even her ex gave her this sort of love and devotion. Lord, she did not know what she was missing this whole time.

CHAPTER FIFTEEN

Three months spun by and Maxine felt as if she had everything under control for the first time in her life. Her new receptionist and secretarial replacement from the temp agency was a fabulous, hard-working older woman who really meshed well with Dream Weddings, Inc.

The new software had some minor teething problems and glitches during the first month up and running but before long Lucas's team helped her set things back on track and business was running smoothly and flowing well once again.

Lucy and Antonio's baby was due any day so the family was excited about the new addition to the Romero dynasty on the horizon.

Maxine was so grateful to Lucas for everything. And since it was his birthday, she was all too glad to take him out for a special dinner for once. Just the two of them.

She discovered with the help of Lucy a renowned plush restaurant in the entertainment district that was exclusive.

"Thank you, Maxine, but you didn't have to do this. I actually do enjoy your cooking." Lucas grinned. He sat across the table from her and had the most beautiful glow on his handsome features from the soy candle in the cozy booth.

She scowled playfully at him. "Very funny, Lucas." He knew full well that she was no Martha Stewart in regards to cuisine. Still, he appreciated her and often showed her stuff he'd learned with preparing certain dishes. Imagine that! He loved her in spite of her imperfections.

"Well, now what should we order?" Maxine picked up the velvet-covered menu.

He looked lovingly into her eyes but did not move. He just gazed intently.

When she opened the menu she was stunned that a silk flower slid out. It looked remarkably similar to the one from the bouquet she'd caught at Lucy's wedding. Her heart pounded hard in her chest.

"But...what is this?" she asked and picked up the flower. Lucas was grinning from ear to ear across the table from her. Did he know? But how could he have known where she'd take him for his birthday?

"I don't get it. Did you put this here? Why?" Oh, right. She forgot that she mentioned it to him last week.

"Well, you caught the bouquet at Antonio's wedding and I caught the garter. So it was only natural."

A lump climbed in her throat. She didn't think she'd be able to breathe again. "What?" she whispered before picking up the flower and taking a closer look. Her heart almost gave out. She reached into the flower and pulled out the most beautiful diamond ring she'd ever seen in her life.

She felt weak, dizzy with excitement. Stunned beyond belief. Her eyes widened as she looked at Lucas with tears misting her eyes.

Lucas got up from where he was seated and went to Maxine's side of the table. He knelt on one knee. Maxine was about to faint.

"I never thought I would ever get married until the day I met you, Maxine. You brought such an unbridled joy to my life that I can never be the same without you with me. I love you. I honor you and I treasure you. Maxine Summers, will you do me the honors of being my loving wife?" he asked humbly.

Maxine was a river of tears but she was so overcome with joy she just kept nodding. "Yes. Yes. Yes," she said as she reached over and hugged him and gave him the biggest squeeze and passionate kiss to seal their love.

CHAPTER SIXTEEN

Maxine felt an unbridled joy she'd never known before. She was on top of the world ever since her engagement to Lucas a week ago. Lucy, of course, was over the moon thrilled for her. They were going to be cousins by marriage. Imagine that!

She parked her car outside the office building at Dream Weddings, Inc. getting ready for a busy day at work when she was swarmed by reporters. What were they doing there?

"Maxine. What do you think about being used by your fiancé for a public relations gimmick?" one reporter called out.

"Maxine! Maxine! Any comment on the recording? Did you see the video?" another shouted from the crowd.

Huh? Video? Recording? What recording?

Maxine thought she was going to lose her mind. What the hell was going on? Did she miss something on the news this morning?

She hurried into her office past the crowd. Her cell phone was buzzing but she decided not to answer it. Her handbag swung from her shoulder as she entered the lobby of the building. The doorman ushered her inside and she paused panting.

"Are you okay, ma'am?" the young man asked her, a look of concern on his face.

Maxine caught her breath. "I...I don't know. I'll be fine. Thank you." She was breathless but made her way up the elevator to her floor.

"Maxine, the phone has been ringing off the hook. Reporters. What's going on?" the new receptionist called out to her as she entered the reception area.

"I'm sorry, I...I don't know."

Once in her office, she closed the door and slumped into her chair. Her heart was racing, pounding hard and fast in her chest. What was going on?

Maxine looked at her smartphone and a text from Lucas showed up on her home screen. "Will be there soon" was all it read.

She switched on the computer on her desk and went to the Yahoo email home to see what was trending in the news. Her heart flip-flopped in her chest.

ROMERO BAD BOY STAGES FAKE ENGAGEMENT IN WAKE OF PATERNITY SCANDAL

The next trending topic:

MAXINE SUMMERS FAKE FIANCEE

And the topic following that:

MAXINE SUMMERS LUCAS ROMERO

Maxine wanted the ground to open up and swallow her whole. She could not believe what her eyes were glaring at on the screen of her computer.

Fake fiancée? Fake wedding? Scandal? That sex scandal again? She was sure her heart rate was beating five times the limit and her blood pressure was probably through the roof. What was Lucas going to do when he arrived? Explain everything away?

Was he really the father of that girl's baby? Was Maxine just a diversion? A publicity stunt?

She reluctantly clicked on one of the links that led to a YouTube channel. Her body went cold when she saw a video recording of a boardroom meeting some time ago at the Romero Corp. When she listened to the recording, sure enough, Toni Romero and Lucas were discussing his image and the possibility of settling down or getting engaged to project the illusion of stability. So that was why he asked Maxine to marry him? To reverse his bad boy image all in the name of business? What a fool she'd been to believe in him.

CHAPTER SEVENTEEN

Lucas felt the heat of his blood boil inside his vessels. He was face to face with Maxine at her office. "Do you really think this was a publicity stunt? It's obvious you don't know me very well, Maxine."

"But you and your grandfather were on the Internet discussing you settling down. How can you deny that, Lucas?"

"I'm not denying anything, Maxine," Lucas said, his voice stern and cold. "I had a discussion with my grandfather, yes, but it wasn't anything to do with fixing a fake wedding to prove anything to anyone."

Lucas was worked up. Maxine saw a muscle twitch in his jaw. He pace with his hands shoved in his pockets. He paused and gave a sigh. He then turned his attention back to Maxine. "I'll be going away for a while."

"Where to?"

"Don't concern yourself. I'll be out of your way." With those words he left the office before Maxine could say anything else. Her mind was numb. Her legs were weak. What just happened? Everything felt wrong, so wrong. Did she just let the love of her life walk out of her life—for good?

***

"I told you I had it covered, Lucas," Zack assured him later in the afternoon at the Romero Estate. "Our men have the dirt on this woman and we'll be able to make a public announcement soon."

"That doesn't matter right now," Lucas answered back. The men were in the study along with Toni and their press secretary, Pamela. "I really don't care what they say."

"You don't mean that, Lucas. We'll get this cleared up."

"Who the devil could have leaked that to the media?"

"Apparently one of the undercover reporters had sneaked on to the premises and pretended to be a temp. They had their cell phone on the boardroom table recording the whole thing. It was by the basket of flowers," Pamela informed them with bitterness in her voice.

"It seems like we just can't trust anyone," Zack shot back. "If we ever catch that person-"

"Don't worry about that now, Zack. They'll get what's coming to them. For now," Toni returned his attention back to Lucas. "Lucas, you are our main concern. You should never have taken it out on Maxine."

"Listen, if she doesn't want to believe in me after all we've been through, that's fine with me."

"You don't mean that, do you?" Toni walked over to his grandson and pressed his hand on his shoulder. Lucas had his hands in his pockets, pain in his eyes. He looked like a broken man. Giving up on everything.

Zack and Pamela excused themselves from the study to give Toni and Lucas some privacy.

"I really love her, Granddad. I want her more than anything in the world but how can I make her understand?"

"You don't have to. I already do," a breathless voice interrupted the men from behind. When Lucas turned, he was stunned to see Maxine standing at the doorway to the study. "I…I'm sorry to interrupt. I just got here and Zack said you were in the study." Maxine looked timid, anxiety racked her body.

Lucas walked up to her immediately, a look of concern on his face but she could see a mild sign of relief. "What made you come?"

"Because I just realized what I was doing. Lucas, sometimes people say stupid things in the heat of the moment. I thought about the past few months we'd spent together and all you've done for me and meant to me. How could I have discounted all those things? I really care about you," she said before pausing. "Besides, love means giving the one you care about the benefit of a doubt, right?"

Lucas reached his arms around her waist, gazed intently into her eyes and a wave of desire and longing slithered through her being.

"I love you, Maxine. I would never do anything to hurt you."

"I...love you, too, Lucas. More than anything in this world."

She rose up to him on her tiptoes as he lowered his head to hers and pressed her lips to his softness. They'd almost forgotten Toni was still in the study with them.

"It's okay. Please don't stop on my behalf." Toni smirked as he walked out of the room. "Please carry on," the old man said as he grinned in approval.

EPILOGUE

A week later...

"Well, look at the new addition to the Romero family," Toni beamed as he cradled his great-grandson in his arms. The family had gathered in the family room at Romero Mansion for the joyous occasion. "You're a god-send and a blessing, do you know that? I'm going to name you Alexander," he cooed to the little newborn who'd arrived in the morning from the hospital.

"Grandfather," Antonio chuckled. "You can't just name him. Lucy and I haven't decided on a name yet."

"Oh, now. I'm only joking. But really, you two need to hurry up and give this little guy a name or else."

"Understood, sir."

"And as for you two," Toni said as he turned to Lucas and Maxine. "You already denied me the pleasure of seeing you get married. The least you can do now is hurry up and give little Romero here a cousin to play with."

"Now, Granddad, I already told you. We just happened to be in Vegas on a getaway and got caught up in the excitement. We'll have a big reception here. We promise." Maxine was gushing as she held her husband's arm by the fireplace. They gazed lovingly in each other's eyes. "I just didn't want to delay sealing our relationship anymore."

Maxine blushed. "Thank you for that kind message you placed in the papers this morning, Toni," Maxine chimed in.

"Well, I mean it. You're welcome, Maxine, and welcome again to the family. This is cause for a celebration!" Toni beamed. He called out to the butler who came in promptly. "Please arrange for the barbecue and break out the champagne."

"Yes, sir," the butler complied happily.

"Two new members to the Romero family."

"And you'll be next, right, bro?" Lucas turned to Zack and gave him a nudge in the arm.

"I don't think so, bro!" Zack shot back. "Seriously. Good for you and Antonio but me and marriage are like fire and ice. No offense, guys."

Lucas grinned.

"Never say never," Toni cautioned.

"Grandfather, that means nothing to me except the title of a good Bond movie. Thanks but no thanks." Zack lifted a glass to his lips from the butler's tray.

"Oh, sir. You have a visitor at the door."

"I do?" Zack said to the butler before placing his glass down on the table. He excused himself and went into the foyer. He froze. What on earth was this woman doing here?

"Hi," the timid woman said as she stood by the main door.

"Please leave." Zack's tone was clipped and stern.

"I don't blame you. But I just want to apologize to you and your family, Zack."

Zack glared at her. She was a very pretty woman. He'd seen her, along with other reporters camped outside on the lawn during one of their media circuses but reports had been confirmed that it was her cell phone that was used to record the private conversation between Lucas and Toni that spurred another media fiasco. Luckily, the woman who had the pregnancy claim was called out as a fraud and admitted she lied about being pregnant by Lucas but the whole thing with the fake engagement claim almost cost his brother his happiness.

"It really wasn't my fault."

"Oh, really?" Zack stood erect with his hands in his pocket, his chin up.

"Yes. I have nothing to gain by being here. I'm no longer working for…any media. But," she paused wringing her hands. Gosh, the girl was a bundle of nerves. Nothing like the story-hungry young reporter he'd seen lingering about in the shadows. "Someone played a practical joke on me and my phone was missing. The next thing I knew, it turned up there in the boardroom."

"Thank you for coming here…" he probed.

"Blue. Blue Monroe."

And what a sexy name that was. Too bad he didn't trust women and he trusted female reporters even less. "Blue Monroe," he continued. "I'll relay the message to my family."

She looked into his eyes almost as if she wanted to say something more. "Thank you. And congratulations on your cousin's birth."

With that, she turned and let herself out of his family's home…and out of his life. There was something challenging and dangerous about her but Zack tried to play it off. Would he ever see her again? Would he want to see her again?

***

THE PLAYBOY BILLIONAIRE (THE ROMERO BROTHERS, BOOK 3)

Blue Monroe needs to get her life together. The once-promising TV reporter was wrongfully fired by *Channel 31 News*, thanks to her jealous ex, and newly hired by the wealthy Romero family. She desperately needs this job. All she's got to do is keep out of sexy, hot playboy Zack's way and everything will be fine. Blue's got other things to worry about like putting food on the table, taking care of her younger sister and keeping her dark family secret secure.

Sexy philanthropist and playboy billionaire Zack Romero's seductive past may soon catch up with him. Skilled in his taste for fine wine as well as fine women, he does a smooth job of running the Romero family's prestigious award-winning winery and vineyard. But his world is soon rocked when a scandalous sex-tape with an ex-girlfriend threatens to surface. Zack's grandfather and the Romero patriarch, Toni's ultimatum…control his love life! No sex for at least thirty days! But when Zack is forced to hire Blue Monroe to work closely with him to produce a documentary for the vineyard, will it be sour grapes or a sweet pairing from heaven?

CHAPTER ONE

The glorious morning sun glowed radiantly over the sprawling estate owned by Mayberry Hill's most affluent family, the Romeros. The breathtaking scenery of the massive Romero Winery and Vineyard in all its miles of fresh green grass that seemed to go on forever into the horizon and vibrant rows of flourishing crops could be seen from the floor-to-ceiling windows of the study at Romero Manor. Toni Romero sat, once again, in the study surrounded by several of his successful grandsons whom he had a hand in raising from their teens to young men. The Romeros were all dressed in their finest suits. Only the growing look of disdain on the elder Romero's face made it evident that this morning's family meeting was not going to be a pleasant one.

Another scandal threatened to mar the reputation of the Romero family. This time, Zack Romero was the target.

"What do you think will happen if the press gets wind of this despicable...video tape, Zack?" Toni growled.

Zack leaned against the study desk with his arms folded across his chest. He was getting ready to give a tour of the winery to a few college students from the class where he was guest lecturing this semester. Nothing seemed to be going good right now.

"I'm sure I can handle it *if* that does happen." Zack answered in a cool, low voice.

"Zack, this is a sex tape. A sex tape! This is much more critical than you could imagine."

Dios Mio. His grandfather had a point. Zack's brother, Lucas, was plagued by some woman who'd claimed he was the father of her unborn child—a huge fiasco last year that almost blew up in his face. But this? This was different. Zack's ex, Selina, had a video recording of their rendezvous in Vegas.

For chrissake. The explicit lovemaking was wild as sin on that video. He'd certainly performed some delicious sexual acts that could very well be illegal in some of the countries that distributed his company's products. The kinky things he'd done with her in that tape were more than X-rated. Heck, if that ever got out there would be no turning back. For the first time during the family meeting Zack felt uncomfortable and loosened his silk Italian designed tie. He slid his fingers through his hair.

"He's right, Zack," Pamela, the family's press secretary intervened. "We need to do pre-emptive damage control in case the tape does get out."

"*If* the tape gets out," Carl shot to his brother's defense.

The young men were dressed in corporate attire and getting ready to venture out to their prospective businesses. But one thing was certain about the Romero family—during times of crisis or impending trouble, they banded together like a pack of protective wolves. They were tight. Family came first. They would drop what they were doing and meet up at the grand estate to deal with matters if at all possible. Currently, Zack's other brothers, Jules, Alonso and Dion, were out of town. Jules was in Europe opening up a franchise, Alonso, who practiced medicine, was in Haiti opening up a clinic; and Dion had flown to New York to deal with a merger. Lucas was with his pregnant wife Maxine but Carl remained by Zack's side, brainstorming on a plan of action. Antonio III was with his wife Lucy and their toddler, Anderson.

"Zack, you really need to get a hold of that tape," Toni pressed. "You're going up for the National Winery Awards for Excellence in Community Service. A high honor. You've created more useful employment for young adults than any other organization. You've provided more guidance and practical skills to help lower the unemployment rate. You deserve it. But this...thing you've done needs to be cleared up or everything you've worked so hard for, dedicated your life to, will be over."

"He's right, Zack," Carl reiterated. "You're teaching at the college, man. Sex tapes and colleges don't mix. Well, they do if you're some stupid jock frat boy, but in this case, the board will have a field day. By the way, I've already contacted the guys down at the office to look into the whereabouts of the video. The tech team is sending out searchers to see if any of it got online."

Zack nodded. "Good. Keep me posted, Carl." Ironically, it was Zack who'd helped Lucas the year before with hunting down the stalker who'd been terrorizing Maxine. Now, Carl was helping Zack while he tended to business matters. The brothers used a contracted detective agency to handle certain security matters from time to time. The head of the agency was a distant cousin of theirs and had office space at Romero Towers in the downtown core of the city.

Toni's lips were pinched with fury. "Why couldn't you settle down with a nice girl? You need to stop dating different women and the wrong kind. You're a Romero and a high profile one at that. I've told you boys before. We Romero men could be easy target and prey for media and publicity seekers. We need to take extra care."

Zack felt a muscle twitch in his jaw. He remained in cool, poised, daring the whole situation not to rile him up too much. He was often the smooth one who could control his emotions, especially his temper. But right now, his mind raced dangerously at the thought of what else was lurking.

Selina was his ex-girlfriend from many years ago. He'd ended it with her. Zack was upfront with her about not wanting to settle down. The trouble was, she had problems, but he never held that against anyone. He wasn't perfect either. But she'd accumulated a lot of debt and played the casinos one too many times. Yeah, he'd helped her out even when they weren't together. That was the Romero bloodline running through his veins.

Romero was a Spanish surname meaning protector or guardian of the sacred place. It was in Zack's (and his siblings to some degree) DNA to always jump at the chance to protect those who were close to him by any means. Even ex-girlfriends. Well, this instance had proved to be a costly mistake. Zack didn't take very well to getting burned. Very few would cross his path if they knew what was good for them.

The last time Selina asked him, he finally told her he would no longer "loan" her money. He told her she needed to get help for her addiction before she saw another shiny dollar coin. So naturally, that revealing video they'd made years ago was going on the bidding block with the highest price from any slimy media outlet that would take it.

Zack grimaced at the thought. But the last thing he wanted was to make it his grandfather's problem or his brothers. He was going to deal with it his way, on his terms. No way in hell did he take to extortionists, but he would think of something fast. Zack always got himself out of his troubles no matter how crazy things seemed. He got himself into it. He'd get himself out of it. Even if it killed him.

But this only served to reinforce his doubts about getting married or settling down with one woman. Ever. Good for his brother Lucas and Maxine. They were a nice pair. And good for his cousin Antonio and his bride Lucy and their lovely little son. But for Zack? No way in hell was he going that route.

Women were nothing but trouble.

"Don't concern yourself any further," Zack finally spoke up as he pushed away from the study desk. He shoved his hands in his pants pockets and lifted his chin as he faced his grandfather and brothers. "I've listened to each of you tell me what I should and should not be doing and I appreciate your input very much. However, I'm man enough to sort this out on my own."

"Oh, no. We're in this together. If your name goes through the dirt, so does the family name." Toni stood up, his cane in one hand.

"I've got it under control," Zack assured, his voice stern. He loved his grandfather but sometimes he felt Toni pushed too hard to keep tabs on the boys.

"Under control? Under control?" Toni's face grew red. "You can't even seem to control the zipper on your pants, Zack."

"Ouch," Carl said in Zack's place.

"What did you just say?" Zack asked, incredulous. His grandfather was known to be a bold man all his life, one who spoke the truth even if it shot out of his mouth like a speeding bullet and woe to whoever was the intended target. But this? This took the prize. His ears must have deceived him because they were buzzing.

"I think I'd better leave," Pamela said, turning the color of the red dress she had on. She turned to leave but then paused at the door and spun around to face them again. "Oh, um...Toni, the writer will be here soon to get set up for the documentary production." Pamela reminded him, "She's the one you hired to work on the vineyard clip with Zack for the National Wine Awards. Her name is Blue."

"Thank you, Pamela," Toni said, his voice brusque.

"Blue?" Zack responded in shock. "Not *that* reporter who tripped up and secretly recorded you speaking with Lucas about an arranged marriage?"

"Yes, that's the one," Toni confirmed, waving dismissively.

"And why?" Zack's lips were pinched in anger.

"She's an excellent writer and I told her it would be fine to work on the special feature story and documentary about the family business in the winery industry with a profile on your commitment to community. You realize that this segment will be featured at the Awards Ceremony so it is crucial that we don't screw it up. And later, she could do a book on the family."

"Don't you think she's done enough damage to the family?"

"I heard her side of the story, Zack, and I am satisfied that it wasn't her fault. She was set up by the boyfriend as a joke. He also worked at the station. Besides, she no longer works there."

Zack shook his head and chuckled. "I'm not working with her. I can handle my own publicity."

Toni shook his head, his eyebrows creased with fury. "Back to the subject at hand." Toni's voice was firm as he made a point to switch the subject back to the reason they had all convened at Romero Manor.

"Back in my day," Toni continued with his verbal lashing against Zack, "men were perfect gentlemen and we didn't feel the need to...record such things as you've done with this Selina woman. What were you recording your business with her for? Educational purposes?"

"Granddad," Carl interjected.

Zack silenced his brother with a raised hand and spoke. "That. Is. Not. Fair." His tone was cool as a jazz musician.

"Not fair?" The old man breathed in deeply and sat back down with an unreadable expression on his face as if he was searching for the right words. "Zack, I'm very sorry to have to be harsh with you...and your brothers but...this is not easy for me."

Emotion rose in Toni's voice. "I love you boys very much. You've been through so much in your lives, from the time I discovered your father was my son and you boys were living out of his car after he lost his job. I was so happy to rear you as my own. But life is not easy in the so-called real world. There are people who would take pleasure in tearing you down because of your success and everything that you've worked so hard to achieve. You've seen it yourself. The press isn't interested in the good things you do to help society, they just love a juicy scandal. They love to see you fall and fail so that their lives look more liveable. They are happy to see successful people hurt."

"Don't they think we have our own suffering? They want to have what I have?" Zack shot back, arching a brow, maintaining his emotion.

"They can walk a mile in my shoes then." Zack's deep voice sharpened with a matter-of-fact tone. "Let them eat expired canned food as a child because their father lost his job and their home and had mouths to feed. Let them take the pleasure of being ridiculed at school because their clothes were ill-fitted because your folks couldn't afford to buy clothes or cut your hair. Because that's the path we took to get where we are." Zack was making a mockery of the situation. His subtle sarcasm was usurping the conversation. His blood was hot. Fire burned in his veins. How dare they? Whoever they were.

He was not going to let the naysayers or future haters stop him from doing what he had to do.

That was the burning passion behind his programs to create more jobs, heck, he even invented jobs so that every student who passed his program had gainful employment, well-paying jobs. Because jobs meant stability. And stability meant no one's family had to suffer—the way he and his brothers did before they'd become so rich and powerful that they became the city's most hated targets of luxury.

"Listen, I'd better leave you two right now." Carl rose from his chair and touched his brother's shoulder as a sign of solidarity before walking out of the study.

Toni turned to face Zack. "Zack. You know I love you, grandson."

"Yeah. I'm just glad you don't hate me or I'd be dead right now with all that verbal lashing."

In spite of himself, his grandfather broke into a smile and Zack grinned slightly. He was still agitated as hell at all that was happening when he should be focusing on the tour later today and the National Winery Awards.

"I'm glad to see you still have your sense of humor about it all. It would kill me if that…tape ever got out. Is there any way…?"

"Granddad, I already told you. I'm not negotiating with an extortionist. Period. If she wants to play hard ball, that's in her court. But she will pay the consequences, and I doubt she'd get rich out of a reality show from that either."

His grandfather grinned again. "Zack, I really hope so, for your sake."

"Now what's that supposed to mean?"

Toni sighed heavily. He looked at the fireplace and lifted his chin. Tears were moistening his eyes. "Zack, this is very hard for me but I have no choice."

"What are you talking about, Grandfather?"

Toni shook his head, full of remorse. "Zack, I've already told you boys. I'm an old man. I don't know how long I'll be around. Or how much longer, I should say." He coughed. "I just want you all to take things seriously. You've each come into your own, making valuable contributions. Lucas with his Healthy Start Software Program; Antonio with his real estate ventures. And what you've done with this vineyard. You've pretty much grown it over the past decade to what it is today. Remarkable."

"But?"

"But you will lose it all if you don't get serious about your private life."

"Grandfather, let me handle my private life."

"Good. Now that's the most sensible thing I've heard all day."

"I don't get it. Where are you going with this, Grandfather?"

"I'm giving you an ultimatum."

"An ultimatum? What ultimatum? Why?" Zack didn't like the way this sounded. His hot defences shot up now and the heat in his blood was burning inside his veins. Zack was a healthy man. He and his brothers worked out hard at the gym, religiously. They took nothing for granted. They were fit as mountain lions, yet a sick feeling settled in his gut about what his grandfather was implying.

"Zack, I want you to settle down or leave the company."

"What?" Zack stood to full height, his eyes filled with rage. "What's that supposed to mean? You want me to get hitched to keep my position?"

"Not exactly. I just don't want you having any more of these types of adventures with women unless it is the one you want to settle down with. Trust me, you'll thank me later. I don't mean to get into your personal life—"

"Too late for that."

Toni held up his hand to silence Zack. "Zack, please allow me to finish. I'm only asking that you focus more on your business and what you are contributing to these wonderful programs that you have and less on...dating. No sex for at least thirty days. Just keep away from these women you meet."

"What?" Zack could not believe his ears. For the first time, his lobes burned as if ice frost had bitten them. "No sex?" Zack chuckled humorlessly in spite of himself. "You're telling me when I can be with a woman? This is ridiculous." Zack began to pace as he fumed.

Zack never slept around. No way in hell. But he always had a "girlfriend" for at least six months. He always treated his women well and let them know the deal up front. He wasn't in it for the long run. They knew it and they wanted to be with him, just the same. Sex was a four or five times a week pleasure for him, at the least. Sometimes four times in a day, depending on his current babe. Heck, he was a healthy, fit man who worked hard as hell. Having a healthy mutually-beneficial sex life with his current woman was a huge deal in his life. If he couldn't have it for a period of time—like say a month—he wouldn't be able to sleep well at night. He loved women.

He showered them with anything they desired and showed them a real good time—treating them like the goddesses they were. He expressed his emotions more with his actions not words. To him, sex was love in motion. Seducing the right woman was his thing. He loved the way the physical contact drove up his body's oxytocin levels in his brain. The feel-good drug. Sex to Zack was a fundamental necessity. Toni was asking his grandson to starve himself of much needed affection the entire month? Was Toni going insane? Or did he want Zack to go there?

Of all the crazy, ridiculous, unreasonable things his grandfather had schemed in the past, this was the lowest and most insane. He did not...could not believe he was having this conversation with his old grandfather. This had to be the worst thing a man could listen to, next to his father wanting to have "the talk" with him.

Zack Romero was a grown man, for heaven's sake. An affluent businessman and influential citizen. He didn't need to take this from anyone. Not even the patriarch of the Romero dynasty.

Toni sighed deeply again, pain reflected in his eyes. This must have been hard for him but it was Zack who was feeling the sucker punch to his gut like an iron fist striking his flesh. "I'm sorry, Zack, but I still have voting power in the estate and am head of the board. If I find out that you have not done what I think is best for you, then I will have no choice but to suggest your removal from the board."

CHAPTER TWO

Blue Monroe fiddled with the cream-colored cotton vest as she pulled it over her head and secured it over her curves. The darn thing was a little too snug, she observed looking into her full-length mirror in the bedroom of her apartment.

"You do realize that's the third change of clothes you've done in the last ten minutes, right?" Blue's eighteen-year-old sister, Courtney, teased her. Courtney stood in the doorway with her hands on her hips and a playful scowl on her face. "You really like this guy, don't you?"

"Courtney." Blue turned to face her sister. "That's not fair. I'm just trying to make a positive impression. You know how badly we need this work."

Courtney rolled her eyes. "Yeah, yeah, sure. Whatever. You like him."

"No. I don't *like* him. And he certainly doesn't like me. I just hope he gives me the job."

"But I thought you already had the job. You said that rich guy Toni Romero hired you, didn't he?"

"Courtney, he's not some rich guy. He's the founder of the Romero Corporation and Realty. His grandson heads the winery and vineyard and pretty much nurtured it from the ground up to what it is today. He told me he wanted me to film the documentary, but Zack, his grandson, has the final say."

"Oh. Well, I'm sure he'll like you."

"Courtney, it's not about him liking me as I want him to understand what my company can do for his image. This is the first real gig for my new production company." Blue swallowed hard. It sure was the break she was looking for. She was fired from Channel 31 News after her conniving ex-boyfriend played a cruel joke on her and stole her cell phone and used it to record a private conversation between the Romero family some time last year in their boardroom. He was getting back at her for ending their tumultuous relationship as kindly as she could. He was emotionally abusive and Blue was sure she did the right thing. But what did he do? Set her up to get fired. Ugh. The recording showed up online and the rest, as they say, was history. She was just glad that Toni Romero, although his grandsons were harsh towards her, forgave her in regards to the scandal.

Blue had accumulated a lot of enemies during her time working at Channel 31. She was an investigative reporter, her first real job after graduation from the Communications and Media Studies program at the college. She had a tough time trying to prove herself. She ended up getting the worst assignments. Like uncovering racketeering schemes from organized crimes and worse, intervening in marriages by exposing cheating politicians. One in particular, a powerful ex-Senator Ryan Aitkin who was up for some lifetime achievement award, was the absolute crud assignment. She knew he was a cheat. The man was as slimy as they came. Blue shuddered at the thought. But now, word got out he was out to get her for trying to ruin his reputation. As if SHE ruined it. Yeah, right.

She reluctantly took the story about Aitkin having an affair with a female subordinate in his office and an intern, on another occasion. His poor wife. Still, meddling in private affairs just wasn't what gave Blue oomph for life. She wanted out of it. Being fired was probably a blessing in disguise. Now she could start her own business. A small production company called Blue Monroe Productions. It was a simple title but it worked. Her name happened to be unique so she didn't mind using it.

"Shouldn't you be heading to class now?"

"It's summer school."

"But you have an exam today, right?"

"I know. I studied hard last night and during the past few weeks thanks to your whip-cracking."

Blue grinned. "You're a smart girl, Courtney. I know I push you hard but education opens the doors to a lot of wonderful things in life. Education and knowledge are the gateway to achievement." The tears almost welled up in her eyes.

Their parents fought so hard to give them good educations. Extremely hard. They'd sacrificed everything. And now look where they were.

"And pray for me that I do get this assignment with Zack Romero and his winery. Your fall tuition is due soon, isn't it? August?"

"Yeah. I know. Look, Blue. You've done so much for me already. I can always get a job and work for a year before heading to college, you know?"

"No. Absolutely not." Blue was adamant. She flung her jacket over her arm and grabbed her bag and keys from the countertop. "You are going to college this year not next year, even if it kills me. I'll come up with the fees. Don't you worry. Okay?" Blue reassured, her voice almost on the verge of cracking. Courtney was a brave one. So brave but she knew it wasn't easy for them. They had to get by on what they had.

"But you've got the rent to pay and the production expenses with your equipment and stuff."

"Don't worry about me, Court. I'll be fine. Besides, my office is in my kitchen. I can use the studio at the college to do final production. I've still got my contacts there. Now go. Go and ace that mid-term exam."

Courtney smiled and gave her sister a firm hug. "And go get that hottie," she teased her older sister and winked.

"Not funny, Courtney. Not funny at all. Besides, I've got to be going. I'm going to see Mom and Dad first then I'm going to the appointment. I've still got an hour and a half."

"You're going to visit Mom and Dad, today?"

"Yes, today. It's Mom's...birthday."

"I know." Courtney said quietly before grabbing her jacket and her backpack. She wore blue jeans and a white plain t-shirt with her sandals.

"I'll give you a ride to school. Come on, let's go."

* * *

Twenty minutes after Blue dropped Courtney at the high school parking lot to go into her summer school class, she drove off to a local florist. When she walked through the door, the door chime sounded. "Hey, my favorite customer," the owner cheerfully greeted her.

"Mr. Lockwin, you say that about all your customers," she playfully dismissed the man.

"Maybe, but I only mean it for some. Here to pick out a nice bunch for your mom, right."

"How did you know?"

"I always remember her birthday. She's a nice lady, she is."

Blue's heart beat raced. A nervous beat entered her body. "Yes. Very nice."

She chose a beautiful lilac arrangement. Her mother's favorite.

After driving up north towards the Romero Winery and Estate she stopped off to drop off her mother's bouquet.

Nervously, she opened the gate. "Why do you and Dad have to be here? It's so not fair." Blue wished in her heart that she didn't have to visit her parents at a place like this. She walked a few steps and stopped. The summer breeze blowing through her hair. Her breath stopped momentarily. This was hard. In reality, it was never going to be easy. She knelt beside the tall marble gravestone with a beautiful picture of her mother and father secured inside the stone with the words: *Mom and Dad. Forever loved.*

Their parents were taken from them so suddenly. It wasn't fair. They were both killed in a deadly fire that was originally suspected to be the result of arson. The kids were away at the time. The pain gripping Blue's heart was unbearable. But she would be brave. She could do this.

She kissed the marble stone where they were buried together underneath, coffin over coffin in a grave for two. She placed the flowers in front. "Happy birthday, Mom." An ache lodged in her throat. "Hey, Dad," she whispered, pain evident. "Courtney and I are fine. We're going to be just fine. Please pray for us up there, that all goes well with...I know you're both looking over us. I love you. Forever."

With those words, Blue left the Pine Berry Cemetery and walked towards her car. But oddly, she heard shuffling behind one of the trees. Was it the strong summer breeze? Or her imagination? Why did she get the sinking feeling she was being watched? This unnerved her very much. She wouldn't dare tell Courtney what was going on but for the last few weeks, she'd been taunted. Not just taunted but harassed. Her cell phone received a multitude of harassing phone calls and hang ups from an unknown number. Blue turned her head in both directions and looked far beyond the many rows of tombstones in the cemetery. She drew in a deep breath.

It was probably just her imagination. Who would follow her here?

CHAPTER THREE

Zack heaved the heavy weights off his muscular chest and replaced them on the bar. He sat up on the bench press seat, breathing deeply after an accelerated exercise regime. After bench pressing a hefty two-hundred-and-sixty pounds of iron weights, he was done with his late morning workout.

Turbulent thoughts raced through his mind. The weights on the barbell were nothing compared to the weight on his shoulders. His thoughts raced dangerously as he considered the future of his winery enterprise and all that he'd worked for to create viable employment and a future for young entrepreneurs who needed a boost in life, like the one he and his brothers were fortunate to receive.

Just then his cell phone vibrated. It was Jen, his latest girl. Well, actually, his latest ex-girlfriend. They called it quits a few days ago. He couldn't answer the phone. But his voicemail came on. He pressed the button to listen.

"Hey, sweetie," the husky voice sounded on the recorder. "I know we're supposed to be uh, not seeing each other right now, but, hmmm, I want you, Zack. Now. Please call me back. I'll meet you anywhere, baby…" she cooed into the phone.

Zack grimaced, pain shooting through his gut. He groaned thinking of the time when he sat at his desk and she sat underneath his desk deep throating him. Something she loved to do. It was her idea to get all kinky in the office during a lunch break. It caught him by pleasant surprise the first time she did that to him.

"One month?" Thirty days of no physical contact with a woman? Was his grandfather out of his ever-loving mind? He couldn't wait until those four weeks were up to prove he could do anything he put his mind to. He was a true Romero. Romero men were tough as hell and could do the impossible.

Zack read somewhere that although it's average to have sex with your partner three times a week, one in five people were having sex less than once a month. Well, typically, he was never in *that* statistic but…one month of no sex shouldn't be hard. He was a man who could master his emotions and control his libido—if need be. It was going to be hard as hell but, surely, he could do it.

That was nothing, Zack thought to himself bitterly as he dried the sweat off his face with the towel in his hand. He could do better than that. Zack was a man who was known for his strength and his stamina both in the boardroom and outside the corporate world. He could do anything he set his mind to. He never lost a bet yet. And this was about his dream, his future, the very essence of who he was. So, the old man wanted him to control himself? Fine. He'd do just that.

Carl entered the Romero private gym with his workout gear and walked over to Zack who was making his way over to the shower.

"Hey, how did the rest of the meeting go with Granddad?"

"Not good."

"No?"

"Nope. He wants me to stay sex free for the next month."

Carl grinned at first. Then he could not help himself and burst into a full-blown, hearty laugh.

"Hey, that's not even remotely funny, bro." Zack cocked a brow, slinging the towel over his shoulder.

"I'm laughing with you, Zack, not at you."

"You know the funny thing about that statement is I'm not even laughing," Zack answered with a humorless expression. "I'm going to hit the shower. I've got a business to run, a tour to do and a young woman to fire."

"You mean that Blue Monroe chick?"

"Yes."

"You can't do that, Zack. You know that would tick off the old man."

"That's not my problem. He should not have hired her during the preliminary interview without my final say. I just don't think she would be suitable for the job."

"You're gonna go with that, huh? Come on, Zack."

"Hey, don't you have to go into the city for that meeting with the investors?"

"The manager of the firm will handle it. I'm giving her more control of the business so I can focus more on civic duties."

"Oh, no. You're still not thinking about running for mayor, are you?"

"You know it's been my dream to make a difference, Zack."

"Aren't we all making a difference?"

"Yes. But politics is where my heart is. By the way, if I never told you before. I'm really proud of you, man."

"For what?"

"For all you're doing. You've really turned this vineyard thing around. Not only have to nailed the market but you've turned it into a lucrative deal for young entrepreneurs and future winery businesses. The National News made you out to be some hero, you know."

"Really?" Zack kept abreast of industry news through his assistants but he'd specifically asked them not to tell him about gossip the press may have on him. He chose to ignore critics concerning his personal life. It just wasn't worth getting worked up about, just in case.

"Yeah, they said you created more jobs, not just in the industry but related to the industry. Some economic growth impact. Good job, bro. You're not as bad as you want us to believe," Carl teased him.

Zack rolled his eyes and shook his head. "Don't work out those muscles too much in your head," Zack joked back.

"Yeah. Whatever."

After Zack showered and changed into another suit, he left to go to the winery building and vineyard on the estate. It was a cool midsummer day, the cloudless blue sky glowed over the vineyard. He paused when he saw a white Ford sedan pull up by the gate.

That must be his guest ... who would soon be leaving.

Blue got out of her car unaware Zack was watching her. She seemed to be having trouble with her skirt. It was a snug fitting gray skirt that was riding up on her. A grin of amusement touched his lips. He leaned back in the office gazing at her.

My God, the woman is...lovely. Damn.

He had met her on many occasions casually whenever she was sent by her news station to cover events hosted by his family. He'd also seen her up close at the house when she came to apologize personally for her cell phone being used to record the private conversation of his brother and grandfather. A heaviness centered on his chest at the thought of that invasion—though she claimed it wasn't her fault. Don't they all?

Blue closed the door of her car and went to the trunk to grab some equipment. She made her way up the stone pathway leading to the vineyard.

Hmm. The woman had one heck of a figure. She was shapely as sin, too. Her smooth, black, below-her-shoulders hair swayed to the smooth rhythm of the summer breeze. Her beautiful, deeply-tanned complexion was exotic and pleasing on the eyes. She was stunning. Damn. He wanted to know what it would feel like to brush his fingers against that delicious caramel-tanned skin of hers.

Zack felt himself getting aroused. Not good. Not good at all. A bad sign. Zack took full note of her shapely legs and naughty thoughts crossed his mind of those slender legs wrapped tightly around his waist as he pleasured the woman to oblivion.

Zack was known to make a woman scream out his name while forgetting her own name during a passionate night of pure erotic love-making.

He squeezed his eyes shut momentarily then opened them up. He had to get a hold of himself. He was on a celibate run right now, anyway. Besides, he had to fire this woman. He was going to let her down gently of course.

He watched as the guard let her through the gates. Any moment now she would be making her way to the building. But gosh, why was he so captivated by this gorgeous woman with the deep, rich, sultry voice. One that sounded like it could be used on an adult phone line. Her voice always had that seductive touch to it from what Zack recalled.

Women were nothing but trouble, he reminded himself. Sure, it always started off good. The sparks. The seduction. The sex. Then the departure because he let them know up from that he was not a guy who did the commitment thing. And it almost always ended terribly because even though he told them and they consented to his terms, they would change their minds and want more from him. Damn.

Well, right now he had a potential sex tape scandal to deal with that could ruin everything for him. So this good-looking princess was going to have to go.

***

Blue sucked in a deep breath as she entered the foyer of the winery building—a converted luxury mansion. It was, completely, utterly intimidating. The office worker let her in and buzzed Zack through the intercom. The woman then handed Blue, as she was probably instructed beforehand, some brochures about the Romero Winery and Vineyard in addition to a map of the grand estate. Blue glanced through the digitally-colored, expensive-looking brochures.

"He's really nice, Blue. You'll like working with him," the young woman told Blue.

"Thank you. I've heard a lot of good things about Mr. Romero in regards to his winery." *And his women.*

"I'm Venus, by the way." The woman extended her hand over the desk.

"Nice to meet you, Venus."

"Blue's a nice name. It's unusual."

"Thank you. Right before I was born, my mom had a fascination with Picasso's Blue Period. So, how long have you worked here?" Blue asked genuinely. May as well start her profile of Zack Romero and his roster of employers.

The woman sighed. "Cute story. Inspiration comes from the oddest of sources, doesn't it? Anyway, to answer your question, not long enough. Wish I started out here. I'm doing my masters degree in business with an emphasize on entrepreneurship. I have a two-year-old so it's really hard to juggle time elsewhere. The Romeros are really sweet about letting my son come by when I can't find a babysitter. Mr. Romero's wife, Toni's wife, she's so sweet and helps out a lot. I hate to sound cliché, but it's like one big family. Zack is so cool with my little guy. Most employers would try to get rid of you or make it an issue but he tells me I can bring my son any time I need to and they'll have someone look after him. How cool is that?"

Blue was beyond impressed. Her eyes widened. She'd heard of Zack-the-smooth-operator, lady's man. But she'd never seen this side to him or read about his compassion towards his employees like this. Wow. Just wow.

"Wonderful. That's...wow. Just amazing."

"I know. I'm so grateful to be working here."

"So you're starting off as a receptionist? Gaining experience in the winery business?"

"Oh, no. Well, yes and no. I'm one of the vineyard workers. That's what I applied for. My great-uncle back home where I'm from used to have a small grape garden, we used to call it. He died a while back and the estate was sold but since we moved to the US when I was a kid, I've always been fascinated by farms and home-grown produce."

"Good," Blue nodded her head, equally enrapt.

"Mr. Romero…I mean, Zack is awesome. He gives all of us experience with every facet of the business. I've never seen anyone like him before. He's like mega rich but he's so down-to-earth. Well there's a lot of rich, self-made businessmen who sort of stay in touch with reality these days. He's one of them. You'll love him."

Oh, I already do.

"Miss Monroe, good of you to come." The silky, deep voice that interrupted their conversation caused a tingling reaction to course through Blue's blood.

Blue's mouth fell open for the first time today.

The man approached her was not really the businessman she expected. He appeared to be something else.

Her breath paused.

Zack Romero.

He was more stunning than she remembered. His dark, shiny, thick hair was brushed off his face with a few tendrils loose at the front. He had a sexy groomed stubble framing his luscious lips that caused her belly to flip flop. The man had the most beautiful face she'd ever seen. Could a man be considered beautiful? This man could. His dark, sexually-charged eyes, complemented by his long, dark lashes, gleamed with awesomeness.

He was taller than Blue remembered, seeing him up close now. He was inches from her. His hands were in his pockets. He wore a crisp dark, Italian cut suit. It was an expensive designer inspired suit. She guessed, maybe Armani, or maybe it was tailored only for him. It had to be. Look at that broad, muscular frame. He looked like a pro athlete filled out in the suit. She could see the firmness of his sculpted build under his suit. His arms must be ripped with muscles she could certainly tell by the way he filled out in the expensive fabric. His posture was erect as a drill sergeant. Confident and powerful.

No way in hell could she work under this man and keep herself under control. Maybe she should turn around and leave. He was already causing her brain to freeze up. Too much of that hormone rushing through her frontal lobe.

Breathe, Blue.

Take a deep breath. He's just a man. Really.

No. He's a sex god and you know it.

Never had Blue reacted that way over a man. He literally stole her breath away. She forgot who she was or why she was there. She'd almost forgotten that Venus was there, until Venus cleared her throat.

Close your mouth, Blue. Stop drooling.

He's a Romero. Romero men can do that to a woman.

Yes, she'd heard of the Romero men having that type of magical, sexually potent effect on the feminine gender. It was no wonder they were always in the tabloid for naughty behavior despite their remarkable accomplishments in various industries.

"Th-th-thank you," Blue managed. Okay, why was she acting like such a love-struck idiot? *Snap back to reality, girl. It's a job. Only a job.*

"Would you care to follow me outside?" he commanded more than questioned. His sexy gaze held hers and she felt giddy all of a sudden.

"S-sure."

Zack escorted her outside of the building. Blue was actually quite grateful. She needed fresh air to level her head. The sweet-smelling fragrance of the vineyard and surrounding land was perfect for her senses. Maybe it would clear the way for her sanity to come back.

She held tightly to her recorder and her notebook, hugging it to her chest. Blue licked her lips, out of nervousness. For heaven's sake, she was a grown woman. A professional. A business owner. A highly educated journalist. She really needed to get herself together. But how could this man's aura and presence cause this sort of reaction inside her?

"I was about to fire you, Miss Monroe."

Blue halted. Zack, who was walking beside her, had a smooth grin on his face as he followed suit and paused. "Something the matter?" he asked casually, looking more amused than anything.

"You were about to fire me? W-why?" Blue could not control the flutter inside her belly. Her heart was beating erratically.

"Because I didn't think it would be a good idea for us to work together. I didn't think we'd have the right...working chemistry."

"And what changed your mind?" Blue asked, as they both continued to walk through the vineyard pathway.

"I overheard your conversation with Venus, one of our finest workers. I was impressed as to your interest in her knowing she was working at reception, before you found out she was working on her masters and working in the vineyard."

"Oh?" Blue flushed. She felt heat rise to her cheeks, yet it had nothing to do with the summer sun beaming overhead.

"You can tell a lot about a person by not how they treat the wealthy and perceived powerful, but how they treat those who aren't. Some, probably most, people don't even think of talking to the cleaners or frontline workers with such intrigue and respect. I like that about you, Blue." His voice was authoritative and sharp. She could not quite read his emotion but he was impressed with her.

"Wow, you really do sum up a person rather quickly."

"In life, you have to. It's too short to go through a long haul. I'm a to-the-point, do-it-now person. I've no time to waste. I want something, I get it now. Period."

"Oh."

"My grandfather always taught us that personality can open many doors, but it is character that will keep those doors open."

Inwardly, Blue felt relieved. So she wasn't going to be fired from this job after all. That was a good thing. She would certainly be able to pay for Courtney's tuition this fall. *Oh, thank you, God.*

But now she had another matter to deal with. Sexy-as-sin Zack Romero. Officially, her new boss.

"I was also intrigued by what you did what covering that Eli Christopher case."

Blue felt her heart turn over in her chest. She remembered that case. A young man had gone missing and so had a few thousand dollars. They suspected he had stolen the funds from his employer and left the country. But her gut was telling her otherwise. She dug up a lot of information on Eli's background and realized the man had a hard life and had been in and out of the foster care system, but there was something in his eyes that touched Blue when she interviewed him once before the fiasco. She kept digging for the truth. Even after his arrest, by doing some investigative reporting, what she uncovered was that he was an immigrant who was set up by his employer to take the fall. The poor guy thought he wouldn't stand a chance and fled. He had been taking care of his disabled mother and little brother on his modest income. Because of what she uncovered, the truth was revealed and Eli's employer went to prison for embezzling funds.

"Well, you know me," she said, sheepishly. Embarrassed that Zack had taken the time to do his due diligence as to her reporting history and background. But she also felt a pang of longing. Deep, gut wrenching loneliness settled over her heart for far too long. One could be in a relationship as she had been with Elliot and still feel alone. Elliot never really cared for her or cared much about how her day at work went or how she felt. They never truly conversed. But Zack? He was only her boss, yet Blue felt that ease around her heart that he actually, genuinely cared about her work and how she felt. It was odd to think it but she felt a little connection with him. She was comfortable and satisfied in telling him about the things that mattered to her. That meant the world to Blue.

"I try to get to the heart of the story," she continued.

"And that's what makes you unique. Most reporters would have just left it at that. Why did you probe further?"

"Because I always believe that news is about people. I care about people, I guess."

"You guess? You need to sound, no, *be* more confident in your convictions, Miss Monroe."

"I care about people," she grinned, cocking her brow. "A lot. And justice."

"It shows."

Blue flushed. This was nice, she thought. Why was it when a man treated her well, she reacted this way? Her ex, Elliot, was nothing like Mr. Romero. Elliot and she had worked at Channel 31 together but instead of commending her on her efforts, he would often try to pick out a fault in the situation. "Oh, you didn't cover this angle of the story," or "You should have asked one more question." Blue wasn't an approval seeker, but neither did she feel any better when her own boyfriend chastised her every move and never missed an opportunity to berate her.

"We have that in common," Zack continued as they strolled through the vineyard.

"We do?"

"Yes. I like to see people do well in life" was all he said in a sturdy, richly deep voice.

"It's good what you do for students and for a lot of aspiring entrepreneurs from the Humanity Program. You help people from all reaches of economic background. That's wonderful."

He grinned.

"What's so funny?"

"Oh, nothing. I was briefed about your work before you got here, just so that we are clear. I wanted the people at human resources to gather as many clips of your work for me to peruse."

"Oh?" Blue felt morbid. What else had he seen in those footage? Of course, a man of Zack's stature would never just trust his grandfather's preliminary interview to agree to work with her.

"There was a clip of you covering the Anti-Poverty Rally at Queen's Park."

"Oh." Her stomach lurched. She was practically inadvertently tossed around from side to side as the protesters rushed to the picket line—it looked comical at first. Then when she got out of their way, she'd backed away slightly...into the water fountain. She came out dripping wet but continued her story as if it was nothing out of the ordinary. All in a day's work.

When she looked at Zack, she noticed his grin fade. "You were not harmed, so that's why it was amusing. You are tenacious. A lesser woman would have stormed out or backed down. I love a woman with tenacity. You stuck it out and you made light of it later at the news desk. It takes a strong, confident woman to humor herself in a...difficult situation."

Strong? Confident? She sure didn't feel like it that day. She merely got on with the job the best way she knew how. Yes, it was comical and it was the only time that a few of the protesters actually grinned when they learned she was okay.

"Everyone falls some times," he continued. "But getting back up and back into the game takes courage." His silky tone rang with seriousness. Blue captured raw hurt glinting in his eyes. What had his heart gone through in the past? Blue wondered. Zack was a mysterious man. But she was somehow in awe of him. She felt connected to him. His very being. She loved the way he took a spin on life. Sure, he had taken some hard knocks according to what she knew about him, but there he was, a true Romero. Those men always seem to get back up fighting. No matter what life dealt them.

Being on the giving end of the camera was one thing, but Blue couldn't handle being on the receiving end of the news. How awful to be captured at any given time for the world to see...in print and online.

"Thank you," she responded to his encouragement. Elliot never championed her, come to think of it. Her ex seemed to take great pleasure in belittling at the most insignificant of foibles, disguising it as jest, humor. But many a truth was spoken in jest as the saying went.

Still, she was glad to have been assigned the human interest stories such as the anti-poverty movement.

She was covering the event but she also felt passionate about the way low-income families could not provide for their children. She was all for raising the minimum wage. She took nothing for granted.

The thought caused moistness to sting her eyes. Blue knew how it felt to not have much. But then, she'd learned about Zack's background, too. He'd been through humbling impoverished times as a youngster before he met his famous grandfather. But she was not about to bring that up. She would allow him to. Since she knew it was a raw spot and it wasn't something that the Romero brothers flaunted when they worked within the community.

Blue learned the Romero brothers were known for their compassionate work, not for their boastful words.

"You can begin recording," Zack ordered her, in his commanding, deep voice. He walked so powerfully and dignified with his shoulders squared.

Conscious of her own posture, Blue straightened up. Her eyes scanned the breathtaking scenery at the estate. It was a massive sea of greenery with fresh grapes tinting the verdant view as they dangled from vines. There was a beautiful mini cottage that was the garden shed but it was more like a beautiful home with its own shrubs, stone pathway and a double French door like the main house. How marvellous they designed it that way. It was Zack's brainchild, apparently.

The scent of his cologne was irresistible to Blue's nose. Everything about the man was. She felt her nipples getting hard, straining under her bra and through her knitted summer top. She prayed Zack would not look directly at them. It would be so embarrassing. Her skirt was beginning to ride up again. The fabric was not one she was used to wearing and had a bit of stretching Lycra material in it to complement her curves. She just wished she'd worn it beforehand to understand how it would behave. What a day to wear this outfit. Blue tried to change the direction of her thoughts back to her work.

"Blue's an intriguing name."

"Thank you. My mother's favorite artist was..." Blue almost choked trying to utter the words. It was so painful to think about Mom. Even now. "Picasso, so I'm Blue, after his Blue Period." She finished her sentence, almost inaudibly.

"Is everything, okay?" Zack asked in a deep, low voice as if he was in tune with her every word, her every tone. Blue really had to be careful around him. She had to keep her emotions in check. She realized that now.

"Yes," she said softly, trying to bring her confidence up a notch. "Mother always told me that Blue was synonymous energy and it also meant calm and relaxation."

"You don't seem relaxed," Zack observed as he stopped walking after they'd reached the plush garden shed cottage. "If you're going to work with me, Blue, as much as I like your aura, you'll need to remain focused on what you're doing. Is that going to be a problem?"

She shook her head. But tears were beginning to form in her tear ducts. "I just had a really busy morning, sir. But I-"

Zack held up his hand to silence her. "Firstly, we'll cut the formalities. Around here, we're on a first name basis."

A grin of amusement touched his lips. "I'll be the exception when I deem it necessary, Miss Monroe." His voice was deep and rich, and so smooth it slid down her spine with a tingle. Was he playing games with her? Was he saying he didn't want them to be on a first name basis? Or he didn't want use a first name when addressing her? What was with him?

Whatever it was, Zack caused a reaction in her like she'd never experienced. She was addicted to him with just one taste of his presence and that was going to be a problem. She knew it. She could feel it. But she had to get on with the job and focus. She already had a crazy ex-boyfriend in her personal-life portfolio. She didn't want or need another one. She knew of Zack Romero's reputation with women. He was the scream-out-loud sexual pleaser who didn't do seconds. She was not going to be another notch on his king-sized bedpost. She assumed he would have a giant bed with silky, expensive fabric and a room with naughty seductive adult toys, probably.

Blue shook her head trying to push the thought out of her mind. How awful to judge this man based solely on his reputation and what was said about him. Even having worked in the media, she knew too well, not every sound bite was captured. There was always more to a story. Always.

But for now, it seemed as if he were making it clear. She would only be Miss Monroe to him. A worker. A contractor. And...to her private disappointment, she could be nothing more to him.

Later that day, after touring the premise, assisting in the vineyard and doing tons of paperwork, Zack and Blue walked through the enchanted-looking garden leading to the driveway where her car was parked. "Are you sure you don't want me to call a car? It's been a long day. You look pretty beat."

"Oh, no. I can get myself home, thank you."

"You know, it's interesting that you left your job at Channel 31. I thought you were the most annoying reporter there, but you were gifted. You often got to the heart of a story."

She turned around looking stunned and surprised, her folders clutched to her chest. "Annoying?"

He grinned. "In a good way, Miss Monroe. People in my position never like to see media personnel swimming around their fish bowl."

She laughed. The wind swept her dark, beautiful strands of hair into her face and he automatically brushed the tresses away before she could. Her hands, after all, were full. An electric surge rushed between them. He wanted to touch more than her hair. He wanted to lower his head to hers and press his mouth to her sweet berry lips.

He realized then that he probably shouldn't have done that. Her eyes widened. But a look of amazement flashed in them. Was she blushing?

"Sorry. Your hands were full." His voice came out more authoritative and rigid than he intended.

She chuckled sheepishly. "Thank you. And to answer your question, I didn't leave Channel 31. They fired me."

"Fired you? Oh. Because of that debacle with your cell phone?"

"Yes. My crazy ex."

"Your crazy ex?" So there was a man in the picture. An ex-boyfriend.

Zack opened the car door for her after she squeezed her starter and remote key from her keychain.

"Thank you." Blue placed the folders and her recorder on the passenger seat of her car. She turned to face Zack. "It's nothing really. Like I said before, he was trying to get back at me for...ending our relationship and...well..."

"The man sounds like a real lowlife." Zack's tone was harsh. His lips curled in disgust. "What kind of man would do that to a woman?"

"Clearly not a gentleman." Blue smiled, though Zack could see the pain in her eyes.

"You deserve better, Miss Monroe."

She seemed surprised at his response. And a smile of appreciation graced her face.

"What is his name?"

"What? Oh, no. It doesn't matter. Leave him be. I'm not like that."

"Like what? Allowing people to walk all over you?"

"No. I'm not about revenge. I have better things to do with my time."

Now it was Zack's turn to be taken aback. His eyes widened with amusement and surprise. He'd met a lot of women in his time but many of them who were wronged had a whole lot of bitterness and revenge seeping through them, so much that it was unattractive. His stomach clenched at the audacity of his ex-girlfriend, Selina. She was a winner in that category for sure. He still had to deal with the ramifications if that sex tape ever got out. God help him.

But Blue? Heck, she was all heart. Here was a man who ruined her reputation and career and she wasn't even the least bit interested in seeing him suffer. The very thought of Blue's delicate, forgiving nature caused more desire to burn through Zack's body.

"You can tell a lot about a person by the way they treat their enemies, Miss Monroe."

"Well, I guess, it's the way I was raised. Revenge is a time waster. Time is better spent trying to get ahead in life."

"Not to mention, harboring resentment is like sipping on a glass of poison and expecting it to lead to the demise of one's wrongdoer."

She grinned. "You're a man of many words, Zack."

"I've been there before, Miss Monroe. You get to meet all kinds of people in my line of work. And in my position. Besides, our experiences of the past are what shapes us into who were are today."

"That's so true," she echoed.

"Still, it's the ones who make the best of their experiences instead of taking the bad, who will go further in life."

"You're so right. There's always two ways of dealing with the past."

"Yes. You can become bitter or strive to become better."

"Hey, I like that. I'm going to write that down and add that to the documentary notes."

Zack grinned. "I'm glad you decided to set up business for yourself, Miss Monroe. I like to support anyone bettering him- or herself and creating his own path in life. Outside of this documentary that you're filming here at the vineyard, you must let me know if there is anything I can do to help you."

"Oh, my. Thank you. I...don't know what to say." Blue swallowed so hard that he could see the lump in her throat move.

The sun in the sky was beaming, a vibrant orange hue amongst the clouds. The breathtaking scenery made it hard to want to go indoors. Zack felt as if he could stay talking with this woman until the sun set. He was actually enjoying her company. Enjoying her aura. Her mannerisms. Her thoughts.

He couldn't remember the last time he was so entertained in the company of a beautiful woman before.

In the past, women often flirted with him and were after his body and his wallet, not about conversations about daily life, living, politics, socializing. Nothing like that. This was...refreshing. For Pete's sake, he'd been saying goodbye to this woman for what? The last twenty minutes? And she didn't seem to want to get to where she was going any time soon either.

"I'm really glad to leave the media. Trust me."

"Why?"

"Well, I've made one too many enemies," she laughed humorlessly.

"Enemies? You? I find that hard to believe."

"Well, unfortunately, I got assigned some dirty stories to dig up on dishonest businessmen and ex-politicians. Sort of an expose segment on our other TV show at the station."

"Oh, right," he groaned. Zack knew the show and hated it with a burning passion. "Thirty-Minutes."

"Yes, The Thirty-Minutes Show. I was working on this one story about a former senator who was caught cheating on his wife and ...well, that's the past now. I've handed over my research to my colleague over there. That's their problem now. Not mine. Well..."

"What is it?" he asked in a low voice. She was holding back again. What was with this woman and her secretive demeanor? "Blue? Are you okay?" She seemed to stare off into space for a moment. That caused a ripple of concern to shoot through his body. What was going on? Zack was often good at reading people. As nice as this young lady was, he could sure as hell tell she had life that was more complicated than what was seen on the surface.

"Thank you for everything Mr...I mean, Zack. I'll be in first thing in the morning."

"Good. Be sure let Venus know if you need anything at all."

"I will," she said but Zack could see a shred of disappointment in her lovely face.

"I'll be off site periodically on meetings and other engagements. But if there is anything critical, she knows how to reach me."

"I'll be sure to do that." Blue gazed into his eyes. Then she started the ignition. He saw that she got off safely before heading back to the main house.

There was something mysterious about Blue Monroe, and one way or another, he was going to uncover it. Ordinarily, Zack would be inside a woman's heart and ultimately her bed within twenty-four hours of meeting her. But thank God, he was going to rise to the occasion for this abstinence challenge. Maybe it was a blessing in disguise and not some curse as he originally thought. He would get a chance, as hard as that would be, to know Blue intimately without getting into her bed, but inside her mind and soul first. If he could do that and still hold interest in her, that would mean a hell of a lot. It could mean, that she could be "the one." Damn.

Zack was officially on a diet of cold showers and probably self-serving gratification for the long haul. He was not going to screw this up. He could do this. *Keep your distance from her, Zack*. Blue was beautifully tempting, a sweet threat to his celibacy run.

His lips curled into a grin.

CHAPTER FOUR

Almost four weeks later, Blue felt as if she was finally getting a grasp on things. It was early in the morning on a clear, cloudless summer day in the country. She could see off in the distance the blueness of the lake blending with the bright horizon. Her eyes drank in the vivid colors of aqua blue and gorgeous turquoise as the sun reflected off the water. She had already set up her tripod, video editing equipment, digital camera and microphone on the site and thought about the subjects she was going to cover during her tenure filming the short documentary.

During the past few weeks, Blue came into work early—before the first sign of dawn to capture footage of the land as the sun rose inviting in warm hues of rouge and orange rays of light blending with the horizon. One day, Zack had turned up and was surprised to see her there at 5:47 a.m. sunrise time. She learned that rising with the sun meant a lot to the brothers, something to do with their mother, who had passed away, but they never got into what really happened to their mom. She knew there were unlocked chambers in Zack's life that would never open. She wondered how badly he was hurt, so bad that he could not even talk about it. Blue's heart ached for him. She knew how that felt, when she lost her own wonderful parents so tragically. There was nothing that could heal some heartbreaks, she figured. Death was so final. All one could do was to focus on the fond memories and be glad that they were a part of one's life.

It was clear Zack was passionate about his work and Blue really wanted to capture that fully. She had grown to genuinely respect Zack based on knowing him personally, as much as he allowed, and learning more about him through his workers. And...best of all, he never tried to get "fresh" with her. So much for his playboy image persona.

Blue was so focused on getting all the footage just right. Her main focus now was to capture hundreds of shots from various angles and then decide on which to narrow them down to and where to tighten the focus.

Blue gazed off at the magnificent scenery of the estate while inhaling the calming scent of the grapes from the vine that filled the atmosphere.

Divine.

She could work here forever.

"This is the Romero Winery and Vineyard," she began recording against the backdrop of the vineyard from up on the hill. The wind rustled her hair as she faced her video camera propped on the tripod. "Thousands of acres of glorious land that stretches across the city of..." Blue bit down on her lip. She shook her head. "No. Wrong." She fiddled with the buttons on the remote to press the pause button on her camera.

And she blew a deep breath of air that caused her bangs to swing up off her face. She then started the recorder again. "This is the fantastic Winery and Vineyard of Romero..." she stopped herself again, then growled while hitting the pause button.

What the hell had gotten into her so suddenly? Zack.

Why was this man possessing her mind again? Because no man had ever made her feel the way smooth, sexy Zack had. And they hadn't even touched...yet.

Not that she thought she could even get there with him. The man clearly had other things on his mind. Blue had been there for four weeks and outside of very brief fly-by conversations, nothing much happened.

Heck, they hadn't even had a chance to spend an ample amount of time alone so that she could really interview him one-on-one.

The summer breeze may be on the calm side today but inwardly she herself was a nervous wreck. This was, after all, her first time actually filming a documentary—even though it had been a few weeks. She started off with bits and pieces of information and capturing different shots of the vineyard and speaking with a myriad of vineyard workers. She saw Zack on a few occasions to her heart's chagrin. Whenever she did catch a few glimpses of him, her heart sped up and it felt like bumblebees were dancing in her belly.

This charming and alluring man was overwhelming her senses. Gorgeous wasn't even the best word to describe his royal handsomeness. Still, he had kept their conversations brief and clipped and she wondered why he was being more distant with her than his other staffers. Did he still, deep down, hold her accountable for what happened to his brother, Lucas, last year?

Why was Zack really distancing himself from her? Blue couldn't help but feel terrible inside. But she mustered up the courage to plug on with a cheery smile. She kept reminding herself she was there to do a job. Nothing more.

She'd overheard him speaking with his brother when she was out in the vineyard capturing the method in which workers pruned vines with grapes. His brother, Carl, had apparently teased him with a "watch out, she's not on the menu, remember?" Not on the menu? And then she'd heard Carl say something about Zack being on a strict diet to which Zack had imparted a scathing look.

Later in the afternoon, her heart turned over in her chest. Zack had returned. They would finally get a chance to sit down for the first time in four weeks since she'd first spoken with him. This was not the casual walk by, idle chitchat but a real sit down conversation.

After Zack participated in a yet another wine tour and showed Blue around another area of the estate, they settled back in his office. No matter how much she thought she saw of the Romero estate, there was much more she hadn't seen. The place was massive. But then it shouldn't surprise her much since Toni Romero was a real estate mogul. Land and property were his business. It looked as if he'd bought up most of the town of Mayberry Hill.

Blue sat down in the plush chair in Zack's spacious office for a follow-up meeting. He was so busy with errands that she barely got a chance to sit down for some quality film time. The sunlit office with windows that stretched from the floor to the ceiling was marvelous. Ample sunlight shone in but that did nothing to warm the nerves in her body.

The man was gorgeous as hell and he made Blue nervous.

Blue Monroe never got nervous around a man. But this wasn't just any man. She watched him as he keyed in some information on his silver laptop on his desk. He had told her he wanted to discuss a few things but decided to respond to some urgent emails. She noted his fingers brushes against the keys. His long fingers were slender and his skin looked smooth, glowing tanned and healthy. His fingernails were a healthy in appearance too. Something she'd learned in a health class in college. You could tell a lot about a person's diet through their fingernails.

"I'm impressed by your work, Miss Monroe. You show up here early before dawn and yet you leave late, which, by the way, is not necessary." She loved the way Zack highlighted all her strong points and encouraged her as he did his employees. She thought she would be working for a boss from hell, but Zack was kind to everyone from the garden help to the garbage men who came to collect the rubbish. A true man treats all people in society well.

That impressed the hell out of Blue. The man was solid with a heart of gold and a body of steel. So...unreachable to her.

Oh, why couldn't she ever land a good guy?

"Thank you. I just want to make sure I get all the work done."

"You are very passionate. I admire that you only proffer kind words. I know some of the older staff members can be quite a challenge to work with."

"I always give people the benefit of the doubt, Zack. Life's too short to..."

Oh, God. That was embarrassing she lost her train of thought. There she went again. Why did Zack have that mind-bending effect on her?

Her eyes kept drawing to his sweet lips. They looked so irresistible. So...kissable. And his classic facial features. His perfect nose, his marvellous chiselled cheekbones and dark, lovely eyes that captivated her. Was this man even aware of how enchantingly gorgeous he was?

Stop it, Blue. Focus on your job. He is so way out of your league. Don't even go there, girl. You'll just be making a damned fool of yourself.

She remembered seeing clippings online of Zack with gorgeous Hollywood actresses, socialites and super models. An actress and super model, Blue was not.

"What are you thinking, Miss Monroe?" Zack's silky, smooth deep voice interrupted her fantasy daydream.

"Um..." She swallowed hard. He caught her gaping at him, didn't he? How embarrassing.

"Excuse me?" she finally squeezed through her nerve-tightened throat. She felt the color drain from her face.

"You seemed to be gazing intently. I want to know what you were thinking about." He leaned back in his leather chair behind his desk. His hair shined as the sun shone through the windowpane behind him creating a divine halo.

She thought she could see his luscious lips curl at the sides slightly. Was he amused by her ogling him? Well, she was not one of his corporate groupies. She was going to keep herself in check and not give him that smug satisfaction.

She cleared her throat and drew in a deep breath, hoping he wouldn't notice how incredibly inadequate she felt. "I was just thinking about the angles of the documentary." Blue shuffled some of her notes in front of her.

Zack casually leaned back further and propped his leg up over his knee. "Go on."

"W-well. I think it's good that we center on the history of the winery and vineyard and the reason you decided to keep everything...contained."

He nodded thoughtfully. A grin of amusement curled his lips again. "Was that all you were thinking?"

"Excuse me?"

"It seemed to me that you had your mouth open," he said, his eyes dropping to her lips, which caused her to subconsciously lick them.

This was not working out very well for her. Blue had never been so hot for a guy like this and he was not making it easy for her. Was this some sort of test?

Have mercy. Please let me not screw this up.

All she could think of was throwing her notes on the ground, leaping over his desk, scattering his notes aside as she did so, and sucking the life out of him with a passionate kiss. She wanted to feel his firm body with her own hands and enjoy pleasuring him but she had to get her mind away from that all.

She clearly must have been working way too hard. She was having uncontrollable erotic thoughts about this man. It both thrilled and frightened her at the same time.

She could feel the sexual power from across the table. It was too palpable. Blue reached for a glass of water on the side table and took a long swig.

"If you're going to work around me, Miss Monroe, you'll need to get used to my...sense of humor. I often put people on the spot to see how they react. It's good practice."

"No, it isn't."

"What makes you say that?"

"Because. It's mind games."

"Who's playing mind games?"

"Well..." *Be careful what you say, Blue.*

"Miss Monroe, life is stressful as it is. Work can be even more so. Our motto here at Romero Winery and Vineyard is 'work hard, play harder.'"

"Of course." Blue pulled out her notepad and began taking notes. "I've read about your philosophies."

"And you've probably heard that as many as ninety-nine percent of doctors' visits stem from stress-related illnesses."

Blue swallowed hard. "Yes."

"Having a sense of humor is not just the ability to tell jokes, but the ability to *take* a joke." Zack's expression melted into a warm smile.

Blue smiled, sheepishly. "Sorry." It was then she remembered not long ago seeing and hearing the vineyard workers cheerfully having fun while pruning the vines. They even enjoyed a laughter session. It was refreshing to see a highly-energized, positive work environment. She had experiences at her job at Channel 31 News as anything but cheerful and positive. There was a whole lot of backbiting, backstabbing and backbreaking work going on there. She loved reporting and worked with some fine co-workers but all it took was a few sour grapes to spoil what could otherwise be a healthy work environment. There didn't seem to be any workplace politics going on at Romero Winery and Vineyard. None that she could sense, anyway. That in and of itself spoke volumes about their boss, Zack Romero.

"No need to be apologetic. I noticed how stressed out you appeared when you got out of your car today."

"You were watching me?" Blue looked out at the window to Zack's left and could see her parked car not far across the lawn in full view. Of course, he had a clear view from his office. And he must have noticed that she was fiddling with her skirt that kept riding up when she moved the first day she arrived to work there a few weeks ago. Oh, heavens.

"When my staffers...and contractors, come to work here, I like positive energy. We give it and we expect it. Negativity breeds illness and we want our crops to flourish, and most importantly, our valuable employees to do so as well."

"I like that," she said. Feeling more foolish than before. There she was thinking, wishfully thinking, that he was making a pass at her when in fact he was just trying to get her to lighten up. He probably read her anxiety-ridden body language. Oh, God.

"I trust that you've tasted Romero Wine by now?" he arched a brow, flirtatiously.

Oh, God. Would I ever love to taste your wine. Blue had heard of Zack Romero's reputation with women. The man had a commanding presence, a killer body and charm to die for. She could imagine what a sexy lover he would be underneath the silky sheets.

"Well, no. Well, yes."

"Oh?" A grin played across Zack's lips. "Which is it, Miss Monroe?"

"Sorry, I'm just..." *a bit flustered right now. I can't even think in your presence for some bizarre reason.*

He pressed a button on his intercom system. "Yes, sir?" The bodiless voice sounded on the other end.

"Please bring the Merlot, 1976."

"Yes, sir. Right away, sir."

"We have a wine tasting room as you know but for the moment I'm going to improvise."

Blue's heart hammered in her chest. Was Mr. Zack Romero about to do what she thought he was about to do?

"I'm going to give you a lesson, Miss Monroe." A smirk curled his sinfully sexy lips.

"A lesson?"

"Yes. I'm going to give you a lesson on how to taste a Romero."

Heat rushed to the soft flesh between her legs. What did he just say?

"I'm going to show you how to capture the true essence of Romero Winery," he continued, grinning slightly. His dark sexy gaze burned into her. "It is an important aspect of working here that you fully appreciate all that we are. Our taste is our business." His eyes drifted to her lips and she subconsciously licked them.

Taste? Your business?

Blue swallowed hard. *Girl, you've handled politicians, gangsters, protesters and dangerous weather conditions as a reporter. You can handle Zack Romero. Alone.*

"Okay," she said, trying to summon her inner confidence.

Moments later, a member of his staff set the table up in his office for some experimental taste testing. The gentleman covered the oak table in a white satin cloth then laid out a few glasses and two bottles of wine.

"Now, remember, Miss Monroe. Wine tasting is not wine drinking. You are only whetting your palate," Zack said, standing at the wine tasting table with Blue at his side, looking on.

He uncorked the first bottle on the table then poured her a glass of red wine. "This is the result of one hundred percent estate-grown grapes from our own vineyard."

Blue had heard a lot about family owned and operated vineyards and the intimacy they often provided but this was...different.

Splendid. Blue was giddy all of a sudden. She didn't know why. A private tasting with Zack Romero? This was not how she had envisioned this day to be. It was thankfully better.

From the first day she had arrived, the air around the estate was filled with the fresh fragrance of juicy grapes and flowers and the breathtaking scenery almost stole her breath away. Blue would volunteer here, never mind work here, just to soak in the delightful views every day. How nice to be able to live on the property.

"Got it," she said, trying to hide her trembling. What was she afraid of? Heck, she'd never done this before. What was he expecting her to say...or do? What was she to look for...to taste for?

"In wine circles, tasting is the sensory evaluation of this magnificent elixir. This practice is as ancient as wine making itself." She loved to hear the sound of Zack's smooth, delicious deep voice. It wasn't just what he said, but the way he said it.

"That's intriguing to know," she said, jotting down some notes on her pad. Blue placed the notepad and pen down on the table and took the wine glass from Zack. She was ever aware of his eyes on her the entire time. That didn't really do much to help her nervousness.

"There are four stages to wine tasting, Miss Monroe," he said in a low voice, his gaze capturing her own.

"The appearance."

"Yes," she said, noting the beautiful, sparkling red liquid in her glass.

"Then there is the aroma of the wine," he said, as he stood close to her with a glass of his own in his hand. He lifted the glass near enough to her nostrils so she could catch the sweet scent.

"Next is my favorite phase. The taste. The sensation in my mouth," he explained in a low voice. "Some tasters spit it out when done. But I'm a man who enjoys swallowing." A sly grin etched his face. "I like the flavor to slide down my throat," he said, dark passion burning in his eyes, his voice smooth, deep and slippery like raw silk.

Blue's body grew weak and flimsy. Her inner thighs throbbed out of control now. *I want you.*

No. Get a hold of yourself, girl, she scolded herself inwardly. Why were her thoughts traveling down the direction of naughty lane? She had thoughts of him sensuously tasting her between her thighs and squeezed her eyes shut momentarily and drew in a deep breath.

Stop thinking, Blue. Don't even go there. You're working.

There was just something so seductive and connecting about sweet wine and smooth sex. *Like you could ever have a chance with Zack.*

Zack's scent was arousing and delicious. Blue had to steer her thoughts away from him.

She sipped from the glass at his insistence and oh, the taste was delicious, sweet, silky, fascinating. "Oh," she moaned in her throat.

"Smooth, isn't it?" Zack said with a satisfactory boyish grin.

"Hmm," she voiced again. That was all she could say.

Zack's gaze followed Blue's luscious lips. Heat surged through his body at her mesmerized gaze. A delicious fire blazed in the darkness of his eyes. The woman looked stunning. His crotch jumped, to his chagrin, at her sexual response to tasting his sweet wine. Oh, the things he could do to her to make her scream out, never mind, moan with delight. He could bet that she would taste of sweet wine.

Control, Zack.

Abstinence. You're not quite done yet. You still have another day to go. It was a crazy few weeks without the silky touch of a beautiful woman, like Blue, in his arms. He'd thought he would have gone crazy out of his mind.

Why surely he could control his feelings towards this stunning woman before him. He was beginning to harden between his loins so he had to trail his mind away from Miss Monroe.

Control.

"Hmm. You have an impressive portfolio of wine, Zack."

"Mastering the art of women…I mean, winetasting, is essential in order to get the most experience of your consumption of fine wine."

Blue stood there grinning. It was obvious to him that she'd caught his Freudian slip of the tongue.

Good. At least she didn't seem the least bit offended.

"The final stage is what we call the finish. The aftertaste."

"Good. That was quite an experience. Sweet, savory. Memorable."

"I like that. I appreciate your comments."

He poured another glass after uncorking the next bottle. Her first glass was, of course, still full, since the intent was not to drink. It was to take a taste. "Now try this one."

"What is this?"

"A dry white wine."

"Now, Miss Monroe, when you take a taste, you take a small sip and let it roll around in your mouth this time."

Why had he told her that? He could visualise her rolling a part of him inside her mouth. Oh, God. He was, of course, referring to the wine.

Enough. He commanded his thoughts back to matters at hand. Not on some fantasy.

Control.

The truth was, Zack was a playboy. He loved women more than he loved fine wine. He just couldn't trust chicks as much these days. Yet, something deep inside him told him that Blue Monroe was different. He'd had women openly flirting with him in situations less intimate than this one. One even playfully tried to rip off his shirt.

Blue was different.

Gracias a Dios.

"You have wine dribbling from your lips, Miss Monroe," he said in a low voice that sent her pulse racing like mad. Her inner thighs tingled. He reached his finger to brush it off her but the electricity pulled her hard in his direction. Before she knew it, Zack had lowered his head to hers. She could feel the heat of his sex. She could almost taste it.

Kiss me. I want to taste you so badly, Zack.

As if he could hear her wishes, Zack softly brushed her lips with his and electrical currents surged through her blood. She shivered uncontrollably at the sensation of his amazing lips on hers as he kissed her seductively. *Wow.* Rainbows seemed to arch inside her belly at his light strokes and oh, so delicious taste. The silky feel of his lips on hers was delightful; it stole her breath away.

Have mercy.

She had never known what it was like to be kissed by a reputed highly experienced lover like this. Zack had the touch. No wonder he was known as a playboy.

They both placed their glasses on the table. Zack snaked his strong arm around her waist. She could feel his power. A potent surge entered her body from his. He slid his warm, moist tongue inside her mouth, swirling so magically and she tilted her head back and moaned in pleasure. She was exploding with fireworks inside from…his passionate kiss. Oh, wow. He pulled her closer to him and lifted his finger to trace the outline of her jaw and lifted her head back up to his. Their tongues danced and became sweetly entwined. Zack tasted delicious like sweet, red wine.

French kissing her until she was dizzy and her legs felt weak, Blue's body continued to heat to scorching levels. She could feel the dampness pooling inside her panties. Her sex pulsed uncontrollably as he held her firm, his hand sliding down cupping her behind as he groaned with pleasure.

Oh, God. I want you. Take me now.

She was enthralled by the magical expert kiss of this…sex god. She was in ecstasy. She was intoxicated with his salacious lovemaking of the lips. She arched her back in delight. Zack leaned her against the table pushed against the wall and like love-hungry animals, he swept the expensive wine glasses aside with one quick motion and shifted her up on the table. She could feel the hardness of his erection pressing through his pants as the heated passion consumed them with delight. His lips followed the sensitive skin on her neck as his hands massaged and held her body. She wrapped her arms around Zack's neck while he continued to pleasure her with his hotness, sucking on her lips causing them to tingle like she'd never felt before. The sensation of his skin on hers was magical.

How could this be?

There was a strong electrical connection between them, an explosive chemical reaction that could not be denied.

She was kissing Zack Romero. Blue was making out with her hot and oh, so sexy boss. She was dreaming. This wasn't real, she mused. She was dreaming.

Oh, sweetness.

She thought she would die from too much excitement pumping her heart.

Heat.

Then, breathless, Zack pulled away. He looked into her eyes and a sudden change in temperate seeped through them. He looked away, clenching his jaw as if cursing under his breath.

"I'm sorry," he said, breathing hard. His voice hoarse. "I should not have done that." A serious look slid across his handsome face.

Sorry?

For kissing me?

Am I that hideous?

"W-what?" Blue whispered, breathless. Blue was trembling inside. Her body was throbbing. She needed release soon but now she would not have that satisfaction. Why did he stop? She straightened her top and drew in a deep breath. She could feel her pulse beating hard in her throat.

Sorry?

He was sorry?

"Is something wrong?" she murmured.

"No. We have work to do, Miss Monroe."

"Now," he said as if nothing happened moments before. Moments ago, he looked disappointed with himself when he had rearranged the table and ensured Blue was okay. "I shouldn't have done that," he admitted again in a smooth, deep voice. "Please forgive my moment of...indiscretion."

"No. I...we...I kissed you. It's okay..." Blue dropped her gaze to her notepad. She was feeling terrible for some reason and she didn't know why. She was disappointed he stopped. Was she ashamed for wanting him? Or for him rejecting her?

"Let's start again then, shall we?" He leaned forward while sitting behind his desk in the sun-filled glass office. His hands were clasped on the desk. His gaze fixed on hers. "First things, first. I will need you to work with Venus tomorrow and she will show you around the office to get a feel of the work that goes on at this end of the business. You'll be spending another two weeks in her section."

"Okay," Blue agreed, scribbling down the notes.

"She'll give you access to some of the material you'll want for the documentary. And trust me, there will be plenty to keep you busy in your research."

"Good. I have a question." Blue could not help but feel an overwhelming sense of rejection that he did not pursue her further. But she was there to do a job. She realized that a man in his position could not afford another family scandal like the one that plagued his brother. In fact, the Romeros always seemed to be in the local news for one thing or another dealing with their love lives or their dating adventures. She really didn't want to be one of them.

Yes, let's pretend it didn't happen. Let's start all over again. She thought the words in her mind but her heart was crushed by the sentiment.

So did this mean she would never again have the pleasure of his lips...or more?

He paused, saying nothing.

There was an awkward silence for a moment and Blue was aware of her own breathing and the sound of her heart pounding in her chest.

"Can I interview you about the special new project that you're working on for the Viticulture program at the college? That's one area we haven't covered yet."

"Yes. But not now. Much later."

"Oh. Okay." Blue spoke softly, trying to hide her disappointment.

"At the end of your research phase, I will take you personally on a few formal wine tastings."

"Oh," was all she could say. What was wrong with her? She was usually way more coherent and talkative than she was now. Holy cow. This man had some bewitching effect on her.

"You will have all the information you need in good time."

She gushed. "I understand." Her lips felt dry again and she nervously ran her tongue over her top lip.

"Can I get you a drink, Miss Monroe?"

"No, thank you." *I'm just having difficulty thinking right now.*

"You seemed to be very talkative when you worked at Channel 31 News."

"Oh. I'm just a little..."

"Nervous?"

"No. Trying to make sense of things. We have only two more months to put this entire film project together and it doesn't leave us much time really. There's editing and mixing to do during production once I've got all the raw footage filmed."

"I know that." He paused for a moment and opened his sweet lips as if he were going to add something else but decided against it.

She had already spoken to him about what she had completed so far and he seemed pleased. A bonus in her books.

"Earlier, you were asking about some statistics on the wine business," he said, seemingly changing the subject.

"Oh, yes. I was impressed with the numbers." She reached into her binder and pulled out some sheets of paper. "It says here that the Canadian Wine and Grape Industry contributes $6.8 billion in economic impact to the Canadian economy alone. That's...very impressive."

"Yes. We do our part." He was sounding modest, but also unimpressed. Why? Did money mean nothing to this man who had an abundance of everything possible—including good genes?

"The wine industry is responsible for creating more than 31,000 jobs," Zack continued, holding her gaze. "We provide employment in manufacturing, agriculture, tourism, research, retail and even medicine."

"Medicine?" she queried, incredulously. Blue had never thought about winery and medicine mixing. She was learning something new. She loved learning new things every day in her line of work.

It pleased Blue that she was beginning to feel more relaxed and more comfortable around Zack again. She knew why. They remained focused on work again. Only work.

Once she stayed focused on only work—and only work, she was not focused on how hard and long Zack's erection could possibly be. And she was not imagining Zack in all his glorious nakedness. Blue saw pictures of him online in nothing but swim trunks after paparazzi had captured images of him swimming at the beach. She had to focus, after all. She had debts from her parents' untimely deaths to settle. She had a sister's college tuition to pay in the fall. She had to survive for her sister and her own sake.

"Yes, we turn surplus grapes into surgical spirits."

"Surgical spirits?" Blue repeated, scribbling her notes in long hand.

"Yes. We send our surplus grapes to distilleries to be turned into surgical spirits and industrial alcohol used in detergents and medicines."

"Awesome. I really don't think the general public knows this."

"You can get the quote on video later when I am interviewed at the end."

"So, will you continue to teach at the college?"

"Well, I'm a guest lecturer for this semester. I'll have to see how it goes."

"How do you like it so far?"

"I enjoy sharing whatever knowledge I have with eager minds that have a thirst for knowledge."

"Nice," she said, writing ferociously on her notepad while Zack continued to survey her. Aware that she was holding her breath, she inhaled deeply.

"Are you okay?"

"I'm good. I think I have enough to go on for now. I'll work with Venus again and interview her and the other workers throughout the week for the next segment of the documentary."

"Good."

"Um. Do you have any questions or requests?" Blue asked her boss.

"Yes."

"Oh?" she asked, breathless. She was caught by surprise because she really hadn't expected him to ask her anything else. Her heart pounded hard and fast in her chest.

"Have dinner with me, tonight?"

Zack's invitation slid off his sexy tongue like melted caramel. His voice was low, silky and deep. The reaction sent shivers of delight running through her belly. Her inner thighs tingled deliciously. *Oh, no.*

Blue felt her breath stop. She could not answer him. She wanted to. So he wasn't rejecting her after all. He just wanted to make it official. But have dinner with him…tonight?

CHAPTER FIVE

"I...I can't," Blue whispered, breathless. Finally, she managed to squeeze a vocal sound through her nerve-constricted throat. What was she saying?

Sexy, sizzling, affluent bachelor, Zack Romero—her boss, just asked her to dinner. Tonight. And she said no. She said *no*. Was she out of her mind? But she could not stop herself. She just wasn't prepared. She couldn't. After that kiss, she wanted to do more with him. But she couldn't. Not tonight.

"No?" he echoed, seductively. A salacious grin touched the corner of Zack's sexy-as-sin lips as he leaned forward in his chair. His brow raised a fraction. It was as if he were amused that someone had declined to dine with him.

"Um...well. I mean..."

His silence, waiting for her to finish her sentence, was overwhelming. Blue perspired in her seat. Her mind was all scrambled. She knew she just couldn't drop everything she had to do tonight to go out with him. To have dinner with him.

It's only dinner, Blue. He wants to have a meal with you. Not have you for his meal.

Blue really didn't want to get into her personal life. She didn't want to tell him the real reason she wasn't free to just do as she pleased right now. But she didn't want to come off as rude either. Should she tell him?

* * *

The woman *actually* said no? Her response to his question rendered Zack off guard. *Sweet*. Despite that tasty kiss a while ago, the woman was not *easy*.

That was a good sign. And it took a minute for him to remember that he was to stay clear of sexual relations for at least another day. Which was also good. But he still had another day of abstinence to go. He groaned inwardly at the thought.

Zack leaned back in his soft leather chair and slid his gaze down this woman's opulent facial features. How intriguing. A woman telling him no was not something he heard, often. Or ever in his recent years. His eyes surveyed Blue Monroe as she sat in her seat across from his desk, practically squirming as if she were his prey. Why did she react that way with him?

She possessed the most delicate, dainty features he'd seen on a woman. Her sweet, fully defined lips looked as red as ripe strawberries and tasted as sweet as the grapes that made the wine in his winery.

But oh, Zack would love to taste much more than just those sexy lips of hers. He wanted to taste all of her. This woman was causing a strangely delicious reaction in his body that was stronger than he had ever had with a woman.

Her caramel skin was enticing to his eyes. The contrast with her beautiful, silky, black hair that had a healthy shine to it brought a warm feeling inside him. My God, this woman was pleasing to his eyes—and he was sure to any man who became captivated by her beauty. Did Blue even know this? Judging by her awkward demeanor, she sure didn't act as if she was a god-gifted beauty. There she was, so educated and talented and yet she never displayed a grain of vanity.

A surge of heat raced through him. He really wanted to hear the reason why she couldn't or wouldn't have dinner with him.

Suddenly the deal he'd made with his grandfather to give up sex for a month had proven to be a learning curve and at the same time major inconvenience—a pain in the butt. He loved to romance and seduce a beautiful, strong woman. He took significant pleasure in pleasing his ladies. And this one before him was stunning. So fascinating that it almost stole his breath away.

Damn that deal he'd made with this grandfather.

By now he would have whisked Miss Monroe off to his waterfront condo in the city for a night of unforgettable passion. The thought irked him that the past few weeks he had to disallow himself to get close to her. And now? Christ, she was rejecting him.

"I trust that you have plans tonight, then?" he asked out of curiosity.

"Um. Well, no. I mean, yes."

He cocked a brow. Was she playing games with him? She certainly seemed as if she wanted him while they were kissing. He could tell these things with women. He loved the chase but he wasn't sure where this Miss Monroe was coming from.

"Well. Is it no, or is it yes?"

"Well," Blue breathed deeply. "I…I've already made plans." She seemed uncomfortable with his silence but he should probably cut her a break from his humor. She had a right to not want dinner with him. He was only pulling her leg. Oh, he would love to do more though.

"I have a younger sister. We live together. Alone. She's my responsibility."

"Oh?" Zack wanted to hear more. The woman was more intriguing every moment he spent with her.

"Yes. This is her last day of summer school. We always discuss her day at school and I don't want to bail out on her tonight."

"I see. That's very noble of you, Miss Monroe. You're a wonderful big sister. One that every sibling should have."

The woman appeared embarrassed and he could see her cheeks turning rouge. "Well, I'm just doing what's right." Blue turning him down for a dinner date after their passionate kiss spoke volumes about her character. He loved that she as not an easy woman. And he delighted more in the fact that she had integrity and she had her priorities straight.

"What about your parents? You never mentioned them."

She looked down. He wondered why the hell he was prying into her personal life. For God's sake, she was his employee. Nothing more. She could be nothing more. Yet, something about her was too compelling for him to pass up the chance.

Was his grandfather right about him? Was he too controlled by the addictive sexual magic of having a beautiful woman in his arms and underneath him in bed?

But this one seemed oddly, different.

He was more than interested in having Miss Monroe in his bed. He wanted to get inside her mind. Her soul. He wanted to know everything about this woman. And he didn't know why. What had gotten into him all of a sudden? This wasn't usually his style. He cared deeply for people. But when it came to attraction, he had often had only one thing on his mind. But not now. He felt, oddly, drawn to Miss Monroe.

"They're no longer around," she said softly, her eyes filled with sorrow.

"I'm truly sorry, Miss Monroe." His gut twisted inside. He could see pain flash in those beautiful dark brown eyes of hers. The large chocolate eyes framed by adorable black curled lashes.

Call it the Romero bloodline in him. The fact that his name meant protector but he wanted to comfort her. He sensed there was a whole lot more to her parents being just "no longer around."

"It's okay. It was…a couple years ago."

"Was it an accident?"

She pressed her lips together firmly and shifted in her seat before answering him. "I don't know."

His brows drew together. "What do you mean, you don't know?"

"The police said it was accidental. But the original fire marshal report suspected arson."

"So you think someone may have tried to kill your parents? Why?"

"I…I don't know. I really don't want to get too much into it right now. I…"

"I'm sorry to probe. I was concerned."

"Oh, no. Please. I'm glad you asked. I mean, thank you for your concern. I…I'd better go now."

He nodded politely and in a gentlemanly fashion rose as she, too, got up from her seat.

CHAPTER SIX

Blue drove down the main road heading into the city, still breathing hard. Her mind was reeling with delight from the passionate kiss with Zack, the electric sensation dancing through her body. She could not believe what had just transpired.

Zack Romero. The notorious playboy with a hard-ass body.

Have mercy, Lord. This man is simply exquisite in every way. Unforgettable. That's what this day will be. Unforgettable.

She pressed her right foot on the gas, glancing at the display clock on her dashboard of her Ford. She also caught the fuel gauge and realized she should have filled up her tank before leaving Mayberry Hill. But it would only be another thirty-five minutes before she would be back in the city. She could refuel at the station near her apartment. The sky was turning a musk color as the late afternoon turned to early evening. Her cell phone buzzed and she instinctively reached for it on her seat. She often placed it by her seat when she was driving so she could see the display in case it was a call from her sister. Whenever she left the phone in her purse while driving, she would let it ring so that she didn't end up taking her eyes off the road to fish for it.

Of course, she could just learn to use her Bluetooth, which would solve all matters.

The caller was an unknown number. Again. She carefully kept her eyes on the road while reaching over and grabbing the phone then hitting the answer button and speaker option.

"Hello?" she answered but the caller hung up.

Again.

It had happened quite a few times in the past week alone. She wondered if it was a wrong number and the person on the other end of the line realized it then dialled the intended number.

Blue shrugged then replaced the phone on the passenger seat. There were very few cars on this stretch of road going into the city. It wasn't a very busy road considering. But she didn't mind being able to drive to the limit with little traffic on the road. The window of her Ford was cracked open and the breeze from the speed of the vehicle whisked her hair and cooled her skin. The air conditioner wasn't working so she was glad to have the gentle breeze from outside.

She enjoyed clear summer days. Blue relished in the thought of no cares for a change. She guessed the magic of excitement did that to a person. Inner excitement over having this wonderful opportunity to work with her new boss—or client, however she looked at it. This was her first major assignment since starting her fledgling production company.

Zack Romero.

"God, you're incredible, Zack," she said to herself, grinning from ear to ear.

Blue's mind drifted back to his alluring face and delicious appeal. Oh, if only she could be with a man like that. She knew that was farfetched. He clearly was a bachelor for life. She'd read about him beforehand. He had given interviews a while back about not being a marrying man. Not that she could possibly have a chance with him.

But, oh, he kissed her. It was as if a part of him stayed with her. The soft tingle of his lips on hers was pleasantly memorable. Zack Romero had kissed her.

Zack had a compelling presence. Mesmerizing. He had that special something about him. Blue couldn't quite put her finger on it. But it wasn't often she met a man who had that raw electrical effect on her. When he shook her hand earlier in the day, there was a surge of power that coursed through her veins. The man oozed charisma from every pore of his body. His hands were strong yet smooth. His eyes, so captivating. She had a chance to finally be up close with him and her body reacted in such a surprising way. Her mind turned to scrambled eggs for one thing. All she could do was gush uncontrollably at his masculine sexiness, his delicious scent, his gorgeous features and strong, tall athletic body.

He was like something out of a magazine, a Hollywood blockbuster action film or something, but not real life. Yet the feelings that pulsed through her body being with him, so close to touch, were mind-blowing. He made her feel giddy with lust all of a sudden.

Blue's crazy ex-boyfriend, Elliot, her former colleague at Channel 31 News, never had that kind of effect on her. There was never any spark, one she'd always read about, with Elliot. She really liked him then. Sure, he was a fair kisser and she enjoyed being around him when they'd first started dating, until she realized that he was a real actor, not a journalist. The guy turned out to be a creep, an emotionally abusive, jealous dude who didn't want her to have any friends. He'd always criticized her weight and told her to lose her "baby fat" and she'd be fine. Her friends at the station warned her that he was seeing other people and she never believed it until she saw it with her own eyes. She'd caught him necking a fellow co-worker in the lunchroom after hours when most people had left the office.

When she tried to end it with him, he turned all crazy on her. Kept calling her and hanging up, telling her co-workers all sorts of crazy lies.

Blue shuddered at the thought. The past was the past. It was dead and gone. Why bring up a dead memory to haunt the present?

Blue was so past that. She had learned to move on earlier. A bit of Yoga and positive thinking exercises really helped pulled her through it all. Of course, the last draw was the cell phone recorder fiasco that cost her a job at the station but now she realized it was a blessing in sweet disguise. She'd never been happier to be her own boss, however challenging it was at times.

Blue remembered reading somewhere in one of her self-help books about when you keep on the positive side of things, you realize nothing happens to you, it happens for you. She wanted to believe that the universe would be good to her. She'd been through so much painful hell, it was insane. Losing her parents still caused her heart to ache as if someone had taken a knife to her and left it impaled in her chest.

Think positive, Blue.

She gazed at the cars speeding past her on the road, the trees whizzing by as she drove 80 km per hour in this zone.

Count your blessings, not your troubles, she reminded herself.

She was blessed to have sought gainful employment in this tough economy. That was a miracle. And this project would be the best thing to boost her business upward, not to mention the credibility it would lend to her business as word got around of her documentary on one of the most prominent families and businesses in the province.

In short, the universe had provided a much needed way out for her at the nick of time. Courtney's tuition was coming up. Not to mention paying off loans and taking care of her parents' affairs since they did not have adequate insurance. She was also able to come up with the rent for at least the next twelve months. Maybe she could even manage scraping together a down payment to finally own her own home. Courtney could have more room for herself, too. It sure was a challenge being cooped up in the little apartment with her young adult sister. But finally, there was hope. A new beginning. A chance to set things right.

Thank you, Universe.

Thank you, Mr. Romero.

Blue surprised herself when her mind drifted again. She had a vision of Zack Romero. She was alone with him in the most fascinating penthouse suite. He was moving his hand slowly down her back making her dizzy with unbridled excitement. Her nipples strained through her bra while he slowly undressed her like James Bond did in one of the earlier movies, smooth and suave. Her dress was on the floor before she knew it and she stood before him as he delighted in her body. He then lowered his head to hers and pressed his luscious lips to hers and kissed her so passionately, she forgot where she was. Heck, she forgot WHO she was. He then slowly unhooked her lace bra and she felt his hand move slowly down her body where he...

Blue shook her head and blinked hard, trying to shift the focus back on the road.

Did he harbor some magical mystique that drew women in to him like a magnet? Everybody's heard of the Romero men's sexual appeal and potency. The reputation of the brothers had been reputed to have spread far and wide for years.

Blue was still grinning while behind the wheel. She'd better keep her focus on the road and her mind out of the naughty gutter or else.

She peered in the rearview mirror and noticed that a blue SUV was driving close behind her. In fact, he'd been tailing her for quite some time now. An uncomfortable feeling befell her and she just couldn't figure out why.

She decided she was going to turn off the main road. Maybe check a few emails on her smartphone then get back on the road. The paranoid princess inside her just wanted to make sure she wasn't being followed. For whatever reason.

She remembered that day at the cemetery, a few weeks ago, she felt as if she were being watched.

You're not being watched or followed, Blue. It's all in your silly imagination.

Blue stopped the car and put her gear into park and waited. She looked at the rearview mirror again. Slowly, the blue SUV, the same vehicle that was shadowing her since she left the Romero estate had turned on the street she was parked.

Oh, God.

Her heart pounded hard, knocking the chest wall inside her with a heavy beat. She felt her body turn cold. Her worst fear confirmed.

She was being followed.

Blue, panting hard, fiddled with the gear shift after turning on the ignition. She quickly reversed then turned her car around. *Should I call 9-1-1?*

And say what, idiot? You think you're being followed while you are safe in your car?

She hit the gas and continued on. Unfortunately, there were no other cars on the road.

Great.

The trouble with travelling out of town from the city was that oftentimes some of the roads could be so isolated. Lonely driving. Thank heavens, the sky was still light enough.

Breathing hard and fast, Blue floored it while glancing up every so often in her rearview mirror. She was going to die tonight, she thought with terror.

Somebody was trying to kill her.

The blue SUV drove faster, tailgating her. She couldn't quite see who it was. Blue couldn't tell if it was a man or a woman or more than one person. The windows of that vehicle were tinted dark.

Crap.

Keep calm, Blue. Nothing gets done in a panic.

Yeah, tell that to her body. She was so tense she could barely steer her car. She pressed the gas pedal harder trying to outrun him. Trying to shake him off. But it was no use.

She felt a bang and her body flung forward in her car. His truck nailed her from behind. The driver struck her bumper on purpose. What the hell was going on?

Who was that crazy person?

Just then she heard the wheels of the SUV screeching as he sped up and rammed her again. This time, Blue saw her life flash before her. Blue lost control of her car and drove off into a ravine.

CHAPTER SEVEN

"Oh, somebody's got a woman on his mind," Carl teased his brother, Zack, as he walked into the foyer at the winery house.

Zack was leaning back on his desk with his arms folded across his chest, peering out at the window. An incredulous look formed on his face at his brother's words. "What are you talking about, Carl?"

"Oh, come on. You were daydreaming about Blue. She's one heck of a gorgeous reporter."

"Film producer," Zack corrected, not amused. "She's only here working on a documentary for the winery, Carl. And no, I was not thinking about her." Zack tried to keep his tone as cool as he could. Truth be told, he was lying right through his teeth. Damn. Blue Monroe was hot as hell. So hot, his body was on fire from the embers of her kiss. He really needed to take a cold shower more than anything. Good thing the main house wasn't too far from the winery house on the estate. He loved working close to home, or at least one of his homes, since Romero Manor was the family estate.

"Well, good, because you know you can't break that deal with Granddad, or he'll have you out of here. You've still got what? Another week."

Zack winced. "Another day," he scowled. Old man Romero was a sturdy, fine man who grew up on principles and loved his family dearly, though at times, he often imposed some childish rules on his grown, accomplished grandchildren. But Zack, like his brothers and cousins, loved Toni Romero without bounds. They would do anything for him.

"Did you find anything else out about that tape?" Zack changed the topic. "I presume you're not here for a brotherly chat."

Carl grinned. Zack's sense of humor was often dry but he tended to make light of most situations.

"Well, yeah. That," Carl said, rubbing his stubble. "There is a digital file in some Cloud storage."

"What? Are you sure about that?"

"Yeah. Sorry, man."

"Right." Zack's jaw clenched. Of all the lowdown things. "Doesn't she realize that Cloud storages can get hacked into?"

"Well," Carl grinned. "First off. No, our men did not hack into her account."

"I didn't think you did. You know I wouldn't stand for that."

"I know. Anyway, our man JoJo mentioned that she sent emails to an associate. They were talking about how much they could potentially get on hot video like that. They're looking at a bidding war of seven figures between several of the leading online news rags."

Zack winced. A sick feeling settled in his gut; he felt acid burning a hole in his heart. *Selina. Nothing but trouble.*

"Just keep me posted, will you?"

"Sure thing."

"And you still want to go into politics, bro? You're crazy," Zack chided, pouring himself a glass of wine. He took out another glass and offered it to his brother one.

"Sounds like a great plan, don't you think?"

"No. Not in the least bit. If you think business can get crazy, politics is way worse, Carl. Just you be careful. We Romeros have to stick together. Too many crazy people out there would like nothing more than to see us trounced."

"I hear ya, bro. I thought about it but, I really want to do something decent in this town. Help those who started out like us—with very little or even nothing. You know, be a voice for the voiceless."

"You're full of crap, you know that?" Zack teased his brother. Truth be told, he loved his family more than the breath in his lungs, but the guys infrequently complimented each other outright or said anything sappy. "But you just might stand a chance. If you can get those skeletons cleared out of your closet in time for election." Zack grinned and took a sip of his Merlot.

Carl, who was standing close by to him, gave him a playful punch in the arm. As if his steel biceps could feel a thing. But it almost knocked the drink out of his hand.

All this time, Venus was still there, working late and knocked on the door to Zack's office.

"Hi, I'm sorry, Zack," she said, breathless.

"Venus, what is it?" Zack asked, concern evident. He cared a lot about his employees. A damn lot and now his level of alertness shot up. She seemed to be in distress.

"Are you okay?" Carl dropped his glass on the table and went over to her.

She shook her head. "No. I mean, yes. It's...I just got a call from security. They spotted Blue Monroe's car in a ditch. Off the main road."

Zack's fingers went numb, which almost never happened, and he dropped his glass on the desk. "What? Are you sure?"

"How far from here?" Zack asked, grabbing his keys and his jacket. Fury fumed through his veins. It was an inferno in his body right now. All he could do was think about lovely Blue, crushed. Hurt. Or worse. Her shiny black hair tangled. God help somebody out there, if a hair was out of place or a scratch was on her skin. Why all of a sudden did he assume it was somebody else's fault? He didn't know why, but he just did.

He cursed under his breath. Damn. Why hadn't she taken him up on his offer to have a car take her home? One of his drivers could have easily done that. She looked so darn tired at the end of the day. Shit! If anything happened to her, he didn't know what the hell he would do with himself.

CHAPTER EIGHT

"You're very lucky, Miss Monroe," Dr. Randall at the Mayberry Hill County Hospital told Blue later while she sat up on a stretcher in the emergency room. The green hospital curtains around her bed were pulled closed for privacy. "It could have been worse. Much worse. No broken bones. No fractures. The nurse will give you something for your headache."

The doctor stood in the private area along with Zack. Carl stayed back at the estate after driving Venus home. She also overheard Zack asking Carl about finding out some information about what happened. Information? Whatever could that mean? Weren't the cops on the case? She'd heard about the men having their own team of investigators who work behind the scenes on projects for them from time to time. They could never have too many or too few enemies and always aimed to stay on top of things as far as dealing with unscrupulous people was concerned.

Regardless, Blue loved the way the Romero family was so down-to-earth and went to great lengths to take care of their staff members. Holy hell. She was grateful to be working with them. What a change from Channel 31 News. She didn't feel like a contracted employee at the Romero Winery and Vineyard. She felt more like a family member. It was as if she had an extended family of her own.

"Thank you," Blue said, her voice hinted at fatigue and she felt so drained. She was glad to have Zack by her side.

"You're very welcome, Miss Monroe. The nurse will give you the discharge papers later. In a few minutes she'll bring you some Tylenol."

The doctor nodded politely to Zack and left the area, pulling the curtains open and closing them behind him.

"Oh, no. Courtney!" Blue said, remembering her sister would be at home worried about not seeing her.

"It's okay," Zack said quietly. "I had Venus call before she left to let your sister know that you were okay. We have someone posted at the building outside on watch to make sure nothing happens."

"You don't need to do that, Mr...Zack."

"After someone tried to kill you just now by forcing your car off the road? Please," he objected, leaning against the wall.

Blue pinched her lips together. Oh, great. Now she might have to tell him...everything. Blue really didn't want to get into her past right now. She didn't want to have to go deeply into all the crap that had happened to her and her family. But then again, she didn't really know who ran her off the road. She never got a license plate or saw a face. What did she really have to go on?

The police had already taken the report on the scene and Zack offered to have his men at their own garage take care of vehicle repairs. It was all she had. She didn't want to report the accident because she knew her insurance would go through the roof. Then how would she afford the monthly premiums? Still, she was glad she got the help when she needed it. Blue always sought to do things on her own. She was an independent woman, who, in the past, would take on three part-time jobs at the same time just to make ends meet. Going from one place of employment and at quitting time, taking the bus to her next job. At one time, she even worked a double-shift, long before she finished college and became a journalist, which ended up being a short-term career thanks to her ex Elliot.

Yet, Zack was not judgmental. He just wanted to be there for her. She wasn't used to being treated like that. She could see the look of genuine concern on his face.

She remembered a while back when she had borrowed Elliot's car to take her sister to the orthodontist. Someone had parked their car beside hers and had opened their door wide and carelessly enough to scratch the car door on the passenger side.

"You idiot," Elliot shouted in a rage at her. He hurled a whole lot of abusive words and Blue failed understand his fury. It was a car. At least she and Courtney were fine. Wasn't that what mattered? Nonetheless, Blue offered to cover the damage done, even though it wasn't her fault. She shouldn't have parked there. She should have checked the licence plate of the car beside her just in case before she drove off. She should have done this, or that. Never, are you okay, honey? Never. He wasn't even concerned about her sister's procedure. He only informed her it was the last time she would drive his car. He obviously had completely forgotten how many times she loaned him her car when his was off the road. He became increasingly horrible towards her. Blue could no longer bear it. What a difference it was to see Zack not scold her for not taking him up on his offer, knowing that she was tired, to take a ride home. Perhaps, if she were more alert, she would have thought to take down the license plate number. Perhaps. Perhaps. Perhaps.

"Yes, you're right, Zack," Blue conceded, getting back to reality and the present moment.

The nurse came in and gave Blue two Tylenol tablets with a cup of water. Blue thanked the woman.

"Thank you," Zack also said to the nurse in a low, deep silky voice while Blue swallowed the water. That was awfully nice of him. He was very gracious, that was evident.

"No worries. I'm glad you'll be leaving soon," the nurse said, turning back to Blue. "For your sake," she corrected. The nurse appeared nervous. She was a young woman with dark brown hair and blue eyes that matched the color of her scrubs. The nurse kept glancing at Zack and gushing. Did she know who Zack was? Or maybe it was the sexual appeal that was so splendidly obvious. A blind woman would notice his sexiness. The way he walked, his smooth voice, his aura, his admirable physique and handsomeness was a gift to behold all eyes that were laid on him.

And oh, he was with her, Blue Monroe.

Not that they were together of course. Like only in her dreams. But he was there, with her and no one else. The thought brought on an a comforting warmth to her stomach.

All her life Blue was the one to rush to the ER for her sister or a friend or when her parents were alive and had sudden chest pains or other ailments that would require a visit. Yep, Blue was often the go-to gal.

But who would be there for her?

It was nice to be the one taken care of and fussed over for a change. Even if Zack was her boss and nothing more.

Moments later when Blue got her things together and her discharge papers, Zack rolled her out to his awaiting SUV. Oh, my. It was evening now but she could still appreciate the fine shiny black vehicle. She felt as if she were a celebrity who'd just gotten out of rehab and had one of those monstrous luxury trucks awaiting them. Only difference, of course, was no reporters or freelance photographers. Ha! Unless, she counted herself.

Zack introduced Blue to a burly man who looked more like a bodyguard.

"Nice to meet you, Hans."

Hans nodded and echoed the sentiment.

She scooped herself into the backseat. The leather interior was plush and opulent. The dim lights inside brought on a soothing ambiance. Oh, what a day it had been. Blue never thought it would end up like this. Alone with billionaire playboy Zack Romero at her side. A headline story if she had to write it herself.

She groaned. Thankfully, Blue was no longer in that awful line of work and didn't have to come up with sensational storylines to sell copies of a newspaper or score viewers for her network.

There was a more pressing thought on her mind, as much as she didn't want to admit it to Zack. She desperately needed to know. Who the hell tried to have her running scared? Zack was right. Courtney had to be protected at all costs. She really didn't know who could have done this to her. Was it some drive by crazy who randomly chose to drive her off the road? Was it Elliot or his guys? Elliot always hung with gangsters outside of his duties at work. Was it the ex-Senator Aitkin? She squeezed her eyes shut, momentarily, and sucked in a deep breath as the vehicle traversed the main road to her home.

She glanced in Zack's direction. He seemed lost in thought as he sat in the seat beside her. She could see raw hurt in his sexy, dark eyes. What was on his mind? He was miles away.

"We're going to pick up your sister. You'll get a chance to gather your things."

"What?" Blue's heart pounded hard and fast in her chest. "What are you talking about?" she queried. She did not like the finality in his tone.

"You don't think I'm going to let either of you stay at your apartment after this, do you?"

"Well, where else would we stay?"

"In one of my apartments in the city, if you wish. Or you could stay in Mayberry." His tone, it was hard, authoritative. Commanding.

Blue was speechless. Her mouth hung open for what seemed like forever. "You're not serious."

"I've never been more serious, Miss Monroe. You are currently in my employ. The incident happened close to the estate. You're my responsibility. Until we find out who did this and get to the bottom of this…" He seemed to be giving her an order like a soldier under command of his higher ranking officer. However, she was not a soldier and he was not her commanding officer.

The memory of Elliot bossing her around, bullying her to do whatever he wanted her to do came crashing down on her mind like a violent tornado whirling her thoughts and emotions all over the place. So Zack was rich and powerful. Did that make him the boss of her life? Hell, no. Was she some cheap, mindless being who when told to jump would ask how high? This was her life he was talking about.

"But you can't just tell me what to do." Blue's ears burned. She could not believe what she was hearing. "You didn't even consult *me* about it first. My sister goes to summer school and I…I'll be fine at home, thank you."

"I'll decide that." Ooh, his tone was clipped and curt.

The hell you will. "Is this how you treat everyone in your life? You just order them around and they do as they're told without question? Well, I'm not one of your pawns. You seriously have control issues, Mr. Romero."

"Ouch. Remind me to send you the bill from my therapist."

Despite herself, Blue giggled. Was this guy for real? Okay, he was hot and sexy and oh, so charming. It was damned hard to stay mad at a guy like that. Okay, maybe she was being a bit harsh.

"I'm sorry, I…I'm not usually this rude."

"Oh, here I thought it was the impact of the accident."

"That's not funny."

"I know. I apologize. And I did not mean to be overbearing, Miss Monroe. It's a very serious thing that happened. Would you and your sister like to stay in a more secure housing complex like the Romero Towers at the waterfront, or at the estate?"

Ooh, now that sounds like an enticing proposition. What could she say to that? "I…I don't know how my sister will feel about that, Zack. I…thank you."

***

"Who the hell are you?" Elliot asked the towering, muscular man in the black suit. He looked like a mob hit man but he couldn't be sure.

"My boss sent me," the man said, closing in on him. "Where were you this evening?"

"What do you mean? I was here. At home." Elliot loosened the tie around his neck. He'd just gotten home from work at the station and turned on the game. He hadn't even changed out of his suit. Who was this monster of a man working for? He'd slept with that model from the club and never called her back. Could she have been a call girl or something? Heck, there were a lot of women who he couldn't care less about calling in the morning once he got what he wanted. They would get over it. He racked his brain trying to figure out which broad he had screwed and couldn't subsequently handle the fact he did not dedicate his life to her.

When he reached his apartment earlier, he'd heard a knock at the door and when he opened it thinking it was the pizza delivery guy, the thug of a bodybuilder barged through the door.

"Never mind that," the man hissed in a dangerously low voice, void of emotions.

"Look, man, what's this about?" Elliot felt his blood pressure climb. Sweat beaded his forehead. He'd run some numbers before, hadn't he? Shit! His past was catching up with him. Was it the money he'd taken from his ex-friend's loan shark business? Shit. What had he done? Who was this man?

"A nice lady named Blue."

"Blue?" Elliot's mind went numb. Blue was probably only the sanest chick he'd been with. As much as she didn't want him. "I got rid...she and I are no longer together."

"You are to stay away from her. Capisce?"

Elliot loosened the tie around his neck, yet again. His throat was expanding with blood pumping hard through his neck. Sweat started to drip from his face. "Understood." *Whatever.*

"Look, man. I don't know what this is about but I don't have anything do with her anymore. I don't even see her since..." he paused. He decided he'd said enough.

Shit! He thought Blue was some kind of loser loner girl. She didn't even have much family or parents, did she? Where the hell did she know this guy or his boss from? And who the hell was this man working for? He certainly wasn't someone Elliot wanted to even deal with. The fact that he had timed his arrival at home and knew who the hell he was and where he lived was terrifying.

Very terrifying.

"You have my word on it. I won't go anywhere near her."

CHAPTER NINE

Courtney looked around the enormous room as if they had won their very own dream home. Her backpack was slung over her shoulder and her jaw dropped. Zack had just escorted Blue and her younger sister to the west wing of the grand Romero Manor and into one of the rooms where they would take up temporary residence.

Romero Manor was a 22-bedroom luxury mansion that had its own sprawling acreage of land and parks in addition to the 16,000-square-foot winery and estate.

Each wing was basically a self-contained home of its own with its own massive granite-top kitchen, games room, in-home theatre, den and living area that was joined by an incredibly huge ballroom and grand foyer that rivaled Buckingham Palace.

It must have cost a fortune to build this place, Blue thought to herself with delight. How marvellous the design was. She felt as if she were in an art gallery rather than a home with its collection of superb paintings on cream-colored walls and the breathtaking views to the gardens and hills in the tall ceiling-to-floor windows that brought in ample sunlight during the day. It was like a North American castle. The vaulted ceilings had Italian-inspired moulding and beautiful paintings above. The ceiling seemed to go on forever.

The floors were marble, exquisite and expensive. A warm golden hue. Zack seemed so hot yet down-to-earth, approachable. As wealthy and affluent as he was, she would never think he was so approachable seeing that he lived like a crown prince.

Blue was enthralled by the whole place. Intimidated. Yet she tried to act more composed. She'd seen many places while working as a reporter. But none like this up close. It was more like a palace. Blue was sure she would get lost trying to find her way around. It was a good thing the estate was equipped with several kitchens and living areas in each quarter so it would be easy to stick to one area of the mansion.

"You really didn't have to do this, Zack," Blue turned to her boss, while Courtney delighted in walking in and out of the huge walk-in closets "wowing" and saying "awesome" and "cool" as she made her way around. Their suitcases were left in the room for them to sort themselves out later.

So this was how the other half lived.

"It's the least I can do until we get things sorted out," Zack said in a low tone, rubbing the stubble on his face. He appeared distracted as if he had the world on his shoulders. The least thing she wanted to do was to add to his troubles. Great. Blue was already becoming a burden to him and she'd only been on the job for a few weeks.

Well, on the plus side, perhaps she could dig into her research while she was there about the winery and estate and gather more background information. After all, she was now officially at work.

"Thank you, Zack. You have no idea what this means to me," Blue said, stepping outside the room and leaving Courtney to get unpacked. "But how long…how long can we stay here?" she said, her brow raised. It wasn't really a question. It was more like a statement. How long did he think he could really keep Blue and her sister living in this sheltered palace?

"As long as you need to be here, Blue." His voice was more curt. Rough. Did he really mean it? Goodness, it was difficult as hell to read this fascinating man. Perhaps that was all part of his allure. He didn't wear his emotions on his tailored sleeves.

"Well…I…thank you, again. I don't know how I will ever repay you," she said, almost breathless.

Zack's dark, sexy gaze caught hers and she thought her breath was stolen away. Her belly caved in with the massive butterflies flapping about inside her. Was he always this irresistible? She had to get hold of herself. Her life was in danger. That was the bottom line.

Her breathing shallowed. His cell phone vibrated in his pocket. Without taking his gaze off Blue, Zack reached into his pocket so smoothly and answered it with a deep, low "yes" to the person on the other end. Whoever it was.

"Good. Keep me posted," Zack said after a moment. He ended the call and replaced the phone in his pocket. He breathed deeply.

"Dinner will be ready at eight. Our chef is preparing seafood tonight. We'll be eating in the east wing. This will give you a chance to meet the rest of the family."

"Oh?" This caught Blue off guard. Family? Dinner? At eight? "I...I don't know what to say."

"You and your sister must be hungry. I'll leave you to change."

Blue realized that she was a guest in his home at the end of the day and she bit down on her lip, trying not to sound ungrateful. After all, this gorgeous businessman who probably had an incredibly full agenda made time for her and her sister on such short notice. He must have shifted plans for them. She was thankful to that at least.

And oh, God! Her stomach squeezed mercilessly. She could still see that blue SUV speeding up behind her and slamming into her bumper. She squeezed her eyes shut trying to block out the gut-wrenching feeling of virtually seeing her life flash before her eyes. If anything had happened to her, what in God's name would happen to Courtney? Her sister was eighteen and at the age of majority but in Blue's eyes, she was still a kid and that would make her an orphan with no family.

Blue snapped back to reality and tried to think positive and worry about the present time. At the moment she was not in any peril. That was what mattered, right? Worrying never solved anything. Most of the time the things one worried about almost never happened. Her father had told her that once, when she was in college.

* * *

Blue's heart hammered against her ribs. She thought she was going to pass out. It was a good thing Courtney was with her walking towards the dining area of the east wing. She was with Louise, the housekeeping staff member. She couldn't call her a maid exactly. She didn't seem as formal though she was dressed in a black flowing skirt and a white shirt wearing a silver necklace with a blue pendant.

"There's nothing to be nervous about. The Romeros are very friendly," Louise said to Blue as if she noticed her silence.

"This is really cool," Courtney said, gaping at the artwork in the corridor as they walked towards the main foyer. "I can't believe you guys live here like this. It's like royalty or something."

Louise laughed heartily. She was an older woman with a very round and friendly face. Her hair had turned silky silver and was tied back neatly in a bun. Blue was grateful to have her escort them to the dining area. She wondered why Zack hadn't suggested that they have something delivered to their rooms. It was more like a grand hotel than a mansion in any case.

As they neared the dining area, Blue could hear the chatter and laughter of a few members of the household. That was when her heart pounded harder and faster. Could she take much more anxiety? She was shy about meeting new faces in a social setting such as this. She'd been working for the past few weeks at the vineyard but went nowhere near the main house on the estate.

What if she didn't use the right forks? Start from the inside and work your way out, she'd read somewhere. Or was that her imagination? Shit! That was a scene from the movie Titanic. Molly Brown was instructing Jack Dawson on the proper way to eat dinner with the rich passengers on the first class deck of the ship.

Way to go, Blue. What if etiquette rules were upgraded since then?

She'd heard of the table setting etiquette of the rich but hadn't studied it in great detail, thinking she would never have to worry about having to dine with royalty or a head of state. Not that the Romeros were royals or heads of state.

They just lived like it.

It must be incredible to have such wealth and power as they had. She wondered how much it would cost to heat a massive entity like Romero Manor. She wondered what their monthly utility bill would set her back. Probably the amount of her annual income times ten thousand.

"Ah, Miss Monroe. Glad you could join us for dinner," Toni Romero's cheery voice greeted her as she and Courtney walked into the dining room.

"Th-thank you," Blue stuttered. She felt flustered and almost lost her ability to breathe. In. Out. In. Out. Well, look at this place, she thought to herself. It was a spacious room with dim lighting provided by the enormous crystal chandelier hanging in the center. An intricately-carved oak dining table was flanked by of rows of neat, matching tall-back chairs. Blue couldn't count the seats but she guessed it could very easily seat twenty people around the long table. What looked like expensive China plates were placed in front of each of the seats in addition to a tall empty glasses and rows of sparkling knives and forks.

Okay. She felt so out of her element here.

Was there a special occasion? Had she intruded on an already planned special family dinner?

"We often get together once a month to have a family dinner," Toni spoke up as if he could somehow read her mind. Not that it did much to ease her anxiety. "You happen to be here at a fortunate time, Blue." Toni continued, motioning Blue and Courtney to be seated.

She was glad there was another young lady who appeared to be Courtney's age. Blue had already been introduced to the Romero family on another occasion so she knew who most of the family members were.

But where was Zack?

Her stomach felt uneasy. She needed Zack to be there. She felt so comfortable around him. Protected. It was weird. Blue couldn't make sense of it. But Zack had that kind of effect on her. A connection. Though he could be distant at times, there was something about his aura and her being that just...clicked.

"Will Zack be here soon?" she asked politely.

Toni paused momentarily.

Blue felt as if she wished the ground could open up and swallow her whole. Did she ask the wrong question? Oh, God. Did she come off as desperate or attracted to Zack?

"He invited us to dinner with you, so I thought..." Blue clarified, trying to win over the moment again.

"Oh, nothing to worry about, dear. Zack had to attend to another matter but he should be joining us shortly," Toni said matter-of-factly. She thought she caught the elder Romero raising a brow to his wife, Shelly. What was that about? Oh, God. Blue hoped they didn't think anything was going on with her and Zack. God forbid. Not that she could ever really be with an out-of-her-league man like Zack.

"Oh, good," she said, trying to hide her relief.

"By the way, we're sorry to hear about what happened to you earlier this evening. How are you feeling, dear?" Toni asked with genuine concern.

"Oh, I'm okay. Just a little shaken. But no broken bones," she said softly, trying to put on a brave face.

"We're glad you're okay. I hope they catch that fool who did that."

Blue smiled appreciatively.

"Hi, I'm Melissa," the young woman at the table said to Courtney as she sat down beside her.

Shelly, Toni's wife, also greeted Courtney. "Courtney, this is my niece. She's staying with us for the summer. We have a program running for young college students."

"Oh, that sounds cool," Courtney chimed in. "I've heard about the Rom Res."

"The what?" Shelly said in unison with Blue.

"Oh, it's what it's called by a group of us. It's a nickname." Melissa playfully rolled her eyes. Courtney grinned. They both seemed to hit it off right away.

Inside, Blue was more than thankful her little sister had made a new friend. Just over an hour ago, Courtney was in such a distress when she found out that Blue was at the ER after the accident. Courtney finally calmed down when Blue had assured her she was safe and everything was okay. She didn't feel the need to get her worried about the other part of the story, so she omitted telling her that someone had tried to kill her.

She and her sister had been through hell and back after their parents' mysterious deaths in that fire. Even though arson was officially ruled out, Blue suspected it was suspicious nonetheless. She didn't get Courtney worked up but always trained her to be on her guard, keep in touch at all times and keep her cell phone turned on in case Blue had to reach her or vice versa.

At least now, she could keep a close eye on her. Courtney knew about the reputation of the Romero Resort or the Rom Res as the young kids were calling it these days. It was as secure as a National Defense camp. She would be fine and that gave Blue a lot of much needed reassurance.

"Yes," Blue grinned, as if she could read her sister's silent pleas. "You can stay at the Res for the rest of the summer as long as we keep in contact."

Courtney playfully rolled her eyes. "Yes, of course."

The mouth-watering aroma of the seafood dishes wafted by Blue's nostrils. Hmm. She realized after her dramatic day that she hadn't really had much to eat and she was famished.

It looked as if Zack would be having dinner with her tonight, after all, she mused trying to avoid grinning. She couldn't wait for his return.

The kitchen staff had soon brought in countless dishes while Blue and the rest of the family including Lucas and Maxine and Antonio and Lucy were engaged in light conversation. She also got a chance to meet Jules and Dion, Zack's other brothers. Troy, apparently, was out of town on a crucial business deal and couldn't make it back in time.

This was marvellous.

Blue loved the way the family lived no matter how busy they were in their daily endeavors and businesses they made time for each other. Especially their elderly grandfather. How admirable. Of course, it was noble that they had not forgotten where they came from. It was Toni who helped them with a boost to give them all a good start in life after learning of their existence. And of course, they hadn't forgotten. The only thing he'd asked of them, she had read once, was that they never forget the importance of family.

Without those you love around you, money and business equate to nothing. It was an empty existence. And if one was too busy for friends and family—then one was just too busy, she remembered a quote from one of the speeches he presented at the Annual Ball that she was sent to cover for Channel 31 News. Those were the days. She was an outsider looking into the world of the Romero family. Covering their every move, some of them. And now? She was amongst them. How strange life could be in throwing some unexpected curve balls.

Never burn your bridges, she'd learned early in life. It was a good thing she had gone out of her way to clear her name with them after that media scandal involving Lucas. Blue would have had enemies from this powerful family instead of being asked to do a documentary about them—and later, dining with them.

"Sorry, we're late," Zack walked into the dining room with his brother, Carl, looking exquisite. He had showered and changed into a crisp shirt and gray pants. He looked magnificent. This man would probably look hot washing dishes.

Washing.

Oh, the sexual thoughts that seeped into her mind as she thought of Zack's hot, muscular body naked with dripping water cascading off his slippery skin.

Blue blinked her eyes emphatically. Oh, no. She was not going there. She really needed to keep her whirling thoughts in control. Not the place. Not the time. Thank God it wasn't possible to read people's minds and vice versa. That was all she could think of. That was one thing she hoped they'd never discover: how to eavesdrop on people's private thoughts.

"You're just in time," Toni called out, his hands clasped in front of him. She caught Toni glancing at her and then to Zack. Blue wondered what that was about but decided to ignore it.

Blue had to keep from looking at Zack who happened to be seated across the table from her. She spoke at great length with Shelly who was beside her. Shelly was such a warm and friendly person. It shouldn't surprise her since she was a new addition to the Romero family herself and it couldn't have been easy marrying an older man with grandchildren almost her age. Blue was sure Shelly had experienced her share of family politics before being accepted into the inner circle.

Blue kept her gaze elsewhere in the room as they devoured their entrees. The sound of knives and forks scraping the plates along with the murmurs of various conversations around the table was welcome from her earlier turbulent moment on the road. She could not believe the family ate dinner like this. A few close friends were also seated around the table. Earlier they were served Caesar salad with fresh Parmesan and house made herb croutons. They finished the evening having been served various seafood dishes that started off with fresh scallops and vegetarian soup. They were also served roasted double ranch prime rib with marinated shrimp, opal basil and mint spring rolls.

Blue felt as if she'd eaten enough to last her the week. There was something soothing about seafood. She often thought of pasta and seafood as her favorite comfort foods. Right now, she could use all the comfort she could get.

"It's so nice, what you're doing," Shelly commented to Blue. "The documentary. We're all excited to see the finished product."

"Thank you. I'm truly grateful for the honor. I've always admired all the wonderful contributions you all have bestowed on the community and in your amazing products."

"Yes, well, excellence is our middle name. If we can't live up to it then we don't do it. Isn't that right, Zack?" Toni commented, turning from Blue to Zack.

"We do our best," Zack assured, a smooth grin curled the corner of his lips.

* * *

"Why can't I go now?"

"Because, Courtney, we just got here," Blue said later to her sister as they got ready for bed. "I'll be in the next room across the hall. Just shout if you need anything."

Courtney folded her arms across her chest. "I'm eighteen-years-old, Blue."

"Yes. That's right. So act responsibly."

"Melissa invited me. There's a few of the girls from my school who will be there. I spoke to Tiffany already. She's in my Bio class."

What was Blue afraid of? She knew at Court's age, she was able to hike across Europe for God's sake. Courtney was just going to the adjacent land next to the Romero Estate to be with the other kids her own age. It sure would be better than hanging out in a vacant wing of a lonely mansion with her older sister.

"You know something? I'm sorry, Courtney," Blue said, plopping herself on the bedside. "You're right. You're eighteen. And you are responsible. I know you are. Just…no drinking or anything okay?"

"You know I'm a teetotaller, right?"

She reached over and hugged her sister. "Enjoy yourself, sis. But not too much."

"Good. We're going camping tomorrow and then we're going to hit the amusement area. You're like the best sister ever with the hottest friends, eh?"

Blue playfully rolled her eyes. "I told you, Courtney, we're just going to stay here until my assignment is over. Then…" Then what? A painful lump settled in Blue's throat. Yes, then what? She sucked in a deep, lung-expanding breath. Yes, what was Blue's plan B? What would happen when Zack decided he no longer needed her around? What if he found out about her past…with the ex-Senator Aitkin?

CHAPTER TEN

Blue tossed and turned beneath the silky sheets on her bed in the guest room at Romero Manor. How could she possible sleep? Who could possibly sleep at a time like this? First, her job with Zack working under his direction for the documentary. And it had to be perfect, too. She still had a whole lot of filming and editing to do. Then...there was that crazy accident.

Somebody *was* following her. It wasn't her imagination, after all.

Her mind was tormented with a whirlwind of confusing thoughts. Her heart pounded like a bass drum inside her chest. She was breathing hard and fast. So hard it was almost painful to inhale and exhale. After gazing up at the magnificent star ceiling art that twinkled in the darkness of the room, the ceiling created the illusion of gazing up at the stars at night on a clear night. It was awe inspiring. Under normal circumstances she would be soothed. But not now.

Blue had one thing on her mind. A crushing, pressing thought.

Zack Romero.

Would she ever be able to break through his barrier and get close enough to him—again? Tonight at dinner, she felt ashamed for the arousal she felt seated across from him. The man was uber sexy in every sense of the word. He was breathtakingly stunning. Why in God's name was her mind so obsessed over this hot man?

She wished she could wipe him out of her mind. Right now she had to be thinking about doing a damn good job in putting together what must be an award-winning documentary on the Romero Winery and Estate for the National Wine Awards show. It was a prestigious industry award and he was selected to be featured. She couldn't afford to screw that up. Then she had to find out who the hell was trying to murder her.

How long could she keep under Zack Romero's protection? Really? Not forever. Then what would happen to her? What would happen to Courtney? Who wanted to run her off the road? Was it her imagination? Zack didn't want to impart too much information on the matter. He told her the police were on the case. He also mentioned he had some men on the case, too. Whatever that meant.

Blue propped herself up on the bed and drew in a deep breath.

"Right, that does it. I'm officially up." She glanced over at the digital display of the clock by her bedside. It read: 11:48 p.m.

She whipped off the sheets and got up out of bed. In the room, there was a sixty-inch flat-screen TV mounted on the wall and a remote control on the nightstand but she decided she couldn't bring herself to watch anything.

Blue was just...restless.

Zack Romero.

Why was he the only thing on her mind? She wondered obsessively what he could be doing. Was he in the west wing nearest her? Or was he in the east wing, or heck, the north or south wing. The mansion was a massive maze. She paced in the room, debating if she should go outside in the hallway or not.

"I need air."

Blue slipped on her flip-flops and fixed her hair in the mirror. She had worn her night t-shirt and matching pink pyjama bottoms. To the casual onlooker her attire could easily pass for summer wear but of course she purchased it in the nightwear department.

She quietly opened the door of her room and peered out into the long, lonely corridor. It appeared the entire residence was asleep. There wasn't a sound to be heard, except for that of her own breathing.

A chill slithered down her spine.

Why was she afraid? She was safe here. She would be okay. Everything would be okay, she kept consoling herself. It had to be.

*　*　*

Zack was a tormented soul. He didn't often fight. But right now he was wrestling with his emotions as he swam in the night-time-only-illuminated pool on the estate. With a vengeance he propelled his body through the water powerfully, making waves and splashes. Swiftly, he'd swam another few laps with ease.

It was almost midnight. But hey, going for a late night swim on a summer night wasn't all that unusual. Especially on his estate. Good thing they didn't have neighbors for miles. He loved the sensation of moving his body through the water. Currently, he had a lot of pent up energy to burn off.

His mind was still swimming with effects of tonight's wine and dinner with their guest, Blue Monroe. What a gal. She was hot. He'd seen beautiful women but she...was stunning. She had the type of skin deep beauty that elegantly shined. She wasn't only physically gorgeous but she had a heart of refined gold. And it was a good thing while he was sitting across from her that she could not see the effect she was having on him below his waistline during their meal. He just kept looking at those precious full, ripe lips of hers. They looked juicy enough for him to want to suck on. The memory of their sweet kiss made Zack hard like steel again.

There he went again. He was supposed to be in control of his libido for a full month. It had only been twenty-nine days. Like hell that was going to be easy. Why was he so obsessed with this woman all of a sudden? It was as if she'd bewitched him with her beautiful charm and demeanor.

The truth was, he had taken a lot of cold showers the past month. That was why he'd kept his distance from her and tried to focus on work at the other site while handing over duties to his deputy manager. He'd better stay the hell away from her until he could master his feelings. Instead of the other way around. What else was he to do?

One month without sex? Without a chance of seducing Blue? *Dios Mio.* He had almost gone crazy out of his mind during that time.

His grandfather was right. He needed to take control of his actions. But face it, beautiful women were his weakness. He was a breathing, healthy man. How could that be so unusual? Yeah, but men often thought with the wrong head. That's what got him into trouble in the first place, wasn't it?

Selina. Shit! He'd done some wicked and wild things with her in Vegas. And yeah, she wanted to film everything. He thought it was kinky as hell, but he loved the idea of capturing it all on video. What an idiotic thing to do. Was it the thrill? The danger he lived for? His old gramps was right, though. Stuff like that could only spell trouble. Now it could ruin his business. He never once thought that she'd betray him or want to expose herself like that. It was true he had met the wrong women in his life. And now that he saw great potential in finding "the one," she was unreachable. Off limits. How pathetic was that? Still, the Selina sex tape drama was still under surveillance. So far nothing had surfaced...yet.

Then Zack's mind drifted further back to the time when he was in high school. Before he'd met his wealthy grandfather. There was a girl he liked in school, Michlene. She was hot—though nowhere near Blue's dazzling appeal. He liked Michlene a lot. Hey, he was young, from a working class family and he liked to date. He had given his virginity to her. He thought she liked him. But then when things got rough with his old man and they ended up losing their home, it all went downhill from there. When the bailiff changed the lock on the door, they'd lost everything, including the clothes for school the next day. It was a disaster. But Zack still looked forward to making his way to class. He walked what seemed like a mile to get there but he just had to have a good friend. But word got out and she turned her back on him. Not only that, she'd taken someone else to the prom. "Mom says it's better that we don't see each other anymore," she had squirmed when she told him, outside his locker one day.

"Why?" he said, hurt in his voice.

"Well, we're not really compatible."

"Oh, I get it. Because my dad's broke? We're no longer compatible." It was one of the first times he remembered crying. Hey, he was a teen. The other kids were not exactly kind about it either. But after that heartbreak, Zack vowed never again was he going to get hung up over any girl. And he also vowed that he would have everything he needed.

Now, funny thing, women wanted to date him for what he had. They practically threw themselves at him. It wasn't just after they'd had the fortune of meeting their grandfather, but he'd busted his butt and worked hard in the family business and discovered a way to turn the unused land at the manor into a successful vineyard. His grandfather never handed them anything on a platter. He told them that earning things in life instead of being handed everything made people more appreciative.

Zack pushed himself from the side of the pool and dipped back into the water, his heart racing as he swam another lap. His mind drifted back on his meeting earlier with the family's press secretary, Pamela. "If you go further with the National Wine Awards, and this tape surfaces," Pamela advised earlier, "it could spell disaster. You would go down as a National Award Winner with a sex tape scandal."

He remembered he had winced at the thought. "On the other hand," Pamela had continued, "if you back out now and keep a low profile and the tape surfaces, no one would be interested. You'd be just another businessman with a tape that is public. And they would see it as a violation of privacy from a private individual."

"Yeah, but there isn't much privacy being a Romero, now, is there?" Zack fired back, annoyed. Not that he was world famous or anything. He was known around town. But the National Wine Awards was an internationally recognized, world renowned organization. The Oscars of the Wine Industry.

He saw her point. "No way in hell, am I going to back out and lay low because of fear of what might happen. We Romeros rule our fear, not the other way around."

"I got it," she replied to him. "I'm proud of you, Zack. For not cowering and turning tail. It was only a suggestion. But I'm glad you decided to stay in the game."

Zack could feel the coolness of the water bathing his skin, heat shot through his muscles as he worked his body in the water. It was as if he was competing. He had a whole lot of time to think.

Then his gut clenched at the thought of some creep trying to snuff out Blue. If he ever caught who was trying to do that...

Zack shifted his focus. He had to focus. What was he going to do about Blue and his feelings for her?

He had the documentary to finish and to ensure that Blue had full access to all the winery's facilities for the production and enough background information in their library. But he still hadn't sat down with her for a heart-to-heart profile to be filmed. A personal question and answer period where she would get to ask him everything about his life growing up and about what it meant to run one of the country's most elite family-owned wineries and vineyards.

When he was done with forty laps in the pool, Zack climbed out at the side and grabbed his towel to dry his face.

He paused when he saw the silhouette of a woman in the moonlit darkness wandering in the near distance. A curvaceous woman. Her wavy dark pair pinned up in a loose ponytail. She was petite in height. That walk. He could recognize the distinctive sway of each woman he'd ever met. He had that recognition gift.

Blue?

What in God's name was she doing up at this hour?

CHAPTER ELEVEN

Blue didn't know what got into her that night but she felt compelled to seek out the fresh summer night's air and inhale the aroma of the vinery that lingered in the atmosphere. She looked up at the dark night and captured the splendor of the tiny dots of white stars glowing against the backdrop of the sky. It was weird but she felt comforted being outside, under the canopy of the heavens. She was glad that she—and her sister, got a chance to get away from the city and stay in Mayberry Hill where she could finish her film project.

Just as Blue walked out to the pool area, her heart jumped.

Zack.

Zack had been swimming; he was sitting at the side of the pool, dripping wet. A towel slung over his shoulder.

Oh, my.

She hadn't really seen him semi-naked before—not in person, anyway. But he saw her. He got up and walked over to her.

The saltwater pool was illuminated by glowing nightlights, so Blue could see the crisp blueness of the water against the darkness of the night. Trees stood as sentinels around the patio. It looked more like a holiday resort than a private home pool. She loved the night illumination of pools. There was something calming, soothing, romantic about it. The Romeros lived very well.

"What are you doing up at this time?" he said in a low voice, slightly breathless after swimming laps she guessed.

Blue could see the ripped muscles on his moist chest, so sculpted and prominent. The excess water glistened on his smooth skin. She fought the urge to reach out and glide her fingers down his taut, sexy muscles to enjoy the silky feel of his smooth, wet skin. The guy was fit like an athlete and ripped like a medium-weight bodybuilder. His muscular body and biceps were to die for. Zack was perfect.

"I was…I…I couldn't sleep," she fumbled with her words. Her gaze dropped slightly to the growing bulge in his swimwear shorts. His dark, sexy hair was moist and sexily wet.

His well-built legs looked the athletic type, muscular and powerful. Holy crap! The man was built like a sex god.

There was a massive whirlpool hot tub adjacent by the pool that was activating a continuous flow of water. She found the gentle swishing of the water as romantic as the dim ambiance of the area.

She wondered how many women had Zack or his brothers taken here at night by the whirlpool or in the hot tub after a swim. She was never much into swimming since she often got "swimmer's ear."

Her heartbeat galloped harder and actually increased. She was ever conscious of breathing hard and a trembling desire slithered through her. She was glad it was dark enough that Zack could not see her aroused nipples through her nightshirt.

Now she was more intimidated seeing him like this.

"You couldn't sleep?" he echoed, his voice smooth and deliciously deep.

Blue's gaze kept surveying the sweetness of this man's powerful semi-naked body. "Sorry, I…I didn't mean to dis…turb you. I…I had no idea you'd be…"

Blue could not think. Her mind was drawing a sweet blank. The kind you get when you are completely enthralled with a gorgeous person. Zack. There was just something about a hot, muscular guy coming out of a swimming pool, dripping wet. Her eyes drank in the beauty of his chest and ripped muscles again, his nipples were hard and erect, as were hers.

He drew in a breath. "It's okay, Blue. Stop apologizing. It's not necessary." A boyish grin touched his lips. He motioned for her to sit by him on the patio chairs. He wrapped a towel around his waist and grabbed a pitcher of water. He offered her a glass.

"No, thank you. I'm good for now," she said, breathless. Her mind still reeling of the gorgeousness of her boss. Zack took a quick drink.

She noticed his gaze swept across her body and she felt more self-conscious. Why had she worn her nightshirt and PJs? She should have put on a robe.

So he wasn't completely annoyed that she'd interrupted his quiet time. He was probably de-stressing after a long day filled with never-ending drama. Most of it caused by her, she could not help but think.

The dark moonlit night air was warm and inviting. A beautiful summer night by the pool area. There was something calming about the water whooshing from the pool's whirlwind hot tub.

Blue sat in a plush patio chair with a high back separated from Zack only by a table.

"I'm going into the hot tub. I often do that after I swim. Do you mind?"

"Oh, no. Of course not." *Can I join you?*

There was something arousing about being neck deep in water with a sexy, well-built man. "Care to join me?" he asked, his voice low and silky.

She froze. What? In a hot tub? With Zack? Her body was screaming yes, go. But then her mind was racing with questions. Should she be naked in a hot tub? Topless? Bathing suit? Why surely he wouldn't want her to…?

"You can come in just as you are," he grinned, as if reading her mind. "Or you can grab your bathing suit."

"Um…well, you know what? I could do with a bit of unwinding." Blue breathed deeply, trying to calm her nerves. "I think the ER doc said water would be therapeutic to ease my muscles. You know how you get all jarred around when you're in an accident." But the truth was she wanted to be close to Zack. She wanted to reach out and hug and rub and squeeze him with all the appreciation in her body for all he'd done for her. He had practically saved her life earlier in more ways than one. Not only did he give her a way out, in her financial crisis, but he protected her and her sister from some lowlife who obviously wanted to harm her.

How could she possibly thank him enough for all he'd done?

"Yes, it would be excellent therapy," he said in a smooth voice, not taking his gaze from her.

A little while later, Blue returned to the pool area wearing her two-piece bathing suit underneath her robe. The swishing of the whirlpool moving the water around in the tub was relaxing as she leaned her head back. Zack seemed to have a lot on his mind. His eyes were closed at the moment and he had his head tilted back. She glanced up at the dark sky and the twinkling smattering of stars. The air was so crisp and clear out in the country. Blue relished it. It was a good thing that a man as busy as Zack had a soothing place to unwind and relax.

"I don't bite, Miss Monroe." Zack grinned, a boyish, cheeky grin. His sweet lips looked inviting to taste. Would she ever have the chance to kiss him again? "Since you started working here, you seem a lot more shy than when I remembered you reporting for Channel 31," he commented.

She could not help but feeling soft inside. He was delicious, appealing. His sexy male scent mixed with the non-chlorinated pool water was tempting her in every way. She could feel it. Magic.

"I…well, I guess looks can be deceiving," she surmised, her eyes drifting down on the bubbling water. My God. What if anyone saw them in the tub at this time of night? They could even assume they were…naked.

Zack tossed his head back and laughed. She loved the sound of his laugh; it was filled with heart and soul. There wasn't anything about this man Blue didn't like.

"Now, that I don't believe for one moment," he said, his arms were stretched out resting on the edge of the tub as he shifted to better enjoy the feel of the water.

"Well, we have to perform whenever we're in the…spotlight. You know, when the cameras are on."

"I see. And what about today?"

"Today?"

"Yes, when you are working behind the cameras. Were you performing then?"

She giggled at his sly humor. "No. I was not." Blue grinned.

His dark, sexy gaze captured and held hers. All she could do was feel her heart explode inside her chest, beating harder and faster. *Oh, kiss me.*

She thought about their earlier meeting during the wine tasting and how much she craved and desired to taste his sweetness on her lips. And how he finally satisfied her craving.

"What's on your mind, Miss Monroe?" Zack arched a brow, playfully.

"You."

A grin of satisfaction touched his lip. "Oh? I like a woman who is honest."

"What's on your mind?" she said in a low voice, breathless, wanting to be closer to him.

She could feel the electricity pulsing between them again. It was unstoppable. Captivating. Magical. They had some sort of chemical reaction she could not fully explain.

He showed her by lowering his head to hers and brushing his lips against hers. Her body shivered uncontrollably with erotic pleasure from his lips. Oh, she missed those lips of his. Hungrily, passionately they kissed and devoured each other's lips while the warm water splashed around them. The feel was so amazingly erotic.

She enjoyed the feel of his soft lips on hers, the heavy breathing.

"Oh, God," he moaned in a hoarse voice. "You have no idea what you do to me, Blue." He called her Blue. He addressed her by her first name.

She moaned in response as she arched her neck back to savor the moment of his wet, hard flesh caressing her.

She was well aware that hot tubs were divine for relaxation and stress relief and sexual touch was always better when extremely relaxed.

The water was like a lubricant and its warmth coupled with the bubbles from the jetstream multiplied her pleasure.

Zack really knew how to excite a woman. She'd never even been in a hot tub before, much less caressed inside one. But oh, the sensual experience.

Zack massaged her skin in circular motion sending currents of desire rushing through her, as he continued to nibble on her neck enjoying the feel of her flesh. Her body felt deeply relaxed and profoundly heightened. Her sex throbbed and pounded between her legs, her nipples were hard and peaked.

He was a skilled lover. He knew how to pleasure a woman passionately.

Blue read that a lot of men go for the nipples or the genitals right away during foreplay, which wasn't always the best way to satisfy a woman. But a man who really took his time and massaged and caressed his lover in other areas had it just right—there was something oddly arousing and calming about that, which heightened the senses even more before going deeper into the sexual experience. There was nothing more sensual than a complete erotic massage, leaving the g-spots and the erotic zones till later when they were ready and primed. The sensation she was feeling was delicious. Unbelievable.

Her body's response to his soft carnal touch was overwhelmingly sweet to her senses. His lips were magic and made her tremble inside with deep, unbridled desire.

"Oh, Blue," he said, kissing her slippery, sensitive skin down her arms and she wrapped her arm around his taut, moist flesh, sliding them up and down. The sensual feel of his warm, wet skin was delightful to her senses. "God, Blue. You're so damn beautiful. I worship your body," he moaned.

Take me now! She was screaming inside. Begging.

As the powerful jets in the tub circulated around them compounding the erotic sensation, the heat between them was explosive and had nothing to do with the warmth of the hot tub.

Zack reached his hand under the water and lifted up her leg. "Oh," she giggled with heightened delight.

Before she realized what he was doing, a wicked grin played on his sweet lips as he lifted her foot to his mouth and began sucking and licking her toe and trailing his soft tongue over her skin making her tingle with ecstasy.

"Oh," she screamed out in delight. She had never had that done to her before…until now. Oh, what had she been missing? She closed her eyes enjoying the incredible manipulation of his hot tongue on her toes one by one. "Oh, Zack, oh," she groaned with an overwhelming want.

Breathing hard and heavy, Zack repositioned himself, enjoying the pleasuring of her body and sucked on her skin going up her leg, massaging her sensuously, passionately. Still, he hadn't yet touched her nipples or her inner thigh, yet she was more aroused than she had ever been. She slid her hands over her breasts as he continued to please her.

"You're a very beautiful woman, Blue," he cooed breathing hard. "You deserve to be treated like a queen."

She moaned in response.

"You like that, don't you?" he continued as he moaned, a satisfied devilish grin on his lips. Blue leaned over to him in the water and held his head and kissed him hungrily while he kissed her. She could feel his manly arousal from underneath the water.

"I love that," she moaned, softly. "Oh, Zack."

And he groaned. "It's after midnight now. It's been thirty days."

"Thirty days?" she whispered, puzzled, while she continued to kiss his neck.

"Oh," he groaned, "Later. I'll…" he said between hungry passionate kisses, "…explain…later," Zack managed to say, hoarsely as he slid his hand under her bikini top back, unhooking her. He slid his soft hands over her mound of flesh massaging her at first and the sensation was incredible. Then, he leaned and he gave a quick flick of his tongue over her nipple and Blue shivered with delight. Breathing hard he ran his tongue over her round, hard nipple in a whirlwind figure eight. How did he do that? Blue cried out with ecstasy. He then covered her breast and sucked soft at first then hard while teasing her other nipple with his finger pads.

She was in deep, warm water in the whirlpool but she was sure that a lot of moisture was coming from between her legs from her own body. Zack reached down with his hand and slid her bikini panties off in the hot tub. Rubbing and massaging her back and sliding lower to her ass and caressing her. Her whole body was treated to a full erotic massage.

Oh, the moment has come. Would she live up to his expectations? Could she? Her body was on fire. Pulsating from her head to her tingling toes. Begging for Zack to take her to obscene heights. She wanted the expert playboy to be inside her, with her…forever.

He pulled back from her momentarily, capturing her gaze with his dark, sexy eyes. Blue shivered uncontrollably, panting, gasping and wanting more from him.

Zack gave her a knowing grin. "I want you to sit up here," he said in a low, silky voice as he cupped her behind and guided her to the edge of the hot tub.

Blue complied and propped herself up, her sex still throbbing hard and fast. As he remained partially in the water up to his waist, she was propped up on the edge, her legs in the warmth of the water, wrapped around him.

He gave her a devilish look before lowering his head between her legs. Blue sucked in a deep breath, her heart beating uncontrollably fast. "Oh," she cried out at the first brush of his lips over the sensitive wetness of her folds. The pleasurable sensation from the touch of Zack's sexy lips down between her legs was delightfully overwhelming. She squeezed her hands tightly on the edge of the hot tub as he wrapped his hands around her hips and sucked and kissed and teased her moist folds.

"Oh, Zack." she cried out, moving her hands to his wet hair and threading her fingers through his silky mane as he continued to hungrily kiss her between her legs, softly, passionately with delightful strokes in naughty places while his finger slid inside her thrusting back and forth at the same time until she came with a violent shudder. Blue screamed out. She kept trembling from the overwhelming pleasurable ecstasy.

"God! Oh, God!" she cried out, breathing hard and fast. Hungrily, she lowered her head to his as he lifted his head and they kissed with an unbridled passion.

"I love that," he groaned as he kissed her. "You came so beautifully, Blue," he said, hoarse with pleasure.

Zack repositioned himself up to her and savored her lips, tenderly kissing her. He guided her out of the water and covered her with a towel sitting by the side. His erection was hard and prominent. "Let's go inside there." He motioned towards the guest house.

Blue had almost forgotten that they were outside, as much as it was a naughty adventure. It was probably for the best.

Luckily there was a guest house near to the pool so they didn't have to go far to continue their prurient adventure.

Once inside, Zack unwrapped the towel from her seductively and she kissed him on his strong, hard chest, sucking his nipple before moving down on him.

"Oh, you're hungry, I see." He grinned playfully.

Blue could not wait. She wanted him inside her so badly. She wanted to pleasure him with her mouth just as he had given her the best orgasm she had ever experienced. His hardness was calling to her.

A wicked grin played on her lips. She didn't know how she'd become so playful, so naughty all of a sudden, but the mood was right. Blue felt comfortable with him. She felt cherished by him. He made her feel appreciated, precious. Priceless. She really wanted to do this.

She freed his erection from his swim trunks and oh, God. He was huge. She wrapped her fingers around his long, thick erection and knelt on the ground, licking her lips first. She wanted to do this right. She wanted to delight him as he had done for her.

"Oh," Zack groaned, closing his eyes, breathing hard as she slowly, like a delightful suction slid him inside her mouth, moving up and down his long, hard shaft. She enjoyed his moans of pleasure as she teased him with her tongue, swirling around and enjoying the splendid feel of him inside her. The more he moaned, the more Blue was turned on. She took him as much as she could while sliding her hand up and down his length.

"Oh, God, Blue," Zack continued to moan. Blue sucked harder and faster. "I'm going to come," he said, pressing his hands on her head motioning her to move but Blue wanted to continue until he released.

"You should stop now, Blue," he groaned, his voice hoarse.

Blue continued, enjoying making Zack crazy.

Zack's body throbbed and went into erotic spasms. He came hard, shuddering. His muscles tensed for a while then relaxed. His silky release covered Blue's voluptuous bosom. "You didn't have to, Blue," Zack said in a low voice, breathing hard.

A grin of delight on her lips, Blue whispered, "I wanted to."

Zack lifted her chin up and pressed his lips to her softness and kissed her sweetly, then hungrily. He could not get enough of her.

Thirty days of celibacy.

Zack could not wait to be inside Blue. All this pent up energy for the past month, his testosterone levels were probably off the charts. "I think I still have a condom in this joint," he moaned in delight as Blue continued to kiss him. He grinned, boyishly.

Perhaps it was good to wait all this time, getting to know Blue on a platonic level. He'd grown to appreciate and respect her more over the past month. He'd grown to cherish every living breathing moment in her presence. There was a connection to Blue he hadn't really experienced with another woman before. And Zack had been with a lot of women in his time. Blue was different. His soul resonated with her. He would never admit it, but the days when she was not at work or that he didn't see her, his thoughts would obsess over her and wonder if she was okay.

Blue Monroe, she didn't know it, yet, but she had him. She had his heart.

"You're trembling," he murmured to her, nibbling on her neck while they relaxed on the bed. Zack had better find that freaking condom ... or else. He had her underneath him while he lay on top of her kissing her, his right arm stretched out over by the side table, fishing in the side drawer for that condom packet. He was sure he had a couple in there. Though it was a guest house, it was often the cottage that Zack used often so most of his things were in there.

Blue was pressing sweet kisses on his neck. Zack grinned in delight.

"Did you find it?" she murmured into his neck.

"Oh, yeah," he groaned. She writhed beneath him, their naked bodies entwined with each other.

"Oh, good," she whispered hoarsely.

"No, I want to do this," she said, stopping him. She propped herself up on the bed, while he moved off her and she hurriedly ripped open the package while Zack watched her with delight, a devilish look on his face. She was so eager, she fumbled with the condom. He also figured she was nervous as hell. He slid his hand up her smooth skin on her arm and she trembled. "You okay?" he said in a low deep voice.

"Yes, I'm...very okay," Blue said, finally freeing the condom from the packaging. She lowered herself to him, eyeing him salaciously and licking her lips while she held his still hard erection in her hand and rolled out the condom, sliding it over his long shaft.

"Oh," Zack moaned in his throat. The more Blue touched him, the more aroused he became. He couldn't wait to have his throbbing manhood inside her.

She glided her hand over his smooth muscles on his chest and then wrapped her arms around his neck, lowering him down to her, while they pressed their lips together in sweet loving harmony.

"Take me, Zack," she purred into his ear, the warmth of her breath on his skin caused him to react.

Zack lowered his head to her breasts and sucked on her nipple, swirling his tongue over her hard tips, teasing them as she arched her back. He loved the feel of her skin.

"God, you're so beautiful, Blue," he moaned with pleasure, while he worshipped her body.

She wrapped her legs around his waist, while he repositioned himself over her, kissing her on her lips again, swirling his tongue inside her sweetness.

Blue writhed beneath him causing his senses to go into overload, the softness of the hairs on her mound touching his as they entwined, moving and grinding their hips together in delicious motion, he slid inside her, her walls tightening around him, so hard he thought he would explode.

He thrust himself inside her, back and forth, first slow and then faster and harder, as she cried out his name, digging her fingernails into his back. Her legs wrapped tighter around his waist and she had an incredible orgasm, exploding, trembling in delight. Soon after, Zack came incredibly hard. His whole body trembled and shuddered until they both collapsed into each other's arms.

Panting and breathing hard, he could hear their heartbeats in their chests, pounding against their ribcages.

The magic of the moment was phenomenal.

Zack had never felt this satisfied with a woman. What was this? Was Blue really the one for him? He was often told by experts, that a man could tell when he found that special woman.

Blue was different. He was already addicted to her sweetness, to her body, to her soul. He was addicted to Blue. *Good God!* Was he in love with her?

Blue lay on the bed, in a dream state. It was in the middle of the night. She was still feeling a bit sore from all that wonderful love making. Her body was on fire—in a good way. She was throbbing, feeling magnificent, her body tingled from her head to her toes. Zack was a master lover. There was a connection she felt to him, being so intimate. *My God, he'd seen every inch of my body. He pleasured every part of me.*

She reached over to his side of the bed but was stunned to see Zack wasn't there. He was sitting up in the dark on a chair by the window. The moonlight from outside the window illuminated his handsome, dark features. He looked as if he were deep in thought. He was gazing in her direction.

"Zack, wh-what's wrong?" she whispered, still hoarse.

"Why didn't you tell me?"

Blue propped herself up on the bed. "Tell you what?"

"That you were a virgin!"

CHAPTER TWELVE

"I...I was..."

"Please don't try to lie to me, Blue. I have enough experience to know these things."

Blue got herself up out of the bed and grabbed the top sheet to cover herself. She moved over by the window and sat on the windowpane bench by Zack's chair.

"Zack, I..."

"Blue, I would never had done those things with you tonight. Not for your first time. It's supposed to be special."

"It was special, Zack. Oh, my God!" Blue grabbed her hair on top of her head. "It was amazing!"

"I thought you had a serious boyfriend before me."

"He was...well, we just didn't go all the way. That was one of the problems. I wasn't ready yet," she said bitterly. She bit down on her lip. "I found out that the reason he was so patient was he was...with some of the other women at work."

"I'm very sorry to hear that, Blue. You deserve better. I'm glad you didn't...go all the way with him. A decent woman should only give her precious self to man who treats her well, loves her, respects her and honors her. Nothing less," Zack pressed, his tone serious, deliciously deep and commanding.

His words reverberated inside her. She hugged herself and tried to push the thought of Elliot out of her mind. She was with Zack now. Or was she? What exactly was Zack saying?

"What about you?" she asked, softly, looking out the window, trying to avoid his dark, sexy gaze. "Do you...honor and respect me?"

"More than you'll ever know," he said in a low, soft voice.

"That's good to know," she murmured.

"Real men are respectful. Real men treat women with the utmost respect they deserve. What few realize is that respect is always a two-way street. You want respect, you give respect. Yeah, I've made a few stupid mistakes in the past but I've always been upfront and open. No deception."

Blue smiled and nodded her head thoughtfully. The man was deep. She had a good feeling about him all this time and now she realized she was right.

"Come here," he said, stretching out his arm to her, a boyish grin on his lips. She walked over to him and sat on his knees. Feeling cozy, comfortable. A wide grin on her face now. "I've never been with a woman I respected more than you, Blue. You mean a lot to me."

"I do?"

"Why does that surprise you?" he murmured.

"I don't know, I just..." she shrugged her shoulders feeling shy.

"You're not shy now after what we've just...had together, are you?" Zack playfully cocked a brow, squeezing her gently around her waist. She felt tickled and giggled.

He seemed to be deep in thought about something for a moment as if making some sort of assessment in his mind. Then he spoke softly to her. "Don't ever do that again, Blue," he said, leaning to her, pressing a soft kiss on her neck that sent her pulse racing.

"Do what?" she whispered, arching her neck, enjoying the silky feel of his touch.

"Surround yourself with people who don't appreciate you," he said.

"Wh-why do you think, I..."

"You have in the past. I can tell. You should never doubt yourself again. Never doubt your inner beauty and power. You're a wonderful woman, Blue. You deserve the best. You're worth it, Blue. You deserve to be only around people who treasure your presence."

Not trash it, like Elliot, she finished for him in her mind.

It was true then, wasn't it? It really showed. All that time with Elliot belittling her subtly and making her feel inadequate any way he could possibly find, wore down on her emotions, on her self-esteem without even realizing. Why? Because she had been too busy trying to please others, trying to make others happy and figuring if she couldn't do that, something must be wrong with her. But it wasn't. Something wasn't wrong with her. Something was wrong with her relationships. But this was a new phase for her. Zack was right.

Blue always gave her best, she deserved better.

Moments later, Zack explained to her about his one month vow of celibacy. Blue didn't know what to think at first. She thought it was some sort of mind game. He had reassured her that it had nothing to do with her. But he did not go further into any details.

"That's remarkable," she commented.

"What's more remarkable is that fact that I've never been more attracted to anyone as you. Even all this time we were platonic."

"Will you try the celibacy thing again?" she queried, looking into his eyes, amused.

"Hell, no! What do I look like to you?"

Blue burst out laughing, tilting her head back. Zack was one heck of a guy. She was glad to be knowing him out of his professional realm. She'd grown to appreciate that Zack may be from an affluent family and have impressive connections given his name, but he was a real guy. A playful guy with a great soul and a genuine warmth that was more sexually gratifying than any thing she'd known.

They embraced each other, gazing out at the moon over the dark sky and the twilight of the stars against the waning night. It was a perfect. Summer. Night.

CHAPTER THIRTEEN

Two more weeks had gone by at Romero Estate and Blue had delighted in her time with Zack. They'd made sweet passionate love every night since then, and each time, he'd shown her new things about her body and her feelings. Zack was truly an oh, so sexy incredible lover. Their bodies truly connected in a fascinating way. Being intimate with Zack was a delicious soul-satisfying experience. Blue felt giddy with radiant joy, every day, as cliché as that sounded. There was something to be said about the gratifying hormones the body releases to the brain to boost one's spirit when in a healthy relationship with someone who cares deeply about you.

Could this be it?

Was there really a chance for her to meet the right guy? After Elliot, Blue doubted her ability to attract a good man in her life, one who respected her, cherished her, understood her and supported her. Zack seemed to offer all of that.

How lucky she was. So there was hope after all.

Zack and Blue continued to work closely with the film project. She interviewed him on several occasions when he wasn't nibbling on her neck or playing games with her. They got a remarkable amount accomplished way ahead of schedule.

To top things off, her sister, Courtney, seemed to be enjoying her time over at the Romero Resort with her new friends. Every day, Courtney would text her that things were cool and show share photo attachments of the two of them.

Blue also had a wonderful chance to sit down again with Toni.

"You are a good luck charm, my dear," Toni had told Blue, his wife sitting by his side.

"Thank you, Toni," she had said. "Thank you for believing in me and giving me a chance to work on the winery."

She couldn't understand at first why Toni was so interested in learning how she truly felt about Zack and her long-term plans relating to marriage but she tried to keep a cool head about it all and not jump to conclusions. She was feeling so good about herself and her life for the first time in her life since her parents died and since her nasty break-up with Elliot.

She just didn't want to jinx herself, God forbid.

* * *

"So?" Courtney teased Blue after she'd gone shopping for back-to-school clothes. Her sister agreed to let Blue take her to the mall in Toronto for lunch so they could have a special sister's day together. Normally, Courtney hung out with her friends and shopped with them. She was excited about going in to college. Blue was even more thrilled that not only was she able to pay for the entire year for her sister, including the cost of those extremely expensive text books, but she had more time now that her project was wrapping up.

"So what?" Blue looked at her sister, incredulous.

"You still haven't told me about you and Zack getting married," she grinned, picking at her chicken fried rice. They decided on Chinese food.

Blue sighed, trying to hide her smile. She playfully rolled her eyes. "Courtney, Zack and I are…seeing each other but we're sensible adults. We're not rushing into anything." Blue took in another mouthful of buttered shrimp, savouring the taste.

"Yeah, whatever." Courtney rolled her eyes. "I see the way you guys look at each other whenever you're together."

"You're not around us much."

"Hmm-mmm. I know. Melissa and I have been visiting the vineyard when you're not there to um...taste some of the grapes. We've heard the staff talk stuff."

"Like what?"

"Oh, nothing, just...nothing." Courtney gave a knowing grin and continued eating.

Gosh, was it that obvious?

Blue should be glad that Courtney was more relaxed now. After all, she was starting college soon and Blue wanted to see her sister safe.

"It's nice, anyway," Courtney continued with a full mouth.

"What's nice?"

"Seeing you...what's the word, happy for a change, sis. I like to see you happy. You deserve it."

Blue fought to keep her eyes from misting. She reached across the table and squeezed her sister's hand lovingly. Courtney squeezed her hand back. They'd been through hell and back since the death of their parents.

"I'm glad that both of us can be happy, Courtney."

Blue didn't know how long this would last with Zack, but for now, she was content.

CHAPTER FOURTEEN

"Channel 31 News, Elliot speaking."

"Hi," the sultry voice sounded on the other end. "I'm...My name is Selina and I was told I could reach this desk to provide...um...a scoop."

Elliot became attentive to the phone caller and peeled his eyes away from the screen of his laptop while he sat in his office. It wasn't all the time that he got "scoops" coming to his news desk since he'd been demoted to covering local community news.

"I'm listening. What type of scoop do you have, Selina, is it?"

"Yes. I can't talk over the phone. Can we meet in person?"

An hour later, Elliot was seated in his office opposite a voluptuous woman with streaked blond wavy hair and bright red lipstick. Her eyes were stunning. But Elliot detected a lot of pain in them. What the hell was this about?

"Well, I have some revealing information about a very prominent family and well, the tape is all yours for the right price."

Elliot leaned forward, bursting with curiosity. "What family?" Clearly, he didn't want anyone wasting his time or teasing him with probably fake information.

"An indecent night in a Vegas hotel room, should I say," the woman raised a brown, her lips pressed into a thin line.

The woman proceeded to tell Elliot about the contents of the tape.

She was jilted. Hurt. She was getting back at her ex.

"Wow," Elliot said, scratching his head. "You still haven't told me the person involved."

"Romero. Zack Romero."

Elliot felt his heart give out. His jaw fell open. "Zack Romero!"

He swallowed hard. His heart was thrashing against his rib cage. His mind flashed back to that night. That thuggish mob-like guy who barged into this apartment, warning him about troubling Blue.

Shit!

No way in hell was he going to touch this one with the proverbial ten-foot pole.

"Do yourself a favour, lady. Run the other way. And burn that tape."

"What?" Selina looked incredulous.

She looked the same way Elliot felt inside. What the hell was he doing? Throwing away a potentially huge story. The decent and well-respected Romero men always made headlines with their sexual escapades. But now? He had taped proof. This could go viral. But hell no! It just wasn't worth it. And if Blue really was seeing this guy—which he had no proof that was the case, she could get hurt as well. Not that he cared too much but deep down inside, he knew he'd really screwed up with Blue. He'd treated her like shit. He knew that now. If he could only make it up to her. She really didn't deserved to be hurt any more.

"Listen, what is it that you really want? You know you could get hurt just as much as he could with this...tape. Not everyone with a sex tape gets paid and lands a reality show and finds fame. It could backfire big time and cause permanent damage to your rep. Do you really want to do that?"

Selina bit her lip and looked out the window behind him.

"Listen, besides, our news shows don't really get into that kind of stuff. It's not like he's running for office or a married man or anything...um...Selina, right?"

"You have a bad memory for names," was all she said, before getting up. "Thanks for wasting my time."

She slammed the door behind her with such a force that it rattled the frame.

Elliot leaned back in his chair. He had no idea what just happened or how the hell she found him. Heck, for all Elliot knew, the Romeros could have set this up to catch him. Maybe it was a trap. Entrapment. Well, it didn't work, if that was the case.

He got back to his computer screen, downloading intriguing pics of women scantily dressed in sportswear bikinis. Heck, he was on break. He needed something to take his mind off his stress. Sometimes it was better to look at women and not get involved.

He just couldn't take that kind of trouble right now.

CHAPTER FIFTEEN

"I'm not to be disturbed, Venus," Zack said through the intercom.

"Sure thing, Zack," Venus's cheerful voice boomed through the speakers. "Oh, and just a reminder that I'll be going on break soon."

"Sure."

Zack sat in his office typing away at his notes on his laptop. He hated to be distracted when he was working on his notes for his upcoming agenda. He needed his full concentration. He was figuring out a new direction for his winery program and wanted to do a detailed proposal. There were some things he assigned to his assistants. But others he preferred to take matters into his own hands.

The doorknob turned and Zack looked up annoyed. Usually, Venus knocked first. Only it wasn't Venus.

Shit.

Selina.

"How did you get in here?" he said, his tone clipped. He rose to his feet, jaw clenched. The nerve of that woman.

"Relax, Zack," Selina said in a low voice. "They're doing a tour at the winery, remember. It's open to the public."

"Then you can leave the same way you came in."

"Zack, Zack, my baby, Zack." Selina smirked as she sashayed up to him. "I don't want things to be bad between us, Zack," Selina whispered in her throaty voice. This time it had no effect on Zack whatsoever. He was so over Selina. He was not addicted to her the way he was before. She used to have some sexual magic power over him but after being with Blue, nothing compared.

"Where's the tape, Selina?" Zack demanded in a cool voice, his hands shoved in the pockets of his pants, his chin tilted up.

Selina feigned innocence. "What tape?"

"Don't test my patience, Selina."

"Okay. I've had a change of heart."

"I didn't realize you had a heart."

"Ouch. Now that really hurt. Okay, so I deserve that, Zack. I'm here to offer a truce, Zack. I just...want to be friends with you. I promise you, I won't try to sell that magical time we had together in Vegas. That will be our little..." she murmured as she leaned over to him, her lips close to his but Zack was not responsive to her. "Secret," she finished her sentence.

Selina unhooked the shirt dress she was wearing and it dropped to the floor. My God! She was stark naked under there.

She wrapped her arms around Zack and slid her hands through his jacket, trying to wiggle it off. "It's over, Selina, please get don't do this to yourself. Get your clothes back on."

"What? No way. Mr. Playboy refusing this? What? Have you turned gay on me, Zack?"

"Do you think because a man is decent enough to not have sex with you at the drop of a hat, he's automatically gay? Please, you're embarrassing yourself." He tilted his head back and chuckled.

Selina was taken aback, fury flared in her eyes.

She hugged her hands around his neck and pulled him to her. "I know you want me. I don't care what you say." She forced a kiss on his lips.

"Oh, God," a voice cried out behind them. It was Blue.

"Oh, fuck, no!" Zack hollered, biting down on his lip. "Blue. It's not what it looks like."

"How could you....I...?" Blue's eyes were tearful, getting red.

Selina was clearly enjoying the little "misunderstanding." Oops!

"It's okay, honey. It was only sex, nothing more."

Blue stormed out and stumbled down the hall. Tears blinded her. Zack tried to reach out to her but Selina held him back. He literally picked up Selina and placed her over by the table to move her out of his way. Blue had managed to make her way to the driveway.

A pretty, scratch that, a gorgeous naked woman was in his office, kissing him. A note was on the reception desk outside his office that he was not to be disturbed. Shit! How the hell could Zack explain this all to Blue?

CHAPTER SIXTEEN

Blue pressed her foot on the gas pedal as she sped down the country road leading out of Mayberry Hill. Her heart was palpitating in her chest.

Oh, what a fool I was.

To think that Zack. To think Zack and I...

Who could blame him? He was just like all the rest. Liars. Cheats. But...what about all that talk? That felt so real. The way he made her feel was real. She should have listened to him but the pain was far too great. Did he think she was an idiot?

The horrible memories of Elliot came rushing to her mind.

Blue caught Elliot near the water cooler with his hand up Emily's dress, making out with her against the wall. "Oh, fuck, Blue. It's not what it looks like," were the words that flew out of Elliot's mouth and stabbed her like a knife to her heart.

So that was what men called it now? "Not what it looks like?" Well, it sure looked like she'd been taken in one too many times.

Just then a silver sedan drove up near her car. Was it Zack in one of his fancy cars? She couldn't tell the model or the make. The windows were tinted dark.

She felt her heart pound hard against her rib cage again. Something told her, it probably wasn't Zack.

This couldn't possibly be déjà vu.

Her car suddenly sputtered and the engine light came on. *Crap!* She was supposed to stop by the gas station to fill up the tank. She had planned to do so but had left her bag at the winery office and had returned earlier to grab it. That's when she decided to surprise Zack in his office. But, oh, the surprise was on her, wasn't it?

Her car slowed. It was grinding and tilted to the side.

Crap. She'd probably run over a nail in the road. She had a flat tire, too. *Great!*

One of the things she was going to do was get a new car. But her father purchased this old car for her. It held such sentimental value to her.

But that wasn't going to help her now. Blue hopped out of the driver's side door and went quickly to the trunk to grab the spare tire and jack. Her father had taught her how to change her own tire if she needed to do so if stranded out and about. She had the tools inside her trunk. But before she could reach into it, a man grabbed her from behind and covered her face with a cloth.

Blue passed out.

CHAPTER SEVENTEEN

Blue woke up, dazed. Where was she? Her head hurt like hangover hell. What the heck had she inhaled in that cloth? Well, she at least remembered that much.

She was in a hospital room.

"You okay?" Zack's soothing voice called to her. His hand was on her forehead gently stroking her head.

"Zack, what happened?" she groaned.

"It's okay; luckily we got to the scene in time."

"Who was that?"

"I guess you were right about that ex-Senator guy."

"What?"

"He was the one who had this all set up. He was trying to...hurt you." Zack's tone was serious, void of emotion. It chilled her to hear him speak in that voice. But he was visibly upset as much as she was.

Zack got up from the side of the bed. It looked as if he'd been there all night. It was three o'clock in the morning. She was at the county hospital.

"Why did you do that, Blue? You just ran off without letting me explain. And you could have gotten yourself hurt out there," he said, looking out the window at the darkness with the city lights. He heaved a sigh.

"Zack."

"Blue, I would kill myself before I hurt you like that, do you understand me? I used to be lady's man, but I would never have two women at the same time. Not all men are like that, Blue."

"Elliot was."

Zack swallowed. His Adam's apple bobbed in this throat. "I'm sorry about what happened between you and that idiot guy, Blue. I'm not an idiot. Romeros don't play that game. We're raised to have respect for our women."

"God, I know how it must have looked, Blue," Zack said in a low voice, leaning against the seat by the window. Zack explained the whole story about Selina and the videotaped recording.

"Oh, no. That's....terrible!" she said, digesting the details.

"I know. But it's over between us and it has been for a long time now. I just wanted her to get help."

"Do you think she's made copies? Do you think she'll ever?"

"She handed over the tape to me. I have to trust the universe that nothing stupid will show up somewhere online in the future. But in the meantime I don't live in the fear of what may never be. Worry never solves anything."

"I know." Blue grinned. She was happy to be okay with Zack again. She went crazy out of her mind thinking that they'd been torn apart. She needed him, craved him, desired him to be in her life, forever.

"Blue, I've never felt this way about anyone before in my life."

"I...I know."

"How do you really know?"

"Your grandfather shared quite a bit about you." She grinned sheepishly.

Zack responded with a smile. "Yeah, my old man is something, isn't he?"

"You mean, your old grandfather." Blue cocked a brow teasing him back.

"Seriously, though. You know a lot about me and I want to know everything there is about you. I need to know that there are no surprises, Blue. I love you, and quite frankly, I want to spend the rest of my life with you."

Blue sat up on the bed, her heart gushing. What had he just said? "You...you do?"

"I can't stop thinking about you, Blue. I don't think I can not have you in my life. We're meant to be together."

"I feel the same way about you, too, Zack. I love you so much," she said, leaning into his firm chest, feeling the warmth and positive energy from him rushing through her body. His currents racing through her.

"Now, why didn't you tell me about that former senator, Aitkin?"

Blue pulled her head away from him to look deep into his eyes. Tears stinging her eyes. "That he's a creep, a lowlife and a wife-cheater?"

"No," Zack said, leaning closer to her. "That he's your father."

CHAPTER EIGHTEEN

Blue covered her face with her hands. She recomposed herself and then got up.

"I...It's a long story, Zack."

"I have all night, Blue. If we're going to be together, I need to know everything. You believe he had something to do with killing your parents, right?"

"Well, no. I mean, yes." Blue drew in a deep breath. She was shaking. Zack motioned to hug her but she stopped him. "I'm fine."

She sat up on the chair and told him everything. Blue's mother worked for the senator and his family as a domestic. He then later seduced her mother. Her mother fell pregnant the same time as the senator's wife. Of course, this would have caused great scandal to the family and the senate.

So naturally, Blue's mother married the man who she grew up to know as her father. As far as Blue was concerned the parents who raised her were her real parents—her only true parents.

"So in other words, you had proof the man was a liar and a cheat," Zack clarified, a disgusted look on his face. "You *were* the proof. And he wanted to silence you."

She nodded solemnly. "My father, my adopted father who is Courtney's real dad, lost his job and he decided to blackmail the senator into supporting all of us since he was my biological dad. You see, only Dad knew the real secret. He'd met and married my mom when she was already two months pregnant with me."

"I see."

"I think he planned to get rid of all of us to cover his tracks but he couldn't do it himself, so he got others to try to do the dirty work."

"Well, you will no longer have to worry about him."

"W-why?"

"He was questioned by police last night. They got a confession out of the thug who tried to kidnap you."

"Oh." Blue felt as if she would faint.

"Don't worry about your family name. My men are on the case. The senator doesn't want any more embarrassment than you do. And your mother's—your parents' good name will be protected. We're seeing to it that nothing gets out in the news. I think he's going to accept a plea bargain on this count. Apparently, leading a double life wasn't his only pastime."

"I see."

"Listen," Zack's voice changed, "we're not going to let anything bother us tonight, right? Let's have a good night sleep in..." Zack looked around at the modest size hospital room.

"You don't have to sleep here, Zack. The bed is like a cot to you." Blue was ever so aware of his six-foot-four frame.

"Baby, as long as we're together, I don't care where we sleep." He nuzzled her on the forehead sending shivers of pleasure down her spine. Oh, she loved to feel Zack against her skin.

She really felt his magic, his warmth, his genuine affection and that was all she needed to get by in life. That was all she needed, period.

In the morning when she woke up, Zack was by her side. She kissed him on the lips as he lay in a dream-state sleep. She giggled at how wonderfully innocent he looked bundled close beside her on the bed. She managed to get off the bed without disturbing him and went into the bathroom. Her eyes widened in shock when she looked at her left hand. Oh. My. God.

How did that get there?

She looked over at Zack who was, probably, pretending to sleep. A grin curled his soft, sexy lips. She tilted her head back and laughed.

"Yes."

He opened his eyes without effort. "I just wanted to surprised you, baby. I'm glad it fits. Do you know how hard it was to get your finger size without you knowing?" Zack cocked a brow.

On her ring finger, during her sleep, Zack probably took his time and placed a beautiful diamond engagement ring on her. The largest, sparkling one she'd ever seen.

"Will you marry, Blue?"

"Oh, my God, are you kidding?" Blue could hardly breathe. She was nodding and tears of delight gushed down her face. "Yes. Yes. Yes." She reached over and grabbed Zack's neck and hugged him to her.

"Yes. I will marry you, Zack."

EPILOGUE

"And this year's honor for the National Wine Awards goes to..." the announcer at the gala event lifted the trophy in her hand. "Zack Romero, president and CEO of Romero Winery and Vineyard."

A round of applause erupted from the packed-to-capacity auditorium at the Trade Center as hundreds of press cameras clicked away. All eyes were fixed on the stage.

Zack was reluctant at first to go to the stage by himself. He said earlier it was a team effort and he wanted Blue by his side for capturing the greatness of the vineyard's legend and the rest of his team for making it all work.

"Wow! Well, here's the thing. I'm not a man who relishes in giving speeches. But today I will make the exception."

Laughter rang from the audience.

"On a serious note, I would like to thank each and every one of you here for this. For making this happen. Just like growing grapes in a vineyard takes a nurturing hand and caring and passion, so does cultivating healthy relationships in our business and in...our lives. And it's all about growth. It's all about not just letting things sit. Everything takes time, care and tending to..." Zack's eyes captured Blue's in the audience. "And just like the time it takes to sow viable seeds that may one day blossom into delightful treasures, anything that you work long and hard for is well worth the wait and worth the effort."

Zack went on to talk about the programs they have in the community to help support other companies. Saying was what set them apart from the others. Caring and sharing go hand in hand. That was how his grandfather raised them and that was what he shared with his team. "Because that, my friends, is true success, giving your best, being your best and sharing...only your best."

A huge round of applause filled the room, once again, and this time the audience stood up in recognition of this year's honorary winner of the National Winery Awards.

It was a truly blessed evening. While at the Romero Estate, prior to the awards, the Romeros, once again, celebrated Zack and Blue's engagement. Carl, Troy, Dion, Alonso and Jules, of course, reiterating that they doubted very much they'd join Lucas, Antonio and Zack in holy matrimony. Toni teased them and said, "Don't count on that, my boys. Don't count on being a true bachelor for too long." He winked knowingly.

Moments earlier they viewed the beautiful documentary of the Vineyard and Winery produced by Blue Monroe and her team. She'd won an award earlier for her work that caught her by surprise. She didn't know it would also be featured in the awards section.

Around the white table-clothed table, guests of honor seated were Jules, Alonso, Carl, Toni, Troy, Shelly, Antonio and Lucy, Lucas and Maxine, who was about to deliver. All dressed to impress in their black tie affair suits. Blue wore a shimmering gown that accentuated her curves. A floor-length flowing ball gown. Zack looked dressed to kill in his tailored tux. The man oozed sexual power, no matter what he had on. Over three thousand affluent guests filled the hall.

Blue noticed Carl glancing over at Venus, the vineyard's receptionist, once every so often. Toni noticed it too, she thought. It was obvious Carl had some feelings for Venus. Blue felt giddy inside for Venus. If anyone deserved love, it was Venus.

She was happy with Zack and she wanted everyone to find someone.

Later, after an exquisite dinner and meal, the ballroom was open for an after-ceremony dance. Blue went into the restroom to powder her face. She could not wait until tonight to have Zack all to herself again. He'd been all worked up about this show because he wanted to announce his new program to honor hard-working, upcoming winery entrepreneurs, too. It would all fall under the umbrella of his company.

Venus was on her cell phone and looked distraught.

"Are you okay?" Blue asked, trying not to pry.

"Oh, I'm fine, thanks," she said, ending her call. "It's never easy when you're all by yourself and doing it all, you know. Sometimes, I wish I had a...partner."

"You've been crying," Blue assessed, her voice comforting.

"Oh, no. I'm just...I have to leave. Tristan is having trouble with the new babysitter. Finding a good caregiver is hard."

"I know. You've always said you wished you were able to afford private daycare. Hopefully, things will work out for you. I hope you do meet the right-"

"Oh, no. Let's not even talk about that," Venus dismissed. "I...I could never get married or settle down. I wish I could but-"

"Never? Why? Are you still...married to Tristan's father?"

"Oh, no. I'm not married. Never was. I'm just saying, oh, Blue. You and Zack look so happy together. Just be glad you are both free to love each other."

"What do you mean by that, Venus? Aren't you free to...be with anyone?"

"No. Blue, I can't really talk about my...past but...I'm just thankful to have a job. But unlike you, my life is...well, I could never get close to any man. I mean, I could but...well, between you and me, it's better that I don't. Anyway, congratulations on the beautiful film and I'm so happy for you and Zack. He's a good guy."

"Thank you," Blue said, softly.

Blue was still puzzled by Venus's anxious behavior and her earlier statement. Venus was such a kind woman, hardworking, single-parent who seemed to love her son so much. And Venus came to Blue's rescue one too many times while Blue was trying to figure her way around getting the right information for the vineyard in the documentary. She couldn't have done it without Venus's dedication and hard work. They'd even shared countless lunches together and became friends. Yet, Venus was always secretive about her background and her home life.

What could have possibly happened in Venus's past that would make her feel she could never be loved?

* * *

*** BONUS SHORT NOVELLA *** (featuring Zack and Blue's Island Wedding!)

THE BILLIONAIRE'S ISLAND ROMANCE (THE ROMERO BROTHERS, BOOK 3.5)

A romance, hotter than the island sun...

Coming from one of the world's wealthiest and most influential families, the Romeros, Christian Romero knows better than to turn down an invitation to a mega family reunion in Jamaica for his cousin's wedding. The family is gathering at the exclusive Duponte Hotel & Resort in Montego Bay for the highly anticipated nuptials of former playboy billionaire Zack Romero and ex-reporter Blue Monroe. Christian's ex-girlfriend, Arianna Duponte, who walked out on him over a month ago just when things were getting hot, happens to be the general manager of the five-star palace resort where the family is gathering. No woman has ever turned him down before. Yet, sweet Arianna wasn't just any woman. She'd given him her virginity and he'd given her his heart. So what went wrong? Will this be a bitter reunion or a better opportunity to find out if there are truly second chances?

Arianna Duponte has always had a special place in her heart for sexy, hot Christian Romero, her first true love, but getting close to him would be too risky given her past and a scandalous family secret. She refuses to break his heart again. She tries to keep her distance while preparing for the big Romero wedding but it's not as easy as it looks. As the wedding bells echo in the sultry island air, will they rekindle the union they once had?

CHAPTER ONE

"Oh, the dress is gorgeous, Blue." Arianna Duponte beamed at her friend Blue Monroe as she held up the white satin and lace gown to marvel at its intricate details. The bright Jamaican island sunlight burst in through the window of the fourth floor bridal suite at Duponte Hotel & Resort in Montego Bay. The water splashing from the pool outside, laughter of guests, and the live reggae band playing Bob Marley's "One Love" could be heard from the open patio door.

"You really think so?" Blue cocked a brow.

"Um, *yeah*," Arianna grinned. "Oh, don't be so nervous, girl. Really. It's fine."

"Thanks, Ari. I totally trust your opinion. And thanks to Venus here for helping me pick out the design." Blue carefully took the dress from her friend and placed it back inside the lace garment bag. She appeared giddy, like a schoolgirl in love. "In seven days, I'm going to be Mrs. Zack Romero," Blue gushed, looking dazed as she sucked in a deep breath.

"Hey, that's what friends are for," Venus chimed in.

"So, are you getting the wedding fever, too?" Arianna turned to Venus.

Venus's smile evaporated. "Um. No," she said quietly. "I...I won't be getting married."

"Never? You sound so final," Arianna said with concern.

"Oh, I'm very happy for Blue but...I..." Venus closed her eyes then opened them again and drew in a deep breath.

Arianna felt terrible for bringing it up. She sensed the topic was painful for Venus.

Venus appeared as if she was trying to lighten the mood. She playfully wrinkled her nose and shook her head. "I don't think I would make the best wife. Besides, my little guy is my world. I just want to raise him the best I can."

"Of course," Blue added.

"By the way, thank you so much for the special daycare program," Venus said to Arianna. "At least I know my son is safe and happy with the other children while I help out with the wedding."

"Oh, no worries," Arianna replied. "That's one of the perks for visitors here. Childcare is free for children of our guests."

"Thank you." Venus glanced down at her watch. "Oh, no. I'd better get my son. Tristan likes me to give him his asthma medication. It was nice meeting you, Arianna."

"Likewise," Arianna said, still looking confused about Venus's previous reaction.

Venus left the hotel suite after she gave Blue a bear hug.

"She's wonderful," Blue commented after Venus left. "She's been working for the Romeros for a while now and she's the sweetest person I know."

"She seems nice."

"Anyway, I'm glad I hit it off with Zack. Being with him and being a part of his family has changed my life, Ari."

Arianna smiled then briefly turned her gaze towards the wonderful view of the glistening bluish-green sea outside the window. The aquamarine water had sparkling diamonds of white dots entwined in its waves from the bright reflection of the sun. The splendid white-crested waves rolled along the sandy beach swirling and crashing into the coast. The Duponte Resort had one of the best beachfront locations in Montego Bay. It was an intimate, five-star hotel and resort property that boasted several massive pools, pool bars, party rooms, snorkelling adventures, tours around Jamaica and ample poolside entertainment. Not to mention the breathtaking view of the green hills, a golf course and a tennis court for guests.

"You can't go wrong with the Romero family, Blue. They're amazing," Arianna murmured, swallowing a painful lump that just climbed in her throat. She then turned to face her friend. Her smile was heartfelt. Arianna knew Blue hadn't had much luck in the past with men. She was glad she'd found someone truly worthy of her heart. She'd heard about how well Zack Romero treated her. If anyone deserved a good man it was Blue.

"Thanks, Arianna." Blue blushed. "I know that. I feel so lucky to have met Zack. Just goes to show that you can't trust rumors."

"Rumors?"

"Oh, some old stuff. I've covered so many events the Romeros held over the past few years when I worked for Channel 31 News, but getting to know them up front was so...different. Special. To be quite honest I hated seeing those online tabloid headlines about his love life and his too-many-to-count girlfriends. Zack is so...romantic. So good to me. He's so...real."

"The Romeros are," Arianna agreed. "They all are," she continued in a low voice.

"I guess you should know." Blue arched a brow playfully.

Was Blue fishing for more information? Arianna drew in a deep breath. Her heart was beating fast and hard again. So hard it burned her chest. "Listen, Blue, I'm not gonna go there again. It's over between Christian and me. End of story. Okay?"

"Okay. It's just that...well, you were so happy when you guys were together. Are you sure you can't work things out?"

"No. I mean, yes. I'm sure."

"Ari, look at me. I'm your girl, remember? You and me go way back. Back to high school. Come on. It's me you're talking to here. What really happened?"

"Nothing. Nothing, Blue. I... Never mind."

"Oh, no. It's not about...your parents, is it?"

"No."

"Why don't you tell him what's up with your mom and dad? I'm sure he'll understand, Arianna. Don't do this to yourself."

"Blue, I know you care about me and I appreciate it. Really, I do but...I think it's best I just stick to my plan and stay a bachelorette. Maybe I'll go visit a sperm bank when I'm ready to have kids."

"Ari!"

"No, seriously, Blue. He wouldn't understand."

"Why don't you try him, Ari? I've interviewed him before. I've gotten a chance to know Christian. I've done a lot of research on most of the Romeros. He's a good man. He really is. And he is so in love with you. I see the way he looks at you whenever you guys are...or I should say, were together."

Arianna's heart sank to the floor. Blue was probably right but she just couldn't handle any kind of rejection. No. He would surely reject her if he found out about her family history. What was worse, she could end up losing everything. Everything! It was a risk she just wasn't willing to take. Not now. No way in hell. But what really crushed her spirit was not being able to have sweet, sexy Christian Romero in her life again. He was...her first love.

He was the first guy she'd really trusted to go all the way with. He'd been so gentle and loving with her. Respectful. He treated her like a treasured queen. She could still feel the silky touch of his warm skin on hers, running her fingers down his smooth, muscular body. The heat of his passion left her begging for more. He pleasured and pleased every inch of her body with his lips, his soft touch and his caresses. She'd never experienced such an erotic avalanche of emotions before meeting him. He was and would always be her one true love.

Yet, sadly, she could never have him again—except in a locked chamber that held her memory of their time together.

"Really, Ari. How long can you really keep this up?"

"As long as I need to, Blue. It's called survival. I can't handle...I mean, I can't...do this. It could destroy my family."

"I understand your fear of losing your family," Blue empathized, her eyes now downcast.

Arianna wanted to curse herself. "I'm sorry, Blue. I know you've had it rough. Oh, God!"

"It's okay, Ari. I've come to terms with things. My mom and dad are no longer around. And I've come to accept it."

"Did you find out about what really happened in that fire? Was it arson or accident?"

"Well, the report said accident and you know what? It doesn't make sense to stress over it. It's not like it would bring them back. In fact, it may bring me closer to them if I stress over it too much, if you know what I mean. Stress can kill!"

"Blue?" Arianna grinned in spite of herself. "Well, it's good to see that you have a good, strong mentality over the whole thing. How's Courtney?"

"Well, you know my little sis. Happy as hell."

Arianna smiled.

"She's just as thrilled as I am, Arianna. They've absorbed her right into their family, too. The Romeros are so amazing and wonderful. They're a close-knit, strong family. Everybody looks out for each other, you know?"

"I know."

"I thank the universe every day that I've come to know them. My God! I lost my family and it's as if I was given a new one—not that anyone could ever replace my mom and dad, but having this love, this void filled by these wonderful people is like...wow, amazing."

Arianna laughed.

"What's funny?" Blue asked, hand on hip.

"Toni Romero. I bet you he's still the same Toni, huh?"

Blue laughed, too. "Oh, God. The family wouldn't be the same without Granddad Romero. I love Toni. He lays it on the line, says whatever is on his mind. And I mean anything. He tells it like he means it."

"I know. But what that man has done for those boys, Zack and his brothers, is amazing. Imagine, he didn't know they existed and then all of a sudden in their teens, he took them in at the right time when they lost everything. Wow. It gives me goose bumps every time I hear the story. Rags to riches. Living out of their dad's car, their mother died mysteriously, the authorities were after them. Then a door opened. And they've worked hard and each came into their own."

"I know. They never forget where they come from. And Toni made sure they each earned his own way in life. God, they're good. Alonso is a successful doctor. Do you know he's opened up some free health clinics in Haiti?"

"Yeah, I read that somewhere."

"And Lucas has his Healthy Start Software program that really took off."

"And Zack, wow, he's really done well for himself and what he's done by creating a program through his winery to boost the careers of thousands of entrepreneurs. I heard he's created more jobs than any other single family-owned business. Is that cool or what? Girl, you should be really proud of your man."

"I am. I just..."

"What?"

"I'm just nervous, Ari. Every time things seem to be going great, something happens."

"Stop that, Blue. What could possibly happen? You're getting married in seven days."

"I know. I just hope nothing steps in to mess it up. I hope Zack doesn't change his mind."

"Blue? Talk about a bad case of pre-wedding jitters. Oh…" Arianna finally realized the source of Blue's jitters. "Those damn articles. I hope you're not reading any of that garbage online about Zack and publicity stunts and sex tapes?"

"No. I'm not…well, I happened to be checking my email once and it popped up on the trending stories but other than that, no."

"Listen, Blue. Whenever miserable people see a good thing going they always take some perverse pleasure in picking it apart and tearing it down. Why can't naysayers leave well alone? Don't read any more of that junk online. It's all tabloid stuff and probably bitter ex-girlfriends who are jealous that you're the one he's walking down the aisle with. And trust me, if I have to drag you two together down the lobby to the gazebo, I'm doing it." Arianna pressed her hands on her hips and gave a mock scowl.

Blue laughed. "Oh, Ari! What would I do without you, girl? You really are a true friend."

"Come on. I'll let you get ready since you just arrived. Then we'll head over to the pool bar. We'll cool off there and take in the sun and water."

A knock sounded on the door.

"Don't worry, Blue," Arianna said after she hugged her friend. "I'll get it on my way out." Then she walked towards the door. When she opened it, kaboom went her heart.

A sinfully gorgeous, tall, dark and deliciously handsome man stood before her. Her eyes caught his dark, sexy gaze, a heated look stole her breath away. There, standing in the doorway, was none other than Christian Romero.

CHAPTER TWO

"Christian," Arianna gasped, almost breathless, too breathless for her liking. The tension increased inside her body as inner torment whirled inside her mind.

Christian. Her heart rate immediately escalated inside her chest, beating hard and pounding fierce. The man always had that effect on her whenever she was near him. It never failed. Adrenaline coursed through her veins. What was Christian doing here?

She had anticipated meeting him sometime during his stay on the island, but not right this minute, so soon. She simply wasn't prepared to see him…now. Emotionally, she didn't know how she would react to him again after their last face-to-face meeting which didn't go all too well.

Things were going fabulously during the time they were dating, so Ari thought. She'd been flying back and forth from Jamaica to New York every other week since she'd taken over more responsibility at the hotel as her father went through a bout of depression. Christian teased her that it was almost like dating a flight attendant. Always on the go! Of course, being from a prominent and wealthy family like the Romeros who were spread out all over North America, travelling on a private plane or commercial jet-first class was not a problem. They'd spent plenty of passionate times together and spoke every day without fail. Her parents had taken over the Duponte Hotel after her grandfather, the founder, died when Arianna was only twelve. The hotel was everything to her parents. Everything. Over the years, they'd fixed it up and turned it around into a world-class hot spot for tourists heading to the Jamaican west coast for an unforgettable vacation.

Being in real estate, Christian and she had so much in common. He'd given her so many tips and valuable advice and even put her in touch with some crucial contacts to help her and her parents renovate the hotel.

Then he'd introduced her to his family when she flew back to Buffalo, New York. Oh, they loved her but she could tell they had standards. Standards that she knew too well, she couldn't meet. They were family-oriented, hardworking, successful people who seemed so together. She wasn't able to reciprocate by introducing Christian to her family. She felt deep down inside that she just wouldn't be…good enough. If they'd learned about her family background, it would cause great embarrassment. He would have left her anyway. She just couldn't risk it. Arianna was hoping that he would have just pretended they'd never met. Lord knew, she tried, but her efforts failed miserably. How could she ever forget the magical touch of his firm, soft skin on hers? The way he made her body climb to escalating levels of mad love-making hormones? The way he treasured her like a goddess? Yet, she knew he could never stay with someone of *her* background.

"Arianna," Christian said, his voice low, deep and captivating. "You're looking well." His dark, sexy brown eyes held her for a moment and she shivered with delight. The Romero effect. Christian was a Romero. Those men had a reputation for being uber sexy and having that sort of captivating effect on their women—heck, on all women. You just couldn't meet one and not fall under the influence of their charm, their aura! Yes, that aura. That's what it was that held her every single time.

Still, Arianna hadn't seen him in over a month, yet there he stood in all his gorgeousness with his buffed body and broad shoulders. The man was fit and had a radiant glow. He towered over her at six foot four inches. His voice was silky deep, rich and his handsome facial features looked robust with a healthy tan. He was wearing a polo shirt, white and crisp that only further accentuated his sensual and beautiful skin. His Ray-Ban sunglasses were propped up on the top of his head of dark, silky, short-cropped hair. He looked toned from head to toe. No doubt, Christian worked out five times a week at the gym for as long as she'd known him. His hands were shoved inside the pockets of his brown khaki shorts that gave him a trendy, relaxed look.

And his lips, perfectly shaped. So kissable. Oh, the hours of pleasure he'd given her with those lips of his. *Oh, God! Christian. I've missed you so much.* Her eyes drank in his handsome face and content gaze that held hers. She could see hurt in those beauteous dark eyes of his.

"Good to see you again," his smooth voice was even. His face unsmiling. "I was told I could find you here."

"Um," she murmured, swallowing hard. She'd just lost her train of thought. Damn it! She was the GM of the hotel. She couldn't afford a train of thought derailment. Ever! "Oh, I thought maybe, you were here to see Blue."

On cue, Blue made her way over to the door. "Hi, Christian!" Blue chimed in. "You guys just arrived?"

"Yeah, we just got in about an hour ago. The rest of the gang's coming in tonight. You're looking well, Blue. Congratulations, again. Being a bride-to-be suits you." His voice beamed a bit brighter when addressing Blue. His smile seemed to warm up to Blue. But of course, he didn't have anything against Blue now, did he?

Blue smiled. "Thank you." Blue then looked from Christian to Arianna. Tension appeared on her face.

"Um, listen. I was just leaving Blue's room, maybe we can talk out here," Arianna murmured.

"Oh, don't worry. I'll be fine," Blue interjected. "Listen, Arianna, my sister Courtney will be here soon. I'll head over to the pool bar with her. I can catch up with you another time."

Another time?

Arianna paused briefly. Blue was giving her a way out of their planned get-together. Did Blue think Arianna needed to be excused so she could speak with Christian? She'd rather sit and chat with her bride-to-be girlfriend, than have to deal with Christian right now. Lord knew, Arianna's emotions were all over the place where Christian was concerned.

"Sure, that will be fine. We'll catch up later," Arianna said quietly and gave Blue a quick hug.

"So, how have you been, Arianna?" Christian queried in a deep, emotionless voice, as he walked down the corridor with her. His hands were still placed in the pockets of his khaki shorts. Her steps were quiet beside his. She wore soft sandals on the job, knowing that she would often find herself running from one end of the hotel to the next every five minutes. Though she practically owned the Duponte Resort, along with her father, the family members took an active role in the day-to-day management making sure operations ran smoothly.

"I've been..." *Missing you, like crazy, Christian.* "Fine, thank you. And you? You look well," she commented, her heartbeat still pounding in her throat. Her chest felt light. When were they going to cut the casual chitchat and get to the heart of why he really wanted to see her? At this moment?

"More screwed up than you can imagine, Arianna." Christian's tone was flat.

Arianna froze. Now that wasn't what she was expecting to hear from Mr. Christian-Got-It-Together-Romero. "Wh-what?"

Christian paused in front of the glass elevators on the floor. "We need to talk, Arianna. Now."

* * *

Christian didn't think this moment would come. But it did, and in this moment he didn't know if he was coming or going. His blood pumped hard in his veins. And like hell, his emotions were zigzagging all over the place, fired up. His gut was telling him that Arianna was in deep trouble and she really needed his help. Romero men always protected their people—lovers, wives, girlfriends, and associates. Period.

Moments later, Christian sat opposite Arianna on the private roof-top patio of her hotel suite and office overlooking the crystal blue sea. He would finally get a chance to confront her about her bizarre behavior. She'd told him that she loved him and wanted to spend her life with him. Heck, her body was screaming it every night they'd made love. Then...it all ended, and she told him it had nothing to do with him.

WTF?

"So, are you going to tell me what's been going on?" Christian interrogated. His tone was a bit more clipped than he had intended, but hell, this girl was the closest thing to him and she just ripped out his heart without so much as an explanation. Things were going so well for them. What the hell had happened? Almost a year of being a couple. They were so good together, the chemistry, the love, the hot sex, the connection. Then, after he'd introduced her to his family and all was going well, she cooled off. No explanation. He'd asked to meet her mother, since he'd already met her father, but she just turned cold and told him it was better that they didn't see each other anymore. He wouldn't even have bothered to try talking to her now if it hadn't been for her sending him mixed signals, like sending him "likes" on his social media posts and dropping subtle hints that she was still interested in him.

Something was metaphorically eating her up inside, bothering her, and he wanted to know what the hell it was—or who the hell it was that terrified this poor girl so that she backed away from a chance at genuine happiness. There wasn't anything in this ever-loving world he wouldn't do for Arianna. He'd told her that many times. He thought he showed her that by his actions. Even now, being here after what she did to him—*to them*—a month ago. He could tell she still wanted him but something was holding her back and he wanted to know what the hell it was. He thought that was reasonable.

"I don't know what you're talking about, Christian," she said in a low voice that hinted at nervousness. He could always tell when she was nervous. Her eyes were fixed on her tall glass of pina colada that was just delivered by the waiter. His own glass was barely touched. Whenever she cast her eyes down, didn't make eye contact with him, he knew then that she was hiding something, lying to cover up something. Whatever it was.

"I think you do." His eyes narrowed.

Watching her pouty, soft lips was hard as hell and made him hard. She was one heck of a kisser. So sweet, so tender. She didn't even have any experience before they'd met. She'd been too busy being a straight-A student and helping out her family to find time to date.

God, she was beautiful. She captivated his eyes and his heart the moment he first laid eyes on her at the Romero's Annual Diamond Ball in Mayberry Hill a few years before. His uncle Toni Romero, the famous real estate mogul and philanthropist, hosted the special black tie affair every year, which also donated millions of dollars worth of scholarships to deserving students to start up their own businesses and further college educations.

Arianna had donated a generous gift from her family business, the Duponte Resorts. They hadn't really gotten close until much later. She was so genuine. A breath of fresh air. So different from all the other women he'd met over the years. She was young and ambitious like Christian and she didn't mess around. She was serious-minded and kind-hearted. She loved her family and that meant a lot to him. He was a family person. They'd dated almost a year before he finally went ring-shopping with his cousin, Carl, to hunt for the best ring for his darling sweetheart.

"What are you hiding, Arianna?"

"Nothing that concerns you."

"I think it does. Anything about you concerns me and you know that."

"Christian, I told you, I...we shouldn't see each other again."

"Are you seeing someone?"

"No."

"Do you really want me out of your life, Arianna? Look at me!" His dark eyes burned into hers.

She couldn't look into his eyes.

"Christian. Please, don't make this harder for me."

Christian got up and walked over to the balcony to watch the turquoise blue waves swoosh and hit the coast below him. The air was warm and gusty and palm trees swayed to the rhythm of the island summer breeze.

Jamaica was one of the most beautiful places he'd frequented. He enjoyed visiting to relax, any time he could get away from his work. Heck, he worked twenty-four hours around the clock in his commercial real estate business. Thanks to his uncle Toni, most of the Romeros were invested in businesses and owned assets around the world. Christian had even teased Ari once about buying her out and turning the Duponte Hotel into a sweet merger.

"Don't you think you owe me an explanation? I think you owe it to us, Arianna."

"Christian, you're right." Arianna got up and moved closer to him. "This is very hard for me."

"What are you afraid of?"

"Being hurt."

"Hurt? By whom?"

"You."

"Me? Are you kidding? Why would you think that?"

"Because I didn't want you to...know about my...my family."

Christian held his head back and chuckled. "You've got to be kidding me, right? What do I look like to you, Arianna? So what if your mother is a recluse. What does that have to do with us?"

Her eyes opened wide.

"Yeah, that's right. I know all about your mother's...illness. I know that my step-mother got a bit...nosy and prying at dinner that night but she really didn't mean it, Arianna. We want to welcome you into our family."

"Christian, it wasn't just that. It's the way people talk about....people like my mom." Arianna looked away then back into his eyes. "Christian, you come from a well-off family. Everybody has opinions. I...just don't think I would fit in." Her eyes were filled with tears.

"Hey," he said softly, tilting her chin up with his finger to face him. "I love you, Arianna. And do you know what love means?"

She gazed into his eyes.

"Love means in spite of, Arianna," he continued. "Nobody's perfect. No one's family is without flaws. And if they try to pretend so, they're lying. We love people *in spite* of their weaknesses. What I have for you is so freaking strong you wouldn't believe it. And if my family didn't accept you, that would be fine with me. Nothing in this world could tear me away from you, girl. I'd abdicate my position in the family if I had to."

Arianna grinned.

Ha! That got her laughing.

"You're not a king, Christian. You can't abdicate."

"You're *my* queen. I can do whatever the hell I please!" He grinned, looking into her eyes. His smiled faded when he could still see raw pain flashing in her pretty brown eyes.

"What else are you hiding from me, Arianna? What else is bothering you?"

She pulled away from him and hugged herself. "Christian. Oh, God! Christian, there's so much more that you don't know about my family and me. So much more," she said, her voice trailing off.

"Like what, Arianna? Why won't you open up to me?"

"I want you, Christian." She turned to him. "Oh, God, Christian. I wish I could tell you everything but I don't think you'd understand. And I couldn't bear it if you didn't respect me anymore."

Christian rubbed his stubble. He was confused as hell. "Why don't you try me, Arianna? I'm sick and tired of you making assumptions about what I will and will not accept about you. Heck, I don't even care if you turned out to be a freaking alien or something. Do you have any idea what you do to me? Over the past month, I could do nothing else but think about you. Every time you left a sign for me online, I wanted to reach for the phone but I just couldn't because I didn't want to deal with the pain of you telling me we shouldn't see each other again. It really messed with my head. Why do you keep doing this to us? To yourself?"

It was true that Christian was a put-together, well-adjusted man. He often didn't give a rat's ass what others thought of him. He was ambitious, confident and did his thing. Being named the youngest real estate mogul to take over one of Mayberry Hill's famous landmarks had earned him many enemies and jealous rivals. He just stuck to his guns and got on with it. Like a true Romero, their skins were smooth and thick as leather. Nothing could penetrate. They never backed down from any pressure—whether in the boardroom or the business world, but Arianna, she really brought him down a notch. Never had he been so wrapped up in another person as he was with Arianna Duponte.

The woman did things to him—to his mind, to his heart, to his very soul that he could not quite understand. All he knew was that she completed him. He would be lost without her. His life wouldn't mean the same without her in it. Strangely enough, he knew that. But oftentimes, one didn't always get that special chance to meet his or her other half—his soul mate, so when one did, the opportunity must not be taken for granted. And now, he was going to do every blessed thing in his power to win back Arianna's love.

Hell, even looking at her now in her pretty summer dress that accentuated her natural curves and her shapely tanned legs caused a rush of heat to surge through his loins. He was getting rock hard just absorbing her beauty with his eyes. Did this woman even know how naturally beautiful and breathtaking she was?

"Because, Christian, I've been hurt before. Badly. And right now, things are just too great a burden to deal with. You wouldn't-"

"Don't tell me I wouldn't understand, Arianna."

"Okay. I don't want to bear the burden of hurting you. I'm not what you think I am, Christian."

"Now what the hell is that supposed to mean?" Christian rubbed his head. "Don't freaking tell me you were born a man."

"No! Oh, God! No. Nothing like that!" Arianna burst out laughing. "Good God, Christian." She reached over and hugged him around his waist and a surge of her magic touched him, again. Why was it so difficult for two people who clearly loved each other to be together? Why the hell did outside factors have to be in the way? "You always come up with the right words to lighten any situation. I've missed you."

"How much?" he probed, leaning closer to her. Her scent. Oh, that sexy, girly fragrance wafted to his nostrils and caused a sweet reaction inside him. Her dark brown hair cascaded down her back. Her pretty feminine face warmed his heart.

He desperately wanted to taste her sweetness again. All he could think about on the flight to Jamaica was how much he couldn't wait to be with her again. To touch her again. To feel and enjoy her magic again. That special connection they had with each other was incredible. That undeniable surge of electrical attraction. They had the right chemistry. There were no two ways about it. He was meant for her and she was meant for him. He knew that, and deep down inside, he felt she knew it too. He could tell by the way she gaped at him when she saw him at the door to Blue's suite. They still had it. There was no denying true love.

Christian lowered his head to hers and tenderly kissed her lips.

CHAPTER THREE

The kiss was oh, so sweet! Christian captured Arianna's lips with his and she tingled from her head right down to her toes peeking out of her sandals. Oh, his magical, loving touch. Arianna never felt it with any other human being before. When she fell in love with Christian over a year ago, she didn't know what had struck her. She couldn't think straight for days. She couldn't focus on anything but his handsome face, his sweet caress, and his aura. She'd never been so captivated, so enthralled by a gorgeous man like Christian before. The memorable times they'd shared over the past year were treasured moments. They had so much in common. That's why it had pained her, ripped her to shreds emotionally when she knew the time had come for it to end. The façade. The fabricated lie she was living had to take its place.

But, oh, Christian. How could she keep away from the one man who rocked her world and showed her how to appreciate the woman she was, or pretended to be?

Her breasts swelled sensually underneath her dress as he continued to brush his lips against hers so tenderly. Her nipples reacted and peaked at the feel of his hand on her back as he leaned her against the balcony tantalizing her lips.

"Oh, God, Arianna. I've missed you so much," he moaned into her neck as his lips trailed down her soft skin.

"Oh," Arianna groaned with pleasure. She always enjoyed the erotic, soft touch of his tongue inside her mouth, teasing and playing with her tongue. Their lips were entwined in a sweet tango of lust. She wrapped her arms around his neck as he held her firmly against the high balcony sucking on her lips then moving his tongue inside her mouth. She could feel his hard erection pressing against her. Oh, how she missed his eager touch. What had she been thinking? How could she live without this man? Christian really knew how to please her. He'd studied her body and knew what she loved and desired. He'd discovered her G-spot and knew how to please her to oblivion. He knew how to kiss. Apparently, not all men did, but he must be an expert. Intermittently, he would kiss her softly, then passionately, thrusting his wet, soft tongue inside her, swirling and teasing in all the right places, while his smooth hands caressed the sensitive parts of her body.

Christian could sure kiss the living breath out of her. Breathless, Arianna arched her neck as he pressed his sweet lips to her throat. "Oh, that feels so good," she moaned, smiling with pleasure. Her body was light now. Her cares suddenly drifted away with the ocean tide.

Christian's soft lips nibbled her neck. "You like that, don't you, baby?" he groaned.

"Hmm-mmm." Her eyes were closed as she fully enjoyed the silky feel of his skin. Her nipples were straining against the fabric of her dress. Her inner thighs moistened with heated anticipation. She wanted Christian now. She needed him. Desired him. Craved him. She'd been starved for his affection for far too long, and now, she finally had her chance with him again.

Christian lifted up her dress and slid his hand up her skin, caressing her. Oh, how she loved the way he pleasured her, massaging her first, but she wanted him inside her. Her heartbeat climbed and escalated.

"Oh, God, Ari. You have no idea how much I love you. You're so beautiful." His voice was hoarse now, his breathing heavy. She delighted in his delicious scent of cologne. It drove her senses wild. She relished in his hard firm flesh as she slid her hands over his smooth muscles on his arms. She moved her hands down his chest and felt his taut nipples underneath his shirt. Oh, his body was firm and gorgeous. His hand moved up her thigh and slid beneath her lace panties. Arianna was already soaked and ready for him. By the feel of his hand and the grin that entered his lips, she could tell he knew it too.

"I want you so badly, girl."

"Oh, Christian. Please, take me now. I need you," she begged, breathless.

At the most inopportune moment, a loud knock rattled the door.

Christian cursed under his breath.

Arianna broke from his embrace, her heart flipped hard and fast. She was dazed, caught off guard by the interruption.

Oh, God! What was she doing? She was at work after all. She was supposed to be overseeing things at the hotel.

Was it a member of her staff? Was there an emergency? She was expecting a delivery of special props for the Romero's themed wedding this morning.

"Who is it?" Arianna called, brushing her hair back with her hands. She straightened her dress and repositioned her panties. Her heart was still beating erratically. She could feel it in her throat. Christian leaned back on the balcony rail while she went to the door, flushed and out of breath. Desire still burned in his eyes as he watched her walk away. She caught his eyes undressing her sexily while she walked off. She grinned, then drew in a deep breath to straighten up her expression. The last thing she wanted was for her staff to feel as if she was messing around in her own office. She just wanted to be professional.

"Sorry, miss," the hotel clerk said apologetically. "It's your father. He's upset again. He's in the hotel lobby."

"Oh, no!" Arianna grabbed her keys off the counter. "I'll be right down."

"What is it?" Christian came in from the balcony, a look of concern on his face.

"It's nothing. Just something I have to handle."

"Is your father all right? I overhead him telling you something's up with him."

Arianna hesitated at first. "Um…It's okay. Really, Christian. Listen, we can catch up later, okay?"

"I'm coming with you." Christian's voice was stern. His tone had an air of finality to it. Dare she try to persuade him to leave her be now? The truth was, she could really do with a bit of support, especially if her father was having one of his…moments again.

"Okay," she finally complied. Arianna swallowed a hard lump in her throat.

* * *

Arianna wasn't prepared for the scene in the hotel lobby. Her sandals made a soft sound as she hurried across the marble floors of the grand lobby. Her father was at the front desk arguing with one of the clerks.

"Dad, what's wrong?" Arianna asked, breathless, as she approached the desk clerk.

"Nothing. Nothing. I just wanted to know why your mother was given the wrong lunch tray. She hates seafood."

Arianna's heart sank. She felt her heart crushing in her chest. Christian stood by her. She felt as if she could melt into his arms. She needed support. "But, Dad, it has nothing to do with the front desk clerk."

"It has everything to do with her." Her old man turned to her. His lips were pinched. "Your mother is allergic to shellfish." He was clearly distressed over the situation.

"I know," she said quietly.

"So why did she get shellfish? Are they trying to kill her?"

"Dad, I'm sure it was a simple, honest mistake. I will take care of it, okay? I'll speak with the head chef. Louise, is Frank in charge today?" Arianna turned to the desk clerk.

"Yes, ma'am. Should I call him?"

"No. I will speak with him later. I'll go to the kitchen myself."

Louise smiled slightly and nodded. "Yes, ma'am."

"Oh, hello there. Christian, right?" Mr. Duponte turned to Christian, extending his hand.

"Yes, sir. We meet again."

"Yes, we do. I've been asking Arianna here about you. Her mother and I have been asking about you actually. You didn't even get a chance to meet my wife yet, did you?"

"Not yet, sir. No." Christian looked uncomfortable for a moment. Arianna drew in a deep breath and closed her eyes momentarily before opening them again. Christian had seen her father on several occasions, briefly, but not her mother. In fact, her father had invited them to dinner but that was when Arianna decided it was time to call it quits. She just didn't want Christian to know everything…yet.

"Why don't you join us now? For lunch. It's," Mr. Duponte said, glancing at his watch, "quarter to twelve. We can have lunch early. We live on the second floor. We also have a cottage over by the west side. It's all part of the hotel, you know."

"I know," Christian said with a warmth befalling his expression. It appeared that Christian understood that her father was…a bit moody at times, even forgetful. Christian seemed quite good about the situation. Arianna was ever so watchful, especially of her father. She'd always been protective in regards to her parents, but Christian seemed okay in dealing with her father's severe mood swings. Her dad was in his sixties. Her parents had her in their forties after years of trying. Her mother had just turned forty when Arianna was born. It had been a miracle for her.

"Listen, Dad. We can all get together some other time. Not now."

"Aren't you going to come and see if your mother's alright?"

"Yes. I'll be there soon. Did she eat any of the fish?"

"No. Thank God I was there." He shook his head, tears in his eyes.

Arianna had to always keep in mind that her father was elderly. He'd suffered with a bout of dementia at one point in his life, but things got better after that. Then…her parents went on a trip to Europe on some Mediterranean island. It all went down hill after that. Things were never the same again.

"Well, I'm going to go back to the room to make sure she's okay," her father said.

"Okay, Dad."

"Your father's looking a little lost these days. Everything okay, dear niece?" A tall, heavy-set man wearing a black shirt, black shorts, and shades walked up to her. She hadn't noticed that he was sitting in the lobby when she went to see her dad. His face lacked empathy. His voice was cold and bitter.

Shivers ran down her spine and not the good kind, either.

"Uncle Ned," she said in a low voice. "I didn't see you there. When did you arrive?"

"Oh, I flew in this morning. You know me. I'm always here every month to ensure things are running smoothly. You know how upset I can get when things are not running well."

Arianna said nothing. That was not the reason he was here.

"Is everything okay?" Christian turned to her, noticing her rigid body language.

"Oh, you have a handsome friend here," he said, his lips curled in disgust. His voice was laced with sarcasm. "And you are?"

"Someone who's concerned about the way you're talking to Arianna."

"Oh, dear. What have we here? A *protective* friend?" Uncle Ned arched a brow. He gave Christian the once-over, eyeing him up and down.

"It's okay, Christian. Uncle Ned was just leaving."

"Oh, but I just got here," he said sarcastically. His speech was slightly slurred. Had he been drinking again at this time of the day? "I'm going to enjoy my stay for the next week or so. Who knows, I may hang around longer." Ned then turned to look around the grand lobby. "You know, I've always thought this place could do with a new coat of paint." His lips were turned up in disgust as he grabbed his jacket and bag and weaved his way towards the elevator.

"Trouble maker," Arianna whispered under her breath. For as long as she could remember, her uncle had always been intoxicated, obnoxious and bitter. Bitter about anything and everything. She tried to warm up to him on many occasions, but to no avail. He had threatened her and lashed out at her in the past when she tried to defend her father in his presence. He had a personal vendetta against her dad, his younger brother. A sibling rivalry that ran so deep and dark it literally tore apart the family.

"And why is this guy here? Don't tell me it's because you share some DNA?"

"No. I just…He's entitled to stay here whenever he wants."

"Arianna, why do I get the feeling there's so much more to this?"

"It's okay, Christian. Listen, I've got to get things prepared for your cousin's wedding. I mean, I have to oversee the shipment coming in and then stock the placeholders," she said nervously as she scanned some notes on her clipboard. Her fingers trembled.

Christian took the clipboard from Arianna and laid it on the desk. He then reached over and lifted her hand to his lips and kissed her skin, sending a pleasing tingle inside her belly. He pulled her close to him and hugged her. She could feel his energy and his support.

"Thank you," she murmured, looking into his dark, sexy eyes.

"For what?" Christian grinned.

"For just being you. For everything."

"That's what I'm here for. Now, what's up with dear old Uncle Ned?"

"Oh, he's quite a character," Arianna said, opening up to him little by little. Her heart thumped erratically in her chest. Her mind still whirled in a daze as to how much she should reveal to Christian about her family and their darkest secrets.

CHAPTER FOUR

"So, your uncle wants to ruin your life, too?" Christian said later that afternoon. He was seated on the private patio overlooking the pool opposite Arianna. He'd convinced her to unwind after a challenging day at work.

"Yeah. He has this terrible gambling addiction. My dad never really got along with him."

"I see."

"He's had a few businesses in the past, under different names."

"Different names?"

"Yeah. I mean, he would open up different kinds of 'fast money-making' businesses as he would call them. He started harassing us and threatening to take the hotel when his businesses went bust and his gambling debts increased. Of course we'd helped him out a bit in the past but…we stopped. We told him he needed to get help. We don't owe him anything but he still tries to…" she hesitated for a moment.

"Wait a minute. Did you say he was trying to take the hotel away from you?"

"Yeah," she sighed, her voice drifting.

"How could he do that?"

"Easy. My grandfather bought and owned this place back in the day. Well, when his wife, my grandmother, died after committing suicide-"

"Oh, God. I'm sorry to hear that."

"It's okay. Anyway, when she died, he decided he was going to leave this hotel to his older son, Ned."

"Oh?"

"Yeah. But as you know, my father ended up taking over the place instead. Ned's gambling addiction revealed itself early on, and I guess Granddad thought it best to hand it over to his youngest son instead. So Ned really got nothing."

"So if your grandfather willed the place to your dad, what's the problem? There's no contesting the will."

"Oh, well. Yeah. There's this little…stipulation. A clause that says Ned can take ownership if Dad…"

"If your dad does what?" Christian delved further.

Arianna drew in a deep breath. She closed her eyes and tried to squeeze out the pain. She couldn't tell him. Not now. No. She didn't want to spoil the moment.

"Listen, let's change the subject. How have you been, Christian, really?"

"Missing you like crazy." He leaned over and kissed her gently.

"Mmm. I've been missing you, too. How has business been going?" Just then, his cell phone rang. Christian excused himself to answer it. "Yeah." He listened for a while before he spoke. "Yeah. Good. Just look into that for me. I need to find out all I can about this guy."

"What are you doing?" Arianna asked, her heart beating heavy and hard in her chest. She had an idea what that call might be about knowing Christian. Knowing how the Romero men were so connected, and so feared.

"It's nothing to worry your pretty little head about," he dismissed her, nuzzling her neck.

"Christian, I need to know."

"Listen, I don't appreciate anyone making idle threats against my girl."

"But…Christian."

What was she going to tell him? From day one her uncle made threats and hurled snide remarks against her father. And God knew what kind of shady characters from his gambling world her uncle knew. What if he'd paid someone to try to bump off her father … or her? All Christian wanted to do was to protect her. It was who the Romero men were. Everyone who knew about the Romeros was well aware of their behavior.

She blew out a breath.

"What were you going to say?" Christian asked.

"Nothing. I can handle things on my own."

"Really now?" He grinned.

"Yes. Really."

"Sometimes, Arianna, it's okay to get a little help from someone who cares deeply about you. Remember that. You're a good girl and a fine woman and from what I've just seen with my own eyes from your uncle, I'm not sure I can say the same about him." Christian looked deeply into her eyes and Arianna shivered with delight. An intense desire burned in her veins for him. Oh, when would she get the chance to have him all to herself again?

"I'll try to remember that, Christian." Arianna smiled and wrapped her arms around his neck as he lowered his lips to hers again to sweetly reclaim them.

"Oh, God, Christian. I want you so badly."

"Mmm," he growled passionately into her neck, sucking on her warm flesh. "I want you, too, baby."

"Oh, but I have to get the theme night stuff set up. I have to make sure the stage is set."

"The stage is set right here, baby," he moaned.

"Seriously," Arianna giggled as he continued to nuzzle her. His lips trailed over her earlobes and she thought she was going to go insane with carnal pleasure. Oh, she loved the way her body heated up and butterflies exploded in her belly when he did that. It was amazing, the least likely sexual parts of the body. When he'd first kissed her ears, she trembled with delight. He'd caressed her nipples simultaneously and brought such pleasure she'd never known could possibly exist. Every inch of her body had been teased, pleasured and caressed sexually by Christian. She couldn't wait until later to have him all to herself. Again.

**

Christian sat at the bar by the pool a while later, his cousin Carl at his side. A live band on the makeshift concert stage by the poolside played the reggae ballad "Three Little Birds" by Bob Marley. The lyrics *"don't worry about a thing, 'cause every little thing gonna be alright,"* boomed through the sound speakers on the stage. Christian wished he could follow Bob Marley's advice right now.

A surge of powerful emotions shot through Christian's body. He was torn with conflicting feelings. First, he was elated that he'd finally made some reconciliation with Arianna. She was at least talking to him again. That was a huge step. It had been way too long—a month, since they'd made direct contact. He thought he'd lost her forever. That would have killed a part of him. He couldn't imagine his life without her.

Second, he was sickened at the thought of her being harassed by her creepy-behaving uncle. He didn't like that someone held an axe over his girl's head. He didn't like it one bit. Anger seethed through his body. He felt a torrent of adrenaline rush through his blood at the memory of the way her uncle looked at her, as if trying to intimidate her. Was she terrified of her uncle?

Christian had an overwhelming urge to find out more about this uncle character. Everything. He didn't take too kindly to threats being made against a nice young lady from a man, especially against *his* lady.

"So you want to know what's the deal with her uncle?" Carl clarified, sipping on his icy drink.

"Yeah. I don't trust him. I need to know everything about him and exactly what he has over Arianna and her parents."

"Did she say anything specific?"

"Not a lot to go on. Just what I've told you so far." Christian gazed into the sparkling pool, his eyes were narrowed and although he was glancing at the water, he wasn't registering the image of the swimming pool. His mind was clouded with visions of Arianna, obviously terrified. Holding some sort of guilt, an onerous burden on her shoulders. Was this the main reason she'd backed off from getting too close to him? Heck, every family had a black sheep, or two, but he wasn't about to let that deter what they could have together.

"No problem, cuz. I've got my men on it. They're doing a background check on this guy as we speak."

"Hell, you made a call already? That was fast."

"Yeah, well, as soon as you told me earlier, I got right on it. Time is everything in this business. Besides, you really sounded pissed off when we first spoke about it. I just gave our man JoJo the details, like his name and his link to this place. A couple small things to go on right now. I'll let you know what they come up with."

"Thanks, cuz."

"Hey, Romeros stick together. We don't take chances with threats, whether to our friends or us, and in your case, your future wife-" Carl grinned and arched his brow.

"What?" Christian turned to his cousin. "Don't you think you're jumping ahead, Carl? Who said anything about marriage?"

"Hey, man, I'm just pulling your leg. Gramps would love to think that all of us will be tying the knot soon." He rolled his eyes, grinning as he shook his head. He lifted his drink to his lips again, taking a long sip.

Christian shifted his gaze to a couple by the poolside, cuddling together on the side. He thought about a time when he'd taken Arianna to the amusement park, they'd held hands and embraced most of the day. They were supposed to be sightseeing and having fun, instead they had turned in early and spent the rest of the evening exploring each other's bodies like an amusement park, enjoying all the rides, experiencing all the excitement, together.

God, they had such a wicked chemistry. He felt it and he knew she sure as hell must have felt it. Then it just stopped abruptly. Something was troubling her. Something deep and terrifying for her. What the heck was it? He would soon find out. He didn't want anything blocking her happiness in life. She deserved it and much more. Whether she was with him or not, he truly wanted Arianna to have the good life she deserved.

"Can't believe Zack's tying the knot, man," Carl commented.

"Yeah, I know." Christian couldn't help but grin. "Never thought that Zack, the ultimate lady's man, would settle down like that, but Blue's a pretty cool gal."

"Yeah. But you know what this means, right?"

"No. What?"

"My grandfather is going to believe that if Zack can settle down, then all of us can settle down."

Christian laughed. "Yeah, that sounds like Uncle Toni all right."

"So we're gonna have to run down that aisle or run away so he doesn't catch us."

Christian laughed out loud. "Yeah, right. Better get your sneakers on, then bolt," he teased his cousin. "You're gonna need to sprint the hell far away. Uncle Toni is fast and he'll catch up with you."

"Oh, I don't think so."

"So, what about you?" Christian asked, holding his drink up to his lips and taking a long, refreshing swig as he sat enjoying his time with Carl.

"What about me?"

"You seeing someone?"

"Nah, not seriously."

"What about that cute assistant you have? Venus. Don't tell me nothing's going on there."

"Oh, no, man. It's nothing like that. She's sweet. She's a good girl."

"Doesn't have to mean she isn't a good girl if something's going on. You're both single, right?"

"Well, that's just it. I don't know what's with her. She's real secretive about her life. Everything."

"Really?"

"Yeah, but that shouldn't surprise you. Women like to keep a lot to themselves for some reason." He arched a brow.

Christian grinned. "Did you find out anything about her?"

"We know all we need to know about her for work. I would only use our men for good reason. Not just to be, well, all up in her business."

"I bet if you two were together, you'd be all up in her business!" Christian delighted in poking fun at his cousin.

Carl looked as if he was far away for a moment. "Yeah, well, she's a nice girl. I really like her. Not saying that I don't. I just…something's just a little mind-boggling about her. But nothing we found out about her seemed odd or out of place, so we're leaving it for now."

"I see."

"Anyway, I'm going for a swim. I need to cool off." Carl placed his glass on the counter.

"I'm with you, man." Christian could do with a few laps right now. He thought about Arianna and couldn't wait to see her again. Now that he'd spent some time with her for the first time in over a month, he just couldn't get enough of her.

CHAPTER FIVE

"Uncle!" Christian beamed as he approached Toni Romero, his favorite elderly uncle, who was seated beside his young wife in the lounge of the hotel. The Sunset Beach room was gorgeous, overlooking the Caribbean Sea soaking in the fiery sun as it set. Guests mingled about in the lounge. It was in the early evening.

"Well, how's my favorite nephew?" Toni grinned and held his arms open. Christian leaned over and hugged him, patting him on the back.

"Shelly, you're looking well."

"Thank you, Christian."

It seemed as if the rest of the Romero crew had touched down in Montego Bay and they all decided to gather in the Sunset Beach lounge. Waiters, dressed in white, walked about offering guests refreshments. Romantic music played over the speakers soft enough that you could still hear conversations of people with whom you were speaking.

Zack and Blue were cuddled together in a corner of the lounge nuzzling each other like soon-to-be newlyweds, while Antonio and Lucy were sitting together hugging. Their toddler, Alexander, was playing with his cousin and new friends in the Duponte Hotel Childcare Play Center. Lucas and Maxine cuddled together whispering in each other's ears. Maxine had given birth to a baby girl just six months earlier (also being entertained at the play center) and this was her first time getting out—so to speak.

Carl was busy flipping through the screens on his smartphone—always dealing business as usual. Carl had long been rumored to be running for mayoral office up in Canada, but everybody told him it would be a challenge being the first bachelor to run. Most candidates were married with families. It was all part of the presentation.

Jules and Dion were by the bar deep in conversation. Troy was speaking with the Romero family's press secretary, Pamela, who had also arrived from Toronto, and Alonso, Dr. Alonso Romero—that is—was sitting by the side enjoying the music and the breathtaking views of the red sunset and the calming waves of the sea.

A pain of longing shot through Christian's veins. He'd never really thought of himself as a marrying man but seeing his cousins so happy—the ones who were hitched or about to get hitched, made him rethink his priorities. He wasn't exactly getting any younger. Sure, he'd be thirty soon, but he really had strong feelings towards Arianna. The question was, did she feel the same about him? She was still holding back and that bugged the hell out of him. Yeah, she said she loved his body and the chemistry between them was out of this world. She even told him that she loved him, for who he was. Yeah, right! Just not enough to trust him. But man, her body caused a reaction in him each and every time, but was that enough. He glanced at his uncle who was in his seventies, married for the fifth time to his young nurse who was in her forties. Heck, even he was getting some regularly. He was blissfully married.

"You know," Toni turned to Shelly, "I love this."

"The vacation?"

"No. Well, yes, that too, and getting together with family. It's one of the most important things to do in life with those close to you."

"I agree. You raised the boys well, Toni."

"I tried." He teetered his hand in a mock so-so gesture. "Some of them are still a little rough around the edges, you know," he teased.

"Hey, what's that supposed to mean?" Carl interjected playfully.

"Well, so far, Lucas and Antonio and now Zack will be married. But what about the rest of you? I told you that having a loving wife by your side and a family to call your own is one of the greatest assets in a civilized society.

Looking at little Alexander today and Mary-Louise made my heart sing for joy," he said, glancing up with a sincere smile on his face. "I'm so happy to see Lucas and Antonio bearing fruit for the Romero family tree."

"Granddad!" Carl voiced.

"Well, come on now. Look at me. Look at my age. I feel blessed to have two beautiful great-grandchildren. But considering my age, I should have more." Toni playfully laughed and winked.

"Besides," he continued. "What type of life do you think I would be having now if I didn't have any children to begin with? I wouldn't have had your father and Antonio's father. And then there would be no you or your brothers, Carl."

"Okay, Granddad, you've got a point."

"Life would be so empty without any family at this juncture."

"Yeah, but you still have my brothers, and me," Christian chimed in with a wink. He held up his beer bottle to his lips to take a swig. "I mean, you forgot you have your younger brother. My father?" Christian cocked a brow.

"Hmm-mmm. If that's how you want to look at it," Toni fumbled for words for the first time. His younger brother, Jackson, had quite a few sons who lovingly called him uncle. One of them was Christian. "But it's still not the same as having your own family tree growing," Toni said, winking back.

Just then, Arianna dropped in to see that everyone was okay. She smiled sheepishly when her eyes caught Christian's. They always seemed to have this little play thing going on. His crotch throbbed when she stepped beside him. There was something about her aura, her presence that always got this reaction in him. God, she looked hot in her red evening dress. Hot as hell! Sinfully sexy.

"So when are you two tying the knot?" Toni asked Christian and Arianna.

"Toni!" Shelly exclaimed beside him.

"Granddad, we're not doing this again, are we?" Carl teased, as he turned off his phone and placed it on the table before him.

"Hey, I'm just saying." Toni shrugged his shoulders innocently. "Come on now. You two look so good together and don't tell me all this talk of wedding doesn't get you in the mood." He winked.

Christian shoved his hands in his pockets and shook his head, grinning.

Arianna looked uncomfortable at first, but then she melted into a grin.

"Why do you always think two people dating will get married?" Shelly playfully rolled her eyes, smiling.

"Because they are more compatible than most couples I see," Toni finished, as if they were not standing there.

"What do you mean by that?" Christian chimed in.

"You're both into commercial real estate for one thing."

"So?" Christian offered up, smiling. Everybody loved to humor Toni, just as he loved to humor them at times.

"Well, that's one sign that it would work out best. It's not just chemistry, you know."

"Oh, boy. Here we go again," Christian said, lifting his beer to his lips.

"No, seriously," Toni continued. "Why do you think movie stars marry each other, doctors usually marry other doctors and artists marry artists? Usually."

"Why?"

"Compatibility. Understanding."

"Understanding?" Christian cocked a brow.

"Yes. You see, when you are in a stressful industry, it's hard to understand your loved one. Let's face it, we're all human. Take Alonso there. He's a doctor who works twenty-four hour shifts at the hospital at times. It would be awfully hard to have a stable relationship if your spouse works nine to five and doesn't understand the struggles of shift work. I do hope he meets another doctor to marry or a nurse," Toni continued, getting slightly off track.

"You know something?" Christian said thoughtfully. "You're on to something, Uncle. I think you have a good point."

"Don't think. Your dear old uncle might be pushing up there in age, but trust me, I have years of wisdom. Not to mention I've made a heck of a lot of mistakes. After my first wife died, I married four times until I hit the jackpot, right, dear?" Toni patted his wife's hand that rested on the table. She smiled.

"And you know what they say? The more mistakes you make, the wiser you become. I made all these mistakes, boys, so you don't have to. Trust me when I give advice."

"You know, Gramps does have a point. He hasn't let us down yet. Though we don't always agree with his methods," Carl said, laughing.

"Anyway, it's so good to see you again, Toni and everyone," Arianna said. "I have to get ready for the themed party tonight. We're getting things set up and then I have to be present to introduce our special guest band."

"Oh?" Toni chimed in. "Themed party? That's sounds good. When is it? What is the theme?"

"Oh," Arianna hesitated. "It's...um...later tonight and it's...a pajama party."

"Oh, that sounds fun." Toni brought his pina colada to his lips and placed it back down. "I'm game. Let's all go."

Arianna flushed.

Carl, and now Zack who had joined them with Blue at his side, grinned. "Um, Granddad, I don't think it's something you would want to go to."

"And why not? Arianna said it was going to be a pajama party, didn't you, dear? I have my PJs."

"Oh, um...well, it's an adult pajama party, Toni. It's going to be adults in sexy nightwear, dancing..." she said, hunching her shoulders. She'd turned the color of the red sunset.

"Oh, dear." Toni looked embarrassed. Then without a thought he opened his mouth again. "I guess you guys are too young to join us then. Shelly and I will let you know how the party is."

They all laughed.

"Yeah, right. Like that's going to happen," Christian teased. He glanced over to Arianna. Man, he couldn't wait until later tonight to be with her.

Venus, who was seated near to Carl, couldn't help but chuckle. Like everybody else, she enjoyed Toni Romero's wild sense of humor. The family was so loving, so close-knit. She was thrilled to be working for the Romeros. At least something was going good for her in her life. That and her son, Tristan. "Your grandfather is really something." She smiled, picking a cherry off her soda.

"Yeah, he's a hoot," Carl commented back.

"What about you? You don't really speak much about your family. You've been working for us for how long now? And you hardly speak about them."

She knew he was just making conversation, but she really didn't want to, or couldn't, get into it with him. As much as she admired Carl and all that he stood for. "Well, there's not much to say really." She hunched her shoulders. "Like I said before, my family pretty much died out." She wanted to cross her fingers under the table. That was only half the truth. "When I moved to Canada from Maryland, I decided we were going to make a fresh new start. And by the way, I love your family. You guys are so... loving. You have so much fun together. You stick together all the time."

"That's the way family should be, isn't it?"

"Yeah, I guess. But it doesn't always turn out that way."

The music played in the background creating a relaxing ambiance. Currently, James Ingram's old tune "Forevermore" beamed through the sound speakers.

"I love this place. Have you guys been here before?"

"Yeah. The Duponte family is pretty cool. Well, Giles Duponte, who owned this joint before his daughter took over, is a cool dude. He did some good business transactions in the past with Granddad."

"What about his wife? I heard no one hardly sees her."

"Ah, now that's a mystery. I've met her before. She seems like a nice lady, but she hardly makes eye contact. I hear she has this phobia. Social phobia or something like that. Anyway, she stays indoors most of the time. She's very shy. Soft spoken."

"Wow. I don't know what to say. It must be awful for her husband and daughter to see her like that."

"I guess people live with all sorts of issues. We have to count our blessings when we can. I don't know what I would do if I didn't want to go outside or around. It must be torture for her."

"I know," Venus said, running her finger around the rim of her glass.

"So, are you coming with us?"

"Where to?"

"The pajama party."

Venus grew nervous. Her inner thighs tingled. Carl? Seeing her half naked, wearing nothing but silky lingerie? She didn't know what she would do.

"Um. No. I'll probably knock off early tonight. Besides, Tristan loves when I sing him *Hush Little Baby* before he goes to sleep."

Carl smiled. His gazed trapped hers and she melted inside. "You know, you're a good mother."

"Thanks, I try to be."

"Well, if you change your mind—after you sing him to sleep, let me know."

Venus smiled. Wishing she could be a part of the Romero family but knowing full well, she could not. Not ever. Blue was so lucky to be in love with Zack and now on the brink of becoming a part of this wonderful, powerful family. Still, a girl could dream, right? "Sure. I will," she answered Carl, before lifting the glass to her lips to take another sip of her drink.

CHAPTER SIX

The women were all dressed, or underdressed, in sexy, elaborate lingerie that would make a Victoria Secret model blush. And the men? Gorgeous, model-like with nothing but shorts and vests or t-shirts showing off their bulging biceps. One of them was Christian.

Oh, God! Christian looked so hunky, it blew Arianna's mind. She was feeling possessive over him suddenly, watching other girls ogle him as he walked by. The music was pumping through the base speakers at the Duponte Resort Clubhouse Dance Hall as the first Sexy Pajama Party theme night got underway.

"So this is your first time attending a pajama party?" Christian turned to Arianna as they stepped inside the hall.

"Well, yes and no. I mean, at this hotel? Yes. I thought it was a good idea when my event planner suggested we incorporate a pajama party themed night at the Duponte since we have a massive couples- only clientele that stay here. It's popular at other resorts."

"I see." Christian grinned. "And of course, you just had to try it out, huh?" he said, pinching his lips. His expression was stone cold. She could tell whenever he was jealous. "I really don't like other men looking at you when you're dressed...or I should say, undressed so beautifully in your lingerie, Ari. I hate it."

Arianna grinned. "It's okay, Christian. There are plenty of other girls for the men to eyeball. I can't dress in my Sunday best to an event like this."

His eyes scanned appreciatively up and down her body and she shivered with delight.

"I'm just here as a guest. I mean, I have to sell the benefits. How would I know what to recommend to my guests if I don't at least try it out?"

He smiled, capturing her figure with his eyes as he held his glass of wine to his lips. "I've missed you," he murmured, leaning closer to her.

"I've missed you, too." She couldn't help but gush. "Oh, wow, it's one of our favorite songs playing."

The speakers played the old hit song "Baby, I Love Your Way" by the reggae group Blue Mountain. "I love it. Let's dance!" He pulled her to the dance floor after setting down his wine glass.

The disco multi-colored strobe lights sparkled in the dark club as couples gyrated and danced closely with each other. Everyone seemed to be having a blast. The warm island breeze blew inside from one of the open doors. The rest of the Romero clan, minus Toni and Shelly, seemed to be at the themed night tonight, also having fun. The place was jam-packed with guests.

Arianna caught glimpses of women gazing in Christian's direction and a twinge of jealousy befell her. That was soon wiped away by the thought that Christian was with her. He had his arms wrapped around her waist from behind and snuggled up to her, nuzzling her neck as they danced the night away. His sweet-scented cologne tantalized her senses. His firm, manly hands held her strong as she swayed into his hips, feeling the hardness of him rising. Oh, no. This was probably not the best place to be bumping and grinding on the dance floor. She was dressed down, but some of the guests would recognize her as part owner of the hotel.

Then, "Tonight, I Celebrate My Love for You" by Peabo Bryson and Roberta Flack came on.

"Oh, God. I'm so turned on, Ari," Christian moaned into her neck as he kissed her gently. Right there. Out in the open.

"Mmm." Arianna turned to face him as they slow danced. "This is our song, isn't it?"

"It sure is," he said in a low, throaty voice. The part in the song about "tonight we will both discover how friends turn into lovers," really gripped her heart. She'd transitioned from being his soul mate, girlfriend to lover one night long ago, when that romantic ballad had played. It held such a significant, special meaning to them both, every time they heard that song—their song.

Christian looked deeply into her eyes and she felt weak and giddy in love. Her stomach flip flopped in her belly, bringing a light tingling feeling. Love.

"You're very beautiful, Arianna," he breathed in a low, deep voice. "You mean the world to me, do you know that?"

Her arms were wrapped around his neck, as he swayed into her. *The man can sure move.* "I...know I do, Christian. You mean the world to me, too."

"I want to make you happy, Ari. I want to spend the rest of my life with you. There's nothing I wouldn't do for you, girl. If only you knew."

She tilted her head up to meet his lips and they kissed softly. She was on the dance floor. She had to leave with Christian now, or she would go crazy. She needed him, like now.

"Let's go...to my room. It's not far from here."

He grinned into her lips. And he kissed her again.

"Oh, God, Ari. Don't ever leave me again," he said in a hoarse voice, kissing her passionately on the sensitive part of her neck, while she arched her back in his arms on the bed. They'd made their way over to one of the suites she occupied at the Duponte near the office. She breathed heavily as he touched her gently.

"I won't, baby, oh," she purred.

"God, I couldn't wait to get you out of your nightie tonight. I was going crazy on the dance floor."

She knew that. A smile touched her lips. She was going crazy inside, too.

He then moved his lips over to hers and sucked on her lower lips causing electrical currents to shoot through her heated body. She loved his touch. She loved the way he took her lips between his soft tender lips and passionately caressed her.

Christian was such a gentle, passionate lover and Arianna loved that about him. He always took his time pleasuring every inch of her. He then moved his lips over to her earlobe and began sucking on her skin again, while his hand slid inside her lace panties. He stroked and teased her throbbing folds as she groaned with ecstasy, digging her fingers into his muscular back.

"Oh, God, you're so wet." Christian smiled salaciously while his fingers slid deeper into her moist, swollen sex, stroking her up and down gently. She writhed underneath him on the bed, groaning in delight at his expert touch. "You're ready for me, aren't you?" he said in a low, hoarse voice, a wicked grin on his sexy lips.

He then lowered his lips to her breasts. She had removed her lace camisole bra. He kissed her mound of flesh and swirled his tongue over her hard nipple, which made her shiver with desire. He took her nipple into his mouth and teased her sensitive bud. A moan of ecstasy slid through her lips. Her body was on fire. Desire burned through her for him to take her. The stroking of his fingers sent pleasant jolts through her body as he hit her G-spot with excitement. She could feel the growing hardness of his erection pressing into her skin.

"Oh, you're so wet," he groaned in a deeper voice as he moved his lips down her body. "Do you want me?"

"Mmm," she groaned. "Yes. Please!"

A wicked grin touched his lips again. He slid off her panties and spread her legs apart and lowered his head to her sex. She gasped when his soft tongue touched her sensitive flesh, brushing his tongue up and down her moist center as she arched and writhed on the bed, groaning with sheer pleasure and excitement. She knew it wouldn't be long before she came hard.

She desperately needed Christian inside her. It had been too long. She'd longed for his touch, ached to hold him during the time they were apart.

"Oh, Christian," she moaned as his gentle massage of her inner thighs sent currents of heat and desire through her body. Thrusting his tongue deeper inside her, she came with a shuddering ecstasy. Breathing hard and fast as her heart sped in her chest, she then collapsed in pleasure, her legs weakened.

He stripped off his shirt, breathing hard and deep, a grin of satisfaction on his sweet lips. "God, you're so beautiful when you come," he groaned with pleasure. His lips moved to hers and he devoured her mouth hungrily, passionately. Still reeling from the delightful magical touch of his lips inside her, Arianna ran her hands over his smooth, hard flesh enjoying the feel of his muscles.

"I love you, Christian," she whispered, breathless. She sucked on the skin of his neck, moving her lips over his flesh. Enjoying the taste of his manliness and the low moans emanating deep within his throat. "Oh, Christian."

Arianna repositioned herself over him when he turned over and laid on his back, kissing him deeply. Her fingers traveled down the smoothness of his body, over his rippled muscles and down towards the soft hairs on his groin. She slid her hands inside his silk boxers delighting in the feel of his long, hard erection.

With a naughty grin she eyed him delightfully.

"My turn, baby," she whispered breathlessly. She kept her eyes locked with his dreamy eyes as she freed his manhood, stroking him gently up and down his shaft while he moaned. She loved the feel of his hardness between her fingers. She wet her lips before extending her tongue first over the head of his manhood then slowly and seductively taking him inside the moist heat of her mouth while he groaned deeply. With long, soft strokes she slid her mouth up and down his shaft while working her hands simultaneously, pleasuring him and kissing him harder and harder and faster until he came hard, his body jerking uncontrollably.

"Oh, God, Ari. I love you so much. You have no idea," he breathed hard, between kisses after she'd repositioned herself up to him.

"Oh, I...I don't have a condom," she said disheartened.

"It's okay, baby. I have one in my pocket," he moaned. "It's good that you don't have one."

"Why do you say that?"

"Because it means that you weren't busy with another man while we were apart," he said, a boyish grin on his face. "I was hoping you wouldn't want to be with anyone else," he finished his train of thought.

Arianna smiled deeply. She was so relieved that he had a condom. She needed him to be inside her so badly. She was dying for this moment to come.

He reached over to his shorts on the floor and retrieved a square golden packet with a latex condom. He proceeded to open it, but Arianna climbed over him playfully and took it from him, opening it herself. "I want to roll it on you," she said, eyeing him seductively.

She leaned over and stroked his manhood again while he groaned, holding her tightly, then she rolled it over his long, hard erection until it was firmly secured. Arianna straddled herself over Christian and moved down on his erection; both gasped with excitement. She enjoyed the magical feel of him inside, filling her completely.

Riding him and grinding her hips into his, they made hot, passionate love and she came first with a shudder and he came soon after. They enjoyed the awesomeness of their heated chemistry and lovemaking. He made love to her over and over through the night. Before long, the early morning sunrise shone in her suite, bathing the room in a soothing hue of orange and red. The palm trees swaying outside to the early morning breeze, while the sound of ocean waves swooshed gently outside the window.

For a fleeting moment, Arianna felt everything in her life was okay. She was safe with Christian, the man who loved her and would do anything to protect her.

Doubt crept into her mind as she watched Christian sleep. His dark long lashes looked enviable with his eyes closed. Would Christian really be able to protect her? Protect her from herself?

CHAPTER SEVEN

"Morning, beautiful!" Christian kissed Arianna on the cheek. He then sat beside her at the breakfast table on her balcony overlooking the sea.

"Morning, hon."

"Why didn't you wake me?" he said in his deep morning voice, rubbing the stubble on his chin.

"I wanted you to sleep in. You earned it!"

"You're the one who should have been sleeping in," he said, smiling as if admiring the vision before him.

"What's that supposed to mean?" she teased him playfully.

"The desk clerk mentioned that you had been working sixteen days straight before I got here. You need a break, Arianna. I'm taking you out today. And I won't take no for an answer. Besides, the wedding is only a few days away, this Saturday."

She smiled. "You're too funny, you know that?"

He leaned closer into her, hugging her. He looked into her eyes. "You were so incredible last night," he said in a low, deep voice.

She smiled sheepishly. "So were you."

He kissed her again and necked her so deliciously. "Oh, Christian," she moaned, smiling.

Just then, there was a knock at the door.

"Who could it be at this hour?"

"Oh, I took the liberty of ordering breakfast for us," she murmured.

"How did you know I wouldn't sleep in until noon?" He grinned.

"Because, I know you, remember?" Ari arched a brow. "The latest you sleep in, Mr. Workaholic, is like eight o'clock on a Saturday morning. About this time." She playfully pointed to the clock.

"I'd better get my pants on then."

"Oh, I'll get the door. No worries. Besides, I don't want the hotel staff talking. You know, you answering the door in nothing but a towel or boxer shorts." She smiled.

"Whatever." He grinned then kissed her cheek.

Later they settled for a typical Jamaican breakfast of Ackee and Saltfish with delicious fluffy fried dumplings and fried plantains. They drank the juice from freshly squeezed oranges and refreshing coconut water.

They made love again while showering together after breakfast. It was a sensual and fulfilling moment for Christian and Arianna. Bathing each other while caressing each other so lovingly. Admiring each other's bodies. Christian could not seem to get enough of his sweet Arianna. Later, they both got dressed. Christian had gone up to his suite to gather some new clothes to put on.

"I can't believe you're taking me out today."

"And why not? If I don't insist on you taking a break, you'll work yourself to death and you know that would drive me crazy, right?" He grinned.

Arianna playfully nudged him in the ribs. "That's not funny, Chris."

At last tearing themselves apart, they headed downstairs to the main foyer of the hotel. The tall green plants were perky from being freshly watered and provided a nice blend with the shiny, recently polished marble floors. Before they walked out of the lobby, Mr. Duponte strolled in.

"Dad? You're up early." Her father often never left the hotel room until well after noon. It was just something that he did, especially as of late, since Arianna had taken over duties at the hotel.

"Oh, I'm fine," he said, dismissively. "It's just your mother. She's a bit moody this morning. I tried everything but..." He shrugged his shoulders.

"Oh, Dad," she said, leaning over to hug him. "Is everything okay?"

"Oh, yes. I said I will give her room to breathe and that was that. I'm going up now. Pray she doesn't kick me out of the room again. Good to see you again, Christian."

"Likewise, sir."

Mr. Duponte nodded and headed toward the elevator to go back to his suite.

"You sure your old man will be okay?"

"Um...yeah."

"What about your mother? Is she alright?"

Arianna hesitated at first. Should she tell him? What could she say? How could she tell him? She nervously glanced around the massive lobby of the hotel to see if her uncle was anywhere nearby. There was that feeling again, that chilling sensation in the pit of her stomach. Her heart was crushing inside her chest. She drew in a deep breath.

Everything will be fine, she coached herself.

It had to be fine.

"Mom's okay," was all she said in a low voice, then continued to walk outside the hotel, toward their waiting car.

CHAPTER EIGHT

Christian drove, with Arianna, up the hillside towards Ocho Rios in his rental convertible. The wind rustled through their hair as they took in the tall green plants and trees dotting the hills. Jamaica was blessed with rich vegetation and colorful plants. Ari admired the mountainous swells and the miles of greenery as they drove by.

"Please tell me that you've been to Dunn's River Falls before." Christian turned to her before fixing his eyes on the road.

"Why?" she asked as she clutched her sun hat as the wind whipped about her hair. She sported her sunglasses but could still appreciate the blueness of the cloudless sky and the bright sun as they drove.

"Because, you can't be in Jamaica and not go to Dunn's River. That would just be crazy. And it would tell me that you've been working way too hard to enjoy yourself."

The Dunn's River Falls were one of the most breathtaking tourist spots and highlights of visiting Jamaica. An angelic place anyone should visit before leaving this earthly plane. A "must-do" fun activity! Who hadn't been there? Tens of thousands of visitors flocked to the site every week. Although there was a small beach at the base of the falls, climbing the massive boulders on the falls was one of the best parts. Arianna couldn't wait to climb with Christian while the cool running water gushed down on their skin.

"That's just it. A lot of people who live close to landmarks don't always visit because they take for granted that they will always be there."

"True," he concurred. "But that's still no excuse." His boyish grin always melted her inside and his cute dimple was adorable. Oh, his sexy dimpled cheek when he was happy got her every time.

"Okay. I've been once. A long time ago."

"Well, we're going together as a couple. And you're really going to have a time to remember."

"I can't wait."

The Satellite radio played some classic R&B tunes. The current song playing was "One Hundred Ways," a sensual, memorable ballad from Grammy award winning singer, James Ingram.

"Oh, I *love* that song!" Arianna reached for the controls and cranked up the volume. "That guy can sure sing. Dad used to play that tune in the house when I was younger."

"Love her today, find one hundred ways," Christian sang out the lyrics, a little out of tune, but sexy as hell. His voice was so deep, soft and sensual.

"Ask her to stay, find one hundred ways," he grinned as he continued to sing. He looked so handsome sporting his Ray-Ban shades over his eyes. His dark, short, silky hair tossed from the breezy hillside drive.

"Hey, I just noticed, you never commented on my singing," Christian teased her.

"Well, I didn't want to spoil the fun we're having, you know." Ari winked.

Christian gave her a mock eye roll and chuckled.

"I'm teasing, hon, you're hot!"

"Yeah, whatever." He broke out into a wide grin. "I love you, you know that?"

"Love you, too, baby," she cooed beside him. She leaned over and planted a warm kiss on his cheek. "Okay, now I don't want to distract you from driving. You have to watch those turns on these hills."

"Yeah, I think I have enough experience to know that, darling."

Arianna felt alive for the first time in such a long while. Her stomach caved in for a moment. *Oh, my God! I almost gave this up. I almost gave up being with Christian. What was I thinking? What was I on?*

She loved the way Christian made her feel. Arianna always enjoyed his warmth, his connection, his crazy-ass laughter and bad singing. God, there wasn't anything about Christian she did not love. She was so grateful to the universe that he had showed up at Blue's door when he did.

Arianna was so elated that Christian hadn't given up on connecting with her, even though she kept her distance during the past month, vowing to never see him or get too close to him. She would give anything for this moment. She would give anything to turn back the hands of time. Just to think that she had hurt him. She hurt this wonderful man beside her who wanted nothing more than to love her, to be with her, to make her happy. How could she not want to be with Christian?

Oh, Christian.

They had already packed what they needed for their trip to the falls. She wore her white string bikini underneath her orange cotton sundress. Of course, her sundress would be removed before her climb up the falls. She applied sunscreen the requisite thirty minutes before departure and had on comfortable footwear. Her towel was packed in her bag. Christian had his bag jammed with his necessary items.

"Got your aqua socks for the climb?" Christian said as he pulled up into the parking lot. He knew this was going to be a fun, physical excursion, climbing up the beautiful rocks on the falls. He was as fit as an Olympic swimmer, but would she be able to handle it?

"Oh, yeah. And I've got my waterproof camera here. I'm going to ask the tour guide to take a picture of us climbing."

Christian smiled as he got out of the car, popping open the trunk. "Good."

Bob Marley's tune, "No Woman, No Cry," was blaring through speakers nearby as they joined in with a group of tourists at the base of the falls getting ready for their climb. The energy was high and pumping with the group they joined. The heavy, whooshing sounds of the waterfalls gushing down on the boulders was refreshing on this hot summer day.

Just the thought of climbing up the six hundred-foot high falls was both thrilling and frightening to Arianna's soul. It would take about forty-five minutes to an hour, an hour of pure entertainment and fun with Christian.

"Ready, baby?" Christian said in a low, deep voice, as he snaked his strong arm around her waist. Ari shivered when his firm flesh touched hers. Christian always had that effect on her.

"Yeah," she said over the roar of the falls. The water cascaded off the boulders at full force and splashed on their skin. She was already knee deep. She had her rubber aqua socks on as she gripped the limestone boulders, walking upwards against the glorious rush of blue water.

She didn't want to admit it to Christian yet that she was part thrilled and part nervous. It had been quite a while since she'd come to the Dunn's River, but then she hadn't climbed up the falls before. She didn't want to reveal that fact to Christian. He would think she was crazy for coming to the falls in the past and missing out on the best part—hiking up the falls.

"God, you look so good in that," Christian whispered in a low, deep voice in her ear as he hugged her. Electricity pumped through her blood.

"Hmm. So do you, hon."

Christian looked so hot in his blue swim shorts. His legs were ultra-muscular. All that leg pressing at the gym paid off for him. He was toned from his upper to his lower body with his rock hard abs and muscular biceps. He was probably the fittest visitor there. He looked even more devilishly handsome here. Christian was one of those drop dead gorgeous men you couldn't tear your eyes away from. Every time Arianna glanced at his radiant good looks, she was awed.

The trip up the falls was probably one of the most romantic things a couple could do. Up, higher they climbed up on the boulders with the force of the water gushing downwards on them. It was a delightful effect. The coolness was so refreshing. Arianna almost stumbled on a boulder and Christian, of course, was there to hold her.

"Thanks," she murmured, almost breathless.

"Welcome, baby. Thought you told me you'd been here before," he said with a cute grin.

"I...I have, just...not up here."

He gave her an odd look. "Not here? Don't tell me you've been to the Dunn's River and forgot to climb the falls. That's the best part!"

She looked back at him and playfully rolled her eyes. "I guess I was waiting for you to be with me."

He chuckled. "Well, I'm here now, baby."

A strong gush of water washed over them from the falls and she gasped. Laughter could be heard from the other visitors who were clearly enjoying the excitement of it all. It was a pleasurable experience.

Arianna giggled when Christian playfully pinched her bottom. "Ah, Christian! There are people around," she scolded him.

"You have the most beautiful smile I've ever seen, you know that?" He pressed a kiss on her cheek. "And ass."

She blushed, leaning into him as he held her. For a moment, Ari embraced him and the water level got higher delightfully flooding them waist high. The sensation was exhilarating. She turned to him and pressed her lips to his, kissing him gently.

"Thank you."

"For what?"

"For this. For teaching me to relax again, to laugh again." They stood on a large boulder for a moment embracing as the water gushed between them. Tourists were around in the near distance, laughing and enjoying themselves as they climbed the rocks. Everyone was enjoying themselves.

Reggae music blared from somewhere. They caught the soft sound of a nice ballad but couldn't place the song. It was uber romantic. She could stay there forever.

"You know I'm always looking out for you, right?" Christian quizzed, his expression serious.

She nodded, her arms wrapped around his neck. Arianna enjoyed the silky feel of his wet skin. His hair was silky damp, sticking to his skin, like hers. They were delightfully soaked. Just like this morning, they were soaked as they had been in the shower. The only difference was that they were not alone now. They were out in the open. Out in public. So no lovemaking here, but, oh, if they were back at the hotel. There was nothing more sensual, more erotic than reveling in intimacy during a soapy wet shower, pool or bath. Right now water gushed and splashed around them as it cascaded off the famous, breathtakingly beautiful falls onto their skins and on the rocks.

"Come on, let's go," he said in a low, sensual voice as he guided her higher on the falls. There was nothing more electrifying than having cool water gush down full force on your body while you had the man of your dreams holding you, by your side.

In this place, in this moment, Arianna was in heaven.

It was breathtaking, one of nature's finest creations. The greenery of the trees nearby provided an awe inspiring sight as they made their way up step by step.

"It's all about the journey, right?" Christian commented, holding her. His eyes were on her the whole time it appeared. As she looked nervously at the rocks walking up, he kept a grin on his lips, enjoying her holding on to him, squeezing his hand as she moved upwards. "Relax, baby, I'm right here."

"I...I know," she said, breathless, enjoying the energy and the walk. This was much needed exercise and movement she craved to energize her body, and what could be better than doing it with Christian?

"Relax, baby, you're so tense," he said, holding her waist again. He was right.

"I...I never said this before," she said over the noise of the falling water. A flicker of apprehension coursed through her veins.

"Tell me what?"

"I...I'm afraid of water," she admitted, her breath burning in her throat. A sense of inadequacy swept over her.

"What?"

"No. I mean, not water but...rivers and stuff."

"Oh, God, Arianna. Why didn't you tell me this before?"

"I don't know. I just thought...well, you know. I didn't want to miss out. I mean, didn't you tell me we shouldn't let fear control our lives?" she said, arching a brow as she paused, turning to him.

"Stop, right here," he said softly. He held her firmly as they reached a pool of water on one of the boulder levels. It was awesome. A steady stream of water gushed down, showering them. "Oh, God, you look, wow..." he said, redirecting his train of thought for a moment. Ari looked down at herself, realizing that the water completely soaked her bathing suit. Her erect nipples were showing clearly through the wetness of her white bikini bra. She blushed, a grin on her lips. Oh, Christian.

"Never mind! What do you mean you're afraid of water? Did something happen before?"

"Well," she said, resting on a boulder as the water drifted past them. "When I was younger, my mother and I went fishing with Dad and...I fell off the boat. I couldn't swim and...neither could Mom."

"What happened?" Christian's facial expression grew more serious. His tone static.

She shook her head. "Well, I obviously didn't drown," she said smiling, trying to lighten the mood and make fun of the situation. She saw how gutted Christian looked, but he was still clearly concerned.

"I can see that," Christian teased back, his handsome face still serious. He waited for her to say more. He obviously had no intention of going farther up the falls with her until he knew more about her newly revealed fear of water.

Christian could not believe what he was hearing. His gut was telling him to do everything in his power to protect Arianna. Why the hell didn't she tell him this before they headed to the falls? What was she afraid of besides the water? He was hoping she would open up to him more. But this?

God, he would kill himself if anything happened to Arianna. She could have had a panic attack here, and he wouldn't have even had a clue as to why. Still, it was good that he knew now.

He thought Arianna looked gorgeous in her string white bikini. Oh, man! He loved the way her body filled out in all the right places. She had the roundest, finest ass he'd ever seen on a woman. Her bottom was perfect. And her waist was nicely curved accentuating her sculpted, child-bearing size hips. Her voluptuous breasts were so full and shapely. She had a heavenly cleavage to die for. Good thing he was with her now though. He would have hated for her to be here so exposed with her assets—and he wasn't nearby. He didn't want any man ogling his woman. He could still taste the sweetness of having her this morning as they made love so hungrily, passionately.

It tortured him to see her looking hot and sexy in nothing but a stringy number like that, knowing full well he couldn't do a damn thing to her or with her out here—in public. Damn, he couldn't wait to get her back to the hotel. His sex was throbbing hard underneath his swim trunks.

Her beautiful dark brown hair was now fully wet and clung to her smooth, wet skin. Christian remembered a scene from an old Bond movie, Dr. No, which happened to be filmed in Jamaica. In the scene that came to his mind, that famous-at-the-time Swiss bombshell Ursula Andress emerged from the sea in her well-known white bikini. She looked hot, but man, those James Bond chicks had nothing on his girl. Arianna looked like a goddess, and she didn't even act like it. She was so sweet and so humble. God, it ached for him to think about her being terrified of water. Instinctively, he wanted to protect Arianna. He just wanted to be there for her anytime whenever she needed him. Heck, even if she didn't need him. Why in God's name hadn't she told him about her fear of rivers before?

"Well," she continued with her story. "I probably got the fear of rivers from my mother. She froze when I fell overboard. Luckily, Dad was nearby and he dove in and swam to save me." She bit down on her lip, looking up at the sky, shaking her head. He could see the hurt in her eyes. "Dad was so upset. He got mad at my mom, saying that she didn't even try to save me. She just froze, but it wasn't her fault. She was just…terrified of rivers. She's had a fear of a lot of things growing up. That was one of them. Anyway," she looked down at the water flowing around her. "I love the water; it's the fear of drowning that's the problem."

Christian sat close to her on the boulder and wrapped his arm around her waist, holding her tightly and firmly to him. "It's okay, baby. I'm here. I'll never let anything happen to you, okay?"

She nodded.

"I'm sorry that happened to you when you were young. It must have been terrifying for your mother," he surmised in a soothing voice.

"Yeah, it was." She looked around at the water gushing around her. "Thanks for not laughing at me."

His brows furrowed. "Why the hell would I laugh?"

"I don't know. Maybe because you thought I was a wuss or something."

"Hey, please don't insult me. You know I would never think that way about you…or anyone who had a fear of anything."

She hugged him and drew in a deep breath. "I know. I was only playing with you."

"Besides, I love a brave gal like you."

"Brave?" Ari pulled herself away from his embrace to glance into his eyes. "But I just told you that I'm terrified of water."

He looked deeply into her eyes and tilted her chin up to his with his finger. "And yet, you came here anyway."

His expression melted into a grin when he saw the stunned look on her face. Ari smiled appreciatively. "Have I told you how much I love you and how awesome I think you are?"

"Not enough," he teased her before lowering his lips to hers and kissing her gently, then passionately.

"Woohoo," a voice sounded from near the trees higher up. A tourist had caught a glimpse of them kissing. Actually, two of them and they both clapped.

Arianna blushed and he felt like a guy crazy in love. He didn't care. He was with the woman of his dreams. So real, so strong, yet she had her own weaknesses, just like a real person. Just like him.

"Come on, before we end up on YouTube from someone filming us on his cell phone," he joked as he guided her up. "You ready to go farther or do you wanna stay here? Just let me know, baby, I'm good with whatever you want to do."

"Just saying that makes me feel okay, Christian. Thank you."

He rubbed her shoulder and squeezed her lovingly before they made their way skyward. "You know," he said as he walked behind her, which did nothing for his growing erection as her ass wiggled and moved in front of him. "They say that being brave isn't the absence of fear."

"Yeah, I know."

"It's taking action, in spite of your fear."

"I know that, too," she said, turning to him with a sheepish grin. "I thought…I had to do this," she continued, breathless. "I wanted to prove something. That I wasn't going to be a prisoner of my fear…like…"

"Like who?" Was she going to say like her mother?

"Nothing," she said, shaking her head. "Let's just get up to the top of the falls."

They climbed up, enjoying periodic breaks soaking in the magnificent flowing water around them.

Christian could not help but feel more admiration for Arianna. He was glad he'd at least achieved something today. He got her to tear herself away from her work, from caring for others, including her parents. He had spent some time talking casually with some of the staff who worked for her. And from what he'd heard—all good things about her hard work ethic and fairness to her staff, she was also a workaholic who took great care of her parents. The fact that she even stepped up to the plate to help run her father's hotel spoke volumes about her. When they met, she was intent on furthering her college education to open up a daycare center. Well, this was a long way away from her dream but at least she was still managing a business that dealt with people. Christian admired her hard work and tenacity. Whenever she was needed, she stepped up to the plate without so much as a flinch. She was all heart and soul.

That was why it was important when he had learned that she had worked sixteen days straight to get her away from it all to take a break. For her own good.

Earlier, he told her that she had a competent staff working with her there, and the hotel already had a manager, so she would be okay to take a day off and do nothing but have fun. Selfless, unadulterated pure "me" time. He was glad he could be a part of it all. Seeing her smile, giddy with excitement and just relaxing brought a radiant smile to his heart.

"So...um...what about you?" Ari turned to him. "Do you have fears?" Her voice was low, breathless from the ongoing hike up the falls.

"'Course I do."

"Such as?" She playfully arched a brow.

"You."

"Me?"

"Yeah. I was really messed up when we were apart, Arianna. I was really afraid of losing you—for good." And, man that was the truth! He was going crazy out of his mind, not being able to reach her. Not knowing the real reason she left him high and dry.

He didn't know what he would have done with himself, if Arianna had refused to see him when he came back to Jamaica.

"We all have fears, Arianna," he said over the thunder of white foaming water smashing against the smooth boulders, as it spilled over the enchanting Dunn's River.

"I know."

"Seriously, I'm afraid of...never having the love of my life with me and dying alone."

She looked surprised. She was caught off guard by his frankness. What was wrong with him? Why was he opening up to her like that? Was it the effect of being amidst one of nature's most awesome spectacles? Was it the effect of the hot sun scorching overhead? Having another chance to be with Arianna?

"Wow," she said quietly. "I don't know what to say, Christian."

"Don't say anything. Just know that I want us to always be together, Arianna. I've never felt this way about anyone before," he confessed to her as they rested on a boulder with the water splashing down on them from all over. The cooling effect of the gushing waterfall over them was refreshing as the sun burned hottest at that time of the day.

"Afraid of dying alone? I never even thought about that," she considered, looking over the falls. They were pretty much midway now. Probably another half hour and they'd reach the top of this magnificent nature wonder. Christian enjoyed the salty spray of water as it showered them. What a day it was.

"Yeah, well, believe it or not. I think about it sometimes."

"Why? I mean, Christian, look at you. You're so...hot!" And he was! Her heart raced hard in her chest whenever her eyes were treated to his lovely physique. There he was dripping with charm and sexiness. The man made her heart throb every time. He was so good with those soft lips of his. Everything about this man oozed sweet sexual power. Her body got aroused more often than not whenever Christian was holding her. His nearness alone caused a sensuous reaction in her body. Hot probably wasn't even good enough a word to describe Christian Romero.

He grinned. "Yeah, so are you," he said, arching a brow.

"It's not easy finding your perfect soul mate. And when you do, you don't want to lose her. It's that simple really," he said, looking out into the distance. Tourists were climbing nearby filling the atmosphere with laughter and chatter as they made their collective way up. Christian saw an older couple with graying hair holding hands. They were dressed in blue bathing suits. The man in his trunks and t-shirt. They looked fit for their age—whatever ages they were. How nice it must be. The dude looked pretty happy. He figured they must be retirees who worked hard all their life, probably had a few kids and grandkids and probably great-grandchildren, too. Who knew? They were having fun—together, in their golden years.

"A dollar for your thoughts?" she said, playfully leaning into him, bringing him back to reality.

"Just a dollar?"

"Yeah. Better than a penny." Ari grinned.

Man, Arianna was really something, wasn't she? He drew in a deep breath. Why now? Why was he so intent on letting this beautiful woman into his heart and his mind? It wasn't like he was the type to spill out what was in his gut, his deepest fears or desires. Arianna had that effect on him. He felt so connected to her in a way that he'd never been with anyone else. That was something, wasn't it? Fate. Kismet. Love. Connection. All those things.

"You know," he said, changing the subject slightly. "Uncle Toni always told us that there are three things in life that are important. He got it from some old saying."

"What's that?" she probed eagerly. Looking up at him admiringly. He was glad that at least she wasn't fearful of the water falls right now. That was a good thing, wasn't it?

"One: To love someone. Two: To have someone love you," he said, smiling.

"And...? What's the third thing?"

"And three: To have one and two happen at the same time."

She melted into a soft laughter that warmed his insides. There was something so innocent and heartfelt about her laughter. He didn't know what it was exactly but he loved it. A lot. Christian pulled her closer to him. "I have to look up that saying. Even though Uncle always tells us these things, he always gets them from these books he reads. Quoting famous people and such."

Ari giggled. "Uncle Toni rocks!"

"I know. Anyway, I changed the subject but you wanted to know why I'm afraid of losing you and being alone?"

"Yeah."

"Well, I told you about my Uncle Everton on my mother's side."

"Oh, right. The one who passed away a couple years ago. You spoke about him a lot."

"I know. He was always good for a laugh. We used to hang out at the bar sometimes, play a few games of pool. In fact, he was the one who taught me about shooting pool."

"And women," she said smiling. "I remember you telling me that he taught you about women, right?"

"Yeah. Whatever. Anyway, he always told me to do everything to make the one I love feel special. He told me I would know when I found that one. That special one. You feel different. You can't stop thinking about them. They make you feel on top of the world, comfortable, and connected to. Alive."

"That's very nice."

"Yeah."

"But what happened to him? He died alone, right?"

"Yeah, he did." The pain of that memory was unbearable. Yet Christian felt he needed to finish that story. "He met this really nice girl he had planned to marry back in Vienna."

"Oh? You never told me that part."

"I know. I don't really talk too much about it. Most of the family—on my mom's side—know about it."

"So what happened to her?"

"They had a really bad argument. Some silly misunderstanding."

"Oh."

"Well, anyway, stubborn as he was he decided to keep his distance. He didn't take her calls. He wanted to, I don't know, get back at her. He said he was being stupid. Stubborn."

"So what happened after that?"

"She met someone else."

"Oh, no."

"Not at first, mind you, but he always regretted not trying to reconcile earlier. He had buried himself in his work and decided that it was better that they took time apart. But weeks became months."

"And then she met and later married someone else?"

"Yeah. He was pretty messed up after that. He dated a lot of girls after that but none came close to her. It just wasn't the same. That's why he always told us, me and my brothers. You find a good girl. You do everything to keep her. Treat her right. Don't ignore her. Don't take anything or anyone for granted."

"Wow, that's so...wow."

"He always had a fear of dying alone, and well, that's what happened."

"Oh, Christian, I'm so sorry. I...I really am. I remember you saying that you were one of the pallbearers."

"Yeah," he paused before speaking again. "You know, after we broke up, I took a lot of time off work, which as you know is something I don't really do."

"I know."

"Then, when everyone started to complain that I wasn't around work much, I decided to bury myself in my work nonstop. I realized what was happening. I thought about Uncle Everton and had nightmares that I was turning into him. God, that was the last thing I wanted."

Arianna wrapped her arm around his waist as she sat beside him.

He held her closer to him. "I love you, Arianna. I don't ever want us to be apart again. There's nothing I wouldn't do for you," he said, looking into her beautiful large brown eyes. She had the loveliest eyes he'd ever seen on a woman. So filled with love, energy and genuine care.

"I love you, too, Christian."

For a moment, they held each other. Just treasuring their time together. Their moment. He loved the saying that life was not about the number of breaths that one took, but the number of moments that took one's breath away. This...was clearly one of those moments. He was never going to lose Arianna again. Not if he could help it.

"Woohoo!" Arianna shouted excitedly. "We did it!" They had finally reached the top of the Dunn's River Falls in all its glory and breathtaking scenery. It was amazing. She didn't think she could do it, but she did. Oh, God! She made it to the top. It had taken them an hour to climb up and it was the best thing she had done in the longest time that she could remember. She made it. She didn't cave in to her fear of rivers or waters. She was okay. She was not a prisoner of her fear.

"Yes!" Christian grinned, hugging her from behind. "You did it, baby. I'm so proud of you." He pressed a soft kiss to the sensitive skin on the side of her neck and she shivered with a surge of pleasure. She had accomplished more than she could have ever imagined today.

She drew in a deep breath. She was actually looking over the glorious Dunn's River Falls. "Oh, God! This is so beautiful."

"Just like you," he said, grinning. He still had his arms wrapped around her waist, swaying with her to the beat of the music playing over some speaker nearby. He kissed the top of her head. "Honey, I'm so proud of you. You have no idea."

"Thanks, baby. Thanks for putting up with me. I'm sure you would have made it to the top in half the time if I wasn't with you."

"And what fun would that be?" he murmured, kissing her again.

"Hmm. Come on, I'm famished."

He laughed. "After climbing the most magnificent falls on the island, you're famished?"

"Yeah, so what?" she toyed with him, winking.

"I'm hungry as hell, too but not for food." Christian looked at her seductively. His dark, sexy eyes locked with hers and she smiled sheepishly.

"Yeah, we can eat again over at the hotel."

Later, after they had dried off, they strolled through the shopping area that was situated at the top of the falls. They purchased a refreshing bottle of water for each of them and chugged it down in no time. Arianna felt so alive, as a tourist, for the first time since she'd arrived on the island to help out at the hotel. She felt as if she didn't have a care in the world when she was with Christian.

Christian and Arianna took a five minute drive to Dolphin Cove where they watched the dolphins at play. Dolphin Cove was the next best activity to experience out in Ocho Rios, next to the famous Dunn's River Falls hiking. The interactive dolphin show was a fun aqua activity that provided crazy entertainment. Seeing the dolphins do their thing totally brought her into a whole new world. She'd even forgotten for a fleeting moment that she was in charge at the Duponte Hotel and that she had the massive Romero wedding to oversee this coming weekend.

They also took a walk along the jungle trail and later soaked up the sun on the white stretch of sandy beach. Ocho Rios had one of the best beaches on the island; miles of white sand and glorious views of the sea. Hugging and kissing like young lovers without a care in the world on the beach, while their eyes drank in the crystal blue water was a magnificent way to end their day.

Why hadn't Ari taken time out for herself like this before? Perhaps having her parents, especially her father, so in need of emotional support had taken its toll on her without even realizing it. Thank God for Christian. If he hadn't pushed her to take the plunge, so to speak, she would have worked her way through another week without a break. She needed this reprieve—badly. Of course, she thought that she and Christian were through, so burying herself in work and making sure her parents were all right had been her top priorities at the time. Well now, she was going to take some time for herself once in a while to debrief. To recharge her energies. Really recharge her energies.

***

What a day it had been. Arianna snuggled up to Christian in the bed as he slept. Thank God, Christian had taken Arianna off the premise for a change in scenery. She really needed that badly. They had taken a fun-filled splash in the famous Dunn's River Falls and soaked up the sights of the west coast and taken in a midafternoon concert and later relaxed by the beach in a secluded area. The dolphin show was a blast! It was a dream.

Christian even gave her a wonderful, and erotic, massage. She hadn't realized how tense her muscles were until he got out most of the kinks. Gosh, he was so good with his hands in every way imaginable.

Everything had been centered on the Duponte premises and she'd been working overtime lately to get caught up with inventory, special events and back orders. Not to mention handling the management that had been placed there long before she came on board. Since her father's health had deteriorated somewhat, Arianna wanted to ensure everything was in order and no one was going to take over.

Especially her debt-ridden, gambling uncle who would like nothing more than to yank the resort from underneath her and sell it off to the highest, or lowest, bidder he could get. He already ran several of his other companies into the ground. No way was her uncle going to take the hotel away from them and do what he pleased with it. It would kill her father. It would kill everything they'd worked so hard for. The Duponte was his whole life. He'd taken the once run-down property, which was willed to him on certain conditions, from a useless property to the five-star exclusive hotel that it was today.

It was more than her parents' dream, it was their life. It was her life. She had moved her world over to help manage things, relocating temporarily from New York, while things got running again smoothly. She had every intention once her staff had a handle on things to shift back to the States, where she could go back to her normal life, overseeing things from abroad. But right now, Arianna had other things to take care of. Her life. Her love life. Her well-being. Christian was right; without taking care of herself first, she didn't have a hope of taking care of others—or her business.

CHAPTER NINE

The following day, things had pretty much returned to normal. Crazy normal. Arianna spent most of the morning going over budgets, staff appraisal comments, making notes for the person who would take over in managing the day-to-day functions of the hotel—someone who had been on staff at the hotel from the beginning, and reviewing upcoming events, like the Romero wedding over the weekend. Inventory was satisfactory, thank heavens.

But oh, last night with Christian was so amazing. Last night and into the early hours of the morning Christian made love to her over and over again until the beautiful glowing sunrise on the beach, warming them into a new day. The cadence of the crickets singing outside, the ocean waves beating against the white sandy beach, the birds chirping, everything was so melodious, calm and perfect. Ari's heart thumped like crazy in her chest just thinking about him. Missing him already when he wasn't in her sight. Oh, how she craved his presence all the time.

Would she ever get enough of hot and sexy-as-sin Christian Romero? A delicious heat enrobed her body. Her pulse leaped with excitement just thinking about spending time with him, knowing that he was hers and she was his. What more could she want from life? When you have love in your life—everything seemed to fall into place. Life didn't have to be perfect, but just having that special person by you, with you, made the journey so much more pleasurable.

Arianna sat at her desk in her office sorting out some paperwork with a huge grin on her face. Christian. Her spine tingled pleasantly thinking about their precious moments together yesterday and early this morning. She wondered what he was up to. Probably with the rest of his family going over some last minute details regarding the wedding. The rehearsal was still a few days away, the evening before the wedding. That would be Friday night.

Christian energized her in a way she never would have thought imaginable. It was true about finding that special soul mate. That special one. Oh, she couldn't wait to see Christian again. Her body tingled from head to toe just thinking about him, the feel of his soft skin on hers. And those lips. Oh, those sweet, sexy, kissable lips of his all over her body. What had she almost given up by breaking off with him a month ago? She didn't want to even entertain that thought. She had to prep for an upcoming board meeting with the department heads at the hotel.

The phone on her desk rang. "Hello."

"Hey, Arianna, just thought I'd let you know that your uncle is heading your way." It was Tiffany, who was known by many as Tiff, her assistant general manager who was on the other end of the phone.

Tiff was an older Jamaican woman who knew the hotel like the back of her own hand. She was always on top of things and was genuinely kind and helpful. Tiff always kept Ari in the loop with tons of stuff happening around the property. In fact, if it hadn't been for Tiff, Arianna didn't know if she would have been able to grasp as much as she had in the short time that she had taken over the reins from her father. Tiff was her dad's assistant for many years since he assumed ownership of the hotel.

Tiff was so down-to-earth, funny and took no nonsense from anyone. She also knew the painful relationship between her uncle and the family. Tiff had seen him on one of his drunken rants before and almost had him thrown out of the hotel for misconduct. She wasn't afraid of dear old Uncle Ned. She was loyal and devout to Arianna's parents, and for that, Arianna was truly appreciative. She wanted to give Tiff more responsibilities as things moved forward. Perhaps promote her to GM eventually.

"Oh, no. Thanks, Tiff."

Just then the door swung open. Uncle Ned had a stiff expression on his face.

"What's going on here, Arianna?"

"What? What do you mean? You can't just barge in here like that without an appointment. I have a meeting to go to and a business to run."

"Oh, no. Not so fast. Your father should be the one running this business. I've been trying to reach him. Where is he?"

"I don't know. Did you try leaving him a message?"

"Don't be smart, my girl. I heard you talking to him on the phone this morning. I think you do know. You also know full well the conditions of your grandfather's will pertaining to this hotel, Arianna. You know full well, I could take over any time now. You better not be hiding anything from me," he sneered, jabbing his finger at her.

"You were listening to my phone calls?" she said with alarm. Now she thought she'd heard enough. "You have no right to be snooping around here, Uncle Ned. You can stay here but only on the condition that you don't harass my..." she paused, biting her lower lip, trying to stifle a tear. "...my parents or me, or our guests!" Arianna was emphatic.

"You know full well, this joint should be mine. And I'm sick and tired of you guys hiding stuff from me." His tone was chilly. So cold, Ari shivered. She knew what he wanted to do. He wanted to use the hotel to pay off one of his gambling debts. He had several failed "gold-rush" businesses that he ran into the ground with reckless management and poor staffing decisions due to his inability to control himself and his alcohol intake. He couldn't care less for the hotel and he'd told her father and her on many occasions in the past. He wanted whatever money he could squeeze out of it.

"Uncle, we're not going to go through this again. You know why grandfather left the hotel to Dad. We've been through this a million times. Besides, this is not about the hotel and you know it."

"Ah, so now we're talking," he mocked her. "Yes, that's right. Money. It's about money. Money that should be mine."

"Uncle, you've had many businesses in the past, on your own. This is all Dad has. Why would you want to take that away from him?"

"Because if he can't run it, I will." His voice was hardened, his eyes cold and calculating. So cold, it made Arianna feel uncomfortable enough to want to call for help or summon backup. She'd heard about her uncle, not just on his boasting sprees in the past, but from others about his evil connections and how he liked to "fix" people who were getting on his nerves. He was all bad. That apple fell far as hell from the family tree. It's no wonder her grandfather didn't want him in charge of anything. Her dad was nothing like her uncle. They were night and day. Fire and Ice. Opposites. Completely.

If Dad can't run it, you will? Yeah, right. Run it into the ground more likely.

"Who's to say he can't run it?"

"You know damn well why he can't. He should be going over inventory and running this place, not you."

"So what if Dad showed me the ropes and he wants me to help out a bit. He's a little tired right now but..." Arianna bit down on her lip again. She hated to not tell the complete truth, but how could she? Her uncle was a shark, a gambler who got in over his head and only wanted to take over to suck more money out of the place to continue with this addiction. The addiction he refused to get help for.

"Uncle, if it's more money you need to borrow..."

"Never mind that. I'm warning you and your old man, don't mess with what's rightfully mine." With those words, he stormed out, slamming the door behind him.

Arianna slumped down in her chair. What had she gotten herself into? What was she going to do now? What was she doing? Who was she protecting?

"You okay?" Tiff came into the office, seeing her slouched in the chair.

Arianna straightened herself up and stood up. She brushed her hair off her face with her hands and picked up her papers. "I'm good, thanks."

"Listen, don't let that man intimidate you, okay?"

"I...I won't. Come on, we've got a meeting to go to," she said breathless, her voice aquiver.

Later, Arianna sat in the boardroom with her department heads and some senior level staff members.

"Everything looks good so far," she said, trying to sound as calm as her nerves would allow while reading over the items on the agenda. "Okay, guys, we're doing well. Our main goal is to continually provide superior customer service and meet and exceed clients' expectations. So far we've had three hundred glowing and complimentary letters over the past year. Let's keep up the good work."

The group cheered around the table.

Ari held up her hand politely to silence them. "But...we've had a few complaints about the rooms, noisy air conditioners and such. So, guys, let's try to reduce the number of complaints in each of our departments. Understood?"

"Yes, ma'am, but it's not always easy when guests put notices on the doors not to be disturbed and then complain when their room isn't cleaned," the senior executive for housekeeping said.

"Okay, fair enough. I will look into that and ensure guests know that the rooms won't be cleaned or entered with the Do Not Disturb sign on the doorknob outside their door."

"Oh, and speaking of which, ma'am. We're still not cleaning your parents' suite. I mean, Mr. Duponte insists on always doing it himself. He tells us to just get the linen and the cleaning supplies. I don't mind but-"

"It's okay, Mara," Arianna interrupted, a lump in her throat. Her mother had agoraphobia for the longest time and didn't want to ever come out of her room for fear of crowds. She'd been to therapists in the past, but Dad was so good to accommodate her for the longest time. That was why when they went on their trip to the Mediterranean last year; it was a huge step—and a huge mistake!

"Thank you," Arianna continued, swallowing the lump in her throat. "Anything else, guys?"

"Don't forget the new dates for the staff training sessions," Tiff chimed in.

"Oh, right. We'll be scheduling some more staff development training sessions in the coming weeks. Tiff and I will go over the program and email each of you. And..." She flipped through some of her notes. Her mind still reeling over her tumultuous morning spat with her uncle. Her fingers were trembling ever so slightly. She hoped no one would notice. She drew in a deep breath and took a glass of water beside her to her lips and tasted the refreshing aqua. She then placed it back down on the table. "...we'll also need to put up the new fire safety plans. We had the graphics department design some eye-catching, new brochures to replace the ones we have up now."

She could do this. She could go through this meeting and forget about her encounter with her uncle. He had threatened to take it all away from them but she was not going to let that bother her. She was sure that legally, he had no right to.

Being brave isn't about not having fear, Christian told her while they hiked up the awesome Dunn's River Falls. *It's about moving forward, in spite of your fear.* She was not about to fear or worry over what may or may not happen. She was not about to let Uncle Ned ruin her morning and sidetrack her from all her goals she needed to accomplish. She had a hotel to help run and staff to manage and guests to take care of.

Focus, girl. Just focus—on the right things! Keep it positive. Positive thinking makes for positive results.

Arianna then went over some more items with the guest services manager, director of operations, rooms coordinator, chief concierge, bell captain and their sales manager. So far the numbers looked adequate. She was satisfied with the way things were moving. The Romero wedding was the biggest highlight this weekend. It was actually bringing in the most revenue and created more contract jobs than any other wedding they'd hosted. The Romeros spared no expense. Whatever they did, they did with class and money was not an object.

The Banquets Captain was ecstatic about the upcoming wedding and assured Arianna that all the supplies, catering and decorations were in place. The wedding was to take place on a custom-designed white gazebo by the sea with floral and white satin decorations entwined on it, in addition to silk and real flowers. Ari couldn't wait. She had already seen some of the shipment that came in early.

She was especially proud of her housekeeping department, who paid close attention to detail. "Continue to live out our motto: Friendliness and Cleanliness," she had praised them earlier.

She was also supplied up-to-date information from Joe, the hotel's chief maintenance engineer, who oversaw the overall operation of the building and parking lot, common areas and had other tasks like maintaining all equipment in guest rooms, monthly safety inspections and training on safety and emergency procedures.

"Great, so we've replaced all the older smoke detector models in all guest suites. Awesome!" Arianna confirmed with Joe. It was also good that they had installed those self-closing doors, which had proven to save lives by confining smoke so that the evacuation routes would be clear.

Before Joe could answer her, the fire alarm sounded.

"Oh, no!" Tiff exclaimed.

"I'll call the fire department," Joe said.

"Good," Arianna said.

Everyone looked around. "It's been a while since we've had an alarm," a member of the board commented as they all got up.

"Okay, guys, you know what to do. Close all doors, ensure everyone's okay until the fire department gets here and let's gather in the lobby."

"I'll make sure the elevators are shut off," Joe told Arianna. He held his cell phone to his ear. He was on the phone with the fire department. Even though they didn't know the source of the fire or if there really was one, they were not going to take any chances. While they got everyone safely out of their rooms, they would investigate to see if everything was okay.

It was a mad rush. Soon hotel guests came out of their rooms and everyone gathered in the plush lobby as per the Duponte Hotel's clearly posted fire safety and escape plan. Some were dressed in their robes, others in shorts and t-shirts. The designated fire wardens did a quick head count while Arianna's assistant grabbed the master guest list.

Just then, she saw Christian rushing towards her. "Arianna, are you okay?"

"Yes, thank you. It's probably nothing. Maybe a drill or someone pulled the alarm by mistake. We're investigating."

"Okay. Anything I can do?" he said, and he scanned to area for anything obvious.

"Joe called the fire department."

Just then, her uncle Ned came out of his suite and into the lobby, looking royally peeved as he eyed Arianna with disdain.

"Well, he looks cheery this morning," Christian commented, his jaw clenched. She could tell Christian saw her uncle's expression and wasn't impressed either.

"Where are your parents?" Uncle Ned demanded bitterly.

"Oh, no. Probably still up in the room." Arianna glanced around quickly, then glanced back down to the master guest list with her pen.

Before she could stop him, Christian left her side. "I'm going to get your parents."

"Okay. Thanks," she said before realizing what he was doing.

"Oh, God! Christian! No!"

He rushed up the steps and had arrived on the second floor in front of the Duponte's main suite where he knew they were staying. Christian was fit and athletic and it was almost impossible to catch up to him. Breathless, Arianna ran after him. "Christian, no. Please!"

He knocked on the door and Mr. Duponte opened the door to his suite. "Oh, Christian, I'm so glad you're here. Please help me convince Mrs. Duponte that we need to evacuate."

"Sure thing." Christian burst into the room.

It was too late. Arianna's legs were weak and she almost collapsed at the door.

"Oh, darling," Mr. Duponte called out to his wife. "It's time to go, dear. Christian is here. You remember the guy I was telling you about. Arianna's nice boyfriend. He's come to help me carry you down the stairs."

Mr. Duponte then turned to Christian with a smile of relief, as he pointed to his wife. "Will you please tell her we need to go now?"

Christian was never more shocked in his life. He felt his gut being ripped out of his body with a sharp knife. He looked in horror at the scene before him.

WTF?

Nothing could have prepared him for what he was seeing with his own eyes. Very few things could ever cause a knife-twisting reaction like that in him, but this did.

"Christian, I'm sorry you had to see that." He heard Arianna's voice beside him but he was too numb to say anything.

Just then the alarm silenced. And an announcement over the speaker sounded that it was a false alarm.

He looked at Arianna, his jaw clenched. He looked at Mr. Duponte and without so much as a word he motioned to walk away.

"Christian, I didn't tell you before because I didn't think you'd understand."

"You're right," he said, his tone chilly. "I. Don't. Understand."

CHAPTER TEN

"What's all this nonsense?" Toni demanded, turning to Carl. "First they tell us there's a fire. Then they inform us there is no fire."

"It's okay, Granddad. It was apparently a false alarm. It happens. We can go back to our rooms."

"Oh, I'm going over to the bar by the pool. Care to join me, Shelly?" Toni turned to his wife.

"Sure. Why not? I could do with a tall pina colada right now."

Just then, Carl spotted Christian. His cousin looked like hell. What had happened to him?

"You okay, man?" Carl turned to Christian. "What's wrong? You were on cloud nine earlier this morning."

"Everything," Christian said in an icy tone, his mind still reeling in shock and disappointment.

Christian walked up to the bar and ordered a non-alcoholic beer. What he really needed was something heavy and intoxicating but it was way too early in the day for that.

Shit!

What just happened? Why did Arianna lie to me like that?

"Seriously, man, your eyes are looking wild and dangerous, cuz. Whatever it is, she loves you. I can see the way she looks at you when you two are together."

"What makes you think this is about Arianna?" he said, not looking at his cousin, taking a swig of his drink.

"Because it usually is about a girl. Besides, only love can fuel those strong emotions. You only get really pissed like that when someone you really care about screws you or screws around with your head, man. That's the look you have right now."

Christian buried his head in his hands and drew in a deep breath. He had to settle his anger and his inner torment. He lifted up his head and rested his chin on his hands. "Screwed up is right, cuz. Things are really screwed up between us."

"Between you and Arianna?"

"Yeah."

"Don't you think you should be with her right now, sorting it out?"

"Not now." Christian shook his head. "She just really messed with my head. I...I can't think straight."

"S'okay. Let's chill for a while." Carl grinned.

"What's so funny?"

"Women. They are the most beautiful, exotic and complicated creatures I've ever known. But ya gotta love 'em."

In spite of himself, as painful as it was, Christian grinned slightly. Yeah, his cousin had *that* right.

CHAPTER ELEVEN

Arianna sat down in her office, a mixture of sadness and shame filled her heart. At least the fire alarm turned out to be a false alarm, but right now she felt as if her whole body was ablaze. Her heart burned in her chest. She needed emotional CPR to resuscitate her spirit.

It was all over. Mixed feelings surged through her body, leaving her bruised and confused. Hurt and dazed. She didn't want Christian to find out like that. Not a chance. What must he think of her? And her family? That they're all a bunch of psychotic weirdos. Oh, great! She'd just ruined her chance with the most perfect man she'd ever met—perfect for her. Her mind swirled with doubts and chaos.

She hung her head in her hands and squeezed her head as if trying to squeeze out the migraine. Earlier, her uncle was standing outside the door to her parents' suite when Christian had come in to help her parents evacuate. Arianna didn't even know when Uncle Ned had snuck up behind her outside her parents' room at the time. Had he followed them up from the lobby? Her uncle would miss nothing of course. He'd obviously heard her screaming after Christian not to go up to the room to help her parents get out. So naturally, he couldn't wait to follow them to nose around to see what was going on.

Now Uncle Ned knew too. He suspected something was up, but now he knew for sure and her whole life was about to be ruined. Right now she was more shaken than she cared to admit. Her entire family's future was about to be crushed in one fell swoop.

CHAPTER TWELVE

A knock sounded from the other side of Arianna's office door as she leaned against the windowpane, deep in thought.

"Who is it?" she uttered, almost under her breath. She didn't have the strength to deal with anything right now.

Christian entered her office. She looked up and there he was standing in his white shirt and dark gray dress pants. She remembered he said he had a business meeting to attend this morning on the island with a client of his that happened to be vacationing in Jamaica.

"Hey," he said quietly. He stood at the door for a moment with his hands shoved in his pants pockets, looking so handsome despite his unreadable expression.

"Hey." She turned to focus outside the window. She couldn't bring herself to look into his eyes again. The hurt. The embarrassment at what he'd seen. It was all too traumatic to relive.

He quietly stepped towards her, and without saying another word, he reached over and pulled her to his chest, wrapping his arms around her in a warm embrace. Arianna wanted to cry; tears moistened her eyes as she sank deep into him hugging him back.

That was all she needed. Christian. His unconditional love again. His understanding. Something she didn't feel she had a while ago. Now everything seemed as if it could be okay. Maybe.

After a while and a good cry, her eyes were dabbed dry with a tissue Christian used to wipe away her tears.

"Hey," he said, tilting her head up to his. "You're way too pretty to be crying like that. Okay?" He kissed her forehead gently, a warm smile on his face. His unreadable expression turned to that of concern.

"I'm sorry I walked out on you like that, Arianna."

"No. It's okay. I don't blame you."

"No, it's not okay. I was in shock but I..." He drew in a deep breath. "I just don't know what got into me. I just couldn't handle it. What's going on, Arianna? The truth. I want to help you...and your family. You mean too much to me. Why didn't you tell me...your mother didn't exist?"

His mind flashed back to what he'd witnessed in her parents' room after the alarm sounded earlier. Mr. Duponte was fussing over a large white pillow with a photo of Mrs. Duponte adhered to it. The pillow had been wrapped with a woman's pink knitted cardigan as if it were a real person. Her father treated the pillow as his wife. His stomach clenched at the sad, heart wrenching, yet tender memory. Nothing would be able to wipe that image out of Christian's mind.

Arianna broke away from him gently, hugging her arms around her chest and hunching her shoulders slightly.

She drew in a deep breath. "Remember the time I told you about my parents' trip?"

"Yeah."

"Well, as you know, my mother was always agoraphobic. Dad loved her so much. Anyway, they took the trip to Murumba and..."

"It's okay. Take your time," he said gently.

"Don't you have a meeting to go to? You said you had a client who was on vacation and wanted to see you, right?"

"You're my priority right now, Arianna. My assistant is here and she can handle things for me. Go on."

"Well, Mom never really wanted to go rafting but Dad thought it would be a good way to...get her out of her shell."

"And?"

Tears welled in Arianna's eyes again. "She panicked and stumbled before falling off the raft."

"Oh, God! Arianna."

"The waves turned harsh and strong at that time."

"But you never mentioned a funeral. So they never found her body?"

She shook her head, fighting back tears. "No. And according to the law in Murumba, a person cannot really be legally declared dead until seven years has passed in absentia. Until then, unless they find her remains, there's nothing we can do. They have strict laws. Dad was a wreck. That's when he had his breakdown," she said in a low tone.

"And that's when you went to be with him?"

She nodded. "Yeah. It ruined him. Emotionally. Psychologically. Guilt destroyed everything he was. The doctor who saw to him said it was a severe form of PTSD, Post-traumatic Stress Disorder. Experts have found a link between that disorder and delusional disorder as some form of coping. But mental illness and depression run in the family so..."

"Oh, God, Arianna. What a horrible thing to happen. You bore this entire burden on your shoulders—alone? Aw, Arianna," he said in a low, deep voice, shaking his head, holding her tighter. She could feel his energy surge through her. "You shouldn't have had to bear that burden alone, girl. You really love your father. You kept up the pretense this whole time so that he wouldn't be embarrassed, hoping that he'd get better."

"I had to. It's all he has. It's all we have—as a family. Anyway, I called the therapist after you left. Dad has agreed to go to Florida to a facility there to help him cope. I'll be going with him. Now that my uncle knows what's going on, now that it's out in the open, my dad can freely get the treatment he needs consistently. He feels guilty, torn up about what happened to Mom. He feels responsible. He loved her so much, he would have given his life for her. So when she...vanished like that, he had to keep her alive in his mind. I've been doing what I could from here with the guidance of the doctor he saw in Murumba, trying to ease him to reality at times, but just letting him go at his pace. I didn't want to push him too hard. But I had to keep up the charade with him right now."

She drew in a deep breath and tried to steady her nerves. Her breathing was labored. It hurt to even breathe, thinking about everything.

"That's why he pretended she was there, taking care of her," she carried on with her painful memory of the events that followed from that fateful trip to Murumba. "Bringing her meal trays, eating her meals...with her. You can't possibly know what's like to feel responsibility for the death of a loved one. Someone you've spent your whole life with... He just snapped."

"God, Arianna! No wonder your father..."

"Lost it?" Uncle Ned waltzed into her office with a smug look on his face.

"What the hell are you doing here?" Christian challenged him, his body rigid, his jaw set.

"I think I should be asking you the same question, Romero. It's officially my hotel now."

"Uncle Ned?"

"Arianna." Ned turned to his niece with a sarcastic look on his face. "So nice of you to hide the truth from me all this time. I knew something was up. You know full well the condition of my father's will."

"What condition?" Christian growled. He then turned to Arianna. "Arianna, what is this man talking about? I'm not gonna just sit here and let him walk all over you."

"It's the will that granted my father—and me the right to this hotel that Grandfather left."

"I don't understand."

"Oh, no. Let me explain." Uncle Ned plopped himself on the chair and grabbed a bowl of raisins popping one at a time into his mouth. "You see, I was the intended heir to this...place, but dear old Dad thought that my younger brother should have it since he believed I wasn't responsible enough. Now, let me see," Ned continued, leaning back, enjoying this situation.

"Now, the will as I remember," Ned continued, "stated that my father should inherit the place instead since he is of sound mind and judgment. And since, as Arianna might have mentioned to you before, mental illness runs in the family with my mother suffering severe depression before she took her own life and Dad having bouts of dementia on and off, dear old Dad stipulated that Giles, Arianna's father, should have this hotel as long as he is of sound mind." Ned popped another raisin in his mouth chewing emphatically and making 'mmm' sounds.

"Now as we all know—and my lawyers will know soon—dear old brother isn't exactly playing with a full deck of cards, if you know what I mean," Ned said, making circular motions with his finger at his temple.

Arianna's heart squeezed. She felt as if her head was about to explode. Her limbs felt weak.

"So that's probably why Ari here didn't want you to know we're a mixed bunch of fruits. But in any case, the will states that if for some reason that Giles is not able to run this place by not being of sound mind or is deceased, then I get the facility."

"And if you can't for whatever reason be in control, then I'm named third in that will, Uncle Ned. You know it."

Ned tilted his head back and laughed, almost choking on a raisin. Christian looked as if he was fuming, his eyes narrowed in contempt for the man.

"You and I both know, darling Arianna, that is not going to happen. Now you have," he glanced at his watch, "twenty-four hours to hand over the papers. I have someone who could be interested in buying this place. We may rip it down and turn it into, oh, I don't know, a strip bar or something. We can do this out of court or in court. Have it your way. But this place is mine. Bear in mind it could take years or a lifetime to contest the will."

"Why would you do that to your own niece? She and her father worked hard for this place. Man, are you crazy?"

"Ha. No. I'm the true owner, and in fact, I don't care for your presence here right now. Romero or not. There's nothing you can do to me."

Christian narrowed his eyes. A wicked grin on his lips. Arianna didn't know what to think of what was going to happen next. He was a hot-blooded Romero and you didn't want to mess with them or challenge them or mess with anyone close to them. That much she already knew.

"What did you just say?" Christian said, his jaw clenched.

"I said, I would like you to leave now and your family, too."

"You can't just take control like that, Uncle Ned. It takes time. There are laws in place."

"Yeah, like laws about deception. You knew full well, your old man had lost his marbles long ago on that island in Europe and you kept it from me. How's that for laws in place?"

"Speaking of which," Christian stroked the stubble on his chin. He leaned back casually against the windowpane. "Didn't you own several businesses in the Cayman Islands and a few up in Canada over the years?"

"Yeah, so what? Ooh, I'm shaking in my boots. You've had your investigators check me out. Good for you. Now get out!"

"But you made how many millions before your companies all went bust?"

"What are you getting at?"

"Didn't you turn a huge profit of over $50 million dollars, putting the businesses in your ex-girlfriends' names and sending them emails that they were not to let on that you were the owner?"

Ned loosened his tie. Sweat glistened obscenely on his face. "So freaking what?"

"Did you…um…" Christian casually picked up a magazine resting on the table and pretended to be interested in it, flipping through it. "…remember to report your earnings to the IRS?"

Ned froze.

Ned's eyes appeared as if they were about to bulge out of his skull. "W-what?"

"The Internal Revenue Service," Christian emphasized, trying not to grin, apparently.

"You know, I hear they can be real sticklers to U.S. citizens who forget to report revenue and evade taxes."

Ned's face went beet red. He looked as if a heart attack besieged him. He shifted uncomfortably in his seat.

"Oh, dear. Was that supposed to be your little secret, Ned?" Christian feigned surprise. "You know, our investigators estimated you owe probably $20 million or so in back taxes and we both know you don't have that. Geez, what do you think the IRS would do to you, Ned, if they found out and you didn't have the funds to pay them back?"

Ned flinched. He got up from his chair stumbling. He straightened himself up. "How did you...you...wouldn't..."

Christian lowered the magazine to his lap and glared dangerously into Ned's eyes. "You're not going to do anything that would hurt Arianna. Understood?"

Ned looked to Arianna and back to Christian, defeat in his eyes. "Understood." He grabbed his jacket from the back of the chair and placed his sun hat on his head. He walked out of her office without so much as a glance back.

CHAPTER THIRTEEN

"Oh, my God! Christian?"

"What? How did you...what just happened?"

"Oh, it's nothing. I just had my guys do a bit of research on your uncle. I wanted to know what he was about and what he was hiding. You should know me by now, Arianna. I'm a Romero, and we don't mess around when it comes to protecting those we love and care about. I'd do damn near anything I had to just to make sure you were okay. Understood?" He arched a brow and looked so sexy when he did. She reached over to hug him.

He embraced her tightly and pressed his lips to her forehead. She felt a delightful spark of energy rush through her from the soft, magical touch of his lips on her skin. God, she loved the way he felt. All the time.

"Oh, Christian. I'm so sorry that I never trusted you before."

"Why wouldn't you?"

"You heard Uncle Ned. Mental illness can run in our bloodline and...I...I mean, you would want to have children with me knowing that...?"

"Hey, don't even finish that sentence. And don't insult me. I love you, Arianna. My love for you is unconditional. Besides, you don't suffer with depression."

"I did once. Not like that. I mean, Dad has delusional disorder and so did Grandma. The trouble with that disorder is that sometimes it can go undetected because, depending on how severe, most people can function in their day-to-day lives. I didn't want it to get out-"

"Hey, it's okay. We're going to make sure your dad gets the best treatment and we're going to move forward, okay?"

She nodded. "Okay."

"God, Arianna. You're so...amazing, you know that? It must have torn you up inside, seeing your father like that. You kept up the pretense with him not just because you didn't want to have him humiliated but you didn't want him to lose his business. You're one brave woman. As painful as that was, you did it for all the right reasons. Who could fault you for that? Heck, if that's the kind of genes you have, I'd be honored to procreate with you."

She smiled appreciatively and hugged him closely.

He glanced at his watch. "Come on. Let's go check on your father."

"I love you, Christian Romero."

"I love you, too, Arianna. Just don't ever hold back on me again. Don't ever take on anything like this on your own without giving me a chance to help you. Promise?"

"That, I promise."

CHAPTER FOURTEEN

The next couple of days, Arianna had addressed some members of the hotel staff, including Tiff, about her father not being well, though not going into details. Many of them had suspected something was wrong. Although her mother rarely left her room when she was…around, the staff never saw her since Dad returned from Murumba. Even during drills in the past, she would explain it off that her mom had stepped out.

Arianna sat at her desk in her office flipping through some files and sifting through invoices while thinking about the events of the past few days. She was more grateful than ever to have Christian by her side, supporting her. He was the greatest thing that had happened to her. She didn't know what she would have done if he wasn't in her world. Oh, God! She could have lost everything. Her father would have been gone completely if her uncle had stepped in with a dramatic hostile takeover of her father's beloved "home."

Thankfully, her uncle agreed to sign official documents, declaring it best that the hotel keep its current management since he would not be in a position to manage the facility. After all, he had new issues surrounding unpaid taxes that he would have to face. Arianna wasn't at all against helping him out whenever she could. He was still her flesh and blood, she just wanted her uncle to get the help HE needed for his gambling addiction and hostile behaviour, or more accurately, anger management shortcomings. She just wanted everyone to be okay. She didn't like to see any one knocked down in life.

For now, her father was her priority—as he'd always been.

The truth was that Arianna had an explosive, crippling fear that her father, if anyone knew the truth about his "bout" of delusion, would be hauled off by men in white jackets and locked away in a padded cell.

The thought imprisoned her, paralyzed her. She would have died if that had happened. She knew from speaking to medical professionals that the delusions he was having could very well be a prolonged denial that would eventually subside.

And the truth was, her mother's body was never found, so they weren't lying overtly. It hadn't even been a full year yet.

The fear of losing her father, too, was so great and painful. So much so that Arianna would do anything she could to make sure that he got the help he needed. She had seen therapists, when he wasn't ready to go in the past, and talked to them about a "friend" who was going through delusional episodes after a tragedy. She had taken their advice and tried her best when not working to work with her dad in orienting him to reality as much as possible. At times, she would go along with him gently in order to not have him traumatized any further. She had spoken at great lengths to the doctor in Murumba who had initially treated him for shock when her mother vanished beneath the water. The doctor knew the truth since he'd seen her father before they left the island.

Thankfully, now her father would get the additional help he needed. Tiff had agreed to handle more responsibility so that Arianna could spend more time in Florida with her father while he went through his treatment.

Currently, Arianna had the wedding to think about, ensuring that the banquet department and event planning department had everything in place. The wedding was taking place soon.

CHAPTER FIFTEEN

There was nothing more romantic than walking on the golden orange sand on the beach. It was Saturday morning and the guests were getting ready to enjoy a memorable beach marriage ceremony, with a sea of aqua in the background, enjoying the soft music playing. The bright sun shone in the cloudless blue sky, as the calming whispers of the waves washed up on the side of the beach shoreline. The white-painted wooden arch of the wedding gazebo was tastefully decorated with pulchritudinous yellow flowers.

Heated anticipation rushed through Arianna's blood, thinking about Christian and how they would enjoy another passionate night after the ceremony. She just couldn't get him out of her mind, for one minute of the day. She straightened out her cream-colored satin dress and took her seat near the front. She reached down and brushed some small grains of sand from the simple, strappy flats she wore. That was the thing about beach weddings, one had to make sure they had the right elegant foot wear so as to keep shoes from sinking in the sand. She learned that the hard way some few years back when she'd attended another friend's wedding on the beach.

What a glorious, cloudless summer day it was to get married by the beach. Thankfully everything was in place. It had been a mad rush that morning getting last minute details together for the event.

Christian looked so hot and delicious as he stood in his tailored white tux along with his brothers and cousins as groomsmen in the wedding party. He always had a compelling presence, even in a crowd. Christian, with his radiant tanned complexion, smooth skin and devilishly handsome face, seized her heart every single time her eyes captured his.

Arianna sat beside Venus on the white satin covered chairs watching. She noticed Venus glancing up at Carl every so often. It was so obvious Venus liked Carl. Why didn't she just admit it? Arianna smiled to herself. There were about two hundred guests present, mostly family members and close intimate friends. The Romeros were extremely popular but wanted to keep this a small—by their definition—and intimate occasion. She didn't blame them. Two hundred guests? Family only? The family was massive on their own. What a close-knit group. She longed to have a large, close family just like the Romeros.

James Ingram's beautiful, romantic soul ballad "Forevermore" played as Blue walked down the rose petal-lined aisle. Blue's sister, Courtney, was her maid of honor. Arianna never heard this song being played as the bride walked down the aisle. It was a classic love song. If only she could walk down the aisle one day. This would definitely be her song to stroll right into the arms of a handsome man who loved her. Christian.

Blue looked so gorgeous and stunning in her elegant beach bridal gown, an A-line strapless chiffon chapel train wedding dress. Classy, magnificent, and Zack, oh, Zack looked so perfect for Blue, handsome in his white tuxedo. He, like his brothers, who were so tall they towered over the minister, lined up waiting for Blue to reach the altar.

An ache crept in Arianna's heart for Blue that Blue's father was no longer around. She wondered if Blue thought about her father as she walked down the sandy pathway alone. The flower petals placed strategically down the walking path, as Blue made her way down, looked so festive.

"Please be seated," the young minister told the rest of the guests.

"We're all here to celebrate the love and union between Zack Romero and Blue Monroe," the minister continued with the ceremony.

Arianna felt joy dance through her heart. She knew how hard it had been for Blue in her life. She couldn't be happier for her. Arianna's eyes then glanced at Christian and her heart jolted again. She wondered if they would ever have a chance to be...joined in holy matrimony. As the waves rolled on the side, beating on the shoreline she continued to watch his sweet physique as he stood by with his other brothers in their white tuxes. To her surprise, he glanced directly into her eyes, as if he could feel her eyes on him. For a moment their eyes locked, and oh, her heart turned over in response. A quiver surged through her blood and she tingled in her belly. *Oh, Christian. You have no idea how much you mean to me.*

His lips curled slightly into a handsome grin and his dimpled cheek caused waves of excitement to rush through her. She glanced around quickly, hoping no one would catch their little exchange, but of course, they were focused on the bride and groom.

Arianna had a vision of Christian up at the altar, only not as one of the groomsmen, but as the groom. Her groom. Would that ever happen?

* * *

The beach ceremony was a blast! Arianna couldn't remember the last time she had so much fun at a high-energized wedding. They'd feasted on an exquisitely prepared dinner in the professional garden at the resort with a captivating view of the sea making the moment all the more memorable. Arianna couldn't keep her eyes off Christian all afternoon.

Later, she slow-danced with Christian at the wedding dance, her arms snaked around his neck as they both swayed to the love song and as usual, Christian flirting with her, singing adoringly off key. She giggled when he nibbled her earlobe. His sexy aftershave scent made her feel so romantic. He smelled, oh, so good. All the time. She enjoyed the heat from the silky feel of his skin on hers as he ran his hand over her back. Her dress at the back revealed a bit of skin in a classy way with its low-cut design. "You are so beautiful, Arianna, do you know that?"

"You tell me all the time!" She grinned sheepishly.

"Believe it," he said in a low, seductive voice, looking deeply into her eyes and heat slithered down her spine. Oh, Christian.

Earlier at the wedding ceremony, Zack and Blue did the romantic unity sand moment. Just like the unity candle, only they each had separate bottles of sand symbolizing their separate lives and all that they were as individuals before today, of course. Then, the romantic part that melted Arianna's heart was when they poured the sand together, the individual containers of sand were no longer in existence but joined together as one. As one. Exactly as marriage should be. It was so magical. Breathtaking. Just as this moment with Christian was, she mused with delight.

They'd danced the night away, pretty much. She had a longing for family again. Before she and Christian headed to her suite, she checked on her father. He was sound asleep in his suite. Toni's wife, Shelly, who was also a nurse, had learned that he hadn't been "feeling well" and had also checked on him. Soon thereafter, Ari would be taking time off from the hotel to take him to a treatment center in Florida, while Tiff managed things at the hotel for a while, and Christian, darling Christian, had insisted that he take the trip with them. He said he didn't want to spend another moment away from Arianna, but that was too much to ask of him, she told him. As usual, he told her not to ever insult him again. He was, after all, the boss. He could hand over duties to his subordinates while he carried on with important matters in his life. She was important to him? The thought caused a rollercoaster wave of emotions to heat through her body. She was important to him, but how much?

She woke up to sunlight piercing hot rays into the room. She glanced around pulling the sheets over her. "Christian?"

She looked around. Where could he be? They had made passionate love despite being a bit tired at first from dancing all night, but oh, their energy kicked up a notch when he got aroused seeing her strip out of her gown. Arianna grinned at the memory.

She brushed her dishevelled mound of morning hair off her face and got up off the bed. She went into the living room of her suite and overheard Christian speaking to his cousin, Carl. "Yeah, cuz. Thanks again. I'll catch up with you later," Christian said just outside the door to his cousin before returning to the suite and coming back inside.

"Christian," she said, turning to him. She was caught by surprise that he was already up...and dressed. *What gives?* "You're up early. Is everything okay?"

"Yeah. Morning, beautiful." He pulled her gently to him and bestowed a soft, tender kiss on her lips. Oh, those sensuous lips of his.

Christian reached for the bouquet she'd caught at Blue's wedding. "Carl just brought this in. You left it at the reception."

"Oh, no. I...I was tired. Thank you. I must tell him thank you."

"No problem. I already thanked him for you." There was something odd about the way Christian uttered those words. She didn't know why but it was just...different. There was a look on Christian's face. A handsome, mysterious poker card-playing look. As if he didn't want her to know what cards he had up his sleeve.

"Okay, what is it? I can tell you're dying to laugh. Is there a gag here?" She held the bouquet away from her chest, just in case. She knew the Romeros often liked to play jokes on each other. Was the bouquet of flowers going to fall apart on her or spew water? She grinned to herself. She then placed it on the table beside her, only to have a small, velvet covered box drop out.

Her heart pounded fierce and hard in her chest, thrashing madly. She could not breathe. She needed oxygen. This couldn't possibly be what she thought it could be—could it?

"W-what is this?" she whispered, breathless, picking up the small jewelry box. She quickly opened the box as swiftly as her heart sped in her chest.

"Oh, God!" Arianna covered her mouth with her free hand. It was the most beautiful sparkling diamond engagement ring she'd ever seen.

"I had my assistant bring it in when she landed a couple days after me."

"Oh, Christian." Arianna was in shock. Her legs felt numb. Weak. Her head felt giddy.

Christian got down on bended knee and tears watered her eyes. "Arianna Marie Duponte, will you marry me?"

Arianna was overcome with emotion; her lungs were squeezing hard for air. She could not speak at first but just nodded repeatedly. "Yes. Yes. Yes," she said, wrapping her arms around Christian after he got up. She embraced him like never before. "Yes, Christian, I will!" She looked into his eyes, those dark, sexy loving eyes of his. "Yes, I will marry you. I love you."

"I love you, too, baby. You mean the world to me. And I'll never leave you, girl. I'll be loving you forever." He pressed his soft lips to hers and kissed her passionately, sealing the deal. Beginning their journey of love...forever!

THE BILLIONAIRE'S PROPOSITION (THE ROMERO BROTHERS, BOOK 4)

Sworn bachelor and sexy charismatic billionaire, Carl Romero, needs to find himself a wife and child before he announces his run for mayor—but only for a one-year commitment. He's determined to win in the next election but being a young, single man is his only obstacle to gaining the voters' confidence. In politics, image is everything. He has his eyes set on his delightful executive assistant, a single mom, Venus Jackson. His troubles compound when he realizes winning votes isn't all he wants, so is winning Venus's heart.

Struggling single parent, Venus Jackson, has a dark secret in her past and too much emotional baggage. She simply can't handle any more drama in her life, but when her irresistible boss, Carl, offers her a proposition to play his doting wife for one year as he embarks on a political career, her mind is telling her to run the other way, yet her heart is pulling her in his charming direction.

CHAPTER ONE

"They can't get away with this!" Carl Romero declared, slamming a copy of *The Hills Times* newspaper on the desk in the study at Romero Manor. His eyes were just assaulted with the latest headline: Party Playboy to Join Mayoral Race –A Joke!

The shock of the morning headline struck him full force in the gut like a steel bat to his flesh. A vein throbbed in his temple. Heat burned through his body while he processed the insulting jab towards him in the news.

"I haven't even officially announced my intention to run yet!" Carl finished. That was true, though he had spoken about it publicly before when interrogated by a reporter. He hadn't made an official announcement but it seemed as if his dirty opponent in the upcoming race, Dayton Leechwood, was intent on having Carl's bridges burned before he had a chance to even cross it. Well, he'd be damned if he let that happen. The current mayor, Ruben Smith, was plagued by scandal and drug use lately and the city of Mayberry was ready for a change in power.

"Calm down, Carl," Toni, his grandfather and patriarch of the Romero dynasty, ordered. Toni was no stranger to conflicts. The widower had married his young nurse, Shelly, to the chagrin of his grandson Antonio. But he loved his boys and he'd be damned if they caved in to pressure like this.

The family had convened, once again, for a family meeting. This happened quite a bit, though the Romeros were successful in various industries, they often gathered when urgent matters arose at the sprawling 16,000-square foot luxury estate with its breathtaking views of the hills of Mayberry Hill and its own winery and vineyard. They also never forgot that family came first in a crisis.

"They want you to react this way. Don't play into their hands," Toni admonished. "Remember that life is ten percent what happens to you and ninety-percent how you respond. That's what makes or breaks you."

Not long ago, family members had convened in the same area of the mansion's luxurious study when Lucas was in hot water with a pregnancy claim from a woman he had allegedly dated. Zack, too, had been the center of undesired media attention when his ex-girlfriend threatened to sell a sex tape of their Vegas rendezvous in a blackmail attempt. Carl was the one to organize a team to dig up the location of said video recording. Never in Carl's mind would he have thought that he, too, would be the victim of harsh and defaming rumors! And now? Right on the verge of his political career.

Dios Mio!

"He's right, bro," Jules added. Not only was Jules Carl's ever-protective brother, he was also co-owner of their successful business, R.M. Fitness Centers. "Just do your stuff. Don't pay any attention to the haters."

"The haters?" Anger flared through Carl's being. "That's easier said than done, Jules. The voters will be reading what those damn haters are saying about me."

Carl leaned against the study desk at Romero Manor, his arms crossed over his chest. He was wearing a black suit with crisp white shirt and blue tie. How appropriate that he'd worn his dark suit today, since his mood was anything but bright.

So what if he was a member of the most prominent family in the province? The Romero family, thanks to their wealthy real estate tycoon and philanthropist grandfather, was popular not just for its contribution to society but also for the headlines the single Romero men often made.

But it didn't start off that way. They had only met their famous grandfather in their teens since their father didn't actually know his real dad, Toni. Before Toni had mentored them into self-made trendsetters in various industries the boys had suffered the tragic loss of their mother and their father lost his job, rendering them desperate and destitute. They'd lost their home and lived out of their father's minivan for a little while until the authorities stepped in. It wasn't all fun and games growing up. But the humility and difficulty during that period taught them to never forget where they came from. They knew in their hearts that a minor setback was a setup for a major comeback. And come back they did. Currently, Carl, along with his six brothers—and their cousin Antonio III, was on the Forbes list of wealthiest entrepreneurs in the world.

Carl knew the haters thought of him as an over-privileged dilettante. But none of the Romero boys coasted through life on their grandfather's back.

His cousin, Antonio III, was a real estate tycoon, like their grandfather. His brother, Lucas, was founder of the popular software and app Healthy Start Program. Zack Romero, often dubbed the real playboy in the family until his recent marriage, owned a successful winery and vineyard and created more jobs than any other family-owned business. Dion and Troy ran the most lucrative international business college that boasted thousands of successful online and in-class graduates, and his younger brother, Dr. Alonso Romero, developed both affordable and state-of-the-art medical and plastic surgery clinics all over the world. The plastic surgery clinics helped burn victims with reasonably-priced reconstructive surgeries.

Carl, though his international health club was flourishing, knew what it meant to be from a low-income family and wanted to do things a lot differently in the city as its mayor. But would he even get the chance? Property taxes were already sky high in the city. How could people afford to pay their mortgages with the skyrocketing taxes on their homes? And what about affordable daycare for families on modest incomes?

"Get this," Carl growled, picking up the newspaper again and reading another paragraph from the article. "What does Carl Romero know about struggling families?...the man is a party prince from a wealthy family who is out of touch with reality."

He threw the paper back down on the desk. "Can you imagine? Me! Out of touch with reality?"

"Man, if they only knew how out of touch with reality we were when we went to bed hungry in Dad's car every night, late at night in the coldest dark days of winter," Jules chuckled, devoid of any humor.

This was not how Carl anticipated his first few days back in Canada to be. The Romeros had recently returned from Jamaica, not even a week, from his brother Zack's island wedding to Blue Monroe. His brother and Blue, an ex-reporter, were still on honeymoon. But, oh, he wished he could get some insider information from his new sister-in-law about the inner workings of the press and their crazy antics.

Right now, Carl was on a mission and he damned well could do without this little tabloid-like reporting fiasco.

Carl, along with his brother Jules, headed R.M. Fitness Centers, which not only had a state-of-the-art run health club facility but they had a morning program for youngsters addressing eating well and trying to get better food choices in the schools. For as long as he'd known he could, Carl always wanted to make a difference. Like always. And his heart had always been in politics. Running a city. Or heck, maybe even a province or the country one day. Who knew? He was young and he was ambitious. His motto was always to live life to the fullest. Work hard, play harder—was how the Romeros ran things and they were rarely intimidated.

"That wasn't all the papers reported." Toni got up from his recliner by the massive stone fireplace that was nestled within the wall of bookshelves.

"What's that supposed to mean?" Carl asked, arching a brow. Oh, no. What was his grandfather getting at now? He had a gut feeling he knew what else his old man was going to chime in with.

"Marriage."

And there it was. The M word always seemed to make its way into conversations where their grandfather was concerned. Toni Romero believed betrothal would solve all of his grandsons' woes.

Jules shook his head, a grin plastered on his face. "Now how did I know Gramps was going to go there?"

Pamela, their young press secretary, was taking notes while she gazed at her own copy of the paper. She had already added her input to the heated discussion earlier. Image. Image was everything, she had rapped to him. Especially in the political arena.

"Marriage?" Carl repeated; he was incredulous. Now he knew he'd heard it all. "Grandfather, what does marriage have to do with any of this? Just because I'm alone, it doesn't mean I'm lonely." And that was the truth. Carl never experienced a deficit when it came to a hot date whenever he wanted, wherever he wanted. Women were often throwing themselves at him in all kinds of social settings.

"Fair enough. But marriage is not just about sex. It's about being with someone committed to you for life, showering you with unconditional love. Someone who brings out the best in you and more importantly, who encourages you and brings you happiness. I know you boys hate to hear it." The old patriarch hunched his shoulders innocently. "But...it is what it is. If you were married, my grandson, they wouldn't be able to call you an out-of-touch-with-reality party boy bachelor, or whatever it is they called you," Toni finished, addressing yet another section of the derogatory article.

Carl leaned back on the study again. Tilting his head back and grinning despite his anger. "Granddad, I think you've gone a bit far. Blaming me for what others are saying about me."

"He does have a point, Carl." Pamela placed her notebook and her copy of *The Hills Times* down on the table beside her and joined in on the conversation. "As I said earlier, public image is everything in politics. You want voters to feel as if they can trust you. Face it, most voters are families struggling with children. There's a reason a lot of presidents and world leaders tend to be married with at least one child. And right here in Canada, most leaders started out their careers always married. I did a study on this. In Mayberry Hill, you would be the very first candidate in your demographics—late twenties to early thirties—and single."

"See," Toni said, arching his brow. "I don't know why you boys have an aversion to marriage. It brings you stability to be with the one you love. You boys look at a wedding band as if it's a tiny handcuff. It's not. It's a joining symbol that frees you to be you, knowing you have love by your side."

"Yeah, I see their point, Carl. Voters want to know you're getting it regularly at home in a monogamous relationship so your attention is not elsewhere trying to sow some wild oats. Not to mention your body will always be charged on endorphins and ready to do your job." Jules grinned, teasing his brother, probably trying to lighten the mood—as was his thing to do.

Only Carl's body was pumped with adrenaline right now. He was feeling anything but light or amused.

"So you're trying to say that Leechwood would make a better mayor than me because he has a wife and kids? You've seen how many times in the past he's been in the papers for cheating on his wife. It's good that she openly forgave him but the guy's a creep," Carl continued, pacing around the fireplace. His dress suit jacket opened up.

"I can't believe the press isn't on to that!" Carl added, "The guy wants to raise property taxes, for Chrissake! He thinks it's better that hard working people foot the bill for a mismanaged city instead of taking it from the surplus and the reserve we never use. I have it all figured out. I can do this and save the city and taxpayers a crap load of money so that nobody has to go to bed at night wondering how the hell to pay their bills."

"Carl, you are so right. I admire your passion, grandson. That's why I want you to be successful, as much as I don't like the dirty games of politics. But we sure could use someone like you in office."

"Good. I'm glad you agree! I don't need to get hitched to prove anything to anyone. I have a campaign to organize. I'm not going to waste another minute talking about a dead topic like getting married. It's done with. I'm not marriage material."

"Oh, nonsense!" Toni snapped. "Carl, your brother Jules is right for a change."

"Hey," Jules feigned being offended.

"Being married shows stability and commitment," Toni continued. "I know you are committed and stable. But, it's not enough to do the right thing, Carl, one must also *appear* to be doing the right thing in life. I know it's not fair, but that's how the world of politics works. But never mind that; I know you won't regret the joys of being in love and married. And look at your cousin, Antonio. He said the same thing about marriage," Toni continued, "and now he is happily married to that nice wedding planner girl, Lucy. And don't tell me you don't love your adorable little cousin, Alexander."

"You know I love my cousin, Gramps!"

"You see, it's all about family. Family is the magical key that opens doors. The building blocks of a healthy society. We all need love. Love is good for us. It's more than that, it's essential! Heck, Antonio was even dead set against me and Shelly getting married. Yet here we are, married. My fifth marriage! And I'm happier now. And then your brother Lucas got married to Maxine. That was beautiful. Though they eloped in Vegas," he frowned.

"Now look at your brother Zack." Toni grinned widely. "Zack surprised the sweet Jesus out of all of us. I never thought he would have settled down. He had a different girlfriend every three months it seemed. He would change them with the season."

Pamela chuckled then quickly wiped the grin off her face.

"And don't tell me you didn't have a nice time in Jamaica."

"Granddad, I did. And good for Antonio, Lucas and Zack, but it's not for me."

"And don't forget, your cousin Christian is now engaged to that nice girl who owned the resort where we had the wedding."

Carl frowned. He drew in a deep breath and gazed out at the breathtaking views of the hills and all its greenery outside the French glass doors of the study.

"If it's any help, Carl," Pamela interjected, "I have the results of the latest opinion poll about what voters expect in the next election. Do you want to hear it?"

"No. Not really," Carl dismissed with a raised brow. His lips were slightly curled up at the side. He knew Pamela didn't fear any of the brothers. She was young and ambitious and worked for them long enough to know she need not tiptoe around them. Not only that. She was damned good at her job and had saved their public butts on many occasions. She was going to tell him the results anyway.

"Well, the results were," Pamela said quietly, ignoring his earlier response, "voters were unanimous with their main criteria. Family-oriented, family-friendly candidate." She then turned to Carl. "Carl, I'm afraid your grandfather's right. We know you'd make the best mayor this town has ever had but right now you have two strikes against you. You're single—and attractive! And you don't have a family of your own."

"She's right, my boy. I know you young men have accomplished much on your own and you know your way around your own business but trust me on this one. Your old grandfather is never wrong in regards to these things."

"So what do you want me to do, Granddad?" he said, turning his attention back to the group. He was beyond fed up. "Go out and buy me a wife and kid?" he continued with a trace of playful sarcasm. "Perhaps I can charge that transaction to my business account under public image. Do you think I'll be able to write it off on my taxes?"

"Now, Carl," Toni scolded, his voice raised a fraction.

Pamela burst out laughing then quieted herself quickly, clearing her throat.

"Sorry," Carl said, "I didn't mean to sound so..." *Sarcastic?* A devilish thought struck Carl. Could he really buy a family? Pay someone to pose as his doting wife? Nah! He couldn't do it. That would be dishonest, and didn't voters value integrity? He wanted to win this race so bad. But not that bad. He wanted to do what those darned opponents didn't want to do—make life easier for working class people. Lower taxes for residents so they could afford to support their families.

No. He was not going to play into political mud-slinging. Politics was deadly. And it could be even deadlier when one wasn't up front about everything.

"Where are you going, Carl?" his grandfather queried as Carl grabbed his keys from the table.

"To work. We have some new equipment coming in to the gym."

"I said earlier that I'd handle it, Carl. I've just got to meet with that supplier from Buffalo," Jules interjected.

"It's okay, Jules. I've got it covered."

Carl then thanked everyone who had turned up this morning to meet and discuss how he was going to deal with this latest debacle in the headline. "I need to clear my mind. To think," he continued, his voice hard and low.

"Carl, do you want me to go ahead with the statement we talked about?" Pamela asked.

"No. Not yet. I...I haven't officially announced my run yet. Right now, I think, no response is the best response. We'll strike back with something better."

"Hey, Carl, I'll have our boys look into who's behind printing up all this junk about you," Jules interjected. The Romeros had their own private detective agency that handled certain situations they often encountered. Least was they often vetted everyone who worked around or near the family. They rarely took chances with business associates ... or competitors. "I'm pretty sure it's Leechwood. That's usually his style. He's as mean and dirty as they come. He's been known to set up his past opponents and competitors in his business dealings."

"I know," Carl said, his jaw clenched. He could taste the bitterness on his tongue, at the mere mention of that man's name. Leechwood. His nemesis.

"I'll see you guys later," Carl continued. "Pamela, I'll be in touch with you this afternoon."

With those words, Carl strode out of the study.

"Hey, bro, are you taking the chopper into Toronto?" his brother Jules called out to him. The Romeros were one of few families that owned a helipad on their sprawling estate. Often as an alternative to the long commute into the city of Toronto from Mayberry Hill. They owned several lakefront condominiums in addition to several skyscrapers on Bay Street in the business district—often dubbed the Wall Street of Toronto. No surprise since Toni Romero was a real estate mogul who owned properties and land all over the nation and even some internationally.

"Nah. I'm good. I'm driving in. I need to think."

"Don't think and drive, bro. Could be dangerous."

Carl rolled his eyes. "Yeah. Whatever."

* * *

Later, Carl drove along the main road in his convertible. He knew his sports car was one luxury that probably had to go, he thought to himself as the summer wind rustled his hair. A young dude like himself driving a luxury convertible would probably send the wrong message to voters.

What was with him? Why did he give a damn what others thought of him? His car had voice-activated controls and he ordered for Venus, his assistant, to be called. Venus was a together, young woman who worked hard as hell. She was all too eager to work with him on his upcoming campaign. She was a single mother with a two-year-old. An odd girl. Quiet, hard working, efficient and always saying a kind word, but distant at times. He would often catch her ogling him but then she would turn her attention elsewhere while blushing whenever their eyes locked.

And man, she was hot. A surge of heat shot through his body thinking of her on their recent trip to Jamaica and how well she filled out her bathing suit while on the beach. Her glowing, tanned complexion, dark, silky, long, thick hair and large brown eyes captivated Carl the most. She was one of the finest women he'd ever set eyes on and yet she never flaunted her assets. And man, what an ass she had. She had a petite waistline that accentuated her wide, curvy hips. Carl was getting hard thinking about her.

He tried to squash the thought of anything that could arouse him sexually right now. He had other things he should be thinking about—like his upcoming bid for mayor.

Focus, Carl.

Carl had noticed in the past that Venus's defenses always seemed to go up whenever he would ask about her family in Kansas or from wherever it was that she had travelled. She was originally from some island in the Mediterranean but rarely spoke about that.

An odd thought crossed his mind. She had been struggling for so long and…he wondered if she would…? No. He wasn't even going to entertain that thought. Heck, he could win this campaign on his own merit. Without a wife and kid.

For some reason, Carl took a detour off the main road and maneuvered down Chancery Lane. His heart was beating thunderously in his chest, bashing against his rib cage. It was almost painful for him to breathe. He pulled up to the curb of number 123. It was a white brick bungalow. Three bedrooms, one and a half bathrooms. He looked over at the side and could still see the tree that had been carved with some initials.

Carl got out of his car and leaned against it. His vision blurred with tears of pain, his lips pinched together into a thin line.

Memories.

Painful, unbearable memories.

He remembered as a youngster, looking out at the window at top. His father had just gotten home from work, dread in his eyes. His mother, who was battling breast cancer, had been suffering from depression. She did her best with her boys. Dad had just lost his job. They were already behind in payments at the bank.

But property taxes had risen, and even if Dad had another job, there was no way in hell he could pay what he owed the municipal government.

It was right there in that very spot where his car was parked across the street that he and his brothers and his parents watched as their home was auctioned off. They had nowhere to go.

His eyes were blurry with salty moisture.

Carl's family had lost their home. Soon after that, they had agonizingly lost their precious mother.

Did the local government even care or assist them in time? Dad did his best. No one could have stepped in to help them at the time. They had a cousin in Virginia but that was a long shot. She couldn't take in his father, not with seven young boys.

Carl wiped his eyes, his anger still seething through his body.

He was damned if he was going to let that scene play out again, whether with himself or another family.

The address at 123 Chancery Lane was one of a few homes they'd had. Their father's car was another home until authorities stepped in. Then they lived in a low-income housing project down the street at number 490 Chancery Lane in apartment 14A. They'd all crammed into that little crap place. Though they were thankful to be out of the old minivan. So they ended up going to the same school, as difficult as that was. But they'd always hoped they would have gotten their home back. That never happened.

Carl glanced at his watch. He didn't know what shot through his body in that moment. But it was a high-powered electrical surge that raced through his blood and pumped some idea into his head!

He changed his mind. Coming down memory lane, as painful as it was, was an omen, he mused. A good omen.

Carl decided just then that he *was* going to announce his candidacy. But he was going to do it, not as a bachelor, but as a doting husband and family man. Of course, marriage could never be on his agenda for long term. His past with women had already dictated his fate. He could never trust a woman—again. But it wasn't just about having had his trust betrayed, was it?

His heart squeezed in his chest at the thought of the hell he had gone through with his ex-girlfriend, Nea. He thought she was *the one*, until he found out that she'd been sleeping with his best friend—his ex-best friend. That really did a number on his nerves and smashed his heart and soul to pieces. Since then, commitment was always an issue with him. He wasn't going to give another woman the chance to hurt him that way again.

Anyway, he wasn't going to waste another thought on it. He had a campaign to run and a plan of action to implement. Marriage to Venus, assuming she accepted his proposition, would be for the purpose of image only. It would be short term. Nothing more. He knew she was going through a difficult patch in her own life and often talked about wishing she had more support. Well, this would be a win-win situation. They would both benefit from being married—to each other.

Hell, he was going to do anything he could to boost his reputation so he could win that seat and make the changes necessary to keep his end of the deal he'd made to his mother on her deathbed.

He was going to run for mayor of the city.

And he was going to win.

CHAPTER TWO

"Okay, sweetie," Venus Jackson directed her two-year-old son, Tristan, "just remember to breathe into this little chamber." She held the Disney designed aero-chamber in front of him. He was always fussy when it came to taking his asthma medication.

She glanced at her watch. It wasn't easy being a single mother who worked outside the home. Venus was constantly juggling between taking care of her sweet little angel with his medical needs and the workload of an executive assistant to an extremely busy employer. A charming boss, but busy nonetheless. She had heard her cell phone ringing moments ago but couldn't answer it. Not while she was giving Tristan his medicine. This part of her morning routine always took forever.

Her little boy shook his head and wrinkled his nose.

Venus was already running late for work. She was supposed to meet Carl Romero in his office at the main office at R.M. Fitness Center. They were expecting the latest state-of-the-art equipment for the facility. But that wasn't all. She was going to be helping him with his campaign. She was all too eager to take on the new role as his assistant campaign manager while transferring her current administrative duties to a fellow employee.

Oh, she daydreamed about Carl sexy-as-sin Romero almost every waking hour. It was as if fantasizing about him kept her going in more ways than one. A grin warmed her face just thinking about Carl with his tall six-foot-two-inch frame. It was no surprise that he would run a successful health and fitness center franchise with his brother since they embodied fitness. Carl was muscular and firm. He was well dressed in his dark designer suits when he attended meetings and filled out deliciously with his broad shoulders and lean frame. But when he was in his gym gear, it was heaven to her eyes. Venus often surreptitiously glanced at him while he worked out in the gym on the weights, his smooth skin and ripped muscles glistened with moisture. The health club was bright and airy and had a unique design with offices overlooking most of the facility. Her office had a window that overlooked part of the main gym. She often saw other female employees ogling her boss, but she never openly let her own feelings about him be known. It wasn't as if she even had a chance with him.

She'd always harboured a secret attraction to her boss. But she could never reveal that. She'd come close to letting herself go in Jamaica at his brother Zack's wedding but she knew that she was destined to be a single mother. She could never be with any man. Not now. Not ever. It would be too dangerous, given her past and the lie she was forced to live.

"Okay, now one, two and three, breathe in," she chanted, pulling a funny face so that Tristen would laugh. It often calmed his nerves down a bit. He giggled at first then he allowed her to place the mask portion of the aero-chamber to cover his mouth and nose so that he could inhale. She squeezed the blue inhaler into the chamber and he inhaled as she counted.

Tristan breathed in and out slowly into the smooth, long, plastic chamber.

"Good, sweetie," Venus praised him. She was just grateful that he was allowing her to give him his medication this morning. At times, she would have tumultuous days when he was literally screaming at the top of his lungs and refusing to put his lips close to the mask. He needed to take his puffers daily for a maintenance dose to keep his lungs from getting inflamed again—according to her son's pediatrician.

After she finished giving him the two required inhalation doses, Venus took Tristan to the bathroom to rinse out his mouth. "Okay, honey, remember what the doctor said. After you have your blue puffer then your orange puffer, you need to rinse your mouth." She helped him onto the stool so that he was at the level for the sink and she reached for a disposable cup from its holder and filled it with tap water.

"Cup!" Tristan shouted.

"Yes, that's right, honey. We're going to fill the little cup with water. And you're going to sip and spit the water back out, okay?"

He nodded, looking more jovial. Tristan loved this part.

While she was assisting Tristan, Venus's cell phone rang again. She wondered who could be trying to reach her so desperately at this time of the morning. It wasn't as if she had plenty of people calling her these days. It had to be her handsome boss, Carl, or perhaps her friend, Blue, who was now married to Carl's brother, Zack.

She smiled at the memory of her time in Jamaica for Blue and Zack's nuptials just a couple of weeks ago. It was much needed rest and relaxation she craved. Aside from Blue's wedding, of course. And Tristan had a wonderful time, too. The island's clean air had done his lungs wonders. The resort where they stayed had a splendid daycare that was free to guests. It was a remarkable package that didn't come cheap. Venus would have been all too glad to pay her own way but the Romeros insisted they pay for everyone.

Prior to working for Carl, Venus was employed by his brother Zack at the Romero Winery and Vineyard after her placement there. She was in college part time advancing her studies in Business but she would often take time off to look after her little guy. Finding affordable daycare was always a bitter challenge. Sometimes, Venus didn't know how she could go on like this. But it was a blessing when the Romero family took her on. They had a reputation for treating their employees like family. At times, when Venus's babysitter did not show up, she would be stuck but Zack and now Carl always insisted that she bring her toddler in. At the Romero Estate, they had someone who could watch over Tristan. And currently at R.M. Fitness, where a daycare was located in the building, Venus often left Tristan there with comfort knowing that her son would only be a few steps away from her and in good hands. Sometimes, she felt indebted to the wonderful and powerful Romeros. Venus was a hard worker and would do almost anything for that family. Almost anything.

Finally, after Venus assisted Tristan with his jacket, she was ready to head out the door. After she buckled him in his stroller, she answered her cell phone that had rung yet again.

"Hello?"

"Hi, Venus."

"Yes?"

"It's Amber Johnson-Murray from the Murumbian Consulate." The young woman on the other end of the phone line had a smooth, low voice that sounded slightly hoarse. Yet, her voice delivered words that Venus did not want to hear.

Venus felt her heart thump hard in her chest. Goose pimples sprang up on her skin. A chill filled her body like nothing she had felt before. Except for...that fateful night. *The Murumbian Consulate?* That could only mean one thing, and one thing only. *Oh, God!* She dreaded the day she would receive a phone call from them.

"Y-yes?" Venus tried to calm the emotion in her voice. Instinctively, Venus knelt beside her son's stroller and placed her hand on his while he played with his soft toys on the hand rest of the pushchair. She remembered meeting Amber once, a long time ago, when Venus arrived in Canada. They had a brief conversation and Amber told her that everything would be okay and that Venus should not hear from them again, unless...

"First of all, how are you and Tristan doing?" Amber sounded calm but Venus wasn't convinced. She knew what was coming. Why didn't Amber just cut the casual chit-chat and tell Venus the real reason for the unexpected phone call?

Venus's fingers were trembling. She looked at her son in the stroller. He was cheerfully playing with his toys and didn't even have a clue that his mother was on edge. That was good. Protecting Tristan's well-being was the only thing that mattered. "We...we're fine," Venus answered, breathless. Her breathing was becoming shallow to her chagrin. Why was she nervous? She knew what she had to do. It would be that simple. She was going to have to run again. So what? She knew this day might come.

"Good to hear that, Venus," Amber continued, breathing a deep sigh over the phone. "Listen, Venus. I'm not going to take up too much of your time but you probably realize the reason for this call."

Venus was silent yet her heart pounded loudly in her chest.

"Well, as we had discussed before, if Eduardo ever got released then-"

"No!" Venus squeezed her eyes shut. Her body trembled. "Don't tell me anymore."

Startled, Tristan looked up from his toys. "Mama?"

She opened her eyes again and tried to put on a courageous face for her son. "It's okay, baby. Mama's fine," she said, her voice soft and wavering.

She stood up with the cell phone pressed to her ear. Her eyes stung with moisture. She would not cry. She was not going to cry today. How could this be? How could Eduardo be released?

"How could they release that...monster?" Venus said, gasping for a satisfying breath. She hugged herself as she leaned against the door for support, facing her son in the stroller. She was supposed to be heading out the door to work but how could she work now?

"He was not released, Venus."

"But you just said-"

"I know," Amber's voice sounded apologetic. "Listen, can we meet sometime today?"

"Why? What is it that you want to tell me?" Venus grew more concerned.

"Venus, Eduardo has escaped. The consulate got the news this morning."

Venus felt her blood run cold.

"Escape? But how? He was supposed to be in maximum security!"

"I'm sorry. You know his background. That's all I have to go on right now. We will update you further but-"

"It's okay. I'm...I have to find another hideout."

"No. Venus, please don't do anything rash. Now, the last time we spoke you told me that you have a wonderful job and career and a safe home. The worst thing you could do is make any drastic changes. There is no way he can find you."

"No way? How can you be sure?"

"We're keeping a very close eye on this situation, Venus. Think about it. He is all the way in Murumba. With the way the new international laws and flight security has been since 9/11, I doubt very much that even if he tried to use his connections to change his identity, he could not receive a valid passport to travel."

Venus slumped to the floor. She held her head down. Amber had a point. What was she worried about? She would be more paranoid than ever and do everything to protect her son but she would not do anything too rash. At least not now.

"Just continue to keep a low profile and everything should be fine. I'll keep you posted on any new developments. Okay?"

Venus nodded. "Okay."

Venus could do this. Eduardo had ruined her life before as well as Tristan's. She was not going to give him the opportunity to do it again. No way! She had to be brave. She couldn't keep running. She would not have any quality of life. What would happen to Tristan?

After Venus hung up, she dried the tears from her face and drew in a deep breath. She was going to march into work and do her job to the best of her ability and carry on as if nothing out of the ordinary just happened. As if her life was still okay. Working for Carl was one of the only things she had to look forward to every day, outside of her miracle son, Tristan.

She wasn't about to give it up now. Eduardo was thousands of miles away across the Atlantic Ocean. He couldn't hurt her. Not anymore.

Off to work, she would go.
To a normal day at the office.

CHAPTER THREE

She's perfect.

The words slid into Carl's mind as he glanced out of his office window at R.M. Fitness Center, his sweet, unsuspecting assistant Venus was on her way to the building from the parking lot. What would he say to her? How would he say it? He had to be very careful about his proposition to her. If it came off wrong, it could blow up in his face and cost him a valuable employee and trustworthy ally and supporter. That was the last thing he wanted. But oh, he wanted Venus. Her long, dark, silky hair rustled in the summer breeze as she strolled up to the main entrance of the facility, her rounded hips wiggling as she walked. She looked so damn cute in her pencil hip hugging gray skirt and white blouse. So professional and neat, yet sexy as hell. A subtle type of sexiness, not in your face. She had class and style. Yet, she was soft in her mannerism and her speech. Damn, she would make a fine political wife. Quiet, polished, discreet yet charming. She was refined in every way. His body always reacted to her when she was nearby. At least if they were ever in public on one of his campaign trips, they would have a natural chemistry. Heck, he felt it every time she looked at him. He knew there was something there with her towards him, too. Carl might not have let on to it that he knew, but men knew things like that. His plan just *had* to work.

Venus would be absolutely perfect for his wife. But would she go along with it? She was a quiet, hard worker who kept her business to herself. Lord only knew what it was that she was hiding about her past. She wasn't a talker or a socializer. That could work to their benefit, if she went along with his scheme.

* * *

"I need a wife and child by tomorrow," Carl asserted in a serious tone. He was seated at his desk in his office, opposite Venus. His finger jabbed the copy of the newspaper on his desk, his image was spattered across the front page.

"Excuse me?" Venus was too stunned for words. Her jaw dropped. Her sexy boss had come up with some off-the-charts marketing ploys in the past where the fitness center was concerned. But this? For his burgeoning political career?

Venus felt for him. She felt his pain of being ridiculed by his future political opponents, especially considering all the good he had done and his accomplishments. One of the outreaches that touched her the most was when his brother Jules and he went out to local area schools last year to personally ensure that healthy snacks and lunches were given to all students, especially homeless pupils or children living in shelters who were attending the school. He had totally flipped out when he found out that some students were forced to go hungry because they couldn't afford lunch. He insisted that the principals take note of the issues and let his foundation know about them so they could personally intervene to make sure there were no hungry students.

How honourable was that?

Carl didn't even care about getting any publicity for his deed.

He deserved to be in office for mayor of Mayberry Hill, but she wasn't sure if this new plan of his would even be work!

"I can't believe those people. Who do they think they are judging me like that?"

A photo of him, along with two women on his arms, appeared on the cover taken at a club that his brothers and he often frequented when they unwind. It appeared Carl had a bit to drink. It was New Year's Eve. One of the women was his girlfriend at the time; the other, a friend who just decided to pose for the camera. It was a

New Year's Eve bash for God's sake! But the reporter conveniently left out that pertinent bit of information. The headline caused Carl's stomach to churn.

Billionaire Party Animal Wants to Run for Office.

Articles were popping up left, right and center since the rumor mill got busy that morning with his intent to run for mayoral office.

The article went on to detail a rumor that Carl Romero wanted to run for office and probably use his status to date single voters. It also reiterated that he wasn't serious and didn't know what else to do with his money. His opponent was quoted: "Carl should leave the mayoral race to serious-minded candidates who care about the issues facing many families struggling for survival. What does a party prince know about that?"

Venus's stomach turned over at the thought of those lies circulating about sweet Carl. They had no idea how far from the truth they were. Sure, he was hot and he dated like any normal, healthy bachelor but he didn't deserve this kind of attention.

"You're right about defending yourself, Carl. You've done so much good in the community, more than any of those guys in office. You're so genuine and caring. God, we need people like you in charge. But, Carl, you can't just...*get* a wife and family." She swallowed hard.

Venus tried hard to not look too deeply into his soft, dark chocolate eyes because she would surely melt. Looking at his handsome face always made her gush. He was so extremely gorgeous, captivating. How could she look at him and not blush? From day one he always had that effect on her but she had always kept her eyes on her notes whenever he was dictating or giving instructions. Her heart would often beat hard and fast in her chest when he was near her. Whenever his eyes captured hers, she could not think; his beautiful face, his charm, and his sweet yet powerful aura often mesmerized her.

And now, she wasn't sure if she could even hold a conversation without reaching out and hugging him. Better to keep her distance. She'd never had this magic cast over her by any man. This was mind-blowing to her. She was torn inside. Her nipples strained under her blouse for his touch, yet she was aching for him in her heart. What was she to do? How could she help him without having further harm done to him through this difficult campaign for mayor? Running for any office was always a risky venture.

Carl paused for a moment. He could palpate the young woman's nervousness. He looked Venus in the eyes. Her soft brown eyes were edged with reddish lines. He got up from his chair and leaned against the front of his desk in front of her, looking deeply into her eyes. A look of concern overcame him.

"What's wrong, Venus?" he asked directly. "Something's happened to you." It was more of a statement than a question. Here he was ranting about his political woes when his assistant clearly was going through some sort of heartache and the hell he was going to let it slide. She had better be truthful with him.

"Oh, it's nothing," she dismissed quietly, looking down at her notepad. She wasn't making any eye contact with him. If someone hurt her, he would...

He leaned down and looked at her eye level, lifting her chin. A mixture of anger and deep concern surged through his blood. If anyone ever attempted to hurt this pretty young thing...they would be more than sorry. "Tell me the truth, Venus. Something's wrong. You've been crying this morning."

"No. I...Well...Please, Carl. There are more important things right now."

"Like hell there is. My employees are my concern. And you're more than just an employee, Venus. You're like family."

"Carl. Thank you. I...Please. I'm fine. Really. I would tell you if I wasn't. I...I did have a rough morning but I'm fine now. I don't want to discuss it." She fumbled at first but then lifted up her notepad and placed her pen over the page where she had already scribbled some notes. "Right now, your mission is very important. You have very good issues you want to tackle for this race. The daycare thing really is going to make voters appreciate you, Carl. Affordable daycare is something many mothers like myself have been fighting for. We need you in office."

"Do you really believe that?" he quizzed in a low voice, still feeling uncomfortable about her not opening up to him about what really went down with her this morning. But he had to learn to let things go sometimes. She said she was fine, so he would keep a close eye on things and trust her words.

"Of course, I believe that, Carl. You know you've got a lot on those opponents. This town has been inundated with so many empty promises from previous mayors. Look what you and Jules did for the homeless students going to school hungry. You personally saw to it that no students in the city had to go hungry by providing healthy lunches. No one else thought of that. Things are getting worse for working-class people. If it hadn't been for your family's kindness, I don't know if I could even afford to work."

"Good, I'm glad you agree," Carl said. "Marry me."

Venus's expression froze on her face.

CHAPTER FOUR

"M-m-marry you?" Venus echoed, her eyes wide with shock. Her heart was pumping fiercely in her chest. Did her boss just ask her what she thought he'd asked her? She must be hallucinating. Perhaps the shock of this morning's phone call from the consulate had been too much for her and taken a toll on her senses more than she realized.

Carl Romero was one of the hottest men she'd ever laid eyes on. This seemed like her deepest, delicious fantasies come true. But this was way out there. He could easily have any gorgeous, eligible bachelorette on this planet by his side.

Either he had taken leave of his senses, or she had.

"Yes," he verified, leaning back in his leather chair behind his desk. His sweet, handsome face had a grin. Was he joking? "You heard me correctly. Marry me. It would be like a contract. I'll draft up the details."

"But. I...I..." Venus choked up. She was also dazed with euphoria. Her wildest fantasy was coming true yet it was so close yet so unattainable because Carl didn't know what on earth he would be getting into by wanting to marry her. She wasn't a simple person. She had a complex past. She had baggage. Too much baggage. Heavy baggage that could literally sink their relationship and all they'd worked for in their lives.

There were things about her that Carl could not even know about. Oh, God! Why did things have to be so difficult? Why couldn't it be simple? Here she was in front of Mr. Right who was asking her to marry him for all the wrong reasons yet she wanted to say yes.

Oh, God, her heart was singing yes, yes, yes. Yet her mind was screaming no, no, no.

"Carl," Venus said, getting up from her chair. She was suffocating in lost thoughts. She needed air to breathe. She couldn't breathe. Marriage? Carl really wanted to marry her? Her heart kept thrusting hard against her rib cage, her flesh felt sore and ached.

Carl also stood up, his arm folded across his chest. He stood in front of her, his eyes capturing her as he leaned against the desk. His silence was filled with expectancy. His expression, charming yet unreadable. His brow was raised slightly, which gave him an adorable, boyish look. This was not a joke. This was a serious matter, yet she could see slight amusement on his face. Did he sense how in love she'd been with him? Did he know? Was he daring her to say no to this...proposition of his?

"Carl, I think we should think this through," she said, breathless. She turned to him and her stomach felt light and giddy inside. Oh, gosh, he was so damn cute! What was she saying? She should be screaming yes to the top of her lungs for this chance to be his wife. Carl Romero's wife!

"Yes, you're right. You have until the end of the day to think it over," Carl said matter-of-factly.

"Carl! The end of the day?"

"You need longer?" he delved, arching a brow as if nothing out of the ordinary was just asked of her. She'd always admired Carl and had never seen this side of him before but she now knew it was true that the Romeros didn't mince their words when they wanted something.

"But, what about...?"

"The fine details? I've already taken care of that."

"You have? What would be involved? I mean. I just can't..."

"I'm sorry. I realize that sometimes I do get ahead of myself. I would never want to put you on the spot. And rest assured, I've taken care of the financial details. You'll be paid very well..."

Venus felt her blood boiled over in her veins. She shot Carl a raged glance. "What?" she said fuming. "Financial?"

"Well, you didn't think I would have you do me this favor for nothing, did you? How does one million dollars sound?"

"One million dollars?" Her eyes widened in shock. "I am not for sale, Carl! Do you think I am some whore?"

"What?" Carl's expression changed quickly. Anger flashed in his dark, handsome eyes. "Who said anything about you being a whore?"

"Well, you want to pay me...for," she said, trailing off, "my commitment."

"Listen, Venus. I didn't mean to come across that way."

"It's okay," she said, hugging herself. She was shivering, not because she was cold but because she was feeling overwhelmed with her feelings for her him. "Besides, one million dollars a year is crazy money. How long would we stay married if I can do this?"

"First of all, it would be one million for each month you are married to me."

"A month?" Venus felt her heart explode in her chest. "A month? One million dollars a month? Carl, that's insane!" She wanted to say that she would do it for free. But she could not even do that. Because it would never work given her past.

She paced in his office, hugging herself. "I...I don't know. I can't do that."

"Where are you going?" he said, watching her as she grabbed her notepad.

"I'm sorry, Carl. I have to...I have to be somewhere. Can we meet later?"

"Sure." His voice was nonchalant and clipped, an amused grin was still on his lips. Did he not realize what he had done? Did he think this was amusing?

Venus left Carl's office and went into her own office. She grabbed her purse from her drawer and fished for her keys and cell phone. She promptly left the building, her heart pounding in her chest. Her throat had virtually closed up. She could barely speak. She whisked past her co-workers and out the door. Would she even return to work at R.M. Fitness Center?

One million dollars?

His wife?

What the?

And for how long could he keep this up?

Then another thought struck her. If she didn't go along with his plan, would he find someone else? She could see a lot of women at the office jumping, no, *throwing* themselves at the chance to share Carl's hot bed and life, and especially for that insane amount of money. Not that Carl needed to pay anyone. As sexy and charming as this beauteous man was, women would gladly pay *him* to be on his arm. But Venus just could not accept his proposition. Besides, she wasn't free to marry anyone—something that Carl didn't even know.

What would Carl expect for one million dollars a month? For her to turn all kinds of tricks in the sack? She didn't think so. No way in hell. She was hot for him, but she had her pride. She had her dignity, damn it. Carl was willing to pay her that amount of money? What must he think of her?

CHAPTER FIVE

Later that afternoon, Carl and Jules sat at an exclusive restaurant in the downtown core in a booth discussing his plans.

"So, you asked her to marry you, and she ran out on you?" Jules couldn't help but grin.

"It's not funny, Jules." Carl was not impressed right now. Though his brother and he often joked and bantered, he was just not in the mood for it.

"I'm sorry, man. I just didn't expect that reaction from her. I know she likes the hell out of you."

"What makes you say that?"

"Oh, come on, you must see the way she ogles you every time your back is turned."

"If my back is turned, genius, how am I supposed to see that?" Carl arched a brow, his lips thinned.

"Very funny, bro. You know you have eyes on the back of your head," Jules teased him, then wiped the smile off his face. "Seriously, though, man, she's been talking about you a lot."

"To whom?"

"To dear old step-grandma Shelly."

"Shelly?" Carl wasn't expecting that. Shelly was his grandfather's young, hip wife in her late forties and she was so good to talk to. In fact, at times, Shelly would step in and babysit Venus's son Tristan whenever she was stuck for a reliable babysitter so that she could go in to work.

"Yeah, Shelly. Apparently, Venus likes you a lot. She talks about you all the time and asks Shelly all kinds of things about you and even asks if you have girlfriend."

"Why would she do that?"

"Well, she's not gonna ask you now, is she?"

Carl grinned, lifting his drink to his lips. "Right."

"Anyway, you'd better have a good plan in place either way, bro. These politicians play nasty as hell."

"Did you find out anything else about my future opponent?"

"Yeah. His campaign platform is to discredit anyone who comes up against him."

"What? Seriously?"

"Wish I was kidding, man. The guy's a mean mother f—"

"Okay, okay. I get it."

"Now on the other hand, he's not exactly squeaky clean."

"Oh, no. I'm not playing their game. If they wanna see if they can sling mud on my reputation, good luck to them. My platform is what I can do for the people, not how much I can tear down my competitors. I trust that people will vote the right way."

"Yeah, just as long as you at least appear competent. They still want a family-friendly mayor, if you know what I mean."

"Yeah, I hear ya!" Carl's lips were pinched tightly. He was thinking. Turbulent thoughts raced through his mind as he recalled his meeting with Venus that morning. Shit! She was hurt. Insulted, even. What the hell had he just done? And all to get into the mayoral seat. He knew what he wanted to do to win and to make a change but hell, if it meant hurting Venus, none of that seemed to matter all of a sudden.

Now wasn't that the craziest thing?

One moment, he was all for winning at any cost. But Venus? She struck a chord inside him. There was something that radiated about her. Damn, he'd do anything to protect her. And if she didn't want to go in with this with him, he just realized that there wasn't anyone else he would want to ask.

Imagine that!

What was this feeling he was having towards Venus? He just couldn't wrap his head around it. It perplexed him. Heck, *she* was perplexing!

None of that mattered now.

Could his grandfather be right? Was love and family far more important than anything else in society? Carl was beginning to feel it deep down in his soul. Their father was more together when their mother was around. His folks may not have had much later in their marriage but they had love and it bonded them and held them together until tragedy struck down their family.

Carl squeezed his eyes shut and opened them again, bringing his drink to his lips and taking a long swig. He could barely taste the fluid going down his throat. He was numb. He was dazed. And all over a woman.

Venus bewitched him—in a good way, of course. There was just something strong about her that resonated with his soul. He couldn't get her out of his system, out of his mind. And it took something like this morning's encounter for him to realize that?

"Well, put it this way, Carl," Jules interrupted his concentration. "At least you know she's a good woman."

"Why do you say that?"

"You know. Most women would have probably jumped at that kind of cash you offered her but she has to think it through. What does that say about her character?" Jules shoved a bite of steak into his mouth.

Carl had also ordered the steak and pasta lunch but hadn't touched a morsel. He had other things eating at him.

"Yeah, you're right, Jules."

His brother was in fact right. Venus not jumping at the chance to take his money proved that she was the woman he wanted, more than anything else in the world right now.

And Carl wasn't going to let Venus go that easily.

CHAPTER SIX

"I'm glad you came here to see me in person, Venus," Amber said at the Murumbian Consulate. "I felt terrible about our phone conversation this morning."

"It's okay," Venus said quietly, sitting in the chair in the bright office at the consulate. It was strange. She hadn't been there since she came to Canada. Seeing her country's orange and green flag on the wall and coat of arms brought a sad feeling to her heart and a sense of longing. She missed her old life. She missed the way things were before…that tragic incident two years earlier that had her flee her homeland and take up residence in Kansas and then now here in Mayberry Hill, a quiet town on the outskirts of the city of Toronto in Canada. What a journey she and Tristan have had during the past two years. But going to college and finding work had kept her going and kept up her spirits. Until this morning. She was torn about what to do.

Never had Venus been in so much emotional turmoil since residing in Canada. What to do? Why had she come to the embassy?

Carl.

She desperately wanted to help him but not on his terms and not until she found out if she was truly free to…marry. Even if it were for a contractual period of time.

"So let me get this straight," Amber clarified after Venus told her that somebody was interested in marrying her. "Someone you like asked you to marry him and you said no?"

"Well, it's not quite like that," Venus murmured.

"What is it then? Venus, what are you worried about?"

"Well, you know about my past. You're one of the few who knows."

"Yes, I know."

"Well, how can I even think about getting married and not tell my…future husband?"

Amber drew in a deep breath. "You're right. It's something you need to think about clearly. But if you're worried about Eduardo, I wouldn't let him keep you from moving forward. You need a life, Venus. Like I said before, he can't come near you to harm you or Tristan. And he doesn't even know that you're in Canada."

"I know. But he could find out."

"Like I said before, once you continue to keep a low profile…"

"But that's just it. It's possible that my…future husband may have a high profile career in the future."

"I see. That could be a problem. But you have to weigh the odds, Venus. Besides, you look so different than when you first came to us two years ago. Your hair color has changed. Your weight is different. You were so emaciated then. You look healthy now. A nice glow about you! It's up to your comfort level, Venus, but…" Amber looked as if she was feeling sorrow or pain, Venus couldn't quite tell which.

"Is everything okay, Amber?" Venus was so grateful for all that Amber did for her and Tristan when they came to Canada to help them get settled when she had to flee her country and find this nice place to reside. She hoped Amber was okay. She was one of the few people who knew about her past, whom she could trust.

"Venus, I shouldn't be telling you this, but it's not every time in life that we meet that special guy. The one who could make our hearts leap in our chest or bring unbridled joy to us. And when he asks you to marry him, well," she shrugged, giving Venus a hopeful look. A smile then crept on her face. "I say, go and follow your heart. I wish I could."

"I'm sure you could. You're attractive and single."

Amber laughed. "Thank you, Venus. But my life's a bit more complicated."

"It can't be more complicated than mine."

"Actually, you'd be surprised." Pain flashed in Amber's eyes. "Take the opportunity when you can to be with the one you love, the one you care about. Let things take care of themselves. I'm telling you this because I believe you deserve to be happy. Since you've spoken to me about your job, you seem to glow when you speak about this man…and I'm assuming that he works with you." Amber grinned. "Anyway, I wish I had the opportunity that you have but…I don't. And I may never get that chance. We women keep denying our chance at being happy for the littlest things sometimes."

"Little? I would hardly call my past little."

"No. And I didn't mean it like that. What I meant was, love is so huge, Venus. Having love in your life is bigger than anything in your life. Remember that. It's always worth fighting for."

Venus swallowed hard. No way in hell was she going to make herself a high-priced "wife" but she wanted to be in Carl's life. She now had to figure out how she was going to do this without getting either of them doing anything they could regret later.

But was Amber right? Was having love in Venus's life bigger than anything else in her life?

CHAPTER SEVEN

Later that afternoon, Carl leaned back in his leather office chair and skimmed over his notes for his upcoming candidacy announcement. He agonized over the fine details and weighed his chances of genuinely winning over voters given his background.

Fellow citizens,

I am honoured and humbled to have this opportunity to represent you in this great city of Mayberry Hill as your mayor.

My friends, we find it is increasingly harder and harder to survive in this economy...

Carl scratched out the last part of that sentence. He knew what it was like growing up in a struggling family home but he sure as hell wasn't struggling now. Would they relate to him?

Well-paying jobs are being eliminated and there is no plan in place to create new ones. Families are finding it more and more difficult to survive. Affordable childcare is becoming unreachable for working class families struggling to make ends meet. Many know how it difficult it is to make ends meet, period.

Carl drew in a deep breath and scrapped the last part of that paragraph. Focus. He needed to focus, but his mind was all over the place.

The right to work for a decent living wage and have universal healthcare is vital and indeed one of our fundamental rights.

Mayberry Hill is ready for a different kind of politics...One that is fair and just...one that puts family first, for survival, for decent living and for betterment.

Family first? What did he know about having a family of his own to raise? Perhaps his grandfather was right about him offering to represent families and being at odds, given that he was a bachelor with personal annual revenue that could very well represent what the average worker would make in a year—he made that in an hour.

His stomach clenched. He felt a knot tighten in his gut. But it wasn't always like that. He wanted to help create more jobs and opportunities for working class families and the poor to get ahead in life. Sure, he got a break when he met his grandfather in his teens but he also worked his butt off on his own merits, just as his father did before his dad fell on hard times—without the Romero name and all its privileges.

I've experienced firsthand the hardship that families can experience, growing up in a working class home. I feel your frustration, I feel your anxiety, your pain...when the mortgage or rent can't be paid, when you have to choose food over shelter, when medical care and bare necessities are out of reach...

Carl's heart was pounding hard in his chest. His mother never stood a chance before her sad passing, battling cancer, not having enough funds or resources. The bitter memory tore a part of his soul. He wanted voters to see that he could not only make a change—a difference, but he truly felt their agony.

I take my job and my duties seriously in helping to bring positive change to the lives of hardworking individuals....I will aim to work with community leaders and local businesses to bring about positive change, to create better-paying job opportunities and affordable childcare for those who work outside the home. We don't need more politicians, we need more leaders. Together, we can make a difference.

Carl thought for a moment. "Together, We Can!" was his new political slogan thanks to Venus, his wonderful, insightful assistant. She came up with the idea during one of their recent brainstorming sessions.

A knock sounded on Carl's office door, interrupting his thoughts. It was already the end of the workday. Since Venus had returned from her late lunch break hours ago, she and Carl hadn't had a chance to converse. She had her reports to finish for him and he was busy engaging with the suppliers on his latest equipment shipped to the gym.

Carl had also spent a great deal of time going over some hand-over stuff with his brother, Jules. Carl was in the process of transferring over more of his duties to his brother while he prepared for his run for mayor. He didn't know what the outcome would be for the mayoral bid but he wanted to devote his full energies to his upcoming campaign—once he made the official announcement regarding his plans to run for office, of course.

"Yes?"

The door pried open. Venus stood there in the doorway, looking more stunning than earlier, if that was at all possible. There was just something enticing and elegant about her presence that captivated him each and every time he laid eyes on her. She had a healthy glow about her, even though it was apparent that she seemed more tired today. Her full lips looked so cute painted in a vibrant red, her large brown eyes framed by long lashes looked so innocent, so inviting, yet he could see apprehension in those dark, beautiful eyes of hers.

"Hi," she said quietly. Her eyes barely met his. This was not like Venus at all. She'd always displayed herself as a strong, feisty woman who got things done around the office. But today? Not a chance. She seemed intimidated. Shy.

Venus squared her shoulders. "Carl, I'm ready for us to discuss your proposition."

"Good." He leaned forward in his chair. Venus came in and sat down in the plush leather seat in front of him. She'd gotten her nerve back. Good.

She heaved a sigh at first then proceeded to talk. "But I will not be paid the sum you had suggested."

Now that had Carl stumped. "And why not?"

"I just don't think it's right. I want to help you win this election, but I don't feel right about that sum of money."

Carl inched forward in his chair, clasping his hands together in front of him on his desk. He was truly amazed at this graceful yet elusive woman before him. What was it she wanted from him then? Another thought rattled him. Surely, she couldn't think they were really getting married—to stay married.

"Venus, perhaps I should make this arrangement clear to you," Carl said in a soft low voice. "This is only a contract. You do realize that, right? It's business."

"Business?"

"Well, yes. You know why I need to do this. I only want to ensure that you are adequately compensated. You can't possibly think that a man in my position would allow you to make such a sacrifice for nothing."

Venus shook her head, a grin finding its way to her lips. "Oh, no, Carl. I know full well what this is about. And trust me. I want you to win. I've seen the other candidates. You're the best man to represent the people of this town, Carl. I consider it my civic duty."

Now Carl was even more confused. "Civic duty?" He arched a brow. Was that all this was about? Why was Carl feeling uncomfortable all of a sudden? Wasn't that what he wanted all along? A trophy wife for his campaign image? Yet, a part of him wanted so much more of her. The truth was, he really felt a strong attraction to Venus. Maybe this could be the beginning of a real relationship, so he wouldn't really be lying about his marriage.

"Well, no," she quickly rebutted, looking more flushed and embarrassed. "Wrong choice of words. Sorry. I meant...I don't want to be paid to do this."

"But surely you could use the resources," Carl continued, trying to sound as discreet as possible, "for your son," he finished, raising a brow. "Think about college tuition when he grows up. And you've been complaining about daycare costs and affordability for the longest time, Venus. Why would you think I want your help but would not help you in return? Venus, from the moment I met you I notice that you always have a tough time asking for help or receiving it. It's okay to allow someone to help you once in a while, you know. Why do you feel you're not worthy of—"

"Oh, no. It's not that," Venus jumped in.

"Then what is it?" He just couldn't figure out this girl, no matter how hard he tried, yet something inside him pulled towards her magical aura. There was something about her alluring beauty and unique grace that captivated him, mesmerized him. Damn, he was falling for her hard.

"Listen, before you answer that," he said, picking up his phone to make a call. "I'm going to arrange for dinner for the two of us so that we can go into greater detail about our...arrangement."

"Dinner?" Venus arched a brow. "I need to get home for Tristan."

"Oh, right. Listen, I'll arrange for childcare at the estate so that we can go on the Janissa."

"The Janissa?"

"Yes, the yacht on the lake by the house. I'll have staff arrange for us to have a private dinner there. That way, Tristan would only be a short distance away while we discuss our business further."

She seemed stunned at first. "Oh. Um...sure. I would like that."

"Good. It's a date then."

A date? Yes, it would be one heck of a business date.

CHAPTER EIGHT

The waterfront property outside the Romero Manor estate was refreshing and serene. The evening summer sky was quickly fading from clear blue into a beautiful blend of orange and red hues in the dusk backdrop. It was alluring cottage country. The warm summer breeze kissed Venus's skin. After a long day at the office and a stressful day after that phone call from the consulate, she felt oddly relaxed, safe in Carl's presence on the lake.

The waves of blue swirled and washed up on the shore as they were seated on the top deck of the customized white yacht. The luxury boat swayed to the rhythm of the motion of water swirling around it. Venus always found water and the sound of waves to be soothing for as long as she could remember. The Janissa was stunning. The glow of the candlelight on the table as well as the dim flood lights on the boat created a calming, romantic ambiance.

Venus could not believe she was there, alone with hot and sexy Carl Romero. This was a dream. It wasn't real. Her eyes captured Carl's handsome features as he surveyed his notes on his laptop. His skin carried a warm glow from the sunset sky, the wind gently rustled his dark, cropped hair and the dim light highlighted his high cheekbones and dark, sensuous eyes. The man was stunning, breathtaking in every way. Her body reacted in his presence. But how could she even help herself? She didn't even want to. She longed for him to touch her, to be close to her and wondered often what it would feel like to be held in his strong, muscular arms and feel the warmth of his body entwined with hers. Oh, gosh, she was feeling heated already.

Her heart pounded hard and fast in her chest. She didn't think she could calm her nerves for one single moment while there with Carl. But wasn't this what she'd always fantasized? She was sure it was the fantasy of every female employee at R. M. Fitness Center the way they often went on about him during lunch breaks and working hours, ogling their hunky boss as he whizzed by in his expensive tailored suits.

"Why the name Janissa?" Venus asked Carl after the waiter had taken their orders. She desperately wanted to get her mind out of her sexual fantasy about him. They were there, after all, to discuss business. Serious business regarding the upcoming election—and nothing more.

"My mother's name was Janissa." Carl's voice was low and deep; there was an air of sadness in his tone. He said nothing more. She'd heard that his mother died tragically when he was young. A pang of empathy stabbed her heart.

"That's a beautiful name," she replied quietly, feeling her gut twisting inside. She knew very well the horrific feeling of losing a loved one, her own mother—and father.

"Thank you."

Not long after, the waiter returned with two delicious dinner trays. It was more like a miniature buffet for two. There were so many choices. She felt overwhelmed and more hungry now, just salivating over the scrumptious entrees.

The large China dishes were filled various offerings. One plate had fresh baby spinach with slices of seasoned tomato. Another dish contained roasted watermelon salad with lime, mint, lemon balm, goat cheese crumbles, fleur de sel and extra virgin olive oil. Their entrees consisted of oven roasted French-cut chicken breast with cherry sauce. Another dish had rack of carved roasted lamb with tomato apricot chutney. The waiter had also served a bottle of fine red Merlot wine from the Romero Winery & Vineyard, of course. The sumptuous aroma of the dinner before her wafted to her nostrils and seeped into her stomach. She didn't realize how hungry she was until now.

But looking across the dimly lit table from her gorgeous boss made her hungry for more than food. She wanted to rinse the naughty thought from her mind. She'd just realized that this was the first time since they'd been working together that they sat down to a dinner together. Just the two of them. Normally, they would sit down to staff dinners at fine restaurants or at the estate with the family—but never alone.

Carl had the most captivating dark, sexy eyes she'd ever seen on a man. His lovely chocolate eyes framed by thick black lashes often entranced her. He was a beautiful man to behold. Waves of desire slid through her every time her eyes locked with his. What was it about him? He was utterly mesmerizing. He had the sort of look that would draw you in and make you want to do anything for him—or to him, in a delightful way.

She shook the mental image of him kissing her passionately out of her mind. This was business. All business. Nothing more could possibly come of it. Venus just didn't want to make a big fool of herself and presume anything more right now. They would only be married contractually for…?

"How long would you…um…require my services?" she asked calmly, dropping her fork on her plate after taking the last bite of her roasted lamb cut. "Well," she chuckled, acutely embarrassed, "perhaps, services is not the right word."

"Oh, that's okay. I understand what you meant." His voice was deep, low and slid through his lips like smooth honey. There was something about his rich, deep voice that always resonated with her. For a man with handsome, boyish looks, she was always surprised at how deep and powerful his voice sounded.

"I'll need you for one year," he instructed. His voice was calm, his gaze intent. Venus shivered inside as heated anticipation shot through her body.

"One year?" she echoed breathlessly.

"One year." His dark, alluring gaze captivated her. She froze for a moment. Her mind processed what that meant. She would be Carl Romero's wife—for one year. One year! And what about Carl's reputation as a hot lover who always had a glowing arm-candy model at his side? What would become of that? Would *Venus* become his…lover?

"Okay," she said, trying to sound as cool as she could. "And, um…what about…arrangements between us? What exactly would be involved?" she finished her sentence, not sure of how to come out and say it. What about sex? Would he expect her to sleep with him during this period? She could think of nothing else. Secretly, she would *want* nothing less.

Carl leaned back in his seat against the rail of the yacht with a mischievous boyish grin.

Please say yes we'll be intimate. Please don't tell me that you already have a girlfriend who you will secretly sleep with on the side. Venus bit down on her lower lip, hoping that he could not possibly read her mind, or her anxious emotions right now. She would just die if he didn't want to "consummate" their fake marriage. God, why was she so desperate to be touched by this man? Why did she crave his silky touch, or the feel of his smooth skin on hers?

Carl heaved a deep sigh. "Don't worry about sleeping arrangements, Venus. I have a lover who will take care of my sexual needs," he said, his tone cool and deep.

Venus's face fell. Her heart smashed against her rib cage, painfully knocking the wind out of her lungs.

Carl's grin widened.

"I'm teasing you, Venus!"

She let a deep breath she didn't realize she was holding and chuckled. She gave him a playful brow bashing before rolling her eyes in return for his practical joke. "That's not very funny, Carl," she chided him.

"I don't think it would be wise for me to have a lover on the side while we are legally married, Venus," he said, his tone more serious. He still had that captivating rich, silky smooth voice.

"That would be the last thing I would want for many reasons," he continued. "Even though the reasons we are getting married are not conventional, I still believe in being faithful to the one I'm with, regardless of why I'm with her. And secondly, an extramarital affair would be very easy for my opposition to track using any old detective agency and that could bring the worst kind of unwanted publicity. So yes," he continued, gazing into her eyes, leaning forward. "I would expect us to consummate our marriage as part of our...arrangement. I'm sure we both have needs, just like everyone else."

She swallowed hard but the lump would not go down her throat. It was closed up from her bungled nerves.

Yes!

This was what she wanted, wasn't it? So why was her mind in a dazed whirlwind? Why was she giddy with a mixture of stirred emotions? Why was her head spinning? She could not believe all of this. Yesterday, she fantasized about her boss, as she had since she'd known him over the past year—and now? She was going to be his lover, his wife. This was all so much to process and she was feeling overwhelmed, in disbelief.

"Y-yes. Of course. I...agree," she said, trying to sound matter-of-factly.

"So," he continued, pulling out some sheets of paper from his case that rested on the empty seat beside them, "the arrangement would be for one year followed by a quiet separation that hopefully the media won't find out about. By then, I should be more settled in my new position as mayor and have implemented all the changes that need to be done. Hopefully, voters won't mind much what goes on in my personal life."

Venus took the sheets of paper Carl handed her. It was in the form of a legal contract, all neatly typed up. This was official, wasn't it? Carl didn't mess around with his business. He never took chances with anything ... or anyone.

Venus's eyes scanned over the first page of the document but reluctantly settled on one word in the bullet form of expectations.

Separation.

Separation? Venus's heart sank even lower than it had when he told her he had another lover a moment ago—which thankfully was not true. Why was she feeling daunted all of a sudden? Did it matter that they would be separated? This was, after all, part of the deal, right? It was not real, she had to remind herself. It was only a contract. A marriage of convenience. Besides, she knew full well that deep down, she could not be married for too long to anyone, lest her secret past surface and ruin everything. It was just that she had never before come so close to happiness and only to be told it was a time-limited experience. How sad was that?

"Yes, hopefully voters won't...mind," she agreed quietly.

"And I have a few other stipulations in our agreement. Though it hasn't been drafted up officially, I expect it to remain a closely guarded secret. As you can see, under the heading of behavioural expectations, I expect that we'll both be mutually respectful to each other both in public and in private. I strongly believe that respect is a two-way street. And we're not to disclose any of this to anyone outside of a few trusted members in the family circle. I know that you're a very discreet person, Venus. So my concern is not that."

"Thank you, Carl. What is your concern then?"

"You."

"Me?"

"Whatever it is that you're hiding. One of the things we need to agree on is not to harbor secrets. Are you going to tell me about your past?"

Venus felt her throat close in again. She could not breathe. Her muscles tensed in her body causing a painful ache.

"M-my past?"

"Yes, Venus." He reached his long, strong arms across the table and held her hands in his. She felt a jolt of his powerful electricity pulse through her veins at the touch of his skin. Oh, God! His firm, silky touch! The energy was deliciously palpable. She wanted him to hold her forever. "I need to know everything."

She drew in a deep breath, trying to squeeze oxygen back into her lungs.

"I...I can't tell you everything, Carl. I....just can't. Please trust me on this. It's better you don't know."

"I think it's better that I do, Venus. How can you ask me to trust you when you don't trust me?"

"Because this is different, Carl."

"But if you're going to be my wife, I need to know about your past. Everything."

"But you're not going to be my real husband. This is only a pretend marriage, isn't it?" she shot back, then she felt like a goose for doing so. Why was she taking it out on Carl? It wasn't his fault what happened to her in her past.

Carl leaned back, removing his hands from hers. He stretched his arms across the rail of the yacht and cocked a knowing grin. "You're really something, you know that?"

What was he getting at? Was he upset about the situation now? Or was he amused? He glanced at the darkening sky then turned his attention back to Venus.

"It's really that bad, is it?"

"Carl, please. Just trust me."

"The last thing I would want is for the press to find out about you before I do, Venus."

"And that's not going to happen."

"It isn't?"

"No. Because, I've taken care of that problem. What's done is done. The past is dead and gone and I'd rather forget about it. You're my...future, my present focus right now. We need to get you in office, Carl. You're the best man for the job. The community needs you. I...need you to be in office, too." Her voice trailed off. She needed him more than just to be in office.

Oh, damn Eduardo!

Why did he have to escape from prison? But Amber at the consulate had assured her that everything was okay, so she would have to take her word for it. She was in Canada now. No one would ever find her. He didn't even know that she was out of the country. The embassy made sure that no one knew she had fled. That was good enough. She and Tristan were safe.

Out of harm's way.

Why bring up the past? It would only create possible danger for Carl if he found out. It would complicate matters. And for what? After the year was up—Carl would be out of her life and not have to bear that burden of her secret. It would be better this way.

"You know you really had me there. Very well. I'm not going to push it. But just tell me one thing. Did he hurt you?" Carl's eyes flashed anger and a dangerous dark look that she'd never seen before.

"Did who h-hurt me?"

"The man you're running from?" His tone was direct and void of emotion.

"Carl, what makes you think it's about a man?" Venus looked down at her almost empty plate.

"Venus, look at me."

Her eyes locked with his again as she raised her head.

"I'll let it go for now. But if I find out that anyone has threatened you or has anything over you or is hurting you in any way, I can't promise you I won't get involved. And it won't be pretty. Okay?"

His smooth, deep words sent a shiver down her spine. His tone was cool as ice, dangerous.

"Okay," she murmured, breathless. She drew in a deep breath to calm her nerves. "Fine. But you won't have to worry, Carl. I...I promise."

"Oh, no. Look at the time," Venus continued. "I must pick up Tristan."

"He should be fine at the estate," Carl said, looking down at his watch. "But I'll take you to pick him up and then I'll take you home." He rose from the table.

"Thank you. And thank you for a lovely dinner, Carl."

"My pleasure, Mrs. Romero," Carl said with a grin.

Mrs. Romero?

The words washed through Venus like a tsunami of emotions. Mrs. Romero? She loved the way that sounded. It finally struck her. She would really become Mrs. Romero, wouldn't she? Even though it was for fabricated reasons. This was going to be the real deal. She was overcome with emotions. Stunned. Amused. Dazed.

There was no other man in the world she wanted to be with more than Carl Romero.

She didn't know what got into her at that instant.

Carl had taken her cardigan off the chair back to place over her shoulders. And she was inches from him facing him, looking up into his gorgeous dark eyes. His hands were still holding the cardigan around her and he gently pulled her closer to him. His smooth cologne danced beneath her nostrils, delighting her senses. What was it about this oh, so sexy man she worked for? There was something so mesmerizing about him, enthralling that made her desire him so much. That made her want to be closer to him in every way possible. That made her forget who she was for a moment and made her feel that all her cares in the world were drifting away.

With just the sound of the waves from the lake swirling against the boat and the sound of her heart pounding hard and fast in her chest, Carl lowered his head to hers and she shivered with delight. His soft finger traced the outline of her jaw and she tingled at his silky feel as he stroked her sending waves of desire through her body.

Oh, Carl. His touch was magical, pleasing to her body.

So this was what it felt like to be touched by…a Romero. She'd heard a lot about the sexual prowess of the Romero men but had to take a moment to process all that was going between them. Was Carl going to kiss her?

"God, Venus, you're so beautiful," Carl said in a low, husky voice as he lifted her chin to his. He softly brushed his lips across hers and a light electrical current bolted through her body.

"Oh, Carl," she moaned, as she pressed her lips to his enjoying the sweet touch of his flesh. His lips parted hers and claimed her tongue with a moist sweep of his. He slid his strong arms around her waist and she felt the heat of his firm hands on her back. She reached her arms up to hug his neck as he continued to pleasure her with his soft lips, kissing her passionately and erotically, sucking on her flesh as she moaned in ecstasy.

Oh, what a kisser, she mused. Venus couldn't believe how good Carl's soft, passionate lips felt on hers.

Heat throbbed between her legs, her nipples tightened at the tenderness of his hungry kiss. Her mind was in a whirlwind daze, her legs felt delightfully weak as she leaned against the rail on the yacht making out like crazy with her hot and magnificent boss.

She relished the sweet taste of his tongue and his lips as they continued to kiss hungrily. She could feel the moisture increase inside her panties. She even hoped he had a condom with him so that they could go much further. That was how badly she wanted to have him—all the way.

Carl. Oh, Carl

She wanted him, craved him. Now. Right there and then on the boat, on the lake. Out in the open. She didn't care about anything else than having Carl make love to her, thrusting inside her. Never before had a desire so strong, so powerful overwhelm her by just a kiss. No. Not just a kiss, a passionate lovemaking of the lips.

He murmured, "Oh, Venus." His breathing was heavy and labored as he moved his hands down her dress, lifting it up. She felt the delight of his hardness tenting his loins. Now. She wanted Carl now. She was going to go crazy inside if she couldn't have him now. Her body pulsed uncontrollably. The anticipation of having passionate sex with Carl sent currents of desire ricocheting through her body. Her emotions whirled and skidded as she thought about consummating their relationship.

The sound of a man clearing his throat interrupted their sensuous lip-locking session. It was the waiter. He was standing a few feet from them looking rather sheepish.

"I'm sorry, sir," the waiter apologized. "Your grandfather has summoned you back at the house. It's rather important."

For some reason, the waiter, or butler, sounded more British than earlier before. Or maybe, Venus simply hadn't noticed before.

"Thank you," Carl said, concern befalling his countenance. He was breathing hard, the passion left him panting as it did she. "My phone was switched off. He must have been trying to reach me."

"Very well, sir."

Venus straightened her dress. She knew from working for the Romeros that if Toni called at a late hour like this, it was often something important. And the Romero family always stuck close together and dropped what they were doing for the elder Romero. No matter what time it was. She respected them for that. Their grandfather had done so much for the brothers over the years and it was a blessing that they never forgot where they came from—no matter how high in life they'd reached.

Still, Venus's mind was reeling from that damn hot kiss.

What just happened?

She was left breathing hard, panting. His electric kiss left her dazed and confused. She reoriented herself to what she was doing on the yacht with Carl. Oh, right. The agreement. The arrangement. The proposition. She knew this was only for a year. A taste of what was to come. But would a year be nearly enough? Could she possibly be his without breaking down and revealing her dark secret to him—something he may very well find...unforgiveable?

"I'm sorry," he said, breathing hard. Hungry passion still blazed in his dark, sexy eyes.

"It's okay. I have to get my son anyway. It's getting late."

"As I said, I'll take you home and the offer still stands," Carl said, reaching for his cell phone and powering it back on. "I just need to make a phone call first." Carl excused himself to make the call while Venus gathered her notes and her contract off the table. Oh, God! Did the waiter see what was on the table when he approached? She immediately dismissed the thought from her mind. Even if he did, the Romeros only hired and vetted discreet and reliable people to work close with them. She should know. They vetted her before she started working for them. Although her past in Murumba was a closed vault that not even the federal government could open.

"Is everything alright?" Venus turned to Carl after he'd finished up with his phone conversation.

"Yes and no. I will explain later," he told her as he guided her down the steps to the lower deck. Her shoes clanked lightly as she stepped down after him. He looked worried, concerned. Oh, dear. She hoped everything was okay with Granddad Romero. She was so fond of that man. If it hadn't been for Toni Romero, she may not have even landed the job at the Romero Estate, first working for the vineyard and winery and now for Carl and Jules in their corporation.

"We still need to go over some fine details about our marriage and arrangements. I will speak to you about that later."

"Okay," Venus said, disturbed by Carl's sudden change of tone and his seriousness. She knew that more than anything else, Toni was an important factor in Carl's life. Period. Then another thought struck her. Would Toni, as much as he always spoke about the boys getting married, agree with their plan to stage a marriage—for a year? Toni always spoke about respect for the institution of marriage as sacred.

Venus swallowed hard.

She hoped Toni would go along with the plan Carl had developed knowing how influential he could be with his grandsons. Venus prayed he would go along with it.

CHAPTER NINE

Carl drove Venus along the country road from the waterfront to the main house in his convertible. He used the automatic power button to close the roof top as night fell over them. The evening breeze began to drop the temperature slightly. Venus felt the temperature inside her body chill at the thought of only having Carl for just one year. Then it would be all over. She tried desperately to squash the thought from of her mind. Instead, she diverted her eyes to the sightseeing of the grand Romero estate.

My God! The Romeros own all of this?

Venus's eyes drank in the massive land and the green mounds of hills on the way to the manor passing by the grand vineyard in the distance. The Romeros owned almost 20,000 acres of magnificent countryside property including the gorgeous wrap-around land by the pristine lake that housed several yachts at the dock. It was a popular waterside getaway—privately owned. It was mind-blowing. Surreal. And...

Where on earth would she and Carl be living while he ran the city—assuming he won the election?

"Carl, where will we live?" she blurted out. "Here? At the manor?"

Carl tilted his head back slightly and chuckled.

"Oh, no, beautiful," he answered. "There's no way I would run a city from this place. Do you think the hard working taxpayers would appreciate it?"

"No," she agreed quietly. "You're right. I guess you think of everything." She admired the way he planned ahead. He was so right. It would send the wrong message—yet again. And that was the last thing Carl would want to do in his run for mayor.

"Unfortunately, Venus, life isn't always simple," Carl opined, steering the car towards the main road leading to the house. "It's not enough to *do* the right thing. One must *appear* to be doing the right thing in life, as Granddad said."

She noticed his grin faded fast, his eyes penetrated the dark roadway ahead of them.

"Of course," she said quietly. Why did life have to always be about appearances? Or keeping up appearances?

"I own a modest property near..." he hesitated for a brief moment. She thought she saw raw pain clouding his eyes. "Near the place where we grew up," Carl said, continuing as they drove closer to the manor. "It's nice in a decent neighbourhood. Four bedrooms, three bathrooms, detached, two-levels. I think it would be perfect for us and we'll be closer to the community I'm going to serve. It also has a good size backyard where Tristan can play."

Yes. It sounded perfect. Perfect for their impending marriage of convenience.

Still, Venus admired him for his purpose and intent on making a difference in the community. "You know that is so commendable of you, Carl. Here you are, ensconced in so much luxury and yet you don't mind living modestly."

"Money isn't everything, Venus."

"Says the man who has all the money in the world," she teased him.

His face melted into that sweet, boyish, handsome grin again. God, he looked so charming, so adorable. And her lips still tingled from the memory of their sweet, passionate kiss only a few precious moments ago. Oh, she couldn't wait to taste his lips again—and so much more.

"Being content with who you are and what you do and what you represent in life means a lot more," he said, arching his brow.

"So true." Her voice trailed off. Was she content with whom she really was? Her heart plummeted again inside her chest. She wasn't even up front with him about her past. She began to feel distressed about her past and what she had become—her belief about being true to herself was not in tune with her actions.

Venus was beginning to experience cognitive dissonance. She detested the feeling. It was unbearable. Distressing. She hated to deceive him. She hated that she could not be upfront about...her past. But it didn't matter now, did it? She was protecting him by not telling him what really happened to her. If he ever found out, which she prayed he would not, perhaps he would forgive her and know that she really had no choice but to leave her past out of the equation. In any case, she was an entirely different person now. That was all that mattered.

At least that's what Venus wanted to believe.

* * *

"Granddad, are you okay?" Carl whispered, leaning over Toni's bed.

"Yes, Carl. I just had another little scare. Nothing to get all up in arms about. I'm not sure why Shelly called everyone here." Toni Romero was reclined up in his special custom-made adjustable bed. Shelly was by his side.

Carl and his brothers Jules and Zack had commissioned the design of the unique bed for their grandfather after his stroke a couple years earlier. The luxury mattress was therapeutic and had a soft memory foam that enabled their grandfather to have the most relaxing, restful night's sleep. Heck, the old man deserved it. He'd worked tirelessly around the clock his whole life just to provide for others. Giving them nothing but the finest he had to offer. He deserved only the best. Anything they could do to make his life a bit easier was good to them.

"Your grandfather had an absence seizure," Shelly clarified, as she lovingly hugged Toni. Being married to a nurse had its advantages for his grandfather. At first when Toni had announced that he was marrying his young nurse, the family was up in arms. And rightfully so. The wealthy tycoon had many previous marriages, not including the one to their beloved, now-deceased biological grandmother. The brothers summed up his previous brides as gold diggers who ended up with the old man paying plenty in alimony soon after the nuptials dissolved.

"Dr. Ademe just left," Shelly continued, rubbing Toni's arm. "He came in to check on your granddad when I called. I didn't know what else to do."

Toni heaved a sigh and rolled his eyes in mock exasperation. "Honestly, I don't know what I'm going to do with her. She gets too worked up about things." A grin played on the old man's lips. That made Carl feel a bit more at ease. At least his grandfather wasn't taking things too seriously.

"What do you mean by absence seizure?" Carl asked.

"I just stared off into space for a bit and Shelly went ballistic because I wasn't paying attention to her," Toni chimed in playfully.

"Now, Toni, you know that is not quite true." Shelly then motioned to Carl. "I'm just going to speak to Carl and Jules for a minute. You need your rest. Okay?" she said, getting up and placing her hands on her hips.

"Fine." Toni picked up the newspaper on the bedside beside him. "I'm going to read a bit more first."

"Toni, I really don't think you should be reading that now."

"Please, woman. Let me be!" Toni waved her off dismissively.

Soon after, Shelly and the boys went out into the hallway outside the room.

"Okay, now tell me what's really going on," Carl demanded.

"Well, Carl," Jules interjected. "Before you got here, Shelly filled me in."

"Oh?"

"Carl, your grandfather is worried sick about you," Shelly explained. "And yes, he has been having these little absence seizures. Nothing to worry about. We just need to monitor him closely. Basically, they are seizures that can last for a few seconds. Sometimes it's hard to detect. It's rare for absence seizures to occur in adults. But it can happen."

"Hard to detect? Few seconds?" Carl repeated in shock. Why the hell wasn't Carl told about this sooner? "And what do you mean, he's worried sick about me?"

"Carl, I noticed your grandfather started to read the newspaper about what the press is saying about you and well, at times, I would be speaking to him while he had the newspaper in his hand and he would suddenly zone out for a few seconds. I wasn't sure what caused it but it's been happening quite a bit. You know your grandfather is already having some challenges with his health," she added.

"I know," he said, still reeling in shock.

"Well, it distresses him when he sees the press taking potshots at you like that. He's worried about you running for mayor."

"But our granddad is always worried about us, doing anything."

"Yes, but politics is a whole different arena, Carl. He kept talking about them making a fool out of you, mocking you, trying to knock you down before you have a chance to accomplish anything. You know your opponents want nothing more than for you to be out of the competition," Shelly continued.

"Yeah, and so what? I'm not backing down that easily," Carl shot back.

"I know, man, but it's really something to think about," Jules added.

"So I'm to just back out and let the incompetent haters take over?" Carl demanded, a bitter taste rising in his throat.

"We're not saying that, it's just…" Shelly hesitated at first. "You see how the media can be with mayors from other cities who get wrapped up in scandals."

Carl rubbed the stubble on his chin. Shelly did have a point. Damn, the media could be darn right brutal!

Then, he thought about Venus for a fleeting second. His mind trailed to the secret she was hiding, whatever the hell it was, and his own background. Were there any proverbial skeletons that he had forgotten about that could resurface from the graveyard of the past?

Not that he had any crazy exes that he was worried about making a name for themselves, but still, one could never be too careful. All it took was for one person to blow things out of proportion with half-truths, untruths and everything but…the truth. The papers fed on scandal and *The Hills Times* was no exception. Heck, they had it out for the Romeros for the longest time dating back to an old family feud with the newspaper's founder and their great-grandfather over some damn land issue.

"Thank you, Shelly," Carl said dismissively. "I'm sure Granddad would appreciate you by his side now."

Shelly appeared stunned at first but took her cue. "Good luck with everything, Carl. Are you going to make the announcement soon?"

"Soon enough."

Shelly left the boys out in the hallway and re-entered the grand master suite, closing the French double doors behind her.

"What was all that about, Carl? You seemed really peeved with her. She was only trying to help."

"It's not that. I was about to tell Grandfather my plans but I don't know how he would take it right now. I'd rather not do anything that could rattle his nerves or get him upset."

"Upset?" Jules appeared puzzled at first. "Oh, wait a minute. You're still going through with that fake wedding, bro? Gotta be careful the press doesn't get wind of that. It wouldn't be pretty."

"I know. But it's not going to be a fake wedding. We will be getting married. And I need you to be there."

"What?"

"Yeah, Venus finally agreed to the arrangement. I'll do whatever it takes, Jules. And besides, I really like Miss Jackson, a lot. She's a good woman. People get married for all kinds of reasons."

"Yeah, but love should be one of them."

Carl grinned. "I know." Who said Carl *didn't* love Venus?

The truth was, Carl was falling for Venus. He was falling damn hard for her. Thinking about her right now got his body aroused. Shit! That kiss was something else. He'd never tasted anything more beautiful, salacious than sweet Venus. She turned him on in every way a man would be turned on by a beautiful woman. This wasn't purely a contractual deal. He really was feeling something for her. Even if it were for just a year—since he could never really do the lifetime commitment thing—he still wanted to have a meaningful temporary relationship with her. He was going to enjoy playing man and wife with darling, marvellous Venus Jackson. And he was all too happy to play the doting father to her adorable son. He felt oddly comfortable in taking on his new role.

"And where is Venus now?" Jules asked, as the brothers walked down the corridor to the grand stairwell.

"She's with her son in the daycare center."

The Romeros had built a twenty-four hour care center for staff who worked for them around the clock but needed the odd assistance with last-minute childcare. Venus at times would always tell him that she didn't want to take advantage and preferred not to use it too much on her off days but it worked well. They had their own screened childcare professionals. Especially since his cousin Antonio and his wife Lucy had their little Alexander. They were often busy taking business trips and in meetings with clients, so it was a convenience. Lucas, his brother, and his wife, Maxine, also used the private care center in the west wing of the Romero Manor for their little girl, Mary-Louise.

"I'm going to take her home but we'll need to get a few documents in place," Carl finished.

"You're really going through with this, aren't you, bro?"

"You know it means a lot to me...and to the people. They deserve the best. If we didn't get lucky with Granddad, what would have happened to us?"

"You don't have to tell me twice," Jules agreed. "Listen, you know I've got your back, regardless, right?"

"I know. And I'm not going to tell Granddad yet. Maybe tomorrow, before we leave. I'd hate for him to read about any weddings in his own family that he wasn't invited to in the newspapers, if you know what I mean."

Jules grinned. "Yeah, I get you. I agree with keeping it from him for now given his recent situation. I just wish Granddad wouldn't read those damn rags."

"I hear ya. So you're with me?"

"Yeah. Just say the word and I'm there, Carl."

"Good. We all leave for Vegas, the day after tomorrow."

Jules appeared caught off guard and almost missed a step on the marble staircase spiralling down. "Man, you really don't waste any time."

Carl grinned. "Time is way too valuable to waste, my brother. Time is all I've got."

CHAPTER TEN

Early on Wednesday morning, a private plane touched down in Las Vegas, Nevada in the United States on a glorious summer day. It was the hottest day in the year thus far in the region. And, it was the beginning of a whirlwind adventure.

Since deplaning, Venus felt shaken inside as they drove in the limousine. Her nerves were a hot mess. And it wasn't the heat from the sun that melted her inside, it was Carl Romero.

Her heart palpated every time she was near the man. At the moment, he looked ravishing in his dark gray business suit, white crisp shirt and navy blue tie. His dark short cropped hair was slicked back and accentuated his beautiful cheekbones and complemented his smooth tanned skin.

The expression on his handsome face was, however, serious. Something was bothering him and Venus wished she knew what it was. Was he having doubts? Or second thoughts about the whole marriage thing? She knew full well that he had a heated conversation with Toni, his grandfather, prior to their departure from Canada for this trip. What had that conversation been about? Carl mentioned to Venus that Toni had finally learned about their plans and intentions as soon as he his condition had become more stable. He told Venus that his grandfather was speechless at first and then scolded Carl for what he was getting into but the elder Romero decided he would leave it be—for now!

If only Venus could have been a proverbial fly on the wall at that time. Carl insisted that everything was still a go and that all was well with Grandpa Romero. He left the conversation at that. There was no room for questions when he had told her. Instead, Carl had immediately turned to his phone at that time which annoyed the heck out of Venus.

But having thought about that, she wasn't exactly open about every aspect of her own life with him, either, was she? That was one heck of a way for a couple to start off a fake relationship, Venus mused, mentally shaking her head at the irony of the whole situation.

Next, Carl and Venus went to the Clark County Building to obtain their marriage license. They had already sped up the process by filling out the online marriage license pre-application form in advance. Since the state of Nevada had no waiting period for couples eager to tie the knot, spur-of-the-moment weddings were as common as playing slots. Nevada was known as a state where weddings happened quickly. Venus's mind was still reeling from this whirlwind pretence romance with her boss. But her mind was still spinning, her heart still galloped hard and fast in her chest. She still couldn't process all that was happening.

It was no secret why it was one of the world's most popular hot spots to tie the knot. Pamela had already given them information about the legalities on getting married in Vegas so that the marriage would be validated once they returned to Canada. The last thing they would need was to have their marriage not recognized—which was rare, after getting married in Vegas.

Talk about a fast-and-easy way to get hitched!

After they left the Clark County Building, Carl glanced in Venus's direction as they sat beside each other in the super stretch Hummer limo heading back to the hotel. Jules had travelled separately with Pamela.

"You seem nervous," Carl commented, his dark, chocolate gaze capturing Venus.

Butterflies fluttered inside her belly again. His voice, his smooth tone always had that effect on her.

"I'm good," she lied, sounding as calm as her voice would allow. The truth was, she was going crazy inside—in a good way. She was just nervous as hell. What was she getting herself into? Good heavens! What was she doing? Getting married to a high-profile mayoral candidate?

Breathe deeply, Venus. Take a deep breath. Everything will work out fine. It has to work out fine.

Long before Venus knew that she could never really get married and have a happily ever after like most women dream about, she had never in her life thought that if she did tie the knot it would be in the famous Sin City! She felt like an A-list celebrity, hiding from the paparazzi and doing a spur of the moment quickie nuptial to escape a possibly media frenzy. This was somebody else's life, Venus thought to herself, not hers. Nothing seemed real about the day—except for the fierce beating of her heart and spine-tingling sensation she was having being near to Carl, knowing that by the end of the day, she would be his lawfully wedded wife.

My goodness!

Her body perspired at the thought. Her sex throbbed just thinking about him. She was having trouble breathing without trembling. Why did the air around her seem too thick to breathe all of a sudden?

Venus was about to become Mrs. Carl Romero. *Have mercy!*

"You sure now?" he asked, raising a brow. "You're not having second thoughts, are you?"

"Well, the only thing I'm not sure about is finding a wedding dress with only a few hours notice. I'm not exactly a supermodel thin type."

"No. You're not," he agreed. "You're so much more beautiful, more shapely." His silky gaze captured hers.

Her stomach flip-flopped. Her heart squeezed. Wow! What a thing for Carl to say. How was it that this man always knew the right words to speak to make a person feel...so good? So appreciated?

"Th-thank you," she said softly, almost breathless, "for the compliment."

"It's the truth," he affirmed, his eyes still engaged with hers.

Venus drew in a deep breath. He wasn't making her nerves any easier to manage, she mused with delight. Carl was so charming, so good in every way.

"I'm sure we'll find something in due time," he continued, turning his attention to his jacket, whipping out his smartphone. The partition of the limo was closed.

Venus didn't know if he was calling the chauffeur, or Pamela, who had taken up a duel role of assistant in addition to being the family's personal press secretary. She was now their official go-to girl and executive assistant whenever they needed. And Pamela was such a darling sweetheart and seemed to enjoy working for the Romeros as much as Venus did.

"Right," he said, after finishing his brief conversation. "There's a wedding boutique off the strip. Pamela will assist you in picking out a gown."

"Wow, thank you. It all seems so...official."

"Well, we need to do this right, don't we? Besides, we need to have official wedding photos up on our mantelpiece of our big day to make it look authentic."

Official wedding photos? Look authentic?

Her head was spinning. She was in a daze again—and this time, not in a good way. Why had her mood just slipped down into oblivion?

Crap!

Just when Venus started to feel so good about herself again, the thought of not having Carl forever, just bumped her right back into reality. *Look authentic?* That was what this was all about after all, wasn't it? Nothing more. Nothing less. This was all just for show. And what better place to have their wedding than in one of the world's top entertainment districts? The dazzling show-girl city. Las Vegas, Nevada!

"Yes," she agreed quietly. "It has to look authentic." Venus swallowed a hard lump in her throat that took forever to go down. Much like the bitter pill of reality. She could never really have Carl to herself—forever. That was her reality and she just had to get used to it. No matter what. She could do this. She could pretend to be his wife. She could pretend that it would mean nothing more. She could pretend...

This was going to be a lot harder than she thought it would be.

CHAPTER ELEVEN

The next day, Venus's heart fluttered in her chest, skipping a beat and thrashing about madly. She was going to implode. This was the day. It was finally happening. She stood in her hotel room on the Vegas strip, sucking in a deep breath while Pamela helped her with last minute finishing touches. As if this were real. As if she would stay married

"You look so beautiful, Venus," Pamela said, gushing over Venus's wedding gown.

"Thank you, Pamela. Thanks for spotting the dress in the boutique. I didn't think I could possibly find something so beautiful that would actually fit on such short notice." She swirled in her silky white floor-length gown.

Her heart was filled with panic. She was revealing an awful lot of herself in this dress.

It was an elegant A-line strapless dress with a plunging sweetheart neckline. *Oh, heavens!* Her cleavage was certainly prominent. The fabric was an organza flange with a wedding gown skirt that she admired the moment her eyes caught it at the store. The back was laced up intricately. The dress also had a natural waist that accentuated her curves. She was nervous thinking about what Carl would think when he first saw her in it.

Still, the gown was perfect for the Vegas summer heat, too. She'd read somewhere that getting dressed in a heavy gown in Vegas was probably not the best thing to do since it made the bride uncomfortable at best. That was the last thing she needed right now, to feel or look uncomfortable.

"Hey, no problem. That's what I'm here for." Pamela paused, looking awkward. "You know, I really do hope this works out for both of you," she said, handing Venus the silk posy bouquet.

Venus took the fragrant arrangement from her and held it in her hand, trembling. The natural stems of her bouquet were wrapped in beautiful satin and embellished in pearl pins and beaded trims. Her mother had held a similar bouquet, she remembered from seeing wedding photos of her now deceased parents. She wished to God she still had them with her. Right now, Venus had the traditional something borrowed—a piece of jewellery from Pamela. Something blue—an aqua-colored broach. Something new—a ribbon from the boutique store. And of course, something old—a beautiful pearl necklace that was her mother's. Her heart ached that her mother would never get to experience being the mother of the bride—even if Venus was only going to be bride for a year! Yet still wearing something that her mother once treasured brought her feeling closer to her mom—wherever her mother was in the spiritual sense.

"Thanks," Venus said. "I hope it works out for Carl, too. He would make the city's best mayor. He's so dedicated to helping the people."

"I know he's wonderful," Pamela said, looking down slightly. "But…I…I also hope it works out for both of you. I mean, after the agreed year together. I know it's not my place to say this but…you two really do make a cute couple. I see the way you look at each other." Pamela had a spark of hope in her eyes. Venus thought she could see a bit of moisture in them, too.

Oh, Lordie. The last thing Venus needed was to get emotional herself. She tried hard not to allow her nerves get the best of her. She was feeling anxious as it was. She drew in a deep breath.

"Well, you know, I like Carl." *Like* was an understatement. "But, I'll let the chips fall where they may," Venus continued, using a bit of Vegas casino talk. "Whatever's meant to be…will be." She hoped.

The ladies grinned and prepared to leave the suite for the chapel in the hotel. So this was it. No wedding rehearsal. No six-month planning. No massive guest list. Just the quick and done deal. She was going to begin her duties as Carl's loving bride. It was show time!

My God! Carl looks…wow! Just…wow!

Venus stood at the tastefully decorated chapel in the hotel with Carl at her side at the altar. The minister had already begun the brief service. Pamela and Jules were, of course, witnesses and the couple's two guests. Everything seemed to be going fine so far.

But Venus was so captivated by Carl. Her eyes kept drifting to her groom. A longing so painful stabbed at her heart. She'd never wanted someone so badly as she wanted Carl Romero. Yet, she was going to be his wife soon, in every sense of the word, for only one year! That was the only catch.

He stood towering over the minister in his six-foot, four-inch frame. His broad shoulders filled out nicely in his gorgeous white tuxedo. He no longer sported his stubble; he had apparently shaved for the ceremony—she guessed for the wedding photos, too.

Hot damn! She was on fire for sweet, sexy Carl. He was devilishly handsome, dripping with charm and sensuality. His dark features, smooth black cropped hair, dark defined eyebrows and beautiful brown eyes framed by long lashes. His lips were so well shaped, enticing. Kissable. Oh, he was so good with his soft, sexually potent lips. She couldn't wait to taste him again. She wished the ceremony would speed up. Yet inside she was a bungle of zigzagging nerves—all over the place. Her legs felt weak as the minister officiated. And Carl could not keep his eyes off her. She ran over the events of the past couple of days in her mind, since Carl's surprise proposal. She was nervous as sin and had her legs waxed, bikini line waxed and even did the American wax thingy before their arrival in Vegas.

Venus, more than ever, really wanted to make sure that she was as groomed underneath her lingerie as she could be. It dawned on her that Carl had been with some top models and rich socialites, none of whom were anything like her. She had a tough competition to follow. Would he be pleased with her in bed? She'd even taken the time to do a bit of Cosmo research on how to please her man in bed. Oh, heaven help her! What had she gotten into? If Carl's sexually-charged, erotic kiss was any indication of his lovemaking, oh, Lord, she didn't know if she would be able to manage him, or die of orgasmic overdose!

Keep your mind clear, Venus. You're in a wedding chapel.

Was she the only bride in the world who thought about what their upcoming honeymoon would be like making love to her groom, and what it would be like if it was to be their first time intimate with each other?

Her mind was spinning.

"Do you, Carl Vincent Romero," the minister said to Carl, "take this woman, whose hand you now hold, to be your true and wedded wife; and do you solemnly promise before God and these witnesses to love, cherish, honor and protect her: to forsake all others for her sake; to cleave unto her, and her only, until death shall part you?"

Carl's blood pumped in his body. Adrenaline coursed through his veins. *Damn!* What was he doing? He'd never desired a woman as much as he craved sweet Venus Jackson, but hot damn! Till *death* does he or shall he, or whatever the minister just said, part? That's one heck of a long time to be bound to a woman if he ever lived to be as old or older than dear old Grandpa.

Wait a minute!

Carl yanked himself back to reality and remembered their agreement. It was only for one year. Nothing more. But who the heck told Carl to make Jules arrange and book the wedding ceremony on his behalf? Why couldn't Jules have chosen an atheist style wedding or something to that effect? At least then he wouldn't feel so damn guilty taking this "holy" vows under God. He was sinning like hell and was going to go there real fast now. Not to mention that deep down Carl felt terrible for having to resort to getting married to improve his public persona as he entered politics. He kept reminding himself that he really did care for Venus and he knew his heart was in the right place in wanting to help taxpayers.

Carl drew in a powerful breath.

"I do," Carl responded, his voice deep and strong. He gazed into Venus's eyes and something weird and strange happened inside his body. He couldn't describe it. The energy he felt was incredible, her hand in his.

Desire burned through his body when his eyes captured his stunning bride. His wife-to-be. But only for one year! God, she was gorgeous. And her breasts practically bulging from her pretty gown with the low neckline. He could think of nothing else but nestling his lips between her bosom, and heck, between her thighs. His lips twitched just thinking about being inside his fascinating woman later. *Mind out of the gutter, Carl!*

Yet, heated anticipation rushed through his body. All this time that he'd known Venus, she'd been as beautiful as she was elusive. A mystery. Always keeping her distance from him, from everyone. Yet she was so loving, kind, graceful, and attractive in every way. He loved the way he felt around her, whether at work or on family occasions. And now. Tonight. He would finally get to be intimate with her. Heat rushed to his loins at the mere thought of taking her, making her his. Finally.

The minister turned to Venus.

"Do you, Venus Marie Jackson, take this man, who holds your hand, to be your true and wedded husband, and do you solemnly promise before God and these witnesses to love, cherish, honor and protect him, to forsake all others for his sake; to cleave unto him and him only...until death shall part you?"

Venus looked uncomfortable for a moment. Damn! That wasn't a good sign. She looked too stunned to speak. She seemed dazed. The minister, an older gentleman with white hair and pale skin that looked even paler against his black gown, looked concerned, too.

"I..." Venus said, swallowing a lump. She seemed to have difficulty speaking. Carl instinctively held her hand firmly, tighter with love.

"It's okay, Venus," he whispered to her. "You don't have to..."

He stopped himself but he was willing to forgo the charade. If she wasn't comfortable doing the whole wedding vows thing, that was okay with him. Maybe getting married was a bad idea after all. What the hell was he thinking that they could pull this off?

He'd just have to win the election on his own merits—as a single guy with a dream, nothing more. The last thing he wanted was for Venus to do something she was not comfortable with.

"Hey, it's okay, sir. The wedding's off," Carl ordered the minister, whose eyes now bulged out of his head.

"No!" Venus shouted.

Wow, what a voice. That really caught Carl and everyone in the chapel off guard.

"I...I'm sorry. I...I...I do," she said more confidently. "I do. I do take Carl to be my husband." Tears moistened her eyes.

The minister seemed as if he was going to have a heart attack. One would think that performing weddings in Vegas that he must have seen all kinds of weird stuff happening in his ceremonies. But Carl guessed not.

Venus squeezed Carl's hand. "Please. I want to do this. I want to," she said to him, her dark beautiful brown eyes pleaded with him.

"Okay," Carl said softly. He took his free hand and stroked the side of her cheek. "You're so beautiful, you know that?"

The minister cleared his throat. Jules and Pamela seemed to let out a collective sigh of relief. Or maybe that was just Carl's overactive imagination in the moment.

Why did he feel as if his world ended when he thought Venus was going to change her mind about marrying him? Heck, she was just doing it for a year contract. A job. Not the real thing.

Yeah, but this whole fake marriage thing might have been the original agenda but there sure as hell wasn't anything fake about the way his body was reacting to his beautiful assistant. Nothing at all. His feelings for her were anything but feigned. His whole body pulsed uncontrollably. Heat rushed through his loins, his veins.

This woman had captivated him … completely. She had his heart in her hands and she didn't even know it. Was he really falling for Venus?

"Okay then, we shall continue," the minister said.

The minister then wrapped up with the wedding vows, and they recited a prayer and did the ring exchange where they pledged their love for one another.

The minister then sealed the rings with a prayer and pronouncement. "In consideration of these pledges, I am authorized by the laws of the state of Nevada in your marriage license to pronounce you husband and wife. As I do this, let me remind you that henceforth, you are one, one in interest, and in reputation, and above all in affection. What God hath joined together, let no man put asunder."

"May I present to you," the minister turned to the tiny congregation of witnesses, "Mr. and Mrs. Carl Romero."

Carl's heart leaped in his chest. Holy! He'd really done this.

They'd sealed their fledgling marriage with a soft kiss at the altar and of course, Jules and Pamela sprinkled confetti over them. What a ceremony! Carl never thought he'd ever tie the knot, not for any reason, but this was different.

This was unbelievable!

CHAPTER TWELVE

"I thought you'd bailed on me there," Carl spoke softly to Venus, after they'd entered the honeymoon suite of the hotel. He'd carried her over the threshold as was tradition and laid her on the bed.

The red satin sheets were sprinkled with soft pink rose petals. Small lilac scented candles burned on the table in the room to create a mellowing romantic ambiance.

He seemed to enjoy her initial reaction of surprise when he carried her into the room and she first saw the decorated bed. He wanted this to be a special for her. It was the least he could do since she'd done him this enormous favor—and the honor of marrying him.

Earlier, after the ceremony, they'd had a brief reception in Pamela's suite. Prior to that, they had hired a photographer to take elegant wedding portraits in the scenic garden on the grounds of the grand hotel. Venus was breathtakingly photogenic. She looked like a royal bride. A princess. And she was all his. For one year! He couldn't wait to taste the sweetness of her juices. A grin of amusement touched his lips thinking about what was to come. His groin ached to be entwined with hers. He found her natural fragrance pleasantly intoxicating.

Carl knew he should be one hundred percent elated but a nagging torment gnawed at him. Why did he secretly wish their arrangement would be longer than one year? A year didn't seem nearly enough time to be with Venus. Maybe he should have considered a renewal option. Damn! Why didn't he think of that earlier? Then a crazy thought entered his mind. After they separated and divorced, would Venus settle with someone else? The thought of her ever being with another man, well, it ripped him to shreds inside.

He squashed the thought. No way was he going to let that notion ruin the beginning of a beautiful night.

"I'm so sorry, Carl. I just got...a bit nervous at the altar. I couldn't believe it was finally happening. I know we spoke about it before but..." Venus stopped herself before saying anything else. Her mind drifted to thoughts about the threat from Eduardo and her tumultuous past. She thought about losing Carl. She thought about not having Carl with her. She thought about all sorts of crazy things. But one thing was for sure. She wanted Mr. Romero more than anything else in the world. She needed Carl in her life, in her heart, in her body like she needed air to breathe. The feelings she had for him were suffocating. Intoxicating.

This man caused all sorts of wild emotions to wash through her, yet he had no idea just how much he meant to her.

"No, don't be sorry," he said gently, his voice husky. He leaned down closer to her, gently pulling her into his embrace on the bed. God, he was stunning. The way his dark, sexy eyes undressed her made her shiver with delight. Venus tingled in all the right places. The sweet scent of his cologne wafted to her nostrils and heightened her senses.

"I want you, Venus," he murmured breathless, his dark eyes penetrating hers. "You look so...beautiful, amazing today. You stole my breath away earlier."

She could feel the hardness of his erection in his dress pants.

"Th-thanks," she whispered, arousal overcoming her. "S-so do you," she murmured. Her skin was getting moist. Heat rushed through her veins. Her heartbeat pounded hard and fierce in her chest. She was sure he could hear it.

He then lowered his sweet lips to hers and gently kissed her, and oh, a tingling desire and excitement rushed through her body again. Her sex pulsed hard between her legs, throbbing and pounding to the beat of her heart.

I need you now, Carl! She screamed inside her head. She was thirsting for him, starved for his affection. She felt as if she were going to go crazy out of her mind, if he wasn't inside her soon.

"If you want, we can hold off until we get back to Canada," he said, pressing his lips, brushing them gently over hers while she tingled all over.

"No, Carl. No. I need you now," she purred as his lips moved to her neck and sucked on her sensitive flesh. "Oh," she moaned in erotic pleasure as his hands slid underneath her gown.

A grin of satisfaction graced his sweet lips as he guided her off the bed. "Do you want me?"

"Oh, yes," she whispered, breathless. "I want you now, Carl."

"How badly do you want me?" he enticed in a low, sultry voice, arching his sexy brow.

"Oh, Carl!" Venus wrapped her arms around his neck, pulling him closer to her. "This much," she said, kissing him hungrily. Her body was on fire. Desiring him. Lusting for him. The pulse between her legs throbbed harder and harder.

He held her chin in his hands and lowered his head to hers again kissing her passionately. He then moved his hands and began to undress her seductively, while kissing every exposed area of her soft naked skin.

She arched her neck back, groaning in pleasure as he eased her out of her dress. He caressed her skin with sweet, soft kisses that made tingles slither down her spine, embracing her firmly, admiring her body. Her nipples tightened when he unhooked her lace bra and exposed her voluptuous breasts. A smile of approval crept on his face as his eyes passionately drank in her beauty.

"God, you're so beautiful, Venus," he groaned, his voice sounding more hoarse and heavy. He lowered his hands to her rear and gave her a good squeeze and sweet electricity jolted through her. Her arms wrapped around his smooth, defined muscles on his arms as he lowered her again to the bed. She ran her hands up his smooth hard biceps.

Carl leaned down and kissed the top of her breast, rubbing his nose gently over her cleavage before going further around her breasts, pressing his lips over her mound of flesh while her nipples continued to tighten and ache for his touch.

"Oh," she moaned in ecstasy while his hand moved around her other breast, massaging and caressing her taut nipple, enjoying the feel of her naked flesh, sending prickles all over her body.

"I want you," he said, intermittently caressing her with his kisses. "I want you so badly, Venus," he groaned, sucking on the sensitive area around her nipple.

Take me! Take me now, she pleaded in her mind. Her nipples strained. Tingling for his touch. Oh, why was he torturing her? Why was he teasing her? She couldn't wait for him to take her into his mouth.

As if he could read her mind, he brushed his soft lips over the tip of her nipple and she tightened her grip on the smooth skin of his muscular back, her inner thighs throbbed with need. She groaned uncontrollably. Carl teased and played with her nipple with his hot, wet tongue, sucking hard then licking the tip softly and then taking her fully into the moist of his mouth. He tantalized, nibbled and stroked her nipple with his tongue as she grabbed the sheets, writhing on the bed, breathing hard.

He seemed to be more turned on by her moans of pleasure. She moved her hands over his smooth biceps and held firmly as he aroused her with his expert kisses. She moved her hand to the back of his head as he continued to tantalize her breasts.

Carl continued to kiss, nip, suck her passionately, hungrily. She was panting harder and wanted him fully. She managed to grab his shirt and ease him out of it. He carried on pleasuring her while together they skilfully undressed. Soon, he was topless and she enjoyed the feel of his smooth, muscular skin as he moved his lips down her body.

"Oh. Oh, no."

"What is it?"

Carl breathed hard, intermittently pressing kisses to the top of her pubic area just over the softness of her hairs.

Oh, God! Was he going to...go down there on her?

Breathing hard, she told him, "Oh, I'm a little nervous."

"I'll stop," he told her.

"No! No, please don't. I...I want to do this, please," she begged him, breathless.

He looked at her lovingly. "You sure?"

"Yes. Oh, yes!"

Carl was going crazy out of his loving mind. He'd never wanted someone so badly as he did Venus. He fiercely wanted to take the time to explore her beautiful body, appreciating her fully then taste the sweetness of her feminine elixir. But it just dawned on him that not all women have had the pleasure of having their sex titillated the right way. Maybe her ex didn't please her there, or maybe he wasn't the orally manipulating type, but Carl sure as hell knew how to bring her carnal pleasure. Heck, some men didn't care enough to study their woman, take their time with her and please her the way she desired to be pleased. It was all about the woman. His lover was his goddess. And she deserved to call the shots.

A grin curled his lips as he watched her before lowering his head to the beautiful mound between her legs. He spread her legs apart and positioned her on the edge of the bed on top of the satin fabric.

He then got up and finished undressing.

She had a sedating, pleasurable expression on her face that delighted him. Good. This beautiful woman turned him on like sin and he wanted to make sure he pleasured her the way she deserved to be.

"What are you doing? Don't stop," she breathed, panting.

A spurt of devilish desire to be adventurous in bed spiralled through Venus. She'd read somewhere that it's sexually arousing to be blindfolded not knowing where the next soft kiss, tingling lick or delicate stroke would be sensed on her body. Ooh, she wanted to explore that with Carl. Mystery foreplay. What had gotten into her all of a sudden? This wasn't like her. Maybe being with Carl made her feel more open to try cool things. Whatever it was, she was delighting in being pleasured by Carl in the most sensuous way.

Wearing a blindfold during foreplay delightfully heightened the senses through pleasure by mystery.

"Oh no, baby," he said in a low voice, "I want to make this good for you."

"Oh?" she sighed, her chest still heaving from the arousal.

"Can we...um...try a blindfold? I really want you to surprise me with your...touch on my body." Her heat throbbed just thinking about it. "Oh, I love surprises," she purred.

"You sure you want me to blindfold you?" he clarified in a low, husky voice.

She nodded, grinning.

"Okay, beautiful. Your wish is my...pleasure. I want you to enjoy me tasting you. I want you to feel everything, but okay, no other senses allowed."

Carl got up and positioned Venus on the bed. "I know they have some kinky toys in the drawer here for honeymooners. They must have a blindfold in there," Carl said.

"I can't wait to pleasure you like you've never been pleasured before," he continued, brushing his lips against her neck, breathing hard.

"Oh, you, naughty thing," she cooed in labored breaths.

"I know!" He moved his lips to hers. God, her lips were so soft, so tingling. This woman could sure kiss, he mused with delight. His body tingled, his erection strained inside his silk boxers. Oh, God, he couldn't wait to have all of her. Every single inch of her sexy body. And now this anticipatory foreplay in the dark was an added touch.

"Do you want me to please you?"

"Yes. Oh, yes. Yes!" she begged, between kissing him passionately, sucking on his lower lip. Oh, God! His erection was hard.

Carl moved from her after pressing his lips to hers one more time before attempting to get the paraphernalia he needed. He went to the drawer and looked for what he thought he would find. The special honeymoon hotel suite was stocked with all kinds of kinky pleasures for newlyweds.

He opened the drawer as Venus lay on the bed, ripe and ready for him. Her legs spread slightly open. He didn't want to keep her waiting. Heck, he was dying to take her all the way. He pulled out a dark, silk scarf. Perfect. The room was dimly lit with only a few candles burning, so he couldn't tell what color it was exactly, not that he cared.

He turned around and propped himself over Venus. His body pulsed uncontrollably as she grinned and moaned her approval. "I'm going to cover your eyes now, baby."

"Mmm, I can't wait," she cooed, smiling.

He kissed her, then tenderly covered her eyes with the fold and wrapped it around, the cool fabric covering her eyes completely.

"You okay?" he said, lowering his lips to her neck and kissing her delicately.

She writhed beneath him, nodding, breathing hard, and licking her lips. *Oh, God! Don't do that*, he thought to himself. Seeing her wet tongue slide across her lips just made his crotch jump hard. He didn't want to drive his full length into her until she was good and came for him first.

Carl ran his eyes down her beautiful body, admiring her, his hands followed the smoothness of her precious flesh.

"Oh, Venus. You are the most beautiful woman I've ever laid my eyes on. You're a goddess."

"Mmm," she moaned, breathing hard.

He lowered his lips to her mound between her legs, brushing his lips over her dark pubic hairs and stroked his fingers down her wet, swollen folds.

"Oh," she moaned with pleasure. Oh, the sensation. The sweet surprise of his wet, soft tongue surprising her, kissing her every way in different sensitive areas around her sex. It was pitch dark, only the sensation her body was treated to the erotic tender touch of Carl's lips sending waves of desire rushing through her flesh.

Good.

He went down on her with his lips sucking her flesh gently at first. "Do you like that?" he asked hoarsely.

She nodded, groaning, breathing hard.

"Good," he moaned. He knew how to be gentle with a woman down there, between her precious and beautiful folds. It was all about the touch, how soft the lady wanted it, how right it had to be for her. Each woman was unique and either wanted it hard or she wanted it soft. There was no in between. He always took his time, getting to know, to feel what a girl desired. But heck, Venus wasn't even just any girl. She was superior to anyone he'd ever been with.

He licked her softly between her folds and slid his moist tongue up and down her wetness, tasting her sweet, clear juices. God, she tasted like honey water. Sweet and pure. His blood pumped hard in his veins and all of the plasma in his body seemed to travel to his erection as he sucked her sex, French kissing her swollen folds with his lips, then with his tongue, thrusting inside her space, getting more aroused by every whimper and uncontrollable spasm she made as he pleasured her. He enjoyed sucking her with overt passion as he held firmly to her curvaceous thighs.

She writhed and moaned, crying out with pleasure as he pressed his lips to hers and licked her with his tongue in all the right places. Knowing she was bravely blindfolded and enjoying the sensation without any interference turned him on even more. He'd intermittently reached his hands to her nipples and stroked them gently at times while he pleasured her between her legs, enjoying the spasm of her body. She arched on the bed, her hips rose upward as she came, crying out his name, breathing hard and fast. Her body shuddered uncontrollably. He could not believe how good she tasted when she came inside his mouth. He was more turned on than he'd ever been. His wife was the most beautiful being he'd ever had.

"Oh, oh, Carl," she groaned. She panted, her breath stolen by the experience. Carl moved over her and slid off her silky blindfold. He gazed intently into her eyes.

"Did you enjoy that?" he murmured.

"Mmm, yes," she uttered, her body limp. Spent ... but ready for more.

He kissed her gently, not being able to get enough of her sweet flesh.

"You looked so beautiful when you came," he whispered into her ears, before sucking on her earlobe. She reached her hands over him and squeezed him tightly.

"Oh, Carl," she said, her hand gliding down his hardness protruding from his silk boxers as Carl lay on top of her, kissing her sweetly.

What just happened?

She'd never experienced such erotic electricity through her body before. The feeling of being in the dark while Carl's soft, magical lips worked their passion, caressing various parts of her tender flesh was incredible! This was mind-blowing sex she never thought she could ever experience. The sensation was so erotic, so naughty. She was deeply satisfied and pleased to oblivion.

Venus was throbbing from the aftereffect of her explosive orgasm. *My goodness, Carl was...amazing!* How on earth did he make her come that way? She badly wanted to taste Carl, all of him just as he'd explored her inner thighs with his beautiful, potent lips. Oh, that magical touch! She was still buzzed between her legs after he made her come so violently with a heated orgasm. She could not believe how explosive his lips and his soft tongue felt between her legs and being in the dark created a wicked, pleasurable element of surprise.

They French kissed, sucking each other's tongues, exploring each other's moistness for a time as Venus massaged Carl's erection, but she was hungry for him and couldn't wait to free him.

She knew that Carl was safe and had a clean bill of health. They'd gone into all that detail with the marriage contract after they'd both taken blood tests and all was fine with their results, but she still knew they would have to use a condom because she was not on any birth control.

But not now. She wanted to take him between her lips. She turned around and repositioned herself on top of him, licking her lips like a ravenous vixen. What had come over her suddenly? Was it the ambiance in the room? Or was it just being with the hottest guy she'd ever had the pleasure of being with—her gorgeous, charming hot lover of a husband.

Still breathing hard, Venus playfully kissed a taut brown nipple on his chest as he moaned and she soon slid her tongue down his firm, muscular flesh. Goodness, he was so...fit! So healthy. His body was ripped and sculpted in all the right places. She leaned down and slid off his boxer shorts and his erection was sprung free.

Oh, God! This man was...blessed with good proportions. She didn't want to seem too surprised and tried but her look of approval and lust caught his attention and a grin of satisfaction curled his lips, she noticed.

She eagerly glided her hand down his hard shaft, admiring his firmness. Venus then extended her wet tongue over the tip gently and he groaned with pleasure. Already, she was hot again, so turned on by his arousal. She wanted to do this right. She needed to please him the way he'd just satiated her.

She kissed the tip of his erection and took him into her deeper and deeper with each suck, stroking his flesh simultaneously, and enjoying his moans of unbridled pleasure. He held onto her head as she bobbed up and down on his shaft, enjoying the taste of him inside her. He tasted clean, like a musky soap and a blend of his own masculine sex. The sensation filled her mouth as she pleasured him and swirled her tongue over the top before going down to the base of his erection.

"Oh, God!" he cried out over and over. "I'm gonna come," he said, motioning her head to shift but she wanted to experience all of him. She sucked harder and deeper until he came with a shudder, his milky release powerfully spilling over on her lips.

"Why didn't you move, baby?" he breathed, now hoarse.

"I wanted to," she said, moving up on him, pressing her lips to his neck and to his cheeks, and then moving over to his lips.

"Oh, God, you're something else, you know that?" he whispered.

"Wanna go gloved or bare? You know I'm clean."

"I know, baby," she whispered, kissing him intermittently. "We should use a condom, I'm…"

He kissed her lips before she could finish her sentence. "Don't explain. Safer is better," he said, reaching over to the side table and opening the drawer. He pulled out a square golden foil packet and unwrapped it immediately.

"No, let me." Venus grinned. "I want to do this; let me put it on."

"Okay," he moaned in a low voice, leaning back with a smile on his face. He seemed to enjoy watching her as she straddled him. She surveyed the condom to make sure she had the right way up before rolling it over his long, hard erection.

"Mmm," he groaned when she touched his length. Nothing pleased her more than to hear her man satisfied in every way.

"Come here, baby," Carl spoke softly, as he positioned her to the side and moved himself over her as if he were about to do push-ups. His arms were so strong, his muscles flexed. He then lowered his body to her while she breathed hard and deep. Her heart was pounding harder and harder in her chest. Beating faster and faster as he kissed her lips tenderly then passionately while he moved over her, he positioned his erection at her opening and gyrating his hips over hers, spreading her legs apart then…he slid deep inside her. Venus jolted. She cried out his name, moaning with delight. He came out slowly for a moment, teasing her. She wanted him back inside her, filling her again. She could not believe how wonderful his large manhood felt inside her moist, throbbing walls.

Venus wrapped her legs around his firm waist crying out for more as blood rushed through her, enjoying the heat of his body on hers, inside her. She moaned uncontrollably as he pounded his hardness back and forth into the pulsing of her sex. She couldn't believe how good he felt inside her, sating her completely. Fulfilling her. Desire shot through her body. She'd never felt so erotic, so in touch, so sexy, so desired. Feeling Carl Romero inside her, thrusting his manhood inside her as she tightened around him sent currents of desire through her body. His hardness inside, electrifying her sweetly.

Soon she came again and again, her body jerking hard on the bed. Carl came hard as his body went into spasm on top of her. They both collapsed into each other's arms in the afterglow of their magnificent love-making. The way newlyweds should be. If only, they could stay in this marriage—forever!

* * *

Venus woke up, a satisfied smile on her face, her body still felt a bit sore in a good way, but still buzzed from Carl's stunning love-making. She'd been so intimate with him last night. It was incredible. Incredible was probably not even the best word to describe what they'd experienced. She reached over to his side of the massive king-sized bed but Carl was not there.

"Carl?" she said, propping herself up on the bed in the dark. The room was darker now since the tiny little love candles had burned out. The moonlight was the only illumination in the grand honeymoon suite. She saw a shadow of a man sitting by the window with his knee propped up.

"Carl?"

"Yes, I'm here."

But something was wrong. Terribly wrong. She turned on the side table light. Carl's expression was nothing like the one she'd seen before. She glanced at the clock on the table. It was four in the morning.

"Is something wrong?" she asked, sitting up on the bed. Her heart was pounding hard and fast. But this time it had nothing to do with the anticipatory passion she'd felt. This time, her heart beat furiously out of fear. Oh, no. Did he find out? But how could he? She'd tried to be so...careful.

Carl had on a pajama bottom. His beautifully ripped chest still bare to her delight. She loved capturing his masculine, naked physique every chance she got.

Hours ago, love shone in his beautiful dark eyes. And now? Anger flashed in the blackness of his eyes. They glowed with a savage inner fire. It brought shivers down her spine. Oh, God! He knew. He knew about her.

"Yes," he said, his voice devoid of warmth or any expression for that matter. "Who the hell are you?"

"W-what?"

His tone chilled her body.

"Who are you and where is Tristan's real mother?"

"Carl, what are you talking about? I...I'm Tristan's mother."

"Don't lie to me, Venus. You know you are not. Did you think I wouldn't know?"

"Know what?"

"That you were a virgin," he said, and he rose from his chair to full height. He placed his hands in the pockets of his silk pajama bottoms and paced by the window, eyeing Venus occasionally. He looked as if someone had punched him in the gut and ripped out his heart. He looked...crushed. Disappointed. In shock.

Venus flinched.

"There's no way you gave birth," he continued. "You sure as hell didn't do it naturally and you have no signs of ever having a surgery or C-section. What's going on? Who are you? You came to work for my family saying that you were a single mother and needed a job. You lied right there. You're not a mother."

Venus trembled inside. "I...I am, Carl." Caught up in her own web of lies. Now what? "Okay, Carl," she said, sitting back down on the side of the bed. She covered her face with her hands and willed her tears to stop. She then looked up and heaved a deep sigh. "Carl, I'm so very sorry, you had to...find out like that. You're right. I'm not Tristan's...real mother."

"What? So it is true," he said, looking more shocked. Finally hearing the truth from her lips knocked reality to him.

"M-my name...is not Venus Jackson."

"Who are you then?"

"M-my real name is Nadya. Nadya Korosokowii."

CHAPTER THIRTEEN

"You know, I'm worried about Carl," Toni said turning to his wife, Shelly. It was four in the morning, but for some reason Toni could not sleep. He was propped up on his side of the automatic reclining bed. Thankfully, it had two power modes where each side of the bed could be lowered or raised separately.

Shelly turned over to face him. The nightlight on his side of the bed was turned on.

"Toni, what are you doing up at this hour?"

"I'm worried about that grandson of mine. You know, him being in Vegas with Venus and...well, planning this one-year marriage for the sake of the election and his public image. I wish he would do this for real."

"I agree," she said, raising her side of the bed. "But I think he knows what he's doing. Carl is a good man, the best man for the job, Toni. We both know that. But we also know that a disadvantage like being single and young can run high, too."

"That's true," Toni admitted, adjusting his glasses over his nose. He dropped the newspaper on his lap. "But right now, the media is saying all kinds of nasty lies about him. I hate it. My blood is boiling over just thinking about them getting away with putting him down before he even has a chance to announce his candidacy. And you know where all this is coming from?" he said, rhetorically. "Those Bronsons! They own half the media outlets in this town and they're always all too happy to put my boys down. They'd done so in the past. Not to mention Carl's potential rivals who are trying to dig up dirt on him so that they can bury him before the election. I tell ya, politics is a dirty game. It's not for the faint of heart."

"Oh, no. You're not still reading all that gossip, are you?" Shelly commented. "Toni, that's going to drive you crazy, up the wall."

"I just need to keep up-to-date on what's being said about my grandson. You know how much that matters to me."

"I know. But you also have your detectives on the case, too. You told me that your men are keeping an eye on what's going on. If they come up with anything libelous then we can go after them."

"I know, I know," he said. "It's just that the boys have been through so much in their lives. They've really had it rough, as you know. They used to be poorer than poor before they came into my life—after they lost their mother and their dad lost their home."

"I know. But they're grown now and doing so much for themselves. God, Toni, those young men have skins more solid than steel. Nothing can penetrate them. You know that. They've accomplished so much, too. You can't keep seeing them as boys, Toni. You have to let go at some point. All you can do is guide them and offer them your opinion and let them do the rest."

"Yes, of course," he said dismissively.

"Why do I get the feeling that's not all that's bothering you?" Shelly probed perceptively, raising her brow.

"You're right, my dear. That's not all that's bothering me."

"Well, what is it then?" she asked softly.

"I just don't want to see my grandsons alone, that's all. I see the way Venus looks at Carl. Just the way Lucy looked at Antonio and Maxine at Lucas. And of course let's not forget Zack who's more happy than he's ever been now that he's married to Blue. Marriage is magical when you're with the one who would do everything in the world to make you happy. Someone who loves you for who you are and cherishes you," he said.

"I agree. Couldn't have said it better!" Shelly smiled.

"Venus seems to care so much for Carl and he doesn't seem to see it. Or at least, he dismisses it. He's been...well, hurt before by a bad relationship with that Nea girl, his first real love, and I think he finds it hard to trust and lose love again. But life is about taking chances. That's what living is—or we'd all be sitting in a closet withering away. I hope and pray that he gives Venus a chance. If nothing else comes out of this...political game. I pray that they will at least find love with each other."

"I hear you," Shelly said.

"I mean, look at us. Who would have ever thought we'd end up together? You worked for me as my nurse, remember?"

"How could I forget?" She grinned. "I'm still your nurse."

He chuckled, momentarily. "Well, you know what I mean. The family didn't think we'd be good together because of our age difference and the fact that you were wife number five but the fact remains is that we gave love a chance."

"I know," she said, and she reached over to him and kissed his cheek.

Toni felt warm inside and patted her arm affectionately. "I don't know what I would do without you, Shelly."

"Probably enjoying a peaceful night sleep without someone nagging you all the time," she teased.

Toni grinned. "Yeah, yeah. I just hope that Carl sees Venus as more than just a meal ticket to a high-profile position."

"Oh, now stop. You don't give those boys much credit sometimes, Toni. You know Carl is a lot more profound than that."

"I know, I know. But I hope he doesn't throw love away. You and I both know that there's a lot of politics in...politics, right?"

"Yeah," she said, "and what are you getting at?"

"Life can be hard sometimes. Any place in life worth going, like the road to happiness, is often paved with a lot of trials and tribulations. It's not always smooth."

"I know," she said, "and having someone by your side makes it all the more worthwhile and tolerable," she said, finishing his sentiment.

"That's right. You know I'm not going to be around forever, you know. I'm getting old. I know the boys keep saying that I'm always nagging them about marriage but marriage is the best partnership a person can have."

"Well said, Toni."

He chuckled. "Well, you know me and philosophy, right?"

"Yes, and you're my modern day Aristotle," she said, playfully.

"I just hope it really does work out for Carl and Venus. I don't know what I would do if it doesn't work out between them."

CHAPTER FOURTEEN

Carl narrowed his eyes, overcome with shock and disbelief. The blood drained from his face. "Nadya. Korosokowii?" he echoed her name.

His gut instinct was right. He'd suspected something about her but nothing close to this. Not even remotely. This woman was a complete fraud. An imposter.

He paced by the fireplace in the hotel room and ran his fingers through his hair, dazed. His heart thumped fierce and hard in his chest. He felt his blood pressure soar. A humorless chuckle parted from his lips.

"It isn't what it looks like, Carl."

"No?" he said indifferently. "Why did you lie about who you were on the job application when you came to work for my family?"

"I...I didn't," she denied.

"Oh? But you just told me you're Nadya whatever."

"Yes. I...mean, no. I mean, yes, I am now," she stuttered. Carl could see terror in her eyes. There was so much more to this. So much more.

"Okay," he said, trying to sound more calm to give this woman a chance to explain herself. "Do you mind explaining to me what's really going on, Venus, or rather, Nadya?"

"I..." she got up, wringing her hands, the sheet tied around her, covering her voluptuous cleavage that hours ago he'd pleasured. *My goodness.* He'd just made love to a stranger.

She drew in a deep breath and gazed out at the window, taking in the city lights in the darkness of the early morning. The city that never slept. And it looked as if they would not be getting any sleep either, any time soon.

"You see, I was born Nadya Kosorokwii and Tristan was born Niko," she paused, breathing hard as if overcome with anxiety.

"Are you going to be all right?"

"Yes," she assured before continuing. "You see, Tristan is not my son. He's my...my baby brother."

"What?" Carl rubbed the top of his head. *Shit, this night's getting crazier by the minute!* "Okay, whoa there. Your *brother*? Tristan is your *brother*?"

Well, now it all made sense why that little kid had her eyes, her nose, her face, and everything about her. They damn well looked alike. But not as mother and son. As sister and brother. What the hell was going on? What had he gotten himself into, marrying this woman with the intent of presenting her to the world as his wife?

"Yes."

"So what about your parents?"

"Well, that's where it gets complicated. Oh, Carl. I'm so sorry I...I didn't tell you but I couldn't before."

"Why, Venus...Nadya...or whoever you are?" *Damn! This is all crazy!*

"You can call me Venus. Please. That is my real name," she said with conviction. "Well, at least now it is."

"So you changed your name and kidnapped your brother."

"No, Carl. I..." Venus drew in a deep breath. Carl sensed this was difficult for her. He felt sorry for her. No matter who the hell she really was, he still had real feelings for her. His body could not deny that. Heck, he couldn't deny it to himself. But he couldn't go further without an explanation. He needed to know what the hell was going on and what he and she had gotten herself into. The press would have a field day with this if word ever got out.

"Are you in trouble?" he asked pointedly. Was she running from someone? Hiding from something?

"No. Yes. I mean, I was but not now."

"Okay, tell me everything, Nad—I mean, Venus."

"Okay. My name was Nadya and my brother's name was Niko. He is now officially my son."

"How come?"

"Well, you see, it all started a few years ago. In Murumba."

"So that's where you're really from. Why did you tell me Kansas?"

"I had been to Kansas once a long time ago, so I thought it would be safe to say I'd spent longer than I had actually stayed there."

"I see." His arms remained folded across his chest; his eyes penetrated her. She was still painstakingly beautiful. But just a beautiful liar now.

"I had to say that so that your men, your people around your family could not pinpoint where I'm really from. My parents were brutally murdered in front of me, and Tristan—but he was just a baby so he wasn't aware of it," she said in a low voice, anger more than sorrow reflected in her voice and her beautiful dark brown eyes.

"Oh, God! Venus, I'm so sorry. When did this happen? How?"

"Well, first I will tell you that I had a part-time job to help make ends meet because my family lived on a substandard income. My employer, Eduardo Meritos," she said.

"Wait a minute. That name sounds familiar. Isn't he some mob boss?"

She nodded, her eyes downcast. "We didn't know what he was about at the time. He offered me a job so that I could help make ends meet for my family. But then he started…making passes at me. And well," she breathed hard.

Carl bowed his head. He didn't think he wanted to hear more. Anger seethed inside him mixed with sorrow. He'd kill anyone who laid a finger on her. "What happened?" his voice was dark, void of emotion. "Did he…?"

"No. But, my father got so upset. And Eduardo threatened to do something if we intervened in whatever he wanted to do."

"What happened next?"

"Well, Eduardo came to the house one night. After I had quit working for him. My father and he argued and then…well, shots were fired …" Her voice trailed off and she covered her face with her hands. Carl reached over to her and wrapped his arms around her.

Venus regained her composure and looked up, straight ahead, her jaw clenched. "Eduardo was a powerful man in the town, everyone knew that. He has connections everywhere. People feared him."

"Enough to get witnesses to say he was somewhere else," Carl said, figuring out the rest.

Venus nodded, slowly.

"So let me guess. You were the only one who could positively, without a shadow of a doubt, identify him as the one who murdered your parents and so you entered into some kind of witness protection program."

"Yes," she said, bitterness spilling over in her voice. "But now he has escaped from prison. He escaped! I feel so responsible for…my parents'…deaths." Her voice was heavy with remorse. "I…I don't deserve to have a family. If only…"

"Whoa, wait a minute. If only what? You'd allowed Eduardo to sexually harass you? Hey, don't ever let the evil actions of others make you feel in any part responsible. You did nothing wrong."

Carl felt his gut clench. *Damn!* If he could just get his hands on that low-life bastard, Eduardo. All this time, he thought Venus was playing him and she was fleeing for her life. Anger knotted inside his gut as he tried to grasp the gravity of this dreadful situation.

"I'm sorry I lashed out at you like that," Carl said darkly. "I'm gonna see to it that asshole is caught," he vowed as fury surged through his blood.

"I'm glad it's all out now," she said with a cool reserve, her eyes vacant.

"So that's why we couldn't locate anything more about you even though we hired you. You have all your documents legal because your government arranged it, including a new birth certificate and passport."

She nodded. "Yes. That's right. But unlike the witness protection program in this country, in my country they give you very little to start your new life. You're on your own. The plan was that I leave the country with no one knowing and take Tristan with me and legally adopt him under secrecy. I was so thankful to be hired by your family. You guys have been more than hospitable, kind, supportive."

"Of course."

"Luckily, Tristan is too young to…know the truth." Venus swallowed hard. "I was told it would be best to come to Canada since no one would ever suspect me coming here. I dyed my hair and changed the texture."

Carl was too stunned to speak at first. He was shocked, trying to process all this information. He drew in a deep breath. "I'll call everything off so you don't need to worry," he said in a deep, low voice.

"What? Your bid for mayor? No, Carl. You must go forth!" she exclaimed.

"Go forth? Are you kidding me?" Carl didn't know what had gotten into him all of a sudden. "You just told me that you're in the witness protection program. Do you really want us to go public about our marriage?" He tried damn hard to keep his feelings from spiralling out of control, but it was too late. He was going crazy out of his mind at the thought of possibly losing Venus, for good.

Their marriage?

Wasn't this supposed to be a fake relationship solely for show-and-tell purposes?

So then why was Carl feeling fiercely protective over her suddenly? The woman just lied the hell out of who she was—even for a good cause but still he had been deceived. He should be thinking about divorcing her and calling it a day—finding another woman to take her place.

But he couldn't. He just couldn't leave sweet Venus on her own to deal with all of this.

"Carl, this woman named Amber at the consulate assured me that everything is okay. Eduardo is still in Murumba. There is no way he'd be able to obtain a fake passport and there is no way he could know that I'm here."

"So somebody knows you're here?"

"Yes, but it's okay. Amber helped me to get myself settled. She's one of the few trusted people at the consulate who knows my real identity."

"So that's why you were terrified of telling me about your past?"

"Yes. I was told to not tell a single soul. And also, Eduardo vowed in the courtroom that I was going to be sorry. He threatened me!"

"What? After what the monster did? He had the gall to threaten you—in court?"

"Yes. Eduardo told me that he would make sure that no one else could have me. He'd kill me and anyone close to me."

"Oh, God! I'm so sorry you had to go through that, Venus. I guess the idiot wanted to kill his chance of ever getting parole with that courtroom fiasco," he said bitterly. His voice was laced with venomous sarcasm.

"Yeah, so that's why even though I agreed to our arrangement. I thought it wasn't important that you be involved with my past. It could have put you in danger."

"But jeez, Venus! We're married! Don't you think I should have least known something? I can take care of myself! And take care of you!"

"Yes, you're right. Thinking back in hindsight I see you're right. It was foolish to think that I could get away with not ever revealing my past. That's why I never thought I could ever get married. Of course, I knew this marriage that we have is only for a year, so I thought it would be different, you know?"

"Venus, I'm not going to announce anything yet, until I know for sure that murderous bastard and his entourage of thugs can't get to you."

Carl got up, looked at the time and grabbed his cell phone. He dialled a number. "Listen, we need to talk. Urgent. And get a D.P."

"D.P.?" Venus echoed. "Who is that?"

"It's a code we use for disposable phone."

"*We* use?"

"Never mind, for now anyway. I need to have some things checked on right away, before we leave Vegas. But not from this phone."

"Why not?"

"My darling, Venus, you must know by now that all phones can be easily traced. Except disposable phones—at least not right away."

"You mean, you're not going to d-divorce me?" Venus could not believe this! After the ugly truth and her scandalous past finally came out, Carl still wanted to be with her? He wanted to protect her? Still, she felt psychologically naked, exposed, vulnerable. Carl knew her true identity. He knew who she really was and what she'd been involved in her past. Something she never knew she could handle, if he found out. What must he think of her? Nothing could rip away the guilt, the torment, the pain and anguish of her parents' deaths. All because her crooked ex-boss wanted to harass her by forcing himself on her.

After she'd posed the question, Carl seemed to hesitate at first before answering. "No," he said quietly. "I'm not going to divorce you—yet," he added.

Yet?

Venus's stomach sank to her knees again. Of course not, yet. But eventually they would end their marriage. Still, she was grateful that he didn't just decide to end their nuptials right there and then. He certainly would be within his right to do so. And who could blame him? Part of her was deeply relieved now that it was all out in the open with Carl, but another part of her was deeply terrified. Her pulse pounded in her throat.

"So what are you—I mean, what are *we* going to do now?" she asked. Her mind was still reeling over the heated discussion of the past few moments. Her emotions were spiralling out of control. Over Carl. She'd had the most passionate night, her very first time, and now this? It was marred by the skeletons of her past.

She'd never seen Carl so worked up before, so infuriated. But he had good reason to be. His anger was now directed at Eduardo. Venus actually feared for Carl. She knew the Romeros were a tough family dynasty, but Eduardo Meritos—the infamous mob boss? Eduardo played dirty. That man could obviously never be trusted.

She still flinched from Eduardo's agonizing words at the trial. "I'll kill you and anyone close to you!" he vowed with a vengeance.

Venus shivered just thinking about it. She closed her eyes and drew in a deep breath, trying to settle her thrashing heartbeat.

Carl was way too caring, too kind. Too noble of a man to be put in harm's way—and all because of her. Just as her family had paid the price because of—her. She didn't want to put Carl at any risk. But then she'd already done so thinking that she could get away with pretending to be his wife—even just for one year.

What if any of Eduardo's people recognized her beneath her disguise—her new look? Assuming she would be public beside her politician husband.

"That's what happens when you come from a poor family," she chuckled, humorlessly.

"What do you mean?" he asked. His gaze still blazed into hers.

"I would have never taken the job to help out with the bills and buying food if we didn't need the money, Carl. But my mom and dad encouraged me at first to work at the store, even knowing it was owned by the

Meritos family. It was our only chance. The store was looking for a young cashier. We...we desperately needed the money. Things were so rough. Mom was so sick after she'd given birth to Niko...to Tristan. She had developed cardiomyopathy right after Tristan's birth. Dad wasn't doing too well with his eyesight. I was the only one who could work at the time."

"What about assistance from your local authority?"

"Pff. That's no good. Useless. No city funds, Carl. It's not like here in the western world. There are no agencies to help poor families."

Carl cursed under his breath. That was exactly the reason he wanted to fight in local government and represent the people. It may be a world of difference between her country and his, but it all boiled to the same sickness. Poverty. No family deserved to live that way.

More than ever, he wanted to fight for people like Venus, Tristan, like his own parents who'd lost everything because of a stroke of bad luck, illness and job loss. Damn! It just wasn't fair. None of it was fair. And the sad irony was that Venus had a similar experience that he had growing up, only difference was, she was left to fend for herself without any help from her government.

"Carl, please don't," Venus finally uttered, interrupting his thoughts. "I don't want you to proceed with me. I can't put you at risk. I just can't!"

"What? Are you kidding me? You think I'm afraid of that bastard Meritos?" Carl raged. He stood by the windowpane. An air of command exuded him. He had an innately captivating presence—even half dressed, his muscular chest exposed, wearing nothing but silk pajama bottoms. "You clearly don't know me that well, Venus." His voice was low, deadly. Anger flashed in his dark eyes.

"I know I don't know you that well, Carl. But...I know of Eduardo. He's lethal. He's crazy. I couldn't bear it if he-"

"Stop that," he said, more gently, his fingers stroked her arm sensuously and she felt his warmth zap into her, calming her. "No one is going to harm you or anyone close to you. Ever again. I promise. Okay?"

Venus nodded slowly.

Carl touched her trembling lips with his soft finger and she tingled with delight. Her fear and anxiety seemed to melt slightly with one tender stroke of his warm flesh. She inched closer to him, needing this intimacy more than ever.

He lowered his head to hers and captured her lips with his and heat exploded between them.

"Oh," she moaned breathlessly, enrapt by his sweet, soft kiss. She wanted to cry, she wanted to scream—if only she could turn back the hands of time and none of this happened. If only she could have erased her past with one strike of a delete button. If only...

He parted from her lips and gazed intently into her eyes. What was he thinking? Funny, but she didn't need to know. She felt it. She felt so connected to what he was feeling in her heart in a way that she could not explain.

In some situations, words were not necessary. Body language, vibes said it all. Reactions spoke volumes. The eyes told plenty in their soulful depths. This was one such situation where words were not adequate for a message to be communicated. For the first time in her life—in a long while, she didn't feel so...alone.

Venus could see raw hurt smoldering in Carl's dark eyes. He was hurt because of her, because of what had been done to her and her family. No one in her life had ever felt her pain the way Carl seemed to.

She reached her arms across his shoulders and hugged him tightly. She did not want to let him go. Her heartbeat pounded furiously inside her, blood roared through her veins. She would die if anything ever happened to Carl.

CHAPTER FIFTEEN

"My God, this is serious!" Pamela exclaimed. She looked as if the blood had been siphoned from her face. Her jaw fell open when Carl and Venus explained the situation.

It was seven o'clock in the morning and Carl, Venus, Jules and Pamela had all convened in Pamela's hotel suite down the main corridor.

"Yeah, tell me about it," Carl said, running his fingers through his hair. It was a mindless habit he'd given up years ago whenever he felt jittery. He hadn't felt that way in years, until last night.

"I dug up some info from an online search under Nadya Kosorokwii, sometimes spelled Nadja," Jules reported, a phone held to his ear.

Jules had followed Carl's early morning instruction and ran to a retailer that was open to get a disposable cell phone so that they could make a few calls to their contacts overseas.

"It's a good thing we're in Vegas," Carl said, "At least when you sent those texts earlier, it could only be traced to the U.S. If anyone of his thugs found out, we'd be long gone to Canada by then."

"Yeah, good thing."

"What are you doing?" Venus interjected.

"We're just making sure we can locate him. We know your country's authorities are searching for him but we just want to make sure he doesn't have any contacts with the local police, if you know what I mean," Carl added.

"Right, I see," Venus said, her voice sounding lifeless.

"Yeah, ever wonder how he was able to escape from maximum security in Murumba?" Jules posed, leaning by the counter.

"I can guess," Venus said bitterly.

"We've heard a lot about corrupt officials in your country being paid huge sums of money to do favors for inmates. We're not going to take any chances. We'll make sure he's caught," Carl vowed.

"Hey," Carl turned his attention to Jules. "Did you get the text image of him?" His lips were curled in disgust.

"Oh, yeah. He's as ugly as he sounds," Jules commented. "Here's his most recent mug shot. Our men are on it now. Even if he tries to use a disguise, we can nail him. He's over six-foot-five and apparently has a huge scar on the side of his face. Can't miss it."

"And a limp," Venus added, anxiety eating her alive inside. "He also limps. He had an injury as a child, so we've learned."

"Okay. That information will help a lot. It won't be too long, trust me," Jules continued. "And even if he'd paid authorities with what limited funds he has left. If it means we outbid them, so be it. Criminals belong behind bars. Period."

"Good," Carl said. Never in his life had he felt bitter anger directed at someone. Anyone who would even think of doing the unspeakable acts that man had done deserved to pay the price in the legal system.

"In the meanwhile," Pamela chimed in, "if you two still want to go ahead as planned for Carl's nomination bid, there is a way around things where Venus is concerned."

"As long as Venus is protected, I'm game," Carl said with an air of authority.

"Well, she will be," Pamela assured. "You have the option of not releasing the names of your wife and children in your run for mayor, Carl. The government does respect the right to privacy for the families of local politicians and candidates."

"Good," Carl said.

"So, what we'll do is just note on your official bio that you are married with a step-son—which you are, so no deception there. No mentions of names at this point. It's not necessary. And of course, if and when you win, we can have Venus dressed in such a way that media attention is not focused on her. Very few people care much for the immediate family members of local politicians—unless, of course, there is controversy … or scandal. But there are strict privacy laws in place. So it's a go."

Carl was relieved. He could see across the room that Venus was content with the arrangement, too. Now all he had to do when he returned to Canada was to announce his intent to run as a married man with a child. And pull out all the stops to make sure the thug that ruined his wife's life was back behind bars—for good.

CHAPTER SIXTEEN

The following week, the headlines were buzzing: Carl Romero announces his run for mayor!

Carl was on his way to Channel 31 Studios for a brief interview. His cell phone was vibrating like crazy, nonstop. The phones at his office and at his official residence were just as hectic. He knew there would be some interest given the family he was a part of and recent press he and his brothers had received, but he could not have imagined the magnitude.

He glanced at the digital display clock on the dashboard of his new Ford Explorer. Okay, so it wasn't his BMW or his Corvette, but he sure as hell wasn't going to be flaunting his riches now that he was an official mayoral candidate. Besides, it wasn't about the money, it was the good things that could be done to help others that counted, that mattered.

A tsunami of thoughts washed through Carl's mind, raising the tide of his emotions. Venus rushed into his mind as well. Sweet innocent Venus, and the hell she'd gone through in her life coming from an impoverished background and living in a society that would not or could not help her. The impact of learning what had happened to her in the past sent shockwaves searing through his body.

And then, there was that Achilles heel of his, Eduardo Meritos. Since Carl had returned to Canada, his mind was obsessed with thoughts of getting even with Eduardo, making sure he paid dearly for what he'd done to Venus—and her family. Still no good news on his whereabouts but Jules assured Carl that leads were in place and they were getting closer to the mystery surrounding Meritos's escape.

Carl pulled up to the curb at 490 Chancery Lane to make his monthly stop. He often came by that address. His brothers and he lived at number 123 and lost that home. He switched off the ignition and reached into his pocket and pulled out an envelope. Another large check was inside it. He wasn't quite up front with Venus either, even though they had a marriage contract. He didn't want Venus to know about Clarissa. Not yet. He would tell Venus when the time was right. She had way too much on her mind at the moment. He only hoped that now that he was running for office, Clarissa would not come public about their—little agreement.

Carl exited the car and looked around. The road was quiet at this time of the day. It was almost the noon hour. He opened the side entrance of the building. Luckily, another resident, an older man, was entering at the same time. He slipped in behind the man. Carl then scooted up to apartment 14A. He stood outside the door, hesitant for a moment, his jaw clenched. He could feel pain stabbing his chest. His eyes stung from moisture. He drew in a deep breath and placed the envelope on the ground before sliding it through the gap at the bottom of the door. He looked around to see if anyone had seen him.

He then walked out casually, as casually as he could considering that he was walking through a low-income building and yet, dressed in an expensive gray suit and silk blue tie. He surely didn't look like he belonged there.

It was time to face the cameras.

"So, it is official then," Breena, the Channel 31 News at Noon host, commented to the cameras in the studio. Carl sat in the guest chair adjacent to her. "Businessman Carl Romero has just filed his formal nomination papers yesterday morning amid considerable media attention. Mr. Romero is here with us today to answer a few questions."

Breena then turned her attention to Carl. "Welcome to News at Noon, Mr. Romero. So glad you could join us today. I know you must be extremely busy right now."

"Glad to be here, Breena, but please, call me Carl."

"Okay, so, Carl, first, let's begin with the first thing you'd like to do if you got into office," Breena adjusted the pink glasses on her face, looking pointedly at Carl. She was an eclectic commentator. He'd been watching her for years. She can be grilling one minute and nice the next. A well-educated journalist with a master's degree in political science from Harvard.

"Well, Breena, the first thing is to freeze property taxes. For the past several years property taxes have been going up yet incomes have remained stagnant. I promise that property taxes will not go up this year. We can make deep cuts to city spending, which is far too excessive."

She nodded thoughtfully. "Right. But you do realize that your opponents have made it clear that you'll need to cut back on valuable municipal services in order to accommodate a property tax freeze?"

"Breena, people want an end to annual tax hikes and they want an end to unnecessary, wasteful spending. There are services that are underused and other services that require much attention. It's all about balancing the budgets and making sure that taxpayers come first and don't end up with unfair expenses."

"Okay. And what is something you can do to help make the city more affordable?"

"We need to create additional better paying jobs and build more affordable housing. Period. We have plenty of vacant plots in the city that would be perfect."

"Now, speaking of plots. It's true that you come from one of the most prominent real estate dynasties in the province. Wouldn't this be a conflict of interest?"

"Oh, no. My grandfather came here as an immigrant and worked tirelessly from an impoverished childhood into a successful businessman and he gave us plenty of insight into working hard to make our own ways in life, not relying on what he's accomplished. He has nothing to do with this. I assure you, we never have ridden on his coattails."

"Right, and you grew up in quite a modest, or should I say, challenging family situation before you came to know your famous grandfather, Antonio Romero."

"Yes. My parents had it hard. My mother spent a great deal of life battling cancer that..." Carl swallowed hard. He had to shift his focus on to the issues. Not on his personal life. "...took her from us," he finished his sentence quietly, fighting to keep his voice calm. "My father ended up losing his job and between that and the property taxes, it was all too much and-"

"You ended up homeless," Breena was all too eager to finish the sentence for him. She had a look of amazement on her face. "Wow, it's such an incredible rags to riches story."

"Well, not rags to riches, Breena. It's all about perseverance. It's about getting that break. We got a break and we...I want to give taxpayers a break, too. There are currently too many people losing their homes because of property taxes going through the roof, as high as seven percent a year. That's ridiculous. Meanwhile, services that are not being used are getting all kinds of money thrown at them." Determination flooded through Carl. "When I'm in office, I'm going to put an end to this mindless misuse of people's hard earned monies and put it where it belongs. With the people. For the people."

Breena nodded, her brow arched slightly. "Oh, we have a caller. Yes, you're live on the air, caller number one."

"H-hi. Am I on the air?" a gruff voice sounded over the speakerphone on the coffee table in front of the host and Carl.

"Yes, you sure are. Do you have a question for our candidate, Carl Romero?"

"Um. Yeah. My name is Dave. I work in a factory. Um...this Carl guy. He's so rich and good looking and famous. What does he know about being a hardworking struggling family man? I have three kids, a wife, and two cats. One of my cats needs surgery. How can we possibly afford that? Sure, Carl makes all these promises. But what does he care if he can't deliver? And what about the crime rate in the city? What's he gonna do about that?" The caller was clearly worked up.

"I'm afraid that's too many questions, Dave. You can only pose one question at a time," Breena interjected.

The caller's words stung Carl for some reason. He knew it would be difficult. He was the youngest contender, and true, the past decade was good for him compared to his earlier life.

"Well, Dave, I can answer a couple of your questions. I know we're pressed for time right now. I'm truly sorry about your situation and your cat." Carl genuinely was. Carl's family dog, a golden retriever named Louis, had died soon after his mother passed away and the heartache never went away. They couldn't afford vet care at the time.

"I can tell you this," Carl continued, his gut ached thinking about Venus and the pain she'd gone through inadvertently forced to work for a guy who ended up being a dangerous crime lord in her town. "My office will be working with members of the community, the police services, and the schools to talk about the wave of gun violence in the city's west end and cleaning up the streets. We need to combat this rash of events we've seen recently. And we will."

"I sure hope so." The man sounded dubious.

"And, Dave, if you leave your phone number, I'll have someone from my office contact you regarding vet services. There are foundations my family sponsors to help fund lower-income families so they can keep their pets, whether it be for basic necessities like food or situations like yours where surgeries are out of reach. My staff can point you in the right direction."

Breena looked shocked.

"You'll help me?"

"Yes. I will. Every resident is important to me. Every family. I want people to know that they can reach me 24/7 and I'll be there, or I'll have my assistant take care of things. You will be heard. Your situation will get my full attention."

"Well...uh...okay," the man sounded as astonished as Breena looked.

Carl was sure he was probably breaking some sort of unwritten code, but damn it, he couldn't help himself. And this had nothing to do with votes. He vowed that when he and his brothers fought their way out of poverty they would help others whenever or however it was possible. Give back. Their mother had always raised them that way, even when they didn't have much growing up. Always be a giver. Always look for ways to be a blessing to others. It might have sounded corny then, but heck, he lived by those words. The caller was right; he had a heck of a lot of advantages over the average taxpayer. Why in God's name wouldn't he want to help make somebody else's burden a little lighter, if he were in a position to do so?

"Okay, that's all the time we have for today," Breena concluded. "Carl, thank you so much for joining us here today. We'll no doubt see much more of you and your opponents as the campaign gets underway."

Carl's heart thumped hard in his chest. He'd faced cameras before but not like this. Not a live show. He glanced over to the side. Standing by the cameras, his brother Jules gave him a thumbs up. Jules insisted on heading down to the studio with him for moral support. Toni wanted to be there, but he decided against it as he didn't want the wrong signal to be given. This was about Carl Romero, mayoral candidate, not Carl Romero, grandson of affluent tycoon Toni (Antonio) Romero, one of the wealthiest real estate moguls in the world.

"Yes, Breena, you will see more of me," Carl said with determination set in his voice.

CHAPTER SEVENTEEN

This was one heck of a long day, Carl thought to himself as he pulled up to his modest four-bedroom home he now shared with Venus. The house was located in the suburbs in a quiet neighbourhood in Mayberry Hill.

Funny thing was he couldn't wait to get home to lovely Venus. What was it about seeing her sweet smile, her large beautiful brown eyes, gazing lovingly into his eyes? He kept reminding himself this was not going to last, so he shouldn't get too attached. Venus was doing a job—as his wife. Nothing more. It was just a job, right? But damn, did she ever seem so genuine. Why did it feel like anything but a job?

He'd given so many interviews and talked to countless reporters. It was crazy. His mind was weary. His body ached, and this time it wasn't from lifting weights at the gym. In fact, he didn't even get to spend much time there this past week. Something he was going to have to incorporate into his increasingly busy schedule.

Heck, running a full-blown corporation was one thing, but running for public office? *Jeez!* He wouldn't wish this type of stress on his worst enemy!

He parked the car and switched off the ignition. It was evening. Where did the time go? He knew that Venus was busy during the day doing administrative hand-over at the R.M. Fitness headquarters so that she could spend more time in his campaign office. God bless her. What would he do without her?

"Honey," Carl called out when he entered through the white French doors to their residence. The home was warm and inviting. Cozy. The hardwood floors were spotless. They were genuine red oak. The windows were double glazed. They had a long driveway of pavers leading up to the main house. The house had everything including the proverbial white picket fence.

The aroma of baked honey chicken and warm apple pie wafted to his nostrils, soothing his senses and arousing his hunger. But he wasn't just hungry for food.

Had he just taken a turn down memory lane? Why did he feel as if he'd just taken a turn down Leave it to Beaver lane? Only a modern-day version of that old black-and-white TV show from the late 1950s.

That was just what he needed right now. He heard the sound of dishes in the kitchen. "Oh, hi, Carl," Venus sung out, wiping down the warm-brown marble stone counter.

"Hey," he said, instinctively wrapping his arms around her waist from behind and kissing her softly on her neck and cheek, inhaling the smooth scent of her shampooed hair. She gushed and nestled into his chest. What was he doing? They were supposed to be a pretend couple—not a real one. Whatever that meant. Then why was he feeling so connected to her? Why couldn't he wait for the day to be done so that he could embrace her and take good care of her? What was with him? Had the pressure of being a public figure usurped his senses? Yet, he couldn't help himself.

"I told you, baby," he said, whispering in her ears. "It's my turn to do the dishes. In fact, I don't care how long I stay at the office. Let me do the dishes for a month."

She grinned and turned around facing him. "Carl. Why?" Venus giggled as he nibbled on her ear. "I get home before you."

"So what? You work hard at the office," he refuted.

"So do you, hon. Really, I don't mind."

Much like Britain's Prince William and his lovely wife, Kate, Carl and Venus decided to forgo having a huge entourage of house staff. They wanted to be intimate and do most chores themselves, enjoying each other's company. Just because they could afford a maid and butler, didn't mean they wanted to.

"Hey," he said, lifting her chin up with his finger. "I don't want you to think you have to do any of the work in here. I live here too. Shared responsibility, remember? We're equal partners. In fact, I want to be the one to take good care of you," he said and a jolt of electricity ran to his heart. Venus had done nothing but make sacrifices to everyone in her life. Taking care of her family back home. Adopting her brother and being the best damn mother to a child anyone could hope for and now—she sacrificed a lot so that Carl could run for mayor. How could he not worship her? She was all heart and soul. Here she had a lot in her life to be bitter about—thinking the world owed her much and all she wanted to do was make it better for others around her.

A sick feeling slid into Carl's gut. He could never let her go. Not now. Not even after the year. She was his close companion and his most fierce supporter. She was golden. Solid. Heck, they'd had great sex every night since they got hitched in Vegas. The sex was amazing! Venus enjoyed trying new things and being pleasured by him in so many erotic ways. There was a radiant glow about her personality, her beauty, her charm. Her beautiful personality shone through her and made her even more breathtaking to his eyes and his soul. Everything about Venus was exceptional. Her subtle sexiness captivated him.

Admittedly, his life would not be the same without her. His grandfather was right. Having love in your life was one of the best things that could happen to a person. They were not playing house. They were a real family. For the past week, they'd taken turns reading a bedtime story to Tristan and Venus would take over singing his favorite lullaby. It was heartwarming. Just as his mother had done for him and his brothers when they were growing up—before her health took a turn for the worse and she was taken from them permanently. He felt like a real father to Tristan and a real husband to Venus. None of that was phony. It was all real to him, right from his heart and soul.

He really meant it. Old-fashioned as it was, Carl really wanted to take good care of her. Always.

"You were wonderful today on the news show, honey." She reached her arms up to hug his neck and pull him closer to her. Her beautiful, recently-coifed dark hair shone under the kitchen light and his nose enjoyed the fragrance of her lilac-scented shampoo. The aroma soothed his senses. She pressed her breasts to his chest and his body reacted. He lowered his lips to hers and softly kissed her. His groin reacted.

"Thank you," he said appreciatively. "I couldn't have done it without you."

"Without me?" She kissed him, intermittently. "But, Carl, I didn't do anything," she whispered breathlessly.

"Oh, but you did. You gave me those tips on doing a sit down interview. You know how much I hate cameras."

And he was right. Carl found the whole thing damn near nerve-racking. But Venus had coached him over the past week while they were naked in bed, of course. Well, hey, he needed a relaxing environment—and he always felt totally cool in bed.

She'd told him the old trick everyone used. Picturing everybody—the interviewer and all the cameramen—naked, which didn't help all that much. In fact, he tried *not* to picture them that way.

Then, the most important thing was that she'd gone over some gruelling questions with Carl, rehearsing backlash and rebuttals. The last thing he would have wanted was to be caught off guard and thrown off his game. His opponents would have loved for that to happen. They already called him out on being a rich boy who was out of touch with reality. Carl had many strengths and could often speak on the spot and come up with all kinds of intelligent comebacks. But there was just something about those darned TV cameras that irked the hell out of him. This was all to do with childhood, when authorities got involved and they'd made the local news: Man living out of van with his sons. It was terrible. It had caused a sad media frenzy at the time. From the perspective of a little boy, seeing tons of TV camera equipment and gigantic microphones poking in your face, not to mention the daunting white flashes of cameras clicking away to capture images of them. It was all overwhelming at the very least. It was terrifying. Carl cringed thinking of that memory during a sad and dark segment of his childhood.

He continued caressing Venus's skin with his lips, planting sweet kisses down her shoulder and arm.

"You know you're so beautiful, Venus."

"Mmm," she moaned into his lips, as he continued to kiss her.

"No seriously," he said, pulling away from her gently. He gazed intently into her eyes. "You know something? There isn't anything about you that I don't love. And no matter how tired at the end of the day I get, I'm always going to make it a point to tell you how much I appreciate you."

"Oh, Carl. That's so sweet of you," she whispered.

"Really. A man lands a beautiful woman and takes her for granted, thinking she can read minds. You women are goddesses but you're not mind readers."

She giggled. He loved her girlish playful chuckle. Her sweet brown eyes crinkled when she smiled and laughed. Her cheeks rouged and glowed. "You're wonderful yourself, Carl. You always shower me with compliments. I appreciate all that you've done for me and Tristan."

Carl was about to say that she and Tristan were his family now. But how could he? He wasn't going to press the issue about their one-year deal, but he wanted so much more than just twelve months with her. He wanted forever.

"Hey, it's the least I can do. Besides, you didn't have to do all of this."

"All of what?" she said, looking puzzled.

He gently ran his fingers through her silky locks. "Your hair is always freshly done. Every day you wear a beautiful sexy outfit that turns me on. Even when you're dressed down, you look good. Fashionable. I've never even seen you with your morning hair. You always rush to the bathroom first thing and style it. Like, I don't care if your hair's a mess, or that you look like you've just rolled out of bed. Because to me, you're my princess. I treasure all that you are."

"Oh, Carl. I...I don't know what to say," she said, then a grin touched her lips.

"What's funny?"

"Oh, nothing. I was told that sometimes men go looking elsewhere when their wives...um...what's the word...? Let themselves go."

"Let themselves go? It's the men who let themselves go by cheating. I would never do that to you, no matter what. Hey, no woman deserves that. Period."

"I know. It's not just that. I think it's important in a relationship that both the husband and the wife always remember that life can get hectic and it's important to keep the romance...the spark alive. I really don't want to see it fade. I mean, my parents fell out of love, I think. It was awful to see that before their deaths. Dad...well, I never told anyone this before, but he was seeing someone else. Mom found out and she was depressed about it. I think they eventually worked things out. That's when they had Niko, I mean, Tristan."

"I see."

"Mom told me this story. It's some old tale about this man," she said animatedly, "who sees this beautiful woman at the village and she does everything for him. She cooks for him, cleans, pampers him, everything."

"Yeah?"

"Well, he eventually married her."

"That's good."

"Not really."

"Why?"

"Because he turned up at a bar one night and said to the bartender that he missed the joys of being married. And the bartender said to him, 'I thought you were married.' The man told the bartender, 'I am married, but so far I miss the joys.'"

"Oh?"

"The man had said that his wife used to do everything when they were dating and when he asked his wife why she stopped being nice to him, she had replied 'I've got you now.' Well that marriage didn't last long after that."

"Ouch."

"Exactly. So the morale of the story is that it's not enough to get married, but staying married takes commitment and work and love and if you want to keep the spark or the flame, you've got to work at it. Make your spouse feel happy since he or she chose to spend the rest of their life with you," she stopped. Her voiced trailed off.

For a moment, there was a long, awkward pause. He knew then that they were both thinking the same thing. Spend the rest of their life with the one they loved. Carl felt a stabbing sharp pain in his gut. He really wanted more than anything to spend the rest of his life with Venus. The question was, did she feel the same?

Later that night, Carl lay awake staring at the ceiling in the dark. Venus was sound asleep beside him. For a while he'd watched her sleep. She looked so beautiful with her long lashes so visible with her eyes closed. She was an earth angel.

One year.

No. One year would not be enough but he didn't want her to feel pressured into committing a lifetime with him if she didn't want to. He should probably ask her point blank. He often communicated very directly with others, never one to mince words. But Venus was different. He hadn't feared anything before in his life before but Venus not wanting to spend forever with him would kill him. Not just the rejection but the painful reality of her going her separate way from him.

His cell phone at the bedside rang, disturbing his thoughts.

"Yeah?" he answered. His voice sounded more groggy than he realized.

"Hey, bro," Jules spoke, "Sorry to wake you but I've got some news on Meritos. I think you should know."

Carl propped himself up on the bed in lightning speed time. "What?"

"It's not good."

"Wait a minute," Carl said, and he soundlessly got up from the bed. He glanced at the digital display clock on the bedside table. It was eleven o'clock at night. He crept out of the room, careful not to wake Venus and went into the guest room down the hall and closed the door behind him.

"Yeah, what is it?" he said, sitting on the bed, his heart was beating like a bass drum.

"It looks as if Eduardo knows Nadya is Venus."

"What? How?"

"Well, apparently, one my sources say that he had connections in the country's so-called justice system."

"Including the witness protection program," Carl finished for him sternly. An ice cold feeling rushed through his blood. He cursed under his breath. So Venus *was* in danger all along. It was only a matter of time.

Who the hell could have known?

"Yeah. I'm sorry, man. But listen, we've got some hot leads right now. His IP address, the one he's currently using is being traced so we should be able to track him down and let the authorities know. We'll also uncover the identity of the spy he has in the agency. It's only a matter of time."

"Good. Keep me posted."

"I will, Carl. And, listen, don't worry. Venus is safe here."

"Oh, I know that. I'll make damn sure of it."

Carl knew that as a public official he'd have no trouble getting police protection but no way in hell was he going that route. He himself would protect the woman he…loved.

"Thanks, Jules," Carl finally said, ending the conversation.

He terminated the call and dropped his cell phone on the bed beside him, then he held his head. What the hell was he going to do now?

* * *

It was eleven o'clock at night but Amber had to get into the office at the consulate when her boss, Vic, would not be there. She'd told the security guard that she'd left something important that should have been secured out on her desk. Her mind was bugging her the entire day about what she'd learned.

Her own boss, Vic, was a crook. She knew he'd been hiding things and peeking into her files when she was not there. But something was very wrong and she sensed it.

She managed to get into his office and into his file cabinet. There was a private file that she'd put together on Venus Jackson but it went missing. Later she learned that Vic lied about not seeing it, when in fact, he'd taken some information from her file. But why?

Amber glanced around to see if anyone was looking. Hopefully, security would not be aware that she was not in her own office, though she'd turn on that light, too.

She rummaged her fingers through the files on his desk and then opened up his drawer. She felt guilty for nosing around, but Venus was her responsibility and if there was any funny business going on, she needed to know.

There was nothing there.

Then she remembered those detective shows she'd seen. "The garbage," she said to herself. There are always clues in the garbage, but not just the physical garbage. The trash can of the computer. She didn't want to take a chance on logging on since the time would be noted. But she did go into the physical garbage and turned over his paper waste basket. She rummaged through bits of papers. And there it was! Her heart almost stopped suddenly in her chest.

Ed Meritos 1-212345-555-458-9586968

Eduardo Meritos.

Good God!

Vic must be working with, or more likely *for*, Eduardo Meritos. Amber covered her mouth in shock. She looked at the time. It was after eleven o'clock. She had to call Venus's residence stat. Maybe she should just stop by. What if Venus's husband answered? But that wouldn't be a bad thing. Amber was aware of the Romeros and their reputation and power. Oh, what to do?

She drew in a deep breath. She was going to let them know … tonight. Then, the police would have to be notified in Murumba.

CHAPTER EIGHTEEN

At ten o'clock the next morning, Venus's heart was palpitating and she had to calm her breathing as she stared out of the window, still reeling in shock. Her body felt numb.

Eduardo had discovered her new identity!

Carl had his arms wrapped around her waist from behind giving her the support she so needed. He smelled so good; the scent of his fresh aftershave was soothing, enticing. Neither of them had much sleep last night.

Luckily, Tristan was already at the daycare at the Romero estate and Carl decided he would go into the office later that day, as did she. Right now, they had other things to tend to.

Last night, Amber from the consulate called and came by. She explained everything to Carl and to Venus as they listened in horror. Venus's blood ran cold just thinking about what they were told. All this while, Eduardo knew her whereabouts—he was just waiting to strike at the right moment when she least expected it. It was good that Carl and the Romeros had their men on the case. It was also good that Amber was able to help them pinpoint the mole in the consulate and the other source in the justice system in Murumba.

"So Vic Damon was arrested this morning," Carl told her. "He also gave the name of the source of the spy in the witness protection program."

"I'm glad," she said, relief evident. Her body was still numb. "Carl, if it hadn't been for you, I don't know what I would have done. Oh, my God!"

"Hey," he murmured to her, "I'm not going to let anything happen to you, okay? Don't worry your pretty head over it. Nothing can ever happen to you or Tristan."

"It's a good thing we met, I guess."

"Hey, I thought you believe in divine intervention or what is called? Fate, right?"

"That's true. Whatever is meant to be will be. My mother used to tell me that sometimes the universe brings the right people in your life and removes the wrong ones from your life, if you believe it."

"If I believe it?"

"Yes. Mom used to tell us that we often receive what we believe in. If we go around only expecting bad things then our lives will be centered on that. We might even miss the good things because we're so programmed to seeing the bad in everything and the opposite is true for expecting good things. Oh, Carl, why does life have to be so-"

"Challenging?" he finished for her, a warm smile on his face.

"Yes," she said softly. "Come, I don't want you to be late going into the office. We have a campaign to run."

"Are you sure you're up to going in today? I can have Shelly come over here."

"Oh, no. It's okay. Really it is. I want to get my mind off things. Especially since Eduardo has not been caught yet."

"He'll be apprehended soon. Don't worry. We've already got his contacts. There are only so many places he can hide."

Venus swallowed hard. "I know. But, Carl, Amber said that he knew about us. He found out that we'd gotten married. He had apparently left some notes online that he was going to destroy us. He had some information. How did he find out so fast?"

"Shh, Venus, worrying is not going to do anything beneficial for you right now. There's nothing he can do to us. Nothing. And whatever he has planned, hopefully it will backfire long before we're involved."

"Oh, Carl. I hope so for your sake. Eduardo is a vile, vindictive person. He knows about politics from back home. He could cause a scandal. Anything. I would die if anything happened to-"

"Hey, no worries, remember? Do I look scared to you?"

"No. You always look brave to me," she teased him.

"Good. Now let's get ready to-" Carl's cell phone just rang, interrupting his sentence. "Hey," he said. His face looked grim. He heaved a sigh. "Thanks. I'll let Venus know."

"What is it?" Anxiety knotted Venus's inside.

"Eduardo."

"What about him?"

"They found him and it wasn't pretty. He resisted arrest. There was some sort of shootout between him and the local police."

She covered her mouth with her hand.

"Yeah," Carl said quietly, as if he could read her mind. They were always in sync with what each other thought, which always amazed her about their relationship. But this time it was more serious. "Eduardo was killed," Carl finished in a low voice. His expression was serious. Carl was truly a man. He never gloated over his enemy's demise. He was just as stunned as Venus was. Even though she wanted Eduardo to pay for what he'd done, it was still a shock.

"He's dead?" she echoed in a whisper, trying to let the news sink in. But somehow, she felt the damage he'd done since his escape had not quite come to pass.

CHAPTER NINETEEN

The next two weeks were incredibly busy for the new mayoral candidate, Carl Romero. Venus sat in the campaign office shuffling some notes on her desk.

She had tried hard to push the events of the past month out of her mind surrounding the breach of security within the consulate and the death of Eduardo Meritos. All she could do was think about Carl and doing everything in her power to assist and support him in his bid for mayor.

Her duties as assistant campaign manager included coordinating the campaign's operations. She wanted to ensure that the fundraising was in place and the advertising budget was properly allocated. She was too busy overseeing various supportive activities to be worried about the after-effect of Eduardo's death.

Carl came into her office. "Are you okay, beautiful?" He handed her a Tim Horton's green tea, extra large with sugar. Just the way she loved it.

"I should be getting *you* a coffee," she teased, taking the cup.

He leaned down and pressed a kiss on her cheek. More and more, she wanted to be Carl's wife forever, but he hadn't said anything about the contract, and she didn't want to push the issue. The last thing she wanted to do was force him to remain married to her after the year was over. But oh, he stirred all kinds of delicious feelings inside her. What would she do without him?

He was a wicked-in-bed kind of lover, so smooth and sexy and always made her come to soaring heights. The thought of not having him for too long brought disturbing quakes in her serenity. A wave of doubt swept through her wondering how long he would remain committed to her.

"Good news. Since your announcement, you've gained lot of favour in the local opinion polls. In fact, seventy percent. That is incredible!"

"Good, but I'm not going to break out the champagne just yet. Those polls can change in a heartbeat."

"True."

"So what else have you got for me?" he said, leaning against her desk.

"Well, you have several interviews tomorrow beginning with the local radio station and ending with the school. I'm going to send out some messages on social media like Twitter, Facebook, Instagram-"

"Whoa, wait a minute. You sure we need to do that?"

"Of course! Besides, I've already set up your accounts. Oh, and don't worry about your old Facebook account, I've already deleted some of your ex-girlfriend's compromising pictures of you at the Christmas party"

"Oh?"

"I'm only teasing," she giggled, trying to lighten the mood. She knew that Carl had been tormented over what had happened to her and her reaction to Eduardo's death. She didn't want him to feel that she wasn't coping with all that had been going on. The only saving grace was that the international media had not captured the story and brought it mainstream. The embarrassed Murumbian government was good at keeping things under wraps.

"I was going to get your approval, of course." Venus smiled sweetly.

He melted into a boyish grin that stirred her very soul. What she wanted more than ever was to throw herself across the desk and playfully rip off his shirt and make sweet, passionate, hot love to him like they'd been doing each and every night. She could not get enough of her sexy-as-sin spouse.

Carl pressed his lips to Venus's sweet lips. A knocking on her open door distracted them.

"I'm sorry, Carl," Jules, his brother, stepped inside, "but there's a commotion outside. The media."

"What?" Carl said, turning his attention to Jules.

"News breaking story!" Jules looked part peeved and part apologetic.

Venus immediately opened up her Internet program on her laptop and typed away ferociously. "Oh, no," she said, her heart pumping hard and fast.

"What is it?" Carl said, glancing at her screen.

"It's all over the news. Everything!"

"Carl, I think it's best we lay low right now until we can come up with a statement," Jules advised. "It's up to you, but if you want I can keep them out. Should I call security?"

"No. I can handle them," he said defiantly.

Before he could say anything more, a barrage of news reporters with TV cameras, microphones and notepads assailed them.

"Carl, do you have any comment about the latest allegations?" one reporter shouted out, pointing a tape recorder in his hand at Carl.

"Carl, is it true that you paid Venus to be your wife for a year so that you could feign being a family man?"

"Carl, is it true there's a link between you and a drug lord in Murumba? Did you have him executed, gang style?"

"There's evidence that you're paying a woman to keep quiet about your affair? Clarissa Bougon. Do you have any comment, Carl? Carl? Why have you been paying Clarissa large sums of money? To keep quiet?"

"Carl, why are you cheating on your wife with Clarissa?"

Anger raged through Carl's blood as he escorted Venus out and pushed his way through the crowd of journalists. "I have no comment at this time." His only concern was getting Venus away from them. He shielded her as he made way to a quiet area in the back of the building and closed the doors. He motioned to his brother that he would be right back prior to that.

"Carl," Venus said, trembling as they stood alone in the dim lit storage area. She was clearly shaken up by this whole thing. "You-you're having an affair?" Her eyes widened, horror and shock flashed within them.

"Listen, Venus. I...I'm sorry I didn't tell you about Clarissa, but-"

"So it's true then?"

"No. I'm not having an affair."

Venus didn't know what to think. Her mind was in a daze. She didn't know if she was coming or going. She didn't even care too much about them finding out that Carl tried to pay her to be his wife. But the thought of him having an affair?

"Venus, don't go. Don't leave me like this. I can deal with anything right now. But I can't cope with you walking out of my life."

The words reverberated inside her. She felt a chill slide down her spine. She didn't know what to think.

"But this thing we have is just a one-year contract, remember?" she said to him hoping that he would change his mind. She wanted to hear it from him that what they had would go longer.

But he said nothing. And her soul was crushed.

"I...I have to go," she said, feeling violently ill. Venus felt her heart squeeze in her chest. She was suffocating. She was going to pass out.

Carl went back into the campaign office to face the hoard of media. The noise level shot up in the room and he hushed the crowd. "Please. I will gladly answer your questions. One at a time. Just a few questions. That's it. I have a campaign to run."

Jules gave him the thumbs-up from the side. Carl was a Romero. They were not easily intimidated and he would face them alone if he had to. Right now, he couldn't care less how they wanted to make him look. His mind was only focused on Venus. The look in her eyes. The pain. Damn! He should have at least told her about Clarissa.

He didn't want to tell anyone about Clarissa. That was supposed to be his own secret. But now? He would have no choice but to let the world know. And let the chips fall where they may.

If he lost the campaign based on this scandal, so be it. But losing Venus would hurt him more!

Just then his eyes caught Clarissa. She made her way over to him. "Please, Carl. Please tell them about us. It's okay. I want them to know. I really do."

Carl said nothing. He turned his attention to the waiting press.

"Carl, is it true that you paid Venus Jackson to be your wife?" a reporter called out.

"No," he answered coldly.

"No?"

"I'll be honest here, because that's the type of guy I am. I fell in love with my assistant and I ended up marrying her. End of story. Yes, I was concerned about the idea that voters may not be comfortable with a single young man running for mayor in this town, but then things worked out differently. I will also note that I'm running for office, not my family. And I would appreciate my wife and son being left out of this from now on." His words were firm and stern.

"So you did not pay her to be with you for one year?"

"No one knows how long they will stay married. But all I can say is that," he swallowed, feeling his gut clench, "I hope that Venus and I stay married forever. She means the world to me as every wife should mean to her husband. Next question."

"Is it true that you were paying a woman by the name of Clarissa to keep quiet about your affair?"

"No." His voice was sharp. He knew that day when he'd slipped Clarissa that last check, after he'd flown in from Vegas that he was followed. The old man who had entered the building before him, was a spy, he'd learned later. Something to do with Eduardo's connection having him and Venus watched the whole time. Luckily, he noticed everything and had studied the man's facial features and memorized them down to the hairy mole at his temple. Carl never took anything for chance. Not in his position.

Carl drew in a deep breath. Not caring what the world thought of him. "The truth is, yes, I've been paying Ms. Bougon money but not to keep quiet."

"Then why?"

"As you know," Carl commenced, the room now silent, "growing up, my brothers and I didn't have much. We lost our family home on Chancery Lane. Then we moved into a low-income building. Well, we spent many nights going to bed hungry. Not having enough. At Christmas, we used to pretend we had money," he said, trying not to get emotional. "Well, we made a vow before our mother...died that no one in our household would ever go hungry again or have to make our own presents or not have enough heat or essentials to live."

"Wow," a voice sounded.

He also spotted Clarissa nodding in approval.

"And we moved out of there, eventually. But we lost mother and I wanted to keep that vow. It might seem stupid to a lot of you but I wanted to keep my promise. That address where Ms. Bougon lives—that's the very apartment we'd occupied when we lived in that building. My brother Jules and I always went back there, first at Christmastime to anonymously drop off presents at the door for whoever lived there. Then we delivered cards and gift cards not knowing still who was living there. That home brought a lot of painful memories but also dreams and hopes. Then Ms. Bougon caught us one day and we told her that we were keeping our promise to our mother. She was struggling just as we were when we lived there. You see, that's why as your mayor, I will make sure that families don't just have the bare minimum to survive but enough to get a good start in life. Affordable daycare so they can work. Well-paying jobs so parents can take the best care of their children and...no unfair tax hikes so they can afford to keep their homes. Now, that's all the time I have to answer questions. As you know, I have a campaign to run. Thank you."

With that, Carl turned and left as reporters continued to hurl questions at him.

"Hey, that was good, bro," Jules commended him as he turned to head back to his office.

"Thanks," he said half-heartedly. None of it seemed to matter now. He was running on autopilot. Venus was gone. And there was nothing he could do about it. Jules then turned back to deal with the media.

Carl went back to his office and was stunned to see Venus sitting in the chair in front of his desk with a notepad in her hand.

"Venus," he said quietly, stunned. "I thought you'd left."

She stood up and faced him. "Now that wouldn't be professional to just quit without giving you notice, would it?" she murmured, her great big beautiful eyes fixed on his. "Did you mean what you said, Carl?"

"That I thought you'd left?" he said innocently, a boyish smirk on his face.

She threw back her head and laughed. She dropped her notepad and pen on the table and reached over to hug him. "Oh, Carl. You're something else, you know? I don't know why but my heart told me to turn back and I'm glad I did. I heard your answers at that...press conference."

"Hey," he said, looking directly into her eyes. He lifted up her chin, feeling a magical pulse between them. "I love you, Venus Jackson or Nadya whatever. You make me so happy. You bring out the best in me—even in my darkest moments. I can't live without you. I don't want to spend the year with you. I want to spend forever with you."

"Oh, Carl. I...I love you so much."

"Will you stay married to me, Venus? None of this matters, my campaign, my work. None of it matters if we can't be together. I don't care if I lose this campaign, but I can't lose you, Venus. I love you too much. "

"Oh, Carl, yes," she said breathlessly. "Yes. Forever. Till death do us part. I want to be with you forever."

He pressed his lips to hers and kissed her passionately.

This would be the sweetest beginning to their forever together.

EPILOGUE

Eight months later...

The large-screen plasma TV on the wall of the campaign headquarters was turned up on full volume. "Carl Romero has been elected as Mayberry Hill's fifty-fourth mayor, winning a staggering sixty-five percent of the vote and leading in forty-one of the city's forty-three wards," the reporter announced.

The loud screams in the campaign room and the confetti raining from the air and party favors popping lent themselves to a joyous occasion.

Venus hugged her husband as he prepared to give his victory speech. "I want you here beside me, baby," he said to her.

"Yes, of course," Venus said, planting a huge kiss on his lips then wiping her lipstick away. The entire Romero family was also present, including his other brothers, Zack, Lucas, Dion, Troy and Alonso.

Carl had won in a historic majority vote for Mayberry Hill. He was also the youngest person elected as mayor in the town's 105-year history.

"Well, Mr. Mayor," Jules playfully punched his brother in the shoulder. "I guess they'll be no more favors, huh?" he teased.

Carl rolled his eyes and grinned.

Carl lifted up Tristan. "Well, little guy, are you ready to see all the wonderful supporters?"

"Yeah!" Tristan yelled, clapping his hands in the air.

The environment was energetic in the hall as they prepared to enter. Venus held the arm of her husband trying to let it all sink in while Carl had Tristan secured in his other arm. They looked like the perfect first family. She was first lady of the city. It didn't seem real. None of it seemed real. And Carl was her number one best friend for life and her loving husband.

"My grandson," Toni said proudly to Carl. The look of pride sparkled in the old man's misty eyes. "My grandson, the mayor! I'm so proud of you, Carl."

"Thanks, Granddad. I have all of you to thank for everything."

"Wish Mom could have been here," Jules added.

"I know," Carl said in a low voice. "I think in a way, she is...with us all."

"Hey, bro," Zack and his wife Blue came into the room. It was a family reunion as well as a loving supportive community of well wishers. "The crowd is screaming for you, man. You're a rock star."

"Hey, thanks, Zack. Blue, you look well."

"So do you," she chimed in.

Blue hugged Venus.

Amber, from the consulate, stood in a corner by the door taking everything in. She looked extremely happy for Venus. She'd done so much to assist Venus, and Carl was very grateful to her for that. Even though she'd lost her job at the consulate after what she'd done to help Venus. It was against regulations to "break in" to search your boss's office so it didn't go down too well with the committee. But Carl offered Amber a job, though she had politely refused it. Still, he hoped Amber was going to be okay. She seemed like a sweet girl, though a little reserved with an air of mystery about her. He was beginning to think all women harbored secrets.

"Well, are you ready?" Carl arched a brow, smiling at his darling wife.

"Ready when you are, Mr. Mayor."

And together they faced the world as Mr. and Mrs. Romero, the first family of Mayberry Hill.

***

THE BILLIONAIRE'S BABY (THE ROMERO BROTHERS, BOOK 5)

Pregnant and alone, Amber Johnson-Murray, aka "Miss Always-Careful," never in her life thought she'd end up single while expecting a child. After leaving an emotionally abusive relationship, she has sworn off men until further notice. That is, until she bumps into an old friend, hot and delicious property developer, Jules Romero. The baby growing inside her is a precious miracle. But how can she control the feelings growing inside her for too-hot-to-handle Jules?

High-flying billionaire Jules Romero is determined to bury himself in his work acquiring properties after suffering injuries from a near-fatal accident, but meeting up with sweet Amber has thrown a kink in his plans. Though Amber is determined to keep the identity of her baby's real father a secret, he wants nothing more than to take care of Amber and her child.

CHAPTER ONE

"My God, Jules, I thought you were dead!" Dr. Alonso Romero uttered to his athletic, carefree brother Jules as he lay on the hospital bed. Alonso's voice rang with authority as he spoke to his younger sibling. "Do you know how lucky you are to even be breathing? When I saw that video of the ski-a-thon on YouTube, I panicked and called Granddad. Took the first flight in from Haiti."

"Thanks, bro," Jules said, grinding his teeth to ease the pain as he clutched the side of his ribs where the incision was. Pain shot through him as he propped himself up on the bed. Even though Alonso and Jules were only two years apart, Alonso was always the protective brother. Jules was glad Alonso flew in to see him considering his medical guru brother was often busy managing operations at one of his international clinics. In fact, Jules was overwhelmed the whole Romero clan stopped by to see him despite their hectic schedules. The room was filled with family members, several of his brothers and his grandfather along with his wife. Just goes to show how really important it was to have family by your side when you're at your lowest, or heck, when you're vulnerable.

"I appreciate you being here," Jules continued, "but, honestly, I don't feel so lucky to be alive, right now." And that was the truth. He felt a jolt of agonizing electricity shoot through his bones. That darn morphine was wearing off too fast for his liking. His tolerance for pain was usually high but not in this case. The impact his body took as he collided on the ski slope was damaging in more ways than one.

The hospital room door flung open and Dion, his other brother, bolted through. "Those damn reporters!"

"What's wrong now?" Jules asked, trying to keep his cool.

"They're everywhere. They're like bugs, in your face, annoying the crap out of you!" Dion announced, leaving a Starbucks grande coffee on Jules's bedside table. "One of the cleaning staff just told me an undercover reporter tried to pay her for some inside information about your progress."

"That's disgusting," Grandpa Toni Romero rebuked. The old man's lips were pinched into a thin line. He was seated near the window beside his considerably younger wife, Shelly.

Toni then waved his cane in the air. "I bet they're from one of those darn gossip rags. You can't trust anyone these days. They'll sell you out for the right price. Good thing we have twenty-four-seven security outside your door, Jules. We Romeros can't be too careful, as you know."

"Grandpa, I don't need security outside my door," Jules replied with potency, heat rushing through his blood. The last thing Jules needed was to feel like some helpless cripple. "Please tell 'em to go away. I can take care of myself!"

"Take care of *yourself*? You mean, like you did out there on the ski slope?" Toni argued, arching a brow over his round-rimmed glasses. "Don't tell me you don't need security, grandson. We don't need to take any more chances. Why do you and your brothers have to be so stubborn at times? Look what we've been through in the past with invasion of our privacy by the press."

"It's okay, Gramps, let it rest," Jules attempted to pacify. He loved his old man to bits and would throw himself under a bus to save his life but sometimes, he could be a bit much. He was beginning to wonder if he should have limited the number of visitors in his room. How the heck was he supposed to recover with all this fussing and commotion?

"Okay? No, it's not okay, Jules," Toni continued. "My God! Why does the media have to be up in our business around the clock? Can't we even get *sick* in peace?"

Zack, Jules's brother who owned the Romero Winery and Vineyard, cleared his throat after unsuccessfully suppressing a chuckle. "Oh, Granddad, you're always the same," Zack commented. He knew what it was like to be on the receiving end of Granddad's strongly-worded chastising when a scandalous sex-tape from Zack's ex threatened to surface and ruin his nomination for a prestigious winery of the year award not so long ago.

Jules glanced out the enormous window viewing the white clouds against the blue sky and scenic garden outside with a breathtaking view of the hills of the town known as Mayberry Hill. His grandfather Toni had donated millions to upgrade the medical facility, especially the flourishing garden to make it enchanting for patients who could do no more than stare out the window while they convalesce in bed.

The Romeros might be known to be enterprising jet-setters from the real estate arena to the corporate boardrooms of Fortune 500 companies but when it came to their own blood and supporting one another, family was first. Each and every time. They were tight as an intricately woven rope and never forgot where they came from in their youth when they had nothing but literally the clothes on their backs and hope in their hearts.

Good thing Jules's private hospital room was massive in space. Seated around his bedside were Shelly and Toni, his grandfather and patriarch of the Romero dynasty, and his brothers Dion and Carl, the recently elected—and youngest—mayor of Mayberry Hill who stopped by from City Hall to see how Jules was doing today. Lucas, his other brother and founder of the renowned Healthy Start software, had showed up earlier that morning.

The surgeon, Dr. Adeem, suspended the two-visitors-only policy for a day since Jules was improving. He was already three days post-op.

The fresh pine scent of hospital disinfectant filled the air. The soft beeping of Jules's monitor could be heard faintly since the overhead pagers were going crazy outside the room as doctors were being summoned.

"I don't know what I would have done with myself, Jules, if we'd lost you," Toni softened his tone slightly. "If you ever pull that stunt again, I'll make sure you live to regret it."

Jules grinned. "If I ever pull that stunt again, Gramps, I won't live to regret it. I'd probably be dead!"

Toni smiled but his eyes were misty and filled with pain. Jules knew his old man had been through so much tragedy and heartache in his life as it was. He knew his grandfather wanted nothing more than the best for his grandsons whom he'd help raise when he learned about their existence in their teens.

The brothers often took part in the annual ski-a-thon to raise tons of dough for underprivileged kids so they could go to school and be able to afford not only supplies, but the basics like food and shelter for their families. The event was sponsored by one of many of Jules's privately-owned companies, R.M. Fitness Centers. But something had gone terribly wrong when Jules lost his balance—something that had never happened before. Long story short, Jules crashed hard and the rest was a blur. He'd blacked out and woke up post-op. But that wasn't all there was to it.

Dr. Adeem also delivered some awful news to him. Jules couldn't bring himself to tell his family just yet. He didn't want to hurt them any further.

At least his family—as much as he wanted to be alone right now—was taking his mind off his real problem. His own private hell.

Zack glanced at his buzzing cell phone and answered it.

"Now aren't you supposed to have that thing switched off?" Toni rebuked Zack. "I don't want anything messing with the equipment in here."

Jules tried to resist the urge to chuckle. Besides, he would have to "guard" his rib cage if he did. "Granddad, it's fine for cell phones to be turned on in here. It's a medical surgical inpatient floor so it's okay."

Toni growled. "Very well, then. I just wish you boys would leave business alone for a change. It's family time now. You'll raise your blood pressure working around the clock."

Zack dramatically placed his hand over his heart, feigning a crushed heart.

"And speaking of family…" Toni continued.

"Oh, boy, here we go again." Dion rolled his eyes and shook his head.

"I've said it before and I will say it again. Family is so vital. Jules, you almost lost your life out there and just to think, if anything had happened to you and you didn't have us here, what would you do? Who would take care of you or visit you and comfort you?"

Jules thought about it for a moment. "But I've got you, Gramps."

"Very funny, Jules. You keep putting off settling down, and look. Look what almost happened to you. Heaven forbid, but you would have no companion to leave behind to mourn your passing or no little ones to carry on your legacy."

Jules felt his breath halt. Heaviness centered on his chest and it had nothing to do with the morphine that had just worn off. His gut clenched so hard he felt his muscle pull.

Loneliness hurt like hell.

Having crushed bones was painful, but nothing compared to the pain of feeling lonely.

His grandfather was right, wasn't he? As much as Jules hated to admit it. He looked around the room and saw the content looks on his brothers' faces. Though his brothers and he vowed they would never marry—at least not until they were well into middle age, he saw how happy Lucas was with Maxine and Zack, oh, Zack the lady's man, finally settled down with a loving wife, Blue. And Carl was now happily wed to Venus. Jules was beginning to feel left out.

When all was said and done, family was number one, but what about when he, as an adult, went home—alone. They all had their own families to tend to. Jules wouldn't want to seem like a burden to anyone or heaven forbid—in the way. Of course, they would never purposely make him feel that way. But he was a man with his pride.

Everything's all good and done when you're up and about. But what about someone to care for and reciprocate that feeling? Heck, just being in love could do wonders for your health. He dated a lot of beautiful women but he never wanted anything more serious in those relationships. Then again, he hadn't met anyone he'd want to be serious with. None who came to mind at the moment—except Amber Johnson-Murray, a friend of Carl's wife. Yeah, Amber was real nice. Only trouble was she was prim and proper so he didn't get too far with her—then again, he alerted her up front he wasn't into permanent relationships. But she probably moved on by now.

How lucky his brothers were to have found "the one." The question was, would Jules ever find "the one" before it was too late?

Just then, the door swung open. "Hi, Jules, it's time for your session today. Is now a good time for you?" the shy physiotherapist queried as she entered the room. Beside her was the occupational therapist. They'd come to see how he was doing and to help him to manage himself in his day-to-day activities as part of his discharge plan.

"Sure," Jules said.

"We'll be out in the hallway, okay, bro?" Dion said for his brothers as the men proceeded to give him space.

"Sure, no probs. Granddad, you don't have to leave."

"Nonsense, you do what you have to do. Shelly and I will be outside in the waiting area." His grandfather had his young wife, wife number five, on his arm as he made his way out of the room. Shelly was great and she was also a nurse, so she had been extra supportive when all this happened.

"It's nice to have a big family like that," Deana, the OT, told him.

"Yeah, when they're not a big pain in the butt," he joked, and he shifted himself on the side of the bed, the way they had showed him earlier.

"Good, Jules. You're doing well."

Jules appreciated Deana cheering him on. But he wasn't used to this one bit. He was strong, independent and could bench press two hundred pounds of iron weights with little effort. Heck, why was he feeling like such a dead weight? Man, being unwell didn't suit him a darn. He would do everything in his power to never end up like that again. Still, he would also never take anything again for granted thinking he was invincible. He should have taken his time on the slopes. Even if it was for a good cause. He was showing off his sports prowess a bit if he was honest with himself. Well, that would teach him.

After his session, Jules sat in a chair alone in his hospital room. Dr. Adeem entered and commented, "You're a healthy man, Jules. Healthy and wealthy."

"Excuse me?" Jules could not believe his ears.

"I'm not referring to being wealthy, money wise, Jules. I'm talking about your family."

"What do you mean by that?"

"Well, I've had patients before who have a lot of money but no visitors, outside of maybe the help."

"Oh?"

"Well, they were very lonely, Jules. Don't take it for granted, those nice guys are surrounding you with positive energy and lots of love. I find in my practice having an abundance of love and support can make a difference. More often than not."

"I hear you."

"There are patients I've had in the past who have told me they would trade all the money in the world they possessed to have someone visit them in hospital as they sat there alone with no one to care about them. If you have family and close friends who love you and support you—count yourself richly blessed." Dr. Adeem smiled. He looked young in the face but his graying hair revealed his age—and wisdom.

"You don't have to tell me twice."

Dr. Adeem smiled but Jules knew what else was coming. "Now, as I spoke to you before, there were some complications as a result of your injuries."

"I know."

"Have you done anything to...?"

"Listen, I haven't spoken to my family about my...situation so I would appreciate it if you didn't say anything."

"I'd never do that, Jules. Even though your brother and I have worked together, it would be a breach of patient-doctor confidentiality."

"Thanks." Jules fought to swallow that gelatinous lump stuck in his throat. "So you're saying I may not ever have kids because of my...injury from the accident?"

"Well, not quite. But it could be risky. We'll do the surgery I spoke to you about as an outpatient but the chances are fifty-fifty of it being successful. You know, having biological children is only one way to be a parent if you ever want to-"

"I know," Jules cut him off, and emotion subsequently climbed in his throat. He came across more curt than he intended. But he was a true Romero. Romero men didn't do weakness and all that other stuff.

His mind ran on Lucas and Maxine and their cute daughter Mary-Louise and his cousin Antonio's son Alexander and how they were adding to the branches of the family tree.

The family tree.

The Romero bloodline.

Jules felt a sudden onset of nausea. Damn, he never cared about having kids before. Heck, marriage wasn't ever on his mind before. But just knowing now that there was a possibility that he may never even have that choice tore a hole in his gut.

How could a woman want to be with him if he couldn't give her—an heir, a child?

No. Don't jump the gun, Jules. Doc didn't write you off just yet. You're not out till the end. And it's nowhere near the end.

"Jules, I know it may be hard now but the best thing to do for your full recovery is to get back to life. You don't want to sink yourself into a depressive state. Not that you would, but as I tell all my patients, it's best to focus on things that bring us contentment."

Jules drew in a deep breath. "Right. I know what I have to do, doc."

"And what is that?"

"Oh, don't worry. When I'm good and ready, I will have kids." Jules didn't know how it was going to happen but Romero men never accepted defeat. Ever. Where there's a Romero, there's a way. Period. "So when can we schedule this...surgery?"

"Well, it can be done in a few weeks. I'll talk with imaging first. We need to do another ultrasound. Then we'll get you to see a reproductive urologist."

"Great!" Jules sounded braver than before. "We need to get this thing done fast. I have a big deal coming up."

"Oh?"

"Well, you just said I need to get back to living my life and work is my life. You've heard about the privatisation of the Mayberry Hill Family Center."

"Yes."

"Well, I'll be putting in a bid, so the sooner I recover the better."

"You boys sure have your hands full running a whole lot of companies. I don't know how you and your family keep up." Dr. Adeem gave Jules a supportive smile. "I'll get the tests booked immediately."

CHAPTER TWO

Six months later...

"I can't believe you're back!" Amber Johnson-Murray announced to her elderly customer as she set a plate of scrambled eggs, toast and slices of bacon in front of her. "It's good to see you up and about again, Mrs. Van Hogen. Here's your order. Just the way you've always liked it. Eggs scrambled and fluffy, two slices of well-done bacon and lightly buttered toast. And it's on me."

Amber got a sudden boost of energy despite feeling nauseated all morning. And in fact, it was her first day back at work since she'd been off sick. Her belly knotted up in nerves. She drew in a deep breath. She was well aware of the stares from some of the other patrons. Her midsection had almost doubled in size from the last time she was there.

Some of the regulars at the café knew she'd broken up with her ex six months ago. He'd made a nasty scene at the café that day. The look of pity on their faces didn't do much to make Amber feel any better. Yeah, he was out of the picture and she was now six-months pregnant. She was going to fight to raise her child—alone.

Mrs. Van Hogen turned to face Amber with a glow on her face. The aged woman's silver short-cropped hair glistened in the early morning sun as she sat in her favorite seat by the window of the Murray Café.

"Why, thank you, Amber! That's so kind of you. And it's so good to be out and about again. Six months is a long time to be housebound after my hip surgery," she said with a wide smile, patting her right hip, her walker by her side. "But this new hip will get me back in action."

Amber smiled and tilted her head. Her customers made her day. Most of the diners were older and had been going there over the years. Just listening to them talk about their lives and families and bringing in wonderful stories warmed Amber's heart and gave her new appreciation for taking it slow.

The Murray Café wasn't making a profit. It was breaking even after paying the wonderful staff and ensuring they had the best home-cooked meals to give the locals. The cafe was just barely making it. It was a family-owned business that felt the effects of popular chain-store coffee shops opening up in the area over the years.

That was one of the reasons Amber worked two jobs at one point. The other job was at the Murumbian Embassy before she got fired for helping her friend Venus, who was in some serious trouble. But Amber was glad to be back at the café full-time. Sometimes money wasn't everything.

Mrs. Van Hogen was one of the original customers of the café since Amber's parents first opened it. Her eyes then drifted to Amber's enormous midsection.

"I see you've been quite busy yourself lately," Mrs. Van Hogen commented, looking at Amber's baby bump. "I didn't know you got married. Congratulations." The woman's voice was full of animation.

"Oh, I...didn't," Amber said, rubbing the enormous swell of her belly.

"Are you engaged?"

"Um. Well, no. The father's not in the picture."

Amber caught the look of sorrow sliding across the old woman's face like a dark cloud moving in on a sunny day.

Oh, no. Please don't feel sorry for me. I'll be okay, really.

From the corner of her eye Amber caught the daggers from her aunt's piercing glare. Her aunt then swiftly made her way to where Amber was standing as she continued to speak with her customer.

"Hi, Mrs. Van Hogen," Mavis Murray interrupted the conversation in a boisterous voice. She placed her hand on Amber's elbow. "If you'll excuse me I need to speak with Amber."

"Oh, fine. No problem," the woman hesitated, looking a bit stunned at the interruption. "Thank you again, Amber. And thank you for those lovely flowers you sent me at the hospital. You're a darling."

"Oh, no worries, Mrs. Van Hogen. Enjoy your meal." Amber tried to keep her calm and hide her annoyance at her aunt's rude intrusion. She knew what was coming.

"Is everything okay, Auntie? You seem upset." Amber asked pointedly when the ladies approached the staff area in back of the café. The kitchen wasn't so busy then. It was just after the morning rush. So things had quieted down. It was a good time for Amber to take her break.

"Must you parade your condition in front of our customers?"

"Excuse me?"

"You heard what I said. Do you have to let everyone know you're...an unwed mother?"

"Mrs. Van Hogen asked a question and I answered it." Amber felt her heart pound hard in her chest. It wasn't her original choice to be a single parent but that was how things worked out. The last thing she needed was someone close to her throwing it back in her face or treating her like an embarrassment.

As much as Amber enjoyed working at the café, working alongside her aunt, who could be a bit overbearing at times, was often a nightmare. But Amber tried to be as understanding as possible. Everybody's personality was different, right? After Amber's parents were killed in a car accident when Amber was much younger, her aunt took her in and raised her. The cafe was willed to Amber, but she was too young at the time, so as guardian her aunt Mavis took responsibility and ever since was active in running the business—it was, after all, her aunt who saved the café from going bust.

Amber tried not to focus on negative behaviour and only on good things as much as possible. She had to for the baby's sake. The last thing she wanted was her blood pressure or anxiety levels to soar.

Amber glanced down at her watch. "I have my prenatal class soon. I'll be away for about an hour and a half and then I'll be back," Amber said, pulling off her white apron and hanging it up on a hook.

Amber rubbed her hand over her swollen belly. She felt a ticklish feeling and a maternal warmth filled her heart. Her little baby had just kicked from inside. At least something was pleasant in her life.

"I'll take you there," Mavis insisted. Perhaps she wanted Amber out of there as fast as possible.

"You don't have to."

"I know that. But I will nonetheless."

Moments later, the car pulled up to the front of the Mayberry Hill Family Resource Center. Amber arrived for her first of many prenatal class visits.

"Thanks but you really didn't have to drop me here," Amber said again to her aunt Mavis who barely spoke a word since they had driven from the Murray Cafe.

"Nonsense. I'm not going to have you hobbling about town like that, alone. You're getting bigger every day!"

Amber felt uneasy and rubbed her belly again. Aunt Mavis and Amber never really got along, though Mavis was Amber's mother's sister.

Amber knew why Mavis was treating her this way. Mavis was head of the Women's Reading Group at the Mayberry Hill First Movement Church, and Amber, being unwed and pregnant, just didn't sit too well with her aunt—or her aunt's group.

Well, Amber had always been the careful one. She only had one real boyfriend with whom she'd been intimate. Unfortunately, he turned out to be the king of jerks. They had lived together and were supposed to get married. But Amber quickly learned that he wasn't what he pretended to be when they'd first met. He was cruel, lying and cheating on her and she was all too glad to end her relationship. Sometimes, things didn't work out the way one intended. But Amber was going to make the best of her life—regardless of what others thought of her.

Amber never wanted to be alone. And it wasn't her preference to be a single parent. Heaviness and pain swirled through her body at the thought.

"It should be the father of your child here with you. Where is he?" Mavis asked rhetorically, her lips pressed together in a thin line. The expression on her face, as often was the case, was stony. She was never one to mince words. Ever.

"I told you, Aunt Mavis. It's a nonissue. I'm not getting into it again. He's not in the picture."

"It's obvious he isn't. You should feel ashamed going to these classes alone."

Amber rolled her eyes and shook her head. She'd learned to try to ignore her auntie's criticism and harsh words. She'd read in one of her self-help books that sometimes you can't control how a person treats you but you can control how you feel about it. Amber thought she was solid in deflecting her aunt's rude demeanor but there had been times, especially while growing up, when it sank into her soul and tore her up. Who knew if that's why Amber spent much of her childhood being an anxious basket case with low self-esteem. Amber ended up being cautious of others and afraid of being hurt so she often kept to herself.

Amber was just grateful her aunt took her in when she lost her family or else she would have been forced into an orphanage. Still, that was no excuse for Mavis's rudeness at times.

"I don't know if I'll be alone, Aunt Mavis. I'm sure I'm not the only single parent in this class."

It was Amber's first time taking the prenatal class at the suggestion of her obstetrician. But she was okay with that. She enrolled late, though she was fortunate to join at all since another couple had dropped out of the class.

Amber made her way out of the car and slammed it shut. "Thanks again, Aunt Mavis. I'll catch a bus back to the café when I'm done."

Amber proceeded into the building and searched the signs looking for Room 15A on the main floor. She found it and saw the orange glossy poster: Mayberry Hill Family Center Prenatal Class. When she made her way towards the door, her heart came to a screeching halt. Standing a few feet away outside another door that was marked Conference Room 16A was a tall, dark and deadly handsome young man looking sexy in his tailored business suit. The man was talking on his cell phone until she came into his view. He promptly told the person on the other end he would have to call back and ended his call to look her square in the face.

Jules Romero.

"Amber?" Jules said cautiously. It was the way her name slid off his smooth tongue, so silky and deep. Oh, his voice got her each and every time. It had been a while since she'd seen Jules. And he looked hotter than Amber remembered. He sported an Italian-designed dark blue suit with a navy blue silk tie and he filled it out so nicely with his broad shoulders. Those Romero men predominantly had athletic builds. Her friend Venus was married to one, Jules's brother Carl, the youngest mayor to ever run the town.

In fact, it was her friend Venus who had introduced Amber to Jules.

"H-hi, Jules," she stuttered, caught off guard as she tried to keep her voice from wavering. His sexiness had always overwhelmed her.

Amber's heart hammered in her chest and a quiver surged through her body at his delightful presence. The man was sexy as hell and always caused that stirring reaction inside her body. The truth was, she'd always been aroused by Jules Romero.

Jules's beautiful eyes drifted to her bulging baby bump. His dark, sexy, brown eyes widened a fraction.

"I know, it's good to see me again, right? You just didn't think you'd be seeing so MUCH of me." Amber grinned, trying to bring some humor to the situation.

This was Jules Romero. Jules hot-as-heaven Romero. They first became friends when her friend Venus was in trouble, then Amber and Jules were a couple but that didn't last long enough. Jules wasn't ready to commit and she wasn't ready to have sex—yet.

Jules's sexy lips curled into a sweet grin and Amber's heart melted. God, he was stunning to behold. Her baby's feet tickled the inside of her belly with some swift kicking movements just then. Butterflies also tickled her midsection.

"That's not what I meant," he answered in his richly deep voice, cocking a brow. "But, you look beautiful, Amber. Congratulations. I didn't know you got married. How many months are you?"

He said she looked beautiful. What a thoughtful thing to say to a pregnant woman who felt as if she was growing like a gigantic watermelon. That thought was soon squashed by a painful reality. He was wrong about the being married part.

"Oh, I'm...six months." Amber's stomach lurched; she felt pain squeeze her heart. "But I...I'm not married."

"Oh?" He seemed a bit caught off guard, which was unusual for Jules. She remembered how brave and take charge he was when his brother Carl had a hell of a fight running for mayor amid scandal and a dirty campaign by his rivals and then there was that whole mess with her friend Venus who ended up marrying Carl during the scandal—as a diversion at first but then it all worked out for them.

Well, talk about a swift kick in the gut. Jules could not believe his eyes or his ears. Amber was pregnant? And single? Despite the sad look in her eyes, her skin had a healthy glow to it. She stood wearing Lycra exercise pants and long-sleeved t-shirt. The air conditioning in the building was cold so he figured that was why she was dressed covering everywhere. But then again she was always conservatively clad, rarely revealing much skin. Always dressed in long sleeves and long pants or skirts.

Heck, she didn't even let him go to second base. Which he respected. Though from her kisses, he could tell she was highly sensual and would make a great partner in bed.

God, he could kick himself for not holding on to Amber—for making sex a priority back then. He liked Amber a lot—possibly even loved her—but he just wasn't into having a serious relationship at the time...and Amber wasn't ready for sex at the time.

He could not control the heaviness that settled in his body.

"You're not married?" Jules was stunned. It killed him inside that she'd chosen someone else to get "intimate" with. But the guy didn't even have the decency to marry her. Call him a bit old-fashioned where babies were concerned, but he'd always been raised that a man should do the right thing and marry the mother of his child. Period. And from the time he'd known Amber, she didn't seem like the reckless type. She appeared much too prim and proper to get herself knocked up outside of marriage. Heck, had he been wrong about her? He thought they'd had good chemistry for the brief period they were an unofficial couple. Amber was the first girl he couldn't even get between his bed sheets and now she was with someone else? WTF! Jules was baffled as sin. He'd seen the way her body reacted to his when they were cuddling in the past. She wanted him as much as he wanted her. Yeah, he was baffled all right. But he suspected there could be more to the situation.

"No," she said quietly, looking off into the distance. He thought he caught the look of pain flashing in her beautiful dark brown eyes. She was a pretty girl and soft spoken, yet hard working. He remembered the time she'd worked her butt off overtime to help his sister-in-law Venus when she was in a heap of trouble. Amber had worked at the embassy but got fired after breaking some rules for the sake of helping her friend. She was a girl with guts when it counted. A woman who put her neck on the line to save a friend. Talk about honor.

"So are you engaged?" Jules probed further. Something in his gut urged him on. He was damned curious. He didn't see any ring. He really wanted to know if there was a guy in the picture. He hoped the dude that had the honor of impregnating her was at least around. Then a sinking feeling entered his body when he glanced at the door sign again. Why the heck was she going to a prenatal class seemingly alone?

"Why the twenty questions?" she zinged him, arching her brow playfully. He could tell she was trying to be brave but tried not to push it, but damn, he was so fascinated by her, always had been.

"Why the avoidance?" he shot back, a warm amusing smile on his face.

"I'm not with the father. I'm single. I...I have a class to go to."

"Oh, sorry to hear that," he said, instinctively. Regarding Amber's delicate condition, he was really sorry to hear that she was alone in all of this. "Do I know the guy?" Jules couldn't help but ask pointedly. "Your ex?"

"No. I doubt you've met Rex. It's no one you know."

"Rex? There must be a thousand Rexes around here. What's his last name?" he asked nicely, arching a brow. He tilted his head to the side.

"It's not important for you to know, Jules." Amber grinned and rolled her eyes.

Okay, he wasn't getting anywhere with this. Amber probably knew Jules well enough to know he could find out if he really wanted to and then he'd give the guy a piece of his mind, leaving Amber pregnant and alone like that.

"Well, I don't want to keep you. Though, I'm sure they won't mind you being late this week. You have a good excuse, being with child and all."

"Well, it's my first time going to this class. They had a space free up. I'm surprised to see you here."

"I have a business meeting. I'm in the process of acquiring this place."

"You are? Congratulations."

"Thanks but the deal's not done yet." A gnawing ache entered Jules's gut.

What had he missed out on? He could have been the father of Amber's child. He was foolish for not wanting to commit to her before. Now she'd gone and gotten pregnant by some other dude. He wondered if Rex was really the guy's first name. Amber seemed so protective about his identity.

"Well, it was nice running into you again, Jules. You're looking well, as usual." Amber smiled appreciatively then opened the glass door to the classroom.

And that was that. Door closed. Conversation closed. For now, anyway.

Just as Jules turned to go back to the boardroom across the hall, something pulled his eyes back to the classroom. He swung around, curiosity getting the best of him, and peeked inside the glass door.

Amber still looked hot as hell. He hadn't been lying about that. And man, it took all the will power he had not to gaze at her voluptuous breasts. Holy! Was it him, or did they swell three times their normal size from what he could remember about her?

Jealousy zapped through him again regarding this mysterious man who got Amber pregnant. Why the hell wouldn't she tell him the father's last name? Why was she protecting his identity? Why couldn't Jules have been the father? When he *could* produce kids? Oh well, missed opportunity.

He should be grateful at least he was still considered a stud in bed by the girls he'd dated since breaking up with Amber. Nothing since the accident affected his sex. *Gracias A Dios!* In fact, he felt his erection tingling just now that was very bad timing.

As he peeked through the glass, he saw Amber introduce herself to the class. He surreptitiously glanced inside through the doors, though not standing directly behind the door so anyone could see him.

He noticed that everybody in that class had a partner—except Amber. It looked as if they were about to perform some breathing exercises. He often sponsored classes offered at the fitness facility he ran with his brother Carl, before he became mayor. He was focusing on acquiring new facilities, while his deputy ran the fitness center. There must have been about a dozen couples in the classroom, Jules assessed, still glancing in. One woman had a motherly figure beside her; the rest had what looked to be the baby daddies at their sides, holding their waists as they sat on the carpet. But Amber was alone. Gazes around the room seem to penetrate her.

Jules's heart muscle tugged just then. He felt deeply sorry for her. Amber looked a bit sheepish in her facial expression. It looked as if the color had drained from her face. Not good. Not good at all. He even caught a pregnant woman whispering to her partner and then gazing back at Amber. The class must have encouraged women to bring their partners. It appeared to him that Amber was trying to put up a brave face or a brave front, by the way she tilted her head up slightly and hugged her chest. And that expression on her face? Oh, he knew it all too well. He had studied her like a charm back when they had dated for that brief period of time.

He turned his face to the boardroom and agonized over what to do. His heart burned in his chest. He pulled his smartphone from his breast jacket pocket and dialed his assistant. "Take over for me. I'll be gone for a little while. Remember, we're not going all in without the daycare center. That's part of the deal."

"Sure thing, boss." It was a good thing he'd trained Brenda, his executive assistant and coordinator in this merger, to handle his affairs while he was busy with other projects. She was a gem.

It looked as if Amber could do with a friend. Not like he was busy or anything, he grinned to himself and rolled his eyes.

Jules opened the door and strode inside to the surprised stares of the group. Did they recognize him? Probably not. It was probably the way he was dressed, not exactly ready to do floor exercises in a room with pregnant ladies and their partners.

"I'm here with Amber," he announced to the instructor.

"Oh...um...wonderful."

Amber's face lit up and a huge smile of appreciation rested on her beautiful soft lips. Okay, it wasn't the way he planned his day. But heck, some things were worth more than money and this was one of those moments.

CHAPTER THREE

Adrenaline pumped through Amber's body as excitement coursed through her veins. Overwhelming emotion fluttered inside her chest. Jules had offered to be her partner for the workshop, even though he had prior commitments.

Though she vowed after her crazy ex, she'd never have a man in her life again, she was grateful like sin to have Jules by her side right now. Really thankful.

Amber would never forget this moment as long as she lived.

"Now," the resource nurse started, "as you know, this is a very special session for moms and dads. The topic of this session is: Parenting Together. Many of you may wonder why a father is important or two parents during the process of childbirth. In this case, dads, the most important thing you can give your partner is support. Just to be there. Nothing is more important than emotional support during this time. Making sure that mom's needs are tended to. The baby, most of all, is the focus and mom is carrying your precious bundle, or bundles, of joy and she really needs that extra care. It is a wonderful, and in some cases, overwhelming journey to bring a baby into the world."

Amber's heart melted. Of course, she could have done this all alone, but the resource nurse was right. Carrying a live human being within her and having to give birth one day was an incredible experience. Life transforming. What had she been thinking? There was nothing like having emotional support by your side. Amber took a quick glance around and saw most of the couples snuggling up to each other.

She glanced at Jules who seemed to be listening intently to the instructor, his arm extending across her back in a supportive position. He seemed to be really taking this all in. Oh, what she would give for him to be the father of her child. Just the mere thought that he wanted to be there to lend her support meant the world to her.

Amber felt her baby swiftly kick about in her belly at that instant. A warm smile crept on her face. She hadn't notice that Jules's attention had turned to her. He was grinning from ear-to-ear.

"I think our little one agrees," he said, gesturing to her belly. He must have seen Amber's abdomen stretch while tiny feet pressed against the inside of her abdominal wall.

Amber smiled but then her smile was replaced with the look of astonishment. *Did Jules just say,* our *little one?*

Jules snaked his arm around Amber and gave her a loving squeeze. A jolt of electricity pumped through her body. Her baby also gave her a pleasant bounce kick below her rib. It seemed as if mom and baby were both enjoying Jules's presence and support. She'd never felt the baby so active.

Amber was tickled inside by this overwhelming show of affection. There was a spark in the air. A connection that was indescribable between the two of them—all *three* of them. She didn't quite know what it was. The faint delicious scent of Jules's aftershave delighted her nostrils when he took one hand and unbuttoned his suit jacket to get more comfortable. His aroma was so pleasurable. It had been a while since she'd inhaled the sexy scent of a man. Since she'd inhaled Jules's sweet essence. It was as if they'd never broken up and they were quickly bonding again—this time over her unborn child.

Ignore that feeling, Amber. You've sworn off men, remember? Look at what Rex did to you in the end. It starts off sweet and charming and then...

But if she were honest with herself, she'd realize that Jules and Rex were two completely different specimens. She should have had Jules as her first love, not Rex the Jerk.

But who was she to question Jules coming to her rescue at just the right time? She would have been so alone—felt so inadequate during this special session today. Of all the prenatal sessions in this program, she had to start with this one. The class that required two parents to be present—or at least a supportive partner for the mom.

During the remainder of the session the instructor guided the couples through loving support techniques, a labor and delivery/birth refresher, comfort measures, parenting together, practice runs on changing the diaper on a lifelike baby doll and coordinated pushing during labor.

Amber felt a fluttery sense in her chest and her internal temperature climb at the thought of having Jules by her side during the class. It was a delight to see him fumble with the practice baby doll, attempting to change its diaper. Amber giggled at times when he pulled his usual funny faces that always got her going. The endorphins rushing through her blood at that time were a pleasant muscle relaxant that Amber really needed. Before Jules came into the classroom, she'd felt herself tensing up again—her nerves had taken hold of her. But not now. She was more relaxed and felt more comfortable than she'd been in a long time.

"Man, I hope the real deal is not going to be as awkward," he commented and she smiled at his response. The other dads were also having a hell of a time getting it right. Changing the diaper for a pretend newborn the way the instructor had demonstrated.

Amber admitted she missed Jules's quirky sense of humor. Rex was always the serious type with an ulterior motive to everything whenever he did lighten up. Rex just never knew how to have sincere fun. Right now he would have made her feel like an idiot if she had screwed up in the diaper-changing lesson in this workshop.

At times Amber gave Jules a sheepish grin and appreciative smile. "Thank you," she'd said so many times, whispering in his ears as she watched lovingly while he proceeded to pat the doll's back gently.

What a full session it was turning out to be.

But then her body core temperature plummeted when she realized Jules was there just to save face. What would she do when the actual due date arrived? It was one thing to plan everything but now seeing how happy all the couples looked in that session and feeling the warmth and support of having Jules by her side, even though it was a prenatal class, caused her muscles to tighten at the thought of not having him with her. Funny thing, even if the father of her child was present, Amber would not feel the same as having Jules by her side. Jules was lovable, warm and had one heck of a sense of ice-breaking humor. He would crack a joke from time to time to get her to loosen up or lighten up, or say something witty and charming to melt her defences.

Amber appreciated the fact that Jules was a natural at this. He was affectionate and protective over her. He always was. That's why it ripped her to shreds when she had to part ways with him before they could become intimate. She really didn't want to but she couldn't risk him finding out about her. It would have been all too painful to go through—at least that's what she believed at the time—thanks to her deranged ex. Talk about making the wrong choice!

"Breathe deeply, Amber," Jules coached, his soft, low voice mellowing inside her. He gave her another affectionate squeeze at her side and she gushed.

"Thanks."

"Now, I know you have something on your mind; you look far away," he continued, whispering to her discreetly.

Then she turned to him and gasped at his boyish grin. His smiles were always infectious and she smiled in response. Suddenly, whatever Amber was thinking about was wiped clear out of her mind at that moment.

"That's better," he said. "And don't let me catch you holding your breath like that again. Our little guy needs as much oxygen as he can get."

She chuckled. "Okay, Jules. I'll try to remember." Amber noted that Jules referred to her baby as "our little guy" again. Of course, Amber realized quickly that couples were seated close to them. Was Jules just keeping up the pretence that he was the baby's real daddy? Or did he really mean what he said? Of course, he could not have. The baby wasn't his and he knew it.

A sinking feeling settled inside Amber. Gosh, she had no idea how emotional this session would be for her.

Jules didn't know what had gotten into him all of a sudden. His mind kept obsessing over Amber's well-being and how she would cope bringing a child into the world alone. What was she thinking? She'd left him to be with some lowlife who didn't even have the decency to stick around? If Jules ever got his hands on that creep! Why was she keeping his identity a secret? He could probably figure it out with the help of his agency but he decided to let it rest—for now.

"Hey, you look as if you're in a different world," Amber commented, as she gathered her bag and her sweater off the table.

The prenatal session had just finished and the rest of the couples proceeded to make their way out of the room.

"Oh, it's nothing," Jules lied. What was he going to say to her? That he was royally peeved that she'd left him for a deadbeat? Some Rex without-a-surname guy. The guy's name might as well have been John Doe. Jules would never have left Amber to attend prenatal classes on her own or removed himself from the picture if she was carrying his child. A guy not sticking around for the mother of his child was just plain wrong in so many ways.

"I'm glad you were able to make it today, Mr. Murray, I presume?" The instructor extended her hand to shake Jules's as they made it to the door to leave.

"Murray?" he said without thinking. Great. Amber's surname was Johnson-Murray. The instructor assumed that he was Mr. Murray!

He was about to correct her but caught the look on Amber's face. Too much information. "Call me Jules," he said, shaking her hand.

"Thank you, Jules," Amber said later. "I really didn't want to get into the name business right now with the nurse."

"Well, I've read somewhere in the world, some men take on the woman's name when married. I sure as hell didn't think I would be one of them." He chuckled.

She playfully rolled her eyes and shook her head. "It's only for the class, Jules. I'm sure she won't remember you as I doubt she'll see you again."

Jules froze.

Something pulled internally and it had nothing to do with his early morning workout that day. Never see him again. Was Amber seriously going to finish the rest of the sessions alone? He couldn't explain what the heck zapped into his body right then and there but something moved him to want to stick around Amber, to make sure she wasn't going to do this whole childbirth thing alone.

Was it because he knew then that his chances of having a biological child were practically slim to none? He didn't know why but he felt connected to Amber's child and reconnected to Amber. They definitely had a strong chemistry before their breakup. He knew that now. If they didn't have that special cosmic magnetic reaction in the first place, they sure wouldn't be able to rekindle their feelings for each other so quickly after meeting up again, would they?

"Where did you park?" Jules asked her before continuing farther down the hall. He wanted to walk her to her car, at least before returning to the boardroom.

"Oh, I'm taking the bus to the café. You know, the Murray Café."

"Taking the bus? In your condition?" He remembered she'd gone back to working for her family-run business, the Murray Cafe, the joint her deceased parents willed to her that her aunt had taken over for her until she was of age. He wanted to ask Amber why she wouldn't take time off from working long, stressful hours at a busy café to nurture her body and the miracle growing inside her. But heck, he was a man, what did he know? He only knew that if she was still his woman, she'd be pampered and catered to, not the one doing the catering.

"Jules, plenty of women take the bus while pregnant. We don't break, you know!"

He excused himself before swiping out his smartphone and dialed his assistant. "How did it go at the meeting?" he asked Brenda. "Good. I'll be back shortly. I've just got to drop a friend somewhere."

Today's meeting was more of an orientation to the facility. Jules had already been there and had instructed his assistant, whom he trained impeccably well, to oversee things while he had urgent matters to tend to.

"I'm taking you to the cafe."

"Jules, no. I don't need you to take me. I'll be fine. Really. You did enough by sticking around for the class. I'm good. Really."

"I don't think so."

Just then, Amber bent over, a look of horror on her face. "Oh, God!"

"Amber, what is it?" Jules reached over to hold her.

She did not look good at all. Her skin paled.

"Are you all right?" the instructor asked as she came rushing out of the classroom. She'd apparently heard the commotion outside the door.

Amber could barely speak. "I'm okay. Just a sharp pain," Amber told the instructor.

"I'm taking you to the ER," Jules said in a finite tone. His heartbeat sped a mile a minute in his chest. What was with him? He'd only just seen Amber for a couple hours today after so long but already his feelings for her had resurged from the last time they'd been together.

"Good. She needs to see a doctor," the instructor agreed, her countenance concerned.

Jules was all too prepared to drop whatever the heck he was doing. This looked damn serious. Amber was his top priority right now. He would take her for medical attention right away!

CHAPTER FOUR

Later, Jules stood by Amber's side in the ultrasound room at the hospital, pacing frantically like a nervous father-to-be. Yeah, right. As if *he* was baby's father. Trouble was, he sure felt like it. Since Amber was already more than six months gestation, they had admitted her to the floor as a precaution. Soon after that, she was taken down to have images done to ensure the baby's position was okay.

What the heck was Jules doing? Agreeing to be there for Amber? Was he losing his ever-loving mind? He swore business would be his only focus right now. So why was he so drawn to helping Amber? He'd make sure she was okay, then he'd leave her be.

"Okay, now. We're just going to have a look at the baby, Mrs....?" the tech said, as she walked into the room.

"Ms.," Amber clarified. "Ms. Johnson-Murray. But Amber is fine."

Jules didn't know what got into him just then but he felt irked at the thought of Amber being a Ms. If it were up to him, she'd be a Mrs. *His* missus!

She should be Mrs. Jules Romero. He kept his tongue restrained while the tech proceeded to prep Amber for her test.

Support. That was what she needed, right? Support. That's what he'd just learned in that unexpected prenatal class he'd just attended.

The room was dark and Jules observed the monitor by the stretcher that he'd helped position Amber on.

"Move a little closer to me, hon," the tech instructed Amber. "Good. Now turn slightly to me."

Just then, the tech helped Amber to pull up her shirt a bit to apply some gel.

Amber looked embarrassed at first and hesitant to lift up her top. "Do you want me to leave and come back, Amber?" Jules offered quietly. Wanting to give her privacy. They weren't, after all, an official couple. So if she was obviously playing shy again in regards to having Jules see her bare skin, that was all good with him. It was all for her comfort. Though he was puzzled since she'd been intimate with another man. She was, after all, pregnant.

"No. No, that's okay. Please stay."

The ultrasound tech looked confused. "I'm sorry, I thought he was the father. I usually ask visitors to stay outside while I do the test."

"No. He's not just a visitor."

"We're together. It's okay," Jules chimed in. Why had he said that? Because he didn't want Amber to feel awkward—again? Not that it was anybody's business who the father was or if he was around.

Amber carefully lifted up her long-sleeved black yoga top and revealed her naked skin over her huge, swollen baby mound.

Jules tried to hide the shock and horror in his eyes.

It took all the strength in his body to remain composed. So was this why Amber didn't want to get intimate with him? Was this what she was hiding all along? But why hadn't she just told him? He looked away then back at Amber as the tech squirted blue gel on Amber's abdomen and rubbed it around before placing the scanner on her belly.

Amber didn't look in Jules's direction. He thought he could see raw hurt clouding her eyes. Was she ashamed? God, there was no need to be.

He moved closer to the table and rubbed her feet, massaging them. She looked at him and her lips curled slightly at the corners into a warm smile of appreciation.

"Okay, as you can see, your baby is here. Right where she should be."

"She?" Jules repeated, rubbing Amber's shoulder now as he stood on the opposite side of the stretcher.

"Yes, I'm having a girl," Amber acknowledged, smiling weakly.

"You look tired, beautiful," Jules commented. "Don't worry, I'm taking you home after the doc gives us the go ahead."

"The doctor will have to see the results first. But I'm sure everything should be fine," the tech responded.

The sound of a galloping horse was the baby's heartbeat. The ultrasound machine was quite high-tech and advanced according to the tech. That was no surprise since the Romeros donated millions to upgrade the hospital's equipment to superior quality and turn it into a state-of-the-art facility.

"So this is the baby's heart rate." The tech showed Amber and Jules a number on the screen below the baby's image.

Jules squeezed Amber's shoulder lovingly. It was all spontaneous. Maybe this was God's way of giving him a second chance since he would never be able to have kids—at least not as of now. He was getting a taste of what it would be like to be a real dad. An expectant father. He couldn't understand why some men didn't want to stick around their pregnant wives or partners. This was like…a miracle. Nothing like he'd ever experienced. His heart turned to mush just watching the monitor with the image of a precious life inside Amber. A baby girl. The little bundle was unaware of being monitored and gaped at—just going about her little business in the warmth and safety of her mother's womb.

"So your baby weighs two pounds," the tech continued as she glided the scanner over Amber's belly while her vision fixed on the screen of the monitor.

"You can tell how much the baby weighs?" Jules was stunned. He wasn't a med specialist or anything, that would be his brother Alonso, but he was always in awe of medical science and the possibilities and amazing capabilities of technology.

"Yes, that's right." The woman continued to move the scanner around the abdomen. "We can tell a whole lot more, too, these days. "The crown to rump length of your baby is about fourteen inches, as you can see here."

Jules could not believe this little precious miracle growing inside Amber and seeing a full color image of the fetus was breathtaking. Just as breathtaking as Amber looked in her awesomeness and expectant motherly glow. Seemed like those pregnancy hormones agreed with her.

After the session, the tech switched off the device and wiped down the scanner. She then offered Amber a paper towel to wipe the gel off her belly.

"I'll take that," Jules said, usurping the cloth from the tech. "Come here, baby, let me clean this gel off you."

Amber's look of surprise melted into a warm smile. "Thank you."

"I'll be right back," the tech said. "I'm just going to get the doctor in to see you. If all is okay, I'm sure you'll be able to go home soon."

"Thank you," Amber reiterated to the tech.

After the woman left the room, Jules couldn't wait to turn to Amber. "Are you okay?" he said while cleaning off her delicate skin.

"Y-yes."

"Why didn't you tell me what was going on before?" he asked, as he carefully swabbed her belly to assure it was clean and dry. He assisted her in pulling her shirt down and covering up her exposed skin.

From what he could ascertain, from her stomach to her back and up to her rib cage were rife with horrific jagged scars and raised abrasions.

"What happened?"

"I didn't want you to see what a mess I am before, Jules. It…it happened when-"

"Oh, God, Amber. I'm so sorry. When your parents…that accident…?"

She nodded. He didn't need to probe any further. He wasn't going to say anything more unless she did. He knew all too well the pain of losing a loved one. But it looked as if Amber lost a whole lot more. So much more.

Anger blazed through Jules like an erupting volcano yet he fought to simmer inside for Amber's sake. He wanted to hunt down that son-of-a-bitch that did this to Amber—to her body.

Amber breathed in deeply and closed her eyes then opened them again. "It was hard for me to...get close to you, Jules. I loved you too much."

"But why? Why did you keep this from me? You think I would have minded?"

"From the corner of my eye, I saw your look of surprise when the tech lifted up my shirt. I don't blame you."

"I was shocked. Yes. But not for the reasons you think, Amber. How could you have judged me that way?"

"Because I was afraid of being judged that way. Again."

"Again?"

Amber swallowed hard. "Jules, you have no idea what I have been through as a child. I only told you some of the story. Yes, the crash that killed my parents left terrible physical scars on me but nothing compared to the emotional scar."

"Emotional scar?"

"I was ostracized. Teased. Because..." she sat up on the stretcher and moved her long, dark hair to the side so he could see down her back. "The scars are everywhere and they don't look pretty. Some folks said I should have seen a plastic surgeon, not a regular surgeon. But anyway, as a kid, do you know what my name was?"

"No."

"Frankenstein or sometimes just the monster."

Jules closed his eyes as he leaned against the wall, twisting his college ring on his finger, anger seething through him like acid. He wished he'd been there to defend Amber. He lowered his head. He tried hard not to feel her pain. But it was all too great. How crazy that she had to go through all that after losing her parents and her younger brother. He remembered the story she'd told him. They were driving home from the cottage when she was a girl. It was a cold, dark, fall night. A heavy downpour fell from the sky. They were hit by another car that sped off without stopping. The car swerved into a ditch, smashed into some trees and overturned. Amber was lucky to be pulled out alive. The others were not so fortunate. Her younger brother who was four at the time and her parents were both killed instantly.

No one ever located that other vehicle.

The wreck that claimed her family turned into another cold case for the police—an unsolved case.

And apparently that coward didn't have a conscience to come forth. Amber suffered selective amnesia at the time and didn't recall as a key witness who that other driver could be or what the other vehicle was, which was tragic in itself. That person would never be found.

How horrific for Amber. She'd gone through so much.

And to make matters worse, she'd been through several life-saving operations at the time. He hadn't realized the scars were the result of surgeries from her scalp to her back and abdomen and upper thighs. No wonder Amber often dressed conservatively and covered up as much as she could. She'd been ostracized. Humiliated. Then she was forced to live with her estranged grandfather who had passed away and then she got bumped into living with her aunt who wasn't even close with Amber's parents to begin with.

"I'm really sorry you went through all that, Amber." His voice was low, almost breaking with emotion. God, it killed him inside to know she'd been through so much hell. And she didn't even let him know the full effects of that crash—until now.

So that's why Amber always covered herself up while they dated.

She was so different from any other woman he'd been with in the past. It was his first platonic relationship with—a girlfriend. Come to think of it, there was a lot of firsts with Amber. She got him into this "try a platonic relationship for a change" line while they were dating saying she wanted to "take time" before getting intimate. Of course, that did nothing for his testosterone levels but he really was into Amber. They had so much more in common. It nearly killed him not to be inside her at the time, but he really got a chance to get inside her mind, her heart and her soul. Especially, her heart of gold. She put her neck on the line for his sister-in-law Venus and his brother Carl. Who could forget that?

Still, he had to remember he told her he wasn't ready to commit to her then so how could he expect them to stay together very long when getting married was what she wanted then?

"I know it's hard for you to understand right now, Jules. I know you're a caring, a kind guy. I really enjoyed spending time with you. I just didn't want you to see how I look underneath my clothes."

"So that's why you didn't want to be intimate with me?"

Amber was beautiful. Scars or no scars.

She recomposed herself. "I'm fine. I'll be fine. I just thought I wasn't good enough. And you said you weren't ready for commitment back then. I later met someone else who said he was ready to commit to a serious relationship. He turned out to be cruel and told me no man would want me and that he was doing me a favour by being with me. I left him faster than you could say YOU'RE FIRED!"

"Not before you...." He gestured to her baby bump.

"When I met Rex I thought maybe I would have a chance to have a family. But...well, it didn't work out with him. And now, here I am, single—and with a baby."

"It's okay, Amber. We all have scars."

"Not everyone."

"Oh, don't kid yourself, Amber. Most people have psychological scars even if they don't admit it. The truth is, nobody is perfect, Amber. None of us. And love means loving a person in spite of his or her faults because we all have them, maybe not the same ones but we all have them." He looked deeply into her eyes and she wrapped her hand around his waist and hugged him. He felt her sweet energy transfer to his body and he reacted.

"Amber, I want to be here for you and your daughter. Please let me."

"Jules. I can't ask you to-"

"You're not asking, I want to be here with you." Oh, boy. Jules was digging himself deeper and deeper. He needed to be focusing his energies on his new acquisition but why didn't that seem like the most important thing to him right now? Why was his heart pulling in the direction of the beautiful, kind-hearted woman who dumped him?

Heck, it wasn't even his kid and already he felt protective of the little miracle and more protective of Amber.

"Besides, I had a little accident a while back and well..." Jules said.

"An accident? Oh my God! Were you hurt?"

"Actually, yeah, it's complicated, too."

"Complicated?"

"Yeah," he hesitated. But deep down inside, he really wanted her to know. "Amber, I sustained some pretty serious injuries. I'm healthy and well but...well, doc said there was some damage done to the area near my vas deferens, the muscular tube that connects my..."

"Oh, God! Jules, I'm so very sorry to hear."

"It's okay. I'm a survivor. I just don't know if I'll ever *have* any survivors if you know what I mean."

"Oh, no."

"Well, I'm kind of glad we met up again. I mean, I didn't realize how much I missed our time together until I spent time with you at the class today—as parents. I thought helping you with your baby was like a blessing in disguise—I could be like a godfather or uncle or something." Okay, he was getting all emotional inside. Time to switch the topic.

"Anyway, enough of that!" he said in a commanding tone. "I want to make sure that you guys are okay, Amber. Where are you staying?"

"First, Jules, I'm fine, really. And as far as your…situation, it wouldn't matter to me. You're a great guy!"

"You're a sweetheart, but let's not worry about me. I'm concerned about your condition. You just had a scare."

"But I'll be all right."

"I won't rest until I know for sure, Amber."

After assuring Jules this, too, would pass and that one baby was plenty for her in her lifetime, the door swiftly opened and the doctor returned with the ultrasound tech.

"The baby's condition looks satisfactory, Ms. Johnson-Murray," the doctor said.

Amber smiled while Jules continued to have his arm wrapped around her shoulder for support.

"Can she go home now, doc?"

"Well, not yet," he hesitated, his face evident with concern. He turned to Amber. "We would like to run a few more tests and monitor you for a while just to make sure. We need to get your blood pressure under control. And I do suggest plenty of rest. You said in the ER that you felt a leg cramp, which is not uncommon at your stage. We took the ultrasound as a precautionary measure to ensure your baby is doing okay. No distress there."

"Oh, good," Amber said, her voice sounded breathless.

Jules truly appreciated what a woman went through more than ever now. She was carrying all this extra weight and still going on about her business while another life was growing inside her. Have mercy!

"Oh, and another thing. Leg cramps during pregnancy are often caused by compressed blood vessels as a result of the extra weight you're carrying. So you can help the blood circulate throughout your body and minimize cramping by putting your feet up whenever you can and drinking plenty of fluids."

Jules took note of what the doctor advised. His mind raced as to his upcoming appointments. Why was Amber dominating his interests all of a sudden? He would rearrange a few meetings and take Amber home then make sure she was settled.

There was no way he was going to let her go through *this* again, alone! Not if he could help it.

CHAPTER FIVE

A week later, Amber was finally ready for discharge. She ended up staying in the hospital for more than seven days and Jules had visited her each and every day in between his business meetings. Her blood pressure was unstable and she wasn't eating due to severe nausea, so IV fluids were her only source of nutrition. The medical team was worried about the baby's well-being given Amber's history of multiple surgeries since her childhood accident. They soon considered her to be a high-risk pregnancy and wanted to take proper precautions.

Jules brought her beautiful flowers and fluffy teddy bears to cheer her. She felt as if her heart melted. Her mood was certainly elevated. Aunt Mavis managed to drop by once, for which Amber was grateful. But Jules had seemingly moved his schedule around to be with her. That meant the world to her. He kept telling her that she had saved his brother and sister-in-law and it was the least he could do. But there was so much more.

Amber hated that she felt a magical spark between them again. A chemical reaction of overwhelming proportions.

Or was that her imagination? Amber fought to ignore the feeling. Back then, Jules was all about sex. It seemed evident that he'd changed. But after that sweet heat turned disaster of an ex, Rex, she did not want to risk having her heart singed again in another failed relationship. She just couldn't bear it—again. Jules was merely being a gentleman. Nothing more. It could never lead to anything more than his friendly support.

People could genuinely tell who cared for them when they were at their lowest. When they were most vulnerable. Jules was that caring person and Amber would be eternally grateful to him. God, what if Jules hadn't been there for her? She would have ended up alone in the ward. Venus just had a baby, so she was unable to visit. Her body was still healing. And Amber's aunt was simply too busy running the café in Amber's absence. And it was a good thing. Amber wanted things to run smoothly at the Murray Café in her absence. Amber enjoyed working at the café and chatting with customers. Sometimes her working relationship with her aunt got a bit out of hand with her aunt's mood swings but the smiles on the faces of satisfied customers who loved to come in and share how their day was going really made Amber's day.

Amber really didn't have a whole lot of close friends. Mostly acquaintances but not the huge lot like the Romeros had.

When she was released from hospital Jules was by her side, amazingly supportive as always. Amber was visibly relieved to have a ride home in Jules's comfortable SUV. He told her he couldn't stand the thought of her having to take the bus in her condition knowing full well that she was having some sort of joint pain related to her pregnancy.

When they finally arrived at Amber's apartment above the café and Amber turned the key in the lock and opened the door, Jules stood there, perplexed. He glanced around the cramped studio apartment. Was Amber crazy? How could she even think of having a baby there? He saw a small, old couch with a couple tears in the fabric and a few stuffed pillows and a throw blanket on it. It looked as if Amber used it as a bed.

The kitchen walls were dotted with grease stains and were so dark he couldn't tell if it was the color of the wall or the stains. A container of cleaning solution sat on the counter along with a cloth. The small window had a crack on the lower left corner and some white duct tape over a part of the broken pane. The carpet was old and tatty. Nothing seemed to be new in the joint. It looked as if frozen in a bad time warp capsule from the 1980s. Amber was staying there? His heart fell to the ground. A sinking feeling slammed into him.

The room was the size of a guest bathroom at Romero Manor, his family's estate. In fact, it was the size of his own bathroom at his penthouse condo on the lakefront. No way in hell was he going to leave Amber there. This was no place for a woman and her growing baby.

"What?" Amber said as she walked into her apartment. She appeared nervous and bit down on her lip, rubbing her belly. "What is it?" she asked, gaping at his expression.

"Since when have you lived in a...bachelor pad?"

"Since I lost my job at the embassy, I had to downsize. And oh, I know the window looks bad. It happened recently. Someone must have tossed a rock and it hit the window. I've already gotten some estimates from a glass replacement company to have that replaced. It should be done by the end of the week. I know it doesn't look like a palace but it's not like I have to pay rent or anything."

"But doesn't your aunt own and live in a nice house on the east side?"

"Well, yes. But she has tenants there, so...it's not an option for me. Aunt Mavis said I could use this space until I get myself back on my feet."

"How sweet of her," Jules said in an acid tone, his voice laced with charming sarcasm. To say he was gutted or appalled was an understatement. Why didn't her aunt just shove her in a dungeon or a prison cell? It would have probably been a step up from *this* place. He had seen farm animals live better than this!

Jules didn't want Amber to feel bad so he altered the subject a bit. "Speaking of getting yourself back on your feet, you should be *off* your feet right now. Here, why don't you sit down while I get your things?" He guided her down on what looked like a sofa bed.

"While you get my things?" she echoed, sitting down on the couch.

"Yeah. I don't think you should stay here tonight, not by yourself, Amber."

"Oh, no. I'm not going through that again. Being told what's best for me without my input. My ex already put me through the spin cycle with *that* controlling vibe! I don't think you should be telling me where I can stay, Jules." Amber's cheeks turned red. "Listen, I'm sorry. All you're doing is being so nice to me and I really appreciate it, Jules. I really do."

"I know you, Amber. You're not used to living like this. Look, most of your things are still in boxes." And who could blame her? He wouldn't want to unpack in this crappy excuse for a residence.

"I know. I haven't had the time to get myself sorted out."

"But how long have you been staying here?"

"Too long," she admitted, looking around, shaking her head. "You're right, Jules. You know me too well. I've had a pretty rough time after I lost my job at the embassy, and well, my savings ran out in no time. The rent on my condo ate up most of my available cash. I knew I wouldn't be able to afford living there too long. I'm thankful Aunt Mavis allowed me to stay here."

Glad her aunt allowed her to stay here? Doesn't she mean, she's appalled her aunt forced her to live here?

"But don't you own the café?" he asked her.

"I do. Sort of. My parents left it to me in their will but I was underage at the time and Aunt Mavis had taken over. Of course, when I reached the age of majority, I didn't think I could run the place so I gave her control over the facility so I could go college. Aunt Mavis was all too happy to take over this place permanently. Still, if it wasn't for her, the café would have closed down and it would have been sad since it was my parents' dream. Right now, it's running on a deficit. I mean most people these days head to Starbucks for their next caffeine fix. The mom-and-pop businesses aren't exactly thriving in this economy."

"I hear ya."

"Besides, if my aunt wasn't around I would have found someone else to help me run this place just to keep it open."

"I know." Jules knelt down beside her. "I didn't mean to sound so...controlling earlier, Amber. I don't know what the hell got into me. I've seen your old place and it was nothing like this. I knew this wasn't you. So, Mother Amber, what do you want to do?"

She smiled. "That's better. Thank you for your support, Jules. I would love to leave here but..."

"Consider it done."

Before she could say anything else, Jules swiped his phone out of his pocket and made a quick call. "Hey, Dion, I've got you on speaker," Jules said, giving him the heads up. "Listen, is the 1201 still available?"

"Yeah, why?"

"Good. You remember Amber, right?"

"Yeah," his brother Dion said on the other end of the phone. Since the Romero family owned multiple real estate investments around the city and across the greater Toronto area, it wasn't a huge undertaking to find Amber a cozy suite that would be appropriate.

"Well, she's looking for a place. I thought that one would be great for her. Listen, I have to take care of a few things. Do you think you could have one of the girls look after it for me?"

"Sure thing, man. By the way, how did that meeting go last week?"

"Oh, it came. And went. It's a nice facility. I had to leave the meeting early but Brenda has taken all the available info. I'm not making any rash decisions yet."

"Good. Well, keep me posted. And oh, yeah, don't forget the dinner next week."

"The dinner?"

"Yeah, you know how Gramps will feel if we miss one of our family dinners. Complete with a sermon."

"Oh, right. I wouldn't want to miss that."

The Romero family gathered a few times during the month for a great feast at the estate to keep everyone together. Since most of their jobs and businesses were spread out virtually all over North America. Toni Romero, the patriarch of the Romero dynasty, had instilled family values first in his grandsons and insisted they do everything to keep the family unit close and strong.

He often told them if they were too busy for friends and family, then it meant they were *too* busy!

"Listen." Jules turned to Amber after he'd finished his phone call. "Would you like to come to dinner next week at the estate?"

"Oh, Jules. That's so nice of you to offer. But I really don't want to impose."

"You're not imposing, Amber. Come on. Besides, you've met Gramps before. He really likes you. And he appreciates what you did for Venus and Carl. He said he'll be forever in your debt."

Amber seemed to give serious thought to the invitation. "Okay, I'll let you know how I feel. I mean, I do have my days, you know." She grinned sheepishly.

"Of course." Jules had to remember that Amber was pregnant and from what he'd seen of his sisters-in-law Lucy and Maxine, it could be one heck of a mood swing one after the other. "Anyway, you must be hungry. Let's go get something to eat and then we'll talk about getting you settled in your new apartment."

"My new apartment? It's new?" she gasped.

"Well, yes. Remember, we own quite a few condos by the waterfront."

"I know. It sounds, great really it does. I'm just...speechless. Jules, I don't know how I'd ever repay you."

"That's what friends are for, right?"

He saw the look of disappointment that flashed briefly on her face. Friends. He said the F word. But wasn't that what she'd wanted all along? Well, maybe she was having second thoughts. Or maybe it was the hormonal changes the instructor mentioned earlier in the prenatal class.

Support, Jules. Amber needs your support. Your undivided emotional support.

And that's what he was going to give her. Nothing less.

* * *

It was one heck of a long day, but later that evening, Jules's soft hands covered Amber's eyes as he stood behind her in suite 1201. "Okay, you can open your eyes," he said, removing his hands.

She opened her eyes and her jaw fell open. "Jules!"

"You like?"

"Jules…I…I love it but…this is too much," she refuted. The fresh leather smell wafted to her nostrils as she glanced around at a lovely set of expensive-looking soft leather couches. Movie-style recliner seats and a large screen TV filled an entire wall. It was like a mega home theatre.

"While we were dining, I had the boys at the club set this up."

"You shouldn't have."

"Please. It's nothing."

"But it isn't nothing, Jules. This stuff must have cost a fortune." Amber reminded herself how Rex tried to own her in so many ways. First, it starts with the ownership thing then it leads to much more.

"Please, Amber. Don't think about the cost of things. Having comfort shouldn't come with a price tag."

"That's easy for you to say," she teased him. Amber recoiled from her own comment. Oh, she wished she could take back her words when she saw a pinch of disappointment shadow Jules's expression.

"Listen, Jules. I…I'm s-sorry. I really do appreciate all you've done. It's just that things are moving so fast in my life right now."

"I just want to make sure that you and baby are fine. Okay?" His voice was stern.

"Okay," she whispered. Just then she yawned and the infectious motion touched Jules and he yawned, too.

"Oh, and what's this?" she said making her way over to the open kitchen. It was high-end designer fridge with a TV on it and an ice-maker. No biggie since she'd seen one before. But there was a computer monitor embedded on the screen.

"Oh, it's just a smart fridge."

"Just? What does it do?" Amber opened the fridge.

"Well, for starters, I think every home should have one. It uses a light sensor to scan the kitchen to see if anyone is present then powers down the electricity if not. Anything that saves the environment is all good for me."

"Hmm."

"And it also, get this, can let you know when food expires."

Amber whipped her head around to face him. "Shut up!"

Jules laughed at her astonishment. "Yeah, you just need to scan every item that you buy and place it inside as usual. It knows the location of the food item and will let you know it's time to remove it."

"Wow! I'm…just wow."

"Yes, you are just…wow!" he repeated, flashing her a knowing grin. "You're amazing, you know that?"

"I am?"

"Yeah, just seeing you so happy and beaming like that really illuminates a room. You deserve it."

"Thank you," Amber replied modestly.

Why was it always hard for her to take compliments and to accept gifts from people? Was it because of what she'd been through in her life? Having to humble herself in the care of relatives who really didn't want to be burdened with her when she was orphaned? She needed to learn to quiet the doubts flooding her mind and simply enjoy each moment. And that's what she was going to do.

Later during the night, Amber slept fitfully. Her mind drifted again…

She was in the backseat of the Honda Civic hatchback with her younger brother who was falling asleep and practically leaning on her shoulder, drooling.

"Yuck! Brian, wake up!" Amber had cried out, but her parents didn't hear. Her brother, adorable as he was, couldn't help it. She didn't move him; she just allowed him to continue drooling all over her cool new cardigan. She rolled her eyes and shook her head gazing out at the pouring rain.

It was late at night. Cold and dark, a torrential downpour crashed down on the windows of the car as her father drove through the flooded roads. They had just spent the weekend at the family's rented cottage up north.

"Slow down, Errol," her mother told her father. Amber knew her mom was always cautious.

"We'll be fine," her father responded. "I know what I'm doing, Jacie. I'm a driver."

"Yes, but the roads, Errol. Slow down."

Her father turned to her mother. "Just let me drive, won't you?"

Just then bright lights flashed in front of them, and their father careened into the other lane. The loud honking of what appeared to be a tractor trailer startled them. Her brother woke up.

Amber screamed. Her father swerved back to his lane and narrowly averted the accident. They pulled over to the side in the heavy rain so that her father could catch his breath and calm his nerves.

"You okay, pumpkin?" her dad asked after turning back to face her. Her mother had apparently covered her face with her hands.

"Yeah," Amber lied. Her heart was pounding hard and fast in her chest by then.

Little Brian rubbed his eyes and opened them up. "What happened?" he asked, his voice soft and small.

"Nothing. Your dad just got a little sidetracked." Her father pulled out a map from the glove compartment. Her mother turned her head away to face outward at her side of the window.

Her mom wasn't speaking to their father. It was going to be one of those nights—again.

He looked at the map. "Okay, it looks like I made a wrong turn off the main road where the lights were out."

There were blackouts along the way due to the storm. Most of the roads looked dark, terrifying. Amber grabbed hold of her brother and they clutched each other in the backseat. She was thankful she had the protection of her parents. What if they were alone in that wooded area? Not that they could ever be left alone. Brian was only four and Amber was twelve.

"Okay, I know where we are now," her father said, looking at a landmark sign that was illuminated by his overhead lights. "Let's roll."

He turned on the ignition and proceeded to drive away. Just then, she heard the screeching of brakes and a car was swerving on the road headed towards them. Was the driver out of control?

She couldn't see much. The rain was pelting. Her father tried to see through the windshield as the wipers madly rushed from side to side trying to keep up with the rain.

The car was coming right at them at they were pulling onto the road from the ditch.

It was coming right at them...

Amber screamed and bolted upright in bed. Her heartbeat pounding hard and fast in her throat. Her blood vessels constricted in her body. She could feel her baby move around rapidly inside her. She nervously turned on the bedside light. Thank God, she was at least in a nice secure apartment. But she felt alone. Very much alone.

She picked up the phone on the nightstand and called Jules. But she swiftly hung up, realizing it was two o'clock in the morning. Oh, God! What was with her? She was a nervous wreck. Again. The anniversary of her family's death was approaching. It was always like this. Would Amber ever escape the torment of that night? Trouble was, she couldn't remember much else after that. She didn't want to recall a single detail. She couldn't remember any more and maybe that was for the best.

Amber got up and went to the kitchen. Admiring, along the way, the beautiful marble stone countertop and the stainless steel appliances that housed her smart fridge and smart everything in that home.

She made herself an instant green tea with her Tassimo machine. Jules had spoken to her about not having too much coffee since she was pregnant, which was fine with her. He was such a sweetie.

Looking around her environment was certainly a mood picker-upper. Everything was so calming and soothing in its cream and earth tone colors. The ginormous screen TV was built into the wall and so was the compact, elite looking fireplace beneath it. The floor was professionally finished oak hardwood and highly polished. The walls were painted in an off-white sheen and adorned with calming artwork of nature, beautiful pictures. Gorgeous and healthy green plants also graced her suite. But how long would she be able to stay there? She was grateful for Jules's generosity. She just wished she could actually repay him.

About five minutes later, the phone rang. Amber glanced at the digital display clock on the fridge as she sat in open-spaced kitchen on a seat around the breakfast island. "Who could that be?"

"Jules Romero calling," the disembodied voice sounded from the telephone speaker.

She quickly got up and answered the phone.

"Jules?"

"Amber, you okay? You tried to call me?" His voice was tired but strong. Alert.

"Oh, it's okay…I'm fine. I didn't realize the time."

"I'll be there in a second," he told her without giving her the chance to rebut.

"You didn't have to come here, Jules," Amber said later when he'd arrived at her door.

"You called for a reason. It's not a big deal."

"Really? You're something else, you know that? You've done so much for me and-"

"What happened?" he quizzed, leaning in closer to her. Amber caught the irresistible scent of his cologne again. God, he was gorgeous and her hormones were going wild for him. She fought the urge to wrap her arms around him and give him a good hug and pull him to her, ripping off his shirt. Jules was strikingly handsome and extremely tall and fit, she noted as he towered over her, giving her a loving grin.

"I just had a bad dream."

"It must have been one heck of a bad dream, Amber. Come on now. It's me you're talking to."

"I know."

Amber shared some parts of the dream, so grateful that she was able to get it off her chest and talk about her fears, her guilt over surviving the accident and wanting so badly to be a good mother to her little girl.

"You'll make the perfect mother, Amber," he told her as he stroked her hair as she laid on the couch curled up into him. She enjoyed the warmth of his firm body as her head rested on his chest. His heartbeat was strong and steady. Oh, heavens.

Amber and Jules, like old times, watched a rerun episode of Dancing with the Stars. She didn't know when but she dozed off for a moment then re-awakened, still in his arms feeling loved. Cared for.

The fact that she could call Jules any time of the night and he didn't mind spoke volumes about the type of chemistry they had. Amber was aware when you found someone who connected to you so well, you didn't take it for granted, you cherished it and nurtured it.

Did Jules want to take another chance on her? She noticed he was trying to get close to her but he wasn't as flirtatious as he'd been in the past but that was probably because of her pregnancy. Most men were cautious around a woman who was expecting. Some women had sexy hormones rushing through their bodies, while others wanted nothing more to do with sex, until after the baby was born.

Hot damn! Jules looked so good in his half open shirt, his sexy stubble on his chin and those muscular arms of his. Right now, Amber could think of nothing else but to have Jules make love to her—for their first time. She wondered what that would be like. Her heart raced like mad in her chest as she visualized his strong, soft hands caressing her body as he made sweet, passionate love to her.

Stop it, Amber. It's not gonna happen, remember? Men are no longer part of your emotional budget. It's just too costly to enter into a relationship again.

Still, Amber couldn't help gravitating towards Jules. And judging by his physique and the sweet memory of his incredible kiss when they had dated in the past, she was filled with all kinds of delicious images of what it would be like to make love to him. That was assuming *if* he would ever make love to her. The man was hot though. Even though it could never lead to anything more than physical. If it ever happened.

Jules was probably just there beside her for pity's sake. She prayed that was not the case. Still, Amber wanted to savor the moment because life was about precious moments and this one with Jules was one she would deposit to her treasure trove of precious memories to never be forgotten.

She wished things had been so different between them. She loved her unborn baby, however, it had always been her dream to have a baby in wedlock. Her father, who died in that horrible crash, had not been her biological father and for some time before her parents' deaths, she was often called a bastard at the school by those who knew her parents and were aware of the truth. She didn't want her child to have to go through that. Not that it should matter these days. But oh, how painful it would be to not be married when she delivered her child into the world. Her heart sank at the feeling that it may never happen the way she planned. Yes, Amber wished everything had turned out differently. But the last thing she wanted to do was to spoil everything that Jules restarted between them.

Besides, she could not really cope with any sort of intimacy right now.

Jules and Amber fell asleep but before long Jules woke up. She felt the soft touch of his lips on her forehead as she nestled on his chest. Her heart fluttered. She felt a tingling sensation between her thighs for the first time since she got pregnant. She couldn't help but smile widely. She tilted her head up to his and looked into his beautiful dark eyes.

Jules stroked her chin gently as he gazed into her eyes. "You are so beautiful, you know that?"

Amber smiled.

She reached up to his lips and pressed hers to his and oh, the magic exploded between them. What was she doing?

No kissing, Amber. Don't get caught up in that emotional trap again.

Hungrily Jules kissed her, a raw lust clawing its way from his core. His tongue slid in between her parted lips and sent shivers of delight racing through her body. It had been too long since she'd experienced the touch of a man. And oh, she missed Jules's amazing passion. She trembled with desire and want as he softly stroked her skin. Her body pulsed uncontrollably.

Jules repositioned himself on the couch and got her into a comfortable position then lowered his head to her arm where her scars were displayed. He gently kissed her wounds, a heightened sensation that made her nerves tingle rushed through her body as he lovingly kissed the blemishes as if they were beauty marks. Jules made her feel so special. Her nipples became erect and strained under the fabric of her top.

"Oh, Jules!" Amber groaned in ecstasy, savoring the pleasure of being loved, treasured.

"You're so beautiful, Amber. I've always loved you," he said, his voice hoarse. He kissed the tip of her nose to the bottom of her earlobe and she felt dizzy with excitement. The touch of his soft lips was a delicious sensation through her body. He didn't just kiss her, he caressed her with his sweet lips. Oh, those magical lips of his. His lips were warm and tender on hers.

Amber could feel the hardness straining in his pants and delight rocked her body. Oh, she wanted him. She craved him so badly. Her hormones were racing all over the place. Her body was aroused for him. And his for hers. Perfect!

She reached down and stroked his erection through his pants enjoying the feel of his powerful hardness while he groaned with pleasure. He lowered his head to her breasts and kissed the mound of sensuous flesh.

Then just like that, Jules pulled away, leaving her breathless, her body throbbing out of control. Stunned, she gaped at him. "Jules," she said, breathing heavy. "Why did you stop? Don't stop. I want you, Jules. I need you!"

Jules got up. "I'm sorry, Amber, I...you really need your sleep," he said, extending his hand to her to help her up.

She was still panting. Amber could see that he, too, was still aroused. She lovingly rubbed her belly and accepted his assistance. She knew he wanted her as much as she wanted him, but she was pregnant and he was obviously nervous about being with her—in her condition. Even if it was deemed safe for pregnant women to be intimate. But it was for the best. She didn't know what she'd been thinking. *No more relationships, Amber. They don't last, remember?*

Amber reached over and snaked her arms around Jules and he held her so firmly, so passionately and they went to bed, sleeping beside each other, holding each other, hugging each other and left it at that. Friends. Nothing more. Taking chances could prove too risky right now. So why did Amber feel like hell?

CHAPTER SIX

A month later, Amber sat in the waiting room of her therapist's office flipping through magazines.

Since she had that dreadful nightmare and Jules ended up coming over in the middle of the night, Jules had stayed with her at the dwelling after she asked him to keep her company. She didn't know why but she really didn't want to be alone and he didn't want her to be alone. He was so kind to follow her to her prenatal visits during the past month since they'd gotten reacquainted. She couldn't express her appreciation enough.

Dr. Danye had been so supportive of Amber after her traumatic experience since the accident. She was dying to speak with him. She had to tell him not just about her progress regarding her coping strategies but also about having Jules back in her life. Amber was still having occasional nightmares of that horrible accident that scarred her body for life and scarred her emotionally so that had to be addressed first.

Amber told her therapist about her rekindled relationship with Jules and how he made her feel these days. She felt completely torn and wasn't ready to accept everything that was happening to her emotionally. Jules knew what Amber looked like underneath her garments, the horrible secret she had hidden from him for fear of rejection and yet he cared about her anyway. He went out of his way to make her feel special. Loved. Appreciated. She, in turn, truly appreciated his kindness. But she'd been through emotional hell with her ex that it was hard to trust again.

At one time she would have been ecstatic over Jules's devotion to her, but now Amber was finding she was a bit afraid of it in addition to finding his obvious love for her—and while she's pregnant with someone else's child!—completely tempting and seductive. How crazy was that?

Jules did everything and anything wonderful for her, from giving her the most amazing soothing, gentle back rubs and relaxing soft massages to getting her desired foods and other odd cravings in the middle of the night when he could have sent someone else or advised her where to go.

Then there was the dinner at Romero Manor with Jules's family a couple weeks ago.

Amber was anxious at first about sitting down to dinner with the entire Romero clan but it was a godsend. A contrast from her emotionally-distant aunt. The Romeros were so giving and kind and loving. She enjoyed the warm family spirit and missed that with her own family after the tragedy. For the first time she'd had a sense of longing in every fiber of her being. Wishing they were her family. Wishing that her child would be a part of that loving bond. Wishing that Jules and she would end up...together forever. *Yeah, right. Only in a perfect world!*

The Romeros, Amber noticed, did a lot of things for themselves and often moved with regular folks as well as fellow wealthy people. Outside of their expensive mansions and impressive properties, luxury vehicles and prestigious businesses, they were actually like normal people. She could so relate to them on many levels. And Jules was no exception.

What had she done to deserve his wonderful attention? Amber was wrong about Jules in the past. She was both thrilled and terrified to be able to have a second chance with him though she wasn't quite sure what their relationship was currently. They were just friends, weren't they? Though deep inside Amber wished they were a couple again. A real couple. Over the past few weeks, Jules was so attentive to her—taking time away from his business to help her. Yet, she always felt that it might not even last because she had been traumatized while growing up into thinking she could never be worthy of being with someone as amazing as Jules.

Her doubts were always getting the best of her. And whenever there was a moment she felt good about herself or her relationships, that doubt would rear its ugly head in her mind and she would promptly back away psychologically.

"Dr. Danye will see you now, Amber," the receptionist came back out into the waiting room to inform Amber.

"Thank you." Amber dropped the magazine back on the table. The general waiting served a few offices in that area and had a few people sitting and waiting to see a professional. She never thought too much of it at the time but today she was acutely aware of being watched. A man with silver-streaked dark hair wearing a long dark trench coat and dark sunglasses apparently was gazing right in her direction. A grim expression pasted on his face. He slowly turned his head away but for some reason, Amber felt a sense of uneasiness creep over her. She rubbed her baby bump protectively and walked cautiously into the doctor's office.

Don't get paranoid, Amber. Nobody is watching you. No one is following you. It's all in your mind. Hence, the reason she was still seeing a therapist so many years after the death of her family members. She hoped she was not having one of those paranoid panic attacks.

Through much counselling and focus on the present moment and psychotherapy, Amber was able to ease her distress. But her selective amnesia hadn't changed surrounding that fatal night. "Maybe you don't want to remember, Amber," Dr. Danye once told her. He told her that sometimes the brain worked to protect a person from unpleasant memories in order to function. Especially if it was something horrific to remember that the victim could not change. Some had dubbed the phenomena "conscious memory loss."

She wouldn't know what she would have done if Dr. Danye wasn't a part of her life. He had rescued her many times.

"Good to see you again, Amber," Dr. Danye said as he walked slowly into his office, limping slightly. From the time she'd known him, he always walked with that odd gait. Something from his childhood. That was one of the reasons she felt so connected to Dr. Danye; he could relate to being scarred from an early age.

Dr. Danye closed the door behind him.

"How's the baby?" He studied her with a warm smile.

"Great. She passed her obstetrician visit with flying colors. The baby is doing fine and is on schedule," Amber beamed.

"Good. Glad to hear it. And how are *you* doing today?" He sat down at his desk. His back faced the door, which Amber found interesting. She'd always been told it was good to have an escape plan if you're ever in a dangerous situation. She'd heard about some patients getting aggressive and lashing out at the doctor and the poor medical professional trapped in his own office without the ability to flee.

Oh, why had that awful thought crossed her mind? Sometimes she had way too much thought traffic traversing her mind. *Think positive, Amber. Think only good thoughts.*

"Getting better and better every day," she chanted with an empowering smile. She was not going let negative thoughts or energy consume her and muddy up her perception of life. In the past she fought hard to overcome negative emotions and bitterness, especially over the unfairness of her family's tragic deaths and the criminals responsible getting away with the murders. Dr. Danye told her that dwelling on that day for the rest of her life would not bring them back, it would only rob her of a future and that to honor their memory it was better that she moved forward because it's what her parents would have wanted. He was probably right.

She'd also read somewhere about the power of positive words to heal. She read one doctor had famously told a patient to repeat the words "every day in every way I'm getting better and better." She wasn't sure how much it would actually help but it couldn't hurt. It truly lifted her mood when she chanted the phrase.

"Good. That's good to hear. Now, tell me what's on your mind," he invited, and he shuffled some notes on his desk.

"Well, I'm still having those dreams."

"Oh?"

"Yeah. They had stopped for a while but then a few weeks ago, it was just terrible. I woke up in a sweat."

"Why didn't you call my office? You know we're on call. If I'm not here, my answering service will pick up."

"It was late at night. It wasn't like I was having a crisis. It's not like in the past. But it seemed so real."

"Was there anything different in this dream?"

"No. Dr. Danye, why can't I remember? I know we've been through this a lot but...I just can't remember anything."

"Maybe there isn't anything to remember, Amber. You said you had blacked out."

"I did. But...I wish there was something I could remember in order to help the case."

"Help the case?"

"Yes. Oh, I forgot to mention. I just learned the police have reopened the investigation. I think a witness may have come forth after watching some cold case program on TV."

"Oh? And how does that make you feel?"

That's what she loved about Dr. Danye. He always asked how she felt. Of course he was paid hundreds of dollars an hour to ask but he genuinely cared.

"I don't know." Amber's voice cracked ever so slightly. She turned her head to gaze out the window. The trees swayed and their green leaves rustled in the wind. It was a calming view of the hills outside. She loved living in Mayberry Hill and was glad Dr. Danye moved his office there from the bustle of the city with the noisy traffic and pollution. But she wasn't feeling very calm right now. She could feel her blood pressure soar. Her body pumped on adrenaline. Amber rubbed her belly and had to remember to think positive thoughts for the sake of her little one. She didn't want her baby to feel any of mommy's distress. In fact, just this week, Jules lovingly chastised her for saying a not-so-nice word when she accidentally dropped a plate on the floor smashing it to pieces. "Not around the baby," he said playing daddy. She smiled at the recollection.

Amber drew in a deep breath. "I don't really want to talk about that right now, Dr. Danye. I...I can't. I don't know how I feel about the case reopening. I don't know what leads they might or might not have and my aunt even told me, it won't bring back my mom and dad anyway."

"But don't you want justice to be served? It could bring you closure." He looked at her with concern from across the desk. Amber always thought before seeing a therapist that one had to lie on a couch and confess all her business to a man sitting with a clipboard on the side. But that image was nothing from reality that she was experiencing. She felt more like an interview. A business meeting with the therapist behind the large oak desk and she seated in a plush executive chair.

"Yes, of course, I want justice to be served but I also don't know what it could do to me to face the past again."

"Understood. It's not easy to face that type of horrible reality, Amber. I'm here for you. Just remember that."

She felt warmth creep over her but then she thought about the man in the waiting room. "There's a guy in the waiting area. He's wearing a long black trench coat and sunglasses and his hair is streaked with silver. He's a patient of yours?"

Dr. Danye looked puzzled. He shook his head. "I don't think so. Why?"

"Well," Amber said, getting up. She went over to the door and opened it and peered out in the reception area in the distance. There were three people earlier but now there were two. An older woman and a young man. Trench coat guy was gone.

Amber's heartbeat escalated in her chest.

"What is it, Amber? Are you all right?" Dr. Danye said behind her. He'd gotten up to see what she was looking at.

Amber walked back into the office. She didn't know why she had done that. "I'm sorry," she said, drawing in a deep breath. "I guess I'm getting a bit paranoid again. I thought...there was a guy...oh, nothing."

She decided to let it go. Maybe he was waiting for someone. The waiting area served more than one specialist.

"He could have gone to see someone else here," Dr. Danye suggested, his tone soothing. "Are you sure you're okay, Amber?"

Dr. Danye was a psychologist and not a psychiatrist. One significant difference was that psychiatrists were medical doctors with advanced specialized training who could prescribe medication, whereas psychologists focused on therapy but were not licensed to prescribe drugs. Not that Amber would feel comfortable taking any meds in her condition for the sake of her unborn child. At least not if she didn't have to.

"I...I'll be fine, really," she reassured him, sitting back down on the seat opposite him. "On the plus side, you remember when I told you I was feeling so lonely and alone?"

"Yes, go on."

"Well, good news. I bumped into an old friend of mine. Well, an ex but we were good friends. He's been nothing but helpful and supportive to me. I mean, especially considering that I'm a complex person with a whole lot of baggage under my belt. He's made me feel special."

"Oh, good. Glad to hear it, Amber. You deserve that."

"Thank you, doctor." Amber told the doctor about their chance meeting at her prenatal class and all they'd shared together during the past month. They'd practically picked up where they left off without missing a beat.

"That sounds like a true friend. When you can just pick up where you left off as if you've never spent time apart means you had something special to begin with. He seems like a really decent guy, Amber," Dr. Danye assessed. He then paused briefly and scrutinized her expression. She was looking down at her hands. "I sense there is some apprehension there, Amber."

"Well, there is. Sort of. He asked about the father of my child."

The doctor looked up, face frozen. "And? What did you tell him?"

"I...I couldn't tell him. I decided that I'm not going to tell anybody. There's no law against it. The truth is, my baby's father is out of the picture and has nothing to do with the child. So that's that."

"But if you want to start an honest and open relationship with this man, don't you think he should know?"

"I suppose. But...I really don't think I'm ready to mention anything yet. Maybe one day but definitely not now. I've been hurt badly in the past. Oh, God. The worst thing that could happen is that he wouldn't understand. I don't want to be judged. I've spent so much of my life—after the accident, being judged."

"Fair enough, Amber. I'm sure if he cares about you the way you say he does he'd understand."

Amber bit down on her lip, rubbing her belly protectively with all the love and warmth in her body. "I sure hope he does."

* * *

"Well, somebody's in a good mood," Lucas called out to his brother Jules as he entered the study at Romero Manor. Jules was speaking with his grandfather Toni and their other brother Zack.

"Hey, Lucas," Jules responded.

"Hey yourself, bro. Look at that cheesy grin on your face. You've been in a good mood lately and something tells me it's not the new deal you landed with the family center."

"Yeah. Very funny." Jules looked out the French glass doors to the verdant garden and scenic hills outside with the panoramic view outside. Truth was, he was obsessing over Amber. Ever since they'd met up over a month ago, he would think of nothing else—even while in meetings and boardrooms.

"Well, why shouldn't he be in a good mood?" Toni chimed in. "Venus told me all about you and Amber, Jules. That's very good of you. I hope you two get back together, especially after that horrible boyfriend of hers left her with that baby she's carrying."

"Gramps!"

"What? Well, that's why she's been accompanying you to our family dinners lately, isn't it? You two have something going, isn't that right?"

"Toni," Shelly chimed in. "Leave Jules alone. You're always on about these boys being in a relationship."

"Oh, not just any relationship, Shelly dear."

And just like that, in unison, the entire group said at the same time, "It's all about marriage. Marriage is the building block of a healthy relationship."

Toni looked stunned and taken aback. He growled playfully under his breath. "That's not funny."

"No offense, Gramps, but you do sound like a broken record."

"A broken record? There's nothing broken about me here. I've never given up on finding true love after your dear grandmother passed away many years ago. It took me five tries but look how happy I am with dear Shelly. If I can do it in my late seventies, by God, what about you handsome, successful boys? Look at Antonio and Lucas and Zack and even your brother, the mayor, Carl. Come on now. You, Dion, Troy and Alonso need to get going. Life is too short to live alone. "

Jules's heart pounded in his chest. A sinking feeling slammed into his gut. He wanted so badly to be a daddy—one day. He just took it for granted that he always would be. He'd been so great with Amber in the past and now?

Even if they got back together she could not have a biological child with him. Yeah, it was a blessing that she was pregnant. It just wasn't his child. He drew in a deep breath and tried to hide the hurt and pain circulating in his blood. The sheer disappointment with himself not listening to his grandfather in the past. He should have acted faster with Amber. If only he had been ready then to make a commitment to her.

Maybe then, before Jules's accident, they would have been married and had a family. But man, it sucked to be wrong. He was typically never wrong about anything. But he looked around and saw how happy Antonio was with Lucy and their little guy Alexander and how Lucas and Maxine had a pretty little girl Mary-Louise. Zack and Blue had Jefferson, and Carl and Venus just gave birth to their second son, Christopher, who was only a couple months old.

Of course, Amber, who was also a friend of Venus, visited the estate in the last week to see Venus and the baby and no doubt got to talking about Amber staying at one of Jules's spare condo suites. Yeah, it was hard to keep a secret around the Romero estate, or Romero city, as the land their grandfather owned that happened to be a huge chunk of the city of Mayberry Hill was often dubbed. Jules shouldn't be that surprised that rumors flew fast to his grandfather's ears about Jules and Amber.

Jules shoved his hands in his pockets and proceeded to leave the study before his emotions got the best of him. He knew his family was only trying to be their usual playful selves but it wasn't helping. Turmoil raged through him.

"What's wrong, my boy?" Toni called out.

"Nothing, Gramps. I'm just heading out for a little fresh air. I'll be back. Got to make a quick call," he told them.

When he walked out at the front grand marble entrance, he made his way down the stone pathway through the front garden and who did he see coming up the pathway? Carl.

"Well, Mr. Mayor. What brings you to this humble part of town? Where's Venus?"

"Venus is at a hair appointment."

"Oh, cool. Listen, Carl. I'm glad we're meeting out here. I need to ask you something."

"Sure, what's up?"

"I see how you get along with Tristan, even though he's...well, you know, not your biological son."

"Yeah?"

"Well, do you feel any different about...?"

"What exactly are you trying to say, Jules?"

Jules drew in a deep breath. He really didn't want to tell anyone. But he had to open up to Carl. He just had to.

"If I tell you something, you've got to swear you won't mention a thing. Not even to Gramps. I don't want him getting all worried."

"You know I'm good to go, bro."

He told Carl about the results of the accident.

"Man, why didn't you say anything before? Jules, I'm real sorry."

"Hey, it's nothing to be sorry about. It is what it is. And besides, nothing's set in stone yet."

"Man, that really sucks! But you've had a few girlfriends since the accident," Carl noted.

"Oh yeah. My sex life hasn't been altered after the accident. Oh, I've got no trouble fulfilling the lovely ladies in *that* department!" Jules grinned. "Amber and I broke up long before that accident but I've dated since then. You know that."

And it was true. Jules had no trouble securing hot dates and a mutually fulfilling sex life with whoever was his current girlfriend. Of course, Amber was the only "girlfriend" he *hadn't* slept with even though they were friends long before they officially dated briefly.

Jules and his brothers often spoke frankly about sex, their sex lives and all kinds of stuff so this conversation was no different.

"Well, that's good to hear. So what's troubling you, then?"

"Well, the girls I dated since the accident understood I wasn't the marrying type and they were okay with it. As was I."

"But Amber is the one you think you want to spend the rest of your life with?" Carl tried to clarify.

"Correction. I don't think I want to spend the rest of my life with her. I know I do. I've just been a bit distant around her, intimacy wise. God, she turns me on and I know she feels the same way about me, but in her condition, I just want to give her space."

"Well, I can tell you hormones can get real crazy for some pregnant women."

"I know. Anyway, I just feel that because of what the doc said-"

"So doc thinks you'll be shooting blanks or something?"

Jules shrugged. "Everything's good with me; you know I'm healthy as an ox. But yeah, there's a possibility I may not be able to get Amber pregnant if our relationship progresses into more and it pisses me off. I mean, we've gotten really close like old times this past month and a half. It's like we reconnected all over again as if we'd never been out of touch. There's something between us. I really want to make this work for us but...I think she'd like to have more kids. She didn't say as such, but I got the feeling."

"I know what you mean. But you know sometimes doctors can be wrong, right? I mean, everything's good with you, right?"

"Yeah. I wouldn't even know I might not have kids if he hadn't told me."

"I really think he's wrong. But if it's any consolation, it doesn't matter anyway. Family is family. And blood doesn't make you family."

"Amen to that."

"Besides, you know I love Tristan as my own."

"I know."

"Well, one day he asked me about his real father and asked how I can be a father."

"What did you tell him?"

"Well, I told him in the best way I could a preschooler, that there are all kinds of daddies."

"Good."

"Truth is, Jules, we both know that blood is thicker than water."

"I know."

"But love is thicker than blood."

"So true, man." Jules nodded in agreement. His brother Carl inherited their grandfather's sense of wisdom and sage advice. No wonder Carl won the mayoral election. He'd always been one heck of a talker. "You're right. There are people who would do things for you that your own family wouldn't and vice versa. Blood doesn't make a family. You know if Amber does give us a second chance, I would love to be daddy to her child. But there's so much about her she won't let me in on."

"Like what?"

"Well, she doesn't want to talk about the baby's father. All I know is that his name is Rex."

Carl had a look of shock on his face. "Why not?"

Jules recalled all too well that Carl had been through a similar experience when Venus didn't want to let on to Tristan's real daddy's identity. Carl rubbed his forehead. "I hope the dude is not some drug cartel or something akin," Carl said.

Jules chuckled. "Very funny. With a name like Rex? I don't think so, bro. He's just not around. Besides, she said not putting a father's name on the birth certificate will mean her child will be deprived of a father, as she was. She didn't want her child suffering the same sort of stigma or embarrassment in showing her birth certificate with that omitted information."

"I see."

Carl had already heard about the scars that Amber was left with emotionally and physically. It was no longer a secret. Amber told Venus and became more open about it and started to wear more comfortable clothing for the weather, revealing some skin appropriately instead of wearing thick sweaters and covering every inch of her body in hot temperatures.

"Listen, I'm going to pick up Amber. She's at an appointment."

"You guys really do look good together, Jules. I really hope you guys hit it off again and walk down that aisle. I was feeling the same way you were at one point. I thought marriage would really tie me down but having Venus at my side day and night and enjoying her company and love is amazing. And as Gramps would say…"

"I know, I know…It's better to *marry* than to burn with passion." Jules grinned and rolled his eyes. "Yeah. Whatever."

"Good luck, man."

"Thanks. Oh, and, Carl?"

"Yeah?" Carl said, turning to face Jules.

"Listen, you know I need to check out a few things regarding that accident that happened to Amber a long time ago. You know, when her folks were killed."

"Yeah?"

"Well, I want to get our boys on the case, too. She just told me the cops reopened the investigation after all these years. I just want to make sure Amber will be protected at all costs."

"Sure. We can get our guys on the job."

"Thanks. She keeps having nightmares about the past and I'm concerned. Her aunt's a real charmer. And I don't mean literally. But there are a lot of things going on I don't like. I'm pretty sure Mavis's constant bickering at

Amber has contributed to Amber's self-esteem issues over the years. But if Amber is going to be part of my future I want to make sure she'll be always safe—from whatever it is she's running or whomever she's afraid of."

"What makes you think she's running?"

"Well, she's got a lot of pent-up emotions about her past. I think her aunt really pulled a number on her with emotional abuse. I don't even like the way she looks at Amber now and the way she talks to her—with no respect. Amber's feeling more uneasy lately. I think she's more worried about how her anxiety could affect the baby's well-being. She even insisted that I stay with her at the condo. Which, of course, is totally cool with me. You know how I feel about her. But I could see terror in her eyes."

"Sure thing, Jules. I'll make sure Dion gets the guys on it. Consider it done. If it hadn't been for Amber, I wouldn't have Venus. Amber practically saved her life in more ways than one. Amber is family now. Don't worry, she'll be good."

"Thanks."

Jules knew he could always count on Carl and his other brother, Dion. They were the closest out of all the brothers. When Carl was in hot water, Jules was right there by his side, especially during the scandalous mud-slinging mayoral campaign that almost knocked Carl out of the game. Jules was there by his side.

Jules was going to make sure Amber was protected … come what may.

CHAPTER SEVEN

Later, Amber arrived at the main entrance French doors at Romero Manor after Jules dropped her off. "I'll be right back, I've just got to pick up something for Gramps," he told her before giving her a peck on the cheek.

"Sure."

She noticed the door was slightly ajar and thought it was odd. But Jules had already driven off. "That's strange." It was late afternoon and the lights seemed to be off in the home. Her heart thumped madly in her chest. Why was she nervous? She was at Romero Manor, right? The home was safe if nothing more. She'd been there many times before including the last time they had a massive family dinner to which she enjoyed being a guest of Jules.

Amber moved the door open and the entrance was dim. She made her way on the marble stone floor towards the living room. That was often the place where everyone gathered before dinner. She frowned at not seeing any signs of life in the residence.

She reached into her bag to call Jules but stopped. Curiosity got the best of her. She walked into the study. "Hello. Anybody here?"

She only heard the echo of her voice. Was she dreaming? What was going on?

She turned around and then saw a light flash over by the study. How odd that nobody was around. The entire family was to be gathered for dinner shortly. Then she saw Jules come in from the study.

"Jules. W-what's going on? What are you doing in the study? I thought you dropped me off and went to get something." Was she losing her ever-loving mind? If she didn't know any better she would have thought she was hallucinating. Oh, boy! She really needed to see a therapist.

"I did, baby," he said, wrapping his arms around her waist and bending down to kiss her forehead. He was ever so tall. She was often mesmerized by his height—that Romero height, all of his brothers were over six feet two inches-and his lean, fit muscular frame. "I parked outside and used the garden entrance to get inside," he said, his cheeks dimpled as he gave her that sweet boyish grin she adored.

"B-but why?"

"Come here, I have something to show you."

He gently led her into the dark study where the lights were off. When he flicked on the light switch, she almost jolted with joy.

"Surprise!!!!" everyone called out. Balloons floated from the air and everyone clapped.

She read the huge banner overhead. "It's A Baby Shower!"

"I'm sorry, hon. I really wanted to tell you but I thought I would surprise you."

"Oh, Jules. I…I don't know what to say," she laughed hysterically. "This is….oh, my goodness!" Her voice was overcome with emotion.

Amber figured Jules knew she was worried about not having enough for the baby and not knowing what to buy for her first child. And look at how he responded. She had confided to him once that she never got a chance to have little girl parties or birthday parties growing up, which was all too sad.

Once her mother held a party for her and none of the kids in the neighbourhood ended up attending. It was the lowest point of her life at that time. She had told Jules that one day and he felt her pain. He kissed her and told her that would never happen again. Ever. From that day in her childhood she vowed she would never invite anyone to her party because she didn't want the embarrassment of nobody showing up again, even for a good reason.

But here, here she was surrounded by good friends and family. Venus, her friend, walked over to her and gave her a compassionate hug. "Congratulations, Amber. You didn't think we would let you have a baby without a shower, did you?"

Amber was almost moved to tears and fought her emotions not to burst into a sobbing river. The last thing she wanted would be to tear up at what should be one of the most joyous occasions in celebrating her new baby—even if they were tears of joy.

Oh, Jules.

She looked up at him again with warmth in her heart and appreciation in her smile. Her heart fluttered inside her chest. She was overcome with unbridled excitement and love. So this was what it felt like to come from a large, close-knit family with tons of support.

She looked around and thanked everybody. She saw Antonio with his wife Lucy, Lucas with his wife Maxine, Zack and Blue and Carl and Venus, Toni and Shelly, Pamela, the family's press secretary who was more like family, Dion and Troy, Jules's other brothers. She noticed Dr. Alonso was absent. He was probably overseas again since he had opened new clinics in Haiti. Oh, what a family!

Amber walked into the study with wonder, like that proverbial kid in a candy store as everyone greeted her. Over near the fireplace, some beautiful children, Jules's nieces and nephews, were playing with toys.

And speaking of toys, there was a table near the fireplace that was brimming in Disney-designed gift bags tied with beautiful large red, blue and pink shiny bows. She saw boxes with baby clothes, diaper genies, newborn diapers, and even gorgeous looking designer maternity clothes laid flat on the grand table, adorned with metallic bows. Not to mention the festive helium balloons everywhere.

Amber covered her mouth with her hands, in awe, overcome with emotion.

"Oh, come now. That's okay," Toni said, hobbling towards her with his cane. He reached over to her and patted her back. "You deserve this, my dear. It's just our little gift to you and your baby. You're family now."

"Th-thank you. Thank you so much, I…I don't know what to say."

"You shouldn't have to say anything," Shelly said with compassion in her voice and her smile. "You've done so much for everybody else, especially Carl and Venus, whose idea this was, and it's okay to get some of that back."

Oh, how wonderful of them to say. They made Amber feel as if she wasn't a mere charity case, but a friend. She wished in her heart she was enjoying this shower as Jules's fiancée, or better yet, his wife! But she had to remember that it was she who didn't want to get physically close to Jules in the past and well, Jules wasn't ready to get serious then, or emotionally close.

"You know, I thought you were having one of your family dinners," she said, looking at Jules with a mock scowl as she placed her hands on her hips.

Amber had already dined with the Romeros at their "big" family dinner not long ago, so she was surprised that the Romero clan was meeting up again so soon. Now she knew why.

"It's the truth, right, Gramps?"

"That's right. We'll be having dinner in the dining room after we play a few games."

"A few games?" she mouthed, totally taken aback.

"Oh, you didn't think I would arrange this baby shower without all the fun, did you?" Shelly beamed. "Come here, Queen Mom, you sit right here on the Mommy Throne." Shelly lovingly guided Amber to a comfortable plush seat that was reminiscent of French provincial furniture that happened to be decorated with beautiful pink and pinker, if possible, ribbons and a few balloons.

Amber gushed.

"Oh, you guys are so amazing. Thank you. You really didn't have to do all this."

"Nonsense. That's how we do things. In style," Toni added.

Jules watched Amber and it seemed as if he couldn't keep his eyes off her. He seemed genuinely thrilled that she was happy. A warm smile relaxed his handsome face. He stood by Amber with his arms crossed over his chest feeling a great sense of satisfaction.

They ended up playing a few fun games as part of the "Jack and Jill" baby shower where a few of the men took part, but mostly the women, Shelly, Lucy, Maxine, Blue and Venus along with Pamela, were involved. The room echoed with laughter, music and chatter. Most of the time, Jules was by Amber's side, sticking closer to her than Velcro. Hugging her and rubbing her arm tenderly. She felt a close connection with him. It was the perfect way to spend her evening. If only they were getting married. If only she was his wife but she wouldn't raise the issue. She was grateful to have his company and his affection.

"Thank you so much. The dinner was delicious," Amber commented to Toni after the baby shower and dinner, rubbing her belly as she sat beside the stone fireplace in the grand family room. The "room" looked more like the size of a luxury hotel lobby. It was her second massive family gathering and she enjoyed it very much. She was beginning to feel more comfortable around the entire Romero clan.

No matter how many times she visited, she was always intrigued with the place. The Romero Manor was impressive in its grandeur. It was 16,000-square-feet of modern luxury with four separate wings or quarters and that ginormous diamond-inspired chandelier mounted on the cathedral ceiling was impressive to the eyes of mere mortals.

"Thank you, Amber. As I mentioned at the last family gathering, we try to get together as often as we can for a good old-fashioned family dinner. Just like in the old days when dinner meant being seated around a table with a four-course, home-prepared meal, not on the couch in front of a TV by yourself with something you shoved in the microwave in a tray," Toni said, shaking his head and rolling his eyes. "Things are different these days, you know."

"Oh, I agree with you there, Toni."

The Romeros were lucky, even though they often did things for themselves, they still had a palace-size kitchen and culinary staff to prepare delectable dinners when a dozen people would be guests.

They enjoyed a deliciously prepared meal of honey ginger chicken served with locally-grown garden vegetables that included baby spinach. The meal was perfect for Amber since it helped curb her nausea. The baked chicken was seasoned with honey, lemon and ginger. She also savored the taste of creamy yogurt spread, one of her favorite cravings.

Jules remembered.

Amber noticed he had kept up with her requirements for the baby and her desires in the types of healthy foods she ate. She knew it was no coincidence that everything at the shower had been just as she wanted. That darn smart fridge also let on to Jules what she liked and didn't like, since she input the data from her digital grocery shopping wish list. Amber smiled to herself at the thought. The table was adorned with sweet-tasting fruit salads containing strawberries, kiwis, bananas, apples, blueberries, raspberries, grapes and peaches, all perfect because she really needed to keep up with her four to six cups of fruit servings a day for the baby's sake, especially.

This was optimal for Amber since she was still experiencing nausea this far into her pregnancy. Some women were freed of morning sickness early on but she was one of the few where it looked as if it would last throughout her pregnancy. Did Jules and the Romeros think of everything?

Amber swore she didn't want a man in her life but she was beginning to rethink having Jules in it.

The Romero family was extremely thoughtful as well as observant. They were very much in tune with a person's needs it seemed. Especially close friends and family. Amber wondered what Christmas would be like around the estate. Particularly with the growing family tree and jolly old Grandpa Romero. Family gatherings were amazing at the estate. She'd never seen so much laughter and joy in one room before with so many people close to each other and loving each other and basking in the moment. Just being cool with each other. They made her feel so welcomed and a part of their family. Amber felt so at ease and comfortable around them. Especially being in her sensitive condition where her emotions were often all over the place. She was feeling happier these days and she had her beautiful baby growing inside her to thank for that. Well, she had Jules and his wonderful family to thank for that, too.

CHAPTER EIGHT

"Thank you so much, Jules," Amber said, leaning into his chest as he wrapped his arms around her from behind. They stood embracing on the Romero family's yacht, named the Janissa after Jules's late mother.

"For what?" he said in a husky voice as he cradled her. Amber could feel the warmth of his breath as he softly kissed her neck then her shoulder. His touch shivered through her spine causing a pleasant tingling sensation.

The soothing sound of the lake's water whooshing against the boat was calming to her nerves. Oddly enough, she didn't even feel tired. Maybe it was the adrenaline rush of the amazing day that got her buzzed.

The late afternoon sky was a calming shade of blue as it morphed into early evening.

"You know what I mean," she teased him. "Hmm, that feels good."

"So do you," he murmured.

"I really appreciate the party, Jules." Part of her was brimming with joy inside and another part was filled with sadness over the fact that when the baby arrived, what would become of Jules and Amber? Was he being nice to her because she was pregnant and alone? Did they even have a future together? She would be heartbroken to lose all of Jules should he decide to marry someone else in the future once they parted ways.

"What's on your mind?" He stroked her arm sensuously.

Waves of desire washed through Amber's veins from his gentle caress. She could feel the sexual magnetism between them. It was empowering, undeniable. Her nipples tightened under the fabric of her black Dolly dress. Yet, there was something amiss. Should she ask him? Should she risk ruining the moment and ask him where they stood as to the future? Could they ever become a couple—again? This time, obviously, an intimate couple.

"I...I don't know," she sighed, her mind racing with all sorts of ideas and scenarios. She really didn't want to spoil the mood, especially after all the trouble Jules and his family had gone through to make the celebration extra special for Amber and her unborn daughter. Talk about a caring, wonderful family. All families should be like the Romeros, wealthy or not. Their strong bond was the cement in their relationships that kept them stuck together in times of thick or thin. That was impressive considering how different, yet alike, they were.

"Oh, I think you do know what's on your mind," he lovingly teased her. "Your mind seems to be racing. I can see your eyes spinning in your head, darling."

He grinned and she smiled at the image. "Jules, you're not that funny!" Amber denied, then playfully slapped his arm.

"Ouch."

"That didn't hurt."

"No, not the slap, the words. Man, you can really kill an aspiring comedian's spirit."

She burst out laughing. "I didn't know you were aspiring to be funny, Jules."

"Good. Now that's the spirit. At least I got you laughing."

"Jules, seriously. I...I want us to talk."

"About what?"

"About us. Our future together. The last couple months were just...amazing."

"I know."

"You said you wanted to be a part of my life."

He gently spun her around to face him and cupped her chin in his soft hands. "I do. I still do," he assured, gazing intently into her eyes. His dark, sexy eyes mesmerized Amber and stirred something in her soul. His eyes were so loving, so passionate, so trusting.

Sure, you want me in your life, Jules. I just wished you wanted to marry me. I wish I could be sure it would even work out between us.

"Well, I care about you, Jules. I always have. I really hope that...oh, it's nothing."

"What were you going to say?"

The tranquility of the moment was then shattered by a loud engine roar of a plane flying low. Talk about bad timing. "Oh, Jules, what's that awful sound?" Amber looked up as Jules continued to hold her snugly.

Her jaw fell open. Up in the late afternoon blue sky, a plane spelled out: AMBER, WILL YOU MARRY ME?

Amber's heart hammered against her ribs. Her pulse leaped in her throat. She covered her mouth with her hands.

Jules reached over to the side of the rail and pulled out a gift basket filled with yummy delicacies and a fluffy brown teddy bear with a blue and pink ribbon tied to it. The bear was holding a small red velvet jewellery box in its hand.

"Sorry for the overkill, Amber. I really wanted to make this a special occasion for a special girl."

"Oh, Jules!" She was overcome with surprise. This was all a dream and she would wake up and be back to her usual self—alone with no support. But this wasn't a dream. Jules was on bended knee.

She hesitated at first then nodded repeatedly, the words caught in her throat.

"God, I hope that's a yes in sign language," he said.

Amber melted into a nervous smile. "Yes. I'd be honored to marry you, Jules!"

She should be honored, yet she was torn. She was crazy about the new Jules. She knew deep down he'd be a great father but—and there was this big but—she felt totally unworthy of him and couldn't imagine he'd be happy making love to her one day, given the extent of her scars. Jules was such a perfect physical specimen. Her ex had given her a traumatic sexual experience. What was she thinking saying "yes"?

Jules helped Amber open the ring box and her eyes almost popped out of her head.

She felt her heart explode with overwhelming emotion as he placed a sparkling French-cut diamond engagement ring on her ring finger. "Jules, this is so beautiful."

"Not half as beautiful as you, Amber." Jules smiled and the warmth in his expression was enough to melt her to tears.

"Oh, no. Don't go crying on me now. It's only for eternity that we'll be together. After that, you won't have to worry about waking up with me every single morning."

Again, the soon-to-be Mrs. Romero gave a nervous chuckle. Jules really had one heck of a wry sense of humor about him.

"I love you, Amber. I know we've been through a lot and spent time apart but all this time I couldn't stop thinking about you. When you came back into my life that time at the Family Center...I knew we were meant to be together. I want to spend the rest of my life with you. I never thought I would say this to another person but...It's true."

Oh, God! That sounds so promising but...can this really work? Honestly? Who am I kidding? But this would be the miracle I've been wanting for my child. For her to have a father.

"Oh, Jules. I...I love you, too. I really want us to work. I...I'm so glad, I hope anyway, that we'll be married before," she lovingly glanced down at her baby bump as she gently rubbed her beach ball belly, "she comes along into this world."

Her daughter deserved to have a father's name on her birth certificate.

"So am I. I agree with you. I love you and want to spend my life with you and our little girl. And I do think it's best that she's born to us as husband and wife."

Did he say spend his life with me? Could they even stay *married together?*

"Thank you for understanding, Jules. It wasn't easy for me growing up, feeling different from the other kids because my real dad wasn't married to my mother or even in the picture. When she married my stepfather, it was a dream. I've always dreamed and prayed that my daughter, my child would be born into wedlock. It's just something that meant the world to me. When I became pregnant I thought I'd lost that dream, Jules. Thank you."

"That's what love is all about, right?" Jules lifted her chin to his and kissed her lips so softly.

He had already given the thumbs-up to the pilot of the plane who did the skywriting proposal and soared off into the distance.

"I know," she agreed quietly. Her baby kicked a few times and Jules melted into a grin. He placed his hand over Amber's and both soothed the belly together.

"I'm going to be the best daddy to our little girl, Amber. It doesn't matter that I'm not the biological father. Blood is thicker than water, but love is thicker than blood."

She tingled at the sound of his empowering words. Sure, Jules would be a great daddy. But she didn't know if she could be a good wife to him. Would they end up splitting up again?

"That's so true. I like that."

"It's the truth, but they aren't my original words. My brother got it from some wisdom website."

She grinned again. Oh, Jules. Always the one to lighten what could be a serious or intense moment. "I still agree, Jules. It is so true."

"Anyway, we'd better move quickly with the date if you want to be married before our little princess makes her grand entrance."

"I know." Amber felt a pang of guilt. She didn't want Jules to feel let down by her. There was so much about herself she could never reveal to him.

"I'll speak to Carl and we'll see what we can do to expedite things at City Hall. We need to get some paperwork completed."

"Okay. That sounds like a plan." A lump climbed into Amber's throat again.

He smiled. "I like the sound of that," he purred in a low, sexy voice.

Jules traced the outline of Amber's jaw with his fingers and she tingled at his soft touch. Waves of pleasure tumbled through her veins.

Oh, Jules. That magic touch.

A part of her was glad her daughter would have a father's name on her birth certificate. Part of her was terrified that Jules and she would regret they rushed into this marriage.

His fingers touched her chin and tilted her head up to his and he pressed his soft lips to hers, brushing her flesh with his. Despite her inner turmoil, she enjoyed the soft erotic touch of his lips as she inhaled the delicious scent of his cologne.

She moaned with ecstasy as he moved his lips to her ear and nibbled on her sensitive flesh. Oh, she loved when Jules did that! It was so magical. So amazing. He then slid his lips to her cheek and kissed her lovingly. His mouth moved to the tip of her nose and she tingled with delight when he pressed his lips to her skin.

"God, you're so beautiful, Amber. Every single inch of you," he murmured as he brushed his soft lips over one of her scars resting on her shoulder. At first she was nervous; her belly exploded into what felt like a thousand tiny butterflies scattering inside her. But then she remembered, he was nothing like her ex. Nothing at all.

"Hmm," she responded as she embraced his body, feeling his warmth and his genuine affection. His feelings for her were almost palpable.

She moaned into his lips as he kissed her passionately, sliding his tongue between her lips and gently twirling his tongue inside while she felt her body throbbing from his desirable stimulation. They kissed hungrily and passionately as he slid his hands down her back holding her firmly as she leaned against the rail of the yacht.

Panting hard, she pulled away from him.

"What is it?"

"Nothing. I just…I love this moment." Amber glanced down lovingly at her baby bump before giving it a good rub. She didn't want to progress any further. Not that anything could happen out there in the open anyway. She just wasn't ready yet.

She turned around to face the water. Jules snaked his strong arms around her. "Okay, beautiful," he said, as if he could read her mind. "We'll take it one step at a time." He pressed his lips to the top of her head as he continued to hold her from behind. There was something soothing and calming about being near the water. Amber closed her eyes for a moment and enjoyed the feel of Jules around her, loving her.

They embraced and held each other glancing up at the beautiful early evening purple sky, the coolness of the water from the lake breezing onto their skin as they savored the moment.

The water might have been calm, but Amber felt anything but serene inside. Why did she feel as if Jules proposed under the excitement of the baby? She felt as if there was something missing. A marriage would not change things. If anything it might reveal things.

* * *

"He said what?" Venus asked Amber over the phone the next day, sounding excited.

"He asked me to marry him, Venus. I'm still reeling with shock. I'm so overcome with emotion, you have no idea. Unless, you knew about this?"

She was overcome with emotion all right. All kinds of emotions.

Venus's voice grew excited. "Oh, Amber, I'm thrilled for you and Jules. I had no idea! Carl didn't say a peep. That's amazing. Welcome to the family, sister-in-law."

Amber sat on the plush patio chair soaking in the warm weather at the cottage at Romero Manor.

"Jules is at City Hall right now. He's applying for the marriage license and seeing what he can do to expedite the ceremony for next week or the week after since I'm due in a few weeks."

Amber's heart pounded hard and fast at the thought. Her nerves were getting the best of her again at the thought of getting married in a few weeks before the baby's due date.

"They're lining up a minister and everything. I just don't know how they're going to find a dress that can accommodate my baby bump. I hope I look all right for the wedding photo. I wouldn't want to ruin that for Jules."

"Oh, you won't. And about that maternity wedding gown, that's nothing to worry about. Believe me, you're not the first one to be married with a bun in the oven! Besides, Pamela's super connected in every walk of life. She's good at finding stuff. In fact, she got my wedding dress at the last minute when Carl and I flew to Vegas on a whim to get married."

"Oh, that's right. I remember you telling me that."

"And besides-"

Amber let out a scream!

"Amber?" Venus cried over the phone. "What is it? Are you all right?"

Amber's heart thumped erratically in her chest. She felt fluid ooze down her leg.

Oh, no!

So much for Amber's dream of having her baby born into wedlock next week. "Venus, I...I need to call Jules. I need to go to the hospital right now. I think my water just broke!"

CHAPTER NINE

"Well, congratulations, bro. Welcome to the wonderful world of wedded life." Carl playfully slugged Jules's arm. Jules had just applied for the marriage license so that he and Amber could exchange vows before the baby arrived. They hoped to tie the knot sometime next week.

The two men were in his office at City Hall following Carl's chamber meeting with the council. Carl then leaned back against his desk and folded his arms across his chest with a proud smile on his face. "Man, I'm so glad you decided you're going to do the right thing. You know Granddad is going to go crazy," Carl continued.

"The right thing?" Jules asked, perplexed.

"Yeah. You know Amber is the right woman for you, I just wasn't sure how you were going to handle this situation with biological kids and everything that you were talking about."

"Well, you know, Carl, I thought about what you said and you're right. I don't want to miss out on something amazing with Amber because of this situation. I already lost her once. I'm not making the same mistake twice."

"What did she say when you told her about…?"

"She looked a little stunned at first but then she shrugged and said it didn't really matter." Jules wiped a smudge off his belt buckle as he stood in front of his brother. "What matters is that we can be a family—together. And we can always adopt if we want more kids."

"Nice. Amber really has a heart of gold."

"Tell me about it." Jules looked out the window, his heart racing hard and fast. The city road was busy with cars zooming by. Construction workers were outside drilling. He felt like there was a drill pressing into him right now. Sure he was happy that Amber said "yes" to his proposal and it was good that she said she didn't mind that they may never have biological kids together but a part of him still didn't sit too well with his situation.

"You look like your mind is somewhere else, Jules. You okay? You're not having second thoughts, are you?" Carl arched a brow.

"Nah. Not a chance, man. Listen, I've got to run. I'm meeting with Brenda so she can brief me on some upcoming changes with the Family Center."

"Oh, and how's that coming along?"

"As expected. The current employees were a little anxious about the change in ownership and worried about layoffs, of course."

"And? You're not going to lay off anyone, are you?"

"Are you kidding me? If I thought I would have to do that, I wouldn't have bothered. You know me, Carl. I'm just as passionate about saving jobs as you are. In fact, they were a bit surprised that frontline workers at the center would be getting raises and there will be job expansion, not decrease."

"Sweet. Now that's called progress. Betcha they're glad a Romero took over the facility."

"Well, the old owners were hoping that I'd have an epic fail so they were the only ones who were reportedly disappointed with all of this."

Just then, Jules's ring tone sounded. The tune "My Girl" played.

Carl couldn't help but chuckle. "Dude, that is so lame. Surely, you can do better than that, Jules."

"Nothing's lame when it comes to…my girl. Besides, it's one of our songs—Amber's a huge oldies fan, you know," he said, answering the phone. It was Venus. Why was Venus calling from Amber's phone?

"Thank God, Jules!" Venus sounded frantic. "I'm with Amber. We're at the hospital. We had to call an ambulance."

Jules's heart exploded in his chest.

CHAPTER TEN

Amber shrieked as she was wheeled into the delivery room on the maternity ward. Her heart raced in her chest, her body felt pumped as if it were on a massive adrenaline spike. The nurses sprung into action while her obstetrician was paged.

"It's okay, baby, I'm right here with you," Jules assured. Amber squeezed his hand. Everything happened so fast. She didn't even remember how many centimeters she was dilated when the nurse did the examination at the emergency room before they sent her to labor and delivery.

Amber was in active phase of labor—the phase before the final stage, which would be the transitional or advanced labor. Still, she felt as if she were about to give birth any time now but the ER nurse said she wasn't dilated enough yet.

Amber's contractions were growing stronger and stronger by the minute and the pain more intense and memorable.

She just moaned and groaned.

"Just breathe like we learned in the classes, Amber," Jules instructed.

"Ah!" she screamed out as another shot of pain crippled her nerve.

"Okay, baby, that's good." Poor Jules didn't know what else to do. She was gripping his hand so tightly, it almost hurt. Good thing he was strong and firm like an impenetrable boulder. She needed him to be her rock.

"Oh, Jules," she finally managed to articulate. "I wanted us to be married first."

"It's okay. It doesn't matter."

"But it *does* matter. I want us to be married first. Please, Jules."

"What?"

Amber cried out, unbearable pressure stabbing her lower back and tightness in her throat.

Dion got there in time and Jules's assistant Brenda was nearby. "Okay, guys, where's the nurse?"

"I'm right here," a woman in blue scrubs called out. She was jotting down notes on a clipboard while watching the monitor with Amber's vital signs.

"What can I do for you?" the nurse asked sweetly. Poor thing. She was probably trained to cater to the needs of expectant mothers providing whatever she could for them; however, she was obviously unaware what this expectant mother needed.

Most women asked for a back rub during this phase of labor or a wash cloth, not a minister who could perform wedding ceremonies.

Amber tried to follow the directions she'd learned in her prenatal class about keeping calm and relaxing her muscles but it was increasingly hard to concentrate when her body was going through an avalanche of painful contractions.

"We're getting married," Amber panted.

"Oh, that's nice," the nurse said. "When is the date?"

"Now!" Amber screamed out as another shot of pain struck her like a lightning bolt. Despite the agony, she tried to contain herself. Tears moistened her eyes. She felt her spine burn as if it were afire.

"Now?!" The nurse's eyes widened. She glanced at her notes as if to see if the mother-to-be had any history of mental illness. Her pupils were probably as dilated as the size of a mother about to give birth.

Amber cried out again as the onslaught of fire blazed through her. She had always prided herself as someone who had a high pain tolerance but that was until she went into labor. It was true then, there was no pain in the world quite like it.

"Do you have a minister on hand at the hospital?" Jules asked.

"Um…I…we…um… do have a chaplain on call," the nurse fumbled. She was almost lost for words.

"Amber, are you sure you want to do this now? I don't mind waiting," Jules reassured her as he leaned over her to hold her hand while stroking her forehead with his other hand.

"Don't you want to marry me?" Amber demanded. Why was she getting so testy all of a sudden? Was it the tsunami of hormones caving down on her from every direction? She wanted this to be a perfect day for her, the baby and for Jules.

Amber so badly wanted her baby to be born in wedlock and she came so close. She didn't want her daughter's birth certificate to resemble her own with the admission of "unknown" where the father's name should be. If Jules and Amber were legally married, then by law, Jules would be named the father. Period. It meant so much to her. She'd lost so much in her life, her parents, her brother… So many things she did not have control over but she wanted to have a little control over the birth of her precious baby. She didn't know why she wanted this now, she just did. Something in her gut was telling her that it would be done and could be done safely. She wasn't even fully dilated yet.

An hour later, Amber was still in the active phase of labor and nearing the advanced phase. It could be at any moment when she would come face to face with her precious little miracle.

Carl had managed to make it in and got an officiant, Mr. James Calderwell, who was also a JP, justice of the peace, on hand to perform the "labor" vows at the bedside. It was a good thing Jules had already applied for the marriage license. Jules was grateful to his brother for being there for him at the right time.

"Right, we're going to do this, honey," Jules reassured her. He never left her side since he got to the hospital. He wished he'd never left her side that morning but he really thought she would be fine. She wasn't due for another few weeks. This was so sudden. But he was a Romero. They always knew how to rise to any challenge, expected or unexpected.

Seeing Amber in so much agonizing pain was like a wrench to his gut. He was pained him to see her like this. Man, he really respected the body of a woman more than ever. Seeing beautiful, sophisticated Amber bravely preparing her body to deliver a human being into the world.

He wondered why more men were not at the bedsides of their wives during this awesome yet emotional time. He was overcome by the spirit in the room. The obstetrician and nurses were preparing to deliver their precious little angel into the world, while the elderly JP—the man who was qualified in the province of Ontario to marry them, dressed in a dark business suit, wiped sweat from his brow with a cloth and adjusted the round-rimmed glasses on his nose as he prepared to race through the vows.

Ordinarily the delivery room would only have those involved with the delivery and the mom and dad but Carl and Venus along with his brother Dion were there as witnesses. The rest of the Romero clan was gathered in the waiting room—those who heard the good news and were able to make it.

"Okay, let's begin," Mr. Calderwell announced as he opened his Bible.

Amber bellowed as the pain hit her full force again. Oh, man! What Jules would do to take away the hurt and go through it himself so she would not have to.

Mr. Calderwell was understandably nervous. Jules remembered Carl saying that old man James admitted he was way beyond retirement. He was also a friend of Toni Romero, Jules's grandfather. They went way back. Jules only hoped that there wouldn't be any colorful language in the room as Amber came close to the delivery phase when she would have to push. He trusted Amber would do just fine. She was strong, and like the majority of women, she could do just about anything.

The physical demands on her body were exhausting Amber, but she had to do this. She must get through this for her baby's sake. It was the right thing to do. She felt it in her body, her bones, in her soul. She wanted the best for her baby. The best start to life.

Amber's mind ran quickly to a TV show she'd seen many years ago, an old re-run. She couldn't remember the name of the show but she remembered that memorable scene with the woman being rushed to the ER and a minister on hand as she was saying her vows—right there before the delivery of her baby. How crazy was that? Amber had thought at the time.

Never in her wildest imagination would Amber have thought that the same darn thing would end up happening to her. Imagine that! That famous scene from that show played out in her own life!

This was real. It was really happening.

The minister started talking nervously. Noise. There was a cacophony from every direction from the doctor and nurses prepping her and monitoring her vital signs. Less unsettling was Jules by her side, stroking her forehead, comforting her while holding her hand. Carl, Dion and Venus were off at the side somewhere in the room out of the way of the bedside to give her privacy but close enough to witness, while the minister looked as embarrassed as could be.

No birth goes exactly according to plan, the prenatal coach had told Jules and Amber. Well, heck! If her prenatal coach could only see *this* birth!

"Do you, Amber, take Jules Romero to be your lawfully wedded husband, promising to love and cherish, through joy and sorrow, sickness and health, and whatever challenges you may face like childbirth, for as long as you both shall live?" the minister said as loudly as he could over her panting and grunting in pain.

"Yes!" Amber cried out as pain shot up through her back and in her groin like no other pain she'd experienced in her life. Oh, dear. The contractions were getting more intense. Any time now. Would they do it in time? Would the baby be born before they said their vows? Or would her child have the same life Amber had grown up to have?

It mattered to Amber a lot to be married to Jules before this innocent baby entered the world. It meant the world to her baby. She really wanted to do what she felt was right for her precious little one.

The doctor told Amber it was time to push. She was fully dilated. The baby had its own plans. "Okay, now push!"

Amber did just that and she could not believe the feeling her body was going through. The overwhelming sensation was physically demanding. Incredible.

"Do you, Jules Romero, take Amber Johnson-Murray to be your lawfully wedded wife, promising to love and cherish, through joy and sorrow, sickness and health, and childbirth, and whatever challenges you may face, for as long as you both shall live?"

"Yes!" Jules said lovingly, yet with conviction. He looked deeply into Amber's eyes, his body close with hers, supporting her. He never once looked at the minister. Jules seemed more concerned with Amber right now. As he should. It was time. She was fully dilated.

"Well, by the power vested in me by the province of Ontario, I hereby pronounce you husband and wife and…"

The baby came with a loud and healthy cry.

"…a beautiful family," the minister continued, wiping a tear from his eye.

Amber's body collapsed in relief and relaxation as the doctor held up the baby. Before the minister could say kiss the bride, Jules had already done that. He was moved to tears, overcome with emotion. The moment overwhelmed Amber. When she became pregnant with her baby, she thought she would be all alone, delivering alone, going through everything alone. But she was wrong. Pleasantly wrong. She could feel the love in the room and couldn't wait to hold her precious miracle. Jules moved from her side momentarily because he wanted to cut the umbilical cord.

Before long, their little girl was resting on Amber's chest during the bonding period, after the nurse cleaned her up and got her ready to be with mom.

"Oh, honey, you were amazing. You're wonderful, Amber. You did so well," Jules said so sincerely, so richly with emotion and love. She felt his words reverberate in her heart.

Jules leaned his head to hers as he wrapped his strong arms around her and their baby. Admiring the vision before him. His eyes were misty. She'd never seen him like this.

"I love you so much with all my heart," he whispered sweetly. His words were choked and filled with emotion, his dark, sexy eyes penetrating her with appreciation and admiration. Amber felt so loved and cherished. She was choked too as she kissed her baby on her forehead, looking at her wonderful little bundle of joy with her cute and pouty pink lips, her adorable cheeks, and a head full of dark, healthy hair. Most babies were born with little or no hair but not her angel.

It certainly ran in her family. She recalled her mother telling her that she, too, had tons of hair at birth. And Amber recalled the birth of her own baby brother. Yep, a head full of dark, curly hair. A blessing. It was a family trait—and a good one at that.

Amber wished her mother, father and her little brother were alive to share in her joy. But she had her own family now—an extension of her family that passed away. Looking down on her from heaven. And little Crystal, the name she secretly chose for her baby, was a true Romero, a legitimate child, unlike Amber. Born to her parents in wedlock.

The minister cleared his throat and Jules and Amber were caught off guard for a moment.

"I'm not quite finished yet," he said with a warm smile and turned to the witnesses in the room then to Amber, Jules and baby. "Family and friends, I present to you for the first time, Mr. and Mrs. Jules Romero and-"

"Crystal," Amber called out the baby's name as she lovingly hugged her bundle of a miracle. She had chosen it, because like Amber, Crystal was a precious and coveted substance from Mother Earth.

"And Crystal Romero," the minister said with a smile, his eyes misty with joy.

Clapping and cheering erupted in the room. Jules smiled and kissed Amber and the baby on top of her head.

Now, her daughter would not have a humiliating blank line on her birth certificate where the father's name should be—like Amber had with her own birth certificate. How awful it was for her when situations presented themselves where she had to show it. Her daughter wouldn't have the burden of being judged as Amber had been.

This delivery did not turn out the way Amber originally planned. Her wedding day did not turn out the way Amber visualized.

Amber was both relieved and terrified at all that had just taken place. In one swift moment her life had been drastically transformed. She was both a mommy and a wife! Did she just tie the knot while in labor?

CHAPTER ELEVEN

Three months later, Amber felt as if she'd been a mommy all her life. It was a boatload more work but what a blessed honor. Sleepless nights, round-the-clock feeding, diaper changes galore. She loved her little angel to bits. She was just so...fatigued. She stood over the kitchen counter sterilizing her baby's bottles in the new sterilizer Jules bought for her on one of his business trips to Paris. He insisted that the staff help her with the work but Amber really wanted to do certain tasks for herself.

They moved to a luxury villa near the lake adjacent to the Romero manor and estate. Not too far from the Romero Winery and Vineyard. The stunning view stole her breath every time she admired it. It was a calm and serene area that gave them enough privacy yet they were still close enough to the family's grand main house. The house where they lived had an adequate family size pool and a sprawling garden on the west side with views of the hills. Amber enjoyed taking little Crystal on walks in the stroller in the countryside with Venus and her little ones. Of all the sisters-in-law she'd inherited by marrying Jules, Venus was the closest.

Since Crystal's birth, Jules had been on long business trips. Was he having second thoughts about their rushed marriage? She tried not to let the thought settle inside her. What good would it do? It wouldn't change anything. No, it would just make her feel terrible.

On the plus side, when he was around, Jules was the doting daddy doing everything to make life good for his daughter. Yes, Jules was right about blood being thicker than water, yet love is thicker than blood. It was as if Crystal was his biological child. He practically worshipped his little daughter—*their* little daughter. Gosh, the thought still tickled Amber to realize that she was a mommy. She was somebody's mother. And she was Jules Romero's wife. Amber had lost her own family and suffered cruelty at the hand of others she had trusted but now—as if the universe had shifted things around for her, she felt a bit insecure and hoped this marriage would work out and last.

Amber continued to wash the remaining dishes in the sink. She didn't want to let negative thoughts dampen her mood.

Crystal just had her evening feeding and was sound asleep. At three months, Amber's little angel was finally sleeping for longer stretches, like six or seven hours at a time, which meant more sleep for Amber, too. It was so hard for her to be intimate with Jules because of the exhaustion she'd experienced with the changes her body had gone through but she was feeling more revitalized these days.

Jules was out of town on business with his brother Dion on an expansion deal in the Mediterranean but would be back sometime that night. Business never ended for the Romero men. It was something that Amber had gotten used to quickly and it helped to have her caring sisters-in-law for support, too. Especially Venus who was already her friend pre-Romeros.

Amber could hardly wait to see Jules! Hopefully, they could start getting close again. Especially now that Crystal was sleeping through the night. She wished he would stay in town more.

Her body was back to its normal size and back in shape—even her tummy was flatter again after so many weeks of giving birth, especially thanks to Jules and his ownership of one of the country's largest healthcare facilities, R.M. Fitness Centers. She had also enrolled in one of the Family Center's Mom and Tots program to meet with other young mommies. Venus had joined her with little son, Christopher-Daniel, while her older son, Tristan, was at preschool. It all worked out to be good timing.

The telephone rang and Amber picked up the cordless handset that rested on the marble stone countertop by the sink.

"Hi, Mrs. Romero," Venus teased her.

"Hi, yourself, Mrs. Romero," Amber bantered back.

"How are you feeling today?"

"Much better," Amber responded, stifling a yawn. Then her stomach did that lurching flip flop all over again. Her heart fluttered in her chest. "Well, almost better," she corrected, her voice trailing off.

"Almost better?" Venus sounded puzzled. "Why? What's wrong?"

"Oh, nothing." Amber sighed heavily as she continued to scrub around the sink. Why was she feeling this way? She should be the happiest woman on the Earth. She was happily married to the hottest, sexiest man alive, in her own humble opinion, and he showered her with love and affection.

"I just feel like I've rushed into everything. The whole marriage thing after having Crystal." *And I have a sinking feeling Jules feels the same way, too.*

"But, Amber, it's what you wanted."

"I know. I just hope it's what Jules wanted, too."

"Well, why do you say that?"

"Well, he's been conveniently busy with business since we tied the knot. I hope he's not having second thoughts."

"Oh, Amber, you know the Romeros—all work and very little play. Jules just launched the Family Center franchise and then he's working with Dion on the international expansion of the business college. You know the Romeros have a lot of business interests. There's no slowing down now."

"I know. I guess I'm feeling overwhelmed. And I feel terrible for feeling that way. I should be so grateful."

"Aw, Amber, don't feel that way. Trust me. I know you feel the guilt thing. Your life is nothing more than sleep, wake, feed baby, change baby, sleep, wake and repeat, right?" Venus said warmly. "It's the joys of early motherhood, girl. There's nothing wrong with wanting to take some time for yourself. And there's nothing wrong with wanting time alone with Jules once in a blue moon. Trust me, it's healthy for the marriage."

Marriage? What marriage? Well, talk about a "shot gun" wedding. Amber practically forced him to push the date of their nuptials earlier than intended—like when she was "pushing" her little angel into the world.

"Why don't you let me babysit for you while you and Jules spend a weekend together?"

"Oh, Venus, I can't ask you to do that!"

"Why not? And you didn't ask, I offered! Shelly did the same for me when Christopher-Daniel was born. It was a life-changer. Trust me. I didn't realize how much we were drifting apart after Daniel was born with my exhaustion and hormonal imbalances. This is a time to really bond with your baby but not forget to cater to your own needs and your husband. It's not like you'll be gone for long."

Just the thought of being away from Crystal and leaving her in someone else's care terrified Amber. Crystal was her little baby. She was all Amber really had in this world—next to being married to Jules, of course. But she was so fiercely protective of her child. That was just it. When Jules had tried, between his visits, to get sexual with her, she was feeling so groggy from the sleepless nights not to mention that her body hadn't quite snapped back into shape until recently, that she was always too tired to really do anything. But now, Crystal, thank heavens, was sleeping through the night and Jules was going to be back in town more. But he seemed to be emotionally distant at times. Something was bothering him and she couldn't quite pinpoint it.

"What about your aunt? She could babysit, too."

"Um. I don't think so, Venus."

"Why not?" Venus paused before answering her own question. "Oh. Never mind."

"Exactly. She's a sweetheart. I mean, she really tries but she's not exactly motherly material. I mean, seriously, she barely likes me. Besides, Jules wasn't all too happy when she visited last month. The way she held Crystal." Amber shook her head at the thought, and her stomach clenched. "Well, let's just say that Jules is just as protective as I am over Crystal and he took Crystal from Aunt Mavis's hands so fast it wasn't even funny." A small grin touched her lips at the memory, knowing Crystal was safe but the way Jules had reacted when they were all in the study. It was quite a sight to see.

"You know Grandpa Toni would love to babysit if I'm not available."

"Oh, don't I know it. I love dear old Gramps. But with his cane and his back…" Amber sighed. "I guess I'm just making all the excuses in the book, aren't I?"

"You are, darling. I hope you're not worried about…?" Venus paused again.

Amber's insides tightened. She knew where Venus was heading with her interrogation. Amber was terrified of getting intimate with Jules right now. She was nervous about not pleasing him, even though he had seen her body with the disfigurement from the accident. Oh, heavens, Amber hoped she wouldn't have any trouble around Jules. But oh, her body cried out to be touched by him when he was near her. Even when he was overseas and she heard the silky, deep voice of his sexiness from their long distance phone calls into the night when he was on one of his business trips.

Oh, Jules.

She craved him, desired his soft hard body over her. But oh, that hesitation, that emotional scar from her past.

Amber closed her eyes tightly and drew in a deep breath before opening them again. Venus was right. Amber deserved to be happy. Jules deserved to have all of her. She was ready. She was not going to put off her innermost desire. What on earth was she afraid of? Not pleasing her husband the way she knew he could pleasure her? Oh, his sexually addictive kisses, like an elixir of desire to drink in and savor. She loved the touch of his lips. Her body was ready. No longer sore from giving birth after a difficult pregnancy.

Things would be different.

"Listen, Venus, I hear a car pulling up in the driveway." Amber's heart galloped in her chest like a school girl about to meet her crush for the very first time face-to-face.

"My prince has arrived."

CHAPTER TWELVE

Though Jules couldn't wait to get back home to see Amber, he was feeling stressed and fatigued right now. Marriage wasn't exactly what he thought it would be. Amber was busy with the baby around the clock—and rightfully so. And well, he just got lost with business and working hard around the clock himself. Still, he obsessed about her on the plane from Europe. Amber and his little angel. His daughter, Crystal. His family meant the world to him. Jules didn't know what he was missing out on until that special day when he made it official with Amber and tied the knot. What a ceremony *that* was! They both welcomed their baby girl into the world at the same time. Well, that was some story he couldn't wait to tell his grandkids one day.

Grand kids.

Imagine that.

Jules still had to get his head around the fact that he was a father. He was a little girl's daddy. Didn't matter that she wasn't biologically related. He still felt an undeniable sense of protection and closeness to her. She was so precious, so adorable. The way she looked into his eyes with her large, brown, innocent eyes made him melt every time. Amber even accused him of spoiling her. Well, she was only three-months-old. Of course he'd spoil her! He'd given her everything a dad could give his baby. She had the most advanced and latest toys on the market and Jules made sure that practically everything in her room was sterilized—even though that was going a bit far and admittedly unnecessary. He'd even set up a scholarship fund for her already even though she hadn't spoken her first word yet.

In the past, Jules thought he would do anything for his brothers and dear old Gramps but having a child and a wife was a different feeling. If anyone so much as caused them to draw a tear, he'd have that sucker for dinner. He was fiercely protective of his little family. He wouldn't hesitate to lay down his life for them if he had to. That was the burning love he felt in his gut, in his soul.

He slammed the car door of his SUV shut after he yanked out his luggage. Dion had already gone to his own place. The meeting in the capital of Lendovia, one of the wealthiest principalities in the Mediterranean, where their latest expansion project to open up educational facilities lay, threw a few kinks in their plans regarding expanding Romero's sponsored colleges and educational programs. But they would deal with that after the weekend, on Monday. Now it was all about family time. Now if he could just fight this fatigue from all that flying and those boardroom meetings.

By the time he turned the key in the lock and entered the foyer of his villa, Jules could smell the aroma of freshly baked apple pie with cinnamon. His favorite.

"Hey, beautiful." Jules made his way into the kitchen and placed his luggage on the tile. He then snaked his arms around Amber's waist. He placed a soft kiss on the side of her neck and she moaned with delight leaning into his body.

"Hi, Jules," she said, turning around to face him and wrapping her arms around his neck. "How was your flight?"

"Hi, Jules? That's all I get?" he teased her. "Well, I've been lonely without you." Jules lowered his head to hers and kissed her gently. God, he loved the feel of her skin, the whisper of her perfume. It drove him crazy each and every time. And he enjoyed the feel of his hands on her fine, rounded, child-bearing hips. She was a healthy, proportionate woman. Curved in all the right places.

"Hmm, you smell so good." He nuzzled her neck. He slid his hands over her behind and gave it a good squeeze. Amber's body responded.

"I love when you do that," she whispered as she arched her neck enjoying his silky kisses. "I...I've missed you."

"Good," he growled in a low voice. Just the sound of her soft, sultry voice drove him wild with erotic thoughts of pleasing her in every way, wanting to hear more of it as she cried out his name with ecstasy. Oh, the things he really wanted to do with her right now.

He'd been away from her for way too long. He just couldn't wait to finally be with his wife. He'd been busy since the birth of their daughter and they never got a chance to be intimate, but then again, how many wives gave birth on their wedding day?

Her body had been sore and fatigued and she was feeling too overwhelmed then, adjusting to sleep-wake intervals of two hours at a time.

Damn, he'd waited so long already. He could tell by the way her body was responding to his, that she was more ready than she was before. It pumped him up as well and his fatigue faded.

He reached his hand up her blouse and underneath the material, feeling the skin on her back, gently caressing her body over her scars.

Just then, she pulled away from him.

"What is it, baby?" he asked gently. He hoped he hadn't done the wrong thing. He wanted her to know that he loved her and that he appreciated everything about her, no matter what.

"It's nothing, I..." she said, her voice trailing off as she hugged herself and looked out through the large kitchen window at the sunset. The view was breathtaking as the kitchen window overlooked the beautiful hills in the countryside.

He drew in a deep breath.

"I know what it is."

"No, you don't. You don't understand." Her gaze failed to meet his as she continued to look outside avoiding his eye contact.

"Whenever we get this close it's always the same, Amber. You need to let go and just be okay. I love you, all of you, just the way you are."

"I...I know." She closed her eyes, breathing deeply then opening them again. "Sometimes, I just can't help it, Jules. I'm sorry."

"No. Don't be. The only person who should be sorry is the coward who did this to you and...your family. What happened to you is not your fault, Amber. But you're still beautiful."

"My skin is not, Jules. I know you're just trying to be kind—"

"What?" Heat rushed through Jules's gut and it had nothing to do with passion. He felt his heart squeeze in his chest. "What are you talking about, Amber? How could you think I'm being patronizing? You should know me better than that by now."

"I know you are a perfect gentleman, Jules. You were raised right. But..."

He could see tears threatening to fill her eyes. He reached over to her and pulled her close. If he could only get his hands on the idiot who killed her parents and brother in the accident and sped off leaving his beautiful wife scarred for life, both in body and psyche. Damn it! It wasn't fair. And the first guy Amber had trusted to sleep with, he let her down even worse, making her even more self-conscious and feeling less worthy, when in fact, she was ten thousand times worthy—she was precious like a rare flawless diamond and she meant the world to Jules.

Yeah, Amber meant the world to him. But would she let him inside *her* world, completely? If he was honest with himself, he'd admit he didn't help matters much being away so much. He could have postponed some of his trips or have one of his senior executives take his place. But maybe he was just too overwhelmed with the changes in his life.

Jules already had his men on the job, looking into the accident case that was reopened recently by the Mayberry Hill Police Department. He had connections and they were already hot on to some leads. Apparently, there had been a witness who had recently come forth after a cold case files program was aired on the local network.

It was bad enough that Amber had to deal with the massive changes to her body during the childbirth process and the after effects of giving birth, but now memories of her past came back to haunt her as she watched herself every day in the mirror. Her more prominent scars since childbirth had her feeling less than sexy. She had already explained that to Jules and he'd tried hard to understand, all the while, feeling contempt for the person, or persons, responsible. He would find that suspect, even if it was the last thing he did.

He loved Amber, more than he'd desired any woman in his life. He couldn't imagine his life without her. A vein throbbed in his temple at the mere thought of losing her again—even emotionally. They'd gotten so far in their relationship since they rekindled what they'd once had—and now this.

"I love you, Amber. I love all of you and I want you to know that you are the most beautiful woman I've had the honor of being with. You're so caring and thoughtful, kind and have a heart of gold." It was true and he loved everything else about her, too.

Her beautiful, large, almond-shaped eyes, framed with long, thick, dark lashes and her heart-melting smile, always ready to brighten a room or cheer up anybody who needed it.

"Not to mention, you're the best mother in the world. You do your work with love and warmth twenty-four-seven. You're amazing, you know that?" he said softly, as he tilted her chin up to look deeply into her eyes.

"Th-thank you, Jules. You're wonderful. Sometimes, I feel as if I don't des—"

"No. Don't say it. You deserve everything good in life, Amber. God knows you've paid the price. Nothing good in life comes easy, remember that. I'm here for you. My family is here for you."

"I know," she said, her voice filled with emotion. "Jules, I'm just so...worked up right now...so on edge. I really want us to be...close but...I need to relax. I wish I had something to help me to relax, Jules. I just wish..."

"Listen, I've got something for you," he said, pulling her gently in his direction. He leaned down and reached into the side of his luggage and pulled out a gift set that contained some sensuous body massage oils. He'd had this in mind while on his trip. Amber had always told him that she enjoyed massage therapy in the past but stopped doing it and right now, she didn't trust anybody to get close to her body, to see her scars. There were times when she was okay with her body and other times when her body image issues got the best of her. "Let's go to the guest room," he said gently.

"But, you must be tired, jet-lagged. You just flew in."

"Oh, please. When am I ever beat?"

"That's true." Amber grinned. "You're all work and...all work."

He chuckled. "Besides, I had plenty of time to rest and shower on the plane."

"Oh, yeah, I forgot, you executive folk travel on those Emirate-like flights with gold-plated faucets, private showers and boardrooms up in the sky while you conduct the next business deal..." she playfully teased him.

"And when you're ready, you'll be flying with me on my trips—you and Crystal. I want to take you all over the world on a sightseeing excursion. You said you wanted to visit every continent, remember?"

"You remembered that?" she gushed. The look of surprise on her face was priceless. Amber told him that when he'd first met her, a while back.

"Honey, I don't miss anything when it comes to you. It was supposed to be a surprise, but I think you could use a little cheering up."

She smiled appreciatively.

Jules led Amber into the guest room, a spare room actually, not far from the nursery, with a gorgeous backdrop of the countryside.

Amber got comfortable on the bed while Jules dimmed the light and powered on the musical stand. A romantic classical piece played over the speakers on low volume.

In spite of her inner doubts and bouts of insecurity, the feeling of desire for Jules overwhelmed her. His sexiness in his tailored dark suit unbuttoned and exposing his white shirt and the way his muscular chest filled out in his attire. She admired his broad shoulders and tall frame. Amber couldn't wait to feel his naked hard muscles on his arms and chest again. This time, not stopping from going all the way. Her eyes explored his dark, sexy-as-sin brown eyes and her heart melted into a warm smile.

Oh, Jules.

There was something so magical about his nearness, his presence, his aura. She just couldn't describe it. There was no other man in her life for whom she'd had this intense feeling. Not even her ex. And it was more than just his delicious physical attributes. He was all heart and soul and that was what turned Amber on the most. The way he went out of his way to make her feel special. The way he was so protective of her. It could not have been easy for a man like that to have to wait so long until her body recovered to get intimate. Yet, like a true gentleman, he'd not only waited patiently but made her feel okay about it all.

Amber couldn't wait to see what Jules had in store. Part of her was thrilled yet another part of her was terrified.

Earlier she could see raw hurt glinting in Jules's lovely dark eyes when she hesitated as he slid his warm hand over her scars. There were times when she felt ugly and unappealing but the way he stroked her skin as if she was a princess changed all that. How could she not trust him? He was nothing like her ex. Nothing at all. Not even close. He was everything and more. If she was honest with herself, as much as Jules told her she was beautiful, she'd been tormented by feelings of worthlessness before but not now. She was who she was. And even though each scar reminded her of that dreadful accident that stole her family and brought on her body image issues, she was a new woman. A mother and a wife. A Romero. And she was darned proud of it, too. She felt blessed to be Jules Romero's wife and Crystal's mommy.

"Jules," she said playfully despite her nervousness. "What do you have in mind?"

"Oh nothing. Just a little massage to help you relax." He grinned, a devilish gaze in his dark, beautiful eyes.

"Oh," she responded, heat surging through her body. For the first time in months, Amber felt sexy. It was just the two of them. Alone. She'd just showered prior to Jules's arrival so she felt refreshed. Just as he had done on the plane before landing in Canada.

"Now, just relax, baby, close your eyes and listen to the music." His voice was deep, sensuous and low. His silky voice always caused a sexual reaction in her body. Her thoughts swirled wondering what type of massage he would give her. She tingled from head to toe at the thought of his soft touch on hers again. Her breath quickened and her heart raced like crazy.

Would she stop him again as she had done in the past when he attempted to seduce her—or even undress her? She prayed not. She was so ready. Her body felt electrical currents zapping through her veins.

There was something magical about her tall, dark and sexy husband that captivated her each and every time. Now, she had nothing to worry about. No interruptions. No sore muscles and the fatigue she'd been feeling during the past few months since the baby was born was finally lifted. She felt revitalized. She was feeling more and more like herself. A delicious heat surged through her at the thought of what was to come.

"Okay," she obeyed him. "I'll relax." She drew a deep breath and exhaled all the worries in her mind. Amber enjoyed the scent of his aftershave as he pressed his lips to her neck again.

Her nose caught a hint of the French vanilla candles that Jules had just ignited in the room. That was all part of the ambiance. A romantic massage wouldn't be the same without the soothing ambiance of tea candles to create a luminous effect. Did Jules always think of everything?

Here he was, just fresh from a business trip and even though he rested on the plane, he was ready and pumped to enjoy the night with her.

Jules guided her down slowly on the bed, admiring her body and kissing her shoulder before easing her out of her clothes and then laying a towel over her back as she lay on her front on top of the silky rose-colored bedspread.

Jules unbuttoned his shirt and slid it off so as to get more comfortable, exposing his rock hard abs and muscular chest. A wide grin of approval touched Amber's lips. She couldn't wait to run her hands down his firm flesh.

He then reached over to the bottle of oil and poured some rose elixir in his hand. Hmm, the scent was delicious and relaxing, sweet. Amber had read somewhere that although lavender oil was recommended for relaxation, rose oil was used more for romance and creating that special sensual feeling. That was just what she craved at the moment. Romance with her sexy husband Jules.

"Oh, Jules," Amber groaned with delight as Jules spread the silky warm oil over her back, then with his strong, soft hands, he massaged her flesh using languid strokes to help relax her muscles. She savored the movements of his strong hands over her naked body as he magically relieved the pent-up pressure she had in her body. Jules really knew how to work those wonderful hands of his. Amber visualized his sexy hands exploring more of her body in the most erotic ways imaginable. Excitement exploded in her belly at the deliciously naughty thought.

"Feel good?" he purred in a sexually-charged deep silky voice.

"Hmm, yes," she murmured, her eyes closed as she enjoyed the flow of energy from his lovely hands to her now deeply relaxed body.

"Good!" Jules continued to delight her body.

Oh, my. This romantic massage thingy was the best thing she'd ever experienced. She was feeling wonderfully sedated, sensual.

Gently, Jules slid his lovely hands down to her buttocks and she jolted with surprise. The way he sensuously eased his hands around her flesh sent currents of desire through her. "You okay, baby?" he asked in a low voice.

"Oh, yes. Please continue," Amber murmured, enjoying the experience.

His hands worked their magic over the mound of flesh on her derriere, kneading and caressing while she felt aroused between her thighs, throbbing with want. "Oh, Jules," she cried out to her amazing husband.

"Hmm, glad you like it." He lowered his head and nipped her on her bottom. She felt a tingling sensation slide through her body, enjoying his playfulness.

She didn't know what got into her all of a sudden but her inhibition evaporated. She felt more free, more relaxed, more desirable.

And she was hungry for Jules. Feeling rejuvenated, she turned on the bed to face him.

"What are you doing? I'm not finished with you yet."

"Oh, yes you are, darling," she whispered, wrapping her arms around his neck and pulling him gently to her. She pressed her lips to his and suckled on his sweet lips. He kissed her tenderly, softly sending shivers of delight down her spine. Oh, his lovely kiss was intoxicating. Her body reacted accordingly.

Amber's hands then moved and slid down his firm, muscular chest enjoying the silky feel of his magnificent, solid body. "Oh, baby, I've missed you so much," she cooed.

"Oh, Amber, I've missed you, too. You have no idea how crazy I've been without you," he growled as he held her firmly and kissed her passionately. And not just any passion, it was the type that virtually melted her inside and sent her heartbeat soaring, all her erogenous areas spinning out of control. Her body shuddered uncontrollably. It had been too long since they'd both been intimate and this was their first time with each other as husband and wife.

Her body pulsated anticipating Jules's passionate seduction. He traced the outline of her jaw with his fingers and she tingled at his soft touch. He stroked her sending waves of pleasure through her veins. His soft lips caressed her neck and she arched her back in ecstasy, moaning in her throat.

He then brought his lips back to hers and hungrily devoured hers as she enjoyed the soft eroticism. His tongue slid inside her parted lips and she moaned with pleasure while his hands explored her body. Jules continued to pleasure her, next he nibbled on her earlobe while his hands squeezed her rounded hips. She desperately wanted to feel him inside her more than anything.

Jules moved down toward her naked breasts and she was turned on by the way he cupped her breast while teasing her hard nipple with his thumb. He moved his lips over to her other breast and slid his tongue over her tight nipple, stroking her gently as she arched her back and gasped uncontrollably with delight. Pulsations rippled through her body as his tongue circled and danced over her nipple, licking and sucking her sensitive bud. The space between her inner thighs pulsed and throbbed in response, desiring his magical penetration.

"Oh, God, you're so beautiful," he groaned in between kissing and sucking on her naked skin.

She whimpered in response, her hands firmly squeezing his muscular back, enjoying his heated passion and the feel of his hard erection pressing through his pants as he leaned over her.

Breathing hard she begged him to take her. Panting, she felt nervous as he slid his tongue further down her body toward her inner thighs. She felt his tongue glide over her scars and drew in a deep breath and closed her eyes then opened them again.

Jules gently moved his hand over her soft hairs between her legs, admiring her body, a wicked grin on his handsome face. He lowered his head to her mound of flesh and slid his tongue out and stroked her gently and she let out a moan of passion, breathing hard. Again, he slid his tongue over her throbbing folds and kissed her gently, then his mouth covered her sex and with more passion he sucked on her sensitive skin, pressing his lips to her inner thighs sending shivers of delight spiraling through her. Amber arched her back on the bed, her hands firmly pressed on his head while he kissed the sensuous swell between her legs, hungrily and then sweetly until he brought her to an orgasmic explosion. Her body trembled and her muscles went into spasms on the bed as he pleasured her to dizzying heights, leaving her breathing hard and fast and incredibly relaxed, deeply sated.

A satisfied grin on his face, Jules used the back of his hand to wipe Amber's love juices dripping from his chin. He then slinked up to Amber and kissed her neck passionately then her lips and they both devoured each other hungrily for a moment, enjoying each other's body. Amber couldn't wait to go down on her husband and she playfully pushed him on his back on the bed, a look of delight on his face as she unzipped his pants and eased him out of his silk boxer shorts, freeing his long, hard erection. She held his throbbing shaft in her hand and stroked it gently up and down, enjoying the low groans coming from his lips. Amber lowered her head to her husband's manhood and extended her wet tongue over his shaft as he moaned in pleasure. She continued to claim his erection between her soft lips, moving up and down his length while moving her hand in motion to the base, sucking hard then soft until he came violently, his warm release spilling over. She moaned with satisfaction.

Amber reached for the condom in the drawer and couldn't wait to rip it open and roll over on Jules's manhood. She wanted him deep inside her. Her body was on fire, sizzling uncontrollably for his sweet invasion. Even though she knew they were both healthy, it seemed like the best way to have intimacy. Besides, she knew it was her only source of birth control—just in case the doc had been wrong about Jules's not being able to impregnate her.

In the romantic candlelit room, they at long last consummated their love. Before long, Jules was inside her, filling her, pleasuring her to soaring heights as he made love to her. Amber tightened around his well-proportioned erection enjoying the feel of him thrusting inside her, moving hard and fast, pounding inside her flesh, shaking the bed and rocking her world. The heat of his passion filled her as he ravenously devoured her with his passion. Amber wrapped her legs around his firm waist and moaned uncontrollably as he pounded with lustful abandon. She could not believe how good Jules felt. What had she been missing out on?

His lovemaking was incredible. Gusts of desire overtook her body. His hardness electrified her. She came, not once, but several times as he pleasured her to carnal heights, loving her body, caressing her and pleasing her with his currents of desire. Oh, God. Jules was an amazing lover. Ecstasy rippled through her entire body.

After she came hard, Jules's body convulsed with orgasmic release as well. Her blood pumped hard and fast in her body as he collapsed on top of her. Both breathing hard and heavy as they embraced each other after their magical experience. Deep sexual gratification assuaged them.

Amber had never experienced such mind-blowing passion that caused a rush of blood to course through her veins like that. She ran her fingers over Jules's taut muscles and sculpted chest, feeling sated and rejuvenated. The pleasure was pure and explosive between them. The chemistry was awesome and unique, especially the way Jules caressed and admired every inch of her body making her feel special and loved in every way. Even *normal*. This was good. This was so good. Her body was pumped. So alive. She felt on top of the world. There could be no other lover like Jules—her incredibly sexy and awesome husband. Her body was still buzzed after their magical love-making while she rested on his muscular chest, listening to the steady beat of his heart, savoring the feeling of satisfaction Jules left her with. So this was what it really felt like to be Mrs. Jules Romero.

CHAPTER THIRTEEN

The next morning, Amber woke up to the sound of the baby cooing in the next room, the scent of baby wash and a man's voice singing—or trying to sing—Twinkle Twinkle Little Star. She felt deeply rested and re-energized. Jules was obviously with the baby. *Oh, no. Crystal needs feeding.* There were still some things daddies were not equipped for.

She whipped the sheets off her and sprung out of bed. Amber grabbed her silky pink dressing gown from the chair by the bed and threw it over her. She glanced at the time. Crystal was sleeping through the night these days but it was time for her to eat. Amber quickly went into the washroom to brush her teeth and freshen up as she prepared to go to the nursery in the next room to feed the baby. Actually, since Crystal was officially three-months-old, she had graduated from baby to "infant" now. Amber could not believe her little baby was officially an infant. Imagine that! It was as if yesterday she was born. My, the time did fly as days turned into weeks then weeks to months.

A smile curved Amber's lips at the lovely memory of Jules last night and their lustful night together.

A part of Amber felt a burning guilt over not telling Jules who Crystal's biological father was. She wondered if she should let him know. But she didn't want to spoil the momentum. Did it really matter? Jules was Crystal's father. Born to Amber and Jules in wedlock. What else could possibly matter? It wasn't as if Crystal's biological father would ever be in the picture. It just wasn't possible at this point. Or was it?

Why was it that when everything seemed to be looking hopeful, there was that stomach-sinking sensation over something about to happen to change all that?

Think positive, Amber. You're in a better place in your life. Let the positive energies of the universe flow through you and in your life. Stop creating so much unnecessary drama in your head.

Amber had to learn to switch off any negativity that sometimes crept into her mind at the most unexpected moments. Dr. Danye was right! As soon as she switched her thinking, her mood and sense of well-being would follow suit. Life was just too short to be creating head drama about something that might never happen. "Live in the moment" were words Dr. Danye often prescribed to her during her therapy sessions with him. And that she would do.

Amber finished in the bathroom and tied the belt around her robe to go into the nursery. And when she walked in through the open French doors of the room Jules and his brother Dion had so artfully decorated for Crystal, her heart melted and a wide grin curled her lips.

Jules was sitting in the rocking chair, holding Crystal, an empty milk bottle on the side table beside them. Amber had expressed her breast milk and left it in the fridge so Crystal could be fed by the nanny in case of emergency or if Amber was on her medical appointments or unable to for some reason. The milk would only be left for twenty-four hours at time and Amber would end up using it beforehand to feed Crystal. But it looked as if doting daddy Jules had already beat her to it.

She folded her arms across her chest and leaned against the doorframe watching him rock and sing to their daughter. What a golden moment. Amber hurried to her room, grabbed her smartphone and returned to the nursery to take a few snapshots of this tender moment of bonding between Crystal and her daddy, something for her baby's photo album and scrapbook. Memories to treasure.

"Nice going, Daddy," Amber said, admiring the memorable vision before her.

Jules looked up, his dark, handsome gaze locking with hers as Crystal rested comfortably on his chest while he gently rubbed her back. He smiled lovingly. "Hey, what are daddies for?"

"You're a wonderful daddy, you know that?" she said. "I thought you would still be jet-lagged."

"Nothing could make me too tired to do my daddy duties. Our daughter will get nothing but the best from her parents. She's even got your beautiful eyes," Jules said, admiring his daughter.

Amber's heart squeezed in her chest. That feeling again. She wished she could say that the baby had something for Jules. But she didn't. Crystal looked like everything Amber was. Amber wondered what Crystal would look like if she were a true Romero. Would she have inherited Jules's mesmerizing eyes, his strong cheekbones and his height when she grew older? Amber would never know. What if, God forbid, Crystal ended up looking more like her biological father? The thought caused Amber's breath to pause.

"You should have seen our daughter this morning when she woke up," Jules continued, unaware of Amber's inner turmoil. "She had a riot looking in that mirror there," Jules continued, stroking Crystal's soft hair.

"Oh, not that funny mirror," Amber teased. Crystal's dear uncle Dion had gifted her one of those lovely child-safe activity mirrors and Jules insisted that it stay pinned at the side of the crib for Crystal to entertain herself looking at her face, exploring those adorable chubby cheeks of hers. She was at the stage where she was fascinated with visuals.

Amber looked around the bursting-at-the-seams nursery. The Romero family was nothing short of kind and generous in their time with Crystal while Jules was away on business. Their affection was endless.

"Grandpa Toni was a hoot yesterday," Amber said as she sat down beside Jules and Crystal.

"Yeah?"

"Oh, yeah," Crystal sighed. "He could not stop singing to her." Amber grinned and shook her head. "Well, I know where your talent came from."

"Are you trying to be funny, Mrs. Romero?"

Amber smiled. "I'm just saying, you Romeros have a very unique...um, let's just say...*style* of singing, that's all." She leaned over to him and planted a sweet kiss on his cheek. "And I love you for it, Jules. Crystal couldn't stop giggling yesterday. You know your family has been nothing but wonderful accepting me and Crystal," she added, her voice trailing off slightly.

"Hey," Jules reproached, "you and Crystal are my family, their family. There's nothing more to accept. When are you going to stop regarding me as her stepdad? I'm her father. Period."

"I know. I just can't help but feeling that...well, they know. They all know that when we met up again, I was already pregnant."

"So?"

"So..." Amber felt her throat close off with overwhelming emotion. Was it her hormones? Oh, heaven help her if she was going through post-partum depression. She prayed not. But she really must stop being so sensitive and self-conscious.

"Listen, Amber. You need to know that we, they don't think that way. No one in my family thinks that way. Wait a minute! Has someone said anything to you?" Jules's voice sounded defensive and sharp.

"N-no! No, of c-course not."

"Good. Then please drop it, okay, baby?" he said gently. His voice so soothing, smooth and filled with warmth. "I know you've been through a lot feeling self-conscious and everything, but trust me, there's no need around here. You and Crystal are a part of me now. I would lay down my life for you in a heartbeat. You're my family. That's all anyone has to know."

But Crystal wasn't his blood and for the first time since their marriage, she felt a piercing pain of regret over it. She really wished Jules was the father. She really prayed that no one or nothing could bring up anything in the future to tarnish what they were building. The painful memory of what happened to her was all too fresh in her mind when the kids at her school found out that she wasn't really her stepfather's daughter. Amber was made to feel like trash in her past. And now, looking at her angelic, chubby-cheeked, innocent-eyed, beautiful daughter caused a gut-wrenching feeling to creep into her soul. She would die if anything like that happened to her precious princess. But Jules was right. The Romeros were not judgmental. Lord knew they've had their own reputations grinded through the gossip mill by the media in the past.

And Amber and Crystal were part of the Romero family. They were Romeros. She would deal with anything that came her way—if it ever did. Until then...

"I'm taking Crystal to the café today."

"You are?"

"Yeah, my aunt told me everyone has been asking to see her. I thought it would be nice to stop by for a few minutes and see the old gang. I really kind of miss them even though I'm on maternity leave."

"I wish I could go with you but I have an important meeting later this morning," Jules said. "You know, you don't have to go back to work."

"Jules, are you saying you want me to be a stay-at-home mom? What if I enjoy running the café with my aunt?"

He looked into her eyes and her body responded. He didn't have to say anything, it was just the way his sexy, dark eyes filled with passion captivated her. A grin of amusement curled his sweet lips. It was the look of I-don't-believe-that-for-a-second.

"All right, I confess. Maybe, I don't want to go back to work right now. And I could think of a hundred different reasons why I don't enjoy working with my aunt, but I do want to take a break and show off little Crystal in her new decked out stroller Toni and Shelly got for her."

Jules laughed. "Yeah, just be careful with my daughter. I'll have our driver take you guys there and wait for you."

"But what if I don't want to have a driver with me?"

"I think it's a good idea, Amber."

Was Jules going to be overprotective of her and the baby forever? Part of Amber appreciated his thoughtfulness but she really craved her independence. She didn't mind driving herself to wherever she and the baby had to go. Plenty of new moms do it all the time.

"Yes, sir, Daddy!" Amber finally responded, giving in. He'd have his way. Just this once.

CHAPTER FOURTEEN

"So, big guy, where's Amber and Crystal? Thought you'd bring them in to the office today," Dion said to his brother, Jules, as he propped up he knee, leaning back in the chair opposite Jules's desk at the headquarters of the Mayberry Hill Family Research Center.

It had been a few months since Jules Romero's company had officially taken over ownership of the not-for-profit organization and added it to his portfolio of family-friendly affordable health centers in the province. As his grandfather would preach to him and his brothers, it wasn't always about ways to make money. It was encouraged to think of ways to give back and help others in need. Jules could certainly relate to a time in his youth when he was in need before he became one of the wealthiest men in the universe.

He was getting ready to meet with his newly hired executive director who would oversee the organization in his place while he oversaw operations of the R.M. Fitness facilities. Did Jules really have his hand in too many projects? Amber had spoken to him about it before and he'd playfully tell her there'd be plenty of time to rest when he was dead.

Jules sighed, multitasking as he flipped through some paperwork on his desk to sign left by his assistant Brenda. "Amber's at the café with Crystal. She wanted to see her colleagues and her aunt."

"Ah, I see." Dion did not sound impressed. "You sure you trust her around Aunt Mavis?"

"Hanz, our driver, is with her. You know he's a good detective and bodyguard. I told him not to leave them alone."

"Good thinking."

"So what did our men come up with? You said you had some concerns over her aunt and some other people in her life." Jules dropped the files on his desk and looked pointedly at his brother, pressing his hands together as he leaned back in his leather executive chair. He was anxious to tie up some loose ends surrounding his wife and now his baby. He wanted to be sure Amber was not in harm's way given the new developments in the accident case surrounding the deaths of her parents.

"Well, Miss Mavis is one unique character, I'll tell you that," Dion said.

"Why do you say that? What have they uncovered?" Jules knew in his heart that Mavis was a bit off, the way she would glare at Amber when her back was turned and just her aloof manner. At first he chalked it up to her personality but then he wondered about her. She had pressed, almost bullied, Amber not to dig too far into the investigation surrounding the demise of Amber's parents, her own sister being Amber's mother. They were apparently not very close growing up and then when Amber became an orphan, Mavis wasn't too thrilled having to take over guardianship. Poor Amber had to feel as if she was a burden, losing her family like that.

Jules was fiercely protective of Amber. She meant the world to him. Just thinking about how fragile she'd become since the accident, yet strong at the same time, willing to put her neck out to save a friend, or hold her own ground. Always trying to be independent and stay intact. She was the real deal. Humble and sweet. He'd teach a lesson to anyone who tried to step into her life and mess it up any more than it already had been since the tragedy that befell her in the past.

"Well," Dion continued. "You know your wife is seeing that therapist, right?"

"So?" Jules was defensive but then mellowed. This was his brother, Dion, he was talking with. "What about it?"

"Well, we have reason to believe that Mavis spoke to the therapist on several occasions regarding Amber's memory."

"Her memory?"

"Yeah, her memory of that night."

"What are they getting at?"

Dion heaved a sigh as if wondering how to tell his brother whatever he had to say. "Man, something's just not adding up."

"Amber told me about her selective amnesia. There's nothing that can bring her memory back of that night, so why does it matter?"

"Oh, but there might be."

"You mean there could be a trigger that could make her remember?"

Dion shrugged, flipping through a magazine that he just swiped off the counter beside him. "Anything is possible."

"You think Mavis might have had something to with the accident?" Jules was dubious.

"I know the cops won't rule anything out. It wasn't as if Mavis and her sister were close and loving. There must be some rivalry or something macabre going on. They're still working on things. I just thought I'd keep you posted. You know we need to keep these things under wraps. Not too much phone discussion."

"Yeah, I know." Jules knew all too well. The brothers always kept a close eye on the safety of those around them and rarely spoke on the phone as to certain sensitive information. And he knew something was bugging him but couldn't quite pinpoint it. The day Amber told him she thought she was being followed while going to the therapist's office raised his defenses even more and he started to have security shadow her from a safe and discreet distance.

The Romeros might be popular but they also had haters amongst their so-called rivals. They left nothing to chance. Just having money and power made them anonymous enemies not to mention the crazies that stalked people like him in his position and those close to him. The investigative agency the Romeros used was highly discreet and very few people knew about the boys inside at the detective firm outside of the family circle. They liked to keep it that way.

Not that the vigilance they took was without merit. In the past, the Romeros were victims of corporate espionage and a kidnap attempt. Besides, Romero was a Spanish name for protector. And Jules had no trouble living up to his surname, especially where his wife and child were concerned. Then another thought bit into Jules. Did this somehow have anything to do with Crystal's biological father? He somehow hoped it didn't. It couldn't. Amber said the father was out of the picture. He decided he was going to respect her privacy until she was good and ready to tell him the truth. The last thing he wanted, as tempted as he was, would be to question her timing and go behind her back to dig up information on this dude. Amber said she would tell him soon enough. He would leave it at that for now.

Jules rubbed his stubble thinking about the explosive revelation his brother Carl discovered about his own wife, Venus. Oh, God, did all women have secrets and skeletons in their past?

There was a knock on his office door. "Come in," Jules called, obviously distracted.

"Good morning, boss!" Brenda, his cheerful executive assistant, came in with some posters in her hand. She was a petite Asian woman with lovely shoulder-length, dark hair and a beautiful smile. She rarely frowned, no matter how hectic things got around the office. Jules was grateful to have her on his team. He had it in mind to promote her. She was excellent at handling many projects on her own and was well-educated and fluent in several languages. Oh, the wonders of overseeing human resources. No wonder Amber told him to slow down and relax and take a break once in a while. He was always working overtime—especially in his mind, thinking of his next strategies, promoting, organizing, delegating. It never stopped. But oh, last night was deeply relaxing. Jules thought of the intense, heated passion he'd experienced with Amber, and that mellowed him a lot. He was ready for everything. He couldn't wait to be alone with Amber again, especially after last night when she opened up to him emotionally.

Amber. From the second he got into the office, his mind ran on her a dozen times in between meetings and business correspondence. He could not get enough of his wife.

"What have you got for me, Brenda?" Jules said, leaning back in his chair while Dion acknowledged her before getting back to reading his magazine.

"Oh, some good news, sir."

"Good, I can never get enough of that."

"Well, you know the Spring Magazine often nominates a few model families to be Family of the Year; it's sort of a monthly thing to inspire and encourage other families."

"Yeah, I'm familiar with Spring Magazine," Jules responded cautiously. What was Brenda getting at? She seemed to have a wicked grin on her face.

"Well, news got around with your um...labor vows and how devoted you two were in having your baby and well, determined to get married and well..." Brenda hesitated, something she rarely did.

"Spill it, Brenda," Jules said quietly with a grin on his face and a puzzled expression.

"Well, they've sort of nominated you, Amber and Crystal—after I submitted your name," she added looking sheepish. "I have a friend who works in their art department. He told me the good news this morning. They're getting ready to send you the forms."

"Oh, no."

"Oh, yes."

"No, Brenda. I'm on the board of the Family Center."

"And that's okay. It's not like that magazine has anything to do with us. The point is, boss, your wedding vows in the labor room thing was so hot when it hit the local news that day."

Jules frowned. But that news story had been carefully edited to not include the identity of said parents—meaning Jules and Amber. The reporter, who happened to be a friend of his sister-in-law, Blue, a former reporter herself, had respected their privacy.

"I'll need to get your answer," Brenda added, "like, in an hour."

"An hour? Why so soon?"

"Well, they're running behind schedule. And...um...they told me that the couple they had slated for this month had just...um...filed for divorce."

"They did?" Jules looked incredulous then sighed heavily. "Well, they might not be the only ones. Amber might want to divorce me, too, if she thinks I'm pushing her into the limelight."

Brenda grinned and shook her head. She seemed amused by her boss's wry sense of humor.

"I'm not sure if Amber will go for it," Jules continued. "Besides, what would be involved?"

"Oh, nothing too inconvenient. Just posing for a family portrait." Brenda unrolled some sample posters, with Dion's assistance on the desk, and showed Jules.

"You see here. Look at all these wonderful hall of fame like portraits. We've had people at the center participate as well. Each one so different and beautiful."

"I see," Jules said, looking at the various family pictures. "Okay, I'll talk with Amber about it, and if she's good with it, it's a go."

Brenda beamed. "Awesome! I'll talk to their PR department to get this set up. It will be just in time for our own Annual Family Center BBQ."

"That's coming up soon, isn't it? Doesn't leave us much time, does it?" Jules said. "Fine," he agreed. "Let me confirm with Amber."

"Great. You won't be sorry." Brenda gathered the material from his desk and whisked out of the office as quickly as she came in.

"Well, seems like you'll be having your hands full, bro," Dion commented with a grin.

"Yeah. Let me call Amber. And keep me posted on those developments."

"Sure thing."

Jules immediately called Amber after Dion left the office. Amber actually sounded pleased about the Family of the Month nod to her little household.

Over the phone, Amber told him it would be wonderful and that Crystal would have this to look back on. She couldn't wait to break the news to her aunt, who was sitting close beside her at the café. Amber appeared to be in good spirits. That made Jules feel settled inside.

Well, as long as Amber was good with the Family of the Month recognition, Jules was good with it as well.

CHAPTER FIFTEEN

The following day, Amber was seated opposite her therapist.

"You're doing very well, Amber," Dr. Danye said, beaming. "Keep up the great work."

"Thanks, doc. But I couldn't have done it without your help." Amber prepared to get up from her seat. She was finished with her session.

"Well, you've been doing all the work, Amber. I'm very proud of you."

"The authorities wanted to see if I could give them a little more information to coincide with some new evidence. At least I'm remembering a little bit more now. It's still hard for me, but the police were talking about using a hypnotherapist. I told them I was seeing you for my regular therapy, but I know that's not your area of expertise."

"Well, just go with your gut. You know how I feel about those sorts of things," he said, adjusting his glasses on his nose. He got up again, grabbing his walking cane. "And don't forget to bring your little one the next time you visit."

"I will. Oh, and before I forget," Amber said, reaching into her Coach tote bag. "Here's a copy of a brochure my husband has been working on. I thought you might like to put it in the reception area for some of your patients. We're having a barbecue at the family center. Of course, you don't have to tell them it's from one of your patients." Amber winked.

Dr. Danye grinned. "I'll put this up."

Dr. Danye often displayed colorful family-friendly brochures and other freebies in his waiting area for people to peruse.

"Imagine that," she said almost at a whisper. "Years ago when you first treated me, I didn't have a family," she continued, hot tears stinging her eyes. Her voice broke off with choking emotion. She was feeling overwhelmed again. But not in a bad way. She just couldn't describe the miracle that captured her life after such horrible tragedy and rejection. Her appreciation to the universe was sincere and humbling. She never thought she would ever be "normal" again. She'd been rejected as an illegitimate kid, then orphaned, scarred for life emotionally and physically, feeling worthless, trying to compensate. And now…it would seem that she'd been given a second chance.

"Well, you deserve happiness, Amber. You really do."

"Thanks, doc." Amber glanced at her watch. "Oh, no. I better get going. I have an appointment at the hairdresser and then I have to pick up Crystal from my in-laws."

"Well, I don't want to keep you." Dr. Danye smiled warmly. "Best of luck, Amber."

"Thank you."

Amber grabbed her tote bag and headed out the door, glancing around in the reception area as she walked out. There was no man in disguise. No one following her. Yet, an odd feeling crept into her stomach. It was just a bunch of nerves. Wasn't that what the doc told her? She washed the doubt from her mind. She was going to focus on making Jules proud at the family barbecue. She felt like the First Lady of the Family Center! Image was everything. Her husband was, after all, the new owner.

* * *

Jules sat in his office at the Family Center tapping away on his laptop when someone knocked on the door. "Enter," he said, not looking up from the screen.

Brenda, his assistant, appeared anxious.

"What is it? You look like you've seen a ghost," he noted. "Scrap that. You look like a ghost, the color has drained from you face. What's wrong?"

"Oh, Jules. I...I'm so sorry. It's all my fault. I hope Amber doesn't see it. I'm trying to speak to the magazine's IT department to do something about it."

"About what?" Jules felt his blood pump hard. Why did he have the sinking his wife may be in danger?

"I...well, have you seen the Spring Magazine's home page?"

Jules quickly switched over to the company's home screen page. There was the image of the month of Jules, Amber and little Crystal in that PR pose for Family of the Month. "What the...?"

Brenda bowed her head in shame.

Below the picture there were rude comments he'd rather not take in. But he couldn't help but scan the screen. One comment in particular, grated on his nerves:

"Some family of the month. He's not even the baby's daddy—LOL!"-K.P.

Who the heck was KP?

There were mostly congratulatory comments but the one caustic comment seemed to stand out and Jules's gut clenched. Anger seethed through his blood. He felt his temperature boil to the point where he felt as if he was in an inferno.

"Damn!"

"I'm sorry this happened, Jules."

"So am I." Jules's tone of voice was razor sharp and pointed. "Get their team on the phone. The last thing I need is for the local press to get wind of this. They'd distort things and that would really piss me off." He then asked Brenda to call his family's press secretary, Pamela, to prepare some damage control statements just in case it was necessary.

The last thing he'd want was for the media to go buzzing about who the biological father of Amber's child was. Damn it! He didn't even know the answer to *that* question.

* * *

Amber sat at the salon, trying to enjoy her treatment. Her mind was on little Crystal. She really needed the break but she was always wondering how her baby was doing. She knew Crystal was in good hands at the Romero residence with her grandparents so she tried to squash any worries.

"Honey, what's this?" Luckella, the hairdresser, said to Amber after she'd finished with her conditioner treatment.

"What's what?" Amber's curiosity was piqued. She had given Luckella a copy of the brochure, inviting her to the community barbecue and had told her about her upcoming photo shoot at Spring Magazine.

Luckella had, of course, gone online to see the photo op on the Spring Magazine website from her smartphone. She then showed the display of her phone to Amber. "Why haters gotta hate like that?" Luckella commented.

Amber felt sick to her stomach. A wave of nausea slammed into her gut. "What?" she said, her hair still dripping. She squeezed her eyes shut then re-opened them.

"You want me to reply to that asshole?" Luckella got her phone ready to rip him (or her) apart.

"No. N-no." Amber couldn't think. She was disgraced. Horrified. Who would have written such a nasty remark?

* * *

An hour later, Jules had his shirtsleeves rolled up. Spring Magazine was on the phone with him apologizing. They knew how generous and influential the Romero family was. It was a small community magazine and often featured locals in the area but had never had this happen on the website before.

The IT team from the magazine traced the IP address from the so-called anonymous commenter.

"Well, you know we have the person's information if you're interested."

"I am," he said, anger curdling his blood. If he ever got his hands on the lowlife who did this.

"Do you know a Mavis Murray?"

Jules almost wasn't surprised but the confirmation still came as a rude awakening. He grabbed his jacket off the counter and told Dion to meet him at the café.

* * *

"Did you have anything to do with Amber's parents' deaths?" Jules challenged Mavis later at the Murray Café. Mavis stood by the window of her office, her chin up, her arms secured across her chest.

"I admit I made a mistake and wrote that…comment. But I…," Mavis appeared shaken and sat down in the chair beside her in her back office at the Murray Café. "But I swear to you, I wasn't the driver of the car who killed my sister and her husband. I…I wasn't." she stammered. Her eyes barely met with Jules.

"Well, you certainly went out of your way to make Amber's life miserable. Why?"

"It's not what it appears. I'm so sorry. You won't tell Amber, will you?"

Jules exchanged an incredulous glance with his brother who stood in the corner like a bad cop while Jules continued to interrogate Mavis.

Dion slid his hand in his pocket and extracted an old newspaper clipping to Jules. Jules took the paper and showed it to Mavis.

Her eyes widened. "H-how did you find this?"

"It wasn't hard, Mavis." Jules's voice softened a fraction but he was still riled up. "I understand your…disappointment in your fiancé."

Mavis snapped the picture from him and glared at it. It was an engagement announcement in the Mayberry Hill Times, over thirty years ago. A picture of Amber's stepfather and a young woman—Mavis.

Mavis swallowed hard and threw the picture on the table. Her lips were thinned but trembling. "Yes, we were supposed to get married. But…" she paused, drawing in a deep breath. "My sister decided my fiancé was good enough for her so she took him instead. How do you think it makes me feel looking at…Amber year in and year out? She was a reminder."

"She was an innocent party to this. She's not even the product of their marriage. You know that."

"I know, but she still looks just like her. My sister. I despise looking at her, okay? It hurts me to look at her every day. And then when her parents got killed, I was forced to look after her."

"You really need to get help, Mavis," Jules said as sincerely as he could.

"I'm not the one with the memory issues. She can't even remember anything that happened that night."

Jules shot Mavis a scorching glance. His patience was stretched to the limit. No more mister nice guy. "You need to get help," he repeated in a controlled voice. "Then you need to stay far away from my wife from now on. Find another job, too. Do you hear me?"

Mavis responded to Jules by glaring at him.

Jules was about to walk away when something in his gut pulled him in a different direction. It was something Mavis said. Mavis had mentioned she wasn't the one driving the car in the crash that killed her sister and her sister's family. What did she mean by that? Something else Amber told Jules was also making things fit into place.

"How old was Amber when she started her therapy?" he asked Mavis. He had his smartphone out of his pocket ready to call JoJo from the agency. Something really wasn't adding up. He didn't like the sinking feeling he was getting at all. But his gut was telling him that Mavis was telling the truth. She was not the one driving the car but she sure as hell could have been in the elusive car.

Just then, his cell phone rang and he answered it. "Yeah?"

"I've got some strong leads. We managed to track down that mystery witness that came forth recently but then backed out of telling the cops everything," his source reported to him over the phone. "The guy was some storm watcher who took snapshots at the time of the accident. Saw the whole thing before he came down with a sudden case of amnesia. It's not good news, Jules."

"I'll be right there," Jules confirmed with his source before finishing his call. "Better let the boys down at the division know what's going on," Jules then said to his brother, Dion.

CHAPTER SIXTEEN

An hour later, after her session at the beauty parlor, Amber felt anything but beautiful. The ugliness of the day clawed its way in. That awful remark. And Jules. Poor Jules. It had to be someone in the family circle who knew about Crystal's real father.

She received a text from her aunt Mavis to meet her at the apartment above the café so she decided to go straight there.

Amber walked up the steps, feeling dreary. Was Aunt Mavis behind the comments? Was she going to apologize? She saw a missed called from Jules but decided she would call him right after she found out what her aunt had to say.

Amber knew she would burst into tears if she spoke to Jules. She should have been upfront about Amber's real father. Was Jules disappointed in her?

She finally reached her old unit and was surprised to see the door ajar. "Aunt Mavis?" Amber continued inside.

She turned around feeling something was a bit off; the place seemed eerily abandoned. But it was too late to act, the door slammed shut behind her.

CHAPTER SEVENTEEN

"You sure you've got this all figured out?" Dion turned to Jules as Jules pushed on the gas pedal of his SUV hoping to reach Amber's old apartment in time. He tried her cell phone again. No answer. That just wasn't like her.

"Yeah," Jules said, distracted. His gaze blazed into the busy road as he weaved through traffic. He'd already called the cops to check out the address at her apartment.

"It all makes sense," Jules said, "Mavis was having an affair with a married man. They were driving from their cottage around the same time Amber and her family were. If they'd done the right thing and stayed at the scene, dude's wife would have taken him to the cleaners with evidence of his unfaithfulness. He and his mistress are in a crash so late into the early hours of the night from his secluded cottage."

"I hear you. But hospital records didn't report anyone coming in around that time with injuries consistent with a car accident."

"Yeah, but he was injured all right."

"Good thing we got the goods on that storm watcher. The vehicle was a white BMW."

"Of course, the guy was loaded so he could have any private mechanic fix it. And as far as his injuries…"

"The man obviously went out of town have his leg operated on. But got a botched job. That's why he ended up with a permanent limp."

"According to that report, he told the officials he was involved in a fishing accident. Yeah, right. Been limping ever since."

"But didn't Amber tell you her doc had the injury from childhood?"

"He had an injury from childhood but not that one. Amber started seeing him around the same time he started using a walking cane."

"So I don't get it. Why did he start treating her?"

"He wasn't a real doctor! He was a fake! And he wanted to make sure her memory never came back," Jules said in a deadly low voice, anger seething through him. Just the mere thought of that hypocritical creep getting near Amber made his blood boil in his veins.

"That's creepy all right. Man, I hope we're wrong. Anyway, if Mavis was in the car with him, she'd be charged as an accessory to manslaughter."

"And so be it," Jules added. "And you know we're not wrong. Our boys were spot-on with the investigation." Jules tried Amber's cell phone again, obsessing over why she wasn't answering, praying she was safe.

Dion flipped through some of the printed notes given to him from their source. "You're right, he's not even a real psychologist. He's a FAKE, that son-of-a-bitch! He flunked out of school somewhere in Europe."

"Maybe that's why the coward didn't want to fess up to the hit and run. He knew his career and his life would be done AND his marriage. But that's too damn bad. Amber's parents and brother are dead. And it's all his fault." The memory of losing his own mother came back and haunted him at that moment. But he could not even begin to imagine how horrible it would be to lose his entire family.

And Amber's body. Her beautiful skin fractured, scarred for life all because of that idiot. He would pay. If it was the last thing he'd do, Jules would make sure. Danye was going to pay.

CHAPTER EIGHTEEN

"Oh, God, you scared me," Amber said, her heart jackhammering in her chest. She was afraid. Very afraid. But she wasn't going to let him know. "W-what are you doing here anyway, Dr. Danye?"

"I....I think we need to talk, Amber."

Amber backed away slowly against the kitchen sink, her eyes scanning for anything to use in her defense. She didn't' have a good feeling at all. "D-did you send me the text message to meet you here, pretending to be my aunt?"

"I'm sorry. Yes, I did." The old man limped two steps towards Amber with his cane, then he paused. "Amber, I know you would probably have it figured out sooner or later."

"Figured out what?"

"That it was me who was driving that car that night."

Amber's eyes widened, her heart exploded in her chest. She couldn't breathe. She struggled to suck in air. "Y-you?" she mouthed. Her heart was beating frantically in her chest.

He nodded slowly.

Amber was cornered. Her cell phone buzzed over by the table on the floor where her bag was dropped after the door slamming startled her. It was no use. Dr. Danye was too close.

"It's okay, Amber. I'm not going to hurt you. I promise."

"Like you didn't mean to hurt my family?"

"I deserve that."

"But why? I don't get it. Why?" Amber's voice was strangled. The pain was too great. Dr. Danye did this to her. He was the one to scar her for life! To take away her family. And he sped off without so much as stopping? It was all too much for her to take in.

Oh, Jules. Where was Jules? Why hadn't she answered his call? Dr. Danye was probably going to kill her to silence her for good. It was obvious now why he'd been treating her—to make sure she never remembered what happened that night. To act on things if her memory ever returned. He hadn't been treating her, he'd been monitoring her for his own interests.

"It's not what it looks like, Amber."

"Are you even a real psychologist?"

"Well. No. I'm not." He looked eerily apologetic. "But that doesn't matter now. Let's worry about you." His expression was unreadable.

Amber shook her head, her mind still reeling in disbelief. "You left the scene of an accident," she said, her voice cracking with emotion. "How could you do that? I could have died as well."

"I'm truly sorry, Amber. And to your parents and your brother. But they are dead. I had my life to think about. I was a coward for the way I left, but I was glad you had survived. I know it seems as if I started seeing you to make sure you couldn't identify me but that's not the case. I really wanted to see if I could help you move forward. I knew you needed a good listener at that time, so-"

"Just as long as I couldn't identify you and put you behind bars," she finished his declaration. Her voice sounded more harsh and was laced with sarcasm. Suddenly her grief was replaced with blind anger.

"Amber," he said moving closer to her, backing her against the sink. "I-"

Before he could finish his sentence, the door was kicked open and Jules and Dion stormed in. "Stay the hell away from her!" Jules made his way in a lightning fast motion and grabbed Dr. Danye, slamming him against the wall. "Stay away from my wife."

"Jules!" Amber cried out.

The police arrived seconds later. Everything had happened so fast.

CHAPTER NINETEEN

Amber sat at the police station, her head resting on Jules's chest as he stroked her hair. They had both given the detectives their report and Dr. Danye had confessed to the crime. But somehow Amber felt as if things were far from over. She'd been betrayed by someone she trusted, not once but twice.

Her aunt was charged as an accessory after the fact. Amber couldn't get her heart or her head around this information. Her body felt cold as a melting icecap in the Arctic. Her breathing was shallow. She was numb with shock, yet burning with anger.

On another note, the police also informed Amber that the mystery man she reported to have been following her was, in fact, an investigator who was on to Dr. Danye and his phony practice. At least there was confirmation that she wasn't going crazy after all thinking she was being followed.

Amber was feeling utterly drained and her energies spent. She just couldn't wait to get back home to see her little gem, Crystal.

"Okay, Mr. Romero, you and your wife are free to go." One of the detectives had come into the interrogation room to give them the green light.

"Good," Jules said, kissing Amber's forehead. "We're more than ready to go." Jules sounded as drained as Amber felt. It had been a long week and she could sense it was going to be longer.

* * *

"How are you feeling?" Jules asked Amber in a controlled voice later that night. She sat up in bed. Jules was sitting up in the chair at her bedside.

"Tired," she said softly. She was feeling more weary than anything else. She knew what was on Jules's mind. "I really don't want to talk anymore about…the past…the accident. I don't want to relive that…"

"I understand, Amber. I don't want you to." His voice was soft but his eyes were filled with pain and disappointment. She could see it. She could feel it.

"I want to know who Crystal's father is, Amber. I need you to tell me everything. I don't want any more surprises. I need you to tell me."

"Jules, I…I…I don't know who he is."

Jules's eyes widened in shock. "You don't know? How could you not know?"

Amber whipped off the sheets and got up, heaving a sigh. "I didn't want to tell you, or anyone for that matter. I swore to myself and to my then unborn child that she was going to have a normal life."

"You're not making any sense, Amber." Jules leaned forward with his elbows pressed on his knees. Even in this moment of frustration, he looked so handsome and appealing, his ripped muscles on his bare arms and chest, wearing nothing but silk pajama bottoms.

"Jules," Amber said, tears filling her eyes. "This is very hard for me to tell you. But…when I was little, after the accident, kids would tease me and tell me that no man would want me or touch me. I felt like a reject, a loser, a monster because of my scars. Can you imagine growing up hearing that?"

Jules frowned, feeling her turmoil and her pain.

"I loved you so much but I was terrified that you'd be grossed out by my disfigurement."

"I would never do that, you know that now," he assured softly.

"I know," she said. "Anyway, I met Rex after you and I broke off. I thought Rex and I would get married. Well, he turned out to be a real jerk and when he was no longer in the picture, I still had the burning desire to be a parent so…I went to the Mayberry Hill Fertility Clinic."

Jules looked up, stunned. "What did you say?"

"I...I had IVF treatment to get pregnant. I didn't want to go through that painful rejection again by a lover and I wanted to be a parent so badly." Amber hugged herself looking out the window at the dark sky and moonlight.

Jules got up. "You what? You had in vitro? That's your secret? That's it?"

Amber nodded slowly. "Can you imagine the shame and disgrace if people found out? They would laugh at me and tell me that they were right about no man wanting me and having to go to a clinic to get pregnant. I know this is all probably in my mind but I've been dealt with such cruelty that I didn't want to give any juice to the gossip mill. It wasn't anybody's business and I didn't want people making fun of my daughter because she wasn't conceived naturally. That she was a product of artificial insemination."

"Oh, honey! But so many couples go that route. It's nothing to be ashamed of, Amber."

"Not if you're voted the winner of most-likely-to-never-be-touched-by-a-man," she replied.

"Ouch. I see your point, Amber. It's nobody's business, and you can't let haters dictate the way you live your life."

"I know. I've grown a lot tougher since then. But I never had an easy childhood, Jules."

"You don't have to tell me that." He moved towards her and gently pulled her into his arms. "Our daughter will have a good childhood. Because she's got us."

"You know something, Jules?"

"What?"

"Let's go forth with the annual barbecue. I still want to take part in it. For the families. I want to be an example that women can have babies naturally or not and it was all okay."

He smiled. "Are you sure you're okay with this?"

"I can't let haters dictate the way I live my life. Someone wise recently told me that. I'm going to respond to that comment and I want you to let them know that we had an IVF baby. So what if I got pregnant through IVF? Countless women have gotten pregnant that way for many different reasons. I've got love and your support, and that's all I need, Jules."

"Have I told you lately, how proud I am of you, Amber?" Jules lowered his head to hers and kissed her tenderly. Amber shivered with delight as his loving energy surfed through her body. Oh, that magical feeling again.

"I don't mind hearing it again," she teased him.

"Good. I love you, Amber."

"I love you, too, Jules."

Amber leaned into his chest and felt that feeling of warm love again. Maybe things would be okay from now on. Jules didn't look down on her for what she had done. And that counted more than anything.

* * *

CHAPTER TWENTY

The following week, the garden at the Mayberry Hill Family Center was filled with hundreds of guests from the community. The energy in the air was electric. A live steel band played in the background as waiters dressed in white came around and offered refreshments to everyone. All families, regardless of how they came to be, were encouraged to attend.

This was another phase in Amber's life. She was not only the first lady of the center but she now had complete control of the Murray Café and Jules had agreed to help her with some renovations on the café while keeping the staff paid through the temporary closure. Amber was going to have some major upgrades done, hire more staff and keep her family's legacy and business going. She was so excited to begin this overdue undertaking. But right now, her thoughts were on the wonderful day celebrating the official first Family Annual Barbecue since her husband Jules took over the Mayberry Hill Family Center.

"You look beautiful, Mrs. Romero," Brenda said, beaming. Amber still loved the sound of that. Mrs. Romero.

"Thank you, Brenda. You've all done a wonderful job."

Amber had been thanking and mingling with tons of guests since midday. She looked around for her busy husband and when she spotted him, she couldn't wait to make her way over to see him.

* * *

Dion Romero was glad to see things working out for his little brother, Jules, at the Mayberry Hill Family Center's Annual Barbecue. He was happy that Jules had acquired this new property to add to his other businesses. And Jules and Amber looked so relaxed together. He sure was glad all that drama with Amber's aunt was out of the way. Man, that woman was a real psycho in a dress!

"Congratulations, bro," Dion added.

"Thanks, Dion. I couldn't have done it without everyone's support. It means a lot," Jules said.

"Yeah, I know. And, congratulations again with Amber, too. Are you two planning on having a big wedding ceremony where Grandpa won't be complaining every year on your anniversary how he wasn't even invited to the original nuptials?"

Jules grinned. "Very funny. I don't think he'd like the idea of being in a labor and delivery room. Besides, you saw how nervous the JP was. And he's Grandpa's age. When the time is right, we'll have a big reception. Besides, why don't you give him what he wants? You know he wants us all married off before he puts one foot in the grave."

"A wedding? I don't think so. You know I'm not a marrying man," Dion felt uneasy. There went his heartbeat again. Pounding hard in his chest. Dion had done the engagement thing once before but caught his now ex with his BFF – backstabbing freaking friend. Currently, ex-friend. He knew then, betrothal wasn't for him. It was a good thing they hadn't walked down the aisle yet.

How could he ever trust that a woman wasn't going to rip out his heart from his chest again after he figuratively handed it to her on a silver platter, with a diamond engagement ring on the side? "Don't get me wrong, I'm happy for you, Lucas, Zack and Carl but I really don't see myself tying the knot."

"I know you had it rough, man. But really, when you meet the right one—"

"Jules, I've been down that road before. I'm not going there again. I dodged that bullet! It's lucky that you and the others found someone special. And I say blessed luck! But I'll continue to keep my relationships temporary, thanks. Physical, hot, and wild, nothing more. As long as I let the pretty ladies know up front I'm not a marrying man, they can take it or leave it."

"Fine. You say that now…"

"And I'll be saying that until my dying breath."

Jules play punched his brother Dion. "Yeah, right. I'll believe that when I see it, man."

Just then his sister-in-law, Amber, showed up beside them. Dion excused himself and headed for the refreshments table. Another man walked over to where Jules and Amber were standing.

* * *

"Hi, honey," Amber said when she got close to Jules.

"Hey, beautiful, have you met Mr. Jackson from the Regent Center?" Jules said, turning to the man beside him.

"No, it's nice to meet you," Amber said. Mr. Jackson took her hand and kissed the back of it.

"Your wife is very gracious and beautiful, Jules. Congratulations."

"I know she is. Thank you."

Amber was happy to see Jules in good spirits. It was a trying month for them.

When she pulled him aside away from the crowd, she couldn't wait to tell him the good news.

"We're having a baby?" He beamed.

She nodded joyfully. "I just got the message and couldn't wait to tell you. It looks as if you're okay after all, baby."

"Amber, you don't know how happy I am to hear that." He wrapped his arms around her and practically picked her up.

"I can't wait to share the good news."

"Neither can I."

"You said you wanted to speak with me tonight about some good news. Well, even though it's not as good as mine."

"Yeah, right."

"Oh, come on. What could be more thrilling than us having a baby … together, honey?"

He leaned her against the wall and looked deeply into her eyes, hunger and passion filled his dark, sexy eyes. "Do you remember the ski accident I had?"

"Of course. That's when the doctor said erroneously you couldn't make babies."

"Yeah, well, at that time, he also told me I could have my sperm surgically removed and stored and so I took him up on the offer at the time and then forgot about it." A wicked grin touched his lips.

Amber's heart fluttered hard in her chest, her throat closed up with emotion. "J-Jules…what are you t-telling me?"

"I didn't want to say anything until I got the confirmation but…as it turned out, the lab staff accidentally took my sample and got a local woman pregnant with it. I should be totally pissed, but turns out, there's more to it."

Amber eyes widened. She was crestfallen another woman could be out there with a little Jules or Julie that was not theirs! "A-and?"

"Well, I had them track down this mystery lady and according to DNA tests, Crystal happens to be my biological daughter! Can you believe that?" Emotion filled his dark, lovely eyes.

Amber could not help but let out a scream of joy, turning heads for a moment. "Ah, that's amazing! The universe definitely works in mysterious ways, doesn't it?""

Amber wrapped her arms around Jules and hugged him with all her strength. They embraced and to their surprise a cheer and round of applause erupted from some of the guests who could not even begin to imagine what they were celebrating. Not just yet. Right now, Jules and Amber were going to enjoy a private victory and memorable celebration of their love.

EPILOGUE

One month later...

Dion Romero couldn't believe his ears. He hated to be deceived, especially by a beautiful woman he trusted. A woman who was close enough to him to hurt him. "Jenna-Lynn?" Dion asked incredulously. Dion looked at his private detective, JoJo, a man who once worked as a bodyguard. "My executive assistant? Are you sure?" he finished his sentence.

"Yes, boss."

"There's gotta be a mistake. I checked her background before I hired her," Dion continued. He should be angry as hell right now because it wouldn't be the first time he'd been stabbed in the heart by a pretty face. But it would be the last time. His mind kept trailing on pretty-faced Jenna-Lynn. She was so cute and innocent in all outward appearances. Yeah, they were the worst kind. When would Dion ever learn?

"I know, boss, but there's something about her that just doesn't check out," JoJo said in a rough voice. The man was a leviathan and looked like a giant at six foot-seven. Considering that Dion was six foot four and well-built, JoJo was still the equivalent of Goliath. Not exactly inconspicuous. But he'd worked for the Romero family for years and always got the job done.

"Like what?" Dion said, pacing in his office, unbuttoning his business suit jacket. "What doesn't check out?"

"Her background doesn't fly. It seems a bit too...perfect."

"That's it?"

"It's too perfect, boss," the man said without smiling. JoJo never smiled. Dion couldn't remember the last time he even smirked. Was he even capable of mirth?

"You mean like fabricated?"

JoJo nodded slowly, his eyes narrowed. "Yes, boss."

Dion remembered all too well, the trouble his brother Carl went through when they found out about the past Venus, Carl's former assistant and now wife, had been hiding.

"And that's not the only thing, boss." "What else is there?" Like Dion really wanted to hear more.

"She's been watching you."

Dion got all soft inside for a moment until he read JoJo's expression.

"You mean...?"

"Bingo! We found out she's had you under surveillance this whole time. You and your family."

Dion felt his core body temperature scorch his body inside. What was she? Some sort of spy? Or cop? Boy, did he know how to pick 'em. Hot babe or not, she was out on her butt. "That's it. She's fired!"

* * *

THE BILLIONAIRE'S ASSISTANT (THE ROMERO BROTHERS, BOOK 6)

When it rains, it pours. Swoon-worthy billionaire bad boy Dion Romero knows this all too well. It's bad enough to get thrown into a crisis that threatens the survival of Rom International, one of his lucrative business interests, but now a frivolous lawsuit by an ex-girlfriend who worked with him has surfaced. He needs to focus on getting his business in order and keep as far away as possible from women. The trouble is, he's falling hard for his wonderful new assistant, Jenna. She's a sweet and innocent, yet deadly distraction to his heart. But he's finding she's too irresistible to avoid.

Jenna-Lynn Macchiasso knows what it means to have a crushed heart and suffer betrayal from those close to her so she no longer has men on her agenda. But her new oh, so sexy boss Dion Romero is giving her a run for her money. The secrets of her past make her life too complicated for her to get close to another man. What should she do? Forfeit her mission to her work, or forfeit her heart's desire?

CHAPTER ONE

"Damage control?" Dion Romero asked Pamela, his press secretary, incredulously.

"Yes. We must do damage control as soon as possible," Pamela warned him. "Pre-emptive. This could get ugly fast, Dion," Pamela finished. She was a petite, very young and feisty press secretary with beautiful shiny jet-black hair. Pam had been with the Romero family for a few years and helped them through many scandals by spinning her wonderful words for their public image campaigns. She herself was practically family at this point. Trusted and always on the mark.

Dion glanced out the French glass doors of the study to the patio and garden and the backdrop of the hills. It sure didn't feel like Monday morning. The dark clouds were gray and the rain pelted the paved patio outside. Thunder rolled in the sky. How appropriate for the way he was feeling inside. Like a raging storm in his very soul.

"She's right, grandson," Toni Romero, Dion's grandfather and the patriarch of the powerful Romero dynasty, agreed. Along with his grandfather and brother, Troy, and the family's press secretary, Pamela, Dion sat in the study at the Romero Manor to address the latest allegation in the media against a member of his family. Unfortunately, this one involved him. "Having a disgruntled ex-employee sue you for sexual harassment is not good," Toni continued.

"Miranda and I dated long before I even got her the job at the Rom, Granddad. She embezzled funds from the company. Plain and simple. I had to fire her. That's the reason she's getting back at me with this...this f—phony suit." Dion had to bite his lip to avoid swearing in front of his grandfather. "She won't have a leg to stand on." Dion could feel his core body temperature climb. He was annoyed as sin. Miranda was doing this on purpose—to generate this reaction from him. Dion was known to keep his cool, but she knew his limits. *Women*. And this one really knew how to get him worked up.

"You see, Grandson, none of this would have happened if you'd follow my advice as your brothers, Lucas, Zack, Carl and Jules, had done."

"Oh, no. Not that again, Gramps. Not now."

"I have to tell it like it is, grandson. If you were married, you wouldn't be in this situation."

Dion rolled his eyes.

"You know how much the press is all over you boys since you've made names for yourselves in the business world. You get all these opportunists at your door. Now, if you were happily married..."

"Granddad, marrying is not the answer to everything. Besides, not everyone's cut out to be chained to one human being."

"A marriage does not equate to life in a jail cell, grandson."

"Yeah, well, it's an institution and you know how I feel about those."

His grandfather frowned, shook his head then hunched his shoulders as if giving up on persisting with the topic. But Dion knew it was coming again, sometime in the future. His grandfather would not give up until all his grandsons were married off.

Back to matters at hand. Unfortunately, being popular in the business world brought out haters from all corners of the corporate world. The Romeros had been there before with espionage and kidnap and extortion attempts and now this.

It wasn't long ago when they had convened regarding his younger brother Lucas who had to face accusations of being a womanizer, and Zack's infamous ex threatening to release a sex tape they'd made in Vegas to ruin his chances of being honored with a prestigious industry award.

Currently, Dion was at the center of what could be a large scandal. Sexual Harassment. A false one at that.

"I don't need this right now," Dion complained, raking his fingers through his hair. He unbuttoned his dark tailored suit jacket and loosened his silk gray tie. "We've got that crisis going on in Lendovia. This is insane. Miranda will just have to have her nervous breakdown some other time. Like, next year."

Troy, Dion's younger brother, grinned.

"I couldn't agree with you more, bro. Talk about bad timing. But seriously, we need to nip this one in the bud fast," Troy added. "It reminds me of that sex scandal with that president. Dude was trying to tell his country they have national security issues and they accused him of wagging the dog's tail to avoid the scandal. Not good."

"Yeah, well, your business interests are at stake so we can't ignore that, either," Pamela commented, biting her lip. She sat holding her laptop in front of her ready to type a statement for the media. The energy in the room was palpable, everyone was riled up.

"Forget the business interests right now. Money can be replaced. People cannot. I'm worried about getting my employees out of that country as fast as humanly possible. It's like that nation's going through some civil war or something."

Never mind his reputation. The safety of those who worked for Dion was paramount. It was everything to him. If any single person he employed had so much as a scratch on his or her skin or a strand of hair rustled from the uproar in Lendovia, he'd wage his own war against those responsible.

Dion's employees were crucial to him, and not just in the workplace. They were friends, extended family. He trusted them and they trusted him. Period. He was responsible for providing a good, safe environment for every person he employed. It was the Romero way. The only way the Romeros knew to run a business or any of their enterprises.

In fact, Romero Corp, the umbrella company founded by his grandfather, Toni, was voted one of the top 100 employers to work for in North America by several prestigious publications. And they came up in the number one spot, every year, consistently. And now this…

"You're right, grandson," Toni said. "Normally, I would criticize you for acting too hastily. But we have no choice at this time. Other countries are talking about closing their embassies and urging citizens to stay indoors until emergency flights become available. It's a good thing you ordered some flights to go there on short notice, ready to pick up any of our people who are ready to leave."

"Yeah," Dion sighed, almost under his breath. His thoughts were still distracted. He was worried about his business situation but he was also riled up thinking about the nerve of Miranda coming up with some lame fake claim against him. Yeah, it was true that hell hath no fury like a woman scorned. Well, he sure as hell felt like he was being torched right now. How could she do this to him? He shook the thought from his mind and turned his attention back to Pamela. "So what's the latest scoop out of Lendovia?"

"Well, as you know the country's monarch, unlike, say, the British monarchy, has full power over the country's economic and political affairs."

"And?"

"Well," Pamela continued, scrolling down the screen on her laptop pulling up the latest information, "the reigning king is a tyrant. We all know that. He treats his own family as horrifically as he does those who work for him, not to mention the people in Lendovia. I'm surprised he's still in power, given the current social climate."

"Yeah, yeah." Dion's impatience waned. "What's new?"

Pamela drew in a deep breath before continuing. "Well, word has it that the king of Lendovia has overthrown his own government over labor disputes."

"In other words, the king believes in slave labor and he doesn't like anyone to tell him what he can and cannot do."

Pamela said nothing, her look of disdain at the ruling king of Lendovia's antics said enough. She looked as disgusted as Dion felt at the moment. He darn well hated having his own crew caught up in the hostile political climate of that nation. It all seemed like a wonderful opportunity at the time to open up a campus of Rom International (formerly Beta Business College Worldwide) in Lendovia. The country had a fantastic track record in regards to superior math and science levels, just not enough support from the federal government to push the students to a higher level. As part of the Romero's world plan to make a difference in as many countries as possible, not just their own country, Lendovia seemed like the best place. Unfortunately, the country had been long divided by staggering economic division. You were either obscenely rich or filthy poor there. A middle class failed to exist it seemed.

Dion cursed under his breath. "Damn it! Why did we even bother opening up a school there?"

"Because you believe in everyone having the right to receive a higher education at the college level without paying ridiculous fees. You were hoping to make a difference," Pamela answered Dion's rhetorical question.

"What are we going to do?" Troy added, leaning his elbow on the mantel of the elegant stone fireplace. Troy had invested as much into Rom International as his brother Dion. Most of the other brothers had ventured off into other businesses: Zack owned the winery and vineyard, Lucas had a successful software company, Carl was the youngest mayor elected to Mayberry Hill, their hometown, and Alonso was a medical doctor who opened up private health clinics in third world countries. The Romero brothers were a rags-to-riches story and they never forgot their humble past. Sure, they were considered hot by the elite scene and often attracted unwanted media attention and pretty women and they even partied hard, but they worked damn hard, too. They didn't compromise their integrity and doing what was right.

It wasn't all about living a good life. If you couldn't give back and help make someone else's life better, what was the point of having all that hard money—or heck, what was the point of existing?

The king of Lendovia could have taken a few pointers from many of the philanthropists Dion knew, including the ones in his own family.

"Well," Pamela said, taking charge, "as I said before, we've got two challenges to tackle. We need to get our people out of there fast and close our offices and the school."

"Close the school?" Toni repeated.

"Yes, sir," Pamela said. "I'm sorry but we have no other choice. There's just too much instability in that country."

"We do have a choice," Dion interjected, his tone sharper than he'd intended. "I don't want us to appear as if we're running scared. We want our people out of there but no way in hell I'm closing down the college. After this uprising thing is over and done, we're opening up for business again and we're gonna do what we set out to do."

"But, grandson, Pamela does have a point. As long as King Lend'or reigns in that country, there is no hope the political or economic climate will ever change."

Dion pinched his lips together. He felt a muscle twitch in his jaw. He damn well wasn't going to back down that easily. He was a full-blooded Romero. Defiance and honor roared through his veins. He remembered all too well the red tape and bureaucratic crap they had to spin through just to get a license to open up business there. He was present when the first enrolled students lined up for their classes. The looks on their faces, having their tuition subsidized and not having to worry about getting a good education at a state-of-the-art glass building facility, world-class college made the struggles worth it to Dion. He had ensured the top tech experts in the field and the best instructors were hired to teach there.

Mi Dios. It would kill him to give in. He'd fought for the right to establish his college there for years. This project was his little baby.

"Don't be stubborn, grandson," Toni continued. "Let's get the employees out of there and the students to safety before the rebel forces try to stage some sort of protest."

"Yeah. We'll get that done," Dion agreed. "Now we've got the week to try to rush things. We need to communicate with the dean."

"Done," Troy chimed in.

"Good," Dion said, gliding his finger down the screen of the tablet he swiped off the desk. "We have 450 college students enrolled right now and twenty-five faculty," he said, scrutinizing the screen. "Let's get the office staff to postpone classes until things are safe."

"Sure thing, boss," Pamela said, typing a memo into her email program on her laptop. "Oh, and good news."

"Good news?"

"Yes. Your new executive assistant Jenna-Lynn starts tomorrow morning. She'll be perfect to help with your overflow in getting all the programs transferred and the changes this week."

"Jenna-Lynn?" Oh, boy. Dion didn't have a good feeling about this at all. Heck, he didn't even like the sound of her name.

"Yes, Jenna-Lynn Macchiasso. She's actually from Lendovia. Remember, we requested someone who could speak the language to help with translation and communicating with their authorities. Well, she's a native. She's young and full of energy and could give us some insight on the current situation. She'll be able to help with everything this week."

"I don't need you to hire a secretary on my behalf, Pamela. I can do that on my own," he growled.

"With all due respect, grandson," Toni chimed in, "you haven't exactly been successful in hiring the right kind of assistant. The last one you hired ended up being an emotionally disturbed kleptomaniac! Give Pamela a chance to at least get someone for you," he finished, clutching his cane.

Dion's brother grinned. Grandpa Toni certainly didn't mince his words. But, oh, he had a point.

Dion blew a deep breath. *Young? Full of energy?* "I don't know about that. Where'd you find her?"

"Dion!" Pamela rebuked, her hand on her hip. "I didn't just *find* her. And, what's to know?" Pamela continued, looking up from her laptop. She sat near the fireplace on a chair nearest to Troy.

"I need to know her background. I don't like the whole 'young and full of energy' vibe right now." That was how it started out with Miranda when he met her at the Luxury Club in Toronto. Maybe that was the trouble. He'd met Miranda at a club. A club for rich men, where young pretty women flocked in herds.

"She was hired from the Box-Worth Office Support Agency."

"Good God, Pamela! You hired a temp from Box-Worth?" Dion paced, his hands shoved in the pockets of his suit pants. "We're dealing with pretty sensitive information here."

"I know that," Pamela defended. "We vetted her, Dion. Besides, she speaks seven languages fluently and types at a speed of 100 words per minute with ninety-nine percent accuracy."

"Only that?" Toni said, a grin of amusement crossed his face. "She sounds perfect!" His expression softened and he then held his chin up with a proud smile. He looked at his grandson, Dion, probably hoping Dion would lighten up a little.

"I'm going to do a run on her background myself," Dion finally said, as he paused from pacing. He'd contact his man JoJo, an ex-military specialist and former bodyguard. One of the Romero's trusted private investigators. "Thanks, Pamela. Not that I don't trust your judgment, but you know how I feel about executive assistants."

"Sorry. I realize you've just had a terrible experience with Miranda. But at least you don't even know Jenna. She really seems sweet and humble."

Dion cocked his brow and gave Pamela a yeah-right look. *They all start out sweet and humble, don't they?* "You should have hired an old man or something. I don't trust young women working with me at the moment." Or maybe he didn't trust himself working with them.

"Dion! That sounds sexist."

"I'm sorry. I just…let's get things rolling."

"Listen, bro, let's go for a drink. We can unwind and brainstorm at the Place. You need a break, man."

"Yeah, maybe I need a change of environment and to rethink what we're going to do," Dion concurred. He turned to Pamela. "Regarding that press statement. Let's wait and see what Miss Miranda does first. Then we'll go on the defensive if necessary."

"Okay, we'll try that," Pamela responded. "I'll keep my sources at the papers close to see if anything comes up."

"Good thinking, grandson. If we talk too soon, you may end up looking guilty. We don't want that. Lord knows we don't need that kind of attention. At the present, your mind should be on Rom International and what's going on in Lendovia. The whole world is watching."

"I know," Dion said under his breath; anger seethed through him. "I know."

CHAPTER TWO

What are you nervous about, Jenna? Dion Romero is just a man. A man. Not a god. Merely a man who'll become your boss for the next few weeks.

Jenna smoothed her dark, silky hair with her right hand. She was more stirred than she cared to admit. Her left hand clutched her tote bag and her umbrella. It was early Tuesday morning. The first day of her three-month assignment as an executive assistant to the CEO of Rom International.

She glanced at her watch. Good. She was fifteen minutes early. Jenna walked through the open glass doors of the main office at Rom International. The sophisticated lobby looked like an art museum with the finest displays and the aroma of fresh cut roses filled the air. It didn't look like a head office of a business college, but then again, didn't Rom International teach courses in architecture and interior design? Well, the Romeros had class. She'd give them that. She immediately felt elevated walking through the lobby on the golden marble floor with bright lights, green plants and priceless artwork on cream-colored walls.

"Hi, I'm Jenna-Lynn," she said to the receptionist sitting behind the glass front desk. "I'm here to see Mr. Romero."

The red-headed woman looked at the display clock then her gaze fixed to Jenna. "Jenna-Lynn?"

"Yes." Jenna's heartbeat pounded fiercely in her throat. "From the agency. I'm here on a temp assignment as an EA. An executive assistant." Why did she get the feeling something was just not right? She always seemed to sense that premonition. She hated that weakness.

"Didn't you get the message?" the receptionist looked puzzled, her blue eyes piercing Jenna.

"Message?" Jenna felt her palms getting moist. "What message?"

"Um, well, we no longer need you. I left a message with your agency."

"Oh?" Jenna felt her heart sink to the ground. "I...I didn't know."

Oh, no. Jenna needed this assignment. She needed this job, badly. Like yesterday. She'd already racked up enough of a balance on her credit cards and depleted most of her savings trying to get by and make ends meet. It wasn't easy staying in a foreign country with limited access to money. The agency assignments were helping her with her bills and her rent until she secured something more permanent. Now what would she do? But it wasn't just the assignment. Jenna had read up about the Romeros. Okay, she had done her research enough to know their businesses were some of the best companies to work for. And the safest. Not to mention, Dion Romero was quite a charming man who was more than easy on the eyes.

Jenna's hopes were dashed by the words: we no longer need you. Did they find someone else who could speak Lendovian? Or type one hundred words per minute? Or...oh, God!

Did someone advise Dion Romero not to hire her?

That's impossible, Jenna. There's no way he could possibly know about your history.

Jenna was beyond puzzled. She not only was crushed and let down but she thought everything was a go when she spoke with Pamela the previous week. She genuinely thought things were beginning to look up.

"I'm sorry for the misunderstanding." The receptionist shrugged. She looked as lost as Jenna felt. What an awkward situation.

Jenna heaved a sigh and squared her shoulder. "Thank you," she said quietly. Before she could turn around, the glass door to the reception area swung open and a tall, sinfully sexy gentleman in a sharp-fitted dark business suit strolled in. Jenna felt her heart lunge out of her chest.

Holy hell.

Was that Dion Romero? He looked even hotter than he did in the images she'd seen of him on the Internet, with his dark, glowing complexion and high chiselled cheekbones and dark, sexually-charged russet eyes. The man commanded respect. His appearance was compelling. And damn, he was a lot taller and well-built than Jenna imagined. He filled out very nicely in his dark business attire. Her heart raced like mad in her chest as he approached reception, not even acknowledging Jenna at first.

"Oh, good morning, Mr. Romero," the receptionist greeted enthusiastically. Her smile was a mile wide. Who could blame her? She got the chance to greet a hot, sexy and delicious looking boss each morning, not to mention work in a breathtaking environment.

"Good morning, Della." Dion's voice sounded a lot deeper than Jenna had imagined. And silky and smooth. He seemed hurried and distracted. Too bad Jenna couldn't be his executive assistant. She would work wonders organizing his work schedule.

Dion Romero then picked up what looked like a newly-delivered package on the reception desk. He extracted a golden letter opener from Della's organizer and proceeded to rip the package open, his eyes fixed on his mission. "I'm expecting the legal team in about an hour. Please have refreshments in the boardroom," he instructed, not looking up as the package opened. He took out the contents and scanned the documents.

"Um…" Della hesitated, looking from Jenna to Dion and back to Jenna again. "Mr. Romero?"

"Hmm?"

"Um…" Della cleared her throat, appearing nervous, "…this is the executive assistant from the agency, sir…she didn't get our message."

* * *

Dion looked up slowly, his dark eyes capturing the woman before him the agency sent. *This is Jenna-Lynn? The temp?*

She sure looked tempting, all right.

His gaze dropped to the woman's beautiful red lips and travelled to her enormously luscious mahogany eyes. Their mesmerizing sparkle immediately stirred a reaction in him. The woman's captivating appearance caught him off guard for a split second.

That virtually never happened to Dion. He'd met beautiful women before, but Jenna-Lynn was…stunning. Breathtaking. And it wasn't merely her physical attributes, as appealing as they were, but there was something alluring about her appearance, her demeanor. He could tell a lot by the way a woman carried herself. She radiated sophistication and humility. A good combination in his humble opinion.

Enough, Dion. You don't even know her. I'm sure she's off limits.

His mind immediately flickered back to Miranda, his ex-girlfriend and ex-executive assistant. Oh, no way in hell was he doing a déjà vu on this lovely lady. As lovely as she was.

"I'm sorry for the inconvenience, Miss…?"

"Jenna-Lynn. My friends call me Jenna."

"Well, Jenna." What was he doing? He should have addressed her Jenna-Lynn. Only her friends called her Jenna, right? How presumptuous. She was certainly no friend of his and never would be. "We'll gladly pay you for the week, for your trouble, but we no longer require your….services. Good day."

The woman parted her beautiful lips as if to protest. She appeared stunned. Maybe he had been too curt with his dismissal. But he was going to pay her for the week for doing nothing, giving her enough time to secure another assignment. Wasn't that enough? He didn't want anything to do with this pretty young woman. Heck, she was a distraction to him right now. He felt his groin react from simply looking at her. His body stirred with all sorts of feelings. What was happening? Whatever it was, he'd put a stop to it!

He glanced at her left hand clutching her oversized handbag that was big enough to cover her left side but not large enough to hide the sensuous curve of her hips. *Have mercy.* He noted that she was filled out quite nicely in her orange-colored knitted close-fit top and her silver-gray pencil skirt that accentuated her hips. Her voluptuous breasts and shapely hips gave her lovely hour-glass contours. She wasn't like those skinny supermodel types he'd seen. She was built like a true woman in Dion's opinion. The way he liked his women—filled out in all the right places.

His heart felt heavy just saying no to this woman. Good God! Was she bewitching him with her innocent-looking eyes? He was captivated by her all right.

"I..." she finally said, "I appreciate that, Mr. Romero, but I don't need to be paid for work I am not doing."

What was she doing? Was she turning down *free* money? Who did that? Well, this was a first for him. Most women would have gladly taken the cash and said adios amigos.

"It's up to you, Miss...Lynn." He knew that was probably not her surname but didn't want to probe any further. He had an urgent meeting in moments. He really should be going back into his office. Yet, it wasn't as easy as it should be. Why was he still fixed at the spot in front of her?

"Macchiasso. My last name is Macchiasso."

Della answered the ringing phone at the reception. "Mr. Romero, it's the Lendovian Embassy. They're saying that we might need to start an evacuation procedure as early as this week. The king has gone against the advice of the government."

"Is this official then?" Dion was concerned.

"Not quite but they said something about we must use our discretion."

"I don't want to take any chances. We can start the process over the next couple of days to ensure there's no chaos."

"With all due respect," Jenna interrupted. "You need to get your employees out of there like yesterday, sir. The king is a tyrant. He's unpredictable. He's been known to flip a switch at the drop of a hat and then it would be too late to evacuate."

Dion turned to the temp beside him, almost too stunned to speak.

"And how do you know this, Miss Macchiasso?"

"I worked for the Lendovian royal family for five years." Her voice was void of emotion.

Well, as much as he hated to hire her, it looked as if he would need her services for at least the week. There was also no denying he was impressed by her knowledge.

"Are you still interested in working the week?" Dion asked Jenna.

"Yes, I am," Jenna asserted, her chin held up slightly. He could see she was somewhat nervous.

"Della, please set up Miss Macchiasso's office and get IT to set up her email."

"Thank you, sir." Jenna's expression melted slightly. She was delighted to land the job after all. Dion didn't have too much time to ponder the sexually-appealing temp right now. Ensuring the four hundred fifty people at the Rom International Lendovia site were safe was his only concern.

Dion's lips twitched. "Oh, don't thank me just yet, Miss Macchiasso. I'm only granting your wish to work out the week of pay I'd offered you."

Jenna frowned slightly but quickly recomposed herself.

He'd keep her for the week since she wanted to work for the money he offered her. God help him, if he lived to regret hiring lovely Miss Macchiasso.

"Oh, and, Della, can you forward a copy of Miss Macchiasso's resume to my desk? The one the agency sent us."

"Yes, sir."

With those words, Dion left the reception area and left Jenna looking stunned. Even if he was going to keep her for the week, he still wanted to see her resume and of course, check out a few things himself.

* * *

"Yes, boss?" the man's gritty baritone voice sounded on the other end of the phone. It was one of the Romero family's trusted private detectives, JoJo.

"I'm having a young woman work the week for me as my personal assistant. She's from Box-Worth. Everything looks fine on her resume but I want you to look into a few things for me. Do a bit of fact checking, will you?"

Dion had good reason not to trust an outside office agency's vetting system. Some workers had contacts and could furnish any kind of reference. He also knew that not all agencies were as meticulous as they were in screening and fact checking. Even in this day of modern Internet communication. Dion was already royally peeved at the family's press secretary, Pamela, for taking it upon herself to hire an EA for him without his knowledge ... or approval.

"Sure thing, boss."

"I need this information by noon."

"I can get you some preliminary stuff by then, boss," JoJo affirmed. "I'll need more time for a thorough background check."

"Good," Dion said.

Dion had been burned, one too many times in the past, trusting people at face value. For one thing, his ex, Miranda, who cajoled him into working for him was now trying to pin some fake harassment claim on him.

Dion grew up poor and knew what it was like to be wrongly judged and even snubbed by the other kids at the school he and his brothers had attended. So after the Romero brothers met their wealthy grandfather and he'd shown them the ropes and they'd ventured off into their own successful enterprises, Dion always went out of his way to give back and to make others feel significant. But, oh, he'd learned quickly, it wasn't wise to trust every single person you met. Trust had to be earned. Miranda had faked everything on her resume.

Heck, she'd even faked bumping into him at the club that time. He'd found out later that she'd waged a bet on a social media site that she could land a famous or rich dude and she had her sights set on the Romero brothers. Didn't matter which one, she "knew" she could land at least one of them, bait them in and get whatever she wanted out of them. It was no secret which elite nightclub he and his brothers frequented to wind down from a busy workweek. She knew that, too.

That's when he realized that some women had a motive behind their actions. That's when he learned that sometimes "chance" encounters weren't always by...chance.

Dion grimaced at the thought.

Deception.

God, he loved women. He just hated when women...deceived him.

So much for trusting a pretty face. Dion had learned early that not everyone had benevolent intentions. His parents couldn't give him much, but they instilled integrity in the boys and told them to be honest with people and not to mask their true feelings. And after his mother died when he was young, living out of his father's car as a kid, really provided a different outlook on living he'd take with him his whole life. Still, business was business and the Romeros didn't get where they were by making uninformed decisions.

"I'll find whatever I can on her, boss," JoJo said, before Dion ended the call.

CHAPTER THREE

Jenna sat alone in her office at her computer. The IT rep had just set up her email system. She entered her new password after the system prompted her. She would be meeting with her new temporary boss in a few minutes.

"After you log in, bring your notepad and come to my office," he'd told her.

That Dion Romero was something else. One week? He'd only keep her for one week? Was he crazy? He'd need her much longer than a week. He had no idea what type of bureaucratic red tape he'd have to cut through to evacuate his business and close his office while the country of Lendovia was in the middle of political unrest.

She quickly glanced at the screen on her computer and a map of Lendovia. Jenna printed off the map that also labeled the Lendovian campus of Rom International Business College. She noted the Lendovian Parliament offices that weren't too far from Rom International. The Imperial Palace was situated on the river bank not far from the campus. Not good. Not good at all. She then printed off a list of helpful numbers in the country for the employees and students of the college. The international airport was a daunting 120 miles from the campus.

Jenna hoped Dion would listen to her advice and not just see her as some lowly assistant. It seemed that he respected his staff, from the little she'd seen so far and from what she'd read online. He was one of the top employers in the world. Highly rated by his employees. That counted for something, didn't it?

Oh, who was she kidding? Sure, he liked his own staff, but he hadn't seemed to take a liking to her. Why did she get the feeling Dion didn't want her around? He barely looked at her—for too long. He was annoying as hell. She could tell she was going to have one hell of a week working for the guy. But oh, boy, was he such a marvellous sight for the eyes.

The man radiated sexual power. The scent of his cologne, his commanding presence in his tailored suit, his confident mien, his deep voice and chiselled model-like features were all oh, so appealing. He had it all going on, all right.

Focus, Jenna.

Her mind kept reeling back to her first meeting with Dion Romero. This had never happened to Jenna. Having such a magical first response to someone she'd just met. As much as this stranger of a man caused an instant reaction in her, Jenna knew all too well, she didn't deserve to have another man in her life. And she would never embark on that painful journey again. Not that she could ever get close to the likes of Dion Romero.

She thought about Juan. Her first and only real boyfriend so far. He was now dead. And it was all her fault. The memory of seeing his lifeless body caused her heart to squeeze hard, pulling her into despair, sucking the air out of her lungs. She could not breathe.

It was all my fault.

She would be forever haunted, tormented by what she'd done. Even, if it was unintentional. A hard and painful lump climbed and lodged itself in her throat. Her heart began to squeeze. Oh, she hated that feeling.

Jenna fought hard to compose herself quickly before her new boss stepped into the office. She removed her fingers from the keyboard and pushed herself away from her desk. She sucked in a deep breath as hard as that was and blew out another one, relaxing her shoulders and her muscles. Her muscles always tensed up when she thought about Juan.

When would she ever get past the pain of losing him? When would she ever cope?

No, she didn't deserve to have a second chance at being happy. She knew that. It was good she could never get close to the likes of Mr. Dion Romero. If he ever found out about her past, not only would he fire her, he'd probably have her thrown in prison.

This is not Lendovia, Jenna. No, he won't.

Jenna had to keep reminding herself that she was in North America at the present time. Women were regarded much differently than in Lendovia.

Jenna's cell phone vibrated in her purse. It was the fourth time. She was tempted to ignore it but she glanced at the display clock on her computer. It was lunchtime so she didn't feel bad answering the call. She fished around her bag and pulled out her phone. It read number unknown. She knew who it could be. The only one who knew she would be where she was.

"Hello, Lasrine," Jenna answered.

"How did you know it was me?"

"Because, you're the only friend I have right now," she chuckled. "Well, that's not true. You're the only friend I can trust to have this number."

Lasrine was everything to Jenna. She had sacrificed so much for Jenna. If it weren't for Lasrine, Jenna might not have escaped Lendovia and made it to Canada. Luckily, with some connections she was able to qualify for a work visa for the temp agency. It was a difficult process, but nonetheless, it worked. When her visa ran out, the owner of the agency sponsored Jenna and for that she was eternally grateful. Little did he know that he'd not only provided her with a means to survive, but he also saved her life. If she returned to Lendovia now, there was no telling what would happen to her.

"You sound good this morning, Jenna. I'm glad you're okay."

"I'm fine, Lasrine, really. You don't need to worry about me."

"How is the new company? Romeri?"

"Romero Corp. It's the division called Rom International. You remember, they have a campus in our capital."

"Yes, that's right."

"Well, I almost didn't get the job."

"What? Why?"

"Oh, it's nothing," Jenna dismissed. "There was some mix-up with the agency booking. But it's all good now. I'm in. I can't explain too much about the work. It's confidential."

"Did you check out their business?" Lasrine asked; her voice sounded nervous.

Jenna heaved a sigh. "Yes. I did some online research."

"Online research? Jenna, you need to be more thorough. Be careful. You need to have them watched. If they ever found about you, Jenna..." Lasrine's voice cracked.

"They won't," Jenna snapped. "They can't. Besides, I've had them watched by one of our contacts. He's really clean. Not an ounce of corruption. He's a good person. His whole family's clean." Jenna looked at the clock. "Okay, Lasrine, it's almost a minute. I'm ending the call."

Jenna was ever careful about how long she stayed on her cell phone. Even though this was her third disposable cell phone this week. It took a minute for a call to be traced and she didn't want to take any chances.

"Be careful, Jenna."

"I will. Bye for now." *Mother.*

When Jenna ended the call, she was stunned to see Dion standing in the doorway. His dark suit jacket unbuttoned, revealing a crisp white shirt and silky blue tie. He had a manila file folder in his hand, while his other hand was shoved in the pocket of his dress pants. The man looked breathtaking. His dark, silky hair was slicked back, accentuating his high cheekbones and complementing his groomed sexy bad-boy stubble. His skin looked perfect. Oh, heavens. How was she going to get any work done during the next few days? She felt as if she was working for a hot movie star, not the CEO of a mega corporation and worldwide educational facility. He radiated sexuality in high levels. She felt her core body temperature climb.

Focus, Jenna. He's way out of your league. Besides, you don't deserve to even look at another man, remember?

Goodness. How could a man have that kind of effect on a woman? It was unbelievable. She'd read about this sort of stuff in romance novels. But never in her life thought she'd experience it herself. She thought it was just pure literary fantasy. But Dion Romero was not fantasy. He was real. As real as they came.

"Miss Macchiasso," he said, his professional tone of voice was silky, deep and smooth.

"Y-yes, sir." How much of her conversation had he heard? She wondered, feeling suddenly ill inside. God, she hoped he didn't hear any of it. But he was standing there, for how long, she did not know, when she ended her call to her mother. He was standing there for a period of time or he'd just arrived. Even so, the man had stealthily quiet footsteps—when he wanted to.

"Della will be orienting you to Rom International after lunch. At that time, I'd like you to look over these notices from the Lendovian government website. And translate as much of it as you can."

"Yes, sir."

"Della will handle screening my calls, so you don't have to worry about that," he continued, standing by the window in Jenna's temporary office cubicle. "I'll need you to oversee communications from Lendovia in addition to handling hotel booking, airfare reservations and all other travel arrangements and evacuation procedures for our members in Lendovia. Will you be okay to handle that?"

"Yes, sir," Jenna said, quickly scribbling down notes in short form on her notepad she'd just picked up from her desk. Her desk was equipped with everything she'd need when she first arrived in her little office.

If there was one thing she'd learned from her years of working in offices, it was that the assistant, a good assistant, was always ready to take orders and implement decisions on the spot. There was no room for trying to memorize everything a boss was saying. No information, no matter how seemingly insignificant, could be missed.

"Della will also show you our filing system and the cabinets in the next room that you will have access to," he said.

"Good," Jenna nodded taking down notes. Why were her hands getting sweaty all of a sudden? Her palms felt so moist, she had to wipe them on her skirt before continuing so the pen would not slip out of her hand.

Jenna, in all her years of working as a personal assistant, had never had that problem before—until now.

"Oh, and before I forget," Jenna said, reaching for the pile of printouts she'd just produced. "I think you should take a look at these, sir."

"What are these?" He took the papers from her. Their hands briefly touched and she felt a delicious electrical current shoot through her blood. Her breath halted temporarily. For a brief second, their eyes locked and Jenna felt ecstasy slide down her spine. Her inner thighs pulsed. *Stop it, Jenna. It's all business and nothing more.*

"Um, this is some information I just gathered. The college is too close to zones of political hotspots, in case a protest arises."

"I see."

"And the nearest international airport will take at least two hours to reach, maybe three. But it only takes five minutes to the border to get your people on a plane at the domestic airport that will fly you into Monaco. They'll be safe there. Then they can take an international flight from there."

Dion looked up, his facial expression unreadable. Was she getting too ahead of herself?

"You seem very passionate about your...mission, Miss Macchiasso."

"It's what I do, sir. I can't just sit back when there's work to be done. Especially when safety might be a concern."

He drew in a deep breath. "It takes a lot to catch me off my guard, Miss..."

"Please, call me Jenna. I never liked my last name."

"Jenna."

"Thanks, sir." And it took a lot for a man in his position to be so honest with his staff. Most men wouldn't even admit to having been caught off guard. But Dion wasn't a stick in the mud, he was all right. Still, not as warm as she'd like him to be with her, but the man had a bit of integrity.

"I never take that for granted, when workers go out of their way to make a difference. No matter how small."

That's very big of him to acknowledge, Jenna thought. "Thank you, sir," she said, almost breathless. Her heart raced like mad in her chest. What was it about having approval from this alluring sophisticated man?

"Okay, make five copies. We'll distribute the details to the board members."

Jenna breathed a sigh of relief. "Anything else, sir?" she asked.

"Yes. Arrange for lunch at the Opal Restaurant for the two of us."

Jenna's mouth fell open.

"L-lunch? F-for us?" Jenna had been taking notes but wasn't sure her ears registered his order correctly.

"Yes, Jenna. Is that a problem?"

"Um, no, sir. No problem at all." Yes, there was. How on earth was she going to eat in front of…too-hot-for-his-own-good Dion Romero? The man made her nervous just being around him. He was friendly, but at the same time, intimidating. Okay, so she might be just a pinch attracted to him. She was hungry like a workhorse right now and was looking forward to devouring a heavy calorie-filled lunch. Now she felt obligated to pick at a salad and eat something that wasn't too messy, and nothing with onions. So much for that greasy home-style grilled quarter pounder hamburger with onions, tomato, relish and mustard she was looking forward to at Beefy Burgers! Looking at Dion's healthy skin, immaculate teeth and well-built form, Jenna had a feeling Mr. Romero wasn't a greasy burger kind of a guy.

Sure. No problem, at all. *Yeah, right! It's a huge problem. I shouldn't be dining in public with my boss.*

CHAPTER FOUR

To say the Opal Restaurant was fancy was an understatement. Jenna's jaw fell open when she arrived at the double glass door entrance to the place. The valet dressed in a sharp red dinner jacket took Dion's keys and parked his Cadillac Escalade SUV.

"Cool ride," Jenna commented on Dion's car.

"It gets me around," he said dismissively. "You drive?"

She grinned. "Yeah, well, I used to."

"Used to?"

"I had a car once, but never again. It was an old banger. The thing should never have been on the road."

"Why do you say that?"

"Because it didn't drive, it crawled. And the whole world could hear me coming from a distance. Everything on the car made a sound—except the horn!"

Dion grinned. "You're funny, ya know that?"

"I try not to be," she teased him. "Anyway, it was all I could afford at the time. I transit it now."

"If you end up staying with us, I can arrange for a company car, Jenna."

"Company car? I…I couldn't. I mean, I'm fine, really."

"We'll see how things go." He grinned. And a cute dimple appeared on his cheek. He was irresistibly adorable.

Dion and Jenna walked to the entrance. The Opal looked more like a diamond palace or an art museum than a restaurant. Nothing like what she'd seen in Lendovia.

"This is nice," she commented.

"It's a good place to eat and do business," Dion opined, almost dismissively. As they walked in, the waiter dressed in a butler-style tuxedo approached them. "Mr. Romero. So good to see you again, sir. We have your table ready."

"Thank you, Charles."

Apparently, Dion was granted special attention there. Jenna learned quickly there was always a private area where the Romeros could meet without a reservation. In other words, no one else could take that spot, ever. Well, if this wasn't high class, she didn't know what was.

The ambiance of the environment was surprisingly relaxing. Classical music played in the background. The German Baroque composer Johann Pachelbel's Canon in D minor played if she wasn't mistaken. Jenna would recognize those soothing violin and strings and noticeable melody anywhere. It was one of her all-time favorite classical pieces.

Dion and Jenna were led past an indoor waterfall.

They were seated in a private cozy area away from the rest of the diners. Jenna could not believe her eyes. The wall had a lovely, calming waterfall. Water flowed gently down the wall, only a dim floodlight at the top to illuminate the mini waves in the falls. Talk about a relaxing way to dine and do business. She thought the décor and environment was almost too relaxing and hoped she would not fall asleep during their business meeting.

The waiter arrived at their private table in no time. "May I take your order, sir?"

"Miss Macchiasso?" Dion prompted. Jenna wondered why Dion didn't use her first name but quickly realized it was better to act professionally in front of wait staff, lest anyone assume she was his girlfriend.

Jenna scanned the royal blue velvet-covered menu. It also listed absolutely no prices. She wasn't surprised. She bet Dion Romero and his family had those exclusive Black Cards. She was well aware of his net worth. She recalled JP Morgan's famous quote, *If you have to ask the price, then you can't afford it.*

Jenna and Dion ordered their entrees and the waiter left the table.

"You seem nervous," he said in a low, deep voice and it caught her off guard. Heck, it sent delightful shivers down her spine. She had been daydreaming, mesmerized by the waterfall on the wall for a split second, thinking of her home in Lendovia. Maybe she looked spaced out to Dion.

"N-no, I'm fine, sir. Thank you."

"Please, call me, Dion," he said, his attention now turned to the wine list. She noted the smooth appeal of his skin. His hands looked meticulously groomed, so soft. She knew they felt soft. She remembered when their fingers briefly touched at the office.

Call him Dion?

She didn't expect *that* so soon.

"I don't really care too much for formality," he continued, as if reading Jenna's mind. "I keep telling the staff to call me Dion but some still insist on calling me Mister Romero." He grinned. For the second time, she noticed Dion's cute dimple on his cheek when he smiled. Jenna couldn't help but be smitten. He was so serious back at the office. Unreadable in his expression. This was a nice change to see him relaxed.

Jenna smiled. "Dion's a beautiful name."

"Thanks."

The waiter returned with two tall glasses of water, a bottle of Romero Merlot Wine and refreshments. "Your entrees will be out momentarily." How nice it must be that Dion's brother owned the famous Romero Winery and Vineyard. She'd sampled their delicious wine before. Not that she would dare drink any now at this time of the day and while still, technically, at work.

Dion thanked the man then returned his attention to Jenna.

"So, Jenna, tell me what made you decide to come to Canada to work."

Jenna almost choked on her glass of water.

"Are you okay?" Dion's brow raised a fraction.

"Yes, I'm fine, thank you." *Not*. She'd rehearsed which version she would ever tell anyone if they asked her why she moved to Canada. But she didn't want to be too dishonest with her boss. Then again, it was only for the week. She couldn't tell him everything. She would have to give him a condensed version that was truthful but at the same time protecting her and her mother.

"Well, I needed a change," she murmured, placing her glass down on the table. That was true, wasn't it? She really did need to change her location and flee the country of Lendovia. Her life depended on it. She would be in danger if she returned. She'd be dead.

Her eyes drifted to the warm candlelit centerpiece on the dinner table.

"You mentioned you worked for the Lendovian Royal family. How did you get to work for them? You must be extremely talented."

"Well," *I was forced to work for them*. "It came about naturally."

"Oh?" he said, leaning forward slightly, the look of intrigue twinkling in his dark, sexy eyes framed by long, thick lashes. She caught the scent of his cologne and it was irresistible to her senses. *Damn! He even smelled real good*.

"I taught myself English and then French. And then with some help..." her voice cracked with overwhelming emotion.

Why was she getting so emotional? Because Juan was a part of all of that, wasn't he? Juan had helped her study and practice the popular foreign language.

Women in Lendovia were not encouraged to read or to pursue educations. Juan would sneak books in to her from the public library. Jenna closed her eyes and pinched her lips together. She then opened them again. Fighting hard to blink back any tears that might surface and unsettle her composure. The last thing she would want right now was to get all emotional at work about her past, about darling Juan. The kind young soldier who had laid down his life for her.

"Is everything okay, Jenna?"

Jenna drew in a deep breath and picked up her glass of water, again. She ran her finger over the rim of the glass. The water inside it sparkled under the light. "Yes, I'm fine, thank you," she said as composed as she could. "I just had a flashback of...something that happened there."

"You seem as if you've had a lot more intense experiences than you're sharing. Are you sure you're okay?"

She nodded. "Yes. You know it isn't easy being a woman in Lendovia, right?"

"Actually, until just recently, I didn't know the situation there. The country seems real good at keeping their oppressive rules quiet on the world stage."

Jenna grinned and shook her head. Dion was right on the mark. "You're correct, Mr...I mean, Dion. The king is very old-fashioned in his views and extremely temperamental."

"So how was it that he hired you?"

"Well, he'd heard about my secret education, as he keeps tabs on villagers and libraries and things like that...and he summoned me. The next thing I knew, I was ordered to do a lot of paperwork for him....away from the palace, of course. He owns many buildings, complete with bars on the windows where he keeps his factory workers," she said, trying hard not to sound bitter.

* * *

Rage filled Dion's body as he listened to Jenna's story. He couldn't believe his ears. "What? You mean to say, he used you? Like slave labor?"

"Well, not exactly. We were paid, barely enough, but we were paid."

Dion had a feeling something was a bit off. He knew a majority of the country's citizens were living below the poverty line. That was why he ensured that many of the students didn't have to pay tuition and every enrolled student was eligible for an unlimited supply of bursaries. That was their promise and their fulfillment to the nation and to future generations of prospective students and graduates. But their darn government was so secretive about sharing certain stats with his company that he'd requested in the beginning when they'd been granted a license to open up a campus in the nation's capital.

"So, there were many of you?"

"Some," Jenna answered quietly. "Have you ever noticed the enrolment breakdown at the Rom International and wondered why most, if not all, enrolments were mostly male?" She arched a brow.

"To be honest with you, we don't list genders on the form and we can't always tell by the names who's male and who's female," Dion admitted.

The waiter came back to their table with a shiny gold dinner cart. When the man opened the cover on the entrees, Jenna's eyes widened and she salivated. They'd ordered the luxury seafood chef's choice of the day. Wood-grilled lobster tail marinated in grapefruit juice served with citrus butter and complemented with thin slices of lemon and pistachio rice. The freshly tossed garden salad was served on a dish on the side. Was it Jenna or did the Opal Restaurant have the finest quality gourmet food she'd ever seen?

Once the waiter left the table, Dion and Jenna resumed their conversation as they dug in to their entrees.

The juicy meat from her dish melted on her tongue and satisfied her craving. She was so caught up in how scrumptious it tasted on her palate she'd almost had a When Harry Met Sally moment as she mmm'd at the delicious taste in her mouth but then stopped.

"You like?" he asked, his deep, commanding voice softened a fraction.

Jenna felt heat climb to her cheeks. Was it that obvious? "It's very good, thanks," she finally whispered, sheepishly. She was hesitant to scoop another bite into her mouth. Why was she feeling like a bundle of nerves all of a sudden? Her senses were heightened to the fact that Dion's delicious dark eyes were on her lips.

Oh, God!

Focus, Jenna. He's just a man. He's only being sociable. What is he supposed to do? Stare at the ceiling?

Jenna couldn't remember the last time she'd gotten so worked up over having a meal with a man.

Jenna was determined to change the subject and hoped and prayed she wasn't showing how nervous she was on the outside. She sure felt flushed right now.

"I think it's wonderful what you've done at the Rom," Jenna commented. "Why did you decide to open a campus in Lendovia?"

"Well," Dion said, picking up his glass of wine and bringing it to his lips. Jenna noticed his lips were sensuously shaped and looked oh, so kissable. She tried to swat any sexual images of him out of her mind but it sure was hard. "I didn't always have access to resources like I do now."

"Oh?"

"No. It's no secret my brothers and I faced challenges growing up. I never even met or knew I had a grandfather until my teens. Anyway, if it weren't for him, we wouldn't have had the means to fund a good education, never mind accomplish what we did. It's the right thing to do to give back and never forget where you come from."

"That's very noble of you," Jenna said softly. She'd seen many titled and privileged people in her line of work but none as humble as Dion Romero, or any of the Romero brothers for that matter, from what she'd read about them.

"I'm not noble, Miss...Jenna," he said, in a stern voice, putting his wine glass down on the table. "I'm just doing what everyone should be doing."

"I know, sir...I mean, Dion. But trust me, not everyone with your...in your position, has that kind of attitude. Some turn up their noses at people who are poor or underprivileged or those who are at great disadvantage."

"I can never understand people who snub others who are struggling," he said while taking a stab at his lunch. "I take nothing for granted. The universe giveth and the universe can taketh away. I've seen many robust, yet foolish, men fall and fall hard."

"That's true." Except in Lendovia. Its barbaric king seemed to be enjoying his brutal reign over the people in his country. How medieval could one get? "Well, I wish all people in your position thought the same way, Dion," she said, twirling her fork in her plate. Her eyes glanced at the waterfall wall beside them. The water shimmered as it fell. It was mesmerizing. Calming. Yet, nothing could quiet the storm brewing inside her. She knew what she had to do. She just hoped that Dion would not get hurt in the process. She was there on a mission. She had to help her mother. She had to do something about the abuses in her country. But...

Oh, what was she doing? She was in way over her head. She never should have come to Canada and try to manifest change from abroad. She could not stand up to the rebel forces in her country. She was only one person. But then her mind drifted back to Juan. Wasn't he one person, too? He'd believed in her. He fought to help her escape. And look at what happened to him. Oh, if only Dion knew the whole story.

Jenna glanced his way and saw how unsuspecting he was, eating his meal, having a conversation with his so-called secretary over lunch. She wished everything was normal between them but how little he knew, things were far from normal.

One step at a time, Jenna.

She could only do what she was capable of doing. First things first. She had to help Dion's company and get their employees out of Lendovia. And fast! If she could at least spare them from heartache and terror, then she'd at least have done something of importance.

"You look far away, Jenna. What's on your mind?"

His words startled her, interrupting her brief daydream. "Oh, nothing. I'm glad I'm getting to work with your company this week. I wish the king was as noble as you are."

Dion grinned. That boyish dimple appeared on his cheek. Gosh, he was so handsome. His smooth goatee groomed stubble gave him the sexiest look. His smile vanished quickly as if a thought had crept into his mind. "In all honesty, Jenna, it sucks to be kicked when you're down. And I've felt the harsh blows of a dark reality back in my youth. I learned quickly, the best investment is not in things, but in people. You know what's the best thing you can give a person?"

"No," she whispered.

"Hope."

"Hope?"

"Yes. I've learned without it, people won't see a way out. They won't feel good about themselves. You can't progress without hope of anything good coming. And hope doesn't have to be about writing a cheque to someone but investing your time, showing them the ropes, giving them a means to survive."

"Oh, God. That is so…nice," she said. "You sound like you should be a professor. I guessed that's why you founded the college."

He clasped his hands together with his elbows on the edge of the table, pondering. "I had a college roommate from Lendovia. He was a cool guy but I remember the stories he'd tell me about the struggles and how lucky he was to have come here. It was then I thought about Rom International."

"So you opened up schools using the same model you use here."

"Yeah, but in your country, the government has been…well, more than trouble. They've insisted students pay minimum fees of some sort, even if they're unable to afford them and they wanted me to change the criteria for grants. Boy, was that a fight."

It was Jenna's turn to grin now. She could just imagine how the establishment felt about that. "Good on you for not giving up, Dion."

"It wasn't easy. But now, it kills me to have to close the college, even if for a little while."

"You're not backing out of the country?"

"Why should I?"

"But I thought….the evacuation plan?"

"Jenna, your duty is to ensure we have a smooth evacuation of employees in the event of civil unrest in the country. But I'm sure as hell not closing down for good."

"You have no idea how the Lendovian ruler can be-"

"And I don't really care too much about his problem right now. He's not going to intimidate me that easily as he has his own government and the people."

Jenna drew in a deep breath, her heartbeat raced. Dion was kind-hearted and cool but he was apparently stubborn as hell. They'd tear down his institution and ruin his company there. Didn't he realize that?

"Well, the first thing we need to do is keep this quiet as possible. We'll do this very strategically."

Dion glanced at Jenna and her heart fluttered inside her chest. "You seem to have a vested interest in getting my members out of there fast, Jenna. That's very noble of *you*," he said, arching a brow. She felt as if he was on to her.

"Thanks," she breathed.

"Now, what exactly happened while you worked for the royal family?"

Her heart smashed in her chest. Was he accusing her of...?

"What's that supposed to mean?" she said, her defenses shooting up.

"Did you have personal relationship with the king?"

"No!" Her tone was as sharp as the carving knife in the gourmet kitchen. Her voice rose so high she felt the entire restaurant must have heard, even though they were in a secluded private area.

Dion said nothing for a moment, his dark, sexy eyes penetrated hers.

"What makes you think that?" she said, placing her hands on her hips.

"You hint as if you have a personal vendetta against him. I'm not as clueless as you believe I am."

"I would never think you're clueless, Dion. Far from it."

"I believe you think I'm clueless about you, Jenna, not about life."

"I don't think you're clueless about me. There isn't much to know, really."

He reached into his pocket and swiped out his smartphone.

"What are you doing?"

"Pulling up your resume."

Jenna swallowed hard. She felt heat climb to her throat.

"We're here to discuss our work but I also like to get to know about the people who work for me, Jenna."

Her palms were getting sweaty again and the fork almost slipped out of her grip.

"That's fine," she said, as coolly as she could. There was nothing to hide. He didn't need to know everything. It wasn't his business. All he had to know was that she could get his job done. Period.

"Impressive," he mused out loud, scrolling down his phone. "You type 100 words per minute error free. Communicate in seven languages fluently..."

"Yes, that's true."

"It says here you deliver high-level executive support in a fast-paced environment, complete lengthy analysis, conduct extensive research and develop reports and perform extremely well under pressure."

"Yes, performing while having a machine gun pointed to your head is real pressure, let me tell you."

Dion's eyes widened.

"I'm only kidding, sir...Dion."

He relaxed his position giving her a silly grin. She got a kick out of getting that reaction from him but only for a split second. She realized that wasn't a very funny joke and wished she could take it back. Maybe her English didn't translate so well with the joke.

"I thought you just wanted to hire me for the week?" Jenna cocked a brow.

"I do."

"You seem to be giving me an intense interview for a week-long assignment. Are you thinking of extending my contract?"

Was she hoping he would? The words flew right out of her mouth, but oh, she wished she could lasso them back in through her lips. What was Jenna thinking? She was getting caught up in the moment, the soothing atmosphere of the place, the relaxing vibe she was getting with Dion. Why did she feel so comfortable with him all of a sudden? This was all absurd.

"Would you like to stay beyond the week?" he asked in a mellow, deep silky tone. His luscious dark gray-brown eyes were piercing into her, captivating her. Those eyes! Gosh, they were mesmerizing. The man was gorgeous in every single way. She was always attracted to a man's eyes first, then his cheekbones, his physique. Those were always the physical attributes that got her every time. And Dion Romero had it all!

CHAPTER FIVE

Jenna's inner thighs tingled and she could not breathe for a moment. She could not think. What on earth was happening to her? She heaved a sigh and fought hard to compose her inner self. *I'd love to stay beyond the week. I'd love to stay with you ... forever.*

"Possibly," she finally uttered. "I like to finish what I start."

A wicked grin touched Dion's sweet, full lips and she was caught off guard momentarily. She thought she caught a look of amusement in his lovely eyes. Oh, God! Her words could have easily been misconstrued. She liked to finish what she started? Sure. Who wouldn't?

"Good. I like to finish what I start, too, Jenna." He looked directly into her eyes when he spoke and she trembled inside. His words slid out through his lips and caught Jenna off guard. Her heart thrashed about like crazy inside her chest. It wasn't just what he said. It was the way he said it.

Dion's lips were oh, so sexy. And those eyes of his. She wondered what it would feel like to be pleasured by lips that looked as soft and kissable as his. She imagined what it would be like being in a relationship with this awesome specimen in front of her. She was willing to bet he was one sexy hell of a lover. She tried hard not to picture him naked. By the way his broad shoulders filled out in his dark business suit, she knew he must work out—a lot. She also imagined he would have a firm abdomen and biceps. The man was built like a sex god.

Oh, boy. What was she in for? Maybe she was reading into things too much. When he said he liked to finish what he started, he probably only meant work-related stuff and nothing more. What else could he mean, right?

Why was her mind plunging into the gutter like that? That was so unlike Jenna. She didn't recognize herself with where her thoughts were going in Dion's presence. It was going to be hard getting any work done with him around.

I like to finish what I start, too.

What could she say after that? She drew in a deep breath, trying to divert her attention elsewhere—just not on Dion Romero. She had sworn off men. She kept trying to remind herself that she really didn't deserve a second chance at love. Her ex-boyfriend was dead. And it was all because of her. She was unequivocally bad luck when it came to men. Period. Not that she could ever be with a man like Dion. He was her temporary boss. Nothing else. All she had to do was keep her mind focused on her mission. Get the information she needed and get business in order back in Lendovia. Then she could get out of Dion's silky dark hair and out of his life. There was no turning back. She had to focus.

"Are you okay, Jenna?" His expression was puzzled. He seemed to be reading her with his eyes. But there was no way she was letting him in her mind.

"Yes," she said, putting her fork beside her plate. Her tummy felt more than full right now. "The meal was great, thank you." And it really was. Great was an understatement. Or maybe, the company she had made it all the more enjoyable.

"You're welcome," he breathed. "Now," he said, his tone changing back to business, "you were discussing earlier that we should have employees evacuate to the closest airport?"

So it was all in her mind then. Of course it was. He wouldn't be interested in her at all. She was only there on business. A temp. Nothing more. *Silly Jenna.*

"Yes, that's right. You're better off getting your people out fast. There's no telling what the king will do next."

"Well, I did in fact check with my sources in Lendovia. You're right about the closest airport is the Island Main Airport and word on the street has it that the king is planning to do something unpredictable."

"I told you," she agreed. "And I'm glad you were able to verify my information." Jenna smiled sweetly. She really didn't think Dion was going to go on her words alone. He seemed like a shrewd businessman, a smart enough man to double check his resources and information. Good for him. Bad for her. What else would Dion check out? Would he try to delve into her past?

No, he couldn't. Why would he? She'd given him no reason to. Unless he tried to verify every single little word on her resume. She hadn't lied, of course. She only…left some information out. Information that was nobody else's business but her own. Information that had nothing to do with her job as an executive assistant.

Dion picked up his cell phone but it wasn't just any cell phone. She noted that it had some signature touch thing on it. R, probably for Romero, was engraved on it.

"Nice phone," she commented, almost automatically. "I've never seen one like it. What is it made of?"

"Titanium," he said dismissively as he typed.

She noticed that the glass was some sort of sapphire-like crystal and it was wrapped in sleek leather. Did the man have to go all out with a phone? Then again, who could blame him?

"It encrypts calls and texts," she commented. "I think I've heard of those phones and the button on the side, the red button calls concierge, I take it."

"Yes, that's right." He seemed surprised. She knew very few people on the planet had such a phone and wondered why Dion was one of the exclusive ones. Most other CEOs were comfortable with regular cell phones off the assembly lines, not custom-made for top intelligence personnel.

She grinned.

"What's so funny?" he asked as he typed a text and pressed send. Jenna was tempted to ask him what he'd just sent. Was it related to what they'd just discussed?

"Oh, nothing, it's just that I wonder why you need an EA like me. You seem to have all the latest gadgets that can do everything and put you through to whomever you need."

"Because technology can never replace the personal touch of a warm human being, Jenna." He grinned. "Besides, don't underestimate the power of a good executive assistant. You provide two-way conversations and the ability to brainstorm ideas. Until they invent a computer that can do all of that, I'll still use the resources of a personal assistant." He winked.

"Well, give it a few more years," she teased. It was good to have a light-hearted moment for a change. Too much of the solemn vibe wasn't doing much for her spirit or her blood pressure, she was sure of that.

"We're working on a virtual robot that looks just like a human. She should be ready in a few years."

Jenna's jaw fell open.

Dion laughed. "You'll forgive my lame sense of humor, Jenna. I'm not serious."

She breathed a sigh of relief. Well, that got her engine going. She admired that he could find levity in a situation like this and not be too much of a stick in the mud.

Dion finished typing some more information and hit send again. His long, slender fingers moved quite fast on the crystal-like display of his phone. She wondered what other magic his soft hands had in store. They seemed so strong, capable of doing virtually anything.

"Okay," he sighed heavily. "I've positioned my people to make arrangements for the Island Main Airport. We have a private plane that will be able to pick up everyone."

"A private plane?" Jenna sounded incredulous. She knew the Romeros were rich and powerful but hadn't thought of them owning their own airline. A passenger jet at that.

"Yes," he said, almost dismissively. "Romero 777. We use it for large passenger travel."

"Oh…um…that's good." She tried not to sound too impressed. "I mean, that's very good that we'll have access to an empty plane to pick up everyone." How incoherent, she thought to herself. Why was her brain turning to mush all of a sudden? Jenna wasn't usually the type to get too enamoured with wealth and power and all that other stuff her friends back home drooled over when they got a chance to look at an old magazine, or heaven forbid, surf the Internet.

My God, this man is powerful. The words flashed across her mind to her chagrin. At the drop of a word, he was able to summon his own massive jet to pick up stranded passengers—or would-be stranded passengers.

What was it about power that turned her on? Was it because Dion Romero, as sexy-as-sin as he was, also seemed so accessible? So down-to-earth?

"How many can it seat?" she asked, curiosity getting the best of her.

"It has a typical seating capacity of 350 to 400 passengers and has computer-mediated controls like all triple seven aircraft."

"Perfect! We can get everyone out of there on one flight by tomorrow." And then some. She was going to ask him a small favor and hoped it would not be too out of line since she was only a temp. She desperately wanted her mother to flee the country, too. Would that be too much to ask of him? she wondered. Now was not the right time to ask, but she would bring it to his attention. Dion seemed like a compassionate man. But would he understand?

"Yes, but not so fast."

"Not so fast?"

"We need to draft a notice to everyone to let them know..."

As he spoke the words, Jenna whipped out her notebook and began jotting down notes.

"...that due to tension in the region," Dion continued, "we'll begin slow evacuation of the facility as a precaution."

Jenna's heart sank as she wrote, her fingers slowed down as she scrawled the words in disbelief. "Slow evacuation?"

"The last thing we need to do is cause mass hysteria or bring unwanted attention to the Rom."

"Yes, but-"

Dion arched a brow, his expression unreadable. "Is there something else you would propose, Jenna?"

The feistiness in her was beginning to surface but it was too late to stop it. She had to have courage. If only she could tell Dion everything but he just had to trust her instincts on this one.

"I really think we should just leave the country right away. I mean, have the staff leave the region and close the school for a while." *Please.*

Dion replaced his cell phone on the table and clasped his hands together leaning forward. "Jenna, unless there is something else you're not telling me, I'm not sure why in the absence of any formal travel advisory warnings that we need to rush out tomorrow." His smiled dropped and his facial expression appeared more impatient.

Jenna fumbled for a moment. What was she getting herself into? For a moment, she started to feel more self-conscious.

If only he wasn't too damned good looking, but oh, man was he stubborn! Was he playing games or did he want to test her to see if she knew what the heck she was babbling about?

"I know that, Dion, but you have to trust me on this one. You have nothing to lose by evacuating right away."

He leaned back and cocked a brow, a slight grin of amusement on his face but then his eyes narrowed slightly. Clearly he was disbelieving her.

"Jenna, I will tell you this," he said, leaning forward again. "I don't like to be deceived." His voice was low and a chill slid out from his expression. The temperature between them dropped so suddenly, she felt the chill slide down her own spine and she shivered. It was the way he said, he didn't like to be deceived. Hurt and pain speared his dark, sexy eyes.

"What makes you think I would deceive you, Dion?"

"For one thing, you just waltz into my office—"

"With all due respect, sir. I did not waltz into your office. I was assigned to work for you."

"Ah, yes. The temporary agency assignment," he said, his voice laced with a tinge of sarcasm. And who could blame him? If she was being honest with herself, she might not believe her in his position either. She was just a temp. A temp with so much vested interest in his company more than a stranger should have.

"I've been burned before," Jenna blurted out, before she could stop herself. Why was she opening up to him? It could be dangerous. But there was just something about him that she trusted. Hell, she'd spent the last few months studying the man, in secret, of course. She knew a lot about him. Probably too much.

"You've been burned before? I assume this has something to do with our discussion."

"Yes. I...I've been hurt by people I entrusted with certain information for their safety. I have insider information about the corruption in Lendovia. I don't want to say anymore. You just have to trust me on this one."

"How do I know you're not pulling one over me? Are you a spy?" he asked pointedly.

His accusation threw her off balance. *Keep your focus, Jenna. Lives are at stake here. And so is your heart. He's only a man. A heart-throb, but still a man.*

Jenna drew in a deep breath and tried to still her thrashing heartbeat.

"I've tried to help people before and they've turned on me, betrayed me."

"I'm sorry to hear that. I know what that's like."

Who could betray Dion? He was so noble. So hot. She couldn't imagine anyone wilfully hurting this gorgeous man with the mesmerizing dark, beautiful eyes.

"Oh," she murmured. "Well, you understand then why I can't reveal too much, right now."

* * *

Dion sighed heavily. "I understand why you don't want to reveal too much right now, Jenna. But you need to understand that if you want me to trust you, you've got to return the favor. Trust is a two-way street," he lectured.

She seemed to back down slightly. "That's true," she murmured, almost pouting. "You-you're right," she conceded. She bit down on her luscious lower lip. *Oh, please don't do that*, he thought to himself. His groin jumped, to his chagrin. That's the last thing he needed, to have his libido taking over the situation.

God, her lips are so fine, he thought to himself. The woman was simply stunning in every way. He fought to remove his focus from her plump, kissable-looking lips. Why couldn't his temp be more homely? Did they have to send a beauty-queen candidate with the shape and sensuality of a centerfold? The thing was, the woman didn't even seem to realize she had that effect on a man—on him!

"Well, all I can say right now is that, I've worked for the king for too long to not know his ways."

"Was he abusive towards you?" Dion asked pointedly, his jaw clenched. If that man laid even a finger on Jenna...

"No," she said quietly. He could see something in her lovely mahogany eyes when she answered. Her eyes were cast down on the table when she answered.

"Are you telling me the truth?"

"Yes, I am." Jenna looked into his eyes now. Dion could see raw pain splintering those pretty eyes of her. There was something deep and dark she was hiding behind them. What? He wished he knew. There was something captivating about his new temporary assistant that held her to him. It was odd, but there wasn't a single soul in the universe he could remember having that kind of reaction on him. Jenna was...different. He wished he knew why the hell he cared about her and her past. She was only a temp, nothing more. But yet, there was some indescribable connection there. He could feel her sorrow. Life could not have been easy living in Lendovia. He guessed she was from a modest background. He wondered if she had a boyfriend. Not that he should be even thinking that way. But if she did, and he wasn't about to step into the unprofessional zone by asking her because it was none of his business, he hoped the guy was treating her the way she deserved to be treated. Like a true lady.

But there was something in her that called to him, that wanted him to get to know her better. Too bad, he wasn't ever going to be in a relationship with a woman he'd worked with.

"Good. I'm glad he didn't lay a hand on you. Because if he did-"

"If he did?" she asked incredulously. Her bright beautiful eyes flashed with surprise. "What do you think you could do about it?"

"You'd be surprised, Jenna. I don't take too kindly to a man laying a finger, or even an unkind word, on a woman. Period."

"Oh," Jenna looked down at her half-empty glass. "That's noble of you, sir. More men should be like you." She stroked her finger around the rim of it, looking as if she was in deep thought. Concerned.

Dion couldn't help but notice her beautiful hands. Her fingernails were clean and short cut but not manicured. The woman looked as if she'd never had professionally done nails before. And that spoke volumes about her personality. Not that Dion minded a woman who liked to pamper and treat herself once in a while. Miranda and his other exes had unnaturally long fake nails and waxed everywhere all the time. But Jenna seemed like a girl who would rather spend more time working hard than pampering herself. He never cared much for fake anything; he actually preferred natural nails, a fresh, makeup-free face and all of that. Jenna seemed to carry the full package.

Dion tried to shake the thought out of his mind. The girl was getting to be too much of a sweet distraction for him and she wasn't even trying to be—that was the part that really had him wrestling with himself.

Dion didn't have much time to ponder the situation in Lendovia. His sources had already advised him that nothing was confirmed about the Department of Foreign Affairs' decision to slap the region with a travel advisory warning. It was strictly up to each business to make that determination about emergency evacuation out of the country to a safer region.

But he just wasn't going to let a pretty face like Miss Jenna-Lynn Macchiasso push him into making a rash decision. His mind wandered on Miranda, his ex. She, too, appeared to be full of energy and ideas. But like hell she was.

Miranda was also full of self-serving schemes he knew nothing about until it was too late. And now...? He had to think about not only getting his employees out of Lendovia but fighting for his reputation with this upcoming possible lawsuit that Miranda had threatened him with. He'd given JoJo enough assignments right now, one being, checking out gaps in Jenna's resume because he could never be too careful about who he let into his inner circle. Even if she came from an agency, he needed to vet her himself as he'd done with all his employees. Dion also kept his men busy seeing what they could get on Miranda's fabricated claim against him.

Women.

He loved them like a fine, aged cognac, but man, were they trouble for him, or what? He'd better stay clear away from them and keep it all business where business was concerned.

It took a lot to get Dion discombobulated. He'd always trusted that women would be up front with him. He'd taking a liking to Miranda, just as he was taking a liking to jolly Jenna. But that could prove too costly, if he was wrong.

Why was he resisting Jenna? She was only trying to help in this potentially urgent situation. But just like Miranda, Jenna had come at just the precise moment. The question begged to be answered. Was it pure coincidence or intentional? Their meeting seemed to be perfect. Almost too perfect.

Yet, something about that savage inner fire of hers resonated with him. Her eyes were like summer lightning. A flash of light shone in those beautiful brown eyes of hers. He recognized what it could possibly be. But what was it exactly? Passion? Desire? Determination?

Her eyes were compelling, magnetic. But sorrow hid behind them. Something very deep. He wanted to go beyond that smokescreen and get to the real person. But he had to be careful. Women and business didn't mix well with him, as much as he was captivated by her presence. The woman seemed determined to get her way.

She reminded him of himself when he was younger.

Before long, Dion paid the bill and they both left the restaurant to head back to the headquarters of Rom International. This was going to be one hell of a week having Jenna-Lynn Macchiasso as his PA, he mused as he escorted her out of the restaurant.

CHAPTER SIX

Jenna wondered where on earth the time had gone. It was already late in the evening at the office. They'd both been working late on communication with the Rom campus in Lendovia and sending faxes back and forth. The lights from the other building outside created a noticeable glow against the dark night sky. It was advantageous to be on one of the high floors of the complex if not for the view. She could see outside since there were no blinds on the floor-to-ceiling windows.

The receptionist had already gone for the day. It was just Dion, his brother Troy, some members of the staff and a detective at the office along with Jenna.

Jenna learned the detective's name was JoJo and apparently he'd given Dion some information about her to confirm certain things on her resume and more. At first Jenna was caught off guard but she understood; they needed to verify references and some of what she'd told him. Dion liked to double check his sources and she couldn't blame the man for that, anything less would have made him reckless, right? At least she got the green light. He even told her he'd spoken to a few of her previous employers this afternoon—one of whom was a trusted associate of his, after they had returned to the office from lunch. That made her feel at least more comfortable during this potential crisis.

"How does this sound?" Jenna asked Dion as he leaned against the front of his desk, speaking with his brother. Even though he was clearly under stress, Dion looked smoking hot as he sat with his shirt sleeves rolled up. There was something oh, so sexy about a man with his silk tie slightly loosened at the neck, his blazer off, white shirt unbuttoned at the top and his sleeves rolled up. His sexy bad boy groomed stubble on his face gave him such an exotic appearance it almost made Jenna's heart stop.

Dion took the sheet of paper from Jenna and read it aloud. "If the situation in Lendovia deteriorates, it may be necessary to implement additional security procedures." He exchanged glances with his brother Troy and then turned his attention back to Jenna, the look of concern shadowed his handsome features.

"Security procedures? If the situation deteriorates?" Dion asked Jenna as if to clarify.

"I think we should go with the more serious assumptions, Dion."

"I don't want to be responsible for creating mass hysteria, Jenna. I understand your concerns."

"Maybe we can reword the statement," Troy added, his arms folded across his chest as he, too, leaned against another table in the room. Did no one sit on chairs in the office?

"Maybe we don't need to do a damn thing," a board member, who walked into Dion's office added his two cents. Jenna recognized him from a meeting earlier in the day. "The Department of Foreign Affairs hasn't issued any travel advisory warnings so why are we all up in arms? Because the temp told us to be?"

"Travis, that's enough!" Dion snapped at the older man. "If Lendovia's situation deteriorates for whatever reason, we need to make sure the safety and security of our employees are in no way compromised." Dion combed his fingers through his hair and pondered for a moment. Jenna felt uneasy and knew full well that many of the staff members were not exactly thrilled that she had come on board so quickly and Dion gave her a little authority to call some shots and offer her feedback into the situation in Lendovia. She was grateful he trusted her. But, oh, God! Was he having doubts now? Second thoughts about trusting her?

She felt her stomach plunge. She needed Dion to trust her. It was for his own benefit. It was for the benefit of his overseas employees. Couldn't he see that?

Dion sighed before speaking. "Listen, I didn't mean to snap at you like that, Travis, but we can't afford to take chances."

"And we can't afford to listen to unfounded information."

"Unfounded?"

"Yes. Forgive me, Dion," the man said, unsmiling, "I've worked for your grandfather for many, many years. Even before you were...known to us. We've just been through the ringer with...well, I'm not going to get into that now or bring up her name. You know who I'm talking about. But I think certain decisions should be left to human resources and finance. My department. And trust me on this one. I think we need to take things a lot slower and wait and see before we become the laughing stock of the corporate world." Travis barely acknowledged Jenna's presence.

Dion looked as if he were royally peeved with Travis's insinuation. Jenna could only guess they were referring to a relationship of some sort that Dion probably had with another employee or ex-employee, judging by his reaction.

Dion grabbed a sheet of paper off the table, clearly unimpressed with Travis. He read a statement Jenna had printed out and given to him from the Department of Foreign Affairs' website. "The actions we take depend on the nature of any given crisis in certain countries. We may only provide information on conditions in the country, warning about areas of unrest, information on where to seek help if necessary and other useful advice." Dion glanced up at Travis, daggers in his eyes. "We may recommend that Canadian citizens leave a foreign country and provide departure assistance, if necessary and depending on resources available."

He threw the sheet of paper back down on the table. "Travis, this has nothing to do with any misinformation. Don't you see that even the federal government can't do anything until there is confirmation? But it doesn't mean that we can't! And even then, they can only give advice to foreign nationals on what to do and there is no guarantee that things can happen as quickly as they could if something unpredictable happens."

"So what does that mean?" Travis challenged Dion. "Shouldn't we assess the situation first then act accordingly?"

"I'm a man who likes to be proactive. You should know that by now." Dion paced by the tall window. "It's not always good to be reactive. If you remember that our own company policy to workers in foreign countries states that if there is any threat to the degree where safety or security is concerned it may be necessary to implement additional security procedures and that includes evacuation of personnel out of the country to a safer region. I agree with Jenna on this one. She's worked for the ruling monarch there in the past."

I agree with Jenna?

Jenna's heart exploded in her chest at Dion's words. He agreed with her. No, he *believed* in her and he wasn't afraid to let his team know. That meant more to Jenna than Dion would ever know. Those words of encouragement would forever be engraved in Jenna's mind.

Travis's face flinched when Dion spoke his words. Travis's lips were pinched tightly, and again, he did not even look in Jenna's direction. Jenna tried to squash the feeling of hurt and reminded herself that at least her boss was on her side and he was the one who mattered in this situation, right? He was calling the shots. But, if she was honest with herself, she knew that it would be nice if the team didn't think she was some pest or nuisance insect that needed to be terminated or squashed.

"Very well," Travis conceded. "Let's get the show on then." He sounded bitter and unconvincing. Jenna only hoped that Travis wouldn't try to do anything like sabotage their efforts. She'd been there before with office politics and the ugly side of running a business with those who were opposed to your views who wanted nothing more than to see you fail miserably. She tried to swing her thoughts out of the negative pool and into optimism. Optimism always gave her that energy boost she needed to fight everyday existence. It was better than feeling sunken and unable to cope.

Later in the evening when the others had left the office, Jenna sat at her desk outside Dion's office typing on her computer. The tension earlier between Dion and the members of the board and other staff members had been almost unbearable for her and probably gave Dion a headache as well. She'd only known him briefly but they'd just spent more time together in this concentrated period of time than she'd done with any other person in a long while.

"We have time for a gradual and phased evacuation, Dion," Jenna called out to the open door of Dion's office. Her voice sounded more hopeful than earlier. Was it because her boss now believed in her and wanted to work together as a team? "All we have to do is send out this memo regarding curtailing normal office operations until further notice as a precaution," she said, her fingers flying off the keyboard as she typed furiously then hit send to her boss.

"Thanks, Jenna. You should be going home," Dion said, as he hurried out of his office with some more papers in tow. "I'll take it from here."

"You've been telling me to go home for the past few hours, boss. Really, I'm here to get a job done. You need me right now."

Dion gave her the "look."

"I need my staff to be well and not overworked. When I spoke to your last employer, he told me you had a penchant for working beyond what's required of you."

"Touché!" Jenna smiled. "It seems like you like to work more than anyone, boss. Besides, it's not like I have anyone who's waiting for me at home—unless you count my bed," Jenna blurted out before flushing. Oh, God! Why on earth did she just say that? Was she insane? She realized too late how awful that must have sounded. Or how desperate!

She didn't dare look at her boss's face.

"Well," he said, cautiously, "when you're ready, let me know and I'll take you home." Thank God, he didn't address her gaffe about no one waiting for her at home except her bed. Ugh. Why did she say that?

Jenna swallowed hard. He said he would take her home. Take her home? She really didn't think that was a good idea but she'd spoken enough so far and didn't want to say anything more that might come out as rude or presumptive. "Thank you," was all she said quietly as she gazed at her screen, her fingers frozen of the keys waiting to type something more. If only her brain wasn't frozen right now. She drew in a deep breath, while Dion walked over to the copier near her desk and photocopied some documents.

She was used to top dogs being hands-on. In the past CEOs would have secretaries do everything but these days, it wasn't uncommon to see a top guy or gal at a mega corp who was more than down-to-earth and knew how to type and use his own gadgets and the copier. Or maybe not. Jenna heard a screech emanating from the machine after Dion grabbed some copies. A light flashed.

She got up from her seat. "Oh, what is it?"

She was often the go-to girl in offices when machines had nervous breakdowns, but before she could say more, Dion pulled the machine out and knew which door to open to look for a paper jam. Okay, so it was just a jam but he knew more about basic machines than other bosses she'd worked for. He whipped the paper out then rebooted the machine as if he did this stuff every day. Jenna was beyond impressed. Not because he could fix a simple office machine but he was so matter-of-fact and down-to-earth about it all. And oh, he looked so hot when he knelt over the machine.

"Anything I can do to help?" she offered.

"Nah, it's good," he said. His tone sounded more relaxed and informal than when she'd first met him, which seemed like forever ago but it was only this morning, when he'd also told her that he no longer needed a personal assistant. Which she could see was true to some degree since he was so efficient in handling most of his own personal affairs, but she was glad he'd taken her on nonetheless.

When she moved over to the machine to see if she could be of any assistance, she leaned over the machine not seeing where his right hand rested on the top, and the back of his hand while gripped on the copier machine top touched her bosom. A delicious heat of electricity pulsed through her body. Her sex jumped. She gasped, surprised, and moved back.

"Are you okay?" he said, getting up, not realizing that she'd accidentally pressed a part of her womanhood to the back of his soft sensual hand on the machine, and she was secretly wishing it had been much more than a casual brush. "You weren't shocked by electricity, were you?"

As he stood in front of her, their eyes locked momentarily. The sweet, irresistible scent of his cologne overwhelmed her senses. Oh, God! The man's sex appeal sent her pulses soaring. He was stunning to look at. Yummy eye-candy.

A voltage of electricity pulsed between them then lingered in the air. It was palpable. Unstoppable. His sweet lips, his chiselled cheekbones and dark, gray-brown sexy eyes were mesmerizing. Not to mention the fact that he really towered over her. He must be well over six feet three inches. She knew this because her late ex was about the same height. She felt the space between her legs pulse hard in Dion's captivating presence.

Her body tingled from head to toe as she observed the desire of heat in his sexy eyes. His closeness sent her libido into overdrive. She was inches from him. Their lips were close enough to brush lightly, she felt almost dizzy with torn emotions. This was straight out of a movie. She had to conquer her involuntary reaction to this stunning man's heated gaze.

It was just the two of them in this dimly lit, now-vacated office late at night. She couldn't help but think there was something naughty about being at the office after hours, alone with a hot, unattached boss.

The hum of the air conditioner was the only sound, not counting the hard, heavy beats of Jenna's heart. There was a compelling magic that danced in the air between them. A pulling desire, she could not describe, only that she'd never experienced it before.

"Um...n-no," she finally said, breathing hard. She felt flushed throughout her entire body. "I-I didn't get shocked." She was sure she didn't sound nearly as convincing as she'd hoped she would. Would he sense that she was drooling over him inwardly? She felt electricity all right. But not the kind he had in mind. It was more like a delicious heat, a surge of power, lust, longing to be held by Dion. And the sensation of her mind spinning out of control wondering what the heck was going on with her all of a sudden. Why did Dion Romero have that kind of lusting effect on her? Why was her mind whirling with thoughts of desire for him, curiosity of what it would be like for him to purposefully touch her and bring her to the brink of unfathomable passion? Wondering if she would ever be close to him, experience his nakedness next to her.

Her nipples strained and ached underneath her blouse, which annoyed the sweetness out of her since she was only there to work. She was an employee, and this man, this too-sexy-for-his-own-good man, was her boss. A serious businessman. Not a serious boyfriend.

She should not even be thinking erotic thoughts about her boss, who obviously had no interest in her whatsoever, and even if he did, she was off the market, for good. Not worthy of being with another man after what happened to Juan. Yet, to her chagrin, her fired-up body was giving her completely opposite signals. If only she could control the feelings she was having around Dion. But the feelings could only be lust, right? She hadn't even known him that long for it to be anything else.

Jenna stood firm, squared her shoulders and drew in a deep breath to recompose herself.

"Good," he said, breathing hard, his voice sounded slightly hoarse. Or was that her imagination? He looked a bit lost at first then recomposed himself. "I think she's good to go now," he said, referring to the equipment. "I'm taking you home. Let's go," he said in a low voice not looking at Jenna. He then slammed the copier machine door closed and powered it down.

Jenna's heart hammered against her chest. Her body felt heavy. She couldn't help feel a little disappointed. Were they going to kiss? If she hadn't opened her big mouth? No, she answered her rhetorical question. He was way out of her league and the situation would have been way too awkward. Stuff like that—the sexy boss throwing his assistant on the copier to make passionate love—happened only in romance novels or movies.

Get your mind out of there, Jenna. It's never going to happen. And you don't deserve it anyway. You could never handle a man as powerful and connected as Dion Romero.

After Dion went back into his office, Jenna walked back to her desk and opened the drawer to retrieve her handbag, feeling utterly humiliated. She'd practically opened up her mouth to kiss him and he left her hanging. At least that's how the past moment was replaying over in her head. Funny how when we replay events in our mind, it's never the same. It becomes more intense and we even add our own spin on it. *Memo to self: Stop living in the past, even if it happened ten minutes ago. Live in the moment. It's way better.*

Still, her mind kept reeling over what just happened or what might have happened. Or what should have happened. Now her thoughts were obsessed with one thing. What must Dion think of her?

CHAPTER SEVEN

Dion couldn't get over what just happened, or *didn't* happen, with Jenna. Man, just looking at that beautiful woman made him hard. Her lips looked so sweet, he fought the urge to pick her up in his arms and pleasure her like she'd never been pleasured before. A surge of heat raced through him. His groin throbbed. This wasn't good. Not good at all.

He sat back in his chair pondering as he powered down his laptop. He thought about his crazy ex and her schemes and what she did to him, but heck, that was all about sex but the feeling he was having towards Jenna was something else and it bothered the hell out of him. Why did he suddenly have the overwhelming urge to make love to her, right then and there, by the copier? For a fleeting moment there, desire burned through his body to rock her world with mind-blowing office sex. Yeah, that would have been smart, too. They would have had photocopied evidence of the event, should her nice round ass end up on the copier while he turned her senses inside out.

Get a grip of yourself, man. Ignore the feeling. It'll pass.

Yeah, it had better pass for his sake and for hers. Dion got up and went to the sink in his office and turned on the faucet. He splashed water on his face. Maybe that would cool him down a bit. Or maybe not. It was probably going to take a lot to bring his core body temperature back down.

He knew Jenna was just outside his door waiting for him to take her home. Boy, would he like to take her to *his* home.

Dion knew what he was going to do. He was determined to ignore the urges he was having, take the young lady to her abode and forget the hell about what just happened or almost happened. Sex with a temp was the last thing he needed do deal with right now. Office romance, especially with a contractual employee he only knew through glowing referrals from past associates of his, and a basic background check, was a bad idea. Period. He would just forget the whole thing and chalk it up to the results of a long, stressful day at the office.

I've gotta get my guys out of Lendovia. That's all that matters, right now. Then, I've got to fight some phony claim Miranda is trying to cough up against me. Yeah, I've got my hands full enough to be even thinking of holding a pretty lady in my arms tonight.

Adrenaline coursed through his veins as he grabbed his keys and his briefcase, ready to take his temp home—to her own place.

Dion pulled up to the address Jenna gave him and for the first time that day, he was almost too stunned to speak.

"You live here?" he asked. He was crestfallen.

"Yeah, why?"

He looked at the building. It wasn't the worst neighbourhood in town but it sure as hell wasn't the nicest either. In fact, it worried him that a nice young girl like Jenna would even think about going home late from the office or any place of work to this joint.

"It's not the same address you have on your resume, Jenna," he finally admitted to her that he'd been checking up on her thoroughly. The address on her resume was from the east side in a nice neighbourhood. A high-rise condominium.

"Why did you lie on your resume?"

"I-I didn't," she said, sounding more nervous than she did earlier. "It was my address but I moved."

"I know it's not my business, but are you in any kind of trouble?"

"No!" she defended. "What makes you think that?"

"Because you've had a few addresses in the past few months, Jenna."

They both sat in his luxury SUV outside the building. It was way too late at night for her to go up to her apartment on her own, even though she said she would be fine.

"How did you know that?" she asked, her eyes wide open with shock.

"I checked your previous employers, remember?"

"And?"

"You're registered with several temp agencies in town, Jenna."

"There's nothing unusual about that," she defended, and man, did she ever look so cute with her pouty full lips. "Jobs are hard to come by these days, you know. It's a competitive market. There are university and college grads competing for jobs since the summer began. The economy is tough. The more I spread out my resources, the better my chances are in keeping a steady flow of assignments."

"I know," he agreed, "I admire a woman who works hard and always has a plan b."

Jenna folded her arms tightly across her chest, still peeved. As if waiting for an apology. But he wasn't going to give her one.

"Is there a reason why you list a different address with each agency?" Dion arched a brow.

She turned to him, looking stunned, or was that the look of disbelief? "How did you know?" Her face flushed.

"I like to do background checks on people who work close to me. I've seen the different versions of your resumes."

"You seem to know a lot about me, Dion. I'm just your employee. Do you think that's fair?"

"Do you think it's fair that those who come to work for me and ultimately are put in positions of trust, know more about me than I do of them?"

She was about to say something as if in protest but closed her sweet lips again. "It's called due diligence, but I guess you do have a point," she finally agreed. "Your business is out there for the whole world to see. I...I know it must be difficult."

He nodded. "And I'm sure you've read about my family. I notice you were reading an article about the Romero family earlier on your coffee break."

She looked stunned that he would know this. "Why are you telling me this?"

"Because as much as I don't like people keeping things from me, I prefer to be upfront."

"It's as if you have a vested interest in me," she commented.

"Maybe, I do!" So there! he wanted to add.

To his amazement, the deer-in-the-headlight look on her face was priceless. She then almost melted into a blushing smile.

This woman was as open as any book he'd ever read. She certainly wasn't a poker player or any kind of player for that matter.

That actually turned him on more. Which was not a good thing. Why the heck did he care so much about Jenna-Lynn Macchiasso? Was it because she seemed vulnerable, yet strong? Because she cared so much about the well-being of others, even putting her own career in jeopardy? But she was also one of the most mysterious creatures he'd ever encountered. She was a mixed bag of what? He didn't really know. But something about her really resonated with him.

Still, it was getting late and they had a whole lot to accomplish this week. "Listen, I'll walk you up," he offered.

"Please, don't. I'm fine, really." She bit her lip, looking out the passenger side window. Jenna was too damn sexy and hot when she bit down on her full, plump lower lip. God, he really wished she wouldn't do that.

"Are you sure you'll be okay to go to your apartment alone at this time of night?" he asked.

She nodded slowly. Almost as if she was trying to put up a brave front but she wasn't really sure herself.

He got out of the Jeep and went to her side to open the door. "With all due respect, Jenna, I'm not letting you go up there alone until I've made sure you're safe. It's my responsibility."

"Your responsibility?" she said, getting out of his SUV. Her foot missed the step of the Jeep climb and she tripped and fell right into his arms, grabbing his waist.

"Hey, are you okay?"

"Um, yeah," she said, leaning into him. And he felt his groin harden. A grin of amusement touched his lips. He found her sweet fragrance heavenly intoxicating. This wasn't going to be easy. A surge of heat raced through Dion as they embraced awkwardly on the street late at night in the Sutton Lo Housing Complex under a street lamp, on the west side.

Every minute he was around this dainty office princess, she stirred up all kinds of raw emotions inside his body. Damn, she was just too fine! Did she have to go and fall right into his body like that? If he didn't know any better, he would say that she allowed herself to be so careless, or maybe it was just the universe trying to hook them up despite his reservations about office staff and physical relations.

He stood her up to make sure she was okay then pulled away from her, as hard as hell as that was. He could see the headlines now: Romero brother seduces office temp – It's all in the family.

Dion cringed at the thought. His own brother had been wrongfully accused of being a womanizer. That was the last thing he needed. Thank God, his family was no longer in the spotlight. He just didn't need that kind of publicity.

"Come on," he said, firmly, his body still reacting to the lovely Miss Jenna. "I'll take you up." What he wanted to do was lay her down. Right underneath the stars, stripping her naked and admiring her soft skin and womanly curves and make love to her over and over again.

"Okay," she said, softly, breathlessly. "I'm sorry, if I grabbed you too hard."

He chuckled. "You didn't grab me, Jenna. You fell."

"Thank you for catching my fall."

"It's nothing," he said, resisting the urge to hug her while he walked her across the dark street. There were no cars driving by. It was so isolated. Only a few rundown looking parked vehicles on the curb. He knew his custom built SUV looked way out of place there. Yet he simply wasn't even concerned that he'd come back and see his car stripped. Call it luck or whatever, but his family was just known somehow on the streets. Dion wanted to turn Jenna around and take her to the new condos his family owned on the east side and put her up for a while. At least while she worked for him.

"I didn't realize how high it was to climb into your Jeep then get back out again. I guess they built the car for your tallness."

He grinned. "You really do have an explanation for everything, don't you?" Dion enjoyed the silly grin on her face. Why was she growing on him so fast? There was just something about Miss Jenna that appealed to him. Her aura, her charm, her dedication to helping others, her body. It was just everything. He wished he *was* taking her home as her boyfriend and not as some temporary boss who probably wouldn't see her or need her beyond next week. He'd really like to date this woman, get to know her better—on a more intimate level. She really seemed to rub off on him in a good way.

Man, things seemed totally unfair. Now, if only, he could create more work for her to stay on with his company. He would have to buy her out from the temp agency but that wouldn't be a problem.

Wait a minute. Dion was trying to cook up a scenario to keep a woman near him? That was so lame, even by his standards. What was he thinking? Why did he care about this woman so much? What was it about her that resonated with every fiber of his being?

Dion and Jenna walked into the lobby of her building and he was not impressed. He took a quick glance at the lobby glass door that apparently had a brick thrown through it.

"What's wrong?" she said, hugging herself.

"Don't you see, you've been hit by vandals?"

"Oh, that's been there for a few days. The building owner was supposed to take care of that like yesterday." She shook her head and rolled her beautiful eyes.

"Not good enough," he said, taking note of the name on the building. "Sinott and Latch Corporation, huh?" He committed the moniker to memory. "I'll get my people in touch with them in the morning."

"Dion?"

"It's not right. I'm a residential building owner, too. I would never expect my residents to live like this or put up with crap like this. It's criminal." He was clearly seething. He felt acid rise in his chest at the thought that lovely Miss Jenna was forced to live like this. "The door doesn't even have any security measures on it. We practically just walked in." He didn't want to get too critical but he wondered why on earth the building still operated on a key system. Anyone could cut a key and have easy access to the building. All his residential facilities had electronic FOB key systems that registered to the owners only and could not be replicated in any way. It was the safest and most secure way to live. Especially these days when criminals were getting more high-tech in gaining access to people's properties.

He was going to make sure that his younger brother, Mayor Carl Romero, got wind of this crazy practice. Municipal bylaws had to be enforced for all buildings for safety and security.

"Okay, Mr. Inspector," Jenna tried to make light of the situation.

When they approached the elevator, there was a handwritten cardboard sign: "Elevator No Working. Use Stairs."

Dion had to fight the rage burning inside him. He bit down on his lip. Anger consumed him. "Right, we are not staying," he fumed.

"What?" The color drained from her pretty oval-shaped face. "What do you mean by we?"

"I mean, I'm not leaving you here," he replied, his tone razor sharp.

"Dion," she said, her arms on her hips, fuming. "This is my home. You can't just decide when I can and can't go home. You're my boss, not my...father."

"You're right about that. If I was your father, you wouldn't be living like this."

She huffed.

"This isn't your home anymore, Jenna. I mean," he said, realizing that he was beginning to sound like a dominant prick. "I have employees overseas in possible danger, Jenna. I don't want to feel that the ones working for me here are living in unsafe conditions."

She sighed. "I know it's not the best place in Mayberry Hill, Dion. And I really do appreciate your concern but...it's all I can afford right now. But..." she said, rebutting his attempt to interrupt her. "It's what I can afford. And I'm okay with it."

"You are?" he asked incredulously, arching a brow.

"Yes. I am. Because...this place may be a dump to you but compared to the way half the people living in poverty live, it's a decent roof over my head. I count my blessings, Dion, not my sorrows. The building might suck, but I keep my unit in good condition."

He'd like to see *that*! Wait a minute. Did she say, she counted her blessings, not her sorrows?

He sighed. "Don't you live on the twenty-second floor?"

"Yes."

"So you're willing to walk up twenty-two flights with a heavy bag?"

She looked at her oversized tote bag stuffed with way too many things. He could tell it was heavy. What on earth did she have in that thing? The solution to all the world's troubles? He could never understand why women had to carry everything with them when they left the house. He'd dated this one chick who carried her makeup bag—and it was heavy; a bottle of painkillers—he guessed for lugging around her life in a bag; a mini family album; can of hairspray; diary-planner and address book; an enormous purse; umbrella; and some books! Man, it made his shoulders ache just to think about it.

He didn't know how women managed. He was good to go with his cell phone and wallet. Nothing more.

"Listen, you're doing a special assignment for the Romero Corp. It's not unusual for us to house employees who are expected to work late hours around the clock for us. In fact, it's part of the deal. Why would we treat you any different?"

"I see," she said softly, biting her lip, glancing into his eyes with a hopeful look, then tearing her gaze away. She appeared as if she was pondering what to do next.

"I'll go up and fetch your things, Jenna," he said, his tone softening. He was really beginning to feel her pain and her dilemma. It couldn't be easy having to live like this. Heck, he'd been there before. Living out of a van when he was a kid wasn't any picnic either. "If you trust me to enter your apartment. I'll take you somewhere safer." And much nicer. Heck, you deserve it, beautiful.

For the first time he could see himself railroading into dangerous territory. Miranda, the fake, had set him up real good. The thought slid into his mind that this whole situation could easily get misconstrued if anything crazy happened. But the truth was, his family did own the Romero Condo Corp and housed many employees, especially foreign workers, putting them up in decent furnished housing. He had good reason to want Jenna closer to the office during this potential crisis overseas. But he hoped he wouldn't have to resort to that.

"What makes you think I won't be safe here? I've been here a few months, Dion."

He pulled out his cell phone and quickly typed the address in the search engine. "Just what I thought."

"What?"

"This joint's been targeted many times. There was even a gang-related shooting. Did you know about that?"

She looked guilty. "I...I might have heard about that."

"You *might* have heard?"

"Okay, so there was an incident in the building a few weeks ago. It could have happened anywhere."

Dion sighed. "But it didn't happen anywhere. It happened here."

Dion didn't want to get too into this woman's business but she was working for him now. Heck, all his employees were like family. He took care of them. He was their boss. People spent more time at work than anywhere else in their life. They gave up their waking hours and their lives for service. "As much as I enjoy your company, Jenna, I'm not going to be talking with you all night in the lobby of this building. Would you like me to get your things?"

"I'm coming with you."

"You're okay to climb twenty-two flights?"

"If you can do it...I can do it."

"I'm an athlete, Jenna. I've trained with pros before. I have the stamina."

"And what makes you think I don't?"

"Fine. I'll pick you up and carry you when you get tired by the second floor!" Dion grinned. "Let's go."

She playfully rolled her eyes and scowled. "I just might let you carry me up all the way."

Why did he get the image of carrying this pretty woman over some threshold, never mind the stairs? Oh, heaven help him. He had to remind himself that she was just an employee, a temp, and nothing more.

CHAPTER EIGHT

"So you've got another chick housed in one of our condos, eh?" Troy teased his brother, Dion. It was late at night and the boys were in the grand study at Romero Manor, having a drink and discussing their next move vis-à-vis the gradual evacuation of their overseas staff in Lendovia.

"Not funny, Troy," Dion shot back. "She's not another chick. She's...an EA with my company, and you *know* that."

"I'm only kidding, bro. You're the one who said after Miranda set you up, you were through with hiring females and helping 'em out of tough times, remember?" Troy took another swig of his drink, while he rested his elbow on the mantelpiece of the stone fireplace between the wall bookshelves. "What ever happened to once bitten, twice shy? Just don't wanna see you get hurt again, Dion. You're an annoying brother, but you're still my brother, man. I've got your back."

"Thanks, Troy." Dion leaned back in the black leather executive chair behind the study desk. His drink and his late night supper prepared by the butler remained untouched. He didn't have much of an appetite. Well, at least not for food. "But she's different," he continued. "I actually have a good feeling about her. I didn't at first when she showed up at the office despite the cancellation with the agency. But I do now. She's golden. Everything she's said so far about the tension in Lendovia checks out. We can get our men out of there faster and before anything really stirs up."

At least Dion hoped Jenna was different. He was really beginning to feel her. She had just the right vibes. And man, was she hot, without even trying. Those soft, large caramel-colored eyes and luscious lips. And boy, did she have a killer body with killer curves. She could send a man into cardiac arrest with those provocatively shaped hips of hers.

Troy sighed heavily. "Well, Pamela did say Jenna had all the right stuff you'd need for the job."

Dion gave him a funny look. "I still don't appreciate people, i.e., *Pamela*, making decisions on my behalf. Pam went and hired Jenna without my consent."

"Relax, man. It's all working out, isn't it?"

If he didn't know any better, Dion would think Troy had a thing for Pamela. He was coming to her defense. Well, at least most of the time. Pamela was young and pretty with the shiniest ebony hair he'd seen on a woman. He wondered why none of his brothers had made a move on her. Not that he was ever interested. Right now, Jenna was the one who caught his attention. And probably not in the best of circumstances.

"Yeah, you're right," Dion agreed softly before another concern pounded hard on his chest. "Any news about Miranda's accusation?" Dion had been so busy working with Jenna on those new memos and instructions for a gradual release plan at the Rom that he didn't have time to sit and discuss the latest development with JoJo. He would have called Miranda himself and asked her what the hell she thought she was up to, but he knew that would be just plain stupid and could lead to further harassment charges. Since the Romero brothers all used JoJo, he didn't mind Troy following up on this situation with their own private detective. After all, he couldn't trust anyone else with this highly sensitive information than his own flesh and blood.

"Spoke to JoJo about it earlier. Word has it that her mother's a lawyer. Or *was* a lawyer."

"Was? What happened?"

"She got disbarred for embezzling funds. Sound familiar?" Troy chuckled. "From an estate of a deceased client. She was, not surprisingly, a disgrace to the family—and to her profession."

"Man, that's crazy."

"Tell me about it. Well, as it turns out her mother's fighting the disbarment with an appeal. Meanwhile, her little offspring, Miranda, didn't fall too far from that family tree. When Miranda hustled her way into your path and that money thing happened before you tossed her out on her ear-"

"Oh, no," Dion cut him off, "don't tell me her mother put her up to it."

Troy shrugged. "Who knows? We only know that her mother's one sly cat with some shady connections. It wouldn't help her mom's court appeal if they found out her daughter was also accused of embezzling funds from a company—your company. So my guess is that her mother might have encouraged her to weave a sexual harassment spin on it after she found out Miranda and you had slept together."

Dion cringed hearing that. Well, if that wasn't the lowest thing a person could do to another. "Thanks for the update," he said bitterly. "Well, keep me posted while I get ready to leave."

"Leave?"

"Yeah, I'm thinking of heading to Lendovia to make sure operations run smoothly during the evacuation and everything's taken care of."

"Do you think that's necessary?"

"Hey, they need me there. This could be huge if things turn worse. I need to be there. Besides, my executive assistant's from Lendovia. She speaks the language and knows the ins and outs."

"She's going with you?"

"Well, I haven't asked her yet," Dion admitted, picking up his glass of wine on the desk and putting it to his lips. "I'm sure there'll be no problem."

"Well, let's hope so." Troy was about to place his glass down but stopped. "Hey, you don't have a thing for her, do you?"

"What?" Dion almost spit out his drink. "Don't even go there, man."

"Seriously, bro. She's hot. Don't tell me you haven't noticed." Troy cocked a brow. That mischievous look plastered on his face. The brothers had always bantered about girls before and teased each other about having hot crushes on the least expected females. One time, Dion ribbed Troy about having a thing for his college professor. So he guessed it was time for him to return the favor. Only, Dion wasn't really up to it right now. Not after what happened to Miranda. But Jenna was different. The feeling he had for her was beyond professional—and currently beyond weird for him.

"Are you fishing for something, Troy?" he asked, putting his glass back down on the table. "I think you've had a bit much too drink, man."

"I think *you* have, if you can't see how she looked at you today in the meeting. I don't want you getting involved and getting your heart trashed. Just don't get too caught up in any moments while you're abroad."

Dion rolled his eyes. "Don't worry about anything happening abroad. We have serious business matters to take care of. Nothing more, Troy." Dion thought long and hard about what Troy said. He was, after all, his brother. Who would know Dion better? Suddenly an image of Jenna crossed his mind. And that damn image of her was fully naked. Her beautiful voluptuous breasts in full view and those curves. Oh, what he would with her if she were in his arms tonight.

Dion blinked hard and tried to squash the image out of his mind. Was it that long since he'd gotten laid?

"I can control myself, you know!" Dion finally got himself out of his little moment or passing daydream. "Unlike some people," Dion added with a sly grin, trying to catch the mood again as he gave his brother a you-know-what-I'm-talking-about glance.

"What's that supposed to mean?"

"Never you mind."

"No. Shoot it out."

"You've been spending a lot of time with Pamela lately, haven't you?"

"Pamela. Please, man. She's family. I wouldn't even take a second look at her."

"Now someone's lying right through their teeth."

"Lying? Who's lying?"

"Come on. Never mind a second look. You've been taking plenty of looks every time I turn away. You've got your eyes glued to her ass."

"Hey," Troy protested, trying to feign a chuckle.

Dion thought for a moment. "Look at us. This is crazy, man."

"What's crazy?"

"Us. Is this what it's going to be like now? Us going in and out of relationships like this? Talking about girls we may or may not be into? We're not in college anymore."

"Oh, no. You're beginning to sound like old man Gramps. No way. We're fine. Okay, so he convinced Lucas, Zack, Carl and Jules to get hitched but he's not getting to us. Well, at least not to me."

"Me neither," Dion declared without much conviction. "It was just a thought." Another thought struck him. He'd had a string of unsuccessful relationships. He had always trusted the wrong type of women. He was good being single and having to only answer to himself.

Heck, if Dion's current woman ever betrayed him, he'd just end it. Plain and simple. Give her walking papers and call it a day. But if he were married to her, it wouldn't be so damned easy to walk away—not without a heavy alimony suit.

Look at what happened to Dion's grandfather, Toni, after his first wife, Dion's biological grandmother, passed away from an inoperable tumor many years ago. Gramps was so lonely and ended up marrying the wrong women afterwards to fill that void—young eligible women who were only so "perfect" and full of energy, wanting to cater to his every whim, whilst they were secretly after his fame and money. It was a wonder Toni hadn't gone bankrupt, after his ex-wives took him to the cleaners, each one of them, after the marriage dissolved. Thankfully, he was in a healthy marriage now.

Nope, that was enough for Dion Romero to know that marriage and Romero men could prove a deadly and costly mistake. He wasn't going to go there. He was glad he'd brought up the subject of marriage and settling down with Troy because sometimes bringing things out in the open helped one clear his mind and set his thinking straight.

"Good for the others," Dion said, "but you're right, Troy. I'm not a marrying man and never will be. They all end up to be the same in the end."

"What's that?"

"Heart breakers."

Dion was never going to give a woman another chance to smash his heart to a million tiny pieces and shatter his hopes and dreams of a lasting monogamous relationship. He wasn't giving up on dating and pleasuring women. He loved women way too much for that. But as far as commitment went, he was determined to be a Romero bachelor for life.

CHAPTER NINE

Jenna tossed and turned in her bed, unable to sleep. The events of the past day rendered her mind numb from too many ideas swirling around in her head. Her thoughts raced like mad so the sleep hormone in her brain wasn't able to kick in and do its job. Darn it! The object of her torment was, of course, Dion Romero. How could she get her sexy enigmatic boss out of her head, her mind? Her sexy *temporary* boss, she should say. She dreaded the day she would no longer be working for Dion Romero and moving on to another short-term administrative assignment.

It was no use, she thought propping herself up in the bed—and a luxurious king sized bed at that. She just couldn't sleep. She looked around the unfamiliar room trying to come to terms with her new surroundings. The room was enormous by any standard. Jenna was grateful to be put up in a luxury high-rise condo suite by the Romero family—namely her boss, Dion, but this was all too overwhelming for her.

She almost cried out in pain when she tried to move. Her legs had really taken a workout from climbing up all those steps. Twenty-two flights! It served her right for not listening to Dion.

She sighed heavily and whipped the sheets off her, getting up out of the bed. Thinking about Dion and what he would be doing now. *He's probably sleeping, Jenna. Something you should be doing.*

"Yeah, right. Fat chance of that happening," she scoffed out loud. She didn't think she could fall asleep when her mind was still in an upheaval over the events of the day. The near miss of not working for Romero Corp and then that near *kiss* with Dion. Or at least she thought they were about to kiss. Her lips still buzzed from the sweet closeness of his to hers. They never touched, yet she felt the heat of electricity between them. Her nipples tightened thinking about what Dion would be like naked, touching her, caressing her. Later, he'd told her that he was an athlete. Oh boy, did he have the body of one. The way he strode up those steps effortlessly without so much as being out of breath, as she was. It was, to say the least, impressive. The man was fit as an Olympic swimmer and looked hot in his suit briskly pacing the flights of stairs to her studio.

She heaved a sigh and exhaled trying to keep her heart from racing like mad in her chest again. It was too unbearable. Besides, she knew she could never get close to Dion and that it would be a mistake. She had to remind herself about Juan.

Jenna closed her eyes and thought about that night, when she went to see him. He was lying on the floor of his apartment. She'd called out his name, screamed his name. No answer. He was lifeless, broken. She'd checked his carotid artery on his neck, hoping to feel a pulse. But nothing. Then she knelt over him and started chest compressions hard and fast in the center of his chest, not even counting, just pumping hoping his heart would start again. His body still felt a bit warm so she felt it had just happened.

A painful lump climbed in Jenna's throat. She closed her eyes and tried not to think about that night. She reached for her cell phone and dialled overseas using a calling card.

Lasrine answered. "What are you doing up at this hour? Isn't it midnight over there?"

"Mo...I mean, Lasrine, I can't sleep." Jenna almost slipped up this time. That was close. Even though she was on a disposable phone, she couldn't take a chance that her mother would be caught talking to her. She was sure the feds in Lendovia had her mother bugged somehow. If not her phone, then some sort of listening device outside her home. She didn't want to take any more chances. She didn't want anyone else dying on account of protecting her whereabouts.

"Can't sleep? Why?"

"Well, I...I've got a lot on my mind," she sighed. "Like the job, for one thing." And her boss.

"The job?" Alarm sounded in Lasrine's voice. "But you said the Romero man hired you, after all."

"I know," Jenna's voice trailed off. "He did." How was Jenna going to explain that she'd only met the man for a short period and had already fallen for him?

"Is everything all right, Jenna? You don't sound okay. I'm concerned."

"Don't be," Jenna said quickly, without realizing how she must have sounded. "I mean, I'm going through with the original plan. We're going to do an operation in the coming days. I'll keep you posted."

Operation was Jenna's term for escape plan. Lasrine knew that. They'd discussed it beforehand.

"I'm nervous, Jenna. I'll be honest with you. It's too risky."

"It's perfect, Lasrine. You'll be safe, once and for all." And away from any more abuse. "I..." Jenna's voice cracked as she glanced at the display clock in the room. "It's almost a full minute. Take good care. I..." *love you, Mom.* "Take good care."

"I will," Lasrine said as she disconnected the line.

Jenna was left with dead air and hung up. She felt alone for the umpteenth time in her life. And it wasn't just the kind of loneliness she'd felt before. It was something else. Seeing Dion with his brother and his family at the office who came by to lend their support in his massive operation plan. It was endearing. She longed for that sort of normal family life. She longed for that sort of togetherness. But that was something Jenna was probably never going to have. And she had to get used to it.

* * *

Jenna was startled in the morning by a knock at the door of her apartment. She was in her room, going through a million different outfits to wear for work. She'd pretty much stuffed most of her wardrobe in her suitcase when Dion said he'd take her to the Romero Condos to stay while she worked for him.

Why are you stressing over what to wear, Jenna? Since when do you care if you're perfectly matched up like a cover girl? Since Dion Romero became her official boss, that was when.

"Just a minute!" she shouted, grabbing her dressing gown. She'd just gotten out of the shower and her hair was still dripping wet. She had a towel wrapped around her head. What an early morning sight.

Jenna was stunned when she opened the door. A delivery man held a decorated tray of freshly baked goods in his hands.

"Oh, what's this? I didn't order anything. Who is it for?" Jenna was certain it was a misdelivery.

"Compliments of Mr. Romero, Miss Macchiasso."

Jenna couldn't believe her eyes, or her ears. "Th-thank you." She reached for her purse on the counter.

"Oh, no, miss. Mr. Romero has taken care of the tip."

Jenna was caught by surprise. A pleasant surprise. She flushed and took the beautifully decorated tray from the man. She opened the card on the tray: "Please don't skip the most important meal of the day. We have a busy day ahead of us."

Jenna couldn't help but grin from ear-to-ear and shake her head. Was Dion Romero always this charming...and unpredictable?

Now how on earth would *he* know if she skipped breakfast or that she would skip breakfast? She glanced at the tray.

Moments later, after she'd finished getting dressed for work, settling on a cream-colored blouse and gray, smooth pencil skirt with silver pair of sandals, she sat down at the breakfast bar to devour her early morning treats, thinking of Dion, wishing he was there with her.

The sun shone through the bright ceiling-to-floor windows. The walls in the condo were bright white in color and the floor, shiny laminate hardwood. If all employees had this kind of morning glory greeting Jenna was sure they'd be skipping in to work in high spirits. The place was...therapeutic, if that was at all possible. It must be nice to live like this, she thought. But then her mind swiftly kicked back to her home, if she could call it that, in Lendovia.

A sinking feeling crept into her stomach. She couldn't wait to help her mother and her family and friends out of the dreadful condition where they were mired. She felt guilty for living like this now, for enjoying a luxury breakfast in an upscale suite. She felt undeserving when her mother was forced to live like a caged animal. But soon that would change. She hoped and prayed it would. Once the evacuation process began in Lendovia with Rom International, she'd beg Dion and hope he'd understand her request, her plea to help those close to her to escape.

After she gulped down her freshly squeezed orange juice, Jenna grabbed the FOB key and her purse off the counter.

Just then, the phone rang. The disembodied speaker on the phone announced it was Dion Romero. Jenna's heart galloped hard in her chest, her pulse raced like mad. Dion Romero calling?

She picked up the phone.

"Good morning, Jenna. I trust you had a restful night sleep." His smooth silky, deep voice resonated with her and instantaneously brought a smile to her face.

"Um, yes, sir. I mean, yes, Dion. And my, what a surprise this morning."

"Surprise?"

"Yes, breakfast. Thank you so much for ordering breakfast for me. Do you treat all your employees like that? No wonder you're listed as the number one employer."

"I'm sorry, Jenna, I'm not sure I follow you."

"The breakfast? You ordered breakfast for me, right?"

"There must be some mistake."

Her body went cold. Then she heard a chuckle.

"I'm sorry, Jenna. Please forgive my dry sense of humor—or poor excuse for humor."

Jenna breathed a sigh of relief.

"From time-to-time, I like to ease the tension with my employees. I don't believe in all work and no play. Humor is healthy. I like healthy employees."

"That's good."

"And, we do have a very busy day ahead of us."

"I know, Dion," she murmured, feeling guilty that she wasn't up front with him about everything. "I'm ready."

"Good. Do you have your passport current?"

"Passport?"

"Yes. We're going to Lendovia ... tomorrow."

Jenna felt her heart come to a screeching halt in her chest. Her body ran cold. It was one thing that she wanted desperately to evacuate the employees out of Lendovia and rescue her own family, but to go there herself? She would be arrested at the airport. There was no way she could go back. Not now. But how on earth could she tell Dion?

CHAPTER TEN

Dion sat in the boardroom surrounded by his team, making every effort to choose his words wisely. The last thing he wanted to do was cause a commotion. "Okay, so as many of you've heard, there is a bit of tension that has gripped Lendovia."

"I heard they could be on the brink of a civil war," Chad, from Advertising, chimed in.

The gasps of several team members were palpable. "Not to worry, Chad," Dion consoled. "We don't have any evidence of that, as of yet. It's only speculation." Yeah, right. He knew as the head of a respected corporation, he had to tread carefully with his words. If anything got on the Internet, it would be there permanently and he didn't want that kind of backlash against the business he took over from his grandfather.

"A few of us will be flying there tomorrow to further assess the situation," Dion continued. "If necessary, we may close down temporarily."

Another cacophony of commotion erupted. This time, whispers and shrugs. "Do you think it's good to close down and disrupt studies?"

"It won't be permanent. Just a temporary precaution. We've already spoken to faculty to ensure staff distributes homework assignments to the students during that period of downtime." Dion drew in a heavy sigh. "Then when things get back to normal-"

"And what if they don't?" Travis's voice, laced with acridity, interrupted Dion. He noticed earlier that Travis had given Jenna, who was seated adjacent to Dion taking notes, a bitter look. Dion was about to say something but decided to hold his tongue—for now.

Suddenly all eyes were on Dion. What if things did not get better in Lendovia? What would happen to the college?

"We'll cross that bridge when or *if* we get to it, Travis," Dion answered in a cool tone. He noticed Jenna smiled slightly but wiped the look off her face immediately. Why was he so protective of Jenna? She'd only been working for him for less than a week. Still, she'd done more than most temps had done in an entire contract, and for that he was grateful.

"And who will be going to Lendovia?" Travis asked, slyly.

"A few of us. Troy, Jenna and myself."

He couldn't help but notice daggers being shot visually at Jenna as all attention turned in her direction. She was the new girl on the block whom he'd asked to take with him to Lendovia.

He felt the need to add more, lest it look odd. "Jenna is from Lendovia, for those who are not aware. In fact, she was here working till late last night on the protocols with a few of us. She's been a valuable part of this operation and is able to give us more insight into situations there." He said it as sternly and with finality as he could, trying not to go on the defensive. Still, he was aware that Travis was quite popular with the team. And rightfully so, since he was, after all, head of HR.

But Travis was also the instigator in many office political games and a gossip queen if he'd ever seen one. Travis was also a long-time friend of his grandfather's, and everyone knew that. Dion had agreed to let Travis stay on with the corporation, when he'd taken over from his grandfather. But if Travis kept up with any passive aggressive bullying around here, especially where Jenna was concerned, Dion would be more than happy to break that promise and show Travis the revolving glass door.

"Jenna has distributed the information you should all have by now, including emergency contact numbers while I'm abroad."

"Will you be gone long?" Chad asked.

"Only the week, maybe two."

"Okay," Chad said, scribbling some notes on his pad.

"Any additional questions?" Dion asked. It had been one heck of a meeting. They'd covered much ground. It was now time to kick things into action.

Everyone looked at each other, unsure of how to proceed. This was unprecedented at Romero Corp. They'd never had to evacuate one of their offices in case of political uprising. But since 9/11, most companies didn't take chances anymore. And they aimed to prepare for anything. Safety was more important than anything else.

"Good. We'll have our next meeting when I get back."

* * *

Jenna knocked on Dion's door. She felt her nerves knot inside her throat, squeezing off her oxygen supply. Her heart tried to compensate for lack of air by beating harder and faster in her chest. She was in a daze as she stood outside Dion's office, ready to confront him about the meeting earlier. Ready to disappoint him.

What would Dion say? He'd just announced to the entire team that she was going with him, with her expertise and all that. As much as she'd love the chance to travel with her hot boss, she just couldn't go back to Lendovia. What would she say to him?

"Come in," he called softly. He sat in his chair, leaned back, pondering over some notes in his hand. Scrutinizing an itinerary. He looked up when she walked in, nervous. His soft, dark sexy eyes captured her, holding her gaze for a moment and she shivered under the powerful heat of his riveting gaze. She just couldn't get over how good looking the man was—so talented and sophisticated, yet the man was a gift for the eyes to behold.

"H-hi, Dion," Jenna said quietly. She felt flushed. She hoped and prayed it wouldn't show in her skin pigment.

"Is everything okay?" he quizzed, looking concerned. Yep, it probably showed in her flushed skin.

"Um," she hesitated.

"Close the door behind you," he said in a serious tone and she complied. She noticed and she'd heard that quite often, Dion left his door opened during any conversations with staff, but this time, he wanted the door closed. What did that mean?

"Now what's on your mind? You look as if you'd seen a ghost."

Seen a ghost? That was close enough. "I-I need to speak to you about our meeting this morning." Why was she getting all flustered? She couldn't even think of the right words to say. Would he fire her? Would he demand to know why the hell she backed out of going when she told him she'd do everything necessary to help him with the situation in Lendovia?

"I can't go with you," she blurted out. She didn't know how else to tell him. She avoided looking into his eyes and kept her gaze straight ahead.

"That's fine. I understand," he said casually, glancing at his notes.

Jenna stood there stunned. Her mouth fell open.

What? That was fine? He understood?

"Th-that's fine?" she echoed to clarify she'd heard correctly. Well, that certainly wasn't the reaction she thought she would get. Why did he seem as if he didn't care? Was this the way Romero men showed their disappointment? They just shrugged it off? She'd heard a lot about their boardroom behaviour. Shrewd businessmen who could be cool and sleek as ice. "Y-you understand?" He understood what? Did he know about her?

"Yes," he said, sighing before putting the papers in his hand down on the desk. He leaned back, grinning and eyed her. Her heart pounded harder in her chest. What was going on? She'd really like to know.

"I don't get it. You told everyone I was going with you earlier and now I'm not going. You're not disappointed or curious as to why?"

"I know why."

Her heart exploded in her chest. Her eyes began to sting. Was she going to get emotional?

"It's because when I mentioned it to the team, I saw the way you squirmed in your chair when the others looked at you. At that time, I realized I probably should have asked you and not jumped the gun."

"I don't get it."

"You have a reputation to protect, as I do. It was a bad idea. You're a new temp, Jenna," he sighed. "It's not a big deal. We'll communicate via email and telephone. I won't be gone for too long."

Jenna's heart fluttered. Did he just say what she heard him say? "I...I don't know what to say, Dion. I'm..."

"Don't say another word. Don't worry about it. In fact, I have a lot of work for you to do here."

"You do?"

"Yes, Jenna. I'm pleased with your work ethic so far and all the work you've put in during the past 48 hours. I don't expect my employees to work around the clock. But if you're interested, the assignment to work for me can be extended to, say, six months. Does that sound good for you?"

"Six months?" Excitement coursed through Jenna's veins. "Oh, my goodness, Dion. Thank you."

"Good. I'm glad you're okay with it," Dion said. "I'll send HR the information."

HR? That meant that not-so-nice Travis guy would get the memo. Oh, great. Travis was going to be thrilled, Jenna thought. For some reason, she felt Travis really had it in for her from the get-go. Then another thought struck Jenna. Dion was a lot smarter than she had originally thought. If Travis knew she was going to be more of a permanent fixture on the scene, he'd cool off on the politics thing. Temps tended to have it much harder than permanent employees when it came to scapegoating.

"That would be fine, Dion. I'm happy to work here," she said. *I'm happy to work here—for you.*

Now, a pressing issue threatened her temporary peace of mind. Her mother. What would she do now? She was hoping to extend some information for Dion to take to Lendovia so that she could give her mother instructions on getting a work visa to come to Canada but since she would be working for Romero Corp for an extended period of time, she didn't want to press her luck and ask too much of her new boss. Because that would mean revealing more about her past. And she just couldn't risk it, not now.

This was a game changer, for sure. Dion was so kind to help her out this way. She would always appreciate it and continue to work hard for him, giving it her all. Later, when they built more of a rapport, she'd feel him out and see if she could open up to him completely. She would tell him the truth, as painful as it would be. But he was putting a lot of trust in her and she deeply appreciated that. He was a good man, and those were far and few in her books, from her past experience. She couldn't wait to brief her mother on the changes. But now she would have to wait longer. Say, in the next few weeks, knowing that she had more time, she would see if he could help her get her family out of Lendovia.

CHAPTER ELEVEN

The next three weeks were a torturous game of wait-and-see for Jenna. It was late in the afternoon at Romero Corp, the headquarters of Rom International. Jenna couldn't wait to go home. She was busy at work filing in Dion's office. Her boss was still in Lendovia. He'd run into some administrative complications while there. But it was all good now. Many of the staff members had already been safely evacuated out of the country. They were back in Canada. But Dion had stayed behind to clear up some work to ensure the facilities, though vacated, would be properly secured while they were shuttered. He was scheduled to come back shortly. It was a good thing he'd traveled on his own airplane.

The truth was, Jenna missed Dion like crazy, even though they'd spoken on the phone each and every single day since he'd left for Lendovia—for three weeks! Sometimes they'd speak for an hour, several times during the day. They never ran out of topics to talk about, and it wasn't only about work. After they'd discussed business matters, they would delve into other interests close to their hearts. Every day for the past few weeks, Jenna actually looked forward to his call from a "private number." Her heart galloped like a wild horse when her phone buzzed, hoping it would be Dion. He even playfully called her his pseudo wife when she'd scold him for not getting enough sleep while there, reminding him like a dutiful personal assistant to take good care of his health. Like he needed reminding anyway. He was the fittest person she knew, except for the workaholic part.

"Well, look at this," she said to herself. She stood in his office by his file cabinet, sorting through some of his documents as he had instructed her to do. A folder caught her attention. It contained items that needed to go to archives under "other activities." No, this wasn't just "other" activities in her books. It should have been labelled "exceptional" activities.

Dion and his brothers had taken part in more humanitarian efforts than she could keep track of. He'd personally donated millions of his own dollars to various organizations in helping countless groups from a program called Seniors Living Alone, and another group called Tomorrow's Leaders, an organization helping disadvantaged youth gain better access to jobs, healthcare, even counseling. There was another non-profit to assist refugees. She was relieved to see that one. Dion seemed to have a heart of gold when it came to helping others in disadvantaged situations. He seemed really nonjudgmental, too.

No one in the office at Romero Corp had anything bad to say about Dion Romero. He was a cool boss and everybody loved him. They often expressed they would gladly give their right hand for him. If he could only take *her* right hand—in marriage, she dreamed.

"Amazing," she sighed. Why was it that she could never be with a good guy? Well, her late ex was a good guy, but he was more of a friend, than a lover. They hadn't actually slept together and when she thought they had moved to another level...

She swallowed hard, trying not to remember the pain of Juan's loss. Why was it that any time a seed of happiness tried to grow in her heart, she would remember Juan? Was it grief? Or was it guilt?

Jenna tried to divert her thoughts again and picked up some more files from Dion's desk to put into certain folders in his file cabinet.

She looked at another folder and a magazine fell out of it. Dion was on the cover and oh, my, he looked handsome as ever. He'd won some sort of championship for a charity and he sported a nice pair of swim trunks, his chest looking buffed and fit. She felt her inner thighs throb at the beautiful image of the sexy man looking back on her from the magazine. *So that's what he looks like underneath his tailored business suits.* Oh, God! Jenna could feel heat climb to her cheeks. A naughty thought then crossed her mind and a wicked grin found its way on her lips.

"Oh, Dion," she moaned as she leaned down and pressed her lips to his photo on the cover, wishing it were Dion in the flesh.

The sound of a person clearing her throat startled Jenna and she dropped the magazine to the floor.

"I'm sorry, I didn't mean to disturb you!" Pamela, the Romero family's PR person, stood at the door, looking surprised. Pamela glanced down at the magazine on the floor.

Talk about major embarrassment. Jenna wondered what Pamela had seen. Jenna kissing a picture of her hot boss?

"Um...it's okay," Jenna said, picking up the magazine off the floor and feeling as if she wished the floor would open up and swallow her whole.

Pamela looked equally embarrassed for Jenna. "Oh, it's nothing. I just wanted to check on you to see how things are going."

"Oh, there...um...great, thanks," Jenna said, hurriedly as she struggled to get the darn magazine back into the folder. Her hands were all thumbs.

"It's okay," Pamela said, a cheeky grin on her lips. "The Romero men have that kind of effect on women."

"Oh," Jenna blushed. "It's n-not what it looks like."

"I've been there before," Pamela shot her an uh-huh-whatever-you-say look.

"You have?" Jenna's defenses shot up. *Pamela likes Dion, too?* Why was Jenna feeling so insecure all of a sudden? That was so unlike her. She wondered if Pamela and Dion had a thing going. Was that why Pamela handpicked her from the agency? To make sure his temp was competent enough to do the job, yet not as good looking as her to avoid competition? Jenna was extremely insecure about her appearance, as many women were.

"Oh, no!" Pamela exclaimed. "Not Dion."

"No?"

"His brother," she admitted. "I think his brother Troy's real cute."

"Oh, you have a crush on Troy?"

"Not officially," Pamela clarified. "He can never know this, by the way." She gave Jenna a stern look but Jenna caught something in Pamela's eyes. Was that regret? Or sorrow? What the heck happened between them? Jenna wondered. She'd heard Pamela had been working for the Romero family as their young and upcoming press secretary for many years. She must be good to hold that position and she couldn't be much older than Jenna.

"Besides, we're complete opposites," Pamela continued, looking out the window, avoiding Jenna's gaze. "It would never work out," she said quietly.

Jenna felt for Pamela. She knew what that felt like. Having a crush on someone unreachable. She hugged the file folder to her chest feeling, for the first time, comfortable around someone else, not counting Dion, of course. Jenna always found it hard to get along with women at work, but Pamela seemed all right. She seemed like the real deal. Genuine and kind.

"Well, I promise not to breathe a word," Jenna teased her, "as long as you, ahem, forget what you just saw."

Pamela grinned and shook her head. "Deal!"

Just then, a knock fell on the door. It was Travis from HR.

"Hey, Travis," Jenna said, cheerfully, riding a true high.

"Oh, there you are, Pamela," Travis said, barely acknowledging Jenna.

Well so much for nice and friendly at the office. Every day since Dion was away, Jenna went out of her way to be nice to Travis, whenever their paths crossed, but the guy was cold as a slab of ice to her. She tried to hide the hurt, pretending it didn't matter. She noticed Pamela seemed a bit uncomfortable at Travis's rude interruption and disrespect of Jenna.

"Didn't you hear Jenna?" Pamela said in Jenna's defense and Jenna couldn't be more grateful. It was rare to find anyone in the office defending another employee, especially against a popular one who called some shots. Pamela was good people.

"Yes, hello, Jenna," Travis said dismissively, turning his attention back to Pamela. "Will you give these to Toni when you see him tonight?" Travis handed Pamela a stack of forms.

"Sure thing. Is everything okay?"

"Oh, it's okay. He just asked to see some stats about the Rom International."

"Great. Thanks."

After Travis left the room, Pamela turned her attention to Jenna. "How have things been around here, Jenna? The truth."

"Oh, good," Jenna said, finishing up the last of the files.

"Are you sure, now?"

"Yes, why?"

"Travis hasn't been giving you any trouble, has he?"

"Oh, Travis. He's all right. I don't let anything bother me."

"No? You have a good attitude, Jenna."

"Hey, you can't please everyone. You can only be the best you can be and just do your thing. Besides, I've got more pressing matters to think about than who likes me or who doesn't." Jenna forced a smile. She didn't want Pamela to get the impression that she was weak or a pushover. "My motto is to work hard and be kind to those I work with. If they don't like it, too bad!" Jenna snapped the file cabinet closed with a thud.

"You are a real prize, you know that?" Pamela commented. "I'm glad you're working for Dion."

"So am I."

Just then, Chad from Advertising ran into the office. "Hey, did you guys hear the breaking news?"

"No, what?" Pamela asked. Concern contorted her countenance.

Chad went over to cabinet and pressed a button where the doors opened up to a flat screen TV. He switched the channel to CNN. "Breaking news. War in Lendovia!"

"What?" Jenna felt her heart smash inside her chest. There it was, rebels fired shots. And some had even surrounded the palace calling for the king to abdicate.

"Oh, my God! Dion's still there!" She thought about her family, her friends, her boss. Jenna's mind was in a whirlwind daze. She thought about Juan's death. It was only the beginning, wasn't it? There was more personal tragedy to come.

"And that's not the only thing," Chad added. "They've closed the airports so no one can leave the region."

Jenna's body went cold.

CHAPTER TWELVE

Miranda sat in her lawyer's office, drawing in a deep breath. She should have known better than to use a lawyer who knew the Romero family. Dion, her ex, was a well-connected guy, no doubt. That was what originally drew her to him. His sex appeal, handsome face, great body. He had it all. And for a time, he was hers. All hers. But now? He'd just tossed her to the curb without so much as a glance. And when she tried to call him, he wouldn't even take her calls. Who did he think he was? She knew the answer to that. He was a Romero. They thought they were better than everyone else.

"Now, I'm going to ask you again, Miranda," Dan Rachfield said. "Did Dion Romero sexually harass you?" His query was pointed, his eyes probing.

"It depends on what you mean by harass." Miranda challenged with sarcasm.

"Miranda, this is no joke. And I'm telling you, if you make a false claim against-"

"A Romero?" she finished his sentence and leaned forward in the chair. She was sick and tired of feeling as if the Romeros could throw their weight around any damn time they pleased. Despite what she thought they thought, they were not above the law.

"It's not about the name. Well, not *just* about their good name. Those people are not the type you want to mess with. They've got a solid reputation and powerful lawyers who could rip your testimony to shreds and make you look bad. This could all backfire on you, Miranda."

"Whose side are you on, Dan?"

"The right side, Miranda. Now, I haven't agreed to represent you just yet."

"Why are you being so difficult?"

"Because, I don't like to be lied to, Miranda."

"Lied to?"

"Yes. Do you realize you've told me twelve different versions of your story?"

Inwardly, she was quivering. He was right. She couldn't keep her deception straight. Not the one her mother had coached her on.

"As Perry Mason once said, you don't want to lie to your doctor or to your lawyer because lying to either one could cost you your life—or in the case of the province of Ontario, lying to your lawyer could cost you your freedom!"

Miranda thought about it for a minute. This was more serious than she'd imagined. Why was she so bent on screwing Dion's reputation? "He lied about me," she mumbled. "Then he refused to see me..."

"What?" Dan looked confused. "Lying outside an oath typically isn't a crime. What do you mean?"

"H-he told me that I embezzled funds from the company and that I'm a thief."

"Did you?"

"No."

"Well, how did the money go missing, Miranda?"

"I...I don't know."

"I think you do know."

"What's that supposed to mean?"

"You do live with your mother, don't you?"

"Leave her out of this, Dan."

"How can I, Miranda? Your mother is a wonderful lawyer. Or at least she was, until she fell into that trap."

"Trap?"

"Miranda, your mother has a substance abuse problem. We've all tried to get her help but she has to take some responsibility for her actions."

"That's got nothing to do with anything, Dan."

"Yes, it does. She'll do anything to support her habit. When she lost her job at the firm, she went on a rampage trying to feed her habit, then using her status to try and swindle money from the estates of her deceased clients." Dan shook his head. "It was all over the news, Miranda. We all know about it. Did you leave any of your work passwords at home?"

Miranda thought about that for a moment. She had, in fact, left herself open, didn't she? She'd brought work home many times. But…how would her mother have gained access to her security information from work? Miranda knew it was a rhetorical question. Her mother was a whiz at cracking codes. Either that, or she just knew her daughter all too well. Miranda had made the mistake many make in using the same password or password combos for all her online stuff. She used her birthdate. Stupidly, she always used her birthdate. Of course, her mother would know her birthdate was her password. Dion had warned her about changing her password every so often. Why hadn't she listened to him? Her mother probably gained access to Miranda's work-related files from Miranda's computer by logging in offsite at the apartment they shared.

Well, duh!

That was why Dion confronted Miranda. He tracked down the source of the breach to her IP address on her home computer. Well, crap!

But when he refused to see her again and presented her with her walking papers, she was lost. She felt ashamed and hurt. And then there was their relationship. That had gone to dust. She missed his touch, his sexual heat and caresses. And the way he felt inside her. No one could bring her erotic pleasure the way Dion did. He was golden. The man had "the" touch. No other man could rival him. Miranda was addicted to Dion's delicious sex and damn hell she didn't want him to spurn her like a used woman. She wondered what lucky secretary he was doing these days. That slut in accounting? Jealousy and rage filled her at the time, that was why she'd gone along with defending herself at all costs and trying to get back at Dion, but Dan was right about not going through with this. She didn't want to end up doing time for perjury. She couldn't handle being locked up in a nine by seven foot cell. She loved her space too much.

She sighed heavily.

"I…I think you're right, Dan. I…I'm going to talk with my mother."

"You are?"

"Yes," Miranda whispered in defeat. "Mom came into a large stash of cash right after…the funds went missing at the Romero Corp." Miranda felt ashamed. "Do you think Dion would ever forgive me?"

"I don't know, Miranda. You'd have to ask him. I do think he's a reasonable man and eventually he'd get over it."

"I'm going to drop the case."

Dan smiled. "You're doing the right thing by telling the truth, Miranda."

"I sure hope so. I'm going to see him."

"I think you should at least try to call him first."

"I will."

"I think he's in Lendovia right now."

"Lendovia?" she said, sounding more alarmed than she'd intended. "I heard something on the news about a war breaking out over there!" Miranda's stomach plummeted to her red-soled Louboutin stilettoes.

CHAPTER THIRTEEN

Jenna tried frantically to reach Dion on his cell phone. She kept redialling his number. Then she tried to send him a text but the darn thing didn't go through. What was happening? "His cell is turned off." She was breathing hard and fast, panic rising in her chest. Her heart bashed against her ribs hard and fast.

"It's no use," Chad said, his eyes glued to the screen. "They said phone lines are down over there."

"Oh, no," Pamela cried out, her eyes wide open as she looked at the images on the TV. She ,too, had her cell out. Pamela called Troy, who was back in town, and he said he was trying to reach Dion or anyone overseas at Rom International College.

"We've got to do something. We can't just sit here," Jenna snapped. Her heart squeezed in her chest. She worried about her mother, her family and Dion. What would happen to Dion? She couldn't bear it if anything happened to him. She would die inside. It would kill her, if…the worst should happen. She thought about the late hours they'd spent together working at the office, the sweet sound of his soothing voice every day. Her heart gave another lurch thinking that it would be all a distant memory and he'd be forever gone.

She squeezed her eyes shut and tried to take a deep breath, but it was so hard to breathe. It hurt to draw in air.

"Are you okay?" Pamela patted Jenna's back and directed her to sit down.

"I'll be fine," she breathed, lying through her teeth. No, she wouldn't be fine. She couldn't take another heartbreak like this one. Oh, God! If anything happened to Dion, she would…

"Let's call an emergency meeting, right now," Travis said as he barged into the office again.

"Good idea," Pamela agreed.

Moments later, everyone gathered in the boardroom. It was decided that they would do nothing but wait. Travis made the decision to let everyone go home early, considering the situation. And to keep Dion and everyone in Lendovia in their thoughts and prayers.

Sure, it was easier said than done to just go home and wait. But Jenna couldn't for the life of her simply sit back. What bothered her was that she couldn't get a hold of her own mother, either. But Lasrine was well aware of the ins and outs of Lendovia. Dion was a foreigner there. God help the authorities if they did anything to her boss. She knew Dion was a martyr type of brave guy, just like Juan. But she just couldn't handle if anything ever happened to him.

She wished she taken him up on his offer of getting a company vehicle. She didn't feel like taking the bus home.

"You need a ride?" Pamela offered, as if reading her mind.

"Um, yes, please," she said quietly, despair raw in her voice.

Jenna was silent during the drive home, her mind still reeled over what had just happened in her home country and the fact that no one had heard from Dion. Every time she thought about that, her heart squeezed hard in her chest as if fighting to pump blood to her body. She hugged herself.

"Are you sure you're going to be okay?" Pamela asked again.

"Yeah," she offered, deep in thought.

Just then, the phone in Pamela's car rang and she promptly answered it, a confused look on her face. "Hello?" Pamela answered. A look of concern shadowed her face as the caller spoke.

"Are you sure?" Pamela asked the person. "Wow, that's…unbelievable. Okay." Pamela ended the call.

""What is it?" Jenna asked.

"I have to go to the manor."

"The manor?"

"Yes, Romero Manor. Do you mind if we stop there first?"

"No, of course not."

They drove silently to the estate. Jenna didn't know why but she had a sinking feeling in the pit of her stomach and dreaded in her heart what was to come next.

CHAPTER FOURTEEN

Pamela and Jenna pulled up to Romero Manor after security cleared them at the gates and they both got out of the car. As they hurried up to the front steps past the water fountain and in front of the white French entrance doors, the butler opened the door for them.

"Miss Martin and Miss Macchiasso," he greeted them. "Toni Romero is waiting for you in the study."

"Thank you," Pamela said.

Jenna was stunned at the beautiful marble foyer, but her appreciative feeling vanished when she realized she was probably there to be the recipient of bad news. They were going to tell her that Dion was dead or in jail or being held hostage, weren't they?

"Ah, ladies, thank you for coming," Toni said, as he stood by the fireplace in the study. His cane in one hand, a cup in the other. There were several other people in the room. Jenna guessed they must be family.

"Do you know what today is?" Toni asked.

"No," Jenna admitted, looking puzzled.

"It's National Secretary's Day!"

Just then a tall, dark and deadly handsome man in a suit walked in to the study. Dion strolled in looking very tired, yet still sexy as sin, with his suitcase and dropped it on the floor. "Actually, it's Administrative Professional's day, Gramps," he clarified, in his smooth deep voice.

Jenna's heart exploded in her chest, and unable to contain herself, she charged over to Dion and hugged him, basking in his energy when he firmly hugged her back. For a man who looked like he just traveled the world on foot, he sure had a lot of strength and power in his grasp.

"Well, in Australia it is, since they're twenty-four hours ahead of us, but tomorrow we officially celebrate it here in Canada," Pamela added with a knowing smile.

Jenna could not contain herself. Her mind was spinning like a whirlwind. "Dion! You're here! What's going on? I thought you were still in Lendovia."

"I managed to get a flight out of there in time," he said, his voice low and rough. "But I'm still in contact with some people there. Anyway, getting our employees safely out in time never would have happened if it wasn't for you, Jenna. I told Granddad and the staff at the agency to make sure you are appreciated tomorrow. I never forget days like…Admin's Day!"

Jenna's heart melted; she felt giddy inside and overwhelmed by his kind and thoughtful words. Still hugging him, she broke free realizing where she was. She was embarrassed and squared her shoulders and composed herself professionally. Why on earth did she reach out to hug Dion as if he were her husband? He was her boss, after all, she chastised herself.

Later that evening, after the Romeros had a special appreciation dinner in Jenna's honor—to her surprise and utter astonishment, Dion drove her home to her new condo compliments of Romero Corp. During their car ride, they discussed the events happening in Lendovia. Jenna told Dion that she'd been concerned about her mother at first, but she'd spoken to her earlier and she was all right. She wanted to tell him more about her situation but decided not to burden him with the whole truth, at least not yet, anyway.

When they arrived past her gated security entrance, Dion switched off the ignition and got out of the car. He opened the passenger side of his SUV.

"And this time, there'll be no tripping and falling out of the car, ma'am. I don't think I have workplace safety insurance for that!"

Jenna laughed, remembering the last time he helped her out of his Jeep, only to see her old rundown building on the west side. The one that was now condemned since the city got called in to do an inspection of the place. Luckily, one of Dion's charitable organizations offered to help tenants relocate to new and better housing. How crazy was that? She was grateful to know a cool guy like Dion. And the real kicker was, he didn't act like he had any special kind of clout or power. He wanted people to believe he was just a regular, hardworking guy. Yeah, right.

"That's fine by me, sir," she joked back.

"Why don't you come up...for tea?" she mumbled, feeling butterflies in her chest at asking him upstairs. She needed to see him, to be with him, alone. To make sure he was all right. She'd lost her ex and she'd gotten so close to Dion over the past month. The terror-laced thought of losing Dion, too, was overwhelming. She would never again take anyone or anything for granted. She'd almost lost him but was determine to let him know how she felt about him, while he was still here.

"You sure you're not tired?"

"I'm good. I mean, you must be tired. It's a bad idea."

He leaned closer to her and her heart thrashed about in her chest, her body pulsed by the magic of his closeness and the brush of his soft finger on her cheek. Delicious electricity zigzagged through her body. The sweet scent of his cologne wafted to her nostrils.

"I've missed you, Jenna," he murmured in a low, hungry voice. A voice that sounded ravenous for passion. Did he feel the same way she felt? They'd had so many intimate conversations over the phone during the past few weeks, every day. She thought it was her imagination at first, but now she knew by the way he looked into her eyes, that he'd felt it there, too. There was something magical between them. It was palpable. Undeniable.

"I've missed you, too, Dion," she whispered, breathless and their lips were practically touching before he pulled away, a wicked grin on his lips.

He looked around the quiet courtyard of the luxury condo complex. "Don't you think we should go inside?"

She was so caught up in the heat of the moment that she forgot she was still outside of the condo. She flushed. "Yeah," she said, hoarse with emotion. The last thing she would want was a passionate kiss with her boss to be caught on surveillance, or worse, someone's cell phone camera if they happened to be up and peeking through the window.

"I know, I know...'Love is blind, but the neighbors ain't.'"

He grinned.

Before long, they were in Jenna's corporate suite, and Dion had taken her in his strong arms. She thought she was going to faint from overexcitement. *Oh, Dion.*

"You meant what you said outside?" he whispered in a low, husky voice that brought shivers down her spine.

She nodded, wrapping her arms around his neck. She wanted to undo his necktie and pull off his suit jacket and rip off his white dress shirt but resisted the urge. If he didn't kiss her soon, she just might go crazy.

As if he read her mind, he did loosen his necktie and slide his blazer off to her amazement. She observed that he filled out nicely in his shirt. The man had the body of an athlete.

"Oh, Jenna," he growled, lowering his head to hers as she leaned against the granite kitchen counter in the open area kitchen living room. It seemed as if neither of them was interested in going into the bedroom. She wanted him there and then and his body communicated the same sentiment to her.

Jenna was on fire for him. Her body reacted as he pressed his lips to hers and softly caressed her lips with his. She'd been dying to taste his sweet lips since the day they first met three weeks earlier. Now she knew what she'd been missing out on. Jenna couldn't believe this was all happening. Her mind was in a whirlwind daze, dizzy with excitement and anticipation of what was to come.

She was kissing Dion Romero! They were passionately locked in an intimate embrace. She'd been waiting for this moment, dreaming about it for what seemed like eternity. And now, her fantasy was becoming a reality. A blessed reality.

She felt his eager erection straining behind the zipper of his dress pants, wanting so badly for him to be inside her, filling her.

She moaned into his lips as she ran her hands down the muscles of his strong arms, feeling his rock-hard firm body. Her spine tingled as Dion licked and sucked on her lips like a skilled lover. Her pulse leaped with excitement as he pleasured with his soft, sensual French kisses. Oh, the man could kiss! It wasn't just any kiss, it was the way his soft, wet tongue entwined with hers, creating delicious spirals of heated passion coursing through her body.

"Oh, I want you, now, Jenna," he groaned in a raspy voice she barely recognized. She could feel his erection harden behind his pants and she rubbed her hand on his manhood, which only increased her own arousal.

Breathing hard like love-starved animals they caressed and kissed moving over to the large sectional sofas in the living area where they continued to make out. She eased him out of his shirt and Dion slid his hand under her blouse caressing her skin, moving up to her hard, erect nipple where he stroked his finger over her tip then gently squeezed her taut bud, making her cry out in ecstasy.

Her inner thighs pulsed like crazy, throbbing with need and desire for Dion. He undressed her quickly and she felt conscious of her body, knowing how fit he was and hoping he wouldn't notice that she was a little more curvaceous than some women. He seemed to enjoy her body, approval on his lips.

"God, you're beautiful, Jenna," he murmured in a hoarse, low whisper. She moved her hands down his firm, muscular chest before wrapping them around his neck again and pulling him down to her. His delicious tongue slid between her parted lips and they kissed each other passionately before he moved his lips to her neck and sucked on her sensitive flesh as she writhed beneath him. He kissed the pulsing hollow at the base of her throat. Her hands trailed down the smooth, firm flesh of his back. She delighted in the heaviness of his body over hers.

His lips moved to her naked breasts and he caressed each one before moving his tongue over the tip of her nipple, swirling and sucking on her as her sex throbbed harder.

"Oh, Dion," she moaned, squeezing her hands over his muscular biceps.

Dion moved down her body, sucking on her flesh, kissing her naked skin. Butterflies exploded in her tummy as he went down on her. "Oh," she groaned out loud. Was he really going to…take her there? She'd read so much about a man pleasuring a woman between her legs with his lips but she'd never experienced that before. She was breathing harder as he slid off her white lace panties. She felt her stomach flip flop wondering what it would feel like. She closed her eyes and relaxed because she didn't want him to sense how nervous she was. She didn't want him to stop. Ever!

"You okay, baby?" he moaned.

She shook her head and a warm smile touched her lips. He stroked her softly with his hands first then he lowered his head to her sex. Jenna spread her legs open for him, holding on to his head as he slid his tongue inside her moistness, kissing her between the legs. Shivers raced up her spine and blood pumped erratically in her body.

"Oh," she groaned out loud. "Oh, God…Dion!" she panted, breathing hard as he passionately stroked her with his tongue between the throbbing wetness of her inner thighs. The way he thrust his tongue inside her like magic made her pulse rush with electrical delight all over her body—like sparks of uncontrollable ecstasy.

He sucked and kissed her sex until she came hard shuddering and jerking her body, arching her back in response to the rush of orgasm ricocheting through her body from his tongue's magic as she cried out his name.

He moved his lips back up to hers and they kissed and made out, caressing each other, enjoying each other's bodies.

Breathing hard, they switched positions and Jenna was on top of him eagerly pulling on his belt and unzipping his pants, hungering for his taste, his passion. Wanting to please Dion as much as he'd pleased her to soaring heights.

She freed his erection and her eyes widened at the enormous size of his manhood. Delight and excitement washed over her, eager to rock his world. She lowered her head to his throbbing sex and extended her tongue over his tip, sliding her wet tongue over his hardness as Dion moaned uncontrollably. She swirled her tongue over him while stroking her hand softly down his hard, heated shaft, savoring the softness of his flesh.

She sucked hard and fast, bobbing her head down him, pleasuring him as he did for her moments earlier until he came with a spasm.

Jenna couldn't wait to have Dion deep inside her but a frown made its way to her face.

"What's wrong?" he murmured, kissing her neck while she arched her back, closing her eyes, enjoying his pleasure.

"I...I don't have a condom," she breathed hard, feeling disheartened. She'd wanted to go all the way with Dion but realized she didn't have any protection in her new apartment. Not that she was planning to have sex in the longest while.

"It's okay," he assured hoarsely, "I've got it covered." A grin touched his sweet, sexy lips and she groaned with pleasure, strapping her arms over his neck.

"I want you so bad, Dion," she purred.

"How much?" he moaned.

"This much," she whispered, breathlessly and brushed her lips against his softly and they kissed passionately for moments before he reached for his wallet in his pocket. He removed a small shiny silver foil wrapped package and Jenna was so glad to see that he did come with a condom.

She thought she was going to go crazy out of her mind if he didn't take her tonight.

Before long, their heated bodies wrapped around each other as Dion pleasured her, moving his hips over hers and spreading her legs with his knee. Dion really had wonderful moves. He kissed her devouringly as he slid his hardness into the pulsing of her opening and a smile curved his luscious lips. "God, you feel so good, Jenna," he whispered in a deep voice as he moved inside her heated walls.

She tightened around him and groaned as he filled her inside, moving around inside her, thrusting his hardness inside her throbbing folds. Blood pumped hard and fast through her body as Dion gratified her sexually leaving her sated. She came first with an uncontrollable spasm. Soon after Dion came groaning and moaning with pleasure. She ran her hands down his back, stroking his firm muscular flesh, feeling unbelievably satisfied and overcome with emotion.

Breathing hard, Dion kissed Jenna softly on her neck and moved his lips to hers and they kissed again before he rolled over on his back. She moved over to him and rested her head on his chest, listening to the hard, thumping rhythm of his heart. Wishing this moment would go on forever. She'd read about mind-blowing sex before, but this...? This was incredible magic with Dion. She wanted him forever. The question was, could she ever have Dion...forever?

The moment just slapped her hard in the face. She'd just slept with her boss. The boss she'd lied to...but she wouldn't think about that now...now that things were so perfect between them.

In the morning, Jenna woke up feeling completely refreshed and in love. She sat at the breakfast bar while Dion showered. His second shower, she mused with delight. Late last night, Dion made love to her, not once but three times. Once in the shower. She made him chuckle when she asked him if a condom would work in the shower. He'd teased her and asked her what assignment did she have in mind for it and what would be the working conditions. She had rolled her eyes in his direction and playfully scowled at him. He'd placed on the

Trojan before he got wet and made sure it didn't slip off. She was glad for this obviously. Jenna never thought it was possible to make love in the shower, both wet naked skins slapping against each other in erotic passion. It was incredible.

Jenna wondered from where Dion drew his stamina but quickly remembered that he was athletic, after all. It was funny, how they'd both made love as if it was the end of the world. In reality, it almost had been the world's end for both of them when Dion was in Lendovia during the crisis and she was…well, in Canada worried that she'd never see him again. Missing their daily hours-long conversations, getting deep into each other's souls, thoughts and emotions. But she didn't have to worry about that now, did she? A funny feeling crept inside her. Why was she getting that eerie feeling about things getting turned upside down between them?

The truth, she had to tell Dion the truth, soon. She'd been so intimate with him. He trusted her. And now…? She felt more at ease with him. But how on earth would he take her story? What would he really think of her?

"Morning, beautiful," he said, kissing her on her cheek.

"Morning, boss," Jenna teased him. Part of her was hoping he'd correct her and tell her that he wasn't there as her boss, but her lover. Her man. But that didn't happen. It was only in her fantasy, she supposed. She wanted to ask him where that left them but decided not to bring that topic up at the present time. She wanted to enjoy the moment with Dion. Whatever that moment was.

"You're going into the office today?" she asked him, bringing her glass of orange juice to her lips, looking over the rim of the glass into his dark, sexy eyes.

"Sure. You don't think I'd miss Admin's Day for the world, do you?"

"I thought we celebrated that yesterday?" she asked, rhetorically, knowing full well, the celebration was today but Dion and his family wanted to give her a special thank you at their family dinner last night.

"Very funny," he said, tying his silk tie around his neck, after putting on his shirt.

The man had a killer body. And he was impressively tall and good-looking in every way. But was he just her boss? Or something more? Was last night a passionate one-night stand? Or did Dion feel for her as much as she felt for him?

Not that she could get serious about him when she'd lied to him about…everything.

"We'd better get to the office before they start the breakfast without us," he said. "I'll get you a ride in. I don't think we should go in together."

Jenna's heart collapsed in her chest. "Of course," she said, almost inaudibly. It was for the best.

"Jenna," he said, after pausing, probably sensing her reaction. "You know how I feel about you."

"I know," she whispered.

"I just don't think it's wise parading our…what happened last night in front of coworkers, do you?"

Dion had a point. It would be on with the show for the two of them. She'd get back to work as if nothing had happened between them last night and fight the aching in her heart that she could never have Dion as anything more than a boss. She'd go through with the Admin's Day celebration with the other staff members and her day-to-day duties as if nothing had gone on behind closed doors.

Jenna's heart sank thinking that what they had was nothing more than an amazing one-night stand. He didn't even know anything about her and it killed her inside not being able to tell him everything. He, at least, deserved that, didn't he? How could she start a relationship founded on lies?

She came out of her daydream and responded to him. "You're right, Dion." *And besides, who am I kidding? You and I can never really be together. I'm fooling myself even believing we can do this. There's so much about me you don't even know. I don't truly deserve you.*

CHAPTER FIFTEEN

The following week, JoJo sat in the corner office in his apartment and looked at the screen of his laptop disbelieving what his eyes were seeing. The glow of the screen was the only illumination in the dark apartment. Even though it was daytime, JoJo had the shades pulled down in case anyone ever got the idea to spy on him with zoom lenses. As he sat down hovered over his computer, he thought to himself that he'd seen a lot of dirt in his days, but none like the stuff before him.

He'd received the final report on Jenna-Lynn Macchiasso. Yeah, even though Dion, his boss, told him last week he didn't feel the need to go ahead with the investigation because he trusted Jenna, JoJo never cancelled anything—Dion didn't actually say to nix what he'd started, he just said, he felt good about Jenna so no need for a report.

He knew what Dion went through with Miranda. He was going to protect his boss at all costs. The Romeros were good to JoJo over the years and he always had their backs. Dion was obviously falling for this chick, and JoJo knew love wasn't just blind—sometimes it was stupid, too. Well, that was what JoJo was paid for. To look out for them when they didn't have eyes to see what was in front of them because they were too busy being busy in their work.

"Oh, hell, this is huge!" JoJo commented to himself, shaking his head. The bitch really had the wool pulled tightly over his boss's eyes. Well, the curtain was finally going to fall on this show! He printed off the information and grabbed his jacket and keys off the counter. It was Saturday but the Romeros had gathered at the manor for some work-related function. And Jenna was supposed to be there, too. Good thing. He could escort her out himself.

* * *

Dion Romero couldn't believe his ears. "Jenna-Lynn?" Dion asked incredulously. Dion looked at his private detective, JoJo, a man who once worked as a bodyguard. "My executive assistant? Are you sure?" he finished his sentence.

"Yes, boss."

"There's gotta be a mistake. I checked her background after I hired her," Dion continued. He should be angry as hell right now because it wouldn't be the first time he'd been stabbed in the heart by a pretty face. But it would be the last time. When would Dion ever learn?

"I know, boss, but there was something about her that just didn't check out," JoJo said in a rough voice befitting his massive stature.

"Like what?" Dion demanded, pacing in his office, unbuttoning his business suit jacket. Even though it was Saturday, he'd stopped by the office to sort through a few things. Jenna was already at Romero Manor, waiting for him along with the family. Pamela invited Jenna to help her with some administrative duties. "What doesn't check out?"

"Her background doesn't fly. It seems a bit too...perfect."

"Her background? What about it?"

"It's too perfect, boss," the man said without smiling. JoJo never smiled. Dion couldn't remember the last time he even smirked. Was he even capable of mirth?

"You mean like fabricated?"

JoJo nodded slowly, his eyes narrowed. "Yes, boss."

Dion remembered all too well, the trouble his brother Carl went through when they found out about the past Venus, Carl's former assistant and now wife, had been hiding.

"And that's not the only thing, boss."

"What else is there?" Like Dion really wanted to hear more.

"She's been watching you."

Dion got all soft inside for a moment until he read JoJo's expression.

"You mean…?"

"Bingo! We found out she's had you under surveillance for a while. You and your family."

Dion felt his core body temperature scorch his body inside. What was she? Some sort of spy? Or cop? Boy, did he know how to pick 'em. Hot babe or not, she was out on her butt.

He thought about their heated lovemaking the night he'd returned from Lendovia and their sexual nights every night since then. Jenna? His trusted assistant? The woman who helped him to rescue and save his overseas employees from danger? No way. He couldn't' believe it.

Then JoJo handed him the proof. The reports were authentic. He took them into his hands and his eyes scanned them in disbelief.

There it was in plain sight. Jenna had forged her documents and changed her name on several occasions. She was wanted by authorities in Lendovia.

"Holy hell, I'd harbored a fugitive from the law? I could go to jail for that!"

JoJo nodded slowly. "In all fairness, boss, it's Lendovia and we don't know if the warrant was justified. The king is one corrupt dude."

Dion didn't even care at that point. Jenna had lied to him. She lied about every damn thing! "That's it. She's fired!" Dion threw the papers down hard on the table, fuming. Anger surged through his veins like an erupting volcano. He grabbed his jacket and stormed out the door when something stopped him.

"What did you just say?"

"About the warrant for her arrest?"

"No. About the king?"

"He's one corrupt dude, boss. The guy would have someone arrested for reading if they weren't on the approved list of people who deserved to be educated."

A sinking feeling entered Dion's gut. He looked as if he'd just fallen into a daze. He was in disbelief. He went to his filing cabinet and retrieved some documents that he'd gotten while in Lendovia and compared some notes.

"Holy Jesus!"

"What is it, boss? You look as if you've seen a ghost."

Dion looked at JoJo. "Let's go to the manor." He needed to see Jenna right away. She had a lot of explaining to do.

CHAPTER SIXTEEN

The Romero family and some staff members including Jenna and Pamela were gathered in the living area when Dion and JoJo arrived. Their eyes were glued to the big screen TV watching CNN. Dion read the notice at the bottom of the screen:

Breaking News! The Royal Family of Lendovia has been executed.

His heart sank hard and fast.

"Can you believe it?" Toni Romero said, shaking his head. "It's a good thing you're here, Dion, and your employees are out of that country. Those rebels killed the king of Lendovia and the entire royal family. It's shocking! Horrible!"

"It's terrible," Pamela cried.

Jenna was in the corner, paralyzed with shock, her eyes glazed over as if life was no longer in her body.

Dion went over to her and hugged her. He led her into the study as the rest of the group continued to watch the newscast.

"Jenna," he said softly, looking into her beautiful eyes. "I'm so sorry about what happened over there."

She said nothing, tears stinging her eyes. She was breathing hard and fast as if she'd been traumatized.

He continued to console her. "The newscast said the entire royal family was dead but that's not true, is it?"

Her eyes focused on him. A confused look on her face.

Dion lifted her chin with his finger and spoke to her gently. "It's okay, Your Highness, you'll be safe here. With me."

CHAPTER SEVENTEEN

"Wh-what?" Jenna stammered, clearly dazed.

"I know your secret, Jenna. Or, should I say, Princess Jaynah."

"H-how did you know?" Jenna sobbed, her voice hoarse from emotion and grief.

"Well, we found out that you'd changed your name and some other stuff but that's not important now. When I was in Lendovia, I was in touch with authorities there who had a lot of colorful things to say about...your father."

"M-my father?"

"Yes, there are countless reports the king was not only a tyrant but he bullied his sons into being militants and hid his daughters away from the world. Locked 'em up in some dungeon-like quarters."

"It's true," she said quietly, raw pain clouding her eyes. She drew in a deep breath and turned her face away from him, looking out into the garden through the study glass doors. "M-my father had some problems. Emotional, psychological, whatever you call it. He tortured all of us. My mother included. Locked us away. He only cared about his male heirs. My sister and I were...just mistakes. Inconveniences. He didn't want us to amount to anything."

"So what happened?"

"Well, after months of being locked away, looking at cemented walls, Mother found a way to sneak books in for us so our minds wouldn't rot away."

"That's when you took up learning so many languages?" he clarified.

She nodded, hugging herself. "Yeah. I learned English and some other languages. Of course, Mom couldn't continue to sneak things in for us so she had...Juan, one of the soldiers at the palace do it for her. He was so...sweet. So kind. So brave and selfless." She buried her head in her hands and wailed. "Oh, my God! My mother's gone! My family's gone!"

Dion moved closer to her and hugged her.

"It's all my fault that Juan was killed. And now...m-my family's dead! It's all my fault."

"No, it's not, Jenna...Jaynah. It's your father's doing."

"For years, I blamed myself over Juan's death. He liked me and we started seeing each other. And when my father caught on that he was spending a longer than usual time in my quarters, Juan didn't even confess that he was helping me and following my mother's orders to sneak educational material to me. My father had him...executed!"

"It's okay," Dion soothed, stroking her hair. "You don't have to say anymore."

"But I want to, Dion. I'm glad this is all out in the open. Well, between us..."

"Don't worry. No one needs to know right now. Maybe never. Only us."

"Thanks, Dion. I...I don't know what to say, really. My father then had me doing a lot of clerical work for the palace since I'd taken up typing during that time when Juan snuck in a laptop computer. So when I said I worked for the royal family, I wasn't completely lying."

"I know that. I understand." Dion looked at her. "You're trembling, Jaynah."

"I'll be fine."

"Are you sure? I'm worried about you."

"Yes," she mouthed. He held her tightly. He knew what it was like to lose someone close. His mother had died after losing her battle to breast cancer but he still couldn't understand what it would be like to have your mother killed by a charging bullet.

"It's all over now, Jenna. Your father, as sad as it is that he's gone, can't hurt you anymore. I want to protect you, Jenna," he said. He lifted up her chin, looking deep into her large, soft brown eyes.

"You do?"

"Yes, Jenna or Jaynah."

Just then, Jenna's cell phone vibrated and she pulled away from Dion to retrieve it. She took the phone out of her purse and glanced at the display in shock.

JAYNAH, IT'S YOUR MOTHER.

ANYA AND I MANAGED TO ESCAPE BEFORE THE ATTACK. WE ARE FINE. WE'RE IN MONACO. WE'LL STAY HERE FOR A WHILE. WE LOVE YOU. GOD BLESS YOU.

"Oh, my God!" Jenna cried out. She stared at the screen in disbelief then she breathed a deep sigh of relief, overcome with emotion. She showed Dion the message on the display, tears streaming down her face. After Dion glanced at the display of her phone, he knew then she had tears of joy.

"Thank God, they're safe. Who's Anya?" he asked.

"My sister," she said, tearfully. "They're alive. Thank God, they made it out."

"But the media said—"

"My father had more than one wife. I'm guessing it was my step-mother who...who was killed." Her voice became choked with emotion.

"Will you be joining your mother and sister?" he asked.

"I...I don't know. I know they're safe in Monaco. They have friends there. I...I have friends *here*. I have you, Dion. At least I hope I do."

Dion was relieved to hear that. He hoped that Jenna would stay in Canada with him.

"I've gotten to know you and your wonderful spirit over the past month and I can't even imagine not seeing you again or being with you," Dion murmured.

He gently pulled her closer to him and held her in his arms.

"So where does that leave us?" she whispered.

"Right here," he said, and he lifted up her chin to meet his gaze and pressed his lips to hers feeling her energy, showing her how much he loved her and cherished her.

EPILOGUE

One year later...

It had been a year and a half since Jenna had lost members of her family during the political unrest in Lendovia, but thankfully, her mother and sister had found refuge in Monaco and were living there in contentment. The miracle of this evening, Christmas Eve, at Romero Manor was that she'd gained a new family. A beautiful, loving, close-knit family that supported and stood up for each other, no matter what. The Romero family.

Snow fell hard and flurries scattered across the window pane of the glass double French doors of the study. Looking out into the night with sprinkles of snow and starlight was wonderful. It gave her a warm and cozy feel inside.

"All right now," Toni Romero announced by the elegantly decorated Christmas tree, his young wife Shelly by his side. "We're going to have a gift exchange soon. Let's all gather by the fireplace."

"That includes you, Jenna-Lynn Romero." Dion walked into the study with his brother Troy. He then offered his wife a hand to help her up.

Dion had surprised Jenna-Lynn with a proposal by the beachside. She was looking over some notes on her iPad when he hugged her from behind and asked her to check something out on a website. When she keyed in the website address, there it was on the screen, Jenna-Lynn: Will You Marry Me? You have my heart, Dion.

Warmth filled her soul thinking back on that day. Her heart had almost stopped at the time. But then Dion was ever the romantic, always surprising her from the first time when he'd ordered breakfast for her in her new corporate condo suite he'd arranged for her. She smiled at the cherished memory.

"Coming, darling," she smiled to him, rubbing her enormous pregnant belly before taking his hand to get up from her seat. She was eight months along. The baby was due any time in the next few weeks. Dion was hoping for a boy but either would do, he'd told her. Yeah, right. He'd already enrolled their unborn child in soccer, football and judo lessons. She rolled her eyes at the memory of the day he'd told her. Not that a girl couldn't join those clubs, of course. If she had a girl, she would name her Cherry-Rose Lasrine Romero. Lasrine being her mother's code name and true middle name.

The whole Romero clan was gathered around the fireplace as Toni had instructed. She'd gotten to know the entire family over the past year. As busy as they each were, they gathered every month or so for one of Toni's big family dinners, and certainly on holidays like Christmas and Easter.

And what a big family! Jenna was so thrilled to know that her little girl or little boy (yes, they refused to learn the gender of the child before it burst into their world) would have many cousins to play with and be close with. At least this family was more functional than her own.

The festive Christmas music played over the speakers: Silver Bells. How beautiful and melodic, she thought. Antonio and Lucy, his wife, were present with their son, Alexander. Lucas and Maxine were there with their daughter, Mary-Louise. Zack and his wife, an ex-reporter, Blue, sat there with their son Jefferson. Carl, the young mayor of Mayberry Hill was with his wife, Venus, and their sons Tristan and Daniel. Jules and his wife, Amber, and their daughters, Crystal and Elita, were there. Everyone seemed to be paired up except Troy and Dr. Alonso, who was in town from his work abroad, providing medical care to disadvantaged residents around the world through his world-renowned healthcare clinics.

Jenna knew how Pamela felt in her heart about Troy. She wished she could play matchmaker for them, since Troy would never admit to liking her since she was an employee and it would be awkward. And Pamela was, well, the Romero family's press secretary. She probably didn't want to go there with making a move on her boss, or one of her bosses.

Jenna smiled to herself. She knew what that must feel like. She'd been there with Dion not so long ago.

* * *

Later, after the dinner and gift exchange, Pamela Alvarado frowned. She didn't see Troy anywhere and wanted to speak with him. She was going to take Jenna's advice and ask him out, God help her. What did she have to lose?

She moved and made her way out into the foyer then to the west wing and when she spotted him, her heart sank.

He was with a strange woman. A woman she'd never seen before. Or wait! It was an old classmate of his. She remembered seeing the woman at one of the family barbecues. But they were standing close to each other. Really close. Troy never mentioned having a current girlfriend. No one else mentioned it either. She walked closer about to interrupt when she heard the words that stung her to her core.

"So, big boy! Are you going to tell your family or am I?" the woman asked.

"Tell them what, Priscilla?"

"That you're my fiancé!"

Pam's heart stopped. She had a gift in her hand for Troy that she'd been saving for this moment. She placed the gift by the cabinet in the hallway and slinked away. Out into the blizzard, tears stinging her eyes.

So much for happy endings. Well, at least for me.

Pamela had been working for the Romero family for many years now and had helped them get out of numerous sticky spots. But it was time to move on. She was going to hand in her resignation from the Romero family soon. She loved them dearly but it was time to go.

She got into the car. The snow fell hard and the wind blew even harder. No one even noticed she'd left. The music was playing loudly enough and the sound of cheers and laughter filled the hallways at Romero Manor as family and friends gathered. Pam heaved a sigh and turned on the ignition to warm the car. It was too bad she hadn't listened to the forecast. The blizzard was moving in fast to the region. She drove away through the gates and along the main road.

The wind blew furiously and the snow pellets slammed against her windshield. Her visibility was decreasing. What was happening?

Suddenly, the city blacked out.

"Oh, no!"

There was no power on the roads. Great! There must be a citywide outage again! Pamela was in trouble. But it was too late to turn back.

* * *

SNOWBOUND WITH THE BILLIONAIRE (THE ROMERO BROTHERS, BOOK 7)

Baby, it's cold outside...

Pamela Alvarado, the Romero family's loyal press secretary, finally plucks up the courage to tell her deliciously gorgeous eligible boss, Troy Romero, how she truly feels about him. But when she goes to share her feelings with him one evening, she bumbles into a humiliating and heartbreaking situation when she learns that he's...getting married!

But it's warm in here...

Sexy billionaire philanthropist, Troy Romero, is reluctantly entering into a loveless marriage to spoiled heiress, Cilla de Montagio, so she can keep her fortune. Yet it is his faithful, yet feisty, press secretary, Pamela, who really has his heart. So, stranded in a blizzard during a power outage with Pamela over the holiday season can only spell trouble. The blizzard brings the chill, but it looks as if Pamela will melt Troy's defenses. Now he's got one heck of a storm brewing inside him, too. Does he fulfill his obligation to the heiress who once saved his life, or does he follow his heart to the woman of his desire?

Chapter One

Pamela Alvarado could feel Troy Romero's positive energy from across the room as he entertained party guests. The man radiated sophistication and delicious charm.

Oh, heavens. Does he always have to look so...stunning?

Every time she saw Troy, she practically drooled over him. The man had that effect on her from day one. And this evening was no exception.

It was Christmas Eve yet he looked sexy as sin in his dark dinner jacket and dress pants. His dark hair was slicked back and his high cheekbones were accentuated by the glow from the fireplace and dim lighting in the room. Troy's alluring sexy eyes sparkled when he grinned. He towered over the other guests, at six feet four inches. Troy stood, holding a glass in one hand with the other hand in his pants pocket, by the grand fireplace in the massive study at Romero Manor.

His grandfather, Toni Romero, and Toni's wife number five, the very much younger Shelly, and some friends were engaged in conversation. Toni, head of the Romero dynasty, seemed joyful at the sight of his ever-expanding family—Pamela had been there when Toni chastised the young bachelors in the past about when they were going to settle down. Currently, six out of his eight grandsons were making him proud in the wedded bliss department.

Pamela drew in a deep breath. Her heart fluttered inside her chest in anticipation of getting a moment alone with Troy, tonight. Finally. But when would that moment arrive?

The place was brimming with Romero family members and their guests. The melody of laughter, mirthful chatter and festive Christmas music filled the air.

Pamela was so appreciative to be a part of all of it. Even as the family's press secretary, she didn't have much family of her own, at least not close family. A beautiful, loving, close-knit family that supported and stood up for each other, no matter what, like the Romero family.

The snow fell heavily and flurries scattered across the panes of the French glass doors of the study at Romero Manor. Pamela was enthralled by the winter wonderland outside as the snow swirled around by the heavy gusts of wind this enchanting evening.

"So, did you get a chance to speak to him, yet?" Jenna-Lynn asked Pamela as she plopped herself on an adjacent cozy chair.

"Not a chance," Pamela answered quietly with a smile. She felt heat rush to her cheeks, embarrassed that she might appear desperate. She took a sip of her eggnog, enjoying the rich creamy smooth libation gliding down her throat. Her heart fluttered. Why was she feeling like a schoolgirl about to meet her crush face-to-face? This was so humiliating. She was the family's public relations specialist, for heaven's sake. Yet, when it came to private relations, Pamela felt way out of her league. She didn't want to make a fool of herself in front of Troy.

"Remember what we talked about," Jenna reminded Pamela with a wink.

"Yes, I remember." Pamela sighed with a warm smile.

"You'll be fine, Pam. You're the family's spin doctor. You always know when to say the right thing to make them look good and you've helped out everyone here from a whole mess of sticky situations. There'll be nothing to it."

Pamela playfully rolled her eyes and shook her head. "Trust me, girl, it's a lot harder to confront your boss about how you feel about him than it is to tell the media what you think of them."

Jenna grinned. "Well, you do have me there, Pam. But look, Dion and I wouldn't be together if we didn't admit how we felt about each other. Not only that...gosh, Pamela, if it weren't for you, I don't even think we would be together."

"Oh, Jenna, that's…so sweet of you to say, but please don't give me all that credit. You guys were destined to be together. I'm so glad it worked out for you."

"I've seen the way Troy looks at you, Pamela. Trust me, you have nothing to worry about."

"I sure hope that's true." Pamela sucked in a deep breath, trying to calm those thousand tiny butterflies that let loose in her stomach.

She looked up at the enormous crystal chandelier dangling from the cathedral ceiling of the study. The whole mansion was spectacular. How long had she been working there, admiring the fixtures and elegant surroundings of one of the wealthiest yet sophisticated and kindest people she'd ever known? Yet there was one precious relationship that she'd treasured more than the material wonders of Romero Estate. It was Troy Romero. He'd captivated her heart the way no other man had. Oh boy, she'd fantasized about what it would feel like to have him with her, moving inside her, bringing her to the soaring heights of carnal pleasure. She knew full well, however, Troy's reputation with the women. Of course, when she'd commenced working for the Romeros, it wasn't something she wanted to think about, especially since he was always with a beautiful model or society girl at one point or another. But now? He was free, wasn't he? He was available. And her body sizzled when he brushed her skin by accident while they were in the middle of approving media briefs or heat rose inside her when their eyes locked. Pamela felt heat rise inside her at the thought.

Okay, Pam, it's Christmas Eve. No time for naughty thoughts. Just give the guy his present and call it a night.

Pamela's heart pounded hard in her chest as she held the glass of eggnog in her hand, waiting for a chance to speak to Troy alone. Waiting for the moment to approach him in the spirit of the holiday with a personal gift. Something she'd been waiting for a long time.

But now…it was too late.

Before she knew it, Troy felt for something in his pocket—a vibrating cellphone call, then he excused himself and left the study. Pamela tried to follow him with her eyes but her view was soon blocked as guests moved around.

"All right now," Toni announced by the elegantly decorated Christmas tree, his young wife by his side. "We're going to have a gift exchange shortly. Let's all gather by the fireplace."

"That includes you, Jenna-Lynn Romero." Dion Romero, Troy's older brother, reached down and hugged his wife after he walked into the study. He then offered her a hand to help her up.

Pamela had been told the story many times from her friend Jenna-Lynn. Dion had surprised Jenna-Lynn with a proposal by the beachside. She was looking over some notes on her iPad when he hugged her from behind and asked her to check something out on a website. When she keyed in the website address, there it was on the screen, Jenna-Lynn: Will You Marry Me? Dion.

Jenna told Pamela her heart almost stopped at the time. Who would have ever thought of such a sweet website proposal? Warmth filled Pamela's soul feeling happy for Jenna, whom she had first contacted via a temp agency on behalf of Dion to be his executive assistant. Dion wasn't too happy at the time, but Pamela saw how well it worked out after all.

"Coming, darling," Jenna smiled to Dion, rubbing her enormous pregnant belly before taking his hand to get up from her seat. She was eight months along. The baby was due any time in the next few weeks, that is. Jenna winked at Pamela. "Good luck," she whispered.

Soon after, members of the Romero clan were gathered around the fireplace as Toni had instructed. Pamela had gotten to know the Romeros over the past seven years since she first started working for them. As busy as they each were, they gathered every month or so for one of Toni's big family dinners, and certainly on holidays like Christmas and Easter.

And what a big family! The soothing Christmas music played over the speakers: Silver Bells. How beautiful and melodic. A festive tune, if Pamela had ever heard one.

Antonio Romero and Lucy, his wife, were present with their son, Alexander. Lucas and Maxine were there with their daughter, Mary-Louise. Zack and his wife, an ex-reporter, Blue, sat on the loveseat with their son, Jefferson. Carl, the young mayor of Mayberry Hill, was with his wife, Venus, and their sons, Tristan and Daniel. Jules and his wife, Amber, and their daughter, Crystal, were also present. Everyone seemed to be paired up except Troy and Dr. Alonso, who was in town taking a break from his work abroad, providing medical care to disadvantaged areas around the world through his world-renowned healthcare clinics.

Pamela had confided in Jenna-Lynn how she felt in her heart about Troy. Still, Pamela didn't want to make a move on her boss. He'd been so good to her over the years. They'd been through a lot together, working on publicity issues for the Romero family late into the night. And oh, she loved the way he addressed her with his "hey, beautiful" whenever he saw her. Then again, he called Mrs. Perkings, the sixty-year-old head maid "beautiful," too! He was ever the charmer. With everyone. So much so that she suddenly realized making a move on him would be stupid. On his part, their relationship was very likely just a friendly one.

But, she had bought him a gift. A nice gift. She would keep it in her purse until she had the chance to be alone with him. It was a set of beautiful gold-plated cuff links specially engraved #1 Boss.

"Where's Troy?" Toni called out. "He should be here!"

"I think he's in the west wing," Zack said. "Come on, Gramps, you're not seriously gonna wait for him. Just hand his gift to me." His wife Blue playfully rolled her eyes and lightly swatted her husband on his muscular arm.

Pamela couldn't help but giggle. But something tugged at her heart. How nice it must be to be a part of this loving, wonderful family of successful tycoons. So powerful, yet down-to-earth at the same time. But still, she'd seen them grapple with their challenges. You didn't want to mess with a Romero. They were nice and friendly but oh, boy, if you wronged them or someone close to them...

Pamela swallowed hard. This Christmas was the hardest for her. Though they'd taken her in like family, she still felt...alone. She looked at Zack and Blue. Things worked out so wonderfully for them after their rocky start.

God, to find love. Someone who loved you for you and treasured you was the best gift any woman could be given.

Too bad it would never happen for her, Pamela thought. Still, she'd secretly fantasized about Troy, who happened to convince his grandfather, Toni, to hire her. For which she was eternally grateful. She'd just earned her bachelor's degree in public relations and media studies, with straight A's but with no job in sight—at least not one in her field. Talk about a tough economy. Too many grads, not enough quality jobs. Troy heard about her from the public relations society debate team. She'd liked him ever since. But he, of course, always had a girlfriend on his arm. A beautiful, model-type, at that.

Pamela smoothed her hand down her red velvet dress, over her full thighs. A model type, nope, she was definitely not!

The Romeros gathered around the festive tree.

"Zack, you know how important it is for each of us to be here around the tree at this time," Toni said. "It's tradition. Your dear grandmother, God rest her soul, always wanted it this way."

And that was true. Pamela hadn't met the original Mrs. Toni Romero, but she had seen pictures of her and heard so many heartwarming stories about how beautiful her soul was. No wonder she and Toni had raised such fine boys when the couple found out about their existence.

Later, after the presents were exchanged, Pamela frowned. She still hadn't seen Troy since the announcement of the gift exchange and wanted to speak with him. She was going to take Jenna's advice and ask him out, God help her. So, she would try to make it out to be a casual date and if anything more came of it...well, that would be her dream come true. What did she have to lose?

Pamela moved and made her way out into the foyer then to the west wing. When she spotted Troy, her heart sank.

He was with a woman Pamela hadn't seen before. She'd heard the doorbell ring many times during the festivities and the butler had ushered in countless late guests. So Pamela figured the woman must have been a latecomer. But why didn't she enter the study with the rest of the guests? The woman started to look a bit familiar to Pamela as she got closer... It was an old classmate of Troy's. She remembered seeing the woman at one of the family barbecues in the garden. And on campus, if she recalled correctly. The woman looked a bit different but Pamela noticed the statuesque height, long face, waist-length auburn hair and the longest diva-like nails that she'd seen on a woman.

Pamela walked closer about to interrupt when she heard the words that stung her heart.

"So, big boy! Are you going to tell your family or am I?" the woman asked.

"Tell them what, Priscilla?"

"That you're my fiancé! And you know I like to be called Cilla. You always call me Cilla unless you're mad at me for something."

"Sorry, *Cilla*!" he emphasized. "Anyway, I thought we were going to wait until the new year to make that announcement." Troy arched his brow as he pulled her closer to him with a big grin.

Fiancé?

Troy was getting married?

But...

Pamela's heart halted along with her footsteps. Her breath became labored. How could she have read Troy so wrong? The feeling of a gigantic sinkhole surfaced in her stomach.

Cilla?

The name finally clicked in Pamela's mind. Cilla de Montagio was that snobby heiress she'd met while working with the university's debate team. Oh, Lord! Cilla was not somebody you wanted to mess with. She was one of the most entitled, cantankerous girls Pamela had ever met while in college. Cilla had given Pamela and her friends a hard time. She'd even gotten one of the professors fired after he'd flunked her. What on earth was Troy doing with her?

Let me guess; she's wealthy, from a prominent family of art dealers and architects and looks like a beauty queen.

Pamela, on the other hand, was none or had none of that. Who was Pamela to think she even stood a chance with Troy? Pamela was an employee, nothing more.

She couldn't wrap her head around the fact that Troy was going to marry Cilla.

Stung with humiliation and feeling dazed, Pamela glanced at Troy's gift in her hand that she'd been saving for this moment. She placed the gift by the cabinet in the hallway for Troy to discover later, and she slowly backed away.

Pamela made her way down the corridor of the west wing oblivious to the festive decorations adorning the walls and strategically placed plants. The butler approached her as she entered the grand foyer. "Are you okay, Miss Pamela?" he asked politely.

She could feel her eyes stinging with tears of pain and embarrassment. How stupid she was to have thought that Troy was ever interested in her? What an idiot she was!

"I'm fine, thanks," she said, her voice almost cracking. "Just a little tired."

"Are you all right?" he persisted, concern evident. "You don't look too well."

"I...I'm fine, Hans, really." Pam tried to sound brave as she bent over to put on her brown leather knee-high boots. "Please tell everyone bye for me." She grabbed her white winter coat and her light blue scarf and matching hat and wrapped the scarf around her neck. The same hat and scarf set Troy gave her as a gift three Christmases ago from Tiffany's in New York on one of their business trips.

She fished around her handbag for her car keys, fumbling to pull them out but finally succeeding as she walked towards the door ignoring the gales of laughter and music coming from the study.

Then...she left. Pamela fought her way outside into the brisk cold and the dark winter stormy night.

Out into the blizzard, tears stinging her eyes. The onslaught of chilly air didn't register with her as the cold snapped at her exposed skin. She quickly pulled her hat on over her long, dark hair. For further warmth Pamela pulled the fur-trimmed hood of the jacket over her head.

So much for happy endings. Well, at least for me.

Pamela had been working for the Romero family for many years and had helped them out of various sticky spots. But it was time to move on. She was going to hand in her resignation to the Romero family soon. She loved them dearly but it was time to move on.

Pamela started her car by remote then popped open her trunk and grabbed the snowbrush. She quickly brushed the snow off the windows so she could see. She then got into the car. The snow fell harder and the wind blew with greater force.

No one, except the butler, even noticed she'd left. The music was playing loudly enough and cheers and laughter filled the hallways at Romero Manor as family and friends gathered. Pamela heaved a sigh and turned on the satellite radio in the car. It was too bad she hadn't listened to the forecast channel beforehand. The blizzard was moving in fast on the region. She drove away through the gates and along the main road, her snow tires grinding on the snow-blanketed road.

The wind continued to blow with tremendous ferocity and the snow pellets slammed against her windshield. Her visibility was decreasing fast. What was happening? Why did she leave like that? She should have at least said good-bye to Grandpa Toni, as she'd affectionately called him over the years.

As Pam drove farther down the side road and approached the main road, the snow fell heavier and faster with fury. The windshield wipers scraped back and forth rapidly but weren't able to keep up with the massive amount of snowfall. The car skidded around a couple corners but she managed to maneuver herself okay, thanks to what Troy had taught her many years ago when she had to drive to a press conference downtown during a snowy day. "Never push too hard on the gas or you'll skid on the snow" he'd told her. Amen for that! His advice saved her life, once. But now...she could not even begin to think about that. She had to try to block Troy out of her mind. He was happy. And she was...would try to be happy for him. As her car continued to plough through the wintery main road, the streetlights began to flicker. Then... suddenly the city blacked out.

"Oh, my God!"

There was no power on the roads. The streetlights had darkened. The houses in the distance were also wiped from her view. *Great! There must be a citywide power outage again!*

Panic swept over Pamela like a gust of tornadic wind. The pounding of her heartbeat reached her throat. She drew in a deep breath. She had no choice but to drive as carefully as she could on the slippery, slushy road. She couldn't see a thing on this main road in the country. No other cars were around. But if she stayed there, she'd be buried under the mountain of falling snow in no time.

Pamela was in trouble. But it was too late to turn back, wasn't it?

Chapter Two

Cilla bestowed a superficial kiss on Troy's cheek. "You're a darling, Troy," she purred.

"And you're a devil, if I've ever seen one." He grinned.

"What's that supposed to mean?" Priscilla pulled away, feigning shock.

"Why don't you just tell the executors of the estate the truth, Cilla?"

"You know I can't do that, Troy. Now don't go backing out on me here. I need you. I was there for you when you needed me."

"All right. All right. I know, and trust me, I appreciate it. But this is crazy," he asserted, running his fingers through his hair. "I've got a rep to protect, you know. I wouldn't want the girls to think I'm off the market." He cocked a brow.

"Fine, Troy. But not now. I've sent out invitations already."

"Invitations? Whoa there. You're moving fast, aren't you?"

"You promised you'd help me out," she pouted. "It has to look real. You know the deal, Troy. We elope by my birthday but we'll have a big wedding reception afterwards. My parents left me the entire estate based on proving my stability, which means to me, once I'm married for at least a year. And I have to be married by my twenty-seventh birthday. And the man has to be of upstanding quality, which means…well, you know. That was in their will. If I don't fulfill those requirements then…I lose everything, Troy. You wouldn't want that, would you? I mean, if it weren't for my mother…" Cilla pouted seductively, tracing her finger along his jaw, looking at him with sad puppy-like eyes. Troy felt sorry for her.

"I know. And I'll go along with this fake engagement…or fake marriage thing if that's what it takes for you to keep your inheritance," he said, his voice trailing off. "I'm a man of my word, Cilla. You know that."

If it weren't for Cilla's mother, a high society woman, God rest her soul, spotting Troy outside the mall one day when he was a young teen and noting his striking resemblance to her longtime business associate, Toni Romero, he might not have even met his famous grandfather and he might not have had the opportunity to be who he was—moving from a life of poverty and heartbreak into one of wealth and power. Not to mention, he was able to go to the best damn college in the country and receive the finest education along with guidance from a man who worked himself from the ground up to build his empire - the Romero Corporation.

How could he, in good conscience, sit back and watch Cilla lose her fortune when it was her mother who helped him find his? Yes, he had to do the right thing.

Troy had always been good with gadgets and his brothers and he were the book types who always looked for ways to earn a living by making other people's lives better. All this while they were living out of his father's van after his mother lost her battle to cancer. But having a boost in life, a break—was all it took to raise them to soaring heights. He didn't mind giving back. In fact, it was the motto he and his brothers lived by, but this marriage thing was some weird way to fulfill that honor. But it couldn't be all that bad, could it? It was only for a year, right?

She reached over and hugged his neck, pulling him closer to him. "I know you're a man of your word, Troy," she cooed, pressing a kiss to his lips.

Just then, darkness fell on the house and the music stopped mid-note.

"Oh, no!" Cilla cried out.

Commotion erupted from the living room. "What happened?"

"Great, the power's out," Troy muttered. Luckily, the backup generator kicked in to illuminate the dim hall lights. They'd had it specially installed after the last ice storm that knocked out power to 300,000 customers in the city of Toronto and surrounding areas.

"Wait here," Troy said to Cilla, before walking back towards the study.

Zack, Carl and Lucas emerged from the study like men on a mission.

"Is everyone okay?" Troy asked.

"Yeah, we're gonna see if we can get some more backup."

"Okay, let's all stay calm now, everyone," Toni called out. "Hopefully, the power will be back on in a few minutes."

Luckily, the place was lighted with tea candles so it wasn't utter darkness.

Hans, the butler, came back into the foyer. "It looks as if the blackout is widespread."

"Well that's not good," Zack said.

"Is everyone accounted for?" Troy asked Zack.

"I think so," Zack said, looking around in the dim lit hallway, where all the guests had surfaced.

"Hans," Troy said, turning to the butler, "can you do a head count and get everyone into the guest quarters? We don't know how long this one's gonna last."

"Yes, sir. Right away."

"Where's Pam?" Troy asked. He noticed Cilla looked uneasy at the mention of Pam's name. "She's usually the first one to get things organized when there's a situation." Just then, Jenna came out with her husband Dion.

"She's probably still on the road. She left not long ago," Hans told Troy.

"Well, that solves that problem," Cilla said enthusiastically, sipping on some wine in the dim light. "We know where she is...or isn't..." Cilla tried to make a joke of the situation, which fell rather flat.

"Left?" Troy asked, perplexed, ignoring Cilla's jest. "Why did she leave so early? Where did she go?"

"I don't know, sir. She didn't look very well. I believe she was looking for you earlier."

Troy was concerned. Why in God's name would Pam just leave? Why was she looking for him? It made no sense to him but his instincts told him something was up and it wasn't good. Ice pellets slammed hard against the windows in the mansion. Troy didn't have a favorable sense about this at all—call it a gut feeling but he needed to get to Pamela soon.

"You didn't get to speak to her?" Jenna asked Troy. "She was looking for you earlier."

"Yeah, Hans told me. Did she tell you why?"

"Well..." Jenna's voice trailed off.

Troy didn't take too long to think and switched his attention back to Hans. "She's crazy for going out in the storm like this. Did she tell you where she was headed, Hans?" Troy wondered if Pamela was going home or to the hospital, since she was supposedly not feeling well according to the butler.

"No, sir."

"She lives twelve miles from here," Troy remembered. "She'll never make it in this weather." He knew Pamela hated driving in stormy conditions. She was brilliant at everything else but she admitted, driving under tough road conditions wasn't her thing. Many times, she would leave her Ford Escort and he'd drive her home in his SUV. Why the change? Why tonight? Couldn't she at least have waited?

Grandpa Romero obviously overheard the whole thing. "Why didn't she at least say good-bye before she left? That's not like Pam."

"Right, I'm heading out." Troy grabbed his jacket.

"Troy, you can't go out in this storm," Toni Romero objected.

"There's a severe storm warning right now. I'm picking up a signal from the disaster-proof radio. They're urging people to stay indoors," Hans added.

Anger surged through Troy. It was fraught with feelings of overwhelming concern. He looked outside at the strong gusts of torrential snow swirling with hailstones. Was she stark mad? "I'm going to find her," he said, his tone final.

"I'm coming with you, bro," Dion said.

"I'm good, Dion, you need to stay with Jenna."

"True, grandson," Toni agreed with Troy and turned to Dion. "Your wife could go into labor at any time, Dion."

"Um...Troy," Cilla called out. When she got closer to Troy, she spoke in a hushed whisper so no one else could hear. "You're not seriously going to go out and look for her," she said, nails digging into his bicep.

"Yes. I am serious." Troy was stung by Cilla's lack of concern. "Pamela could get hurt out there. Can't you see how violent the winds are?"

Cilla rolled her eyes and took another sip of her wine.

Troy quickly pulled out his keys and went to the main door, opening it and walking out, slamming the door behind him before anyone else could delay him. His blood was scorching in his veins, furious that Pamela would put herself in danger like that. He'd told her earlier he'd take her home when she was ready.

He had to find her. And when he did, she was going to have a whole lot of explaining to do, pulling a crazy, dangerous stunt like that.

* * *

Pamela's car started to act up on the icy road as gusts of heavy winds and snow blasted her windshield. Winter hit the city hard this year, and in fact, it spread across the entire southern Ontario region. And now her windshield wipers couldn't move fast enough to clear the hard falling snow and ice pellets to clear her view.

She inched over to the side of the road, skidding slightly, remembering not to push too hard on the gas, as Troy had once told her, but gently guiding her little four-wheeled friend over to the side where it would be safer.

Oh, she wished Troy was with her. But, he wasn't and he could never be. Not anymore, anyway. He was officially taken. Her mind flickered back to the house when he was with his fiancée, holding her gently. It looked as if they were about to...kiss. Lucky Cilla.

Pamela tried to ease her mind back to the moment but it was too late; it kept slipping on to thoughts of Troy. For years since she'd worked for him and spent late nights at the office, she'd fantasized about...being with him. But now, that would never happen. Not in a million years. Troy was keeper material. And for as long as Pam had known him, he was a one-woman man, which was good, of course. Because she wasn't into other people's properties. Troy had always been devoted to whichever woman he was with at the moment.

Pamela never told a soul this, but Troy and she had kissed once. They'd gotten close at the office at the manor, but then she'd pulled back quickly, afraid to go any further. Her body had pulsed in all kinds of places, electricity coursed through her body at the soft touch of his sweet lips. Oh, what a kiss that was. He tasted so good, like fresh mint and his own sweetness. Troy was a tender kisser and she'd wondered, fantasized about what he would be like between the sheets, moving inside her.

She'd had a craving for him since then, but she was too afraid to do anything more about it, until this eve. Yes, tonight, was supposed to be the night when she would give him a Christmas gift and later after he'd driven her home as he'd promised he would, she was going to invite him upstairs to her apartment and have a good chat with him and somehow get around to talking about that beautiful night they'd had in the study. Pamela even made sure her bikini line waxing was done yesterday, should anything ever happen with Troy.

Pamela even caught many glimpses of Troy wearing nothing but a T-shirt and dark jeans at one of the Romero family barbecues. And oh my, those strong arms and prominent biceps. The man had a body of a Greek god. No, a sex god. His broad shoulders and firm abs were a treat to her vision. She'd never met a man as fit as Troy—or any of his brothers—before.

The sweet kiss that night, which meant the world to her, had awakened her senses and spoken to her soul. She'd never been pleasured that way by any man before. Not by one kiss. Troy's lips were magical, sexually potent. Loving. That kiss told her something about him. That moment had been engraved on her mind and in her heart ever since, lingering in the middle of her sweetest memory, waiting to resurface to finish what they'd started or tried to start.

Pamela had been on the verge of letting herself go completely. They were alone in the study at the manor during a heated media circus involving one of his brothers, working on a PR campaign to restore the Romero name's reputation after it was marred. She'd worked with her media contacts and Troy was very grateful to her. He didn't push the issue either. "My old man would kill me if I dated you," he'd once told her.

"Why?" she'd asked him, breathing heavy, still buzzed from his soft tender kiss. The man had a caring way about him, the way he'd held her so gently and passionately. Oh my, Troy was addictive. She'd heard of that Romero charm before, but never had experienced it until that night. And it was...like Troy, unforgettable!

"Because he knows me. I'm not permanent relationship material, Pam," he had said to her, his dark sexy eyes penetrating her, making her feel giddy all over. "And if it didn't work out between us and you left..."

Had he forgotten about that conversation or had he tried to shrug it off as nothing? Pamela was no idiot. She just wasn't the permanent type of material for him. He'd found the right one to give his heart to. And it wasn't her.

How could Pamela have thought she'd had a chance with a Romero? Hot, handsome and eligible Troy Romero.

Pam shivered inside, feeling cold and hurt. Loneliness crept over her like a shadow in the night, darkening her spirit.

She just thought there'd always be a chance with Troy. They connected so well on every level. They hung out together a lot. Well, mostly to do with work. He'd never kissed her since then, but many times, their eyes locked and she thought there was something there. Well, now she knew it was only her overactive imagination or wishful thinking.

How could I have read him so wrong?

Now, there would be no more fantasizing about being with Troy or changing him into a "permanent" kind of relationship guy. Because somebody else managed to capture his heart in a way she'd never done.

So all that talk about "beautiful" was nothing more than just...talk?

Boy, did Pam feel stupid. And so rejected.

"Doesn't matter who accepts you, as long as you accept yourself and love yourself," she remembered Troy telling her on one of their walks. He'd given that same speech at the Boys and Girls Club where Pamela was a volunteer youth leader. She'd asked him to give a talk about helping young entrepreneurs. Troy ended up spending a ton of time preparing and setting up workshops for the youth in the community. It was a blast. He always had something to say, and boy, did he always know how to bring a smile to her face, even when she was so serious and uptight about deadlines.

Pamela kept the ignition running but glanced at her gas gauge needle on the dashboard in horror. It was pointing to the bottom of the gauge at the large E in the red zone.

"Oh, crap! It's on empty."

She forgot to get gas when she pulled out of Romero Manor. Of course, Troy had promised to take her home after the party, so she didn't remember that her car was almost out of fuel. It wouldn't be the first time she'd left it overnight at the estate while working late for the family. And whenever her tank was low, she'd had CAA deliver gas to her vehicle.

Right now, she needed a whole lot of coverage. Like shelter … or she was going to die from the frigid temperatures.

The powerful winds violently rocked her compact vehicle from side to side. The howling gusts were all she could hear right now. And her visibility was practically shot to hell. She could see nothing but darkness and hail falling. All she could see was white swirling snow in the darkness with the faint moonlight in the dark sky.

What had she gotten herself into?

Pamela switched on her radio but wasn't getting a signal. She realized that she would run out of fuel soon if she kept the heat on, yet she didn't want to die from hypothermia either.

Pamela's heart pounded hard and fast in her chest. "Okay, stay calm, Pam. You can do this. It's not the end of the world." *Yet*.

She reached into her handbag and pulled out her cell phone. When she powered it on, like the radio, there was no signal. Nada. "What?"

Her heart pumped harder. Goose bumps sprang up all over her body. She could feel it even though she wore a heavy coat. She remembered the great blackout of 2003 when fifty million customers in Ontario and New York had no electricity at all due to a widespread generator problem. The main controls for cell phones had died too. So no one had an operating mobile phone service. But those days were long gone. She hoped. What if the power was knocked out to her cell phone provider? Then what would she do?

Pamela turned on her hazard lights. She was out of gas and out of everything. And she was probably too far away to attempt walking back to the manor in this whopping snowstorm. The frigid blast of Arctic air, along with reduced visibility to see where she was going, would be her demise. She'd drop before she reached the first mile. The windchills were in the minus forties Celsius and plummeting. She tried to look outside. The city was blanketed with heavy snow. The roads were going to be un-drivable as every minute clicked by. Time was running out fast.

The pumping of her heart and heavy breathing made Pam feel queasy. Then a sinking feeling overwhelmed her.

She was going to die tonight.

Chapter Three

Troy cursed under his breath as he used his shovel to clear the accumulated snow from the wheels and the underside of his SUV. A sense of urgency rushed through his blood. He had to reach Pamela and soon. He'd lose it if anything happened to her. Right now, her safety was the only thing he thought about. He was filled with torment thinking about what the hell had gone through Pamela's mind to take off like that, without even saying she was leaving. That simply wasn't like her.

With the wind blowing fiercely in the darkness of the wintery night, he marched through the thick snow to the rear of his SUV and replaced his shovel in the back then made his way to the front of his vehicle. The snow was falling heavy as it swirled in the heavy gusts. He turned on the ignition and started the engine. Good thing he had a four-wheel power drive and the most rugged snow tires money could buy. He liked to always be prepared in any type of weather condition. Not that he'd planned on driving out in the middle of a brutal ice storm.

Troy gave a light touch on the gas to carefully push his way out of the driveway so as to avoid skidding. He turned on his headlights to increase his visibility. The snow could be dangerous when it fell fresh on the ground because it made for more slippery road conditions. Not the kind of conditions Pamela should be driving on right now. Why was Troy being so protective of her? She was just an employee of the family. Yeah, but the Romeros treated their employees like family.

She's a grown woman, Troy. She can take care of herself.

Oh, yeah, she was grown all right. In all the right places. It was cold as sin outside, but thinking about sweet Pamela made Troy feel hot like a furnace.

Yet, he still couldn't help himself, and man, he couldn't get her out of his mind. Heat surged through him. His crotch ached just thinking about her and where he'd rather be, cozying up inside beside her.

Get your mind out of there, Troy. She's off limits, remember? Besides, you have a business deal with Cilla. A marriage business deal.

Man, he must have been crazy to agree to that deal with Cilla.

He remembered what his grandfather had told him about settling down. And when he'd expressed interest in Pamela, Toni warned him not to even bother unless he had plans to make an honest woman of her. But now look at this. He was getting married. Only under false pretenses to Cilla. But Cilla had nothing on sweet Pamela Alvarado. Why couldn't his first time saying "I do" be with Pamela?

A grin came to his lips, thinking about that one night when he had shared a heated and passionate kiss with Pamela in the study. No one knew about it, of course.

Not that much could ever come of it, though. They'd already discussed the implications of Troy dating an employee. It just wasn't gonna happen anytime soon. It would really complicate things. Besides, he wasn't a stick-around type of guy and he was always straight up with the women he dated. Good for his brothers for finding the "one" and settling down but there was no way he was planning on joining them now or ever. He'd much rather remain a bachelor for life. He'd had his heart trashed one too many times in the past. It just wasn't worth it to give his heart to one woman forever.

Troy should have been thinking of nothing but driving safely on the road, but his mind kept running on Pamela and hoping she'd be all right until he got to her—wherever she was. He'd helped her out of a ditch a while back. Luckily, he wasn't too far away when she'd called him and told him where she was. They'd just finished working a long weekend on a PR campaign for his brother, Carl. "What's the best advice you've got for a girl like me in bad winter weather?" she'd asked him sweetly. God, he loved looking at those kissable lips of hers.

"The best advice for driving in bad weather is not to drive at all," he'd teased her then. She'd rolled her lovely mahogany-colored eyes at him and shook her head. He couldn't help but grin at the time. But right now, a smile was the furthest thing from his face. Pamela obviously hadn't taken his advice about not driving when dangerous road conditions were predicted.

"She wasn't looking very well," Hans had told Troy at the house. So what the hell was that supposed to mean? *Not looking very well?*

She looked fine earlier when he had surreptitiously ogled her while she was talking to Jenna at the party in the study. She'd been breathtaking in her dark red velvet dress that caressed her curves in all the right places. He'd even caught her looking back at him, from the corner of his eye.

Troy shook the thought from his mind as he looked out at the horrible visibility with blowing snow pelting his windshield.

He had a sinking feeling in his gut that she was in some kind of trouble. Just looking at the roads gave him a sense of urgency to get to Pam as fast as possible.

* * *

Pamela's mind froze. She couldn't think straight. What was she going to do? How was she going to get out of there alive? They'd find her frozen in her car, dead from hypothermia in the morning.

She tried to use her cell phone again but the darn screen was dark.

"Oh, come on," she whispered to herself, as if speaking to her cell phone would make it work. Nothing happened. It was dead. She blew out a tired breath, then popped open the trunk from the car's inside control knob. Then she opened the car door and got out, forcing herself to move to the back of the vehicle, leaning into heavy blusters. The wind blew violently pushing her hair into her face. She brushed it back trying to clear her view to see where she was going. She looked around and saw darkness mixed with blowing snow. The naked ice-covered tree branches were bending back from the force of the howling wind.

She had to get her emergency kit from the boot with her blanket, flashlight and all the other safety stuff, in the case. Pamela kept it in the back of her car in case she was ever stranded on the roadside, waiting for help. The trouble was, if no one saw her blinkers, she might not get help in time.

Just then, Pamela slipped on some black ice under the snow and fell hard into the snow bank, hitting her rear on solid ice. She cried out in excruciating pain and tried to get back up but the crippling pain shot through her. The frozen ice pellets slammed hard on her. Her skin prickled from the sharp stabbing pain of ice on her flesh.

She felt as if she was going to die.

Considering the wind speed and windchill factor, the exposed skin on her face could get some serious frostbite in a matter of minutes. She breathed heavy and slow, trying not to focus on the numbing of her skin against the frigid weather but it was no use. She was a good as gone and she knew it. No one would find her.

* * *

Pamela didn't know how long she'd blacked out until she heard a car door slam and her name called out.

"Pamela! Are you here?"

It was a man's voice. She thought she recognized the hoarse sound over the wind.

"Troy!" she cried out weakly, breathing hard. Her lungs burned from the cold air. "Troy," she whimpered again.

Before long, strong arms grabbed hold of her. "Oh, God, Pamela. Are you hurt?"

"No, I...just...slipped," she answered, breathless. Intense relief washed over her. "How did you find me?"

"It wasn't hard. I know you always take this route to go home," he said, giving her a scolding look. Troy was ever the cautious type and had always warned Pamela about taking the same route home lest she be followed. And of course, she had scolded him and told him not to tell her what to do because she liked familiarity and going the same way worked for her. Well, it certainly worked well in this situation. What if she'd taken some back street route to get home? Not that she'd probably gotten very far. Especially with the blackout in the area.

Pamela's heart leaped in her chest. Troy was there. He'd come to her rescue. It was like a dream. She just hoped it wasn't a dream.

Oh, thank God, Troy found her in time.

Troy helped her up as gusts of blowing snow and wind blasted them. It was a nasty, wintery night. Ice and snow mixed with freezing rain swirled around them as Troy led her to his vehicle. The area was still without power so it was dark. No street lights to guide the way. Only the headlights from Troy's SUV.

"My...my car!" Pamela cried out.

"Come on, Pam. We'll have to get it picked up in the morning," Troy said, as he opened his car door and helped her into his vehicle. "I'm taking you back to the house. Do you need anything from your car?"

"Just my bag," she said, her voice weak and hoarse.

"I'll get it, then I'll lock your car doors."

Pamela nodded as she hugged herself in the front seat of Troy's SUV. She was deeply relieved to come out of the freezing cold and into a warm vehicle. Troy, thankfully, had the heat jacked up. At least she could defrost, so to speak. It was warm in the car but right now it was even warmer in her heart. The feeling of having Troy there when she most needed overwhelmed Pam. Troy came out in the dangerous icy conditions to rescue her? Well, if that wasn't a noble man.

God, what would she have done if he hadn't found her? She could not wrap her head around the idea. Then another thought struck her. He probably wanted to make sure she was okay then return to the manor to his darling fiancée. That Cilla was one lucky lady. Pamela hoped Cilla was aware of that.

When she looked at Troy through the window as he went to her car, grabbed her bag, turned off the ignition and slammed the door shut, she thought of how lucky his fiancée was. Pamela never desired another man as much as she did Troy. Oh, she wished he was more than just an associate, a professional acquaintance. She relished her slender, sexy-as-hell boss with the captivating dreamy eyes and charming persona.

Troy was tall and handsome and oh, so sexy and strong in every way. He was built like a quarterback. Broad shoulders and a fine body with killer abs and biceps. He was always the take-charge kind of guy. She wondered if the Cilla *really* knew how lucky she was to have landed Troy Romero, the once self-professed bachelor of Mayberry Hill.

She heard Troy crunching through the snow. The white stuff really did a number on the visibility outside the window. She saw Troy's large frame walking back towards the SUV. She leaned over to the driver's side and reached her hand over to open the door for him.

"Thanks," he breathed hard as he climbed inside the SUV, slamming his door shut as flurries blew into the car.

Troy then handed her handbag to her but he did not have a trace of happiness on his face. He was clearly peeved at something...or someone. Pamela.

"Thanks, so much, Troy. I don't know what-"

"What you were thinking?" he interrupted as he fiddled with the defroster button on his dashboard. His tone was hard and caught her off guard for a split second but then who could blame him? He kept the ignition running as he glared outside at the blowing snow.

"I needed to get home, Troy," she whispered, out of breath, afraid to look into his eyes. Troy was always one of those intense lookers who could capture your glance and hold it. And when he did, he often had a gift of being able to tell a lot from a person's return gaze. Were they lying? Were they telling the truth? Well, she was not about to take any chances by looking into his dark, sexy eyes now. His lovable, gorgeous eyes.

"Really? Without saying good-bye? You know I said I would take you home, Pamela." His tone was curt, yet a delicious caring undertone resonated as well.

Yeah, I wanted you to take me home tonight, too. But that was before I found out you have a fiancée.

"I know but I changed my mind." Pamela sighed heavily.

His expression softened when he noticed she was shivering again. He immediately reached over to his heat knob and cranked up the warmth. His arm brushed hers and she felt a delicious spark come between them. Did he even notice? Probably not.

"Are you sure you're okay?" he asked again in his deep, silky voice.

She tried to throttle that dizzying current coursing through her veins but failed miserably.

"You're shivering again," he murmured. The scent of his sexy cologne wafted over her nostrils and sent her senses into overdrive. Whenever she got this close to him, those sensuous feelings overtook her. But tonight was different. He belonged to someone else.

He was no longer the carefree bachelor boss she'd worked for all these years. The one she'd often playfully tease by making comments about their closeness as he would do the same.

"I didn't realize it was so crazy outside."

"You must have heard the storm warning." His gaze turned to the outside as the heavy gusts of winds blew menacingly. The sound of the wind as it literally bent tree branches before their eyes was frightening. Her own car a few feet from them was practically buried beneath a drift. Troy drew in a deep breath while the windshield wipers worked ferociously to clear the snow on his front and back windshields. At first the vehicle got stuck and he pressed on the gas a bit as he reversed out to the sound of grinding tires on the slushy snow. His expression was serious as he glanced at his side mirrors to check his blind spot then made his way out away from the snowbank. "You won't get CAA right now so we'll just have to go for your car later after it clears."

"That's fine by me," she breathed as she leaned back into the soft, warm leather of the passenger seat.

"Right now, your safety is more important," he said, not looking at her but driving as slow as speed dictated in the icy, blizzard-like conditions.

What was she thinking, coming out like this? And to put Troy in danger, too. She blinked hard then shook her head in disbelief as the weather worsened before her eyes.

"Where are you taking me?" Pam asked.

"Back to the house, of course. It's closer and safe. You know you can stay in one of the guest rooms."

"I know," she murmured, feeling more embarrassed by the minute. How stupid she was to think she could pull off a covert getaway.

"Is your cell working?" she asked, changing the subject. She turned to her blank cell phone screen again, fiddling with the buttons, trying to get a signal or power it on.

"Nah. No signal, just like the last blackout. Looks like the cell providers are knocked out of power, too. I wish they'd come up with a better backup support system."

"I know. Tell me about it. I panicked when I couldn't even call anyone for help." Pam realized she would have been in grave danger if Troy hadn't found her. She'd be stuck. What if danger had approached her? What would she do then?

She felt a deep sense of gratitude to Troy. Then, a disturbing thought blew into her mind to cloud that sentiment. The image of Troy hugging his fiancée at the manor. She swallowed the hard lump in her throat. Her chest started to get that squeezing feeling again and the loneliness settled in. Troy was with someone else now. Not that he was ever really hers.

Pamela remembered Cilla's personality and her reputation from college. It was all coming back to her. Cilla would never in a million years allow Troy to have any female friends. Cilla was the jealous, possessive type of girl who had a knack for stirring up rumors about anyone she perceived as a rival. Well, she wouldn't have Pamela to worry about, that's for sure. Pamela was set on getting as far away as possible from Mayberry Hill after this storm blew over. Pamela had to just wait for the right moment to let Troy know. And that moment wasn't now. No way in hell would she be telling him "Hi, thanks so much for rescuing me, boss. By the way, I'm quitting!"

She would have to find a way to slide Troy's sexy memory out of her mind and out of her life. No more would he dominate her secret fantasies. No more would she figure out ways of romantically colliding paths with him. But damn! That was going to be hard as hell to do. Right now her emotions were all over the place. She was riding her own personal blizzard of emotions.

"You're quiet," he observed in his sexy tone. That low smooth voice he'd had whenever they were alone and having one of those close friends with unspoken benefits moments on those late nights on the job. Her body reacted but Pam fought hard to ignore the emotions he stirred inside her.

Cilla.

Her mind ran on his fiancée. How could he even think about taking on that smooth tone of voice with her after he'd just been with his fiancée? Was he crazy?

"Don't you think that tone's inappropriate?" she blurted out.

"What tone?" he asked, as if perplexed. His tone was sharp and assessing.

"You know," she whispered quietly, her expression remained deceptively calm as she brewed inside.

"No, I don't. You don't seem yourself tonight. What's up with you? You were okay when I first saw you this evening. Now you're...well, I'm sure it's warmer outside compared to that vibe you're giving me right now!"

"What?" she scoffed incredulously. She turned to face him with disbelief written on her face. She felt the muscles in her face twitching.

He grinned that sexy bad boy smirk as if nothing was out of the ordinary. Often she would just melt at the sight of his handsome face. But this just riled her up even more.

Pamela folded her arms tightly across her chest, her lips pinched, anger seething through her.

"You know I like it when you get like that, Pam," he whispered.

Oh, God! He was turning her on again.

No. No. No. I will not be turned on by you, Troy. I refuse to listen to my body's response to you.

"Don't call me Pam," she snapped at him, shaking her head. "How dare you!" she said.

"You didn't mind a few hours ago when you arrived for the party." He didn't seem too fazed by her anger, which was pretty much Troy all over. For all the years she'd known him through college and working for him and his family, she'd never really seen him lose his cool.

Shame on you flirting with me when you have a fiancée back at the mansion.

"Yeah, well...earlier at the manor, I didn't damn well know that you were getting—"

She was cut off by a heavy disturbance. Just as they were turning on to the road leading to Romero Manor, a large thud sounded and Pamela screamed. A tree had crashed down in their path. Her heart pounded a mile a second. She thought she couldn't breathe.

"Damn!" Troy swore.

It was too late. They were stuck right on the icy dark road. No other sign of life or cars nearby. No light emitting from any of the dark cottages nearby. And the heavy gusts of wind continued to howl as they smashed through the area, blowing heavy amounts of snow all around them as their visibility plummeted. What was going to happen to them?

Chapter Four

"What are we going to do?" Pamela gasped, feeling more terrible and guilt-ridden than before.

Troy blew out a deep breath. Pam heard him cursing under his breath. "Wait here," he ordered, before opening the driver's side door. Another strong gust of wind blew snowflakes and blowing snow into the SUV before he closed the door. He was outside, surveying what damage had been done to the vehicle.

Pamela hugged herself, worried about Troy and what fate was going to befall them. It was all her fault. *Crap!* Why didn't she just stay at the manor as she'd done many times when she'd worked very late into the night or was caught up working during adverse weather conditions like this?

She couldn't help herself. She just couldn't sit still while Troy was out there in the freezing blizzard. Something bad had happened to the SUV. She felt it. She had to get out to help Troy. Pamela opened the passenger side door and stepped outside, careful not to slip on the foot stand. The wind blew gusts of what felt like ice pellets on her face, slamming her skin like needles prickling her flesh.

"Troy?" she called out, walking towards the front of the vehicle. He was bent over looking at the front wheel.

"We'd better walk to the guest cottage. It's closer," he voiced over the howling wind and blowing snow.

"What?" she called out, holding her hat from being blown by the heavy gusts.

"Let's go," he voiced again. Annoyance swept across his face.

"But your ride! We can't leave it."

"Doesn't matter," Troy said, as he firmly and gently took her arm to guide her along the road. The sidewalks were too high with three feet of accumulated snow. It would not be ploughed probably until tomorrow.

"How close is the cottage?" she belted out, trying to be heard over the loud sounds of nature's blizzard conditions.

"Much closer than the house. We own these cottages right on this street. Just another couple more minutes and we'll be there," he said, holding her. She couldn't see ahead of her with the blowing snow virtually blinding her. She kept her face buried in Troy's jacket. How on earth could he move his way around in this condition?

Then Pamela remembered Troy and his brothers were athletic types. They always did outdoor adventure stuff like mountain climbing in the Alps. Once they'd climbed the world's tallest mountain, Mount Everest, a few years ago. Imagine 8,848 meters above sea level, he once told her. The snow was incredibly deep and the oxygen levels were thin. He'd told her the air was so thin, it was difficult for some climbers to breathe. A lot of climbers needed supplementary oxygen. But Troy did not. They'd faced the dangers of wind-blown snow and the realization that if they weren't careful they could plunge more than 3,000 meters to their deaths. Troy survived all of that. All for a good cause, for a charity close to his heart.

He'd told her once that never in his life was he more proud than climbing that week and being able to raise a staggering amount of funds for the Palliative Care Children's Center in Mayberry Hill. They'd managed to raise millions of dollars during that adventurous feat to build a new wing and a brand new theatre for children to watch the latest blockbuster Disney films. Children who were too ill to go to a regular theatre.

The million-dollar facility could accommodate not just the terminally ill young patients but their families and nurses, too. They even had state-of-the-art seats complete with IV pole holders and oxygen place holders so the kids could be comfortable as they were entertained. Pamela's heart sank for the little ones and gratitude for what the Romeros did for the kids filled her heart. Her little brother Nian had been diagnosed with a rare form of Leukemia when he was five-years-old and it had been emotionally hard on her family, especially when he died so young. She'd always remember that painful period from her teens.

Troy sponsored one of the hospital wings at the facility and named it the Nian Center for Care. It delighted Pam's soul. In a strange way, it was as if Nian could live on in memory at the center, one of the facilities she happened to be a co-patron to now. Thanks to her work with Troy Romero. She didn't have much family. Her parents died a year apart a few years back so that essentially made her the last Alvarado in her father's family line. She had a few distant cousins and aunts and uncles back in Madrid but they weren't really close.

Coming from a small family was so very different from the wonders of a large close-knit family like the Romeros. It was a godsend that she'd met Troy in college and they'd become friends and later she was his employee. It was as if they were her second family and they treated her as such.

As they continued to move through the blizzard with the heavy winds blowing hard snow in her face, Pamela blindly followed Troy as she huddled with him while he practically carried her, ambulating against the gusty wind in the direction of the guest cottage near the Romero Manor grounds. What would she do without him right now?

"We're almost there," Troy called out over the sound of howling wind and blowing snow.

"Okay," she responded, holding tightly on to Troy. She could feel that zap of energy from his warm body as he held her oh, so tightly. Oh, she loved the feel of his strength around her waist.

Stop it, Pamela. He's only helping you. It means nothing.

Sadly, she realized she was getting a firm sample of what it would be like to be held tightly and affectionately by Troy. A mere sample of something she would never have the pleasure of experiencing.

Okay, she really needed to get a life or land a man. It had been way, way too long since she'd dated, she realized.

Finally, they stopped outside the cottage gates. Troy pulled away from Pam and took out some sort of key device to press against the gate. Luckily, it snapped open.

"I guess it has some backup power."

"You better believe it. After the last storm, we didn't take any chances with our smart homes. We made sure that things like the door and gate entries have at least one backup energy source."

"Good thinking," she called out.

They both walked through and the gate snapped shut behind them. They climbed up a long snow-filled pathway, their boots crunching through the hills of snow. She didn't know how on earth Troy managed to move so fast in the accumulated snow, but, of course, if he could climb Mount Everest, this would be a piece of cake. Sadly to say, not for her.

She pretty much fell over and Troy picked her up and helped her along the way. She felt like klutz tonight. Talk about disorientation.

As they walked up to the main door of the cottage, Troy dug into his pocket for his entry key. "Oh, great. I have the gate key but not the key for the main door," he cursed under his breath.

"What?" Pamela cried out, horror seizing her. Now she knew for sure, they were both going to freeze to death.

Chapter Five

"I'm worried about Troy," Cilla said at the manor, looking out through the window of the study. Most of the guests had already gone to their guest quarters but Toni, Zack and Cilla stayed back to see what they could do. "He should have never gone out for that stupid Pamela," she mumbled under her breath.

"I beg your pardon?" Toni Romero asked, disbelief lacing his tone.

Cilla had to bite her lip and remember that the Romeros were quite fond of Pamela.

"Um...Oh, nothing, Toni," Cilla tried to correct herself. Cilla was going to be a part of the Romero family. She had to at least pretend to like the people they liked. For now. Until she got her sweet little foot firmly planted inside their circle. Toni loved the hell out of Cilla because of what happened many years ago when she was with her mother and they'd spotted a young Troy outside the mall, then later, his brothers. But she hadn't really been around them much the past few years. She'd been busy travelling through Europe and Japan and really doing what her parents should have been doing during their later years. Living it up and enjoying their wealth. "It's just that I'm worried that something might have happened to Troy when he went looking for her. I'm sure she made it to wherever she had to go."

"Troy can handle anything," Zack said firmly and confidently, walking back into the dark study illuminated only by tea candles in the blackout. "He climbed Mount Everest in much worse conditions than this. He can handle a little Canadian blizzard."

Cilla had a bad feeling. Troy was her key to her fortune. And the hell was she going to sit back idly and watch that nobody of a loser Pamela take that all away.

Chapter Six

"You don't have the key?" Pamela cried out again, her heart was thumping like mad in her chest. She felt her legs get so weak, she was sure she was going to pass out. The authorities would probably find her and maybe Troy, too, buried under the snow in ice boxes thanks to the pelting of mixed freezing rain. "Troy, I can't take the cold anymore. I….I can't even feel my fingers and I'm wearing gloves."

"Aww. My bad, Pam. You should know me already." A sweet, boyish grin slid across his handsome face. "I just couldn't resist a little ice-breaker," he murmured in his charming voice and pulled out his entry key for the cottage door.

Relief washed over Pamela then when reality settled in, she growled at her intoxicatingly gorgeous boss. Even with the snow flurries blowing across his face, his good looks and charm melted her inside. He had the loveliest dark eyes she'd ever seen on a man. And beautiful long lashes that framed his sexy eyes. But what a time to break the ice when the ice storm was breaking down her nerves. Still, Troy was being Troy. She should have known.

The cottage was a part of the more than 3,000-acre estate belonging to the Romero family that extended from a large portion of the east side of Mayberry Hill. The main house or mansion, Romero Manor, would probably take them a good hour to walk to in this crazy weather. It was a good thing the Romero family owned many residences on their sprawling estate including several guest cottages to be enjoyed by visitors and family members. In the spring and summer, it was a beautiful oasis of green tranquility and professional landscapes, now the place was wrapped with a thick blanket of snow and blowing flurries like a winter wonderland fantasy.

Troy opened the creaky door. The place was dark of course. He led Pamela inside then felt around for a flashlight. She remembered that the Romeros usually equipped each of their cottages with flashlights near the coat closet by the entrance. A damn good idea. Safety-smart, too. If there ever was a power cut or an intruder inside who cut off electricity like in those spy thrillers she'd seen, they'd immediately have access to light so they wouldn't have to feel their way around the dark.

Pamela blew out a visible puff of air through her lips. Yep, the place was as frigid as an igloo. Well, naturally. Nobody had been there for at least a week during this brittle cold snap. The Romero's close family friend Stanley and his wife and kids visited last weekend as a mini retreat and spent some time there away from the kids who stayed back at the manor with their dear "Grandpa Toni." So obviously, the heat was turned off during this time while it sat vacant. But Pamela was so thankful to be indoors.

On any other night, she would have been ecstatic to be alone snowbound with Troy Romero in this cozy stone cottage hideaway near the Romero estate, but not now. Tonight, she learned he would be married soon. So that major finding changed everything. Pamela tried not to let her mood plummet any more than it had already.

And speaking of being dampened, Pam was soaked even though she had on her coat. It didn't help much in this blizzard. Her waterproof boots were soaked because she was knee high in slush from toppling over by the snowbank. The gusts of wind blew off her hood, so the snow drenched her hat and her hair. So much for that.

Troy finally turned on the flashlight he found by the breakfast bar near the main entrance by the open concept kitchen where some decorative candles inside tea light glass cups and a box of matches lay. He struck the match and lit up a few of the candles, about three or four glass covered tapers, and a nice warm orange glow lit up the area.

"How long will they burn?" she asked, trying to hide her nervousness.

"About four hours," he said, as he busied himself looking in draws for something.

"Four hours? That doesn't give us much time."

"We should have the fireplace lit by then." Troy sounded confident and authoritative. It was a good thing Troy was an outdoorsy man who could apparently survive in harsh wilderness conditions. Well, thank heavens she had him around her during a time like this, or she might have one heck of a night in this dangerous blizzard.

Pamela caught her reflection in the mirror on the wall by the breakfast bar and noted that she looked more like a drenched puppy in a winter coat than a young woman. Troy, on the other hand, resembled a hot stud dripping with charm and sexiness. His silky dark hair was damp and clung to his forehead. His handsome facial features were even more accentuated in the glow of the candles. His groomed stubble was more prominent and deliciously attractive. His full, perfectly shaped lips were moist from the melted snow and oh, so kissable.

Pamela wondered for a moment if Troy even knew just how damned good looking he really was. She had to fight the urge to strip off his jacket and his shirt and get all warm and cozy and physical with him by the as-yet-unlit fireplace. The image of him coming out from a hot, steamy shower crossed her mind just then. Seeing his rock hard wet abs as he towelled himself off. Yeah, like she would ever see that happen in real life. Especially now. Pamela tried to tamp down the sexual images as her heart raced in her throat.

"At least this should keep some light in here until the power comes back on," Troy said, his smooth, deep voice interrupting her naughty thoughts about him.

"Good," she said, hugging herself. "That's just what we need. I wish we could call the house to see how everybody's doing."

"It's no use," Troy answered, "We have phone service but the digital phones won't work." He picked up one of the dead phones by the breakfast table and replaced the receiver promptly. "I should have followed your advice and put one of those old-fashioned non-digital phones back in here. We had an antique dial phone in here once."

"Oh, I remember that!" Pamela chuckled, remembering that black rotary dial phone with fondness. "That was Grandpa Toni's favorite, wasn't it?"

"Oh, yeah. Too bad, he removed it from this cottage to have it refurbished. We could have used it right now."

"I know," she murmured, her heart pounding in her chest. "I just hope the power comes back on soon."

"Good thing you're not *alone*," he said. A serious expression dressed his handsome face. He was still mad as hell with her for running off like that into the blizzard. And right now, she was royally peeved with him, too, for hiding his engagement from her, but she could see his point about her putting her life in danger.

She rolled her eyes and shook her head. "Okay, so you can rub it in all you like. I should have stayed back at the house and called a cab or something." Why did she say that? Oh, how she wished she could pull those words back in through her lips.

"Call a cab? Are you kidding me? Not only would you not find one on Christmas Eve in this blizzard but I thought we'd agreed I would take you home."

"Yes, but..." she stopped herself mid-sentence. Emotion climbed into her throat again. She just couldn't bring herself to confront the reality that he was going to get married. Why did she feel as if she'd been stabbed in the back by this handsome man before her? It didn't seem fair in her mind yet she couldn't help herself. Was it because they had spent so many intimate moments together or had so many close encounters? Was it because she thought she and Troy were closer than close and then wham!? He blindsided her and pulled a major surprise on her like this.

You could have said "By the way, Pamela, I'm getting married!" You've shared more revealing secrets about yourself than that to me. Why am I the last to know? Why haven't you even told me already?

"Yeah, I guess it's just the two of us right now," she said quietly, trying to hide the sorrow in her voice. She also felt a pang of guilt. Troy had to abandon his SUV because of her coming out into the storm.

Pamela walked toward the unlit fireplace, hugging herself, avoiding eye contact with Troy. She found herself in the living area and sank down on the leather recliner.

He followed her with one of the warm glowing candles and placed it on the table near her.

"You're soaked. I don't want you catching a death of a cold on me here. You should go upstairs and change."

"I should?" she said, arching a brow. "Oh, so now you're giving me orders, are you?"

"I just don't want you catching pneumonia, okay?" he said in a firm voice that sent her pulse racing and her heart pounding. It was hard as hell to stay mad at her gorgeous now-spoken-for boss when all he cared about was her health and well-being.

She got up from the recliner.

"I believe there are some new T-shirts from the camp sponsorship programs," Troy added. "We've got a stack of them in a box in one of the guest rooms."

"You've still got those?" She had worked with Troy and the Romero family on a mega camp program for inner city youth to encourage positive self-esteem and pursuing entrepreneurial interests. They'd had a blast. The kids enjoyed it and the event was a huge success. That's one of the things she loved about Troy. He was never at a loss of ideas for how to creatively give back, every time he could.

Cilla was one lucky gal. She'd better be good to Troy, or else.

Pamela had so many fond memories of the past with Troy working on so many community and public service projects that she'd lost count. She worried that those days would be long gone. She was certain Cilla would limit the time Troy spent with any females after they became husband and wife.

She sighed heavily. "Aren't you going to change, too?" she murmured as she found her way to the dimly lit staircase.

"Ladies first," he said, fiddling with the breaker panel in the kitchen.

"What are you doing? The whole city's probably knocked out of power."

"I know. Just checking on something," he said, directing his flashlight to the panel. He then shut the panel and switched off and unplugged appliances in the kitchen.

"Checking on what?"

He moved over to the thermostat next and moved the control knob down. "Rule number one during an outage, always make sure equipment is unplugged and thermostats down so that nothing gets damaged from a power surge when power is restored."

"Ah, right, of course. You think of everything, don't you?" she said. "Never mind, I know the answer to that question." Well, he thought of everything except telling her one heartbreakingly important detail this evening. Like he was in fact getting married to another woman.

"You know Granddad likes to keep his cottages like hotels. You'll also find a supply of clean towels upstairs and freshly pressed towel robes. The robe will keep you warm over the T-shirt while the fire warms up the place," he added.

"Of course, Grandpa Toni thinks of everything," Pamela agreed.

* * *

Troy opened the freezer and fridge to survey their contents. He knew that food in the freezer would be good for up to twenty-four or thirty-six hours after power was cut off. He saw some instant TV dinners, desserts, frozen strawberries and vegetables, an ice tray and ice cream. Sweet. "It's a good thing we've still got some food in here."

"Or what?" Pamela teased in her sweet, sensuous voice. "Or, we'd probably end up eating each other tonight?"

Oh, dear God! Troy's groin throbbed and stiffened. Did she have to go and say "eating each other"? All he could do was visualize Pamela purely naked and him sucking on her sensual juices and tasting the life out of her womanhood as she groaned and writhed beneath him into his mouth. Or maybe he could take her on the marble counter by the breakfast bar.

His mouth salivated at the naughty erotic scenario. He drew in a deep breath and tried to switch the image out for one of the current situation at hand. Pamela and Troy alone in a dark cottage with no power or heat in the middle of a blizzard. No heat, except for the one climbing in his groin. Okay, that was a bad idea. Nothing was working right now.

Get your mind out of there, Troy. This is no time to be thinking dirty thoughts about Pamela. Or ever! She's your employee, damn it! One close call was more than enough. Don't even go there.

He hoped she couldn't see his crotch. Good thing she was standing by the staircase and Troy had the breakfast bar to hide behind.

"There'll be no eating each other tonight. I can assure you," he declared, perhaps a little too curtly. He saw her expression fall.

This whole night was going to be torture for him. Truth was, he'd always been sweetly attracted to innocent, lovable Pamela but she was not someone he could be intimate with because he just wasn't a committing kind of guy—except for this one year fake marriage gig, which he'd agreed to with Cilla. And Pamela deserved more. She deserved a guy who would stick around for the long haul. And that guy just wasn't him.

He'd had a close girlfriend once. In fact, the first girl he'd made love to was a college senior when he was a freshman. Erika Pendelin, the captain of the girl's cheerleading squad.

Erika had cajoled him to give her his virginity then smashed his heart into a million tiny pieces. He believed she was in love with him at the time. But boy, had he been wrong. Up to this day, he never shared the embarrassment with his brothers. It was something he hadn't shared with a single soul and never would. A man had his pride. And Troy had his.

He chalked it up to one hell of a lesson and moved on. He was too young and naïve then. But to him, being in a relationship meant a lot.

Erika and he had been dating for a few months before they ended up in the backseat of her brand new red convertible. They committed all kinds of weird and crazy acts that night. But as soon as he had been intimate, she pulled the very same trick that guys who just wanna get laid pull. She didn't call him the next day or the day after that or the week thereafter. She avoided his calls. He learned later that she had a bet with her friends that she could get him, the guy voted "cutest and sweetest" at the college to give it up to her. *Man, that hurt like hell!*

Well, talk about the tables turning. Only, he would never do that to a woman. Sure, he'd had plenty of beautiful girls since then but he would let them know up front he wasn't into long-term commitments.

Years later, Erika claimed to be sorry and wanted to get with him again, saying that she had been pressured to do that but he didn't even give her the time of day. She'd only come after him again—practically thrown herself at him—when she realized she really lost a "great catch." He'd just made his first billion on his own developing a popular innovative educational app for college programs worldwide, the same app he'd ended up using for Rom International, the college he founded with his brother, Dion.

Troy vowed then that he would never give his heart to any woman ever again. Period. That heartbreaking pain almost killed him. And he would never commit to a woman either because he wouldn't want her to go through what he had gone through.

So there it was. So much for ever getting into a committed relationship. And as his grandfather had already forewarned him, he needed to keep away from sleeping with the employees. It was bad for business, especially if it didn't work out.

"I'm gonna go check on the carbon monoxide detector to make sure the battery-powered backup still works," he said, trying to distract himself. "Here, take one of the candles upstairs so you can see," he continued. "By the time you're done showering and changing, I should have a fire started."

"Yeah, of course. We need to get some heat in here," she said quietly.

Heat? Oh, God! He sure as hell didn't need any heat tonight from the fireplace. His whole body was on fire over thoughts of caressing Pamela and pressing his lips to hers again as he'd done in the past and she didn't have the slightest idea of the turmoil going on inside his mind and body.

Troy figured he'd need to take a very cold shower after Pamela was done with hers.

There was an awkward silence between them for a brief moment then Pamela turned to go upstairs with the tea candle and glass holder in her hand. He tried not to watch to make sure she'd get upstairs safely but it was too late. That sweet wiggle of her rounded ass got his erection jumping. This night was going to be one hell of a torture session for him, keeping his hands off his pretty, loyal assistant and erasing all thoughts of pleasuring her tonight—or ever.

Chapter Seven

Pamela didn't waste any time when she reached the top landing of the steps. She had the candle in her hand to light her path as she made her way into the bathroom. Troy was right. She was drenched and needed to change into something dry right away. Her cold, damp clothes clung to her skin at the moment, thanks to slipping and falling in that slushy snow bank courtesy of the gust of frigid wind. That was a recipe for pneumonia waiting to happen.

She absentmindedly reached for the light switch on the landing only to realize that, duh, of course it wouldn't work. There were in the middle of a power outage caused by the ice storm and blizzard. Funny how people often did things on autopilot without realizing it.

She finally made her way into the bathroom and stripped off her wet clothes. She could hear Troy downstairs fiddling with something, presumably finding kindling to get the fireplace going. And speaking of getting the fire going, boy, did he stir up some deliciously hot feelings inside of her. She blew out a puff of air, trying to throttle the butterflies tickling her belly. She always got the giddy tingling in her lower belly when she was near Troy. But he was going to be married to Cilla, she thought as her heart squeezed inside her chest.

Pamela noticed the stall was massive and had two showerheads on adjacent walls of the shower. It also had a nice marble built-in seat. Talk about luxury. She turned on the shower faucet to lukewarm then braced herself before stepping inside, feeling crazily erotic thinking about Troy who was not far from her downstairs. She enjoyed the splash of the water on her skin, wishfully thinking, hoping Troy would magically appear then climb in the stall behind her and slide his hands all over her naked body and...

Pamela was getting hot inside, her nipples tightened at the thought of what Troy would look like naked and wet in a shower. She visualized sitting on top of Troy's lap riding him as water splashed off her back.

Yeah, like that would ever happen now. She shook her head and swallowed hard.

Nice try, Pam. No more hot boss fantasies for you. Troy was probably too busy thinking how he'd rather be back at the manor with his sexy, rich fiancée than being snowbound with his too-dumb-to-realize-she'd-get-stuck-in-this-blizzard assistant.

She still couldn't wrap her head around that one. Why would he want to marry Cilla? What did she have that Pamela didn't have? Oh, right. Wealth, wealth and more wealth. But then again, Troy had his own massive fortune. Perhaps it was because Cilla came from a privileged family and was thus a more suitable match for him.

Pamela turned off the faucet, frustrated that Troy was downstairs going on about his business when she really wanted him inside her business. She hated herself for having lustful feelings about her newly engaged-to-another-woman boss. She dried herself off and looked around in the candlelit bathroom for the robe Troy mentioned earlier. No robe in sight. She wrapped the towel around her body after drying off and went into the guest bedroom adjacent to the bathroom and found the box of T-shirts. She immediately rummaged through the opened box and pulled out a crisp new T-shirt still in the packaging. Pamela shivered as she ripped open the plastic and pulled the T-shirt over her body. *Well,* she thought, *don't I look sophisticated?* The oversized T-shirt clearly wasn't her size but it at least covered her butt and upper thighs. That's all that counted right now. The sleeves were long enough, too. Thank heavens! She was wearing clean, and more importantly, dry clothing.

She heard Troy whistling downstairs and the sound of crackling wood. *Did he get the fireplace lit already?*

He certainly was a handy man to have around. She heard the wind howling outside the window and snow pellets still slamming against the glass panes. She was thankful to be cozy inside the cottage. As she walked down the staircase, still drying her hair with a small white towel, she couldn't wait to get by the fireplace to keep warm.

* * *

Hot damn!

Troy fought the urge to drool as Pamela walked down the steps in her above-the-knee make-do nightshirt. He felt like a steak on a grill - burning up and sizzling inside. The dark cottage, dim ambiance gave him just the right setting to sweetly seduce his beautiful assistant. Yet he just couldn't. Even though he was going to be involved in a fake marriage with Cilla, it still wouldn't be right. He hated himself for thinking impure thoughts but he just couldn't help himself. Any man with a pulse would be turned on by Pamela's appearance. Besides, what else would come of this night? He couldn't commit to any woman right now—for real.

And oh, Pamela in that practically see-through T-shirt with the silhouette of her voluptuous breasts and hard round nipples showing made him hard like a rock. He wanted to take her nipples between his lips. He just didn't need this type of distraction at the moment. He could feel heat and blood rushing to his loins. But he knew what he had to do. He was going to keep the situation under control. He kept reminding himself that he was Pamela's boss. And nothing more. He couldn't wait until the storm passed and the power came back on so that he could get the hell out of her beautiful presence and back to family business.

Ah, hell. Who was he kidding? He was hot for Pamela, and he knew it. Heck, they both could have died out there in the ice storm if the tree that got knocked over struck their windshield instead of falling right in front of the vehicle like it did while he was driving.

Thank you, Universe!

The thought crossed his mind earlier that it could have been a lot worse. Hell, he didn't know what he would have done with himself had something happened to Pamela. Thankfully, they had been at a close enough distance to walk to the cottage without getting blown away by the heavy gusts of wind and blowing snow.

* * *

"Are you cold?" Troy asked Pamela in his low, deep and oh, so sexy voice. His delicious dark gaze caught hers. A pleasant tickle danced down her spine at the sound of his silky deep voice. It got her each and every time he spoke. She could never get tired of it. But she had to learn how to do that, given the circumstances.

The fireplace crackling was the only thing she heard after that.

Oh, no. I'm not cold. I'm hot, baby. Hot for you.

"No, I'm fine," she murmured, hugging herself looking into the fire. She then blew warm air into her hands, shivering slightly as the room grew warmer.

Pamela was not about to share her feelings with Troy. Not now. Not ever. He was spoken for. Well, he would be soon. He was off limits. The last thing she wanted to be was a home wrecker.

"You sure?" he said, inching closer to her as butterflies exploded in her belly. There was that sweet magical pulse between them again. The same pulse that transferred to the space between her thighs. Her heart pounded hard and fast in her chest. This was the moment she'd been waiting for all night until, of course, she found out that Troy had been betrothed to another woman.

Troy and Pamela were alone in a dark cottage on Christmas Eve with the power out and nothing more than a fireplace glowing its natural light and old-school warmth to keep them cozy. The world outside was quiet, dark and cold. The wind was howling outside, the shutters making a lulling banging sound. It would have been the perfect setup, but it was a nightmare of guilt and awkwardness. Pam was with her steaming hot boss, Troy Romero. No one would bother them for hours.

It was just the two of them, stranded in the middle of an ice storm.

Oh, stop it, girl. Squash those thoughts out of your head. He's off limits. He's engaged. He's engaged to Cilla, of all women, but he's engaged.

"Please, Troy." She turned around and his lips were close to hers. Her inner thighs throbbed mercilessly. Damn it! Why did that man always have that effect on her? If only her body paid attention to what her conscience was saying.

He inched closer to her and oh, she wanted to grab him and press her lips to his soft sweet lips, just as they had in the past, that one time at the study in Romero Manor. She was breathing hard, about to lose herself in Troy but she pulled back, dizzy and confused.

"What is it?" he said in a low voice, concern dressed his handsome face. He looked so beautiful in the warm orange glow of the fireplace in the dark cottage.

"You just left me hanging, girl." Troy grinned and a boyish dimple appeared on his cheek.

"You deserve it!"

"Ouch!" He feigned being hurt by her reaction. "What was that for?"

"I...I mean how could you, Troy?"

"How could I what? How could I want to kiss you and taste your sweet lips again?"

"Troy, this is different. Much different than last time." Her face was turned to the fireplace. She fought to contain herself and her overwhelming emotions for Troy. Oh, God, this was hard. She loved him. She always had since the day she'd met him in college.

"What do you mean things are different?"

"You know what I mean. You...you're getting married." There! She finally spilled it. Well, one of them had to get it out in the open tonight.

"Getting what? Married!?" Troy slapped his forehead with his hand, a chuckle erupted in his throat.

"What's so funny?" she asked, mouth agape. Her heart was racing in her chest.

"Oh, God! Pamela, it's all my fault. I guess I do deserve that."

She turned to face him, looking puzzled, her arms folded tightly across her chest.

"What?" she asked softly.

He drew in a deep breath. "I wasn't going to mention this to...well, to everyone just yet, but I guess you saw me with Cilla tonight in the west wing corridor. I knew a few people were walking by in the distance. I guess I never figured one of them could be you. Yeah, Cilla and are getting married."

Her heart plunged in her chest. She felt her lungs spasm. She felt as if she could faint at any second. Confirmation of her suspicion. So it *was* true! There was nothing like good old-fashioned confirmation. *Yeah, right.* The truth hurt. And it hurt like hell. If an icicle had slammed hard into her chest right now, she didn't think she could feel any more excruciating pain than she did at this moment. The moment of truth.

Maybe a part of her, a small hopeful part of her had been secretly wishing that what she'd overheard had been wrong. That maybe Troy was not engaged to another woman, but he'd just confirmed it, didn't he?

She tried to swallow the hard lump wedging itself in her throat but it was no use. She was choked up with emotion.

"G-good for you," her voice sounded more cracked than she had realized. "C-c-congratulations," she finally managed to eke out, sadness filling her voice but she tried to bounce back up. "I guess you are the marrying type after all," she tried to joke, but oh, God, it hurt like hell. She really was losing Troy. They could never be together. Ever.

"Thanks, but..." Troy bit down on his lip, looking profoundly into her eyes. "I can tell you this because you're my confidante and PR person."

"And?"

"Cilla and I are entering into a business arrangement and that's all I can say about the matter, okay? No one outside the clan is supposed to know." His tone was so stern, almost devoid of emotion. She'd never seen Troy so serious...

"A business arrangement?" Pamela echoed dubiously. Her pulse raced. "What?"

"It's not something I wanna get into right now, Pam."

"But...I don't get it. Are you putting me on, Troy?"

He looked at her, regarding her with disbelief. "Hey, you know I joke around a lot, but you should know me by now that I would never kid around about something like that. Do you think I'm trying pull a fast one over you so I can get with you tonight?"

"Yes," she said, her arms folded across her chest. "Well, I...what else am I to think?"

"I can't believe you think I would lie to you about that!"

Oh, no. Great going, Pam. She was clearly getting under his skin. She was ticking off her sexy bad boy boss. And they only had each other tonight to comfort each other through this crazy ice storm and power outage.

She gave him an I-don't-believe-you raised brow look. "Well, I hope you would never cheat on whom you're with because winners never cheat and cheaters never win. And I'm no cheater and I don't like cheaters."

"I think you mean, 'Quitters never win and winners never quit.' That's how the saying goes," he corrected with levity in his tone and a charming grin.

"Whatever..." she murmured, "Same thing."

"Oh, hell no," Troy said, as if he'd just caught on to what she was finally getting at. "Whoa there. Wait a minute! I'm a lot of things, Pam, but I would never cheat on someone I'm with. You should know that by now. You've worked with me as a PA in the past. You've seen my dates. I'm a one-woman man."

"But you're with Cilla. I mean, you guys were close tonight. I don't want to be the backup girl or other woman, Troy. I respect myself too much for that. And furthermore, I respect relationships. I wouldn't want to be cheated on so I wouldn't do it to another woman's man."

And the truth was, her happy family home was trashed by her father's infidelity to her mother. He ended up running off with his secretary and shattered all their dreams. Her mother was never the same after that and had suffered a nervous breakdown. Pamela was never the same after that. She never looked at couples the same way.

"Good."

"Good?" she echoed.

He grinned knowingly. "I like that in a woman." His silky tone deepened. God, he always sounded sexy as hell. Could he not just turn off the sexiness for a minute so she could continue being angry with him?

"You do?"

"Yes, Pamela. That's what I've always loved about you. You're different from other girls I've met or dated. You have a heart. You have values. You're good people. And I'd kill any man who tried to hurt you or take advantage of your kindness."

"Y-you would?"

He nodded moving closer to her, holding her gazing with his sizzling heated gaze. Never mind the windchill outside, it was hot right now between them.

"Yes, Pam. You're the type of woman a guy would be crazy to give up. You have high moral values and you're sweet and kind and very caring. You're pure and honest. And you think good thoughts about other people. You're golden, Pam. A treasure."

Pamela gushed. What could she say in response? She stammered to get her words out but nothing came forth. So much for being a trained spokesperson.

Troy neared her and lifted her chin and softly brushed his lips over hers and a silky feeling of ecstasy slithered down her spine. She moaned into his sweet lips as he caressed her flesh with his warmth. She arched her neck to savor his touch. The silky feel of his mouth over hers was oh, so delightful as he caressed her with his sweet, soft lips, sucking and teasing her with his skilled French kisses.

Pamela's inner thighs throbbed. Oh, no. She didn't have any panties on underneath her nightshirt. She could feel sweet moisture between her legs as she became more aroused by Troy's seductive, passionate kiss. The man really knew how to pleasure a woman with those lips of his.

Oh, it was so hot in there. Hot like sin.

Troy's strong hands softly touched her back and slid down to her hips and electricity pulsed inside her body and spasmed between her legs. Her nipples were tight and erect from his sensuality. His cologne was overwhelming her senses. Oh, he smelled so, so good. She loved the feel of her boss on her skin. She wanted so much more of him.

Just then a loud crash stabbed the silence and they pulled apart, still panting from that incredibly hot and delicious kiss.

"What was that?" she cried out, almost breathless, her heartbeat galloped like mad.

The loud howl of the wind came through as the window inside the kitchen near the pantry had cracked.

"Looks like a branch broke off from the wind and ice."

Pamela's body was still buzzed from Troy's sweet, delicious kiss. She was still delightfully overheated from his magical, sexual touch. What would have happened if they hadn't been interrupted? She sucked in a deep breath and followed Troy into the pantry. Pamela was horribly upset with the storm and Mother Nature, for all the wrong reasons.

"You stay in here," Troy directed as he grabbed his jacket.

"Oh, no, Troy! Don't go outside."

"I have to. I need to close the shutter from outside."

"But you could get hurt," she said, hugging herself, wanting to follow him.

"I'll just be a second. I'm also going to check to make sure no live wires are near the house or we'll be in real trouble."

Oh, great. This night was turning out to be more dangerous than she could possibly imagine. What was going to happen to them? The night could get more dangerous for more reasons than one...

Chapter Eight

Troy combed his fingers through his damp hair as the gusts of wind blew harder. This damn storm wasn't letting up any time soon. And looking around, it didn't seem as if anyone had any power on in their homes for miles. Like the turbulent winds, Troy's emotions were all over the place.

What should he do? His erection was straining inside his pants. Good thing for that distraction or who knew what would have happened as he tasted Pamela's sweet lips. He had Cilla to think about, too. The girl (along with her mother) who led him to his grandfather when he had been a poor boy living out of his father's van after his mother died. They'd just lost their home at the time, too. They were down and out and meeting Cilla with her mom at the mall was heaven sent. She'd led him to his grandfather and a life of luxury and privilege after that. He and his brothers would never in a million years forget where they came from and those who were there for them in their past. Cilla led him to his fortune, so he couldn't possibly prevent her from keeping her own in a bizarre twist of fate. He could just see Cilla's face if she even knew he and Pamela were alone in the cottage.

He couldn't let down a good family friend who pretty much turned his life around—thanks to her mother. But then again, he didn't want to lose what could be the greatest love of his life in Pamela. She was the real deal. His gut felt it with those lips of hers. There was something so sincere, so innocent, and so connecting with being with Pamela. Imagine that! They hadn't even slept together, yet he'd felt so much in love with her, a part of her.

The truth was, his heart was with Pamela—all the way. He could do nothing less than think about her day and night, fantasize about her.

Damn, if Troy were honest with himself, he just couldn't see himself living without Pamela. She had to be in his future. He needed her like he needed air to breathe. But what would he do about Cilla? Their arrangement was to be married for at least a year. That meant appearing as a happily-married couple. He'd have to stay away from Pam, though, for fear of someone seeing them together.

It was no use to see other people if they were to convince the estate that Cilla was in a real marriage. After all, from what she'd told him, the executors of the estate didn't think much of her and would like nothing more than to withhold her inheritance if they so much as suspected she was not truly married as per the weird conditions of her parents' will.

The last thing Troy would want to do was have Cilla's cover blown. If anything had happened tonight between him and Pamela, it would only be the one night. There could be no repeats. Would Pamela even be okay with that? Would he feel good about himself if he'd taken her just then for just one night? It would be their first night together being intimate. Could he even take her once without the temptation and fighting his will power to not want to keep on making love to her night after night? He didn't believe in permanent relationships. He'd had the worst experience in his past.

The whole town looked as if it had no power. But he sure could use some will power.

Chapter Nine

Cilla paced frantically in the guest room, arms folded across her chest, lips pinched together. Her room was located on the ground floor of Romero Manor. Where the heck was Troy? She glared out the window into the dark, snow-blowing night. It was crazy as hell out there. And Troy still hadn't returned to the manor.

"That dim-witted Pamela would have to do something to mess up what should be the best night of my life," she growled to herself.

Cilla thought that Pamela was always a loser since she'd met her at the university. Always wearing the tackiest ill-fitting department chain-store clothes she could buy or find, or so it looked like. It was as if the girl had no fashion sense. She'd apparently never met a manicurist in her life, either, Cilla mused, chuckling bitterly to herself.

Pamela always grated under Cilla's skin without even realizing it. Always thinking she was a Miss Know-it-all because she could turn statements into poetic lies or whatever it was she did as the Romero's spokesperson. Heck, Cilla's cocker spaniel could do a better job with press statements. Why the Romeros kept that fashion-challenged girl on, she had no idea.

Cilla could not for the life of her figure out why Troy even liked having her around as a friend. Then Troy went and hired the homely girl and brought her into Romero Manor to work for the family.

Well, duh! If she couldn't get a job out of college, that meant she wasn't that much of a catch then, Troy.

She sighed heavily. She was going to put a stop to this thing once and for all. She noticed the way Troy looked at Pamela when her back was turned. Like he had some sort of respect for her. Yeah, right!

She was engaged to Troy. Okay, so it was a fake engagement, but still, she was looking forward to the admiration of others by being in the Romero clique. Cilla wanted nothing more than for this crap game to go through for her.

She was a businesswoman and she would do anything to keep her fortune. And right now, Troy was hers. All hers. At least for the next year, possibly more.

Enough already!

Cilla stopped pacing and reached for her purse and car keys. She was going to go and find Troy and bring him back to the manor. Like now.

Chapter Ten

By the time Troy had gotten back inside, Pamela was already upstairs. She knew it wouldn't take him long to close the shutters over the windows downstairs from the outside. But she had to do something about her aroused state before he got back in. The last thing she would have wanted him to see was her intense bodily reaction to his sexual charm. She knew he was to be married to Cilla soon. Even though it was a fake relationship and business arrangement, it was still going to be a marriage and that would mean that lucky-as-hell Cilla was going to have full access to Troy in her bed. Troy was a one-woman man. He didn't even have to remind her, even though she had been snarky to insinuate that he was trying to get with her even though he was taken. The thought caused her stomach to tighten in knots.

She'd hop back in the shower to cool off. Imagine that. Two showers in one night. What was wrong with her? Why was Troy having this crazy yet magical effect on her? And why was it stronger tonight? She'd felt as if there had been some sort of a magnetic pull between them. An intense energy force that neither one of them could deny. She had felt his hardness earlier when they were kissing in the kitchen before that gust of wind blew the tree branch into the kitchen window.

Damn!

What would have happened had they not been interrupted? Pamela felt heat climb inside her as the thought penetrated her mind.

Still, she had to wipe away that naughty thought. It wasn't gonna happen tonight, that's for darn sure.

She heard the door slam shut downstairs and knew Troy had returned. She then quickly turned on the faucet. She had to cool off and clean up...again.

Pamela allowed the lukewarm water to trickle down her skin and splash all over her body. The bathroom and shower stall were dark except for the warm glow from the tea candle on the marble sink countertop nearby.

She heard the sound of knocking on the bathroom door and instinctively answered it. "Come in," she called out before it was too late. Why on earth did she say to come it? Because her body wanted Troy inside there with her and there was no denying it. They were two mature adults who'd come to respect each other and had grown close together over the past few years.

Troy opened the door with a seductive grin on his sweet lips. The lips that just moments ago pleasured her and oh, boy, her body heated up again. So much for cooling off in the shower.

"Do you think that was safe, answering the door like that, telling me to come in?" He grinned and arched his brow. She loved the way his dark sexy eyes slid down her naked body being that he could see her clearly through the glass shower door that was partly slid open.

Was he playing with her? "Well, what else was I supposed to do?" she murmured.

"What if it was an intruder knocking at the door?" he posed.

"Would a criminal have the manners to knock first?" she replied, arching her brow and giving him a wicked grin. Her inner thighs throbbed with want, just looking at Troy as he leaned against the door. For some reason, she didn't feel as shy as she thought she would with Troy there. They'd been so close over the years and she felt oddly comfortable.

"You've got me there," he admitted in a low, sexy voice and moved closer to her.

Oh, God! Troy, I need you now...

As the water slid down her body, she could think of nothing more than having Troy right inside the shower stall with her.

"So...um...is everything okay out there?" she asked.

"Yeah, I managed to get the shutter closed. We're good for now. But...you want to know something?"

"What?"

"The water is controlled by electricity. We could lose precious water supply soon, while the main power's out." Troy grinned.

"Oh, right. You should probably, um...come inside, the water is beginning to trickle," she said. "I'd feel so bad if you didn't get your...um....shower tonight."

"Come inside?" he murmured in a husky voice. "Oh, Pam, are you teasing me?"

"No, Troy. We're two sensible adults in the middle of a crisis."

"Are you sure?"

I couldn't be more sure, Troy. God, I want you. I want you so badly, you have no idea.

"Y-yes, I'm sure," she said softly. Her voice hoarse. Her body was on fire.

"Well," he answered, "let's not waste any more time...I mean, water..." He smiled and his dark eyes crinkled with amusement.

Soon after, Troy had ripped off his shirt and undressed entirely. Pamela's inner thighs throbbed like crazy. Her pulse raced like a galloping horse, her breath became more labored and shallow. This was like a fantasy. She could not believe that she and Troy were...both naked, together in the shower. This was a dream. This wasn't happening. She was going to wake up soon to reality and Troy would not be there with her. She'd still be stuck on the roadside in the middle of the blizzard, not inside a warm luxury shower stall complete with built-in marble seat in a fancy cottage off the Romero estate.

Have mercy! She didn't think she'd be able to control herself any longer. She was just going to jump his bones like there was no tomorrow, if he didn't touch her body soon.

The man was built like a glorious sex god. *Oh, help me heaven!* Pamela was about to faint.

His hardness was huge. Her belly exploded into a million butterflies and she had to remember to keep her jaw-off-the-floor look at bay. His enormous manhood was beautifully framed by soft groomed hair around it.

Troy slid inside the stall behind her and she her mind froze. She could not think about anything right now but Troy naked beside her in all his heavenly glory.

She moved slightly so the water force of the showerhead could blast him with wetness until she recalled the luxury shower stall had not one but two showerheads with its dual plumbing design. *Well, talk about how the mighty live well!*

She could not breathe. She needed oxygen.

Her eyes were treated to a gorgeous visual of his well-sculpted body.

Stop, drooling, Pamela. Even in the candlelight, he can still see you!

For the first time she got a good look at his pecs up close. He was what the girls would call "ripped" in all the right places. Sleek muscles on his chest, a nicely defined six-pack on his abs, smooth skin, hard biceps and broad shoulders. She knew that he and his brothers often worked out regularly, four or five times a week between meetings and business engagements, religiously. Well, she could now see that it certainly paid off big time. The man took great care of his body.

He grabbed the soap from its holder and immediately lathered himself and got washed. Oh, how she would love to lather herself all over his gorgeous...

"You're a beautiful woman, Pamela, do you know that?" he said softly, as he stood in front of her surveying her body. He was now rinsing off the soap from his sexy-as-hell body. Did the man even know what kind of effect he was having on her senses?

"Do you need me to wash your back?" he asked her gently, his voice was low and silky.

You can wash anywhere you please, Troy.

"Um…yeah, sure," she whispered, almost out of breath as the water from her own showerhead rolled down her back.

"Oh, God, you're trembling, Pamela," he said in a low, soft voice that sent shivers racing down her spine. "Are you okay?"

She nodded. "Yeah, I'm just a bit…" she bit down on her lip, her heart fluttered in her chest. "…nervous."

"Nervous?" he murmured. "What for?" He caressed her back with his soft fingers. Oh, she loved the feel of his body on hers. "You know I wouldn't do anything to hurt you, Pamela. You mean the world to me."

"I do?"

"Yes. Why does that surprise you?" he murmured, his voice, low and sensuously hoarse. "Just being here with you blows my mind, Pam. I've been so into you for so long, you have no idea."

"Well, you didn't let on to it while we worked together…except that one time…" She felt heat rise to her cheeks.

Yeah, that one time in the study at Romero Manor when they'd just finished working the longest night ever. They were both so exhausted that the sleep hormone melatonin was kicking in. Was that also responsible for their mellow mood? After that night, to her chagrin, there was no repeat. Oh, God, had she wished there was a repeat of that salacious kiss that made her head spin.

She didn't know what had gotten to her but she couldn't help herself, she reached her arms around the back of his neck and pulled him closer to her, kissing him, pressing her lips to his and he immediately responded and caressed her with his sweet, French kisses. They were going to go crazy in there tonight. There was no holding back the unbridled passion and heat that existed between them. The heat of desire that had long burned between them that was now too overwhelming, too great to deny.

"Oh, God! I want you, Troy," she purred, caressing his firm, smooth muscles as she ran her hands down his hard flesh savoring the feel of his masculinity.

"How much?" he teased her in a low, hoarse voice, breathing as hard and heavy as she was while he pressed sizzling erotic kisses to her neck, sucking on her flesh as she arched her head back and moaned with ecstasy.

"Oh," she gasped out loud, grabbing his shoulder blade as he leaned her against the wall.

He flashed a devilish smile as he continued to sweetly and tenderly press his eager hips to her naked wet flesh and oh, the electricity that pulsed between their bodies was incredible.

Troy gently ran his fingers down her body and she shivered as he slid his firm hands over her rounded breasts, massaging her bosom and caressing her. He then glided his fingers over one of her hard, round nipples, thumbing and stroking her taut bud, caressing and teasing while pressing kisses to her lips.

"Oh, Troy," she cried out with delight, the folds between her legs, throbbing and aching to be touched by him.

"Oh, God, Pam, I wanna have you, right now. Right here, baby. I need you."

"Oh," she moaned uncontrollably, arching her back. She nodded. "Yes, Troy, now," she whispered. "Please, now."

Troy sat her down on the built-in shower seat and spread her legs. He moved down on her and extended his smooth tongue between her folds and she cried out with sheer carnal pleasure. Unable to contain her body's delight from his touch, she held onto his damp hair, arching her back against the smooth acrylic wall in the spacious shower stall.

Troy moved down on her body sucking her wet flesh and his hands slid down her body to her soft pubic hairs and she jolted with delight as he gently stroked her inner thighs, sliding his fingers up and down then in between her folds. He slid his finger inside her and she felt herself pulse uncontrollably. Gently, he moved another finger inside and started to thrust inside her before putting his lips again to her soft heat, caressing her with his lips while he moved inside her she arched her back and spread her legs even wider, calling out his name.

Troy gently licked and teased the sensitive flesh of her folds before sliding his tongue inside her, tasting her juices, sliding his wet tongue in and out and sucking on her flesh, first soft then hard while she dug her finger pads into the top of his head. She could not believe the feeling of having Troy down there, pleasing her the way he did. She'd never felt this way before with any other man in her life.

Troy was oh, so…hmm, good. She dreamed of a moment like this with her hot, sexy boss for too long now but she'd never thought it would ever happen. Not in her wildest fantasy. And this was…greater than her wildest fantasy that she'd ever had about Troy. It was as if he knew her body better than she did. He knew just where her erotic zones were…

Breathing heavy and fast, overcome with the sensation of his skilled touch, Pamela came hard and fast, her body went into spasms and jerked from the electrifying release of her heated orgasm until her legs felt weak and limp. She couldn't believe how incredibly amazing he felt inside her and he hadn't even penetrated her with his manhood … yet.

"God, I love you, Pam," he said hoarsely, while he moved back up to face her, breathless, pressing his sweet lips to hers. She could taste the fresh soapy scent of her own sex on his lips. They passionately brushed their lips as she slid her hands over his muscular flesh. "You're so beautiful, baby," he groaned.

"Oh, Troy, I want you so bad. I…I've. Always. Wanted. You," she breathed between salacious kisses.

Simultaneously, she reached down to hold his hard, long erection as water splashed down on their naked bodies. She stroked him and savored the feel of his length, enjoying his low groans of pleasure. She was so turned on by his moans and couldn't wait to please him the way he'd done for her. While she was still seated, he stood. His impressive length was right where she wanted it, in front of her. She continued to slide her hand up and down his manhood, enjoying the hard long feel as the water sprinkled over them. She was turned on by the sensation of the wetness of their hot bodies. And there was something so sexy about a muscular man being wet and naked. She pressed her lips to his base and sucked on him while he moaned. He felt so incredibly good. She extended her tongue over his tip while holding him firmly, gently sucking and licking over his extension, savoring the feel and the fresh taste of him. She couldn't wait to get to the next step and opened her mouth and took him inside her, going as deep as she could and closing herself around him while he held her tightly.

She wanted to do this as well as she could. She wanted to please him so badly, just as he'd done for her. She wrapped her lips over her teeth so that he would only feel the softness of her lips on his sensitive skin.

She had read somewhere that was the best way to give oral to a man. Up and down his length she bobbed her head moving slowly first then faster, sucking him and kissing him intermittently while moving her hand up and down his hard shaft. He completely filled her mouth and she enjoyed his taste as he pulsated inside her. She couldn't believe she was pleasuring her boss this way. She couldn't believe that Troy and she were sharing something so intimate, so personal, so deliciously erotic. But she enjoyed every ounce of this moment. She sucked and savored his erection until he went into a spasm, groaning with pleasure as he came hard and fast, his silky release spilling over her lips and dripping down her chin.

Breathing hard, he collapsed back onto the wall. "God, you're amazing, Pam," he moaned, his voice hoarse and unrecognizable. Pamela got up and embraced him and he hugged her so passionately.

"I've got a condom, if you want to go all the way," he breathed, his chest still heaving. She could hear the hard and fast pounding of his heartbeat as she pressed her head to his chest.

"Oh, yes," she moaned, lifting her chin up to kiss him. "I want you so badly, Troy."

He grinned, lust overtaking his countenance. He led her out of the stall and they both dried off with the towel hanging over the door, kissing each other as if they were love-hungry animals who just couldn't get enough of each other. He picked up his pants from the floor and reached his hand into the pocket and pulled out a square silver packet.

Thank God, Troy had a condom with him.

It would have been a hell of a shame to stop at the wonderful foreplay.

Before long, they found themselves in the guest bedroom adjacent to the bathroom and Troy led her to the bed in the candlelit room. He laid her on her back and pressed kisses to her skin, from her lips to the sensitive part of her neck to her shoulder blade and to her breasts sucking on her nipple. Troy took his time with her, admiring her body, making her feel like a princess. She appreciated the time he took with her, the love and respect he'd showed her. He was so gentle with her yet a spectacular lover at the same time.

Have mercy. She was sure she would probably die from orgasmic overload tonight!

Troy lay on top of her and gently kissed her lips and she melted into his passionate lips. He then carefully spread her legs with his knee and moved his hips over hers while he moved over her. "I love you, Pamela," he said, in a low, hoarse voice before sliding his hard long erection inside her, first slowly in between her moist, throbbing folds and moving around inside her back and forth, then harder and faster. She couldn't believe how incredibly amazing he felt inside her. Her blood pumped hard and fast as ecstasy consumed her body.

He continued to thrust his hardness inside her moistness, penetrating deeper and deeper, while currents of desire rushed through her blood. She had dreamed of Troy being inside her for so long and now...it was an amazing dream come true.

Pamela ran her fingers over the smooth muscles on his back as he pounded inside her walls. She tightened around his delicious length as he filled her, moving inside her until she cried out with deep pleasure and satisfaction. Her orgasm washed over her body, leaving her sated and deeply relaxed. Soon after, Troy shuddered as he came hard and fast, groaning with delight and erotic satisfaction. He collapsed on top of her, breathing hard, holding her tightly as they both enjoyed the magic of their precious union.

Chapter Eleven

"And where do you think you're going?" Toni Romero asked Cilla, hobbling with his walking stick into the grand foyer. He was wearing a velvet robe over his pajamas and black leather slippers.

Cilla had on her winter coat along with her scarf, hat and leather gloves. Weren't Toni and the rest of the clan supposed to be getting ready for bed? Apparently not. Probably they were still up in the study trying to get a cell phone signal for Troy. "I can't just sit here and do nothing, Toni. Troy could be hurt out there!"

She was worried about Troy because she truly cared for him, but also because he was the ticket to her billion-dollar fortune.

"And Pamela! Pamela could be hurt, too," Toni added. "But trust me, I'm sure they are going to be just fine."

Cilla resisted the urge to blurt out that it would probably serve Pamela right for rushing out into the ice storm like a crazy-ass woman and then having Cilla's fiancé go look for her. "Yes, I almost forgot. Poor Pamela." Cilla couldn't care less about Pamela.

She had to keep reminding herself that the Romeros liked Pamela so she had to be careful what she said about her. Well, that would change when she married Troy. Then as Mrs. Troy Romero, they would all have to pay more attention to *her* feelings instead of outsiders like Pamela. Even if she was going to be a fake Mrs. Troy Romero.

Cilla hesitated. She really wanted to go out there and find out what the hell happened to Troy. But Toni was right. A quick glance out the window proved that it was going to be one hell of a ride out there. The wind howled and strong gusts of blowing snow swept the area away. She could see the trees practically bending outside. What would those strong gusts of wind do to her?

"Fine," she finally agreed, pulling off her coat. "I'll leave it for now but..."

Just then she was almost blinded by bright lights as the power surged back on. She could hear beeping and clicking of appliances as the power reignited in the house. When she turned to look outside through the grand window in the foyer, she could see in the distance city lights were back on, too.

"Well, look at that," Toni commented. "I guess we're not having one of those three-day blackouts again. Thank goodness it was only for a few hours."

"Well, that's good," Cilla chimed in. She immediately reached for her cell phone. "We should be able to call Troy."

"Good thinking," Toni agreed.

Cilla heard ringing when calling Troy's cell phone. At least it was ringing on the other end. She also put her coat back on with the phone still pressed to her ear.

"Why are you putting your coat back on?" Toni queried.

"I'm going to make sure Troy's okay. The street lights will be working so I should be fine on the road."

"But in this storm?"

"It's dying down, Toni."

The old man looked out the window then shrugged. "I don't think so, but then again, love is blind." He grinned.

"What?"

There was still no answer on Troy's cell phone. Just then, Zack came out from the kitchen. "Looks like the power's gonna stay on." He had his cell phone pressed to his ear. "My contact at the hydro company says they're working overtime until power is restored to the entire city."

"Entire city?" Toni echoed.

"Yes, sir. It looks as if power was knocked out everywhere not just in the area."

"Good God! And Cilla wants to still go out now, to look for Troy," Toni added.

"Look for Troy?" Zack echoed.

"Yes, I need to know he's okay, Zack. I can't get a hold of him. His phone keeps going to voicemail."

Zack looked at the time on his cell. "Listen, I'll go out and make sure he's fine. I was going to do it anyway."

"I'm coming with you," Cilla announced.

"Oh, no, you're not, Miss Cilla," Zack said firmly.

"Oh, yes, I am. Troy and I are getting married. I need to make sure he's okay."

Zack opened his mouth as if he was about to protest, but Cilla stuck to her guns. He sighed deeply. Sure, he knew that Cilla and Troy were entering into an arrangement since Troy had already told him about it but he couldn't argue with her tenacity right now. "You sure are taking this business arrangement seriously," he chuckled. "Well, who could blame you? Let's go."

She followed Zack through the side entrance to the garage. She couldn't wait to see Troy again tonight.

Chapter Twelve

Zack and Cilla drove down the road. The wind speed seemed to have died down and the snow wasn't blowing as hard as it had been earlier in the evening. It wasn't too long before they spotted Troy's abandoned SUV on the road side with a gigantic birch tree lying dead in front of the vehicle.

"Shit!"

"Oh, my God!" Cilla exclaimed. Zack parked on the side of the road and got out of his Jeep quickly. He moved through the high snow and over to Troy's SUV. He pulled out his flashlight and surveyed the vehicle.

Cilla huddled beside him. "What happened?"

Zack looked down the road and saw that Pamela's car was not far from Troy's SUV. "It looks as if Troy found Pam and they probably took off on foot."

"Where to? And where are the footprints?"

"Nah, you wouldn't find foot prints now, not with all that snow that's been falling all evening."

"That's true," Cilla agreed, rubbing her arms. Even though she had on her winter coat, it did little against the windchill.

"Wait a minute," Zack added. He directed his flashlight further up a pathway through the trees and a grin touched his lips. He saw the silhouette of the cottage in the distance with a few dim lights at the windows.

"What is it?" Cilla asked.

"They're at the guest cottage. I'm sure they're fine, Cilla. Let's go home."

"What? No! I need to make sure Troy is okay."

"And Pamela," Zack added.

"I don't really care too much about Pamela," Cilla snapped and admitted to Zack.

"Hey, you don't have to worry about anything going on between those two," Zack said.

"I'm not worried about that. I just..." Cilla didn't know what to say. She was just eager to get to Troy. She didn't want to risk anything screwing up her fake marriage to him. She needed her inheritance and she would do damn near anything to keep it. Besides, why did Zack just mention nothing was going on between Troy and Pamela? She suspected something just might be going on between them.

* * *

Troy pressed his lips to Pamela's forehead as they lay in each other's arms by the warm crackling fireplace in the living room. They lay on a colorful duvet on the rug and had another silk comforter thrown over them.

Even though the power unexpectedly came back on, they decided to turn off most of the lights in the home and savor the enjoyment of the two of them alone, with little interference. They shared a fine glass of Romero Merlot that had been in the kitchen and celebrated their golden moment. Whatever that golden moment could really be called.

"Hmm, you feel so good," Pamela cooed, her eyes closed enjoying his silky touch, snuggling up to him.

"So do you, baby," he groaned. "You were amazing, you know that? You have no idea how much you mean to me, Pam."

They had made love three times in the space of time they'd been together. The night was perfect. Pamela told him she felt so treasured more than she'd ever felt in her life. Troy shared his feelings with her again about how much she meant to him and always had over the years but he'd been too cowardly to share his feelings then, not feeling he could ever commit to a woman for life.

Then another hard feeling wedged between his feelings for Pamela. What about his fake marriage plan to Cilla? What was going to happen there? What would become of Troy and Pamela? Now that he'd tasted her, and pleasured her and felt her inside, he couldn't get enough of her. He couldn't dream about spending the year apart while he was married to Cilla so that she could claim her billion dollar fortune. Troy ended up explaining the whole thing to Pamela.

Talk about one hell of a dilemma.

Why did life have to be so darn cruel when it came to choices like that? What was he going to do? He looked at Pamela; her eyes looked so relaxed, so dreamy. This was the woman he'd spent the last several years with as a close friend, devoted public relations assistant and confidante—and now lover. No way in hell was he about to lose that last credential. He wanted Pamela more than anything in his life. After last night, he didn't want what they'd had to end.

"You know it's technically Christmas morning, right?" he said.

"I know," she said quietly. "I was just thinking the same thing. Merry Christmas, boss."

"Please don't call me boss, not tonight. You," he said, looking deep into her eyes, "are the most beautiful Christmas present I've ever been honored with."

She smiled warmly, but she noticed his changed expression. "What's wrong?" she asked.

"Oh, it's nothing. Just a thought that crossed my mind."

He glanced over at the clock on the wall. It was three o'clock in the morning. He had just made love to his assistant. What had he done? The mere fact that she called him boss reminded him of his duties. It reminded him of the warning from his grandfather to never sleep with an employee unless he was in a permanent relationship with her.

The word boss stabbed at his heart as he realized he had just overstepped his self-imposed boundaries.

Chapter Thirteen

There was a knock on the door, actually, more like a hard pounding. Pamela jolted up and covered her chest with the blanket. "Oh, no."

Troy got up and wrapped a sheet around his waist. "I'll see who it is."

"Like *that*, Troy?"

He grinned. Then the smile was wiped clearly off his face. What if it was Cilla? Not that she would have that powerful knock. "You're right."

Troy was more swept away with feelings of guilt. What had he just done? He'd slept with Pamela, his employee. Troy wasn't a permanent relationship guy. Who was he kidding? Pamela deserved so much better. Where would that leave them? And what about his deal with Cilla?

The knock continued on the door. Pamela got up and made her way upstairs to find her robe.

Troy pulled on his T-shirt and shorts and made his way to the door. He looked outside and saw Zack's Jeep. "Good ol' Zack, coming to make sure I'm still alive," he told himself.

He pulled the door open and was stunned to see Cilla there, too. "Cilla. Zack," he formally greeted them.

"Hey, bro. Glad to see you made it okay. Well, better than your SUV."

"Yeah, tell me about it. Better for the car to get stuck in the snow than me, right?"

Zack grinned.

Cilla walked past Troy and inside without saying a word and looked around. "Where's Pamela?" she asked, sternly as if she couldn't wait to scold her or rip her to shreds for her serious lack of judgment.

"Nice to see you, too, darling," Troy replied in his most charming voice. Cilla's arms were defensively folded across her chest. Her lips were pinched. He surveyed his fake fiancée and couldn't believe how different she was from Pamela. Pamela was sweet, gentle and caring. And Cilla? Well, self-centered and always hostile.

Troy sighed. He was about to say Pamela was sleeping but Pamela was already coming down the stairs.

* * *

"Hi, Cilla. Hi, Zack," Pamela said as calmly as she could. She tried hard not to look into either's eyes or Troy's for that matter.

This was beyond crazy. What had she done? Slept with her boss? He was getting married soon—even if it was a fake marriage. Guilt gnawed at her stomach. Confusion whirled inside her mind. She didn't know if she was coming or going. All she knew was that her body was still buzzing from the passionate intimacy with Troy. But she could not have him. He wasn't available. And of course, their business relationship could never be the same.

Why did she feel guilty as hell? She shouldn't be, should she? Troy and Cilla were entering into a fake arrangement so she could fool the executors of her parents' estate. She knew Cilla hated her guts and always had since college but this didn't help matters.

"I'm glad to see you are both safe and sound," Cilla said, ice dripping from her tone.

"Troy, let's go back to the house." Cilla turned to Troy.

Was it obvious? Did Pamela look as if she'd had the wildest lovemaking with Troy a few hours prior during the blackout? She'd tried to smooth her hair back to a civilized state but she was sure she looked as if she'd just made love. Her skin was flushed, for one thing.

"Yes, we should probably head back to the house," Troy agreed. "The roads are clearer, right?" Troy asked Zack.

"Well, it's still pretty rough but not as bad as when you guys left. The winds aren't blowing crazy snow around for one thing."

"Good."

"I see you two have been busy," Cilla commented, eyeing Pamela up and down.

"We both ended up in the snow bank," Troy came to Pamela's defense, his voice stern. "We had to change off clothes or we'd catch the death of a cold."

"Of course," Cilla said, not convinced. "Well, I'll be in the car." She turned to head out.

"We'll have to get CAA out to get to your SUV, bro," Zack said. "It'll all be good."

"Yeah," Troy responded, overtly distracted. Not good. Not good at all. He looked the same way how Pamela felt inside. *Oh, no.* What trouble had their lovemaking stirred up?

Chapter Fourteen

Hours later, Cilla and Pamela were in the study at Romero Manor.

"Oh, I wouldn't get too comfortable, if I were you," Cilla warned. She was facing Pamela by the grand fireplace. The snow continued to fall hard outside blowing against the windowpane of the French doors. The early morning sun reflected on the blanket of whiteness outside, illuminating the entire room of the study.

"What do you mean by that, Cilla?" Pamela asked, trying to stay cool. Her tummy was knotting up in a bundle of nerves. Did Cilla know about her one passionate night with Troy at the cottage? Was she aware of Pamela's feelings for Troy? They never should have slept together. It was a mistake. Even though Cilla and Troy were entering into a fake marriage and were not in a relationship, Pamela still felt riddled with regret. She loved Troy and she believed he felt the same but they were employer and employee, superior and subordinate.

"Come on now," Cilla said, moving towards the bookshelf by the fireplace. She removed a tome from the shelf. Pamela glanced at the book in her hand. The title was Deception Point by Dan Brown. Did Cilla pull out that one by chance or was she trying to tell Pamela something? Well, there was no deception going on where Pamela was concerned.

Cilla was the one who was trying to deceive the executors of her parents' estate by marrying Troy. Not that two wrongs make a right. Pamela felt terrible inside, guilt and remorse tore through her. This could mess things up for Cilla's inheritance.

"We're both smart women, Pamela. We're adults. Even a blind person can see how much you're in love with Troy." Cilla flipped the pages of the book to the middle. She held it up so that Pamela could see its title clearly.

"I...I don't know what you're talking about, Cilla."

Cilla glared at Pam, annoyance aflame on her face. "Oh, really?" she said tossing the book on the chair by the fireplace. She folded her arms across her chest and held her chin up. "Well, let me spell it out for you then. Troy is off limits, okay?"

Pamela swallowed hard but the darn lump seemed wedged in her throat. "I...I'm aware of your situation, Cilla. It's okay. I know that you need to be married for the year," she said bravely. "If you're worried about me and Troy-"

Cilla laughed out loud. And it wasn't the jolly, heartfelt kind of laugh either. "Yeah, whatever. Girl, I've got news for you. Troy ain't interested in you. Never will be."

"Excuse me?"

"You heard me." Cilla walked confidently to the glass doors, looking at the snow covered terrace outside. She then spun around to face Pamela. "I've got news for you, Pammy. Whatever might have happened last night in the cabin was nothing more than a one-night stand."

"What makes you think...?"

"Oh, come on now. I can read it on your face. But let me tell you this," she said, jabbing her finger at Pamela. "Troy and I will not only be married for the year, but a whole lot can happen in 365 nights. I doubt very much he'll even want to be with you after a year with me. And don't you even try to interfere with our arrangement. So help me God, I'll destroy-"

"You'll destroy what?" Troy said as he strolled into the study.

"Oh, Troy!" Cilla changed her expression and ran into Troy's arms. She planted a sweet kiss on his lips. "Oh, Troy. I'm so glad to see you. Pam and I were just discussing how perfect our wedding day has to be. And you know Toni will be so happy to see another wedding in the family. You know how much that means to him. Just like the day when my mother and I spotted you at the mall and told him about how much you resemble him and he found out about you and your brothers. Oh, Troy," she said, hugging him. "Thank you so much for doing this for me. And for Toni."

With a puzzled expression on his handsome face, Troy gently pulled away from Cilla and looked at Pamela. A moment later, his eyes trailed back to Cilla then Pamela again. Curiosity appeared to get the best of him. "What exactly were you ladies talking about?" he asked in an authoritative tone. He didn't seem to fall for Cilla's nice girl talk all of sudden. And what a speech that was. Pamela had learned in communication class that sometimes people babbled nonstop for a variety of reasons including insecurity or trying to cover up something by distraction. Either way, Troy was smart enough not to just take Cilla at face value.

"Um...nothing, Troy. I...I've got some errands to run for your grandfather," Pamela replied with a brave smile, trying to hide the hurt in her eyes. She walked out of the study before Troy could stop her. It was Christmas Day yet it didn't feel one bit festive. Still, the Romero family was going to gather later in the day for their traditional dinner, but this year Pam thought it best to skip out. She was going to get a ride to go home and celebrate the holiday...alone.

* * *

The following week, Jenna met with Pamela for lunch in town. Jenna wanted to get out and do other things while she happily waited for her baby to be born.

"Why didn't you tell Troy what really happened between you two, Pamela?" Jenna asked, rubbing her enormous belly. The waitress at the Murray Café had just placed their orders in front of them. The Murray Café was owned by Amber Johnson-Murray-Romero, Jenna's sister-in-law, who married Jules Romero in a wild ceremony at the hospital birthing center a couple years earlier. Amber had given up on finding true love and was about to become a single parent until she'd met up with Jules Romero one day outside of a workshop for expectant mothers. Thinking about that story made Pamela's heart warm but also fuel longing in her soul. She wished she could be so happy or lucky in love or lucky with love. But she knew now that was not about to happen.

"It doesn't matter, Jenna," Pamela said, stirring her mug of caramel cappuccino. She sighed heavily. "I don't want to interfere with what they have going. Troy is a man of honor. Cilla helped him find his grandfather, and well, she needs him to return the favor to...well, you know...I'm not going to say it in public."

"I hear you." Jenna sounded as defeated as Pamela felt.

A benefit of the Romero family was that they knew how to keep the others' secrets. And Pamela was so appreciative that they'd accepted her in their inner circle as family, even though she wasn't blood or even married to a Romero, like Jenna. Jenna was already aware of the deal with Troy and Cilla. The Romeros were all aware by now. He didn't want to deceive his family into thinking he was really in love with Cilla. But still, they also had to keep up a solid pretense to help Cilla with the executors of her family's estate since she had to "prove" to them that she was in a stable relationship to keep her inheritance. That would mean Pamela would have no more hot, passionate nights with Troy Romero.

Pamela blew out a puff of air and slouched in the chair at the café. "It's no use, Jenna. I can't turn off my feelings for Troy and he's going to be married for a year. And the truth is, marriage is marriage. Anything can happen during that time. They just might fall in love. I mean, he's known her many years since his youth. Who am I to wait around like a woman with no self-respect?"

"But, it's a...you know...not a conventional marriage, Pamela," Jenna whispered across the table. Pamela knew Jenna wanted to say it was a business arrangement but couldn't do so in public, just in case they were overheard.

"I know. But I think the universe is trying to tell me that Troy and I will never be. I think it's time I move on to another job. You know, a fresh start all around."

Jenna almost spewed her orange juice on the table.

"Are you okay, Jenna?"

"Yeah, I'm okay." She mopped at her mouth with the napkin from the table. "Are *you* all right?"

"Of course," Pamela murmured.

"Oh, good. Because it sounded like you said you were going to move on to another job, girlfriend. I'm like, I don't think so."

"But why not? I've worked for the Romeros for many years and…well, I've gained a lot of experience. I've always wanted to move to the Big Apple and check out some PR agencies there. You know, branch out a bit. Explore other industries." Pamela played with the handle of the oversized coffee mug. Running her finger up and down the ceramic texture. Her eyelids felt heavy, not so much from fatigue but a profound sadness she could not describe.

She remembered the feel of Troy on her body, inside her, moving inside her, pleasuring her, caressing her and making her feel as if she were the most beautiful, precious woman in his life—in the world. She missed that magical feeling. How on earth could she have gotten it wrong? But then again, she knew he had strong feelings for her, too, but he just wasn't the settling down type. And she would have to be okay with that, wouldn't she? Cilla had him, even if it were a fake marriage that they would be entering into. Cilla was in. Pamela was out. It was no use trying to believe otherwise. She would just have to lick her wounds and move along.

As painful as it was, Pamela tried to make light of the situation so Jenna didn't end up feeling terribly sorry for her. "It's like every time I think things are going great, they just…keep on going…"

Jenna chuckled. "Oh, Pamela. How could you make light of this? Really, I think you should-"

"Should what, Jenna?" Pamela said softly. "I really appreciate you being a great friend, but there's no way out of this. It's a done deal. Even Toni Romero is happy Troy is helping Cilla in this matter and that Cilla had brought him and his brothers to him. It would break his heart to see Troy let her down. Toni even said he thinks they could truly fall in love."

"But the girl is a witch!" Jenna blurted out to Pamela's surprise. She guessed she wasn't the only who noticed Cilla's personality. "The girl is seriously demented. How could they not see that? She's always making snarky comments and looking down on other people. I'm really sorry she's going to be in the family and not you, Pamela. Life seems so unfair sometimes."

"It's okay," Pamela murmured.

"No. It's not okay. I believe that goodness does follow good people. Maybe not right away but I hope the universe works things around the way they should be. And I'm just not feeling that girl. Something seems off about her." Jenna shook her head and pinched her lips. Her expression was almost humorous but Pamela resisted the urge to chuckle.

"Anyway, I'm going to be leaving tomorrow."

"Tomorrow? So soon?"

"Well, I didn't mention this but I have an interview with a prestigious school for ballet dancers."

"Oh, that sounds dreamy. You love the ballet!"

"I know. I was all too glad to find out they needed a PR person. As a bonus, I get access to free tickets to the ballet and everything. It's a dream. Plus, I'll be right near Broadway. They have a nice high-rise condo on Park Avenue as part of the contract." Maybe this would help her get over Troy quicker. She could lose herself in a performance of Romeo and Juliet. Or maybe not! The words "Romero" and Juliet just entered her mind instead of Romeo and Juliet. She shook her head. She had to get Troy out of her system. For good. It was for the best.

* * *

"What?" Troy asked his grandfather, stunned at the news.

"You heard me correctly. Pamela is leaving us," Toni Romero repeated. His tone was brusque, his expression stony. The old man hobbled to the fireplace with his cane before placing it by the bookshelf and seating himself. Troy could always tell when his grandfather was royally peeved with him. And he could honestly say that he deserved it this time.

Troy combed his fingers through his hair and paced in the study.

"I warned you, Troy. Do not sleep with Pamela. Not unless you intend to marry her. It gets too complicated when things don't work out," Toni continued. "Now look at what you've done. She's leaving us for good. She's been a part of our family for many years. Where can we ever find such a loyal and caring executive like her again?"

Troy didn't say anything. He reached into his pocket and took out his cell phone and auto-dialled her number. It kept ringing. Usually she would pick up immediately whenever he called, especially at this time of the day. No answer. Troy's heart sank so low it hurt. Why did he do it? That night at the cottage had meant so much to him but he knew he wouldn't be able to continue a relationship with her. Besides, he didn't believe in real marriage. He could never commit to a long-term relationship with any woman.

"I messed up, Granddad. I'm sorry. Trust me, I never meant for this to happen."

"Yes, you're sorry all right. Sorry it didn't work out that you could have your cake and eat it too." His grandfather's voice was stern. He wasn't letting up on how badly Troy messed up but Troy couldn't blame him.

"Do you think I wanted to hurt Pamela?" Troy challenged defiantly. "I care about her."

"Yes, I'm sure you care about her, Troy. Just not enough to set boundaries. You messed up a good working relationship. Not to mention Cilla's fortune," Toni continued, his eyes gazing into the fireplace. "She's worth billions and you could ruin that for her, too, if her estate finds out she's in a fabricated relationship. Why can't you boys control your libidos?" Toni was never the one to mince his words. "You only sleep with a woman you intend to marry. Period."

Like Troy could feel any lower than he already did. "I know how you feel about relationships, Granddad. But what Pamela and I had that night was mutual. I know I was wrong to sleep with her but it was something we both felt at the time."

"And just what do you plan to do now?"

"Go ahead with the plan to marry Cilla. The deal's been made. I can't renege. I'll have to try to make it up to Pamela. I have to find her."

"Don't bother, Troy. Just go ahead with the arrangement to marry Cilla. Pamela is long gone. The damage has been done." Toni's eyes watered. This hurt him as much as it hurt Troy. If only Troy could turn back time. If only he hadn't promised Cilla he'd marry her by her birthday, which was very soon, so she could keep her inheritance. The woman who'd helped bring him to his own fortune and introduced him to his grandfather.

"She's gone," Toni said again, his voice a mere whisper.

Chapter Fifteen

The following week, Troy and Cilla were in Vegas.

"What did you say to Pamela that night?" Troy quizzed Cilla, loosening his blue silk tie. They were at a five-star luxury hotel on the Vegas strip. Tomorrow they would tie the knot.

"What are you talking about?" she said, acting innocent. Cilla was a cool girl, but Troy was also aware she could be sly at times. Pamela was a shy, sweet kitten compared to the tigress before him. Yeah, Cilla was well behaved around him but he judged people not so much by how they treated him but how they treated those who they felt were not important to them.

"You heard me, Cilla."

"What? Did she say something?" Cilla said, snarling the word "she."

"*She* has a name."

Cilla huffed and locked her arms across her chest. "Did Pamela tell you anything?"

"No. Are you going to tell me what went on between you two? Pamela is good people, Cilla. She's been there for my family over the years."

"And I *haven't*?"

"You know what I mean. I'll always be in debt to you for what you and your mother have done but this is beyond ridiculous. After that night, Pamela hasn't returned my calls. What did you say to her?"

"It's nothing. Don't worry. We just had a little *girl* chat." Cilla reached her hands over his shoulders and seductively ran her fingers up and down his arms.

Troy didn't feel anything for Cilla. When Pamela touched him with clothes on or without, his blood warmed. Parts of his body awakened to attention. But with Cilla? Nothing. He couldn't quite believe he had to do this fake marriage thing and miss out on being with Pamela. What would happen if she met someone else over the next year?

God, that would kill him inside if another man touched Pam. It pained him to even think about it. He felt like only he could give Pamela what she truly deserved. Yet, he was throwing it all away by marrying Cilla in a business deal—the woman who helped him to be what he was today.

Troy looked into Cilla's eyes. "Are you telling me the truth?" Troy could tell when someone was trying to pull a fast one on him by looking deeply into his or her eyes when he asked a question.

Cilla pulled away, defensively hugging herself. "Yes," she said, not daring to look into his eyes.

* * *

"Yes, boss?" JoJo said to Troy. They were in the bar at the hotel near the casino. The noise, music and loud chatter from patrons almost drowned out their conversation.

"I need you to look into something for me."

"Sure. Who's the girl?"

Troy grinned. "Now what makes you think it's a girl?"

"Isn't it always, boss?"

"Well, you got me there. Nine times out of ten, yeah, it is about a girl, isn't it? I'm getting married tomorrow night at the Little White Wedding Chapel on the Vegas Strip but I need some info first."

"Sure. Just tell me what you need to know. Or what it is you're looking for."

"That's just it. I don't really know what I'm looking for. I just have a sinking feeling about something. About what Cilla might have said to Pamela during that storm."

"Do you think that's why she left us?" JoJo probed.

"Yeah." Troy almost choked on emotion. "I wish I knew where she was. She hasn't been at her apartment for days according to her concierge."

"You didn't hear, boss?"

"Hear what?"

"She's landed some job in the Big Apple. She's gonna do PR for some ballet school."

Troy's blood ran cold. Pamela really did quit on him, didn't she? "Why didn't I hear about her new job? She works for me. She didn't even give me official notice."

"In all fairness, boss, she works for—or *worked* for your grandpa. Pamela told him not to mention anything to you since you're busy with the wedding and everything. She didn't want to interfere in your plans with Cilla."

Troy felt as if someone drove a barbed knife into his heart. His mind was thrown into a disturbing whirlwind of emotions. "What?" he echoed in disbelief. He felt as if he couldn't breathe. Pamela was leaving. Or left, really. She was truly going to be out of his life. For good.

He got up from the chair and took out a few bills from his wallet and placed them on the counter. He had to marry Cilla tomorrow. He couldn't back down now. He had to be loyal to those who gave everything for him. But then what about Pamela, the woman who really owned his heart?

"What are you going to do, boss?"

"Just try to get to the heart of what went down with Pam and Cilla and…I…I'll try to reach Pam."

And do what? Tell her to come back to Canada and wait for him while he got married to a phony bride? Troy combed his fingers through his hair, loosened his silk tie around his neck, which was beginning to feel more like a noose of guilt. He then sat back down, defeated. No matter which way he looked at it, Pamela was gone! Out of his life.

Chapter Sixteen

Hours later, Troy was alone in his Vegas hotel suite.

In an hour, Troy would be married to Cilla. He had to get used to it. He glanced at the clock in the room. Seven o'clock. The small ceremony complete with two witnesses would start shortly. Cilla would turn twenty-seven the next day so she had to be married today. Then they would have the grand ceremony next week. But Troy felt his heart weaken. His heart was with Pamela. Sweet, loving Pamela. What was he doing? Throwing it all away? But then he reminded himself. He had no choice. He would be a heel to let Cilla down and cost her to lose her fortune after she'd helped him gain his. It would just be bad universal karma.

With a heavy heart and profound sadness, he affixed the cuff links on his sleeves. Just then a knock sounded at the door.

"Who is it?"

"JoJo."

Troy went to the door and opened it. "The ceremony starts soon."

"No, it doesn't, boss."

"What? What are you talking about? Where's Cilla?"

"Oh, she's waiting for you in her gown. She's waiting for you to marry her."

"So why is the wedding off?"

JoJo came inside and closed the door behind him. Troy had seen JoJo upset before but he wasn't a man you would want to upset. The expression on JoJo's face as he handed Troy some documents was dangerous.

"What the hell's going on?" Troy fumed as he glanced over the documents.

"Sorry to be the one to tell you this, boss, but Cilla's been playing you."

"Playing me?" He looked up at JoJo.

"Yes, boss."

"What's that supposed to mean? And why would she do that?"

"This whole wedding gig was nothing but a plan."

"Okay, JoJo, first and foremost, I'm already aware of Cilla's situation with her parents' will. She needs to be married or she could lose her inheritance."

"She already has."

"What?" Troy's eyes narrowed. "What the heck are you talking about? Do you realize the de Montagios are richer and more powerful than the Romeros? They've been around forever."

"They *were* rich and powerful, Troy. But your family owns that title now."

"What? JoJo, you're not making any sense, man. Spill it out." Troy could feel his blood pumping erratically in his veins. He wasn't so much angry with JoJo as he was with himself and with Cilla. He had a sick feeling about where this conversation was headed but didn't want confirmation of it. The truth hurt like hell, didn't it? He hated to think he had been deceived by someone who was supposed to be a close and trusted family friend. But...

"The money's gone, boss. She told you she needed to marry you to fulfill some will requirement to keep her inheritance. But the truth is, the de Montagios lost a lot of their fortune in bad investments a long time ago, long before their deaths in Denver. What they once owned in historical buildings belong to the municipal government. Liquid assets? Nada. And what Cilla, or should I say, Lady Priscilla had, she squandered it away, spent money she didn't have while racking up a lot of gambling debts in the process. She owes $800,000 in credit card and casino debt. There's a lien on her residence. She's overdrawn at the bank and owes $4 million in unpaid taxes. She's got nothing. *You* were her last hope."

"What?" Troy felt sick. He could not believe his ears. He paced frantically, disbelief washed over him. "What!?" He stopped pacing and froze on the spot, trying to soak all of this in. "Why would she go through the trouble of pretending to marry me to keep an inheritance that doesn't exist? It makes no sense."

"She needed a rich dude, like you, to sustain her lifestyle—keep her from being homeless. Her plan was to marry you then trap you with a pregnancy either by you or her...boyfriend."

"Boyfriend?"

"Yes, sir. She's still seeing that biker dude—on the side, of course. You told me to investigate her conversation with Pam but I took it a bit further, boss. I knew you were too trusting of her to even investigate her background for yourself to make sure she's legit with you, being she's been a family friend for so long and she was supposed to be as wealthy as you... well, that's when I found out about her financial background. She just filed for bankruptcy, by the way."

"What!? Well, if this isn't the craziest—"

A gold-digging heiress? Imagine that! He'd thought he'd heard it all but this one...*this* one took the gold medal.

"That's not all, boss. She was hoping that *you* would be her fortune. I'm sorry, boss, and I know you're grateful to her mom for locating you when you were a kid, but she is not like her mother. That apple fell far from the tree, if you know what I mean."

"Yeah," Troy murmured, running his fingers through his hair. "So that's why she's had it out for Pamela. And poor Pam didn't even want to get involved with me because she felt Cilla and I were getting married for real. She said she didn't want to be the other woman. I guess you can't put a price tag on having class. Money, apparently, doesn't give all women class."

Troy saw red. His mind flickered back to Erika. His conniving first real girlfriend back in college. The one who'd deceived the hell out of him, played him for a fool. Well, Troy was nobody's fool. That was why when a man saw a good woman, like Pamela, he should hold on to her for dear life because they were clearly precious jewels. Few and far between.

"I hear you, boss," JoJo agreed. "Now, what do you want me to do about Ms. de Montagio?"

"We've got to be careful how we handle this. Gramps is getting old. His heart's not so good these days. He really worshipped at Mrs. de Montagio's feet since the day she led him to my brothers and me. I wouldn't want him to know de Montagio's daughter was a fraud who would pull a fast one like this on the family. First she squandered what was left of her family's fortune then she tries to scam me into getting inside mine. No worries, JoJo. I'll deal with her."

"You sure, boss?"

"I've never been more sure," he said in a dangerously low voice. "In the meantime, I've got to get to Pam before it's too late. She means the world to me. I don't want to lose a good woman."

* * *

Troy handed Cilla the documents as she stood in her hotel suite in a long, flowing Vera Wang designed wedding dress.

The expression on her face said it all. She looked terrified. Her eyes widened in shock as she clutched the notes with a death grip and looked over the pages in front of her. She looked as if she was afraid to glance into Troy's eyes. As if someone had pulled the sheep's clothing off her lying back.

Deception.

She was busted. And she knew it, Troy thought to himself. How was she going to wiggle out of this one?

The evidence was overwhelmingly in front of her. "Well," he finally said. "Don't you have something to tell me?"

"I...I...Troy," she stuttered. "You...where did you get these from?" Just then her expression changed from shock and fear to anger. "Don't tell me. That bitch Pamela. I bet her contacts did some digging on me."

He could not believe his ears. She actually had the audacity to blame poor, innocent Pamela. "No!" he answered. "You couldn't be more wrong, Cilla. Pamela had nothing to do with this. You pretty much don't need any help to expose yourself. You did it all on your own. You get all the credit."

"What?"

"I don't get you. What do you have against Pamela? The fact is, she wouldn't even dream of digging up anything on you. But I can't say the same about you if the tables were turned. She's good people."

"And I'm not?"

"I don't know. You're full of so much hatred and bitterness, Cilla. That's what tripped you up. I wanted to find out why you were hating on Pamela so much and what happened why she decided to run away and it all came back to your scheming lies. If you were a different person, maybe things wouldn't have turned out the way they did. But I'm glad they did."

"If it's money you wanted all you had to do was ask!" Troy tried to soften his tone. "I would have given you what you wanted. In fact, I can still help you. First, I'll pay off that lien you have on your house." That was the least he could do, he thought to himself. The last thing he would want was to see Cilla homeless. She might not have the best personality in the world, but he wasn't a spiteful man. After all, he never forgot when someone did a good deed for him, even if it was just the one. He probably wouldn't be where he was today if it wasn't for her and her mother. His mother once told him that if somebody did you ninety-nine bad things and one good thing, never forget the good thing.

"Then, I'll give you a million to get you back on your feet and help you get a good job. But no more gambling!" he continued. "I have contacts. That's not an issue. But to lie to get me to marry you under false pretenses to keep a fortune you don't even have...?"

"That's not true...okay, so what if it's true? That's how the world works, Troy."

"No. It isn't. Not everybody's like that. And if they are, they get what's coming to them eventually. The universe gives you what you give out. Doesn't matter how long. Time is just a false sense of security that you're getting away with hurting others."

"Oh, really? Is that what your grandfather told you, Mr. philosophical-know-it-all? If it weren't for me, you'd be still sleeping in your loser of a dad's van."

Troy seethed inside. A muscle twitched in his jaw. "Don't you talk about my old man like that. He was a good person. Which is more than I can say about you."

"Oh, really?"

"You need help, Cilla. Get help. And I don't want you near my family. In fact, if my grandfather asks, you let him know you've changed your mind."

"And if I don't?"

"I guess the whole world will know about your little money problem. Who's to stop JoJo from sending a copy of this report to the most popular gossip websites? You know, the sites you often visit every day on your computer to indulge yourself in other people's misfortunes. The comments there could be pretty brutal. I know you care what the haters think of you. That would really make their day, wouldn't it?"

"You wouldn't!"

"You hurt my family or anyone close to me and I'll make you live to regret it. Understood?" His tone was dangerously low and void of emotion.

Cilla kept her arms folded tightly across her chest with her chin up and a smirk on her face. "Understood. And I'll take the million in cash!"

Troy gave her one last look before turning towards the door. He was about to say something but decided to let it go. He had more important things to settle.

Pamela.

Chapter Seventeen

Pamela drew in a deep breath and tried to knock the feeling of impending doom out of her mind. But it was hard. It was hard as hell. She sat at her desk going through some notes in the office at the school. It was her first day at the Crenye & Crenye Ballet Institute. The sound of classical music flowing from the corridor soothed her soul. But a sad longing settled in not long after. The institute was practically empty since it was still officially winter break. Classes didn't resume until the following week. But some students were in practicing for the recital. The music that played was, ironically, from Tchaikovsky's *Romeo and Juliet*.

How tragic. Pamela's real life Romeo, or Romero, married someone else while this Juliet died inside. Pamela felt as if she were an empty shell of the person she used to be.

Cilla had made it clear after the year was done she was going to fight to keep Troy—and who could blame her?

Pamela's heart plunged in her chest. Her blood felt icy cold—so cold, she shivered at the thought of never having Troy in her life again. She could not even think about it. Even if it was a fake marriage. They were still legally bound.

It was over.

A done deal.

Pamela had spent Saturday night in her apartment, under the blankets. She hadn't gotten up out of bed except to use the bathroom. She had a bottle of water at her bedside that day. Her appetite was shot to hell. There was nothing anyone could have done to cheer her up. That was why she had her phone turned off all weekend. Until this morning. She slept away the weekend as the world carried on with its business and the one man she ever loved married someone else.

A knock sounded at the door.

"Come in," Pamela called softly.

"Hi, Pamela," an older woman with bright red hair and a jolly smile said to her as she walked in. "I'm Mrs. Adrenov from the academic department. We're so thrilled to have you here with us."

"Thank you. I'm happy to be here. I've always loved the ballet. They're playing Romeo and Juliet, I hear."

"Yes, it has become one of the most beloved ballets of all time."

"I can imagine."

"Would you like to see a rehearsal? A sneak peek?"

"Sure," Pamela said. She really didn't feel in the mood to watch Romeo and Juliet, but it was her all-time favorite so perhaps that would cheer her up. Maybe it would awaken her soul again so she could appreciate other things in life, like the gift of music and appreciation of the arts and a good love story, albeit a tragic one. Much like her own love life.

When she entered the gymnasium, she saw a few students on the stage rehearsing. It was delightful. The soft sounds of the string quartet played over the speakers and her heart began to sink again. What was that feeling? Melancholy?

"Beautiful, isn't it?" Mrs. Adrenov commented while watching from the back of the empty auditorium with Pamela.

"Yes, it is." Pamela's heart was still in Canada with Troy but she had to get over it. She had to learn to get over herself. She was in New York. Her new home.

Just then, something very odd happened. "I don't remember this part," Pamela commented as a few other dancers came on to the stage holding a whiteboard with a jumble of magnetic words on it. "This is weird."

Mrs. Adrenov looked at Pamela and grinned.

Pamela thought that was odd, too, but when she glanced at what the dancers were holding in their hands, she almost fainted. Each dancer lined up on the stage with a word in their hands from the whiteboard they were holding. Pamela walked closer to see the message on the boards. Her heart thumped hard and fast in her chest.

PAMELA

WILL

YOU

MARRY

ME?

LOVE

TROY

Pamela covered her open mouth with both hands, her eyes widened in shock and disbelief. "W-what? Is this a j-joke?"

Just then, a tall, dark and deadly handsome man sauntered on to the stage dressed in a sharp, tailored business suit.

Troy!

Pamela froze on the spot. The lights dimmed in the auditorium with two spotlights illuminated. One spotlight shone on each of them. It was like out of a romance movie. This was totally beyond belief.

"T-Troy?"

She was dreaming. She had to be dreaming.

He grinned. His eyes caught her from across the room as the ballet dancers quietly bowed and left the stage. Mrs. Adrenov also walked to the side and out the side entrance door of the auditorium.

"Troy," she said, breathless as he neared her. He had probably a dozen long-stemmed red roses in his hand.

"To the most beautiful woman in the world!" He handed her the roses, and she went all crazy inside her body, her pulse racing.

She slowly took the flowers, the scent beautiful but not nearly as sexy as his delicious cologne. "I don't get it," she said, literally out of breath. "Where's Cilla? I thought you two were…"

He shook his head. "No," he whispered. "It's not gonna happen. I'll explain later, but, Pamela, from the day I met you in college, I've always wanted you. I just didn't know it then or I would have married you on the spot."

Pamela felt her heart turn over in her chest.

"I never thought I'd settle down for real until that night we were stranded together in the storm," he continued. "It was then I realized I couldn't bear to not be with you. Oh, Pam, you mean the world to me."

"I've always wanted you, too, Troy," she murmured. "You have no idea."

"I do know," he said softly. "A woman as beautiful, kind and caring and passionate as you deserves the best in life. I only hope I can make you as happy every day of your life as you deserve to be, as you do for others. You are always giving of yourself not expecting anything in return. Always putting out your best and…" his voice almost broke off and that stirred a reaction inside her. Pamela had never seen Troy so emotional before. "I…just can't believe I almost let you get away. Will you forgive me?"

"Forgive you? For what? Trying to help a friend in need?"

He grinned. "Oh, Pamela. You're something else, you know that?" he whispered, and a dimple appeared on his handsome face. God, he was stunning in every way. Every day.

Just then, Troy got down on bended knee. "Pamela Marie Alvarado, will you marry me?"

Pamela was overcome with emotion, joyful tears trickled from her eyes. Her heart fluttered in her chest so hard, she could hardly contain herself. She just kept nodding as if she could not speak.

He looked into her eyes and smiled. "I'm not fluent in mime, but I hope that's a yes."

Pamela melted into relief and laughter. "Yes. Yes. Yes," she finally blurted out. Before she knew it, he was back up on his feet and gently pulled her to him and pressed his sweet lips to hers, pleasuring her with his soft touch and his magical kiss. She felt as if she were on top of the world.

He then reached into his pocket and pulled out a silver velvet jewelry box and opened it. A glowing diamond ring sparkled. Pam gazed in amazement as he took the ring out and showed her the engraving before placing it on her ring finger: To P. My #1 Girl.

Her heart squeezed. It was just as she'd given him the cufflinks for Christmas engraved: To T. My #1 Boss.

To her surprise, applause erupted from the side of the auditorium. "What?"

"I'm so sorry," Mrs. Adrenov said. "I know I should have left but I...I needed to know everything was going to work out all right."

Pamela and Troy turned to her and laughed as they hugged each other. Just then the speakers from the side of the stage played an instrumental song. She recognized the tune. Oh, my. Did Troy think of everything? It was the song *Your Love* by Michelle Wright and Jim Brickman. Talk about a romantic ballad. One of the most beautiful love songs she'd listened to. And the words echoed her exact sentiments. Right now in her life, she couldn't ask for more. Troy's love was...the greatest gift of all.

Pamela was certain for the first time in a long time that everything was going to work out just fine.

Epilogue

Six weeks later...

"Ooh, let me see the ring," Jenna said, looking at Pamela's engagement ring. It was a beautiful eleven-carat natural pink pear-cut diamond ring. Stunning. Breathtaking. Worth half a fortune. "It's gorgeous."

"Not a fraction as gorgeous as Pam, of course." Troy grinned, holding Pamela's shoulder. He gave her a heartfelt squeeze and her body reacted. Earlier Troy had told her that unlike the jewel, Pamela was a priceless treasure he was lucky to have in his life.

"Thank you," she murmured as they sat in the grand study, after dinner.

"Well, this is cause for a major celebration," Toni Romero commented as the entire clan gathered in the study after one of his famous dinners. He held in his hand his six-week old granddaughter Cherry-Rose, Dion and Jenna-Lynn's little bundle of joy. All week, Toni had been showing off the baby to friends who visited. "Two new additions to the family. Cherry Rose, my blessed great-granddaughter, and now a new granddaughter-in-law, Pamela."

Everyone raised a glass to Troy and Pamela. She didn't like to be put on the spot. She was always in the study weaving press reports and PR releases for the Romeros. Now, she was going to be the subject of said news features. But a blessed one. As Troy's wife. Her heart squeezed with emotion and pure unadulterated joy.

* * *

Dr. Alonso Romero finished his dictation in his office and logged off his computer. The thought of having to take three weeks off work for a so-called much needed vacation according to his chief of staff irked him. But truth be told, he was a workaholic and burnout wouldn't do him any good. He hadn't taken a real break from work for the longest time. But he would have to get away and leave his clinics and his patients in the care of his associates. He could only do so much. He just wanted to make sure his patients would be well taken care of.

"Don't you have any hobbies?" his associate once asked him.

"Yeah, medicine, taking care of people."

"No, really, man. You need a life. Or a wife!"

"I don't think so," Alonso had shot back. And he meant it. He was married to his passion—helping to build affordable healthcare for everyone. His own mother lost her battle to cancer when he and his brothers were young and too poor to be able to afford her medications. That tragic loss fueled his desire to save lives and help those who couldn't afford excellent medical care. But he was also a businessman, like all the Romeros. And buying rundown clinics and transforming them was his dream. He even attended auctions almost every month just so he could see what rough gem he could acquire and fix up.

Alonso yawned and stretched. He'd had what felt like the longest shift of his medical career. He had just spent the day fighting in court for one of his patients, Bria, to get the unconventional medical treatment she needed. His mind drifted back to the conversation he'd had with his grandfather and brothers. Good on them for getting hitched. His medical career was his mistress. He was never getting married.

How could a woman possibly understand him not being home nights and being on call practically twenty-four hours a day? Yeah, money wasn't everything. Sure, he had enough wealth to own his own island and an empire but there was more to life than material gain. Like doing good. That's how he got his kicks and no woman was going to take that joy away from him.

He heard shuffling in the reception area after he powered off his lights and walked out of his office, closing the door behind him.

He saw a dainty woman who had the curves of a well-endowed movie star in the reception area though she was dressed much more humbly, wearing a lavender cardigan that hugged her body and a simple pencil skirt that covered her knees. She gazed at him with an unreadable expression, her lips parted as if she wanted to say something but didn't know how to say it. Her soft brown eyes were mesmerizing against her high cheekbones and tanned skin. Her dark hair cascaded down her back. He had the sudden urge to run his fingers through it. He was captivated by her.

"Can I help you?" he asked, caught off guard by her stunning beauty.

"Yes, I think you can." The woman's voice was smooth like velvet, and oh, God, sexy as hell. His groin reacted. That never happened. Not so instantly with a stranger.

Who was this woman?

"Do you know who I am?" she asked pointedly.

Oh, heck. Was this one of the women he'd dated in the past? Please tell him she was not carrying his unborn child—or had a surprise kid at home who shared his DNA. Alonso never took chances and always used a condom. But he also knew that condoms could fail, if not carefully used.

"No," he said, eyeing her carefully. He never forgot a face. And this one he just plain didn't remember. "Should I?"

She stared at him as if he'd done something to her. The woman looked crestfallen and hugged herself. Tears tainting her tired-looking goddess eyes.

"What is it?" he asked. "Are you okay, miss?"

She shook her head. "I was hoping you would know."

"Know what?"

"My real identity. I don't know…who I am. I was a patient at one of your plastic surgery clinics—I had some minor work done after an accident. I thought you'd have the key to my past, but I guess I was wrong."

* * *

THE BILLIONAIRE'S MARRIAGE PROPOSAL

(The Romero Brothers, Book 8)

Sexy, tall, dark and handsome Dr. Alonso Romero was scarred in childhood from losing those close to him, including his first girlfriend, to whom he'd proposed marriage. When she died, he took that as a sign he should never marry. Losing a loved one hurt too much. His remedy? Never get close to another woman—and never wed. To his tycoon grandfather, Toni Romero, Alonso is the only disappointment in the family who has not tied the knot and settled down like his other once-professed bachelor brothers. But that's just fine with Alonso, until...

Beautiful and feisty street nurse, Britney Andropolous, walks into Alonso's office late one night and straight into his heart. She's on the run from a dangerous past. He wants to help her but the trouble is, he's falling for her. Will he keep his distance and his declaration to never get close? Or will Britney's dainty curves and warm heart melt Alonso's defenses?

Prologue

"It's about time you settled down, grandson," Toni Romero chastised Dr. Alonso Romero. A few hours earlier, Alonso attended a ground-breaking ceremony for the new building for the Children's Trauma Center of Mayberry Hill. It would become a part of his special Juliana Center for Children.

Alonso and his brothers were seated in the study at the family's grand mansion, Romero Manor.

"Grandddad, we're not seriously getting into that debate again, are we?" Alonso arched a brow.

"Yes, we seriously are, Alonso."

Alonso could feel his heart muscle squeeze. He glanced around the room. His other brothers, all formerly sworn bachelors who'd had their own share of heartache and scandalous relationships, were settled down with their beautiful, loving wives who were also their best friends, and with their adorable offspring.

Who did Alonso have?

He was wedded to his profession. His passion entailed making great strides in the healthcare industry. And his desire to turn old, rundown buildings into massive, smart-clinics for people from all economic backgrounds.

A woman wouldn't be able to understand his long hours or his unsociable and workaholic personality. Not to mention his travel all over the world, to establish similar affordable healthcare facilities.

Besides, he'd suffered enough heartbreak and traumatic loss in his life. It was better to keep his distance from women. But now that his brothers were settled down, his dear old grandfather would never allow him to get out of his marriage-is-the-best-thing-to-happen-to-a-man sermon so easily.

"Hey, you have seven out of eight of your grandsons married, isn't that enough?" Alonso added. "That's more than an eighty-seven percent success rate. I'd say you should be proud."

"Not until I get the other thirteen percent, grandson," Toni played along. "I don't want to depart this life without seeing you settled down, Alonso. You boys have come along so far. I told you marriage…"

"Is the best thing that could happen to a person," Alonso finished his grandfather's sentence in jest. "I really don't need to hear it, Gramps. Besides, not everyone's meant to be hooked up like that."

"Look at your brother, Zack," Toni continued. "Who would have ever thought *he'd* end up married?"

"You do realize I'm still in the room, right, Gramps?" A questioning grin touched Zack's face.

"Yes, yes," Toni dismissed.

"Gramps, listen up here," Alonso said, trying to sound as gentle as he could, knowing his grandfather only wanted the best for him and his brothers. "I really appreciate you and all you've done for the guys and me. We would be nothing without you. And I often agree with everything you say, but not this time. I will never get married or settle down. Women and I just don't…well, it never turns out the way I expect it to. My commitment is to my work in helping others."

"You'll change your mind," Toni assured, a smug grin on his face. "I know what this is about, Alonso. You keep losing people close to you but I've lost your grandmother and she is now with the Lord, but I got married again since then."

"Yeah, five times after that!" Alonso bit his lip. "Sorry, Gramps."

"No. Please don't be. We're all grown men here. I expect honesty. I know I've made some mistakes, marrying those younger women. But look at my dear Shelly. You guys never liked her because she was my young nurse. But look now. So many years later and we're still happily married. Nothing beats love, Alonso. Please don't give up."

"It's not that easy, Gramps."

"I know. You've lost your mother. That was very painful, I know. Then you lost your best friend in school and then you lost your girlfriend in college."

"Stop there, Gramps. I'm not going there, not today."

Alonso felt his heart shrivel in his chest. All the people in his life he loved died and there was nothing he could do to bring them back. Nothing. He'd attended so many funerals as a youth it wasn't even funny. He'd begun to feel as if he was just bad luck when it came to close relationships. First, his mother, then his childhood girlfriend, Juliana—to whom he'd proposed, then his girlfriend Jennifer in college.

He'd become so numb and never wanted to get close again. He drew in a deep breath and tried to keep control of the conversation.

"I think you will change your mind, Grandson. I just know you will. I see the way you care about others. You have so much love to give. It'd be a shame to not have that special someone to love and those darling little children to bring into the world."

"Are you betting me, old man?" Alonso lovingly teased his grandfather.

"Yes!" Toni's smile widened. "I'll bet you'll get married by the end of the year."

"What are you going to do? Set me up on a blind date or something?"

The old man shrugged.

"Well, all right then," Alonso agreed. "If I end up getting married within a year from today, I'll give up my practice and give up my work as a doc. How's that?"

Toni looked stunned for a moment but then his expression shifted slightly. "I know you love your work, Alonso. What are you saying?"

"I'm saying that I'm serious about not getting married. Ever. It's not for me. But if you feel I'll change my mind, then fair enough. I'll give up my dream of expanding my vision in medicine."

"Fine then." Toni seemed to hesitate at first but finally gave in. "It's a deal."

"Get ready to lose, Gramps. I'm not getting married. And you can quote me on that."

Chapter 1

Dr. Alonso finished his dictation in his office and logged off his computer. The thought of having to take off three weeks work for a much needed vacation, according to his chief of staff, irked him. But truth be told, he was a workaholic and burn out wouldn't do him any good. He hadn't taken a real break from work for the longest time. But he would have to get away and leave his clinics and his patients to the care of his associates. He could only do so much. He just wanted to make sure his patients would be well taken care of.

"Don't you have any hobbies?" an associate once asked him.

"Yeah, taking care of people."

"No, really, man. You need a life. Or a wife!"

"I don't think so," Alonso had said. And he meant it. He was married to his passion—helping to build affordable healthcare for everyone. His own mother lost her battle to cancer when he and his brothers were young and their parents were too poor to be able to afford her medications. That tragic loss fueled his desire to save lives and help those who couldn't afford excellent medical care. But he was also a businessman, much like all the Romeros. And buying rundown clinics and transforming them was his dream.

Alonso yawned and stretched. He'd had what felt like the longest shift of his medical career. He had just spent the day fighting in court for one of his patients, Bria, to get the unconventional medical treatment she needed. His mind drifted back to the conversation he'd had with his grandfather and brothers. Good on them for getting hitched. His medical career was his relationship. He was never getting married.

How could a woman possibly understand him not being home nights and being on call practically twenty-four hours a day? Yeah, money wasn't everything. Sure, he had enough wealth to own his own island and an empire but there was more to life than material gain. Like doing good. That's how he got his kicks and no woman was going to take that joy away from him.

Alonso heard shuffling in the reception area after he powered off the lights and walked out of his office, closing the door behind him.

He saw a dainty woman who had the curves of a love goddess in the reception area though she was dressed much more humbly, wearing a lavender cardigan that hugged her body and a simple pencil skirt that covered her knees. She gazed at him with an unreadable expression, her lips parted as if she wanted to say something but didn't know how to say it. Her soft grayish brown eyes were mesmerizing against her high cheekbones and tanned skin. Her dark hair cascaded down her back. He had the sudden urge to run his fingers through it. He was captivated by her.

"Can I help you?" he asked, caught off guard by her stunning beauty.

"Yes, I think you can." The woman's voice was smooth like velvet, and oh, God, sexy as hell. His groin reacted. That never happened before. Not so instantly with a stranger.

Who was this woman?

"Do you know who I am?" she asked, pointedly.

Oh, heck. Was this one of the women he'd dated in the past? Please tell him she was not carrying his unborn child—or had a surprise kid at home that shared his DNA. Alonso never took chances and always used a condom. But he also knew that condoms could sometimes fail, if not carefully used.

"No," he said, eyeing her carefully. He never forgot a face. And this one he just plain didn't remember. "Should I?"

She stared at him as if he'd done something to her. The woman looked crestfallen and hugged herself. Tears reddening her fatigued yet still lionesque eyes.

"What is it?" he asked. "Are you okay, ma'am?"

She shook her head. "I was hoping you would know."

"Know what?"

"My real identity. I don't know...who I am. I was a patient at one of your plastic surgery clinics. I had some minor reconstructive surgery done a while back. I thought you'd have the key to my past, but I guess I was wrong."

Plastic surgery clinic?

She turned to leave and something inside Alonso pulled him to her.

"Whoa there, wait a minute," he said, going after her. "You mean the Janissa Clinic for Reconstructive Plastic Surgery?" He had taken over the clinic from renowned surgeon Dr. Miles Worthrop and converted it into one of his Romero Health Centers.

Was this woman part of a witness protection program?

He'd offered many special services, including those for witnesses involved in high-profile organized crime cases whose lives were in grave danger and required complete changes in their appearances. Those cases were rare but happened, nonetheless.

"Yes, that clinic," she confirmed solemnly.

"Were you in one of the *programs*?" Alonso hinted he understood she may not be able to go into detail.

She looked overwhelmed and sighed heavily. She seemed to have the world on her shoulders. Alonso felt sorry for her. He didn't know why. He just did.

"Maybe," she said quietly.

"Maybe?" he echoed, incredulously. "Here, you'd better take a seat." He motioned to the plush chair in the reception area in front of a coffee table with a few magazines on it. It was after hours so the office was secure and private. The soothing trickle of the waterfall by the now empty receptionist desk provided a lulling effect to the atmosphere.

"Can I get you some coffee?"

"No, thank you."

Alonso noticed she had a ubiquitous bright orange rubber wristband on her right arm. The inscription read: Nurse Care Corp (NCC).

"Hey, are you part of that group of street nurses helping the homeless?" He was familiar with the organization. He'd donated to them many times. He and his brothers had participated in one of their ice bucket challenges and other activities to raise awareness of various issues and raised a whole lot of funds for their cause.

This woman was a nurse? And an active community nurse, too. Those nurses at Nurse Care Corp worked damned hard and put their lives on the line every day doing what they did best, caring for the most vulnerable in society when everyone else was too damn busy.

She glanced down at her wristband. "Yes, I am. I work there. I'm one of the community leaders," she said.

"Wait a minute. I was under the impression you had amnesia."

She shook her head. "My name is Britney Andropolous," she said. "I'm a registered nurse. I know who I am and what I do for a living." She hesitated. "Or at least, I know who I *think* I am."

"I don't get it," he said, clearly confused. She was as mysterious as they came. "Okay, I think you'd better start at the top."

She hugged herself and hunched her shoulders drawing in a deep breath. She looked so adorable when she did that. Her eyes were a beautiful shade of gray mixed with mahogany.

To say Britney was beautiful was an understatement.

She had smooth lovely dark skin and dark hair but her exotic eyes mesmerized and captivated him. What a striking combination of prominent features.

This woman had cosmetic surgery? He certainly saw no obvious signs of anything done to her face, except maybe on her left cheek and the left side of her forehead.

Alonso noted the subtle incision scar. Whoever did her surgery did an amazing job. Her nose seemed untouched and her chiseled cheekbones were perfect.

She leaned forward on the chair, clasping her hands in front of her. "My mother had...passed away recently," she began, her voice breaking.

Just then Alonso closed his eyes for a brief moment. "I'm sorry to hear that."

He knew firsthand the excruciating pain of losing a mother. He was deprived of a mom when he was only a teenager. He never saw life the same way again. It hurt too much to this day to even think about it.

His mother gave so much to him and his brothers, love and acceptance. When she died, she left a gaping hole in Alonso's heart. Now that he and his brothers were beyond wealthy and living well, it pained them that she never lived to experience this. That she never lived to see what they'd become.

Alonso never got a chance to give her the good life she worked so hard to give him and his brothers so that they could do good for her.

"It's okay," she said, looking down at a magazine cover. "It was a few months ago." She swallowed hard. He could see the pain in her eyes and wanted to hold her, to comfort her.

"Anyway," she continued. "That's when I found out things weren't what I thought they were."

"How so?"

"I was going through my mother's belongings at the rehab center—where she passed away—and I saw some old newspaper clippings. Some articles on organized crime."

"And...?" Alonso probed gently, wanting so badly to help this beautiful, soft-spoken woman before him. There was just something about her that connected with him. It was crazy because he'd just met her, yet there was some indescribable bond he felt with her.

Did she feel the same?

He couldn't be sure, but when she first walked in, her body language was very reserved, defensive almost. But now? She seemed a bit more comfortable in sharing her information.

"Well..." she hesitated again. "I...I think I've told you too much." She rose from the chair.

"You haven't told me *anything*," he said gently.

She paused, taken aback. "Are you trying to be funny?"

"No," he said, matter-of-factly. "But I could ask you the same thing, Britney. With all due respect, you've come into my office and asked me if I know who you are and that I should know your real identity. You tell me half a story and then you want to just up and leave. What am I supposed to think? Now, I want to help you, but-"

"Really. It's okay. I don't want to cause you any more trouble."

"I think it's too late for that."

"What's that supposed to mean?"

"I'm a doctor, Britney. I help people. It's a little hard to have someone come in here asking for help then walking away, expecting me not to care about what happens to them. The fact that you're a nurse, you should understand that." He arched a brow.

Britney thought for a minute then turned to walk out the door.

Chapter 2

Britney felt her heart squeeze. She stopped at the door. She couldn't just walk away. But it had clearly been a mistake coming to Dr. Romero's office. It wasn't as if he could help identify who she was. It wasn't as if he'd done her surgery. It was the previous owner of the Janissa Clinic.

But it was something else that made her stop at the door. Her heart had exploded in her chest seeing that gorgeous hunk of a doctor. She had no idea he was so stunning. She had never seen a picture of him.

What was that feeling she was having? Dr. Alonso Romero was tall, strikingly handsome and oh, so sexy. Have mercy! He was an earth angel. Hot, sexy and gifted. A talented doctor and successful tycoon who owned some of the world's most popular healthcare clinics on several continents. And he was young, too.

"You're right," she agreed to his earlier statement. "I find it hard to not want to help those who come to me for assistance."

She had to remain focused. Terror ripped through her veins when she realized she'd almost given the gorgeous stranger-to-her TMI. *Way* too much information. She could put herself in danger, or worse, innocent Dr. Romero.

"Well, okay. Care to tell me anything else?" he probed, firmly but gently. "Look, Britney, there's obviously some connection to your conundrum and my clinic. You've already established that."

She sighed. "Yes."

"I've dealt with all kinds of sensitive cases in my line of work and at my clinics. Maybe there's something I can help you with."

"You're a decent man, Dr. Romero. Not many men in your position would want to sit and talk with a total stranger."

"Well, you're not quite a stranger now, are you?"

"Of course, I am."

"You're a client of one of my clinics. So you *are* someone to me. A special someone. All my clients and patients are extremely important to me, Britney."

He gazed into her eyes and her knees felt weak as if they wouldn't be able to hold her up in standing position much longer.

Those eyes. Oh, my. Those aqua blue eyes and those high chiseled cheekbones and beautiful dark tanned skin. His eyes were so dreamy she was mesmerized, in a daze. That tingling sensation in her belly got her feeling all giddy. She was sure her breathing had changed. She could feel her breath quickening. Was it getting hot in there?

His hair was dark and slicked back. The guy was gifted with nature's best in the good looks department. He also sported a groomed stubble. A five o'clock shadow, rendering him uber handsome.

Obviously he'd been working hard. She'd worked with many doctors before. They rarely got enough sleep. Working around-the-clock, up early, with unsociable hours preparing for their busy day ahead. They worked twenty-four hours without a decent break.

She knew firsthand nurses had it crazy with the shift work but at least they were required to work 12-hour shifts max in her area, not twenty-four hour shifts.

"Thank you, Dr. Romero."

"Please, call me Alonso."

"Alonso."

"I'd like to think we can be on first-name basis, one professional healthcare worker to another."

"Healthcare worker?" she repeated. "I wouldn't class you as just a healthcare worker, Dr...I mean, Alonso. You own all the Romero worldwide healthcare clinics. You're a gifted visionary. A mastermind."

"Oh, please, Britney. The real gifted people, or I should say, heroes, are the frontline workers. I'm so honored to work alongside them when I get the chance. I love working directly with patients. I'll never give that up. No matter how successful the clinics become."

Well, that warmed her heart. But then a sick feeling soon replaced her warm and cozy one. She could be putting Alonso in danger.

"Would you like to get something to eat?" Alonso offered. His voice was so deep and smooth like raw silk. Beautiful.

"You know we shouldn't be eating at this time, doctor."

"As long as we don't go to bed soon after eating, we'll be fine."

Bed?

The sound of his silky voice stirred a reaction inside Britney.

Now, why did her mind conjure up a naughty image of this sexy hunk of a doctor, naked over her in a king sized bed with red satin sheets around them as he made love to her? Oh, she'd love to go to bed with him after dinner.

Britney's heart turned over in her chest.

Get a hold of yourself, Britney. He's a doctor. You need his help, not his sex.

What came over Britney all of a sudden? This was so unlike her. She wasn't some love-starved prude, but one would think so—if they could read her mind. She was overwhelmed by Dr. Romero's sexually charged appearance and aura. She'd never met a man like him before, one who made her pulse pirouette with excitement.

In any case, she knew she could not get close to any man right now. It would be too risky. Too dangerous. She had far too many secrets cowering in her closet. She couldn't bear to have anyone open the door to her past. The last thing she wanted to do was to expose herself to a man who clearly could not help her to uncover the truth about her past.

Right now, Britney needed to get a grip on herself and find out the truth about her history. She was certain a nice guy like Dr. Alonso Romero didn't need a woman with a whole lot of baggage weighing down their relationship. Not that she could ever be in a relationship with someone as affluent as he was.

"I think dinner would be fine. I haven't eaten since this morning," she blurted out. Now why did she say that? Even if it were the truth. What must he think of her?

"Since this *morning?*" His deep, smooth voice sounded alarmed. "You know you shouldn't run yourself on empty like that."

Britney felt sheepish. She was a nurse. She should know better. "You're right. It's been a busy day," she explained, biting down on her lower lip. "Typical habit. I'm always making sure others are fine but when it comes to me..." She shrugged.

"Well, you really need to take care of yourself first, so that you *can* be in a good position to take care of others." He gave her a charming scold.

"Yes, sir. I'll try to remember that." Britney grinned. Her mother gave her the same advice, too. Britney used to go to the rehab center morning and night to spend time with her mother, making sure she was well taken care of, tending to her mother's needs and doing every thing possible to ensure she was comfortable. She would go early in the morning at five o'clock to stay with her mother, who never liked being alone, before heading to work her dayshift at the nursing street mission. Then at lunch break, she went back to feed her mother.

Since her mother had suffered bouts of dementia and became increasingly agitated towards the nursing staff at the center before her death, Britney visited the facility during meal times to make sure she was tended to, and bathed and groomed for the day.

Britney would lovingly take her mother on strolls through the facility's garden in her wheelchair to get some fresh air. If she had the money to buy the equipment her mother needed at home, she would have kept her there instead. It was painful to see the woman who had raised her and given her everything she could, including all the love in the world that a child can receive from a parent, end up spending her last days in an institution.

It was a difficult period for Britney, after her mother's stroke, to have her in rehab care. Luckily, the street mission she worked for was close by to the rehab center. Britney had selected the center and paid the monthly fees for a private room so her mother could get the best care possible. That alone took up most of her paycheck.

Never mind having a social life—even if she could afford to have one, after paying the hospital fees and sometimes hiring a private support worker to sit with her mom when she could not be there. Her mother's well-being was the only thing that mattered to Britney. Mom and daughter were very close. They only had each other.

"I'll get my jacket," Alonso said, interrupting her thoughts. He went into his office and came back out pulling a blazer over his crisp blue shirt and navy blue silk tie. She observed his tall, well-built physique. The man had the body of a star football player. Sure, he was a medical specialist, but those biceps were built for pro sports—and he was probably a skilled lover between the sheets, she thought to herself. Lucky for the woman he was probably dating right now.

It seemed obvious the man took great care of his appearance and he probably worked out at the gym—a lot.

Alonso led Britney through the marble floor foyer to the glass elevators. The office was plush considering it was a medical center. She admired what he and his medical team had done for the industry. Not only that, but if she recalled correctly, the largest donations to her street mission came from Romero Healthcare Clinics. To that she would be eternally grateful. They were always the first to participate in any campaign the street mission ran, without hesitation. Since Dr. Romero headed the clinics, Britney knew it all came from the top. That was one of the reasons she'd felt comfortable coming to him on this night.

That, and the fact there were some confidential papers his clinic had in its archives that she desperately needed to get hold of. She felt a huge pang of guilt stab into her heart at having to not be completely upfront with Alonso.

He seemed like a genuinely nice guy. She felt an instant connection to him. She liked him a lot already and prayed he wouldn't get hurt in the process of her obtaining the files she needed.

Chapter 3

The cool evening breeze kissed their skin while orange and brown fall leaves danced in the wind as they walked down the street out of the office complex towards Alonso's parked SUV.

"Nice ride," Britney commented as he opened the passenger side door of his massive black vehicle with the tinted windows.

"Thanks. She gets me around," he said before closing the door as she sat down.

"*She*?" Britney cocked a brow when Alonso got into the driver's side. He pressed his finger to the engine start button to bring the motor to life.

"What's wrong with my ride being female?"

"Nothing," Britney chuckled. She was beginning to feel oddly comfortable around Alonso, which tore her apart even more. *Don't fall for this guy, Britney. You've got a mission to accomplish. Nothing more.* "It's just that I assumed guys would call their rides...um, male, whatever," she fumbled for words. Okay, now she was really not sounding very coherent.

Alonso rolled his eyes. "The most beautiful, strong things I know are female."

"Oh? Is that so?" A warm feeling crept into Britney's tummy. It was the way he said it. His voice was deep, yet silky smooth like warm caramel melting on the tongue.

"Yes. I'm surprised you don't agree." Alonso gave her a knowing smirk.

"I'm not saying that I don't agree. It's just that most guys aren't like that. You seem like some sort of male feminist."

He paused briefly and gave her a funny look. "What the heck is that?"

"I don't know. I just heard the term once." She was really taking a liking to this guy. He wasn't a bad person at all. And speaking about nice rides—an image of her riding him slid into her brain before she blinked hard to wipe it away.

Why couldn't I have met you back in college? When my world was not so complicated?

Clearly, it had been way too long since Britney had been on a date. She couldn't remember the last time it was. In college? She'd recently graduated from nursing school but even during that time and before that, most of her time had been caring for her ailing mother.

The only romance she experienced up to that point was from reading romance novels or watching rom-coms starring her favorite Hollywood stud, wishing she was his leading lady. Boy, she really needed to get a life.

What had gotten into her all of a sudden? She'd just met a gorgeous hunky doctor and all of a sudden, her mind turned to mush. Sweet, naughty thoughts dominating her brain. This was utter insanity. Maybe, she'd just had a stressful day. Britney chalked it up to not getting enough sleep.

They drove down the lakeside street with a beautiful evening view of the water as the moonlight and the streetlights shone on the dark waves providing a glittering reflection of light on the surface. It was breathtaking. Britney loved being near water. She didn't know what it was, maybe the soothing sound of the lake as the waves moved or the whooshing sound of water.

She leaned back into the plush heated leather seat, enjoying the quiet drive while her mind raced.

The interior of the vehicle smelled like a mixture of new leather and intoxicating manly cologne. The windows were wound down slightly so they could enjoy the evening breeze. Britney glanced at Alonso while he drove. A serious expression dressed his face. His eyes seemed focused on the road yet his mind seemed like he had a million things running through it.

She wondered what it could be. Did he have someone at home waiting for him? Was he bothered by her taking up his evening and changing whatever plans he might have had?

"Where are we going?" Britney broke the silence.

"To a cozy restaurant on the east side. It's private so we can talk."

"Private? What is it called?"

"The Place," he said smoothly.

"The Place?" she parroted.

He gave her a warm smile and his eyes held hers for a minute. Her heart flip-flopped in her chest. Okay, she was really falling for this sexy blue-eyed, brown-skinned doctor. That was so not good. She had to focus. But, oh, God, his eyes were so mesmerizing and warm. They were magnetic. Drawing her to him whenever she met his gaze.

Before long, he entered a pass code at the gated entrance. The gates opened and they pulled into a parking lot on Riverside Drive next to a glass building. Alonso pressed his forefinger on the engine button to power it down. He got out of the vehicle and came to the other side to open the door for her.

Britney looked at one of the many modern streetlights lining the striking gardens in front of the building. She was willing to bet cameras were hidden in those lamps. It was quiet and the autumn wind howling through the tree branches was the only sound she heard. The air was crisp.

"Are you okay?" Alonso asked.

She nodded.

His cell phone rang and he slid it out of his pocket to answer it. "Yes?" he said. "No, I can't right now. I have an important meeting. I'll get back to you soon."

An important meeting? Was this what she was to him? A *meeting*? In all fairness at least he told the person on the other end of the phone line that it was important. Important was a good thing, wasn't it?

That thought soon faded, and Britney felt self-conscious and overwhelmed. He'd brought her to one of his other office buildings. A place where he probably met patients. She wondered if he was just cautious, and if he felt sorry for her.

Oh, what must he think of her?

She looked around and noticed there were also visible cameras everywhere. They walked up to an unmarked glass and steel door. Alonso pressed a button that recognized his fingerprint and a disembodied woman's voice acknowledged him. "Thank you, Dr. Romero."

Britney's jaw fell open. The door swung open to her utter amazement. Okay, she was so not expecting that. She was a well-educated woman who had seen quite a lot in her line of work, yet this was not something she was expecting from what seemed like an ordinary guy—who just happened to be one of those down-to-earth billionaires from a prominent family of tycoons. Yet, she had no idea they lived like *that*!

What on earth was she doing with him? She felt so oddly intimidated in his presence. The guy was obviously well connected in every way. Beyond what she'd read up on his worldwide clinics. Another thought struck her. For a guy so gifted in the good looks department, it was odd there were so few photos of him online.

Britney had to remember to ask him about that when they settled down to eat. She thought *she* had a mysterious past. Now she was eager to not only have him help her but to find out more about *him*. Curiosity was getting the best of her. There was something about Alonso that was just so…elusive.

Chapter 4

"I'm speechless," Britney said, gaping around the plush restaurant where Alonso brought her. "You really didn't have to bring me here, Dr...I mean, Alonso."

"And why not, Nurse Britney?" he said, as they were seated.

The waiter had already brought their orders, two scrumptious plates of honey-glazed grilled chicken with sautéed vegetables and a plate of healthy tossed salad on the side.

Alonso enjoyed watching her expression over the intricately decorated plates and fine cuisine. The Place had a reputation for the most expensive gourmet dinners in the country. A chilled bottle of Romero Merlot wine was placed on the table.

They had one of the best private views in the venue with a glowing lakeside view. Their table on the terrace was candlelit. The nearby water whooshing on the shore was relaxing. Just what Alonso needed after one heck of a long day at work and he was sure that Britney, like all hard-working nurses, could use a relaxing evening, too.

He'd worked with many nurses and appreciated their selfless dedication and tireless efforts in helping others. Especially the nurses at the street mission.

"Let me guess," he continued. "You love taking care of others but you're not used to being taken care of."

She grinned sheepishly and tilted her head to the side. "I guess it shows," she said in her velvet voice.

"Yes, it does."

"I could say the same about you, too, sir."

"What about me?" Alonso brought the glass of wine to his lips.

"For a successful businessman, you sure do work hard. *Unnecessarily* hard. You have a whole team of staff who can do your work for you. I mean, you still do hands-on patient care."

"How did you know that?"

"I read about the work you do, plus I've heard from some of your patients. Even though you rarely have a photo of yourself online," she added, almost under her breath. "It's not necessary to be a workaholic in your position."

"What's wrong with that?"

"You don't have to work so hard with all that...um...wealth."

He placed his glass down scrutinizing her. A grin curved his lips. "You really think that's what life's about? Making enough money so you don't have to do anything?" He narrowed his eyes.

"I didn't mean it like that."

"Why do you think the late Steve Jobs worked hard all his life improving Apple products? Or Bill Gates works hard even today? So they can continue the very things that launched them—their passion for helping to improve the lives of others. That never ends when you, what's the word you used, become wealthy, or make it, so to speak. I'm always driven by the passion to help others. That will never change. That's who I am. We all have a purpose in life and being active keeps us sharp...and healthy," he added with a charming grin.

She gushed. He could see her cheeks rouging. It looked like he inadvertently embarrassed his lovely guest. But oh, she was so cute when she blushed. Her soft gray-brown eyes looked down at the table, her fork in her hand.

"I guess I sound a little stupid to you."

"No. I like it when people speak their minds." Their eyes locked momentarily and he saw a beautiful spark that resonated with him. He felt his heart flutter and that was something that never happened to him.

There was something very attractive about young nurse Britney. He was really beginning to take a liking to her. Not just the fact that she worked as hard as he did, helping the unfortunate, but she wasn't all arrogant like some women he'd met.

She had a lot of humility. She was humble. Beautiful like a pageant queen, yet humble about her appearance and so upfront.

"I'm glad you came to my office when you did."

"Why?"

"I'll be taking a vacation from all that *unnecessary* hard work you say I do." He stifled a chuckle.

"I'm sorry," she said sheepishly. "But, I'm glad I came to your office, too. I need to solve a puzzle about my past. And I think you'll be able to help steer me in the right direction."

"Go on." Alonso turned serious all of a sudden.

"After my mother died, I found some documents pertaining to change of name forms for both of us. And letters about a new identity and some papers about how to create a new life and erase the past. I also found some articles about mobsters hiring hit men to eliminate witnesses. It's all so crazy. Mom always told me she was in a dangerous line of work and that we could be in peril so we kept to ourselves most of the time."

"That's awful. I'm sorry you went through all that."

"I find it extremely hard to trust anyone. And I've always found it difficult to open up, so please forgive my...um...my manners at times. Some people think I have a chip on my shoulder sometimes. But I don't. I'm just always looking over it, questioning people's motives."

"Well, you don't have to worry about mine. I really do want to help you."

"I just want to know the truth. I want to know everything about my mother's past as well as my own. How can I move forward if someone's out to get me? I need to know exactly who we were before Mom thought it was best we changed our identities."

"If you're saying her identity change happened at one of my clinics, I can certainly try to find whatever information you need. It might take a bit of time."

"I...know...thank you."

Alonso glanced at his watch. "Is there someone waiting for you at home?"

"Yes," she said. "Max."

Max? Why did his stomach just sink like a heavy brick in the water? Well, what did he expect? A gorgeous, well-educated young woman like Britney would have to have someone in her life, wouldn't she?

"Lucky Max," he said, feeling cold. Was he jealous that this lovely woman before him had a man waiting for her at home? Why did he wish it were he, waiting at home for her?

Suddenly, the thoughts of what his grandfather told him slid into his mind. He'd made a deal, hadn't he? He'd promised he would never get married or find a woman who could tear his interests away from his work. Well, he knew he'd make good on it. All the good women were taken. The gold diggers and opportunists were plentiful. He could tell that Britney wasn't one of them.

Well, if she were *his* woman, he wouldn't let her wander in office buildings late at night searching for information about her past, alone.

"Thanks. But I think I'm the lucky one really."

"Well, it's obvious you've found at least one person you can trust and open up to," he said. "Your boyfriend."

"What?" she said as she tossed her head back and giggled. It was a hearty, innocent laughter that rang true and brought a smile to his face.

"What's so funny?" he said.

"I'm sorry, Alonso, it's just that...well, Max is my cat," she clarified. "You're right; I don't trust anyone unless they have four furry legs."

"You're beginning to sound like those characters in Animal Farm now: Four legs good, two legs bad."

She grinned. "That was one of my all-time favorite books. I read it over and over when I was in high school."

"Me too," he said, warmth centering in his heart. They shared an interest in literary classics.

"Anyway, he's with my elderly neighbor. She's a sweetie. I don't like to leave Max at home alone for too long. Even if I have to work long shifts. He gets lonely. He's all I've got now. I love him to bits." She paused looking thoughtful then took a sip of her drink.

"Do you have anyone waiting for *you* at home?" Britney asked. "I mean, I don't want to take you away from any plans tonight." She sounded genuine and those kissable pouty lips of hers were stirring some kind of reaction in him. He had better be careful around this beautiful yet elusive woman.

Was she feeling for him? Did she genuinely care about him? Or was she checking him out to see if he was seeing anyone? Who could blame her for turning the tables on him? He didn't want to come off as lame but the truth was, he'd just gotten out of a crazy sex-dominated relationship with Bianca. They really didn't connect except on the physical level. But it was mutual. He wasn't ready to commit emotionally. But it all ended with Bianca when he'd found out she was doing the head chief of staff at one of his medical clinics in Brooklyn. Well, that really burned the hell out of his trust line.

He'd felt so empty before meeting Bianca. He'd lost his college girlfriend Jennifer to breast cancer. It tore at his gut to even think about it. If he'd ever thought about getting married then it would have been to Jen, sweet Jen. They'd gone to med school together. But she was always missing classes because of one ill episode or another. God rest her angelic soul. She would have made a great doctor.

"I don't do relationships." *Sex, yes. Relationships, no.*

"Oh? I'm sorry to hear that. I mean, you must have been hurt real bad." She was empathetic. She really knew how to connect with Alonso. She didn't judge him like everybody else did or ridicule him, she simply empathized with him. Wasn't that what all human beings needed? Empathy? She was a good nurse. She was a good person. He could tell.

"Thank you for your empathy. And yes, you're right. I was hurt really badly."

"Do you want to talk about it?"

"Am I not supposed to be the one helping you?"

"I thought you said we're both healthcare professionals. One healthcare worker to another. Are you saying we're on different levels now?" she said, playfully.

God, she was so easy to speak with. He'd never met a beautiful woman like Britney before. A beautiful soul. That's what she was.

"Right!" He grinned. So she was giving him a taste of his own medicine. He liked that about her. He liked that a lot.

"Death is a funny thing," he said.

"Oh, how so?"

"I've lost a lot of people I cared about in my life. It makes us re-think things like relationships."

"I understand."

Alonso drew in a deep breath. Why was he feeling okay to talk to her about his lost love? Was it because he'd suppressed his emotions all this time and didn't want to talk about it? Was it because she was a caring nurse who really wanted him to share his feelings with her, to let it out? Whatever it was, it felt right at this time to express his feelings about relationships.

"I've been hurt by a woman before but that was nothing compared to the loss I suffered when my girlfriend died."

"Oh, God!" Britney gasped with alarm. "I'm so very sorry about that, Alonso. How horrible."

"It's okay. I guess I never got over any losses in my life. When I get close to someone I truly care about, they die. Or so it seems."

"You've had more than one girlfriend who died?"

"Yes. And I'm not going to chance it again either. Not to mention the first death I experienced was my mother. She'd lost her battle to cancer."

"Oh, that's awful. And being so young, I can't imagine losing a parent so young. I mean, my dad died before I was born so that was different. I was an adult when my mother passed. How did you manage?"

"It wasn't easy. My father lost it, his job, and later his mind. We lost our home shortly thereafter. So it was rough but then someone heaven-sent came to us. We were discovered by a grandfather who didn't know we existed—and whom we didn't know about."

"Oh, right. The famous Toni Romero."

"Yes, I'll always be thankful to the universe for showing us mercy after all that stuff that happened."

"You said you lost a lot of people," she probed, genuinely interested.

"Yes, my mother was my greatest loss. Then I had a really cool childhood friend named Juliana. I guess you could say she was my first girlfriend, and we were supposed to get married," Alonso said, a nostalgic smile curved his lips.

"Get married?"

"You know how kids play these silly games."

"What games?"

"Marriage games. I wrote a note in grade five. 'Will you marry me?'"

"And?"

"She wrote back to me and snuck the note on my desk. She said: 'Yes. Not now, though, we have a math test.'"

"Aww, that is so sweet!" Britney smiled, chuckling. "I can't get over this marriage proposal. A marriage proposal in grade five? Unbelievable."

"I guess it would be the only marriage proposal I would ever extend."

"Why do you say that? What happened to Juliana?"

"She..." Alonso swallowed a hard emotional lump that surfaced in his throat. "She died in a freak accident in the lake." His heart felt heavy just uttering those words—she died. It was painful. It would always be painful. He would never marry. He would never give another marriage proposal to another girl—well, to a woman.

"Oh, no!" Britney's voice was choked with emotion. Alonso genuinely appreciated her empathy though it did nothing for his emotional state speaking about Juliana. "I'm so sorry, Alonso."

He could feel the sensation of tears stinging his eyes.

Maybe Juliana would have been his only chance at getting married—if she had lived. Alonso and Juliana would have been childhood sweethearts. He often wondered what would have happened if she hadn't died so young. Would she have gone to medical school, too? Would she have been a teacher? A lawyer? Or an entrepreneur? He remembered he cried for days, weeks after her funeral.

Children weren't supposed to die. Not in his book. That was one of the reasons he fought hard to provide competent medical care to children at his clinics regardless of their parents' socioeconomic backgrounds and not only that—to provide safe practices for parents of young children and accident prevention workshops.

Juliana didn't have to die that day at the lake with no adult supervision. Then of course, his thoughts and fears were substantiated when his college girlfriend died, too. There was no hope for him where that department concerned. It was better to lose himself in his mission in helping to heal others, not relationships. They didn't last. They would never last.

Imagine that—a marriage proposal in his childhood. What was he thinking? Oh, right. He was only a kid. A silly child.

"Then, there was my late girlfriend, Jennifer, as I'd mentioned before," he continued, trying to contain his emotions.

Why was he opening up to Britney so easily? Because she was a nurse. A caring and compassionate nurse who well knew death and he felt her concern.

"And yes, their names all began with J. Three Js coincidentally," he added.

"Wow! Wait a minute. You have clinics named after them? The Janissa Clinic for Reconstructive Plastic Surgery, the Jennifer Center and the Juliana Center for Children. Please tell me that wasn't a coincidence."

"No, it wasn't."

"How sweet. I mean," she placed her hand on her chest, tears misting her eyes. "That is so kind of you to honor their memories like that. I'm sure they're smiling down on you every blessed day."

"I don't know about that, but I do know that I vow to help others in their names since I wasn't able to help them."

"But that's not fair, Alonso. You were a kid when your mother and childhood friend died. And when your girlfriend died you were still in med school. You can't save the world, you know."

"I know, but it still hurt like hell, being helpless when there was nothing I could do to save them."

"That's why you became a doctor," she confirmed.

"Yes. Is that why you became a nurse? To right something you felt was wrong in your life?" Alonso turned the conversation to her direction, wanting badly to erase the heaviness that was centering in his heart again. Wanting to bounce back into the present.

"Yes. My mother had battles with depression during her lifetime. Like I said, we were always on the run. And then, later in life she'd taken a turn for the worse. She didn't really trust anyone and always told me not to trust because our lives could be in danger." She looked intently down at her glass.

"Now I know why," Britney continued. "At least I have some part of the puzzle. Just not all. Anyway, as she battled illnesses over the years, I was desperate to help her and wanted to learn how to care for her and for anyone who was ill. And there was a period when we lost our home, too."

"Oh, I'm truly sorry to hear that."

"I guess we have a lot in common. Having been homeless, losing people close to us. Anyway, when an opportunity came up at the homeless shelter for a vacant position for a street nurse, I jumped at the chance."

"Good for you."

"Thank you, I—" At that moment, Britney's cell phone buzzed. She pulled it out of her purse, excusing herself and glancing at the screen. Her eyes widened. The message read:

Your time is up

Chapter 5

Britney was alarmed but didn't want Alonso to see the message or suspect anything was up. She was reminded again by that message about her purpose for seeing Alonso tonight, yet she had been enjoying his company, wishing things weren't so complicated for her. Wishing they had met under normal circumstances. What was Lilly doing texting her at this time?

She had to make an excuse to get up from the table. "I...I need to go to the powder room," she said, getting up, feeling terrible inside.

The troubled look on Alonso's face made her feel more torn but she couldn't bear to look into his eyes.

"Um, where is the washroom?"

"The ladies room is on the far right." He stood in gentlemanly fashion and pointed when she rose from the table to leave.

"Thank you." Britney made her way in that direction, her purse strap swinging from her left shoulder.

When she arrived in the luxurious powder room with the gold-tinted mirrors, she took a quick look around to ensure she was alone.

The washroom area was in the far back. The countertops in the waiting area had gold marble stone tops with a candle on each side. She noticed a chandelier hanging from the ceiling. The seating area had cushions. She hadn't anticipated this. She really felt out of place in...Alonso's world.

Oh, why couldn't she have met him under different circumstances?

She slid out her cell phone and pressed autodial. Lilly answered immediately. "What is wrong with you? Did you get the information?"

"No. Not yet."

"Not yet?" Lilly's voice was impatient. "Britney, you don't have much time. I need the document by morning."

"You won't get it by morning, Lilly. I need more time."

"More time?"

"Yes," Britney said, trying to keep her voice steady. Her nerves were getting the best of her. Why did Alonso's handsome face sweep into her mind—and into her conscience? She didn't deserve his kindness. She didn't deserve to even be dining in such a fine, exquisite place like this, with him.

Britney closed her eyes and opened them again, trying to blink away any painful tears. "I'll talk to you tomorrow, Lilly." She hung up the phone without giving Lilly a chance for rebuttal. She could only do what she could do.

Britney glanced in the mirror over the sink and turned on the tap. She splashed cold water on her face, trying to wash away any signs of distress. She grabbed a paper towel from the gold dispenser and dabbed her face dry.

I can do this.

I must do this.

She tried to remember the techniques she'd learned from one of her drama therapy workshops. Happy face. Smile and you'll feel better, she'd been told. She curved her lips into a smile and tried to think, as hard as it was, of something pleasant. Like the delicious Alonso Romero. Even his name sounded sexy as sin.

Then a sinking feeling struck down that warm and fuzzy feeling about him. Yeah, he was hot all right. But she was so not being totally upfront with him. She was planning to tell him everything at a later time. But just not now. She needed to get an important piece of information from his office first. Or her life would be over.

She squared her shoulders, drew in a deep breath and grabbed her bag to return to the dining table.

"Everything okay?" Alonso asked, getting up to pull out her chair for her. The guy had class.

"Thank you. Yes, everything's okay." Not.

"Well, you had me concerned for a minute," he said, observantly. "You get a text message then run off to the powder room with all your stuff."

Okay, that looked bad, didn't it? "Yes, you're right. My apologies if I worried you."

"Accepted. But you've really got me concerned."

"You? Concerned about me?"

"What's wrong with that?"

"We haven't known each other very long and well...I don't get it. Knowing who you are and how powerful you are, why do you make yourself so accessible?"

"You mean, how did you get past security to show up at my office?"

"Actually, yes. I could have been an intruder."

"Are you?"

"No. Of course not. But aren't you ever worried?"

"The only thing I fear is fear itself. Besides, you underestimate me, Britney. What makes you think I don't have enough security? If I thought you were dangerous, trust me, you wouldn't have been able to get within a mile of me."

"Okay, I guess you're not going to elaborate on your hidden high-tech security features. I'm sure your smart office is well equipped. Not to mention all those cameras about."

He leaned back surveying her as if utterly amused.

"And while we're here, we need to get down to business," he said.

"Business?"

"The real reason you came into my office tonight." He arched a brow. He watched as she swallowed hard. "Why did you lie to me, Britney?"

Chapter 6

"Why did I *lie*?" Britney echoed; she was shocked.

"Yes, lie. I checked on some of your background information."

"But how? When?"

"While you were in the powder room, I took the opportunity to do some fact checking. You should know that technology moves very quickly. At least you didn't lie about being a nurse. You're a nurse in good standing with the College of Nurses. And you've worked at the NCC Street Mission for many years, giving back to the community."

"I see you have one of those apps that can get you access to any database. It didn't take you too long, did it?"

"You sought me out on purpose," he accused.

Britney's throat closed up, her heart pounded like a base drum in her chest. "Yes, but...Dr...Alonso, I needed to speak with you."

"You were accused of stalking Dr. Worthrop—one of the doctors who worked for the Janissa Clinic. Why?"

She drew in a deep breath. "Because, I...He had some information I needed. And I wasn't stalking him, Alonso. You have to believe me. He had accused me of that to cover up—"

"To cover up what?"

"It's a long story."

"The Place is open twenty-four hours," he said, leaning forward, his hands clasped in front of him, his jaw set. A serious gaze from his electric blue eyes met hers. "We've got time."

She seemed caught off guard. "Time?"

"Yes. *Time* is something you'd better spend with me explaining yourself...or you'll find yourself spending it in prison."

"What?" Her eyes widened. Would he really call the police? "You wouldn't."

"Someone breaks into one of my clinics then years later comes into the head office trying to lie their way into-"

"Wait a minute," she raised her voice, luckily the place was quiet and he was sure some of the staff overhead even though they were in a secluded area. "I really don't know who I am. But Dr. Worthrop knows. Or at least he knew."

Alonso clasped his hands together. "I really don't like being lied to, Britney."

"My mother and I had our identities changed. I didn't lie about that."

"What makes you think he would know?"

"I didn't get around to telling you that Dr. Worthrop had performed my mother's surgery. He also did mine."

"You've had plastic surgery done to your face?" Alonso asked.

She shook her head. "No, I haven't. Well, I did get into an accident a long time ago and received a nasty gash on the side of my face. He did the operation to reconstruct this area," she said, pointing to her scalp line.

"I see. I noticed that earlier."

"Yes, well, Dr. Worthrop, who had already seen my mother, was referred to help me."

"Now you said he did your mother's plastic surgery. Was that part of an identity change? He's worked with clients who happened to be in witness protection programs."

"Well, yes and no."

"What exactly are you saying?"

She drew in a deep breath. "You're right about Dr. Worthrop filing charges against me but he later had them dropped."

"And?"

"I hadn't really broken into your clinic that night a year ago. I...I needed to get some answers from him. He'd been seeing my mother after her surgery. And there was a heated argument between them. I'm not sure what it was about but my mother asked him for her files back. Some papers had some of her original information and he refused."

"He refused?"

"Yes."

"Well, you do know that doctors in this country aren't allowed to just hand over certain types of medical records directly to patients for security reasons and fear that it would end up in the wrong hands. We could be held liable, you know."

"I know that. I know that all too well, Alonso. But that wasn't the case. This wasn't just about medical records. This was about some information he'd taken from my mother when we showed up at the clinic."

"What are you saying?"

"I'm not here to bad-mouth any of your doctors who work under you."

"And you're not. Besides, Dr. Worthrop, as you know, has long retired."

"I know."

"So you figured I wouldn't know about that incident a year ago and you could come back to see if you can find any files in his office?"

"No. Not at all."

"Then what are you saying?"

"I think he might have been threatened."

"Threatened? By whom?"

"One of the crime bosses my mother helped put away."

"I see."

"You see, it's no secret that he's done quite a bit of work for some people who have gone through the witness protection program to have their identities completely changed."

Alonso nodded thoughtfully, but didn't want to let on too much. Anger seethed through him. He'd known something was not quite right with Dr. Miles Worthrop when he started to postpone and/or cancel surgeries. The man seemed jittery and later quit outright. He'd left his wife and practically disappeared. Miles had told Alonso he wanted to retire in the Caribbean somewhere and enjoy the rest of his life stress free. But that just didn't seem like him. Did this have something to do with Britney's mother and from whomever she was hiding?

"So what made you choose this night, Britney?"

"Because...it would have been my mother's birthday."

"I'm sorry."

"It's okay. On her deathbed she managed to tell me that it was all a lie—she wouldn't elaborate on what exactly the lie was, so I don't quite know what to think. She did say, however, that Dr. Worthrop knows the truth."

Alonso's eyes widened. "She did?"

"Yes, she did. I wasn't going to mention this but...I'm desperate, Alonso. I feel as if I can't go on not knowing the truth. I'm at work and constantly looking over my shoulders."

"What do you mean?"

"Well, you know I work at the NCC Street Mission."

"Yes."

"We get all sorts of people coming in for treatment as well as some referrals. Well, one day, I get a strange look from one of the clients. He left a note for me on the table at the center saying that Britney Andropolous doesn't exist. Then later that afternoon while I was walking home from work after the clinic closed..." she hesitated for a moment, twisting her hands in her lap.

"And?"

"Well, I was sort of mugged."

"Mugged? What do you mean sort of?"

"Well, I didn't have anything taken from me. Just...well, this guy attacked me, yanked my hair. Took a good clump of hair out." She touched the side of her head. "My scalp is still tender."

"What?" Alonso was vexed hearing someone had touched this beautiful woman in such a violent way. If he ever got his hands on that creep... "Did you go to the police?" he demanded, looking directly into her eyes.

"No. I was too afraid."

"That's when you *should* go." His voice was curter than he had intended. He didn't take too kindly to a man laying a finger on a girl. Didn't matter what the situation.

Anger scorched his veins. His voice was alarmed, yet it was as if he was holding back.

"I went back to the clinic immediately. The nurse manager helped me nurse my scalp. I just left it at that. It's a crazy location where we work."

"That's no excuse." Alonso got up and immediately went over to her head. "When did this happen?"

"Yesterday," she said softly.

He observed her scalp after gently moving some of her hair to the side. He clenched his jaw, anger burning inside him.

"We're going to do something about this, Britney."

"You don't have to ... really."

"The area still looks sore. I can prescribe something to make it heal faster," he said.

"Thank you. I feel like such a bother to you right now."

"Hey, I care about people. I care about what happens to you," he added. "And it bothers me that some low-life creep did this to you. Did you get a good look at him?"

"Not really. It all happened so fast. When I looked up, he ran off. He had on a dark jacket and jeans. That could be anybody, but I couldn't see anything else. I don't even know how old he was. Probably just pulling some prank."

"Pulling a woman's hair or touching her in any way is no prank, Britney. This is serious. Where did it happen exactly?"

"Right outside the clinic."

Alonso keyed something into his phone.

"What are you doing?" she asked.

"I'm going to get some information about what happened. I believe there are security cameras in that area. I'll get my men to do some digging and check it out. Someone must have recorded something."

Britney's jaw fell open. "Alonso," she swallowed a bundle of nerves. "I...I don't want to cause any trouble."

"It's too late, someone already caused trouble. For you," he added sharply. "I will make sure he gets caught and pays for what he did."

"I don't know what to say," she murmured.

"You don't need to say anything else about the situation."

"I'll admit I felt so unsafe at work for the first time and Lord knows if someone's out to get me, I don't want any of my clients getting in the middle."

"So you left the job?"

"No. I just took a day off. I told my boss, I was going to take a personal leave day."

"I see."

"Anyway, I was led to you when I went through my mother's belongings that were given to me from the nursing home. I found that she'd had a list of people written down. Dr. Worthrop had an x beside his name. So did a few others. Except you."

"Me?"

"Yes, you. Alonso Romero had a tick beside the name and I figured that you were good in her books. I had my surgery done at your clinic—the minor surgery and of course, my mother had been to your clinic over the years to have her surgery touched up—not by you but by Dr. Worthrop."

Alonso drew in a deep breath. "I'm taking you home right now then first thing in the morning, we'll go to the clinic."

"Why not now?"

"You need to get some sleep, Nurse Britney."

The fatigue in her eyes told it all.

"I guess I do."

Alonso slid out his cell phone to make a call. He was going to get Britney home where she could get some rest but rest was the last thing on his mind. Her situation was his business now.

And what made this taste more critical was the fact that somehow one of his own doctors had been wrapped up in this. He knew it would be a bit risky having high-profile patients from mob trials who needed identity changes. He'd warned Miles about the risks involved in taking on such cases but damn it. He came into the profession to change lives. And it didn't matter who came to him for help. Alonso Romero wasn't going to discriminate. He'd take all clients regardless of the security risks involved.

Britney watched. Her luscious lips partially opened. "Who are you calling?"

"My detective. We'll get you home then I'm going back to the office."

"The office? I'm coming with you."

"Oh no, you're not. I need to check out a few things."

"But, Alonso, I don't want you to be working late at the office on my account. You looked as if you were heading home. It's all my fault you never got there."

"Hey, nothing's your fault. The fact that you're mixed up with one of my former employees and now you've gotten threats at your workplace is my business." His voice was lethally low and fierce.

"Hey, JoJo, I've got you on speakerphone. Someone's with me. I need you to look into something for me. Are you busy now?" Luckily no one else was near them while they were seated in the restaurant.

"At this time of night?" the man's deep, rough voice sounded through the speakerphone. "Do you ever sleep, doc?" The man's tone became lighter with amusement though still deep and intimidating.

"Not really," Alonso said. "My guest will be heading home soon. Make sure there's backup there. I want her home watched."

"Got it. What's the address?"

Britney recited her address.

"Good, I'll check it out first then get back to you."

The men ended their call.

Britney tried to hide her astonishment. It was harder than she thought.

"Everything okay?" he asked.

"Um…yeah, fine. Thanks." She sounded more lost than she'd intended. She could not believe the access to twenty-four hour support this man obviously had. Why couldn't her life be like that? Of course, she'd heard about the Romeros. Who hadn't? They were well connected. She just didn't know they were literally a digit away from any kind of help or assistance they needed.

He was going to have guys watching her home? This was unreal. Unbelievable. But clearly Alonso seemed royally peeved and only he knew why. Britney was overwhelmed with the kind of protectiveness he was showing to her and they'd barely known each other.

Apparently, the fact that she was a former patient at one of his clinics was enough, not to mention that somehow one of his formerly employed doctors had information that was obviously critical for her.

God, this man was really a take-charge kind of person.

Yet, she was concerned for him. Very concerned. First of all, he'd probably not slept since last night and now he'd be working late at his clinic trying to find some information to help her.

Oh, God! Should she tell him about Lilly? But that could really complicate things for her confidential source.

Britney would have to tell him. Or he'd find out in no time, it appeared. But she wouldn't tell him about Lilly just yet. It could put her source—the one person who helped her and her mother—in great danger.

Chapter 7

Alonso was uneasy about letting Britney go to her own home—alone. Albeit, his security team would be staked out at her place to ensure she was okay.

They drove quietly in his SUV for the first part of the journey to the west side. He really had a bad feeling about something going down with Britney and some obscure mob boss. He couldn't wait to get his hands on additional information.

"So what was your mother's name?"

"The name she wrote under?"

"Yes."

"Anna Andropolous."

"I see. What paper?"

"The Sutton Mirror."

"Sutton? That's way up north."

"I know. We lived out there for a while. We moved around quite a bit, always losing our place," she lamented, looking out the window.

Alonso's heart sank for her. He could tell the pain was deep. He knew what it was like to have parents going through a rough patch with job loss, illness and having to raise kids and move around to find affordable housing. There was something about Britney that resonated with him.

"Sorry to hear that. I know how that is."

"Of course," she said. "I'm not complaining," she added. "Everything that's happened to me has made me a stronger person. A better person. I take nothing for granted and I always try to hold my own."

"I appreciate your spirit."

"Thanks."

Alonso glanced at Britney then fixed his eyes back on the road. He'd never met anyone like her. The girl had a lot of spunk and class.

"And that means caring for those around me, doctor."

"What's that supposed to mean?"

"I mean, I'm serious about you heading home to rest. I hope you're not going to do any research without me at the office. I'm off tomorrow."

He grinned. "You don't know me, Britney. When I'm charged about doing something, I don't like to put it off."

"But you can't put off sleep, either."

"I'm stubborn, Britney. A true workaholic. I'm not perfect. That's why I could never be in a relationship."

Oh, God help him. Was he really destined to end up alone in life? If he did in fact have someone waiting for him at home, would he still want to go back to the office to dig up more information to help Britney?

"I'm only speaking from experience when I say sleep is important."

"Oh?"

"Yes. When I first started nursing, mom got real sick. We couldn't keep up with the medical bills, paying for private care, so I ended up working double shifts."

"Now that's not safe."

"*You* do it."

"I'm a doctor."

"You're human."

"And just how do you know that?" he teased her.

She laughed out loud again. It sounded so warm and friendly.

"Don't ever stop."

"Stop what?" she said. "Laughing?"

"Yeah. I mean, no. Well, you have a wonderful laugh, it's infectious. Childlike. Don't ever lose it. And that smile. It's golden."

"Thanks." Britney looked embarrassed.

Moments later, a call came in on Alonso's cell phone. He answered it and spoke to JoJo briefly before ending the call.

"Right, someone's guarding your apartment building. We'll watch for anyone entering or leaving the building."

"Thanks, Alonso. But is this really necessary?"

"You were attacked recently, so yes." His tone was final. He still wished he could take this pretty lady home with him instead.

"Do you remember the name of the crime boss your mother reported on?" he asked.

"Yes. Jim. I forgot his last name, though. I think it might be Jackson or Jenkins or something like that."

"Okay. Where are the articles?"

Britney seemed uncomfortable for a moment. They pulled up to her apartment building complex. "In my apartment."

"Good, I'll walk you up then I'll take what you've got and do some comparisons."

Alonso switched off his engine and got out of the SUV. He walked to the other side and opened the passenger door. A man in a dark car near to them gave a nod. It was one of the detectives from JoJo's agency. Good.

Alonso never took chances with situations such as these. He'd done a lot and seen a lot. Organized crime was prevalent in certain areas. He'd seen too many people get caught up in the wrong situation. He had a feeling a long time ago that Miles had been involved in some payoffs in the past, too. But he wasn't about to tell Britney since he was never able to prove anything—yet.

They entered the lobby of the building moments later. "On what floor do you live?" Alonso asked.

"Twelve," she said.

"I usually walk up to where I'm going up to a certain floor level, but if you want, we can take the elevator."

"Oh, I don't mind at all. I'm a health-conscious nut. I always walk up to my apartment."

"You do?"

"Yes, doctor. I do. I'm not a member at a gym. It's the only way I get my much needed exercise."

He chuckled. A woman after his own heart.

"What's funny?" she asked, clearly puzzled.

"The fact that you're the first woman I've met who doesn't mind walking up a few flights of stairs."

She smiled. "I'm not this size by accident. I have to keep myself fit."

Britney shared the same interests and crazy ideas he had about life and living. He actually led a workshop to curb the alarming rates of obesity in young adults and encouraged all sorts of little things that people could do on a day-to-day basis to maintain a healthy weight and cardiovascular system.

He was really taking a liking to Ms. Britney. A lot. But a nagging feeling soon entered his gut as they climbed each level, talking about different interests and ideas on promoting health in the community: don't get too attached, something prompted him.

She was just a former client who needed a bit of help. Nothing more could or would come of this. He had to get that idea through his head.

"I just have to stop at the eleventh floor to get Max."

"Right. I thought you said Max was with a neighbor."

"Oh, he is. Well, he's with a neighbor in the building. Mrs. Dawes who lives in 1101. I'm right above her in 1201."

Moments later, they had collected Britney's furry friend—a fluffy, long-haired ginger Persian kitty and headed up from the eleventh floor to the twelfth.

"He's adorable," Alonso commented and stroked Max's long fur. The cat stared at him for a minute, then warmed up to him. Alonso loved cats and dogs. His ex, Bianca detested cats and dogs. That should have been a sign that their relationship wouldn't last.

The fact that Britney held her little furry friend close to her, protectively, like a mother would hold a newborn baby, stroking and kissing his forehead spoke volumes about her. He had a soft spot for animal lovers. Another plus in his book for his enigmatic friend.

By the time Britney got to the twelfth floor, Alonso instinctively stood by her side as she walked up to her door. He had a sinking feeling in the dark corridor. And he was right. Her door looked as if partially open.

When they got closer, Britney gasped. "Oh, no. Someone's broken in."

Alonso carefully pushed the door open wider and walked inside cautiously. Ready for anything. Whoever did this was long gone it seemed. This all seemed like too much of a coincidence. First, Britney took a chance to come in to see him tonight about someone trailing her, attacking her after work. Then, her place gets trashed. What the hell was going on?

"Don't touch anything," he said. "We'll call the police."

"No."

"No?"

Britney cuddled Max to her chest and immediately walked over to her dining table. "Oh, great," she said.

"What is it?"

"They've taken the articles."

"What?"

"Yes, the press clippings I had pulled out. I laid them on the table last night. I was going to run through them again." She leaned down on her knees, overcome with emotion.

Alonso went over to her to help her. He comforted her. "It's okay, Britney. We'll find out who did this, okay?" He reached into his pocket and called JoJo. "We need to call the police, Britney. You do need to file a report."

"I know," she said, defeated and at her wits' end. Then she stood up, still clutching Max. "I'm so glad I didn't leave Max alone."

"Me, too."

"I would go crazy if anything had happened to him."

So would Alonso. He was glad she was the type of pet owner who never left her furry family member alone for too long. A few hours were okay, but more than twelve hours—the length of typical nursing shifts Britney worked, would have been disastrous.

"You're coming home with me," he said firmly.

"No, I'm not."

"Yes, you are, Britney. Someone wants to hurt you. I'm involved now. You're my responsibility."

Chapter 8

Someone wants to hurt me?

Britney was too shaken to disagree with Alonso. He was right. Some maniac apparently really had it in for her. She couldn't stay in her apartment. Not after it was broken into. First, that supposed random attack yesterday, and then her apartment gets trashed the next day. This was not a coincidence. It didn't take Sherlock Holmes to figure that one out.

It was becoming obvious she was getting too close to something dangerous lurking in her past.

"I'm going to arrange twenty-four hour security for you." Alonso's tone was final.

"What?" Britney was alarmed. "I don't need twenty-four hour security, Alonso."

"Yes, you do."

Was Alonso going to take charge of her life now? He might be the owner of one of the most prominent worldwide healthcare centers, but on a personal level, she barely knew him. "I know you're trying to be nice, Alonso, but..."

"Do you really think it's wise to stay here, even after the police come?"

She thought for a moment as she held Max in her arms, a quick sweep of the apartment, looking at her personal effects scattered about made her queasy. She felt violated, yet again. She heaved a sigh. She should be just grateful that she'd met a powerful man like Dr. Romero and that he wanted to help her.

"Fine," Britney finally uttered. "You're right. I don't want to stay here. I guess I'll have to pack a few of my things, assuming my clothes are still in the closet," she said wryly.

What was she afraid of? Being alone with this tall, dark and stunningly handsome businessman and medical professional? What did she have to lose? She cuddled Max in her arms.

Be careful who you trust, her mother's voice echoed in her mind.

Should she trust Dr. Alonso Romero?

Two hours later, Alonso opened the door to one of the penthouse suites at Romero Corp Residential Buildings. The Romeros owned a great deal of real estate not just in Mayberry Hill but all over the country. It was truly a luxurious convenience that she would have a place like this to stay. When she'd approached Dr. Romero that evening, she had no idea the night would turn out the way it did.

"The condo has a twenty-four hour concierge and we also have pet sitters available if you need."

"You do?" Britney's eyes widened as she cuddled Max.

Max couldn't wait to pull away from her, so she gently let him down. He moved around on the floor in the room.

"I think Max approves of the place," Britney said, feeling a little more comfortable. "That's a good sign."

"Good. And what about Max's mother?" Alonso hitched a brow, his gaze intense on Britney.

"It's a nice place to stay, Alonso. I'm not sure I can afford it."

Alonso frowned. "You do realize you won't have to pay a thing, don't you?"

She turned around. "I don't take handouts, Alonso."

"This is not a handout or charity, Britney. You're an acquaintance of mine now and you can use a place to stay. There's nothing to it."

"Okay," she said, too weary to argue. She really did need a safe place to stay. And this place must be more than two thousand square feet of wall-to-ceiling window luxury. She glanced around at the beautiful hardwood floors and saw the open concept kitchen with its granite countertops and high-end cabinetry. She felt so out of her league. Her little apartment would be the size of the kitchen alone.

"Thank you, Alonso. I know it probably seems like I don't appreciate what you've done but I do. It's just that everything's happening so fast."

"I understand, Britney. Don't worry about anything right now. Just get some rest," he said, as if speaking with a patient. His voice was silky and smooth, yet commanding.

Alonso gave Britney a quick tour of her new facility. "You can stay here as long as you need to."

"I was hoping to go back home soon."

"I really don't think that's a good idea, even if the cops find out who broke in. Not for now, anyway. Let's find out who's really behind all this. There's probably a link to what happened to you after work last night."

"Right," she said.

"If you need anything, here's my number," he said, offering his business card. She took it and tucked it away. It was unlike any card she'd ever seen. It just had his initials and a number. Did she now have his private cell phone number?

"Thank you. I don't think I'll be needing anything tonight but thank you."

With those words, Alonso left and Britney felt the void instantly. It wasn't until Alonso came into her life that she'd really realized just how much she'd missed, never allowing herself to get close to anyone, never revealing anything about herself.

She went into the kitchen to make herself a cup of coffee. Just then her phone rang.

"Hello?" Britney answered.

"Britney, it's me, Lilly."

"Oh, Lilly, thank God. I was going to call you."

"What's wrong? I tried to reach you at the apartment."

"It's a long story." Britney told Lilly what had happened.

"That's terrible," Lilly said, after a long pause. "But did you tell Alonso about me?"

"No. Not yet. I'll have to."

"Britney, I'm not sure if that's a good idea."

"Why not?"

"For one thing, you need to get the forms fast. As I told you before, Dr. Worthrop has been under investigation for a while, that's the real reason he sold his shares in the clinic to Dr. Romero before demoting himself to a minor role in it."

"But why doesn't Dr. Romero know about this yet?"

"He will soon. The cops have the information they need but they'll be doing some sort of search soon. That's what my source told me."

"I see," Britney said, feeling hopeless. She knew what Lilly was going to say next.

"And you know if they do and they seize all of Dr. Worthrop's files, you'll never get hold of the information you need. It'll be too late. It might get tied up in court and then everything might become public."

Britney felt her heart explode in her chest. Her lungs squeezed. That would be a disaster. She had to get to the office before the police searched Dr. Worthrop's documents and fast. But Alonso was trying to help her. How was she to tell him that there was a possibility of Dr. Worthrop's records being searched when she didn't have confirmation firsthand? Lilly made it clear she wanted to be kept out of it.

"Thanks, Lilly," Britney sighed heavily. "I'll figure out what to do next."

"You're not going in to work tomorrow, are you? Not after all that's happened and then after that attack?"

"No. As a matter of fact, thanks for reminding me. I'm going to take that overdue vacation time that's been due to me. I have over five weeks banked time, too, from all that overtime and filling in for other staff members' sick calls."

"Good, you do that."

"I will. Right now, I don't want to risk anything happening at work."

"Of course. Smart thinking. Anyway, good luck with Dr. Romero tomorrow. But don't mention my name. Remember to keep me out of it, okay? I'm just helping you out but I don't want to get into any trouble."

"No, Lilly, I'll keep you out of it. I'll do my best."

After Britney hung up the phone, she called work. She explained that she needed to take a leave of absence, and if they could, use her vacation time. They were all too glad to help her out and give her the time off.

"Suzie's been asking for shifts lately since she got laid off from her other job. This works out great," the night supervisor said to Britney.

"Perfect." Britney at least felt settled about work. The last thing she would want to do was leave them in the lurch. At least her part-time co-worker could get the hours and Britney could get her life sorted out.

She poured herself a cup of java and sat down at the kitchen bar to think. Max cuddled up on the sofa as if he was right at home, as if he didn't have a care in the world. Britney smiled warmly. Max was about the only comfort in her life right now.

She decided as she took a sip that she was going to take a hot shower then go to bed and think about her situation in the morning. Right now, her head hurt too much. And besides, Alonso was going to take care of things for her...

Chapter 9

The next day, Alonso sat in his office rummaging through old files he'd pulled from the archives. Dr. Worthrop's office files were transferred to Romero Healthcare Clinics headquarters where Alonso's own office was situated.

Alonso knew he should have been on vacation but he decided to do some extra work instead. And why not? It wasn't as if he had anyone to go home to.

There was that sudden stab of loneliness again.

He tried to thwart that feeling and continued to immerse himself in what he was doing.

Alonso wasted no time arranging for security for Britney. He could not believe someone was out to get the lovely, shy nurse. What kind of twisted crazy fool would trash her apartment like that and go through her belongings?

The next item on his agenda was to go through each and every one of Dr. Worthrop's records to retrieve Britney's old files. At least she wouldn't have to worry about access to her own records illegally.

Now the other question that still lingered was if Britney was planning to tell him about Lilly DuMarco. It seemed as if Britney was willing to protect Lilly even at a cost to her own self.

After speaking with his detective, he realized the source of Britney's claim against Dr. Worthrop was Lilly. She was a retired medical secretary who'd worked with Dr. Worthrop for many years. Apparently, she might know something about the circumstances involving Britney's mother and the Janissa Clinic.

Alonso picked up the phone and called Britney on her cell.

"Hello?" Her silky morning voice stirred a sensual reaction in Alonso. It was soft, slightly husky and mellow. This woman oozed sexuality and she probably didn't even know it.

Was there anything about this mysterious woman he didn't like?

Focus, Alonso. She's a former client. Those feelings will pass.

He drew a deep breath and gathered his bearings. No woman had ever had that kind of effect on him before and all from the word hello.

"Good morning, Britney, it's Alonso."

"Hi, Alonso," she said.

"Did you sleep all right last night?"

"Better than I've ever slept, Alonso. Thank you so much. I don't know what I would have done if it hadn't been for you."

"It's no trouble," he assured, trying very hard not to picture Britney in bed. Did she have her hair down or pulled up in a bun? Did she sleep in a silk nightie or a nightshirt?

Focus, Alonso.

"And that bed. Oh, my God. What is it made of?" she continued. "It's so comfortable. I've never slept on a bed like that before."

"It's got a unique spring system designed for optimal comfort. We only give our guests the best."

"I am truly appreciative. I can't remember when the last time was I had such a good sleep. I almost forgot about all my troubles. I guess you could call it the memory foam mattress designed to soak up your bad memories to have a good night's sleep."

Alonso chuckled. "I've never heard it called that before." He had to take charge of the conversation. He held in his hand the copy of one of Dr. Worthrop's client sheet.

"Britney, you and I will have to meet sometime next week."

"Next week?"

"Yes. What are you planning to do about work?"

"I've already arranged to take some time off."

"Good. We need to track down who attacked you and who trashed your apartment. I'm also working on a few things dealing with Dr. Worthrop's clinic where your mother had surgery and where you visited."

"Okay," her voice sounded more doubtful.

"Not to worry."

"Um…Dr…Alonso, there's something I probably need to share with you, but I can't mention any names."

"Is it about Ms. DuMarco?" he asked pointedly. He wasn't one to mince words.

There was a lingering silence that hung on the other end of the phone.

"It's okay, Britney," Alonso broke the silence. "I'm aware that Ms. DuMarco has been helping you."

"How did you know?"

"My men never sleep. I'm always on top of things. Even if it takes a while to get information, I usually do in the end. I've also been in talks with the police."

More silence.

"What did they say?" she finally asked.

"All I can say for now is that it's okay for me to go through some documents but eventually they will need to be handed over—should the situation call for it."

"So I was right then. Dr. Worthrop will be under investigation."

"Let's just say that everything is moving along." Alonso had his suspicions about Miles Worthrop long before the investigation, and long before Britney walked into his office.

It was very possible that Worthrop had inadvertently helped a mob boss change his identity and facial features in the past. But nothing could be proven at this stage.

Now that Britney was in the picture, Alonso had a feeling that there was a connection between Worthrop, the mob boss, Britney and her mom.

"I want you to just relax right now at the complex. There are restaurants on the main floor and retail stores in that complex. You'll be fine. There's also a gym and recreation room and pool. Just let me get through this week and see what information we can come up with that may provide some help to you. Everything will be fine."

"Thank you." Britney sounded weak and unconvinced.

Chapter 10

The following week, Britney sat in the plush reception area of Dr. Romero's office, mindlessly flipping through a magazine. He had told her over the phone that there wasn't much in the way of new a development except they were trying to track down Dr. Worthrop in the Caribbean. She wanted to see Alonso face-to-face. If just to see his handsome face again.

She could not get over how much he'd helped her over the past week.

She was glad she'd taken the time off from work after the assault on her the prior week. But she felt utterly terrible that Alonso had given up on his own vacation.

Britney couldn't fathom Alonso had already tracked down the suspect. Unbelievable. What had she done to deserve this man's dedicated attention? It was as if he'd taken up a personal vendetta over what had happened to her. A chill slithered up her spine at the thought of it. She saw how dangerous those icy blue eyes of his got when she'd told him about the assault. True to his word, like vengeance, he obsessed over it day and night until he found out who pulled her hair in the parking lot after work last week.

She was feeling for him. Her body was going through a whirlwind of erotic emotions over this handsome and tall, dark Greek god with the medical degree.

She didn't know why but she was beginning to feel overwhelmed over his protectiveness of her.

She felt so...underserving, yet so secure around Alonso. And for the first time in her life since her mother's death, Britney felt completely secure. No more running from a crazy dangerous past, changing addresses or phone numbers every six months.

Alonso had undercover security around Britney twenty-four seven.

How crazy was that? She felt as if she was a first lady or a member of the royal family.

Britney became restless and got up. She just couldn't settle herself down. Her mind raced as thoughts flooded in each minute. It was overwhelming.

And how could she not be when there were so many crazy things happening in her life right now? So many mysterious pieces to the puzzle surrounding her mother and her past that were missing. Would Alonso really be able to help her sort out her past?

"Can I get you anything?" the blond receptionist asked.

"No. I'm just waiting for Alons...I mean, Dr. Romero."

"He'll be with you shortly. He mentioned you'd be here. He had another appointment."

"Thank you," Britney said. "I thought he was supposed to be on vacation."

"Yeah, but we all know Dr. R." The blonde dramatically rolled her eyes. "That man never really takes a vacation. He says he does then he comes in to check on some paperwork then the next thing you know, he's back into the full swing of things. We love him. He's dedicated to his work, that's for sure."

"Wow, he really is busy." Yet another pang of guilt assailed Britney. She knew Alonso was busy working on pulling up some missing files from her mother's case a long time ago. He was helping her, and yet, he should have been working on relaxing and de-stressing. She knew the full effects of working too hard all the time, especially in the medical field that never sleeps. Round-the-clock patient care is inevitable. And sometimes it's not so easy for doctors to turn off completely, especially if their patients needed them on-call. But did she add to his silent troubles by walking into his life and into his office that night?

Britney knew what she must do to rectify the situation.

"You must love working here," Britney commented, trying to switch the subject. The beautiful reception area with the flowing waterfall and lush green plants were enchanting, relaxing. And from what Britney had seen so far of Alonso, he was a really cool guy. She was certain he was a caring boss.

"Actually, this is the third place I've worked since graduating with my medical secretary diploma. And let me tell you, Dr. R. is the best. He really does care. He's not cantankerous or uptight like some of the other staff I've worked with at the other clinics."

"That's the best."

"Yes, it is," she said, very excited to speak of her boss. "He always has staff appreciation days here and when I was new, I made a mistake with the files and I thought I would be fired for sure."

"Oh, no. What happened?"

"Nothing. He took me into his office and told me what went wrong and said that we all make mistakes but he showed me how to use the new online filing system and everything was okay after that."

"Amazing. Now that's a boss everyone should work for."

"I know. I just hope he takes care of himself."

"What do you mean?"

"He needs to take a break."

"Right." Britney thought for a moment. She pulled out her phone and scrolled down the screen looking for an address.

"Is everything okay?" the receptionist queried, apparently noticing the concern on Britney's face.

"No. It's not. Not really. Listen," Britney said, taking a screen shot on her phone of the address she had been searching for. "The address is 1500 Pearl Chester Way, right at the intersection of Pearl Chester Way and Main Street at the northwest corner. I need you to take this address down. Please tell Dr. Romero to meet me there as soon as he's done with his appointment. It's extremely important."

"Oh, um...okay." The receptionist took down the number on her notepad promptly.

"I have to go now, but please let him know that's where I'll be."

"Okay. Is everything all right?" she asked again, sounding more alarmed.

Britney drew in a deep breath. "He needs to meet me there as soon as he's done. I'll be waiting."

"Okay."

"She said what?" Alonso asked as the receptionist handed him the note. Britney perplexed him. Why on earth would she want to meet him there instead of at his office? Was she in trouble?

"When did she leave?" Curiosity and concern got the best of him.

"I'd say about fifteen minutes ago. She was just staring at the screen on her phone then-"

"That's enough. I'll take it from here," he said, drawing his own conclusion as he quickly texted JoJo to meet him at the location just in case Britney was in trouble. He wondered if she'd received another threatening text message like the one she'd gotten at the restaurant. Maybe her life was in danger.

Anger coursed through Alonso's veins. So help him, if anyone laid a finger on Britney—again.

Chapter 11

When Alonso arrived at the northwest corner of Pearl Chester Way and Main Street, JoJo in his SUV beside him, his jaw fell open. There was Britney, looking beautiful and innocent in her purple cardigan and two cotton candies in her hand and a silky grin on her luscious lips that almost melted his heart.

"I hope I didn't cause you any stress, Dr. Romero, but I really think you needed to be here. With me."

Alonso grinned. "It's okay, JoJo. I think we're good here," he said, turning to JoJo, then back to Britney.

"Sure thing, boss," JoJo said, getting back into his unmarked car.

Alonso walked over to the young, pretty nurse. He wanted so badly to be angry with her for tricking him like this, raising his blood pressure a notch, but how could he be upset, looking into her dainty, gray-brown innocent wide eyes? She was irresistible in every way. She was probably the only woman who could have gotten him to come back here. In all these years, he'd never been back. Not since the year he was at the park and heard his best friend from childhood, Juliana, had died. Since that day, the Mayberry Hill Park had been a place of hauntingly sad memories. It was the place Juliana and he had always visited after school.

"And by the way," she added, with her free hand on her hip, "we're not here to discuss the case or anything to do with the clinic or work. That's on nurse's orders."

"Nurse's orders, huh?"

She nodded, her jaw set. Oh, she was cute when she tried to look mean and serious.

"I can't believe you convinced me to come here, Britney," Alonso said, as they walked through the Mayberry Hill Fair. The more he walked through the themed park, taking in the sights, the more his thoughts trailed back down memory lane. When life was simpler. When people didn't die. When his mother was alive, his best friend—or girlfriend, however you looked at it, was still around.

"And what's so bad about that?" she asked with an amused grin. She handed him one of the cotton candies. "Don't worry, Mr. Health-conscious, it's gluten-free," she added with a wink.

"Thank you." Alonso rolled his eyes and took the pink fluffy air-spun candy from her. He'd remembered when he was younger, he'd shared one with Juliana, their parents couldn't afford at the time to buy more than one.

"Bet you haven't had that in a while," she said with an innocent smile.

"Too long. I try to stay away from sweets—and so should you. I don't want you getting all hyper on me now." He gave her a smirk.

"Once in a blue moon won't do anything to your physique. All those muscles under there will burn it off in no time. And you do realize that even doctors need time out, right?" she continued.

"You told me you needed to meet me at this address," he told her, his tone more serious. "You tricked me. I don't like being tricked."

"Oh, come now, it's not really a trick. It's a treat."

He couldn't help but grin over her determination and spunk. She was really something else. She hardly knew him, yet...there she was treating him as if she genuinely knew him—or what was good for him.

"As a nurse who once trained in wellness and health promotion, I highly recommend leading a balanced life to reduce stress levels," she said, matter-of-factly.

"Very well," he was almost dismissive. He wasn't going to win this one. He was often one who never backed down from a discussion but something inside him told him he really didn't want to be in a heated discussion with lovely, unpredictable Britney. She was just—something else.

"I knew the park was around here, but I thought the address you gave me was for a house or office next to it," he said, his tone softening slightly.

"You wouldn't have come," Britney shot back knowingly.

"Darn right, I wouldn't." He couldn't believe he was back at Mayberry Hill Fair. What in God's name was he doing there? He should be following up on reports dealing with Britney's case. But he had to admit, the energetic, fun environment was beginning to calm him in an unexpected way. That and casually strolling through the fair with Britney. There was something enchanting about her presence and her lively spirit.

"Do you even know how to relax, doctor?" she interrogated.

"No. And that's okay." Alonso inhaled the fresh cinnamon scents of candy apple vendors nearby. "There's too much work to be done."

"And it will get done," she promised, over the sound of loud music playing. "Right now, I don't want you to think about work, or my case, or anything to do with the office, Alonso. You work too hard for that. You deserve a mental vacation—at the very least. You deserve fun."

"Fun?"

"Yes. By the time we're done, you're going to want to come back here every weekend."

"I seriously doubt it," he said over the loud music, laughter and joyful screams nearby from the Dunking Duck Pond attraction. Everyone seemed to be having a blast there, carefree fun. But Alonso had ambivalent feelings. Mixed emotions surged through him. No woman had ever even thought to bring him there to wind down, knowing how worked up and engrossed in business matters he was. And you know something, it was working. Slowly, the upbeat tempo of the amusement park and fair was seeping into him. He knew better, of course, knew one should play as hard as one worked, but too often, he found it hard to pull himself away from his files.

Hiding.

Maybe he was simply hiding from his fears in his work. Burying himself under a heavy patient and project load so that he didn't have to be reminded of the disasters that could result from a close relationship—or fear of getting too close to anyone who could potentially cause him heartbreak down the road. But Britney, God bless her, was doing something to him. She was forcing him to relax, even in the midst of her own troubles and her situation with her past.

They strolled through the themed fun fair through the crowds, enjoying the crisp autumn breeze and picturesque trees with the orange and brown leaf colors that signified the beginning of fall. They walked past the large Ferris wheel while music and laughter filled the air. Mayberry Hill Fair was always the fair to go to back in the day and even now. Both adults and children alike had fun on all the rides.

"Oh, you don't know me at all."

"Evidently not," he admitted.

They reached a park bench with a tree right near the lake and stopped.

"You know, I once had a patient who became blind and you know what he told me?"

"No. What did he say?"

"That if he'd known he would have lost his sense of sight, he'd have taken more time to appreciate the beautiful trees and sky and generally enjoyed nature more."

Alonso's gut twisted. "I'm sorry to hear about his blindness. It's so true we take a lot for granted."

"That's why it's important to stop and smell the roses so to speak."

"It's funny that you brought me here today. I was actually telling a patient who'd been recently diagnosed with a treatable form of cancer that it is important to take each day as a gift. We all have to do that. Every one of us. It's a present, that's why it's called the present. We spend so much time fretting over the past or worrying about the future and yet, all we are guaranteed and have is right now, the moment."

"I know. I like that poster you have in the wall in your office. The one with the lake scene and the leaves, just like this one."

He grinned. "Oh, that one. Life is not measured by the number of breaths we take but by the number of moments that take our breath away."

"Yes, that one."

"What are you trying to tell me, Ms. Britney?"

"That you're a hero to everyone else but yourself, Alonso. Even with me. You should have been on vacation, yet you can't stop and you're working around the clock to help me and yet you barely know me."

Alonso didn't say anything.

"I want you to be around for a long time, so you're going to have to relax and have fun once in a while." Britney playfully bumped him with her shoulder.

He glanced into the glistening water of the lake. It was delightful as the afternoon sun set in. The vibrant colors of the trees created a spectacular sight. Britney was right. It was like heaven. A breath of fresh air.

"So are you going to tell me the real reason you wanted me here?"

"I already told you," she said. "To have fun. Why do you think there's an ulterior motive?"

"There always is, isn't there?"

"Not with me."

"Not with you?" he said, evidently dubious. "Oh, come now, Britney. Who walked into my office the other night with a half-story to keep me guessing for a lifetime?"

"Okay, so I made one little slipup."

"One?" he said, arching his brow, trying not to laugh. "Little?" Britney looked adorable with her luscious lips and oh, the way she licked and devoured her cotton candy. He really had to get a life. He really needed to focus his eyes anywhere else but on Britney's soft sensuous lips. It was turning him on and stirring some wild emotions inside his body.

"Yes, one," she said with an air of determination. She tried to give him a mean look but she just ended up looking even more adorable as she wrinkled her brow, with a little grin curving her soft, shapely lips. "Haven't you made a little slipup ever before?"

He thought for a moment. "Not to my recollection," he declared smugly.

She growled.

"Okay, I have made slipups. A lot, actually," he admitted. "Who hasn't? It's not the mistakes you make, it's learning from them and not repeating them that counts."

"Now, that, I agree with, Alonso. I think I read a quote somewhere: The more mistakes we make, the wiser we become."

"So we agree about something." He tore off a hunk of cotton candy and jammed it in his mouth, despite his reservations about junk food. He only ever ate real food. He hadn't had this sweet stuff since his teens. And man, it was weird, having that soft candy melt right on your tongue.

"A lot, actually."

They strolled along the concrete walkway of the fair looking at the different attractions. They passed the grand Ferris wheel, but Britney told him she couldn't bear the feeling of her stomach falling out riding those things, so they moved on. After they'd finished their cotton candies, Britney hooked her arm through his and he felt a silky sensation in his gut. Was he getting completely aroused by this woman? Why was she having this kind of effect on him?

The feeling will diminish, Alonso. She's a former client of your clinic. It can't progress any further.

And he wouldn't allow it to.

The evening was turning out to be just what he'd needed—even if he didn't want to admit it to himself. But what was he going to do about Ms. Britney? Not to mention the growing attraction he was having towards her?

Chapter 12

"We *must* go on the Haunted Tunnel ride, Alonso," Britney said with unbridled excitement. Her soft brown-gray eyes lit up with joy.

"We must?" He arched a brow.

"Yeah, of course," she said, giving him the you-must-be-kidding-by-not-thinking-of-going-on-the-ride-of-the-century look. "Anyone who's anyone goes on the Haunted Tunnel ride. It's the best ride here."

"I'm sure it is. But are you sure you can handle it?" he asked, amusement in his tone.

She rolled her eyes and placed and her hands on her curvaceous hips, before uttering: "I think I can take it, Alonso. I'm not afraid of anything."

"Good."

"That is, I won't be afraid if I'm with you."

He grinned. "Honesty at last."

The whole environment at the fair was striking. It was hard not to want to enjoy yourself. The sound system at the fair blazed popular songs over the speakers with heavy bass. At the moment, the old tune by Shanice *I Love Your Smile* was playing. How appropriate. Her smile was beginning to rub off on him. How was he going to resist her charm?

"I'll go—only because you need me with you," he added.

She rolled her eyes again and grinned. As they walked closer to the Haunted Tunnel with the line up of people, he pulled out his wallet to pay for the tickets.

He wanted to discuss about the latest findings of her case, but he figured it could wait.

Life is not measured by the number of breaths we take, but by the number of moments that take our breath away, he recited the famous quote in his mind.

Wasn't that was life was about?

Yet, it took the young miss Britney to help him to rekindle something he didn't realize he'd lost a long time ago.

She was right. He'd been quite a dud—not that she'd told him that. All work and no play made for a terrible way to live.

He'd spent most of his adult life caring for people who were vulnerable, all the while dating infrequently and breaking it off before anything ever got serious with whichever woman he'd been dating.

"You ready?" he said, turning to her as they sat in the carriage of the train before chugging into the tunnel.

"Sure," she said casually. "Nothing to it."

He smirked. *Sure, we'll see.*

As the train carriage moved slowly into the tunnel, the darkness fell over them. Alonso grinned and rolled his eyes as Britney cuddled beside him. *Yeah, sure, you're not afraid.*

Nothing could be seen around them, so it sure was eerie. Alonso actually thought it was pretty cool. He could feel Britney's fingers digging into his bicep as the strange sounds came over the speakers inside the tunnel.

Then the train picked up speed. After a while, as expected, creepy objects and figurines started to pop up around them. Just then, something reached over and touched Britney's shoulder. Her shrill scream pierced the air, and Britney clung to him more desperately. The culprit was a piece of fabric from one of the mannequins in the dark tunnel.

Britney snuggled into him, her arms squeezed around his abs. And man, did his groin stiffen.

Why did she have to hold him so firmly and so intimately? Did she realize what kind of effect she was having on him?

Alonso was so aroused by the feel of her arms around his waist. They were in a dark tunnel, alone—well, pretty much alone, and she was holding him.

He instinctively put his arms around her. He stroked her head enjoying the feel of her silky, smooth hair. It felt good to touch her. Something got into him and he just leaned his head down to kiss the top of her head. "It's okay," he said, comforting her. "I'm right here with you, Brit."

Brit?

Why did he call her Brit?

Or the question should be, why did he feel so comfortable calling her Brit? You only shortened someone's name with whom you're involved. But oddly, the protective feeling swept over him. It was a fun ride at an amusement park, but they were cuddling like a young couple in love. A young couple who knew each other very well.

Did she even hear him? She seemed so preoccupied with the spookiness of the tunnel, her head still buried in his chest, anxiously waiting for the ride to be over. The more she held tightly onto him, the more he enjoyed holding firmly onto her. Like lovers in the dark.

Just then the very thought of her being naked and resting on top of him slid into his mind. He felt his groin pulse more. There they were in a dark, cold tunnel that was meant to be some horror show and he was feeling all kinds of erotic feelings of lust for Britney.

Why was she having this effect on his body? Whatever the feeling was, to his chagrin, part of him didn't want it to stop. Did she feel the same way about him? Alonso wondered.

Chapter 13

"Thought you said you could handle it?" Alonso said to Britney, after the Haunted Tunnel ride. He looked down upon her with a feigned air of superiority.

Britney and Alonso stood outside the carnival exit door of the ride.

His handsome, dark features were accentuated by the warm glow of the evening sun setting in the distance. The man was strikingly good looking, she noted. He was delicious. Tall, dark and sexy. He towered over her as he faced her. For a minute, a beautiful silence lingered between them. Then her nerves tensed. What was she doing? Falling for this handsome doctor before her?

Why had she suggested the tunnel in the first place? It served her right. She knew full well that as much as she was a nurse and could stand the sight of many things, horror shows weren't one of them. But oh, it felt good for strong, hunky Alonso to be there for her, cuddling her and making her feel okay.

Britney waved him off. "Sure, I was just pretending to be afraid. You know, to give effect."

He shook his head. "Yeah, okay," he uttered, obviously dubious.

They both stopped outside a colorful booth with few people around. "Hey, this looks good. You can raise money for the Children's Center here," he said. "Now that's my kind of game."

"You don't even know what it is."

"We'll find out," he said. A poster of two cuddly bears hugging was displayed before them. "Well, will you look at this!"

The poster read: Hugging Booth. For every minute you hug your partner without moving, you raise a dollar for the Children's Center.

"How sweet," she said. "We *must* do this one."

He grinned. "Now how did I know you were going to say that?"

He pulled out his wallet and dropped an amazing amount of cash on the counter for the cashier.

"At least this time," he said, turning to Britney, "when you squeeze the dear life out of me, it will be for a good cause."

She pursed her lips and folded her arms across her chest. "You're not funny, you know that?"

"Right, I forgot. I'll try not to tell any more jokes, then."

"Oh, sir, that's very generous of you but...wow..." the cashier interrupted, her eyes wide as Frisbees. "You'll have to be hugging for a long time," she finished.

"No problem. I'm donating for a good cause. Doesn't matter if I hug long enough or not. Keep it."

"Thank you, sir. Thank you very much."

Britney and Alonso went into the bright orange-colored booth and commenced an embrace. "How weird, but it's for a good cause."

Other couples were in booths also, hugging as the music played. A park employee watched each couple to see that no one moved before the bell went off in each booth.

"How long do you think you can last without moving?"

"Long enough. I know you'll probably end up twitching first though."

"Is that a bet?"

"Sure is."

"We're on then."

And on they were. Alonso put his arms around Britney and she snaked her arms around his firm waist. Oh my, he felt so good. The delicious scent of his cologne wafted to her nostrils driving her senses wild. How on earth could she possibly hug this guy for minutes without moving? It would be impossible!

"A minute is a long time, you know," he murmured.

"Shush! Every minute counts. I'm game," she challenged.

The bell sounded and they were on. Alonso hugged her and oh, there was that delicious warm feeling again.

Britney thought she was going to lose control gazing into those sinfully sexy blue eyes of his. His touch sent her pulses racing.

The man was drop-dead gorgeous. Oh, heavens. How was it that he was still single? Amazing. And yet, he was so unreachable. She felt his hardness in his pants. Oh, God! She was going to lose it soon. She felt the area between her legs throb and pulse with want. She couldn't remember the last time she'd felt this way. Her lips were dry and she licked them.

She tried to swallow hard but it was no use.

Just then, a sensuous silence lingered between them as Alonso held her gaze with his sexy, ocean-blue eyes that made her legs weak with delight. Then he lowered his head to hers and the buzzer went off—he'd moved; they both moved at the same time. But so what? She didn't care about anything that moment, except Alonso. Alonso and Britney.

Her heart raced, her thoughts spun, her stomach exploded with tiny butterflies. She was breathless as he captured her lips with his and oh, the currents of desire that rushed through her body were electrifying. He kissed her devouringly as he brushed his sweet, heavenly lips over hers, sucking on them, then sliding his tongue inside her mouth as he passionately caressed her with his sweet lips. She heard the sound of someone clearing his throat and they both pulled away from each other, breathless, almost forgetting they were still in the hugging booth.

"Nice to see young people in love," the old man who worked at the booth said with a wink. "You remind me of my grandson and granddaughter-in-law."

Sheepishly, Britney was about to say they were not in a relationship but decided not to.

"Thanks."

"By the way, you two were in the wrong booth. The kissing booth is a few doors down."

Alonso grinned.

Britney felt heat rise to her cheeks and down her throat.

"So, um. It's funny what he said," Britney commented as she and Alonso walked towards the exit.

"About us being young lovers?"

"Yeah. How crazy was that? Why didn't you correct him?" she asked out of curiosity. What was she hoping by asking Alonso that question? That he'd admit he felt something between them, just as she did?

"Oh, one thing I've learned is never let a nice old person down. Why ruin his hopes? It's not like he knows us or will ever see us again."

Her stomach fell. She tried to turn her face so he wouldn't see the disappointment that must have been evident on her face.

"By the way, I'm sorry," he murmured.

"Sorry? For what?" she said, still breathless, as they walked away from that seductive kiss at the booth.

She was still buzzing from that kiss. Oh, my God! That kiss! Where did Alonso learn to kiss like that? She'd almost come right there and then. That had never happened to her before. Ever.

"For what went on back there at the hugging booth. I don't know what came over me. That wasn't very...professional."

So was that all she was to him or could ever be? Professional? Nothing more?

"No worries. It takes two to tango," she said, her voice almost cracking with emotion. *Why are you so upset, Britney? He's just a man. You were a client at one of his clinics. Nothing more.*

"Are you all right?" Alonso was quite perceptive.

"Oh, sure. Um…yeah. Very."

"Well, this is not how I thought today would turn out. I was supposed to update you on—"

"Hey, bro," a voice called out from the crowd. "What are you doing here?"

Chapter 14

Well, this is great, Alonso thought to himself.

Not that he didn't love his brothers and mind seeing them often, but after that passionate kiss with Britney right up there on the booth stage in front of so many witnesses, the last person he wanted to run into was his brother Zack ready to poke fun at him.

Alonso was, after all, still pretty much aroused by Britney. But he didn't want to give his brother, or any of his family members, who'd soon no doubt find out that he'd been there with a beautiful woman, the wrong impression. It wasn't as if anything could ever come out of what just happened at the booth.

Zack was with his beautiful wife, Blue, and their spirited little son, Jefferson.

"Having fun, what else?" Alonso answered with as much charm and matter-of-fact tone as he could muster, given the circumstance. "Nice to see you again, Blue. You're looking beautiful as always."

The two brothers patted each other on the back.

"Hey, you," Alonso said, gathering up his nephew in an exaggerated bear hug, "ready to go on all the rides?"

"Yeah!" Jefferson responded with animated enthusiasm. He had a cotton candy in his hand and had already taken a few bites. The little tyke looked the perfect blend of his parents. He had Blue's soft, tightly curled ebony locks and her flawless mahogany complexion along with his father's eyes and chin, only his eyes were more gray than brown.

"Since when do you have fun?" Zack interrupted, landing a playful slug on Alonso's shoulder—as if he suspected something just went down at the booth. Zack then turned to face Britney, a wide grin on his face.

"This is Britney," Alonso answered his brother's expression. "She's a street nurse from the Nurses Mission. We just decided to stop by the fair for a quick break."

"Nice to meet you, Britney."

"Thanks," she said. "Nice to meet you, too. And you, too, Blue." Britney said hi to Jefferson in a big smiley face like a preschool teacher to a pupil.

After introductions were out of the way, Alonso wanted to make his way out to get back to business matters with Britney and avoid any further questions from Zack but it was too late.

Zack pulled Alonso to the side while the girls chatted.

"So, that was some kiss there," Zack said, taking Jefferson back in his arms.

"You saw that?" Alonso asked, disbelief reigning inside him. Of course, nothing would ever get past Zack. He had eyes like an eagle and spotted almost anything, anywhere.

"Come on, bro. Who didn't?"

"Very funny."

"Nice to see you back in love again. She's pretty. Seems like a nice girl. You are bringing her as your date to Troy's wedding, right?"

"Who said anything about that?"

Zack grinned. "I'll make sure Troy and Pamela amend your invitation to add her name. What was it again, Britney?"

Alonso's face was stern, yet he couldn't stifle his grin. But of course, good ol' Zack loved to play around with his brothers. "I don't think so, bro. We're not a couple."

"Yeah, sure. Right. Anyone could see that."

"By the way, how are things going with the repairs at the manor?" Alonso asked. "Troy's reception's supposed to be in the ballroom, right?"

"Nice attempt to change the subject, dude. Anyway, as you know the engineers are still trying to fix the problem in the roof over the ballroom. Looks like we'll have to have the reception elsewhere."

"Right. Well, Chase is back in town. You know, Chase Belmont?"

"Yeah."

"I'll ask him to pull a favor for us and get one of their ballrooms reserved just in case."

"You know that'll be a lifesaver, right?"

"No problem, Zack. Granddad should know by now we get things done either way."

"Too right."

"And how's Gramps doing with his leg?"

"Not bad. Shelly was supposed to do that special leg massage therapy with him, but she sprained her wrist and now he won't let any other nurse near him unless they've been personally vetted by the family. You know how picky he can get. He wants to wait until Shelly's better."

"Can't blame him, but that's not good," Alonso said. "Wait a minute! I can get a nurse from the office to assist him."

"That might work."

Britney couldn't help but overhear the last part of Alonso's conversation with his brother. "Did someone say they need a nurse?" she offered, hopefully.

"Oh, no. I don't—" Alonso paused. "Wait a minute, do you know how to do that special leg massage they're doing for patients with arthritis?"

"Sure, I do it all the time. I've done agency work at the seniors' home many times. And…I have my certificate in massage therapy. But I haven't really practiced that as my main profession. I just do it on the job once in a while. And I do healing touch therapy and therapeutic touch."

"That's amazing," Alonso said. "You never told me you did all that."

She smiled. Inwardly, she was beaming as if it meant the world to her to impress Alonso. She could tell he wasn't a man who impressed easily.

"How would you like to do a special assignment at the manor? At my family's residence?"

"I'd absolutely love to. That would be awesome. Who and when does he or she need it done?"

Zack looked at Alonso and back to Britney. "Well, as soon as possible would be great. It's our granddad and he'll need someone for the next few weeks, until his wife, who's a nurse, gets better. Her wrist is sprained. Would that be all right?"

"Perfect. I'd be honored."

"Thanks, Britney. We really appreciate it."

"No problem." Britney was thrilled. The truth was, she loved to do special assignments, especially with seniors.

* * *

The next couple weeks, Britney spent more time around Alonso and the Romero family as she went three times a week to the manor to do Toni Romero's special leg therapy. Each time, she grew fonder of Alonso and all the work he did, not just at the clinic but his interaction with the family. She'd been invited to be a guest at his brother Troy and his fiancée, Pamela's wedding. It was unbelievable. She felt a longing inside her soul. She hoped and prayed as they worked behind the scenes to find the missing puzzle surrounding her mother's past that she could continue to see Alonso Romero. But that was probably asking too much from the universe, she thought to herself. But a girl could dream, right? Even if her fantasy of being part of Alonso's life was only that. A dream. Nothing more.

Chapter 15

"I'm sorry, sir," Hans said to Toni in the study while the Romero brothers sat down to a family meeting. "The contractors advised the earliest they can complete the renovation would be November."

"Well, that's not good," Toni said, sitting by the fireplace with his cane by his side. "I want Troy and Pamela's wedding to be special. All wedding receptions happen here in the ballroom."

"It's okay, Gramps," Troy said.

"No, it's not okay, Troy."

"Listen, Granddad, I already told you that Chase said we can have the Queen Ballroom at the Belmont Hotel," Alonso added.

"But on such short notice?"

"Yes. He said he'll move things around to make sure we get it."

"That sounds fabulous," Pamela interjected. "I really don't mind, Toni," she said, sitting on the couch. Troy was sitting on the arm rest of her chair hugging her. "As long as we have each other, it doesn't matter where we have a reception. I'm really good with it."

"Oh, Pamela, you're a champ. But it's your wedding day," Toni reminded her, before turning to Alonso. "Okay, Alonso, you talk to Chase and tell him it's a go. And tell him thank you for doing this for us."

"No worries," Alonso said.

"And is Britney still coming today?" Toni asked, full of hope.

"She'll be here soon, Gramps. She's been enjoying her sessions with you."

"Great. I really like Britney. She seems like she has a good head on her shoulders. She's delightful to be around. I have a good feeling about her and I think you two—"

"Okay, Gramps, you've said enough." Alonso grinned with amusement, hands up in mock surrender.

"But I haven't said anything; I'm just saying."

"I don't think I want to hear anymore. We're friends. That's it. Speak of the angel," Alonso said, noticing through the window of the study that Britney had just pulled up. "I'm going to meet her at the door. I'll be right back."

"Don't rush," Toni said, grinning.

"Who's that?" Britney asked Alonso, while they stood on the front lawn in front of Romero Manor.

She observed a tall, slender and pretty good looking stranger sporting a navy blue Italian designed business suit, sunglasses and slicked back dark hair getting out of an expensive-looking, luxury black SUV with tinted windows.

"Oh, that's my friend, Chase. Chase Belmont."

"Chase Belmont?" Britney asked incredulously. "*The* Chase Belmont, one of the heirs to the Belmont Hotel empire? You're kidding me, right?"

"Now, why would I kid about that?"

"I've read a lot about him in tabloids. He's, like, really famous. Remember that sex tape scandal with that supermodel a few years back?"

"I think we'd *all* like to forget that, Britney. Especially Chase," Alonso said, suppressing his urge to laugh. "Besides, there are always two sides to a story."

"Of course, and you rich folks probably stick together." Britney placed her hands on her hip, pretending to scowl at him.

He grinned. "Let's just say, we understand how vulnerable we become when we acquire certain wealth and become public targets. But if you must know, I've known him a while. We met in college."

"In college?"

"Yes, Britney. Don't judge him because he was born into a wealthy family. I've never seen anyone work harder than Chase. He's hands-on and doesn't sit on laurels taking for granted what he has. He goes out there and does it all—like the rest of us. Some of these rich kids actually do get an education and work. We're not all trust fund babies. Besides, if you've read anything about their history, you'll realize they all had to learn how to work and appreciate money just like most kids. Their dad had them take minimum wage jobs at the hotels to learn what it feels like to get your hands dirty at all levels."

"Well, that's good," she said, sounding rather amused.

"He was studying for his MBA in Business Administration at the faculty of business at the university while I was registered in the faculty of medicine. We met at a college football game in freshman year."

"I see." Britney nodded thoughtfully.

"The Belmonts are much like the Romeros. They don't live off their name; they live off their hard work and experience. They're very hands-on in managing their worldwide hotels. There's so many of them. Most of them have regular jobs in management or marketing and are always in on boardroom meetings. That's what makes them different from other luxury hotel chains.

"Our families are quite close," he continued. "Granddad and *his* grandfather were, as it turned out, mutual associates back in the day. Granddad assisted the family in revamping and redesigning one of their newer resorts that just opened. I think he invested in some property there. The founder, Joseph Belmont, their great-grandfather, left them a legacy of working hard and never forgetting from where they come."

"How cool is that?"

"See? Bet you the press didn't report any of that stuff," he said, a grin of amusement on his lips. Of course, Alonso was a Romero. He knew firsthand what it was like to be judged in the media and only have scandalous stuff written about you or your family, not normal day-to-day positive things. "Anyway, Granddad's been looking forward to his next therapy session with you. I don't want to hold you up. I need to speak with Chase. We've got some business to discuss."

"Sure, whatever you say, doc."

"Chase, thanks for coming, man." Alonso extended his hand as Chase got closer to him on the lawn. "I really appreciate it."

"Hey, no problem." Chase clasped Alonso's hand. "You said it was urgent. JoJo filled me in on some details."

"Yeah," Alonso said, eyes riveted to the ground, not sure of how to proceed. "Before I get into that, Granddad and the family have agreed to have the reception at the Belmont if that's still okay with you on such short notice. We know the Queen Ballroom is the most sought-after and always backlogged with bookings."

"Hey, you guys are family. You want it? It's yours."

"We really appreciate it, Chase."

"No worries. You guys have always looked out for us. It's nothing. Anyway, what's this other problem you have?"

"I know you manage the day-to-day operations at the Belmont in Rosedale. So I figure you can get me some information I need to solve a puzzle."

"Yeah, sure," he said, his hands shoved in the pockets of his dress pants. Clad in his business suit, he was ready to go to an important meeting, no doubt.

"Hey, wait a minute," Chase said, changing the subject. "Before we go on, what are you doing here? You're not at work. Is something wrong?"

"Wrong? No. Why?"

"Oh, it's just that I'm not used to seeing you out and about on a weekday. You're always at the clinic or busy launching some venture or another," he commented. "Must be a nice girl you've met."

Alonso smiled. "No. Not really. Well, I have a friend, I'm helping her out. But as you know, I'm on vacation."

"Like that ever stopped you before." Chase said, raising a brow. "Come on. You can tell me. How long have we known each other?"

"Too long, apparently." Alonso grinned.

"And your face. You have that look, man. It's crazy."

"What look?"

"Like someone's who's in love or at least in lust."

"You're crazy, Chase."

"Least I'm not crazy in love," Chase teased him.

"Anyway, you mentioned you did have information on Jim Jenkins who incurred some gambling debt at one of your hotel casinos in Vegas."

"Yeah. The guy's a real character, too. He tried to mess with one of the waitresses—tried to hit on her and all that. Luckily, I was on duty at the time and really put him in his place. He's lucky that's all I did."

"Unbelievable. I know how much your staff means to you. The guy's out of line."

"He sure is. Well, we kept a close eye on him from that time and it appears that your hunch is right. He does have some sort of search going on for a girl or a woman. He's been looking for someone. Asking a lot of questions."

"And?"

"Nothing we have confirmed yet, but he's been seen showing some pictures of a woman around. I'll follow up with you when I get more information from the guys."

"Good. Thanks again, Chase."

* * *

The next week flew by like the autumn breeze. Each day, Britney was glad to be practicing her skills in a safe, controlled environment—a private home setting, if you could call the massive Romero mansion a mere home.

She'd had a memorable time going to Romero Manor to do Toni Romero's therapy treatments and enjoyed the lovely old man's sense of humor and stories from his past—not to mention the funny lessons he'd learned while growing up in the "old" days. He was a blast. And never at a loss for words.

Britney loved the interactions of the Romero family. They were loving and tight. His grandson Jules was the mayor of Mayberry Hill and would show up periodically to check on his grandfather between meetings at City Hall.

It was the perfect distraction to get her mind off her own problems and keep her anxiety levels low.

Her mind ran on the time Toni had invited her to Troy and Pamela's wedding.

"We would love to have you at the wedding, Britney," Toni had said, after one of their morning sessions.

"Thank you for the invitation, Mr. Romero, but-"

"Please. Call me Toni."

"Toni," she'd said softly, intimidation getting the best of her. She felt so awkward calling the legendary Antonio Romero by his nickname. She'd read so much about him.

"And I insist that you come as our guest."

"I'm not sure if Alonso would want me to come."

"Nonsense," he dismissed her worries, leaning forward. He adjusted his glasses on his nose and whispered to her as if he was telling her a secret. "I heard about the fair."

"You did?" She felt morbid. What must he think of her, publicly kissing Alonso at the hugging booth?

"I've been told that Alonso never looked better that day."

"You have?" she said, sheepishly.

"Yes. Do you know how hard it is to get my grandson to go out and enjoy himself?"

"I can imagine." Britney smiled, overcome by the warmth and caring that Toni showed for his grandsons.

"You're good for him, Britney. You're the perfect prescription for him. He needs to enjoy living once in a while." The man shot her a funny expression and caused Britney to chuckle. "Anyway, your invitation is already printed and is now in proverbial stone. Thus, we've accepted your reply." He wore a smug grin on his adorable face.

"I take it that is confirmation then."

"Yes. You could say so. Besides, it is good therapy for me."

"Oh? How so?" Britney playfully placed her hands on her hips and grinned.

"It's good for my heart to see the family relaxed and happy."

Britney grinned and shook her head. "Mr. Romero, you are really something."

"I know," he agreed. "So my grandchildren tell me all the time." He leaned back in this chair by the fireplace with a smug expression on his face as he gazed at the fire. She hoped he was not trying to set Britney and Alonso up on a blind date. She knew Alonso wasn't a relationship kind of guy. He'd admitted it to her. And she was not in a position to date anyone. Not when she didn't even know who she was...

* * *

JoJo did a double take as he studied the screen on his computer. His hand shot to his forehead.

He'd done many jobs for the Romero family over the years and he'd seen a lot of crazy things come up about suspicious people in their circle but this one was probably the most troubling.

"You want to know if there's a link between Jim Jenkins and Anna Andropolous?" the voice on the other end of the phone inquired.

"What do you have, Kris?" JoJo asked his source.

"Well, Jim hired detectives in the past to find out where Anna lived. However, the real Anna Andropolous died in a car accident many years ago."

"And?"

"It looks as if Britney's mother, whose real name is Aisha, scouted the obituaries to find out who died and had similar attributes as herself."

"I see; so she went to the registrar to get a birth certificate in Anna's name."

"It looks that way."

"Why did she pretend to be part of a witness protection program when she came to the Janissa Clinic to have her face done?"

"She needed a good cover."

"Are you saying she testified against Jim Jenkins and the state didn't give her any protection? She had to find it herself?"

"No. There's still a lot missing to the puzzle, JoJo. But Jim Jenkins had been seeking her out. She apparently has something on him. As far as those old newspaper articles, we're still scouting them for some helpful information."

"So she didn't write the articles, she just collected them but since she used the name Anna Andropolous, when her daughter found them in her mother's safety box, she assumed her mother was the same Anna Andropolous?" JoJo sounded dubious. "You do realize this sounds very complicated and none of it makes any sense."

"I know. But one thing is for sure. Jim doesn't have much time."

"What's that supposed to mean?"

"He's dying. He was a heavy drinker and his liver's toast now. He knows it. Why he's trying to reach Britney makes no sense to me. But we'll find out and let you know as soon as possible."

"Good. You do that."

JoJo glanced over some additional documents and compared pictures of Anna Andropolous with another picture that Jim Jenkins had apparently shopped around looking for her. Someone was trying exceptionally hard to cover up certain information, but what, he would soon find out. JoJo always uncovered out the truth—sooner or later.

Chapter 16

A few weeks later, the Queen Ballroom at the luxury Belmont Hotel was overflowing with hundreds of guests attending Troy and Pamela's wedding reception.

The wedding of the century had already arrived according to Alonso's grandfather. Whenever one of his grandsons tied the knot, it was considered to be the wedding of the century to Toni Romero. Alonso grinned, bringing his glass of champagne to his lips as he watched from the bar as the guests broke out their moves in the middle of the dance floor.

Just then, Alonso's breath was stolen looking at Britney across the dance floor in her beautiful red flowing evening gown. He'd had the pleasure of waltzing with her earlier. The closeness sent his body into overdrive. He'd felt himself getting hard so he politely ended after the second dance and told her he was going to sit the rest of the dances out.

Little did she know the real reason. The closer their bodies touched, the harder his erection became. It would have been impossible to hide it. The heat of her lovely gaze sent his body pulsing with arousal. The trouble was, he was still having a hard time cooling down.

Britney was simply magnificent in every way. The sway of her curvaceous hips and the way she moved into him was incredible.

The grand ballroom at the prestigious Belmont Hotel was a golden palace inside, a stunning work of marble art but it had nothing compared to the vision of loveliness that was Britney Andropolous.

Man, she looked sinfully stunning. Breathtaking. Alonso's body was reacting like crazy as his eyes penetrated her from the distance between them.

Her curves filled out so scrumptiously in that gown. It was crazy what she was doing from across the ballroom and she didn't even realize it. What was he feeling? No woman had ever had that kind of pulsing effect on his body before. Not like that. And he'd met, and even dated, plenty of hot babes before.

"You like her, don't you?" Toni said with a sly grin as the live band played an instrumental version of *Endless Love*. He had a glass of champagne in his hand, his chin up. He stood beside his grandson, observing the other dancers.

"She's a good person, Granddad. And I'm helping her out. But nothing's going on between us."

"Oh come now. I see the way you look at her when her back is turned, Alonso. We all see it. Even Mr. Petro—our retired gardener there with the bad eyes can see it, too."

"We? Who're we?" Alonso couldn't help but grinning. His grandfather was smooth all right. He remembered the bet they had about finding the perfect one and settling down. But every time Alonso entertained the idea, the thought of losing someone close to him terrified him again. It paralyzed him with fear.

First his childhood girlfriend, Juliana. Then later his college girlfriend. Yeah, love was great, but he would go insane if anything happened to the love of his life. Alonso was jinxed in that department and that was the end of discussion for him where marriage was concerned. Losing patients was bad enough, if that ever happened, but losing the love of your life, your soul mate, your very heart, he could not deal with that excruciating pain again.

"Your brothers and I see it, Alonso. You've changed over the past few weeks since you've been spending time with Britney. It's as if she's breathed life into you."

"What?" Alonso almost choked on the champagne he'd just sipped. "Breathed life into me? Are you trying to say that I was a lifeless dud?"

Toni Romero shrugged his shoulders and fixed a smug grin on his face. "Your words, not mine, grandson," the old man teased him. "Let's just say you've been all too serious. All work and no play. Then Britney comes along and all of a sudden, you're going to fairs and amusement parks and partaking of other recreational activities. You're even leaving the office early. You're not working twenty-four hours at the clinic anymore. You've been a workaholic, Alonso. You've always been busy helping others, saving lives, saving foreclosed houses for people down on their luck, campaigning for this cause and that cause. I don't think there's a cause under the sun you haven't championed. I think you might very well hold the Guinness record for that."

"Is there a category for that?"

Toni shrugged, an innocent expression on his face. "Who knows? There's a category for everything these days."

"Oh, is there now?"

"Yes, not to mention, you probably hold the record for dumping more women in a year. You date a girl then you don't want to see her again."

"Hey, I'm a decent guy. I don't use women. You know that," Alonso refuted sternly.

"No, no, no. I don't mean that. I know you wouldn't be so low as to use a girl like that. I know I've raised you boys way better than that. Respect for a woman is everything or you're nothing. I mean, you let them know it will only be a date, nothing more. You don't even want to get close to them. You won't give a girl a chance to get close to you, Alonso. And what about Bianca?"

Bitterness assaulted his taste buds at the sound of her name. "She wasn't what I thought she was." And that was the truth, but Alonso didn't want to spoil the moment by explaining to his grandfather that she'd cheated on him. Still, the old man was right. Where was his life headed? He looked around the Belmont Hotel ballroom. Hundreds of happy guests. All couples.

And the most beaming couple, of course, was his brother Troy and the Romero family's beloved press secretary and PR girl, Pamela. Boy, was he ever glad they tied the knot. She was good as gold. A true, loyal girl who loved Troy as much as she loved the family.

Pamela had helped his brothers out of many near public scandals in the past. Alonso was as thrilled as his grandfather that Troy scooped up Pam when he did. They'd bonded with her over the years like a sister, except Troy, of course, who had a different kind of interest in her. But Alonso sure was glad it had worked out so well for them.

Troy was engaged to marry someone else—a business arrangement—more like it, to one of the family's friends, an heiress, when Pamela and Troy ended up getting stranded together in that awful blizzard that knocked out power to the city last Christmas. It worked out okay in the end. But fate kind of stepped in and brought those two together. Would that ever happen for Alonso? Probably not, he thought taking another sip of his glass of effervescent champagne.

A weird thought crept into Alonso's mind just then: Britney was wearing a long, flowing designer wedding gown with rose petals in her bouquet and in her hair. She looked like a goddess in his mind's image. She was getting married. He was on the dance floor with her and took her hand. He was wearing a white tuxedo with a boutonniere in his left breast jacket. They both showed off their sparkling matching wedding bands as the live band played and his brothers cheered them on.

Alonso blinked to delete the reverie. What was wrong with him? It was only a vision. But why did such a vision slide into his brain? Why was his heart galloping in his chest?

Britney.

From the day he'd met her all he could do was dream about her, obsess over her, drool over her. And that was completely, utterly, totally unlike him. As much as he hated to admit it, even with his late girlfriend from college, he'd never felt this way about any woman. There was some sort of magical connection with Britney.

Alonso never clicked with another soul since his childhood girlfriend died. How crazy was that?

He glanced at the glass of champagne in his hand. That's why he never really drank much. Maybe it was time to lay off the alcohol. It was making him delusional with all kinds of weird romantic fantasies—all involving his lovely, delicate nurse, of course.

His mind kept racing back to the pain of losing a girlfriend. He just couldn't handle anything happening to someone he loved again. Yet, Britney was making it very difficult for him. She was forcing him, inadvertently, to rethink his motivations for not falling in love. And she didn't even realize the effect she had on him. Was it really better to love and lose than to never have loved at all?

Oh, Britney, Alonso thought glancing at her dancing to the music, *you have no idea what you do to me, girl.*

Was his grandfather right? Was he changing his ways since cheerful and energetic Britney, with the mysterious past, whisked into his life a few weeks ago? Was Britney really rubbing off on him? Why on earth did he connect with her unlike any woman he'd ever dated? It was unbelievable. Surreal. He didn't know what to think.

Alonso put his glass down on the table near to where the men were standing.

"Where are you going?" Toni asked.

"To see the woman who breathed life into me." He winked. "I think I need another liter of oxygen from her."

His grandfather grinned.

Alonso wanted to turn in for the night but he wanted to see if his lovely date for his brother's wedding reception was interested in calling it an early night. He had a busy day ahead of him upcoming. Since he'd been drinking, like the rest of his family and the guests, they'd already made arrangements to either have guests chauffeured home or stay in the block of booked rooms for invitees of the wedding. Britney told him she would stay at the hotel. That worked out well, since his room would be down the hall from hers.

Weddings.

Alonso couldn't wrap his head around the fact that his brothers were all married now—and his cousin Antonio III, too. Unbelievable. What ever happened to staying a true bachelor for life? Did they not swear to it in their youth with a blood brothers pact? Seeing how their grandfather had been through five marriages and their own father lost his mind after the death of their mother—it made sense then. Even at that early age. Now Alonso was the only one left on the bachelor platform. An easy target for his grandfather to pick on.

"I had a fabulous evening," Britney said to Alonso after the last dance of the evening. The dance floor in the ballroom was still packed considering the time of the morning.

"I'm glad you did. So did I."

"Good. And look, it's three o'clock in the morning and you're not at the office. Isn't that remarkable? Some sort of record, ay?" Britney teased.

He smiled. "You're really something, you know that?"

"As long as I know you, I'm going to make sure you never spend late nights at the office again. Unless there's an urgent situation. I want you to be around for your patients for a long time, doctor."

"Oh, please. Don't call me doc tonight, Nurse Britney."

"Fine then. But please don't call me Nurse Britney," she said playfully. "You're a good man, Alonso. You've just got to pull yourself away from work once in a while. It's called balance."

She glanced at her watch and stifled a yawn.

"Hey, what are you doing? I thought you were just talking about balance."

"I know," she said. "I guess I need to get some sleep. I'm beat!"

"So you're staying here tonight?"

"Yes."

"I'll walk you to your suite. I'm on the eleventh floor."

"Smart. I'm glad you agreed to all stay here since you'd all be drinking. It's better. Safer."

"You know safety is everything to us."

They were leaving the ballroom together to go to their respective suites, but Britney had a wishful thought, hoping the night would not end—not just yet.

Chapter 17

Alonso and Britney left the reception together and took the glass elevator in the ornate marble gold-plated grand lobby to her floor. The Belmont Hotel was stunning in its elaborate features and elegant design.

"Your brother looks so happy, Alonso. Your whole family's so sweet," she remarked leaning back on the elevator wall, tired from all the dancing and drinking.

"Thanks. They're okay."

"Okay? Just okay? You have all those wonderful brothers."

"Yes. But, trust me, it's not easy growing up with so many brothers."

"It's not? I don't believe it," she said. "God, what I would do to have a big family like that. You guys are all so close. You're so successful and have your own lives but you stick together and look out for each other. And most of all, you know how to have fun together. Trust me, not all families are like that, Alonso. I know. My family, as small as it was, was nothing like that. Mom couldn't turn to anyone when she was going through stuff."

"That's not good."

"I know, but I'm glad you have that. And thank you for making me feel welcomed like part of the family," she said, feeling a pull at her heart. She longed to have close relations like how the Romeros had each other. She felt a pang of loneliness assail her. Then she tried to shift her mood and lighten things up, worried that Alonso would pick up on her sadness. "And by the way, your grandfather is a hoot. Those funny speeches he gave at the dinner were off the wall."

He grinned. "I know. He's great, isn't he? Still, if it weren't for him, I don't know where my brothers and I would have ended up."

"I see. I understand."

The elevator stopped at the eleventh floor. The bell dinged and the glass double doors slid open.

"After you, princess," he said, holding his hand out to guide her out.

"Thank you, my prince," she said playfully.

He walked her to her door and watched to make sure her key card worked. She slid the card through the slot and opened her door. "Will you be okay?" he said, by the door, looking around to make sure she was safe.

"Yes," she said hesitantly.

"You seem as if you're not sure." Alonso immediately picked up on her anxiety.

Oh, why was she feeling the way she was? Why was it so darn hard for her to let him leave?

Oh, make a move on me, Alonso. Please! I want you so badly, you have no idea.

Her body reacted to the memory of their last kiss at the Mayberry Hill Fair. A kiss she wished was longer. A kiss she wished she could have him repeat over and over again. Her body tingled in all the right places just thinking about Alonso's soft lips on hers.

It was funny but it was as if that time was the first time she'd had her first, real soul-touching, orgasmic-inducing kiss.

Britney had never been kissed by a gorgeous man like that before. And a stunning, breathtakingly gorgeous man at that.

Oh, those soft, sensuous lips of his.

Kiss me again, Alonso.

Goodness, the man wasn't even touching her and her body felt on fire for him. Just his aura, his beautiful masculine scent that drove her senses wild. Just his smooth, chiseled cheekbones and heavenly blue eyes had her in a trance.

But oh, the one guy she was really feeling for happened to be the most too-perfect gentleman she'd ever met in her life. Her body was still buzzing from the last dance they'd shared. She felt his magic, she even felt his hardness as he pressed his hips into hers.

And now they were alone—in her hotel suite. And she had to fight the urge not to wrap her arms around his neck, pull him to her and French kiss him goodnight.

"I'm fine, really."

"I'm not leaving you here alone until I'm sure. What is it?"

"Nothing. I..." Britney hugged herself and moved over by the window looking out at the city lights below and the night sky.

He walked closer to her. "You want to talk?" His voice was smooth and silky.

She turned to face his tall frame that towered over her, forcing her to look up into his amazing ocean-blue eyes. His dark hair and silky dark complexion, again, always gave him that mystical exotic look.

No, I want to do more than just talk.

How could she tell him she felt all alone right now? Like a pitiful loner. That after feeling the buzz of togetherness with Alonso downstairs, she wanted more of him. She couldn't bear to spend another night without him. And she knew darn well, it wasn't the champagne talking.

"Hey, it's okay," he said softly, perceptively moving closer to her, wrapping his strong warm arms around her. She felt the heat of his energy flowing through her. Amazing.

And oh, she was going to go insane if she couldn't strip off his sexy tux and get him in the bed with her.

"You've had a rough few weeks," Alonso continued, his voice warm. "You don't need to say anything, Britney. I'll be here for you."

"Oh, Alonso. That's so nice of you. But that's the trouble."

"The trouble?"

"Yes, Alonso, I'm..." *falling for you. But you're too nice. Too good for me.* "So torn about everything right now."

"Shh," he said, capturing her gaze with his steel blue eyes that made her heart flutter and her lungs squeeze.

"You're so beautiful, Britney. You're amazing, you know that?" He traced her jaw with his fingers. She tingled at his tender silky strokes on her skin. The man had quite a magical touch. She'd never been touched by someone with skin as smooth as his. Alonso was dripping with charm in every way. "I've never met anyone like you before, girl. You blow my mind," he said, then slowly and seductively he pressed his lips to her skin and sucked on the base of her neck sending shivers of delight soaring through her. She felt her legs weaken.

"Oh, Alonso," she moaned as her inner thighs pulsed spasmodically at the reaction from his sensuous touch. She was going crazy out of her mind.

He stroked her cheek with his soft finger and shivers of delight slid down her spine. She felt her knees buckle. Oh, so weak. He then lowered his head to hers and the electric pulse that lingered between them for that split second before he brushed his soft lips to hers, almost sent her senses overboard.

A delicious shudder ricocheted through her body as he slid his tongue over her lip then into her mouth, claiming her, pressing his warm lips to hers in a magical sweet kiss.

She moaned into his lips at the electric sensation from kissing Alonso. He tasted of sweet, fine red wine mixed with a minty freshness. Before long, they hungrily kissed, as he slid his hands down the curves of her thighs to her bottom, squeezing her so gently she almost went out of her head. Her arms reached up to hug him, caressing his muscular arms.

She was going to lose herself completely in the rapture of his sexual power. She had been longing for this moment from the minute she'd first laid eyes on Alonso a few weeks earlier. Were they going to go far tonight? God, Britney hoped so.

Then the thought entered her mind: Did Alonso bring a condom?

She really hoped he did because she didn't want this magical moment to stop. Her body was on fire. Her nipples ached for his touch. The flesh between her thighs throbbed with want. She wanted all of him. Right there. Right now.

Alonso's soft lips caressed her neck as he nuzzled her, enjoying her flesh. She dug her fingers into his strong, broad shoulders, her head tilted back in delight, her sex pulsing uncontrollably, silky moisture pooling between her thighs. How did he know the flesh on her neck would be so heightened by his touch? How did he know where to softly kiss her to make the sensation of heat rush through her body? It was as if he was gifted to know exactly the right pleasure zones in her body. And he knew how to apply just the right touch.

"Oh, Alonso, I...I need you," she moaned. Britney didn't know what got into her but she wanted him right now and was fighting the urge to not rip off his tuxedo straight away. "Hmm, please don't stop," she said between his intermittent caresses. Oh God, his touch. Alonso's kisses sent sensational shivers of sensuality soaring through her body. He then moved his lips to hers again.

"Oh God, you're so beautiful," he murmured between kisses, his voice hoarse and unrecognizable. His lips, warm and sweet, recaptured hers and became more demanding and passionate with each salacious brush. His gentle lip massage sent currents of desire rushing through her. She couldn't remember a time when she'd felt so loved, so treasured, so good.

Just then, a knock sounded on the door and Alonso pulled away, breathless.

What the heck just happened? Alonso thought to himself, realizing he was in Britney's hotel room. That should not have happened.

"What is it?" Britney said, out of breath, her chest heaving from the effect of their passionate kissing. And what a kiss that was. His body was still buzzing. His erection was straining inside his pants.

"You'd better see who's at the door," he said, his voice raspy. "I shouldn't even be in here with you, Britney."

He could see the crushing disappointment on her face. Clearly, she wanted this as much as he did. Oh God, did he want her badly. Right now. So was he being too direct when he told her he shouldn't be in here with her? The truth was, that was the only place he really wanted to be. With her. Alone. Beside her. Inside her.

The last thing he wanted to do was hurt her feelings. But no good could come from what just happened. Alonso wasn't into permanent relationships. He just couldn't bear it if anything should ever happen to someone he loved—again. The paralyzing fear and unresolved grief over his past girlfriends were enough to prevent him from falling in love.

Was that what was happening? Was he falling in love with Britney?

It was probably for the best that they'd been interrupted.

Britney walked over to the door, a dazed expression settled on her pretty face. Alonso felt profound regret over breaking away from her so abruptly; he could feel his heart sink.

"On second thought, I'll get it," Alonso said, walking over toward the door, taking charge of the situation.

"I can answer my own door, Alonso."

"I'm sure you can, but I want to see who would be knocking on a young woman's door at this time of night, even if we're in a hotel."

Britney frowned. Her arms folded tightly across her chest.

"Fine. You get the door."

Alonso looked through the peephole then opened the door, looking stunned.

"How did you know I was here?" he said to his brother Dion who stood by the door, a grin on his lips.

"So, it's true then what Granddad said." Dion smirked. He then turned to acknowledge Britney. "Hello, Britney."

"Dion," Britney greeted. She noted Dion looked as if he'd just finished a hard night of steady dancing. He was always with his wife, Jenna-Lynn, of course. His tuxedo was creased and his necktie loosened. Those two seemed to be made for each other.

"You still haven't answered my question, Dion," Alonso said, impatience in his silky, deep voice.

"Who said anything about me coming to see you?" Dion shot back with a grin.

A puzzled expression crept on Alonso's face.

"Relax, man, Britney left her purse at the buffet table. I'm just here to bring it to her."

"Oh, no," Britney said, covering her mouth with her hands. "Thank you, Dion." She reclaimed her handbag. "It's not like there was anything in it, really. It just matched the dress."

"Of course," Dion said. "Well, I don't want to disturb you two."

"Nothing's going on," Alonso denied. "I just walked Britney up to her room."

Britney felt her stomach cave.

Nothing's going on? He just walked me up to my room?

Was Alonso sorry he'd kissed her? But her body was still intoxicated from that sensational, magnetic kiss. Didn't he feel anything? Was he having second thoughts? Or was he just being a gentleman by dismissing what just happened between them?

Oh, great. She would never know now. She'd never felt this way before about any man in her life. Her body felt so at ease in Alonso's presence. The feeling was indescribable. The one man she wanted really didn't want her at all. Boy, she made a fool of herself.

She was so sure she'd felt something between them. She was certain he felt the same way she did. Britney was even hoping, fantasizing that the night between them would progress. But now she knew that would not happen.

Now she knew that he had *other* things on his mind and a night of seduction and passion—at least with Britney, wasn't one of them.

"Sure, whatever you say, bro." Dion winked.

Alonso shoved his brother out with a chuckle and closed the door.

Little did Alonso know he'd just closed the door on any hope Britney had of them together.

Chapter 18

"I guess you'll be leaving now," Britney said to Alonso, her body still on fire from his delicious sexually-charged kiss. And what a kiss that was! Did the man even know how sensually potent his lips were? Never mind that, she was addicted to him. She craved his touch. But she was a lady and she wasn't going to go begging for it. If he wanted to leave, that would be fine with her. Not.

She could feel the magnetism between them. It was undeniable.

Slowly, his sexy azure gaze captured hers and her legs grew weak again. How on earth did he manage to get that kind of reaction from her body each and every time they got closer to each other?

"No," he said, in a low sexy voice. "I can't leave."

"You can't?"

"I need you right now, Britney. I want you….Unless you want me to go," he said, his voice husky and sweetly sexy. He had that look in his eyes. That disarming and charming grin.

"No," she blurted, sounding a little more desperate than she'd intended. She saw the adorable boyish grin of satisfaction curve his oh, so sexy lips and she melted in his arms. He must have sensed her body's reaction to his. He must have known she couldn't breathe without him right now.

She was so relieved the night wasn't going to end.

He neared her and gently led her to the plush king sized bed. He guided her down upon it.

"Britney, I need you to know something," he said.

"Oh, God, what is it?"

"Nothing to be alarmed about. It's just that," he paused, as if agonized over what he was about to say. "I'm not looking for a permanent relationship."

"I don't care. I'm not either!" She didn't care, she wanted him inside her, needed to be with him.

"Do you really want me to stay with you tonight?" he said huskily, as he nibbled her neck with his lips again. She dug her fingers into his arms and arched her back as she lay on the bed, enjoying the silky feel of his lips.

"Yes, oh, yes," she moaned.

"Good," he murmured. "I want you so badly, Britney," he groaned with pleasure as he slowly eased her dress off her, stripping her down sensuously while admiring her body. His lips moved down to her voluptuous breasts and she tingled with delight.

He got up and removed his tux jacket and loosened his silky black bow tie. She could see raw hunger and desire burning in his beautiful eyes. When he unbuttoned his shirt, her eyes widened. She sensed he was well built beneath his clothes, but his body was…wow, incredible. The man had ripped abs and muscular chest and arms. A sculpted body. And the impressive bulge in his pants made her salivate.

While he positioned himself atop her he slowly brushed his lips over the tip of her breast and sucked on her taut nipple. He circled his tongue over her bud as she squeezed her fingers into his arms.

Alonso then moved his sweet lips over her other breast, caressing the swell of her flesh before teasing her nipple with his tongue and devouring her. Britney groaned with ecstasy, moaning as he pleasured her.

Alonso then moved down on Britney, removing her lace panties while she breathed heavy, her body pulsing and anticipating what was next to come. Her heart hammered in her chest. The prolonged anticipation was almost unbearable.

"God, you're beautiful," he groaned, and he stroked her sensuously between her folds. She arched her back on the bed, moaning with delight.

"You like that?" he said, his voice hoarse.

She nodded.

He then lowered his lips to where her soft flesh was and gently stroked her with his tongue and she cried out, overcome with erotic delight. He kissed her softly then hard intermittently until she came with a fury as she cried out his name. Breathing hard, her limbs felt lifeless, her body ravenous for more.

Alonso moved back on top of her and kissed her passionately. She couldn't wait to pleasure him the way he'd sated her.

When he undid his zipper and pulled down his pants, her eyes widened at the sight of the large bulge from his tented silk boxers.

Oh, heavens. The man had it all.

Her heart fluttered in her chest. She was more nervous than she'd thought she would be.

Britney moved her lips over his erection and caressed him, enjoying the low groans escaping his throat. Her hand slid up and down his shaft softly as she took him in further and savored his hardness until he came with a shudder.

Alonso wasted no time in pulling out a square silver condom packet from his pants pocket that was on the bed.

After sliding the condom on his impressive erection, he positioned himself back on top of her.

The moment she'd been waiting for. Britney's body was dying for his intimate penetration. Her sex throbbed uncontrollably, anticipating the thrust of his manhood inside her.

She'd fantasized about being intimate with this hot, sexy heartthrob for so long and now the moment had come. Her body tingled as she observed the hungry passion in his desire-filled eyes.

She inhaled as he moved on top of her, his warm hard body over her while he moved his hips over hers, spreading her legs apart; he soon slid his throbbing hardness inside her and she gasped with delight. He moved inside her and she could not believe how good he felt, filling her completely as she tightened around him. The rush of blood pumped to her sex.

Alonso moved expertly inside her slow and smooth then faster and harder.

He thrust inside her back and forth until she came first then soon after a rush of orgasmic lust assailed him and they both went into delightful spasms before collapsing into each other's arms, hearts pounding hard, breathing heavy, sated by their Edenic heaven as they held each other, deeply satisfied and pleasured.

* * *

"Why didn't you tell me you were a virgin, Britney?" Alonso asked the next morning, his expression was dangerously serious. It was five o'clock in the morning on Sunday. He rubbed his stubble as he stood by the window. He had already showered and was dressed in his suit. Room service had just brought in their early breakfast trays and Britney was still lying on the bed. She'd just woken up. And God, she looked beautiful, like an angel, while she slept. He didn't want to wake her.

"What difference would it have made, Alonso?" she said. "I know you care about me and I care about you. I wanted us to be together last night."

"It would have made a world of difference," he said, pacing by the window, combing his hand through his hair. "This complicates things. You know I'm not a permanent relationship guy."

"I know," she said quietly, the bed sheets wrapped around her voluptuous bosom as she sat up in the bed. And boy, what a killer body she had. His body was still feeling intense desire for her after their wild night of passionate love-making.

"God, this is not how your first time should be."

"How should it be?"

"Not in a hotel."

"Not even a fancy five-star like the Belmont with a handsome, talented visionary?"

"It's not funny, Britney."

The truth was, Alonso could deal with an experienced woman not expecting him to call back. But Britney? It was her first time. All virgins remember their first time. The guilt tore through him like a tornado, messing up his emotions. He really was falling for Britney, but he simply couldn't commit to her. His fear of ever losing her as he'd lost every other woman he'd cared about was too great. Far too great. It was a risk his heart couldn't take.

"Is it about your childhood friend, Juliana?" she asked pointedly. "Then your college girlfriend, Jennifer?"

He turned to her, his expression blank. He stood by the window, with his hands in the pockets of his dress pants. "It doesn't matter."

"Yes, it does. Alonso, I want to be there for you. I know it must be difficult having to deal with that awful period in your past."

"I don't want to discuss the past right now, Britney."

She frowned. The spunky caregiver in her was coming out again.

God, he loved her take-charge, no-nonsense attitude. He couldn't get his head around the fact that someone so beautiful and sensuous and talented was still a virgin. Well, up until last night. He'd met many virgins her age. It wasn't uncommon but he was still stunned by Britney's beauty and her charm.

"By the way, how did you manage to..."

"Stay a virgin so long?"

"I wasn't going to phrase it that way."

"Well, like I said, I pretty much led a sheltered life growing up. Mom and I were always on the run from our past. It wasn't easy to trust anyone."

"I see what you mean."

"So where does that leave us, Alonso?" she delved, hopefulness in her eyes. How could he not resist the charm in her beautiful wide eyes?

"We have a few more things to sort out, Britney. First, we'll finish what we started with the investigation into what happened to you."

"And then?"

"Then..." Alonso drew a deep breath. "We'll see what happens next."

Chapter 19

The following Monday, Alonso was back in the office. He could not keep his mind from running on Britney. The crazy things she was doing to his head. No other woman had ever dominated his thoughts before the way she did.

My God, she was a virgin.

But he could not be close to her. He couldn't bear getting close to any woman again. Yet he was falling for her. He couldn't stop thinking about her. His body was telling him that he wanted to be with her more than anything else, yet his mind was still torn in two directions.

Right now, he had to focus. And the more he kept his distance from Britney, the better in the long run it would be for both of them.

Alonso's mind replayed the unexpected call from one of his private detectives earlier this morning. The shocker of the day. "Miles Worthrop turned up. In the obits," the detective in the Caribbean said to him.

"What? He's dead?" Alonso clarified, disbelief in his voice. "How could that be?"

"He died suddenly. Police don't suspect foul play or anything out of the ordinary. He died a few weeks back."

"Well, that explains why we haven't been able to reach him," Alonso surmised, sorrow in his voice. He was truly sorry Miles was dead. The man wasn't that old. In his seventies and still very active. "Thanks for keeping me posted," Alonso told the man. But unfortunately, the unfolding discoveries that were coming up didn't change anything. And the police were still going to need Miles Worthrop's old records to continue their investigation into a larger case of which Miles was only a small part.

Alonso went into the storage room to sift through the documents Miles had left there. He noticed the late doctor had stacks and stacks of magazines from his subscription to Hypnosis.

"Hypnosis?" Alonso muttered to himself. He remembered having a discussion, or rather, an argument with Miles about not tampering with patients' memories and the hidden dangers of hypnosis. Yet, there it was—the evidence before him. Not just the magazines but ripped out passages on how to hypnotize patients so they forget certain elements of their past, but printed out emails to another doctor who happened to be located in Colorado, about running into some complications while hypnotizing another patient.

Alonso clenched his jaw. He felt his muscle twitch. "Right. That does it." He slid out his cell phone and called his brother, Lucas, who was the tech whiz in the family. Lucas was the founder and developer for many life-changing apps, including the world renowned Healthy Start app. In fact, it was how he'd met his wife, Maxine. She ran the wedding planning company that she took over from her friend and now sister-in-law Lucy but needed to have the company's digital brand revamped.

"Hey, bro. What's doing?" Lucas answered the phone.

"Lucas, I need your help."

"Sure. You sound desperate. You need to know how to talk to a lady."

"Not funny, Lucas. I'm serious. This is about Miles Worthrop, who used to work for me. The doctor who sold his shares in the clinic to me."

"Right. What about?"

"He was doing some unauthorized stuff in the past. And I think it may have somehow involved Britney. But he's dead, by the way."

"Really? Oh, no. I'll be right there." Lucas disconnected the call. Alonso knew that he and his brothers didn't mess around when it came to being there for one another. They could always count on each other.

Later, Lucas sat at the desk with an old laptop of Dr. Worthrop's, keying in codes on a screen.

"Do you really think you can access his old emails?"

"Sure thing, bro. What people fail to realize is that nothing truly gets deleted when it's in cyberspace. You can always pull things up."

"I feel like such a hacker."

"Why?"

"Because we're going through his email."

"We're not, bro. Relax. This is the company's email, right?"

"True."

"So you've suspected illegal activity that might have happened on your watch by someone using the company's email system. Besides, you've already set up a disclaimer that anyone who uses the company's email has to abide by certain rules and that all incoming and outgoing emails may be screened to avoid abuse."

"Okay. You've got a point," Alonso said.

"The trouble is, before you came on board, nobody seemed to be screening or watching this guy's communication. Whoa. Will you look at this?"

"What is it?"

"Looks like someone tried to complain about old Worthrop but he suggested they meet instead, off premise so he could...um...what is this? Make it up to them. Keep it under wraps."

"That really doesn't sound like Worthrop. He was a lot of things, but that?" Alonso said.

Lucas shrugged. "Oh, wait. Here's something," he said, scrolling down the screen. Lucas drew in a deep breath. "I think you'd better read this, bro."

Alonso read the message that was sent to Miles. It had to do with a change in identity and some initials. Were these the initials of the patient he'd hypnotized. Alonso looked again. "I need to get a list of all clients with those initials," he said, stern urgency in voice.

"I think I can answer your question, doc," JoJo said as he entered the room. His expression was grim.

"What's that supposed to mean?" Alonso said as he stood up.

"I think you'd better sit down for this," JoJo advised Alonso.

Chapter 20

Alonso didn't know how he was going to approach Britney. It would be too damned hard. He was still reeling in shock himself. Shock, anger, fury. How could Miles Worthrop stoop to such a thing? If he weren't dead, he would have lost his license for sure.

"What is it?" Britney asked, later that afternoon, her voice soft and trusting. Her eyes wide and captivating. He felt like he would have done anything to protect this dainty princess before him when he'd first met her. But now, he was even more protective of her. He'd had a sweet connection with her from day one.

"I think you'd better sit down," he told her gently. He felt like his heart was about to explode inside his chest.

He wanted her from day one. But now, he wanted her even more. Even though it could mean losing her one day. But then again, sometimes fate had a weird way of correcting what was once wrong in a person's life and making it right again, didn't it? He certainly felt that now.

"It's okay. I'll stand." Anticipation racked her voice and her expression. Her sweet lips parted in expectancy.

"Oh, Britney," he said, reaching over and hugging her to him, feeling the sweetness of her warm body and inhaling the subtle flowery scent of her perfume. "I love you, you know that? I love everything about you. I love your spirit, your personality. You have no idea just what you do to me."

"I love you, too, Alonso." Her words set his soul ablaze. He knew she meant it more than any other woman who'd ever told him those words.

He pressed his lips to her forehead than leaned back to look her directly in her large, soft brown-gray eyes.

"Britney, you were right about suspecting something that had gone wrong when you first came to the clinic with your mother."

"I was?" Britney was breathless.

"Yes," he said, hesitating as to how to proceed. He knew he'd risk sounding crazy but he had to blurt it out. "You were right. Dr. Worthrop had done some things that I didn't agree with. That the clinic did not allow."

"What was that?"

"Hypnosis."

"Hypnosis?"

"Yes, but it wasn't just any hypnosis."

"I don't follow."

"Britney, your real father never died."

Her eyes widened with shock. "My dad's alive?" she asked incredulously.

Alonso was torn about how to proceed. Lie to spare her feelings or console her with the truth?

He nodded. "Your father didn't die, Britney. *You* did?"

"What?" she pulled away from him, as if he were crazy. "What are you talking about, Alonso? Obviously I am alive and well."

"I didn't mean it like that, Britney. I just…" Alonso drew in a deep breath, trying to break it to her without freaking her out too much. "I just meant that was the cover-up with your history."

"Cover-up? What cover-up?"

"You see, your mother was married to Jim Jenkins. And when they were married, they had you."

"What? No. I don't believe it. That low-life creep is my father?"

"Britney."

"No. Leave me alone. I can't believe you'd make something up like that!"

"Britney, listen to me. I'm not making it up."

"That makes no sense. Why would my mother lie about that?"

"To save you."

"Save me?"

"We'd dug up some information on Jim Jenkins. He had a wife and daughter he had abused. Children's Aid Society was called in on numerous occasions beforehand. Anyway, your mother was desperate."

"Is that why she had those newspaper articles? But she wrote them."

"No, she didn't. She changed her name to Anna Andropolous, after the…reporter was killed in an accident. She figured it would be a good cover."

"What? But…that makes no sense."

Alonso's heart crushed and splattered into a million pieces watching Britney in torment. How could he or anyone have expected her to accept this? Her entire life had been one big complicated lie. A fabrication of cover-ups.

"Britney, your mother faked your death and her own by staging the accident at the lake so she could escape your father. That was the only way she could get away from a mobster husband without him hunting her down."

Britney froze. Her eyes welled with tears. Alonso's body tensed, emotion gripping his whole being. He was feeling very tearful, too, and it took a lot to make him get that emotional, especially since he'd seen a lot of heartbreaking situations in his line of work.

He swallowed a hard lump that had climbed in his throat. His heartbeat raced. "Britney, your mother was afraid of you remembering anything from the past so she arranged for Dr. Worthrop, who'd done her own cosmetic surgery, to do a procedure called hypnotic amnesia. She didn't really worry about changing your looks, only mending the gash to the side of your face. She knew that children change rapidly while growing up. But she wanted to make sure you didn't recollect the past. Then she fed you the information that your father had died. All this through hypnotic amnesia."

"M-my mother? Hypnotic amnesia?" Britney looked lost, in a daze. She became unsteady. She looked as if her mind was spinning. Alonso wanted so badly to hold her in his arms and tell her that everything was okay. He wished somehow he could have erased the past and everything that had happened to her. He wished none of this had happened to her. Britney didn't deserve this.

"Yes. I'm not sure if you're familiar with it but it's a controversial technique designed to help patients forget traumatic events. But my belief is that it doesn't take away the feeling associated with the event. You'll be feeling anxious about something without having factual information why you're feeling that way. I never liked the procedure and I warned staff about utilizing such techniques."

"But…I don't understand."

"That's why you couldn't recollect anything. You couldn't trust anyone. And…" he swallowed hard. "You didn't remember when I'd proposed to you in grade five, J-Juliana," his voice broke off with emotion.

He could see goose bumps spread all over her delicate skin. He could not help but feel teary-eyed. To hell with emotion. He didn't care if she saw him shed tears for her. Besides, she was a compassionate nurse who encouraged people to share their feelings, to not hide behind a curtain of pride.

The truth was, he loved her. He'd always loved her. But he'd believed she'd died. And even as Britney, he'd fallen in love with her.

"Your body was never found," he told her gently. "So a memorial was held in your honor. Your mother then staged her own death by the lake after your funeral, pretending to be overwhelmed with your passing and going out there on her own to look for you, knowing you weren't really there. It was a perfect cover."

Britney looked as if she was about to faint, her legs buckled under her, but Alonso caught her in time, holding her gently and lovingly in his arms.

"I don't get it. Why would my own father have me assaulted? That guy who yanked my hair out, was put up to it by Jim Jenkins?"

"It wasn't meant to be an assault, Britney."

"No?" she sounded dubious. He heard the chill of shock in her voice.

"No. You see, he wanted to be sure you were his daughter. He had his suspicions but he figured he'd get a DNA sample by having your hair pulled out with follicles intact. It's a lame and illegal way to try to test someone's DNA without their consent. By the way, he was recently picked up for an unrelated assault. He's in custody right now."

"What?" Britney sounded as outraged as he himself felt at that moment. He could see the color drain from her beautiful face.

She automatically lifted her hand to the once tender part of her scalp where the clump of hair had been yanked out.

"Sure enough, he'd gotten the results back that you were his and of course, it all hit the fan, didn't it? He knew then that he'd been betrayed. He was worried you would know something about his past. I don't think he was on to the whole hypnotic amnesia thing your mother had done on you."

Britney hugged herself. Alonso placed his arms around her to comfort her as best as he could considering the circumstances.

"So, I...I....I'm this n-nice girl, you spoke about in grade school. Y-your childhood sweetheart who...had died? I...I'm Juliana?"

He nodded and gently guided her head to his chest. "It's okay, Juliana ... or Britney. I've always loved you and I always will. It's not your fault that you'd forgotten." His voice was soft and gentle yet hurt hid behind his tone.

Yet, how could Alonso make this better for her? He'd spent his whole life healing patients, but with all this craziness that had been revealed to her, could he possibly heal Juliana's—or Britney's heart?

Chapter 21

The shock of this discovery hit Britney full force. Her nerves tensed. A cold knot formed in her stomach. Her thoughts were sinking into a drain of confusion. What was going on? She could not have possibly seen this coming.

Juliana Jenkins?

She was Juliana Jenkins?

Impossible.

Her stomach churned with anxiety and bewilderment. She must be dreaming. There was no way this could be true. And sweet, charming Alonso Romero—was her first ever boyfriend?

A mixture of anger and perplexity assailed her. How could they have stripped away her memory like that? It was as if she'd had her mind ripped out of her head. It was inhumane. It was wrong. All wrong. She was angry with her mother, though she knew her mother tried to do her best to protect her. But hypnotic amnesia? Was her mother that desperate, or paranoid, that she felt she had no other recourse but to turn to hypnotic amnesia to ensure Britney would forget her past—and her criminal father?

"I guess that's why my spirit connected with you instantly," she said, still dazed and trying to grasp the situation that unfolded before her very eyes. "You're right about forgetting things but not the emotion attached with the event. I guess I've always had good feelings towards you without knowing why."

"But your subconscious mind knew."

"So did my heart," she murmured.

Alonso hugged her and she felt his energy, his love. "I thought it was really odd that I took a liking to you right away, not realizing who you were at first. I didn't have any pictures of you as a child. Never had a camera or anything like that, so my only recollection of you was in memory and as the years went by, you, like all kids, changed in appearance." He chuckled.

"What's funny?"

"Fate."

"Fate?"

"Yes. We'd read Animal Farm together in the library and did that school book report together. Remember, you were my partner?"

She laughed. "I think I do remember now. Vaguely."

"No wonder you and I, now, like the same types of books, the same old movies and the same stuff. We were so much alike back in school. Even though you've been hypnotized to forget certain events of the past, some things stayed with you."

"I know. We have so much in common. And now I know why we feel so good around each other. It's like we're lifelong friends."

"Separated by time but not love. I knew you were the one for me, Britney. After I thought you'd died, that killed any desire I had to get married, even though I was young. I hated the pain of losing someone I cared about. And when my other girlfriend died, I believed it really wasn't meant for me to marry. It was as if I couldn't be with any other woman, but you. It's funny how destiny works. It's crazy to think that when two people are meant to be together, the universe will move things around to make it happen—eventually. What's meant to be—will be."

"Que sera, sera," she laughed, as painful as it was given the situation at hand. "Whatever will be, will be." Her voice broke off with emotion.

"Amen to that," he said softly, before pressing his lips to hers. Britney enjoyed the silky feel of his lips on hers and his soft tongue entwining with hers.

"And that note?" she said, pulling away, breathless. "The note you gave to me in class."

"I have it."

"You do?"

"I'd kept it all these years and forgotten about until that day after we went to the fair and you told me to let go of the past. I went back into the attic and found it among some of my stuff from the old days. Your mother had given it to me after your...funeral. It had my name on it and your name in a heart."

"She gave it back to you?"

"Yes. She always remembered me when I used to walk you home from school and carry your books. I guess that's why I was on her list of people. She knew after coming to my clinic years later—the one I'd happened to take over that there might be a possibility that I'd remember her, but of course, I was so young then I didn't know her. Not to mention she'd changed her appearance by the time I assumed ownership of the clinic. But, apparently, she remembered my name. Because she had asked me quite a few questions about where I went to school and where I grew up. I never understood why she had such an interest in my past until now, of course."

"It's all crazy, Alonso," Britney said, shaking her head. "I don't know what to say, or how to think."

"When your father was told, about a month ago, that he only had a few more months to live," Alonso said, "I think that's one of the reasons he wanted to reach you."

"To say he was sorry?"

"Maybe. Maybe he wanted your forgiveness before he eventually passes on."

Britney hugged herself. "I've already forgiven him. I've made it a point to forgive everyone who'd ever hurt me so that I won't get hurt twice."

"I'm sorry."

"You and I both know, hate and anger are toxic poisons that eat away and kill the holder of the feeling, not the target. I'm not going to be eaten up inside over what someone else did to me. I'm angry—but I'll get over it. I'm not going to hold onto it forever. Life is too short to live in bitterness and unhappiness. I'm moving forward from this day. Besides, something great came out of this."

"Oh?"

"Yes. You."

He grinned, his loving smile so authentic. "Come here," he said, holding her gently. "I need to take you somewhere later this afternoon."

"You do? Where to?"

"You'll see," he said.

Alonso didn't know what got into him that moment, but he had the sudden urge to do something spontaneous. Britney always told him to be spontaneous from time to time because life was too short not to go after what you wanted. Well, she was right.

Chapter 22

Later that afternoon, they'd arrived at the Mayberry Hill Fair by the large Ferris wheel—the very place where they were a few weeks earlier. The place where Britney reintroduced Alonso to his childhood and taking time to enjoy the small wonders in life. The very place where he'd kissed her so passionately in public, not caring that others were around.

"Do you remember the first time we came here?" he asked.

"That was a few weeks ago. Of course, I remember."

"No," he said. "We came here back in grade five, remember?"

"Not...I think..."

"It's okay," he gently hushed her. "I guess maybe I shouldn't have asked you that. It will be some time for some of your memory to return but with gentle prompting it can happen. I'm going to do everything to take good care of you and make sure that when you're good and ready you'll have your memory back. We came here in grade five after school one afternoon," he said.

Alonso then reached into his pocket and pulled out a jewelry box.

"What is this?" she said, almost intoxicated with emotion.

"Something I thought I could never do again. But I am. I love you, Britney, or Juliana. And I always have. You know what's really funny?" he asked.

"What?"

"Even before I discovered your true identity, I felt in my heart that you, as Britney, were the one I was going to give my heart to. I just knew it. You're the one I want to spend the rest of my life with. I was planning to bring you back here and do what I'm about to do—with you—as Britney. But now it has another special meaning. Now that I know who you really are, I most definitely won't let you get away from me again."

Alonso got down on bended knee.

Britney covered her mouth with her hands. Her eyes were misty with tears of joy. "Oh, Alonso."

"Britney Andropolous, aka, Juliana Jenkins, will you marry me?"

"Yes, yes. I will marry you, Alonso Romero. I love you," she gushed.

He opened the box with a beautiful diamond ring in it. The box also had a piece of crumpled paper inside which fell out. "What's this?" she said, as he picked it up to give to her.

"Something I gave you back in grade five."

It was a note with the words Will You Marry Me, Juliana?"

"Oh, my God! Alonso, this is so cute. But your handwriting is...terrible." She wrinkled her nose, a funny expression on her face.

"I know. Apparently I was destined to be a doctor back then with the sloppy handwriting!" he agreed with a chuckle. "And you sure know how to speak what's on your mind, baby. I love it. Don't ever change."

"Oh, no. I didn't mean it like that. I mean, well, most doctors I know have illegible handwriting. So that must be a good sign, right?"

Alonso couldn't stop laughing and got up and hugged her.

"It's your handwriting," she said, "and you know something? It's the most horribly beautiful piece of art I've ever laid eyes on."

"And you, my dear, are a beautiful work of art," he said, amusement crinkling his soft blue eyes. And they kissed passionately, sweetly, as the Ferris wheel moved in circular motion behind them. A round of applause sounded from some of the customers waiting in line to go on the ride.

They smiled, sheepishly at the crowd then they kissed each other, sealing their love. They knew that their life together was going to be one joyous and adventurous ride together as husband and wife.

Epilogue

"Four sons. Eight grandsons. Nine lovely great-grandchildren. And eight beautiful granddaughters-in law," Toni Romero said, misty-eyed at the reception at the prestigious five-star Belmont Hotel & Resort where Dr. Alonso Romero and his new wife, Juliana "Britney" Romero were betrothed in a lavish ceremony by the lake. He wore a tailored tuxedo with a carnation in his breast pocket. His gold-plated cane by his side.

Toni held up a glass of sparkling Romero wine produced from the finest grapes at the Romero Winery and Vineyard owned by his grandson Zack, to toast the newly wedded couple. "I never thought I'd live to see this day. What a true blessing to the Romero family line."

Everyone raised a glass to cheer. The atmosphere was so alive with positive energy and laughter.

"And I'm sure the Belmonts never thought they would see two Romero weddings here in such a short space of time," Lucas joked.

Alonso grinned, though overcome with emotion. Neither had he imagined that one day he'd end up tying the knot like his brothers Lucas, Zack, Carl, Jules, Dion, Troy, and his cousin Antonio. But boy, did fate have a strange way of aligning the universe to work in your favor.

And on top of that, Alonso didn't have to give up his practice. Britney encouraged him to continue his lifelong passion of hands-on patient care. Sure they had lavish villas and fabulous mansions and condos on the lake, but there was so much more to life than living for oneself. They both shared the adventure of worldwide travel while helping to heal communities. It was a dream come true.

Alonso and Britney had a shared passion of building safe clinics overseas. Their dream was to travel the globe together and improve the healthcare systems in underdeveloped countries. He could not believe he'd met, or re-met, someone who shared his same burning passions in the medical field. And someone who was qualified to work towards his vision and his goal.

He had already paid Britney's tuition to go to the top university in the country for med school training so that she could advance her career and go from registered nurse to medical physician. She'd told him she'd always wanted to be a doctor and go to medical school but couldn't afford it, not to mention that scholarships wouldn't have covered all her expenses when she'd applied in the past. But things were different now, of course. Alonso gave her the world—anything she needed would be a phone call away. She had access to the finest of everything and all that money could buy.

Alonso was overwhelmed just thinking about her desire to become a doctor to help him in his world mission to heal broken communities and assist poor patients.

She was his equal. His better half. The love of his life. The woman who made his heart leap in his chest. The woman he looked forward to waking up with each and every morning for the rest of his life. She made his heart smile, whenever she laughed uncontrollably or said something witty or funny to him. She was never at a loss for cute words to put a positive spin on an otherwise average day. Her enthusiasm for life was blessedly contagious.

What more could a man ask for? Alonso just wanted to make sure that every day of her life, he was going to assure she was happy and loved. There wasn't anything he would not do for his bride.

Alonso never thought this day would come. He never thought he'd join his brothers and enter into the blessed union of marriage. But as the saying goes: Never Say Never. Alonso had finally found the love of his life and he couldn't wait to spend his forever with Britney.

Available now...the hot Belmont brothers in the new Billionaires of Belmont Series/The Belmont Family

Books by Shadonna Richards

THE ROMERO BROTHERS
The Billionaire's Second-Chance Bride, #1 (Antonio III & Lucy)
A Bride for the Billionaire Bad Boy, #2 (Lucas & Maxine)
The Playboy Billionaire, #3 (Zack & Blue)
The Billionaire's Island Romance, #3.5 (Christian & Arianna)
The Billionaire's Proposition, #4 (Carl & Venus)
The Billionaire's Baby, #5 (Jules & Amber)
The Billionaire's Assistant, #6 (Dion & Jenna-Lynn)
Snowbound with the Billionaire, #7 (Troy & Pamela)
The Billionaire's Marriage Proposal, #8 (Alonso & Britney)
BILLIONAIRES OF BELMONT (The Belmont Family)
The Billionaire's Bride for a Day #1 (Dane & Olivia)
The Billionaire's Promise #2 (Brandon & Faith)
The Billionaire's Housekeeper #3 (Chase & Abbi)
The Billionaire's Lost & Found Love #4 (Cole & Hope)
The Billionaire's Redemption #5 (Leo & Honesty)

THE BRIDE SERIES
    An Unexpected Bride
    The Jilted Bride
    The Matchmaker Bride
    His Island Bride (Free)
    An Unexpected Baby *(The sequel to An Unexpected Bride)*
    The Billionaire's Second Chance Bride
    The Belmont Christmas Bride
THE BRIDE SERIES COLLECTION (Books 1-5 and other stories)
WHIRLWIND ROMANCE SERIES
Accidentally Flirting with the CEO (Free)
Accidentally Married to the Billionaire
Accidentally Falling for the Tycoon
Accidentally Flirting with the CEO 2
Accidentally Flirting with the CEO 3
THE BILLIONAIRE'S WHIRLWIND ROMANCE (Books 1-3)

ABOUT THE AUTHOR

SHADONNA RICHARDS is a *USA Today* bestselling author who enjoys reading and writing about the magic of romance and the power of love. She has written more than 100 books and is the author of over 25 contemporary romance novels including books from The Bride Series, The Romero Brothers, Whirlwind Romance, and Billionaires of Belmont. Additionally, she wrote the non-fiction books A Gift of Hope, Count Your Blessings, and Think & Be Happy. She has over 500,000 downloads of her ebooks. Born in London, England, she has a B.A. Degree in Psychology.

Winner of Harlequin's So You Think You Can Write 2010 Day Two Challenge, she believes in the importance of promoting literacy. She's a proud mommy and wife and lives with her husband and son.

AUTHOR CONTACT:

Email: shadonna@ymail.com

Website: www.shadonnarichards.blogspot.com

Facebook: www.facebook.com/authorshadonnarichards

Milton Keynes UK
Ingram Content Group UK Ltd.
UKHW031444261124
451530UK00011B/104